Begyn ye now de Secta Avataris, de Way of the Avatar, de Pilgrimage yon de Shrines of de Sacred Worlds.

Behold ye de Deepstone, de Fiery Rift, de Flowery Altar un de Starry Chalice, de Hexagons, de Skybridge, de Fat Omne, de Core Dungeons, de Labyrinth, de Avatar Throne of de Regium basilica.

But alak on yeer journi, bewari ye of de unbelievers: de Worms, de Ghasts, un de unholi magik of de Mucktu.

LEGENDS OF THE KNOWN ARC

BOOK ONE

GRONE

a novel by Patrick Cumby

Broken Monolith Press
ASHEVILLE

First published by Broken Monolith Press in 2023

Copyright © 2023 Patrick Cumby

All rights reserved. No part of this publication may be reproduced, stored or transmitted in any form by any means without written permission from the author. It is illegal to copy this book, post it to a website, or distribute it by any other means without permission.

Greetings, readers. For hints to the puzzles that may or may not be embedded in this book, go to patrickcumby.com/grone-puzzle.

This is a work of fiction. Names, characters, places, and incidents are either a product of the author's imagination or are used ficticiously. Any resemblance to actual events, locales, companies, or persons, living or dead, is entirely coincidental.

Legends of the Known Arc Book 1: GRONE
ISBN: 979-8-9875227-0-7 (eBook)
ISBN: 979-8-9875227-1-4 (Trade Paperback)

First Edition

Edited by Christine Crabbe
Cover art by Patrick Cumby
www.PatrickCumby.com

*Deeply dedicated to my family,
without whom this particular
dream would never have escaped
into the real world.*

discontinuity | TIMELINE

part 1 | MIGRATION	11
part 2 | EASTER EGG	83
part 3 | GAMEMASTER	147
part 4 | HACKER	257
part 5 | LOADOUT	339
part 6 | SPAWN	437
part 7 | GAMECHANGER	499
part 8 | BOSS	527
part 9 | LEVEL UP	593

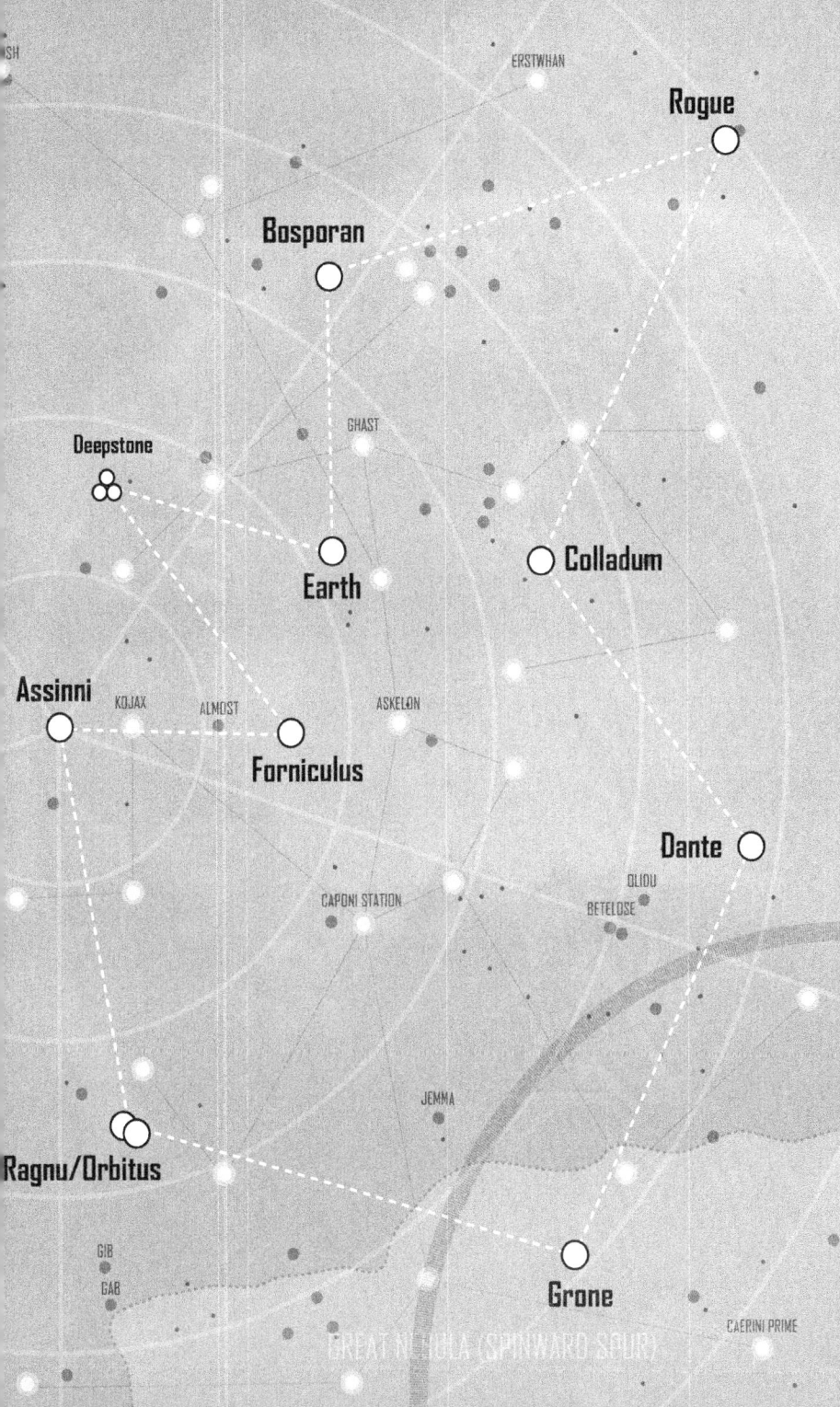

havencosm | MANHATTAN

On his way home from Wednesday mass, Brother Jerome was accosted by a trio of AONs. The oldest looked to be about eighteen; he wore a cheap hoodie printed to resemble a Dei Militans tacsuit. His two companions were twins, dirty-faced mopheads no older than twelve or thirteen. All three had scratched the vulgar symbols of the All-Or-Nothing Party into the iron of their purity collars, and all three wore the dull and belligerent expressions so common to the party faithful.

The older boy carried a nasty-looking curved knife of expensive design on his belt, not something a kid from the river tenements would've come by normally. He'd stolen it, or worse, and his eyes were filled with an unusual malice. He sneered at Brother Jerome. "Hey, bumblebee, where you headed?"

Jerome ignored the taunt, pretending to be lost in thought, hoping the boy would lose interest. Normally he wouldn't be worried. It was common these days to see small gangs of AONs on the streets, mostly rough men and boys from the sprawling church-run tenements that lined the East River. They usually gave Janga monks a wide berth, out of respect or fear, though they would sometimes shout and jeer from a distance. Things were changing, though. The fiery rhetoric of the church's new Father Regis had emboldened the city's poor to demand better. This would be a positive result had it not given the brutes and the sociopaths who

Prologue

lurked in their ranks tacit permission to wreak havoc and terrorize the innocent.

Sure enough, the younger twins moved into positions on either side of him, as if escorting him along the sidewalk. Oncoming pedestrians saw the situation and either ducked into storefronts or crossed the street. At this point, ignoring the boys would only provoke them further. He smiled down at one of the mop-headed twins. "What's your name, boy?"

The boy tried to mimic his older friend's sneer. He sang scornfully:

> *"Janga janga joo joo,*
> *bumble's got a boo boo,*
> *hit 'em up, knock 'em down,*
> *Nothin's gonna change their frown."*

He reached out and gave Jerome's black-and-yellow robe a violent jerk, almost enough to make him stumble. Jerome didn't react. He knew the strategy. The younger boy was trying to distract him, giving the older boy an opening for whatever mischief he intended. Most likely, they were only trying to humiliate him, though they might be after his purse or his faith-relic. It was also possible they meant to harm him, especially given the dangerous light in the older boy's eye and the nasty dagger at his belt.

Now all three were singing, their voices boisterous and taunting. The leader leaped in front of Jerome and walked backward, grinning obscenely:

> *"Janga janga my my,*
> *bumble canna fly fly,*
> *on the ground, pound him down,*
> *Stinkin' maggot crawlin' round."*

Jerome glanced at the lead boy's belt, saw that his knife was missing, and realized what was coming. The song was a two-hundred-year-old rhyme from the time of the Schism, when the Janga sect broke away from the mainstream church. It was phrased like a nursery song, and indeed had been taught to children, but it referred to a massacre of peaceful Janga monks at a monastery on Assinni by the orthodoxy.

> *"Janga janga ping ping,*
> *bumble lost his sting sting,*
> *yellow black, yellow black,*
> *Gonna stab him in the back."*

Jerome was ready. As soon as the boys screamed out the last line, he spun to the side, his robe swinging widely. Sure enough, one of the twins was lunging from behind, the curved knife thrust forward by a stiff arm. Its blade snagged in the fabric of his robe, and it clattered to the concrete sidewalk. The boy's harsh grin became a wide-eyed expression of panic as Jerome fell to one knee, pulled his faith-relic from the folds of his frock and pressed it against the brand on his forehead. He chanted forcefully in High Tang:

"*Signa redita Oa! As circula Matu! Al triangula Jeru! Al quadrata Spiritu!*"

He paused and glared at his assailants with all the theatrical fire he could muster. To the litany verse, which he knew they would recognize, he added a random, scary-sounding line from one of the volumes of *Rebahm's Curses*, shouting thunderously like a brimstone priest. The younger boys he taught at the Brotherhood School called it his "scary voice," and were always delighted when he used it during story time:

"*Sit tibun a dæmoni vexbata,*" he cried. "*Cui poteri confraxus en cor tu'um, Terra vestra in plactum en traxit!*"

Even though the words were silly nonsense, his delivery had the desired effect. The twins bolted away, dodging through street traffic as if they might outrun whatever awful curse he had cast upon them.

The older boy, to his credit, lurched to retrieve his fancy knife, but pulled back when Jerome's heavy boot slammed down on the blade.

"I don't want to hurt you," Jerome growled. "Go home."

The boy grimaced, shot a yearning look at the knife beneath Jerome's heel, then turned and sped away after his companions. The bystanders who had witnessed the brief altercation looked away when Jerome met their eyes. One of them pulled out a komnic, probably to summon the police. Jerome bent to retrieve the dagger and slipped it into his robes, along with the faith-relic he'd used to frighten the boys.

———

He hurried along, his hands shaking, his heart racing. The boy had meant to stab him. In broad daylight. On a busy sidewalk, with dozens of witnesses. It wasn't his first brush with street violence, but it had been so blatant, so unexpected. They'd been boys. Children.

As he neared the school, he considered his options. If he went to the abbot's office to report the incident, he'd miss his afternoon classes. Brother O'Lear would teach in his stead. The boys all hated O'Lear. Perhaps it would be best not to mention the altercation at all.

He walked another two blocks before realizing there were more AONs on the corner ahead of him. Two men, one wearing an AON T-shirt, the other the dark denim coverall of a factory worker. Behind the men huddled the oldest of the three boys who'd attacked him. The boy pointed at Jerome. The man in the coverall pulled out a komnic, made a call. He spoke softly, nodded at the reply, his eyes never leaving the monk.

Jerome quickened his pace, crossed the street, turned at the next junction. He waited until he'd walked a full block before looking back.

The man in the coveralls was following. He was trying to be discreet, but Jerome could read his intentions by the set of his shoulders.

Had this man put the boys up to their mischief? Had he given the older boy the fancy dagger? If so, maybe he wanted it back, and that was why he was following. Or maybe he wanted to finish the job. Maybe he was the boys' kammat, their AON cell-mentor. If so, wounding or even killing a Janga monk in broad daylight on the streets of Manhattan would make him a hero to his young followers and fellow radicals.

Jerome increased his pace again, striding with purposeful steps along the sidewalk, the outer cloak of his robe snapping in the wind of his passage. He turned south onto St. James.

There were more AONs ahead. Little groups of them, spreading along the sidewalks, stationing themselves at every street corner, peering into every shop window, watching the cars and taxis. Mostly men, as was usual for AON gatherings, but Jerome spotted a few women too. The AONs were dressed in everyday clothes, but their affiliation was clear. It was obvious from their edgy postures, the way they stiffened when they saw him. Something was definitely up, but if they were about to stage one of their violent political rallies, then where were their flags and banners?

No, this was different. The All-Or-Nothing Party had called its members out on the streets, but not to start a riot. They were alert, tense, and attentive, of a single mind and purpose. They seemed to be searching for something. Or somebody.

At the corner of St. James and Madison, he ducked into the park, then doubled back behind the row of shrubs, waiting for the man in the coveralls.

It didn't take long. The man approached and paused at the park entrance. His face was set, determined. Whatever he wanted, he was serious about it. Best to disappoint him. Jerome slipped around the shrubs and hurried unseen along one of the hidden routes out of the park, startling an old man feeding the pigeons.

Prologue

He didn't make directly for the school gates. Instead, he angled south down Pearl Street and past the Fat Omne statue at the entrance to the school grounds. It wouldn't do for him to have a confrontation within sight of the students or the other monks. He didn't think the man was still following, but his natural caution told him to continue evading until he was sure.

Pearl Street led beneath the Brooklyn Bridge two blocks west of where the bridge emptied its traffic onto the streets of Manhattan. It was cool in the shade beneath the bridge, and Jerome ducked into a deep, trash-filled recess between two concrete pylons. He tried to calm his breath, slow his racing heartbeat. A group of pedestrians passed, unaware of the anxious monk hidden in the shadows.

A heavy transport rumbled across the bridge. His eyes turned upward to follow the sound of its progress but paused when he noticed movement in the shadows between the steel beams that supported the bridge roadway. At the top of the sloped concrete embankment, a thin, bearded man, one of the city's many homeless, stared down at Jerome. He was no doubt wondering why a Janga monk was crouching in a filthy alcove beneath the bridge.

It was a good question. Jerome had obviously lost his pursuer, so there was no reason to continue skulking. He straightened and stepped out of the shadows onto the sidewalk. A taxi was approaching from the south, but there was no other traffic and the nearby sidewalks were empty. He turned north, intending to hurry to the school gates.

A sound like the basso rumble of a pipe organ's lowest note gave him pause. He thought it must be the growl of a wheeled vehicle up on the bridge roadway, but when it suddenly modulated into an ear-piercing whine he traced the direction of the noise to the street in front of him.

He blinked. On the street's centerline, a shimmer of sparkling light had appeared, a small, spinning dust devil of glitter. It grew denser and brighter, as if illuminated by a hidden spotlight. The whine increased in frequency until it approached the upper limits of his hearing, and the light became so bright he had to shield his eyes.

With an ear-cracking *pop*, the whine stopped, replaced by the bark of a horn and a frightened yelp. A man's voice loudly cursed, "Get the hell out of the middle of the road, you fucking moron!"

The swirling column of light was gone. Standing in front of a hovering taxi, blocking the road, was a naked girl.

Jerome squeezed his eyes shut, reopened them.

The girl was still there.

The taxi driver blew his horn and cursed again. The girl didn't respond. She extended her arms in front of her, examining her hands as if she were seeing them for the first time.

Jerome found his voice. He called out. "Are you okay?"

The girl turned toward him. She was young, a teenager, with straight hair that fell in a dark cascade almost to her waist. She seemed oblivious to her nudity. She gaped at the yellow-and-black stripes of his Janga robe and the faith marks on his forehead. She took a step backwards.

The driver blew his horn again, and the girl jerked toward the sound. She stared at the floating vehicle like she'd never seen a taxi before. Jerome moved toward her. The taxi sped away, the driver sounding his horn in one last spurt of admonition.

"You should get off the road," Jerome said gently. She nodded, but her expression was dazed. He touched her shoulder. It was solid, warm flesh. She was real. She slapped at him clumsily and made a throaty sound that might have held words.

"Okay, okay." He held his hands up in a gesture of nonaggression. "I won't hurt you. You're safe."

She inhaled raggedly, as if catching her breath after a long sprint. At a sudden, distant rumble, she spun to watch the afternoon shuttle ascend on a column of fire from the Brooklyn spaceport, across the river.

He swept off his outer cloak and draped it over her shoulders. She accepted it, pulled it tight. She wasn't wearing a purity collar, and although she looked old enough to have completed the Sacraments, her forehead had no markings. Eventually, she spoke, but he couldn't understand her slurred words. He patted her forearm. "It's okay. Take your time."

She tried again. This time her voice was clearer, though her accent was heavy and strange. "Where am I?"

"You're safe," he repeated.

She shook her head. "No, no. Where *am* I? Is this... New York?"

She must be high on something, he thought. He tried to sound reassuring. "Yes. This is New York."

Another taxi sped by, and she watched it with apprehension. "Flying cars," she murmured.

She stumbled. He gripped her arm and she leaned into him, as if her knees had buckled. He guided her toward the sidewalk and helped her lower herself to the curb.

A voice. Jerome turned toward it. The AON man in the coveralls stood in the sunlight beyond the shadow of the bridge, staring at the girl with wide eyes. He was speaking rapidly into his komnic. Jerome couldn't make out the words, but the man's agitation was plain. His eyes met Jerome's.

Jerome plunged his hand into his robes, found his faith relic. He thrust it high into the air and shouted, *"Cered yan cears'd, or be ye ruin'd mind yan soul."*

The man's face whitened. He turned and fled.

"Shit," muttered Jerome. His faith-relic had saved him twice in one morning. He kissed it, shoved it into its pouch, and turned to the girl.

She seemed far more curious about her own body than his antics. She ran her hands down her legs to her feet, staring at her wiggling toes with delight. She discovered her hair and became instantly obsessed with it. She pulled it over her shoulder and draped it reverently down her chest, stroking it like a lost kitten. Thick, black, and lustrous, it gleamed with reflected light. She looked up at him and he saw tears spilling down her cheeks.

He was unprepared when she flung herself at him, embracing him with the fierceness of boundless joy. He tentatively returned the embrace. Her hair smelled sweet, like that of a newborn.

Another taxi sped by, pulling his eyes to the road and the spot on its centerline where she had materialized. Where had she come from, and how? He'd never seen anything like the whirlwind of sparkles in which she had appeared. A pillar of fire.

He gripped her shoulders, gently pushed her away.

"Who are you?"

She winced. Dribbles of tears accelerated into a stream that she wiped away with the back of her hand. Instead of answering, she raised her face to the sky and released a savage howl of triumph.

meatspace | FIONA

Grone

Fiona couldn't stop staring at the planet's scars. She knew its history, of course, having watched and rewatched the old TV episodes and read every wild speculation that had ever been published about this place. Even so, she'd been completely unprepared for the visceral jolt she'd felt upon arrival. Old videos were one thing, but seeing it up close and high-def, well, *that* was something else entirely.

In the eons since the moonfall, the chain of impact craters had cooled and filled with groundwater to form a necklace of equatorial lakes and seas. From her vantage point in low orbit, the crater seas were immense blue pearls, each set into a ring of mountains as if crafted by a master jeweler, splendid reminders of the fiery apocalypse that had almost—but not quite—taken the world's life. Her throat tightened. Grone was a spectacular planet, but its beauty had come at a terrible price.

A jab from her brother ended her reverie. "Which one is it?" Francis demanded. "They all look the same."

She gestured toward the screen. "There. See the two craters that overlap a little? Check the smaller one." Her brother zoomed the image, revealing a circle of mountains that towered like fortifications around a deep lake. An island rose steeply in the center. Atop the island was the geometric outline of an artificial structure. "That's it. Hurry."

Over her headset she heard their teammate Tremendo express doubt, but her brother didn't hesitate. His fingers darted across his controller, and the needle-nosed *Dagger* dove into the atmosphere at a dangerously low angle, trailing flaming plasma like a meteor. To avoid being seen, he hugged the terrain as they rocketed toward the crater and, at Fiona's suggestion, landed the *Dagger* on the outside flank of the encircling rim mountains, on a narrow ledge above the tree line but below the glaciated peaks.

At the landing site, the four members of their team piled onto the ship's crawler. They took it as high as they could, following a route of natural switchbacks that curled alongside a noisy waterfall. When the ascent became too steep for the rugged vehicle, they continued on foot toward the ridgetop crags, where they hoped to find a pass leading into the interior basin.

It took fifteen precious minutes to climb the crater's rim wall, scrabbling on loose shale, hoping they didn't dislodge a landslide that might bury the crawler, or God forbid, damage the *Dagger*. Eventually Francis led them into a steep-sided gap between two icy peaks, where he stopped and cursed. A smooth cliff face blocked their way, a slab of bedrock upended a million years ago by the moonfall bombardment. They wasted several minutes trying to find a way around, but deep tongues of glacial ice surrounded the cliff on both sides and the vertical surface was too smooth to climb.

Francis was furiously impatient, knowing their head start was a fragile and precious thing. Hundreds of ships would soon be dropping from the sky to compete for this planet's treasures. He ordered the team to hurry back down to the crawler and look for another way over the rim wall. "Maybe there's a tunnel or something," he said.

When Fiona hesitated, the others noticed. They'd elected Francis as the team leader, but in situations like this they usually looked to Fiona for guidance—a fact that seemed incomprehensible to her brother. He was right, of course—there was undoubtedly another way into the crater's interior—but she suspected that the gamemaster hadn't created the obvious path they'd been following simply as a red herring. She had a sixth sense for these things, an ability to recognize the subtlest hints of purpose in the terrain around her. This massive wall of stone wasn't just a random geological feature, she knew. It was a *puzzle*, placed here with delightfully malicious intent, the trademark of a master game designer.

Unlike Francis, who quickly grew bored when there wasn't something to shoot at, she thrived on the long, complex stratagem campaigns that required clue gathering and problem-solving. Her avatar's name never appeared on leaderboards, and who in their right mind would watch her game-stream even if she had one? She was terrible at combat, not at all surprising since her injuries meant she couldn't use the complex handheld controller and headset normally required for this game. The only reason she could play at all was the controller Francis had helped her rig, an oversized trackball they'd Velcroed to the arm of her wheelchair.

She stared at the image of the icy cliff on the television. Next to her, perched on the couch in their basement, her brother muted his headset microphone. "Hurry up," he hissed. "You're slowing us down, again!"

In response she hit a button on her controller to switch the television from split screen, which showed the perspectives of both their avatars, to single screen, enlarging her avatar's view. When Francis started to protest, she shushed him. "Give me a second," she whispered. She rotated the trackball, silently cursing her clumsiness, and on the TV screen her avatar scanned its surroundings, zooming in on several apparently blank sections of the sheer cliff. She leaned forward and pointed. "What's that?"

Before Francis could respond, she tapped her controller to open her item stash. A list of her avatar's inventory appeared. She rotated through its contents until it displayed the flamethrower she'd found in the dungeon during the Borwhan campaign. She selected it, and on the television screen it appeared in the hands of her avatar. "Y'all stand back," she announced into her headset's microphone, mimicking Tremendo's drawl. She leveled the flamethrower toward a patch of blue that was just a tiny bit darker than the surrounding glacier. The weapon roared, spewing a gout of fire that exploded onto the ice. She winced as an illusion of blistering heat seemed to radiate from the TV screen. Holding the button on the game controller, she watched the flamethrower's fuel supply dwindle until the flames sputtered and died.

Her companions peered into the cloud of steam. Tremendo made a pleased grunting sound. Their fourth teammate, a Ghast bot named Gal'Blad, smiled with gaping mandibles. Francis's avatar was smiling too, mirroring her brother's real-world facial expression as captured by his gaming headset's sensors.

The others loved Francis and his avatar, Lord Geo, but they'd been together long enough to know that when Fiona's avatar, the thoughtful and serene Lady Gaia, pulled out her giant flamethrower and wasted its entire fuel supply on a mountain of ice, she had a very good reason for it. As the dark opening of a natural stone fissure began to take shape behind the dissipating cloud of steam, she heard her brother sigh. "How do you always know?"

She shrugged. He gave her a fist bump on her good shoulder and reactivated his microphone. "Change of plans," he announced to the team. "We're going through that crevice my sis just found."

The three of them followed Geo through the narrow ridgetop cleft, eventually emerging into sunlight on a high rocky ledge. The crater's impact basin spread before them like a massive geological bowl, cradling the circular lake and the central island peak they'd seen from orbit. A dark alpine forest blanketed the bowl of the crater around the shoreline. The lake itself was quicksilver smooth, a perfect mirror for the thunderheads gathering above. Fiona felt a deep pang of yearning.

The places her avatar could visit in the game were so much more beautiful than anything in the real world.

From orbit, peering down through the *Dagger*'s telescopes, they'd studied the flooded basin and the citadel fortress at its center, but the view from space hadn't seemed nearly as daunting as the vista spread out before them. This was going to be tougher than she had expected. Via his avatar, Lord Geo, Francis was already giving instructions to the team. That was his way. She called it *ready, fire, aim*. The instant he saw a challenge he tended to leap at it, guns blazing. "Shoot 'em all and let God sort them out later," he would say, laughing.

Not her. She was a *ready, aim, fire* kind of girl. When she'd once told this to Francis, he'd scoffed and laughed at her. "More like ready, ready, ready, aim, aim, aim, then step back and think about it, then find a side door to sneak through." She'd laughed too. He was right. More often than not, she found a way to reach the campaign objective by completely avoiding combat. Despite the fact they were twins, their respective approaches to the game were complete opposites. "It's why we make such a good team," Francis had once proclaimed.

Francis and the others ignored the vista. It wasn't the artistry of the lush forest or the glimmering lake that held their attention, or even the central island that rose from the water like a titanic stone spike. It was the citadel built upon the tip of the spike, where they knew a Bolo warlord named Jaspaar hoarded a stockpile of timedust. Smoke and intermittent tiny flashes could be seen around the base of the citadel. At least one competing team was already there, trying to gain entrance from the fortress defenders.

Francis cursed. He turned to her with an earnest look. "What do you think, Fi?"

A familiar wave of affection surged through her. Her brother was the only person on the planet who still treated her like a normal person. From the moment he'd first seen her at the hospital after the accident, he'd acknowledged her wounds as if they were nothing more serious than a skinned knee. Even after a year, Mama still sometimes stifled her tears whenever she saw Fiona. Not Francis. He'd told her over and over that it was *tough*, what had happened to her. *Tough.* That was the word he used. When he'd first said it to her, she'd choked back tears. *It's a little more than tough*, she'd wanted to scream. *Tough* was a word jocks like Francis used when consoling a friend who'd just lost a tennis match. *Tough* was the way you described failing an algebra test you'd studied hard for.

At first, she'd hated him for not appreciating the magnitude of her suffering. The way he'd smiled at her as if nothing were wrong at all. The way he'd pretended what had happened was a completely normal occurrence in the life of a teenager. Then, as the months had passed and her friends vanished because they couldn't look at her without crying, and as Mama was completely eaten by grief, only Francis had remained steady. He'd started going with her to the endless physical therapy sessions. He'd dropped out of soccer so he could help Mama with her home care. He'd even started sleeping in her room so he could help with the middle-of-the-night medicines and bloody dressing changes. As twins they shared a rare blood type, and he insisted on being the donor for her transfusions. Once the bandages and casts had come off, he'd discouraged her from covering the scars or wearing any of the prosthetics when they were alone together. He'd never once looked at her with horror or pity, even when the full extent of her transformation was revealed. He'd looked at her melted face with his clear brown eyes and simply said, "You're a mess, Fi."

In return, she felt a bewildering jumble of emotions toward her brother: guilt and gratitude, resentment and appreciation, jealousy and bitter remorse. Most of all, she felt overwhelming love. Even today, he wasn't here in their basement just to play this stupid video game. He was at her side on this couch because she needed him to be here with her. He was the nail to which the entire family's sanity hung like a framed photo, askew, but still clinging to the wall.

He was staring at her, waiting for an answer. She returned her attention to the television screen. She could see that from Jaspaar's vantage point on the tip of the central peak, he could easily target any boat on the sea, any climber on the central cone, and any approach by air. An overt attack wouldn't last five minutes. That left subterfuge. She pointed down the long slope of the crater wall toward a series of villages nestled along the lakeshore. "See that town? See the hoverbarge at the pier? I'll bet it's the supply boat for the citadel, and it looks like they're loading it now. If we can take that boat, we might be able to get across the lake without Jaspaar noticing."

They scrambled down the crater's rocky slope, eventually reaching the treeline and plunging into the forest that surrounded the lake. The landscape was rendered with exquisite detail, rough tree boles and mossy mounds amidst an understory of delicate plants and shrubs. The hushed sounds of her companions' movements filled her ears, prompting her imagination to provide the sensory inputs that her headset lacked: the sharp fragrance of fir trees, the softness of pine needles cushioning Gaia's feet.

Geo led the way, followed by Gaia and Tremendo. Their team bot, Gal'Blad, trailed in the manner of her kind, silent as a breeze, darting from tree to tree like a woodland ghost. In a clearing about halfway down, they paused and looked up as the shriek of a descending ship pierced the air. It was coming in fast, dropping recklessly from orbit and diving straight for the island citadel. Francis cursed. Another competing team had arrived.

A contrail of white rocket exhaust shot from the citadel and arced upwards. At the contrail's tip was the bright spark of an antiship missile. It moved with breathless speed, shrinking to a pinprick against the sky. With a tiny puff of smoke, it dissolved into a hundred glinting shards. The shards intersected the path of the descending ship.

Nothing happened, and Francis grimaced. Then the ship bloomed into a billowing smoke-cloud lit from within by orange flashes. Specks of debris mushroomed away from the detonation. Moments later, the thunder of the distant explosion rumbled the sky.

Francis gave her a wry, appreciative grin. Her insistence that they land the *Dagger* outside the crater had probably spared them a similar fate. "Let's go," he said into his headset. "They'll be more teams arriving soon, and Jaspaar won't be able to stop them all."

Bots

In the village they met their first native Gronean, a pale-skinned human named Reikan who was rushing to depart for the besieged island fortress along with a group of fisherfolk and merchants. The villagers had seen the attack on the citadel, Reikan explained, and even though they were not soldiers, they were compelled as subjects of their warlord to go and assist in its defense.

Fiona recognized Reikan and her companions as computer-generated, AI-controlled characters, commonly called *NPCs* (non-player characters) in other online roleplaying games but referred to as *bots* by the players of *Longstar*. If she and Francis had been playing this same campaign three months earlier, it would have been a simple matter to board the hoverbarge and ride along with the villagers. Until recently, bots had been like extras in a movie scene, background characters to provide a realistic atmosphere. You could talk to some of them, but they would respond only with canned replies that were preprogrammed. Sometimes you could learn useful information from a bot, but mostly their responses were just meaningless banter.

Two months earlier, all that had changed. The game designers at Orbital Arena had surprised their millions of subscribers with an unannounced and controversial update to the core AI systems. Now bots like Reikan and the villagers were so interactive that it was sometimes hard to tell them from a player avatar. You could have a complete conversation and forget that you were talking to the game's AI software instead of another player. They had personalities. They had memories. They could hold a grudge. Or, in this case, they could be suspicious of a bunch of heavily armed strangers who'd shown up without warning in their remote village. This meant that Francis's team couldn't just board the hoverbarge without negotiating with the wary villagers first.

Francis pulled Reikan to the side and spoke earnestly. He touched her shoulder a few times—quite awkwardly, Fiona thought—but eventually Reikan's frown became a cagey grin, and she shook Geo's hand. Even with the fluid controls of the game's specialized hand controller, it was still amazing to Fiona how her brother managed to broadcast his real-life charm through his avatar.

"What did you tell her?" Gal'Blad asked when Geo returned to the group.

"I told her we're mercenaries hired by Jaspaar, and that we've been called to help defend the citadel."

Gal'Blad twisted her mouthparts in the Ghast expression of doubt. "She bought that?"

"Yeah, well, I'm very persuasive."

"You promised her a cut of our loot, didn't you?"

"Maybe. Don't worry, I wasn't serious. She's just a bot."

The Ghast's frown deepened. "*Just* a bot?"

Next to her on the couch, Francis cursed softly. It was easy to forget that Gal'Blad was a bot, too, the only bot on their team of avatars. Before the controversial AI update, you never had to worry about hurting the feelings of the computer-controlled game characters. Back then, your team bot would mindlessly follow you around, carry whatever heavy load you gave it, and shoot at any enemy you designated. Now, they complained and griped and often had to be convinced to follow orders. A year ago, the highest-scoring players were those who, like Francis, had the fastest reflexes and had best mastered the combat aspects of the game. Since the update, the balance of power was quickly shifting to those players who could empathize and negotiate with the game's vast populations of bots.

Francis grimaced, and his on-screen avatar matched the expression. "Sorry, I didn't mean it that way."

Gal'Blad didn't reply, just clicked her mandibles in frustration and shook her head.

—

Movement. Gravity. Sound. Light and shadow. As always, the motions of the sky and forest obeyed the real-world rules of physics. This realism, though, came with a catch: the game ran only in real time, and often it took an annoyingly long time to get an avatar from point A to point B. The game designers usually compensated for this by providing instantaneous travel shortcuts like beamriders or jumpgates. Sometimes, though, you just had to endure excruciatingly long waits. The hoverbarge was faster than it looked, so the trip across the lake only lasted about ten minutes, during which time Francis used his avatar's electrospecs to zoom in on the citadel.

"Ah, crap," he muttered. "They've got Mucktu bots with them."

The villagers crowded around Geo, and he passed the electrospecs to Fiona's avatar, Gaia. She zoomed in on the citadel, its sun-bleached ramparts outlined starkly against the dark clouds of the approaching thunderstorm. Sure enough, most of the tiny figures crouching in the rocks around the citadel's base wore gray capes and colorful sashes over their battlesuits. That didn't prove that they were Mucktu, as the game had an infinite variety of costumes, but one of them was brandishing something that looked like a three-foot-long holiday sparkler. Showers of cinders and droplets of liquid fire defined the wide arcs of its swing. That settled it. It was a magical weapon, and only a Mucktu bot could use magic. The entire concept of magic was a recent and unexpected addition to the game, which had never before had fantasy elements. Gamers were complaining, but the magic-wielding bots kept popping up, so players were having to develop new tactics to deal with them.

"Yeah, they're definitely Mucktu," Fiona said. "One of them has a flickerblade."

Tremendo, a burly Forniculan avatar and the most unpredictable member of their team, loudly chambered a shell in his shotgun. "Been hoping to run into one of those creepy motherfuckers," he snarled.

The game hid the true genders and identities of their teammates and masked their voices with audio filters, but Fiona suspected that the player controlling Tremendo was some middle-school boy out in the sticks. His adolescent, trash-talking bravado was tiresome, but it didn't seem to bother Francis, so she put up with it. Tremendo had high marks in agility and strength and was good in close combat, better than anyone else on the team, so as far as Francis was concerned, his skill made up for his immaturity. "His avatar is Forniculan," her brother had once said with a wry grin. "From the Planet of Righteous Rage, right? They're supposed to be obnoxious. He's just roleplaying." Fiona wasn't sure it was just roleplaying, but Francis was right: Tremendo was good to have at your side in a scrap.

She heard an irritated alien growl in her headphones. Gal'Blad was gesturing toward the electrospecs. Fiona shook her head at the team bot, mouthing *sorry*. In the hands of a bot like Gal'Blad, the electrospecs would be useless. Players could share game items with a simple flick of the thumb on the game controller, but weapons and technological devices designed for avatars went completely inert and inoperative when given to a bot. This meant that while Gal'Blad could carry their heavy equipment and weapons, she could never use them. Since the recent AI upgrade, this had become a source of great frustration and resentment for their team bot. With a few exceptions, avatar weapons were far superior to those available to bots like her.

Fiona returned the device to her eyes. "I see at least a dozen Mucktu warlocks," she reported, "but I don't see any avatars leading the attack."

Next to her, on the couch, her brother looked nervous. "That's not right," he muttered. "Why would bots attack the citadel by themselves?"

As they approached the island, Reikan and the other villager bots took cover behind the raised steel ramp at the front of the hoverbarge. Fiona watched in fascination as they clutched their weapons and whispered to one another. She still wasn't accustomed to bots showing emotion, and she certainly wasn't used to them talking to each other. She couldn't hear their words over the rush of wind and the roar of the hoverbarge's engines, and she wondered, *What do computer-controlled characters say to each other? It's just the game's AI talking to itself, isn't it?*

She'd assumed that the new bot behaviors had been introduced to enhance the realism of the game experience, but that still didn't make it any less weird to watch them share anxious glances or show other subtle mannerisms, like nervously licking their lips or absently drumming their fingers on their knees. In some ways, the rendering of bot emotions was better than that of player avatars. Even though the headset face-cams did a pretty good job of translating a wearer's facial expressions to their avatar, sometimes the results were just a little *off*, just enough to be disconcerting. With the newly upgraded bots, though, there was no sign of this awkwardness. They looked completely and utterly natural, all of them showing a complex mix of fright and apprehension and determination.

A hundred yards from the island's landing pier, the hoverbarge slowed and sank to the water's surface. The concrete pier had been built at the water level and served as the foundation for a large, tracked elevator that rose up the steep mountainside to the citadel. Oddly, the pier was deserted. A flatbed cargo hauler had been wheeled to one corner near a few stacks of fishing nets. The dockmaster's shack was empty, and there were no other boats or any signs of workers or soldiers from the citadel. The gated elevator platform was locked, and the elevator car was absent, presumably at the top. The Mucktu they'd seen through the electrospecs had probably taken it up to the citadel.

Other than the soft lapping of lake water, the scene was silent. Unlike most video games, this one had no background music to set the tone. In other games, she'd learned to recognize cues in the music that inevitably hinted at what her avatar would encounter as she approached a new situation. When the music turned dark and scary, or suddenly increased in tempo, she knew to be on the lookout for trouble. When the music relaxed, she knew her avatar was in the clear. For whatever reason, the designers of *Longstar* had chosen to omit music, instead focusing on realistic environmental sounds that were much harder to interpret.

The sky rumbled with distant thunder, and Francis frowned. Gal'Blad absently rubbed her toxin sacs while her eyestalks scanned the scene. Even Tremendo seemed pensive. Something was wrong, and it didn't take Fiona's subtle sixth sense to know it.

"Where is everybody?" shouted Tremendo. He gestured toward the empty pier. "Hey, y'all assholes, show yourselves!"

The villagers glared and muttered at him. Francis shushed him angrily: "Quiet!" Her brother muted his mic and turned to her. "Okay, Fi, what do you think?"

—

They approached the pier. When no threats materialized, they pulled alongside and tied the hoverbarge to a concrete piling. The thundercloud they'd first seen looming over the far crater rim was almost upon them. Wind began to stir small waves in the lake as the forefront of the storm hove into view above the island peak. The clouds rumbled again, now much louder, and when she heard a blistering *crack! crack!*, Fiona assumed that lightning had struck the mountainside. It wasn't until Tremendo shouted that she looked up to see a pair of white contrails zooming away from the island peak and vanishing into the belly of the storm. A moment later the entire cloud glowed orange as the antiship missiles found their mark. A great, rolling *boom*, louder than thunder, echoed down. Moments later, a massive burning hulk fell out of the cloud and crashed into the lake halfway to the shore.

Francis eyed the wreckage as it vanished beneath the lake's surface. "We need to hurry." He glanced at the empty elevator platform, then up to the top of the peak, where the walls of the citadel were barely visible. Turning to Reikan, he asked, "How do we get up there?"

The villager bot looked scared. "I will summon the elevator."

Francis grimaced. The elevator ascended an exposed track up the side of the mountain. A shoulder-fired missile from a competing team could easily take it out. "Fi, there's gotta be another way, right?"

Fiona nodded. Most dungeons had multiple entrances. Some were more dangerous than others, with more traps and pitfalls. Some were time-wasting mazes or simple dead ends. Sometimes, if you were clever enough or knew a cheat code, you could find a back door that avoided most of the perils of the more obvious pathways. She scanned the mountainside above the pier. Too steep, too exposed. "Let's check the dockmaster's shed," she said. "It might have something useful."

They approached the structure carefully, weapons ready. Tremendo pointed. "Hey, what's that?"

Behind the shed, a metal bulkhead jutted from the rock face of the mountainside. On closer inspection they discovered that it held a rusted steel hatch embossed with the sigil of Jaspaar: a planet impaled on a sword.

Fiona nodded to Tremendo. His avatar grinned, tore the round handle from the hatch cover, and flung it out over the lake, Frisbee-style. The hatch creaked open a few inches. Tremendo counted silently to three, giving the others time to prepare, then slammed it fully open and thrust his shotgun into the darkness beyond.

Reikan and the villagers stared doubtfully toward the opening. Francis peeked inside. "Looks clear."

Fiona turned her avatar toward Tremendo. "Nice work."

His thick Forniculan face broke into a toothy smile.

Francis grimaced. "We're running out of time. Follow me."

They filed through the opening into a rough-hewn passageway. Francis and Reikan led the villagers, with Gal'Blad and Tremendo trailing the group as rear guard. Fiona immediately wished she'd taken more time to look for a different entrance. Choosing the most obvious route into a game dungeon was often a very bad idea.

The tunnel's walls were lumpy and corded with natural veins of volcanic rock, but the floor was smooth concrete, tracked and scuffed from passing feet and the tires of the cargo hauler they'd seen out on the pier. A brown stain streaked along the center of the floor from whatever leaky cargo had regularly passed through the tunnel. Above, an electrical cable had been strung along the ceiling, and at every few paces a dangling fixture dropped a pool of light onto the concrete.

Fiona tucked her avatar into its customary position behind Lord Geo. A villager bot fell into step beside her, a young man with sandy hair and the deeply tanned skin of a fisherman. He clutched an old-style hunting rifle. It would be useless against the futuristic sci-fi weapons of competing avatars they were sure to face, not to mention whatever nasty surprises the magic-wielding Mucktu bots might have in store.

She glanced at the boy, considered his work clothes and sun cap and determined expression. He wouldn't stand a chance. In this game, just like in most other online roleplaying games, AI-controlled bots like this boy were cannon fodder. They were the flying bodies in the backgrounds of battle scenes, the moaning and wounded soldiers you stepped on as you advanced across the field of play. Unlike avatars, bots didn't respawn. When you wasted a bot, it was gone forever. It didn't matter, though. The game produced what seemed like an endless supply. There were always more bots.

She almost jerked to a stop when the sandy-haired bot returned her stare and gave her a boldly flirtatious smile. She spun away, embarrassed, then cursed softly. This wasn't how Gaia should react. It's what Fiona would have done if a real boy in the real world had smiled at her. Truth be told, she'd never exactly been Miss Popularity at school, even before her injuries. She'd been the girl in a middle row of the classroom, the girl nobody ever noticed, the girl reading ahead in the textbook because the teacher was going too slowly.

It was a different story here in the gameworld. Her avatar, Gaia, was a lithe and cunning Dryan-scout with flowing hair, piercing eyes, and an athletic body she'd spent hours shaping and decorating with camouflaged war paint. Gaia wore neither bulky armor nor a battlesuit. If an attacker got past Francis, she'd be toast anyway, so why bother? Her only defense, which Francis had insisted upon, was a sleekly molded breastplate with delicate, winglike shoulder guards that doubled as stealthshield generators. That, and a pair of steel gauntlets that adorned her forearms simply because they looked cool.

The sandy-haired bot continued to steal glances at her. Fiona felt her face flush. She almost laughed at herself. She was reacting to an artificially generated character in a video game. She scowled at the TV screen. "What are you looking at?"

The bot's eyes sprang wide, and he almost stumbled. He was *afraid* of her. Afraid of Gaia's dangerous beauty. Fiona tried to smile at him, but something all too familiar echoed hollowly inside her chest, a soundless scream, the same scream that had been trapped inside her since the accident. She wasn't Gaia. She could never be Gaia. She was a fourth-degree burn survivor with permanently scorched lungs. She would forever require supplemental oxygen to breathe, a catheter to pee, and a wheelchair to get around.

Early on at the hospital, she and Francis had overheard a doctor tell Mama that due to the severity of her injuries she would never be eligible for a lung transplant. He'd tried to sound reassuring and optimistic, but his words had been chilling: *there are several excellent continual care facilities near your home, Mrs. Martinez. They have everything your daughter will need.*

Continual care. The doctor had been hinting that Mama didn't have the resources at home to properly care for her. That she'd be better off in a nursing home. And it was true. Just keeping up with her meds was a full-time job. Juggling her homeschooling, her physical therapy and occupational therapy sessions, her meetings with the psychologist and the endless trips to various doctor's offices was more than anyone could manage.

Francis put his hand on her shoulder. "Don't get distracted," he said gently. "We need you."

Cavern

The foamy volcanic rock of the tunnel walls absorbed the clatter of their footsteps as they led the villagers deeper into the mountain. Fiona kept her avatar close behind Francis, moving warily but quickly. Both of them knew this wouldn't be an ordinary game dungeon, because Grone wasn't an ordinary planet.

The Grone expansion had been teased for months on Orbital Arena's social media, but today's release had come as a complete surprise. Normally, the company issued small updates every Friday afternoon, timed to allow a full weekend's play. Two or three times a year, however, Orbital Arena surprised the player community by releasing a major expansion to the game map at a random time on a random day. It was a *big* deal when this happened. Fiona had seen news stories about how the last couple of surprise releases had caused a measurable dip in the national economy as millions of players had neglected their weekday jobs to log on and play the update.

The real surprise had come when Francis's phone had buzzed during his bus ride home from school. Due to some miracle, or maybe because of his recent high scores, Francis had received a prenotification from the game company, two hours earlier than the public notice. Knowing they had a head start, the moment he'd arrived home, he and Fiona had frantically logged on to the game and tried to gather their teammates aboard the *Dagger*. Unfortunately, the timing of the surprise announcement meant that most of their regular teammates were caught offline. Only Tremendo had been available—he'd claimed he was home sick—and there'd been no time to wait for the others. The three of them—Geo, Gaia, and Tremendo—plus their team bot, Gal'Blad, had made a mad dash to the planet Grone, arriving a full hour before the raging masses even knew it existed.

It was a rare opportunity to be the first on scene at a new campaign world and its dozens of unspoiled game dungeons. Fiona knew their advantage wouldn't last. In living rooms and dorms and basements all over the world, gamers were logging on to discover the new campaign. Over the next few hours, thousands of players would be descending from orbit to raid the planet's treasures, the first waves of many to come. If previous map expansions were any indication, the coming days and weeks would see a series of massive battles in orbit and planetside between the game's top teams as they fought to capture the planet and its hidden treasures for their respective virtual empires.

Grone was an even more exciting expansion than most. Not only had the planet been featured in an episode of *Longstar's Rangers*, the television series on which the game was based, but it had been the setting for the season 1 finale, a cliffhanger episode called "Game Changer." Knowing this, as soon as the *Dagger* had made orbit around Grone, Fiona had quickly pointed out the crater citadel among the many potential dungeon sites. "That's the boss dungeon," she'd said with complete certainty.

While dozens of lesser dungeons lay scattered across a gameworld like Grone, there was always only one boss dungeon, and the first teams to successfully complete its challenges came away vastly enriched. The boss dungeon was where the Gamemaster hid the best loot, but it was also the lair of the baddest baddies and the most puzzling puzzles. For Grone, the location of the boss dungeon could only be the crater citadel of the villainous Jaspaar, as seen in the "Game Changer" episode.

Normally, Francis would never attempt a boss dungeon with less than a dozen high-level avatars on his team. Today, they would try it with only three, plus the capable Gal'Blad. It was a pitifully small force, but if they moved fast, they had a decent chance to snag a few of the citadel's choicest treasures. They wouldn't have time to delve too deeply or locate the boss monster they knew lurked in the deepest crypts, but it didn't matter. In the *Longstar* game, it usually took the coordinated efforts of many teams and often multiple attempts over weeks of time to defeat a boss. Based on "Game Changer," Fiona suspected that the boss beneath Jaspaar's citadel would be difficult indeed. Best to avoid it completely—as first on scene, they would have their pick of the dungeon's lesser treasures without risking a confrontation they could not win. By the time the avatar empires and their galactic fleets arrived to mount a serious challenge to the boss, they would be long gone, the *Dagger*'s holds stuffed with loot, including, hopefully, some of the stuff of legend, the most valuable substance in the game universe: *timedust*.

The tunnel bored straight and level into the core of the mountain. There were no side junctions from which enemies might spring. There were no pitfalls or traps. This worried Fiona. The most valuable treasures in a game dungeon were usually reached through a complex maze, not a straight tunnel, and were guarded by an increasingly dangerous array of defenses. They should've encountered at least a few of the citadel's defenders by now. She knew from the TV episode that Jaspaar had a powerful army to protect his huge deposits of timedust and the subterranean lab where his most horrific secret was concealed.

The ease of their progress might also be good news, as sometimes game designers included a back door through which a clever avatar might bypass the worst of a game's traps. Unfortunately, she wasn't feeling especially clever, and as their passage through the tunnel continued without event, she began to suspect they'd been lured into a time-wasting dead end.

When the end of the corridor appeared in the distance, she felt both relief and apprehension. Geo motioned for the rear guard to move to the front. Tremendo and Gal'Blad hurried to his side, the villagers spreading apart to give the Forniculan and the Ghast a wide berth. Geo whispered something to Tremendo and they both raised their weapons. Gal'Blad's throat turned a bright yellow as her toxin sacs began to inflate. A wave of nervous chatter passed through the villagers. Geo motioned for silence.

The passage ended at an open doorway. The thick metal door, corroded by rust, looked like it had been propped open a century ago and not closed since. Geo pointed his flashlight into the opening. Beyond the doorway lay a natural cavern as big as a high-school gymnasium. It formed a perfect sphere, like an air bubble frozen within the gut of the mountain, perhaps a result of the same molten volcanic burps that had formed the tunnel through which they'd just passed. Once again, Fiona marveled at the game designer's skill and attention to detail. She was no geology nerd, but the moisture-glistened walls of ropey volcanic rock looked perfectly real.

At a gesture from Geo, the others moved aside for Fiona's avatar. She crouched and directed the beam of her flashlight into the cavern, searching for clues left by the Gamemaster. The passageway opened into the spherical cavity near its bottom. Her flashlight had range enough to illuminate most of the rugged bowl-shape beneath her, but the widening dome above was mostly shadows.

A concrete ramp angled down from her position toward a circular pool at the bottom of the bubble-cave. The ramp continued into the pool and emerged from the other side, rising up to another door on the opposite wall of the cave. A smooth-sided stone spike about the height of a person rose from the center of the pool. Dank, irregular lumps of some soggy material lay scattered in the dark water, half submerged. The stain that they'd followed along the tunnel floor continued down the ramp to the pool. Over the years, many somethings had been dragged from the water and carted through the tunnel, dripping along the way.

Fiona frowned. This cavern had not appeared in the TV episode. On the show, most of the action had taken place up in the mountaintop citadel, though in the final act, the villain Jaspaar had revealed underground passages that led to his secret laboratory. That meant this cave came solely from the mind of the Gamemaster, and Fiona knew his trademark tricks. There would be something out of place, some faint clue, carefully obscured but visible to anybody who looked hard enough.

She swept her flashlight around the periphery of the cave. Other than the doorway in the opposite wall, there were no other exits. Her glance rose to the top center of the cavern, directly above the spike. Barely visible was a dark, circular opening, about a yard across and obviously leading up into the core of the mountain. She suspected it led all the way to the citadel on the summit, through hundreds of feet of solid rock. She stuck out her bottom lip, an expression that was faithfully mirrored by her avatar.

"Careful. Something's not right."

"Yeah, it stinks," said Gal'Blad. "It's worse than the toilet in the *Dagger*."

"You can *smell?*"

The Ghost shrugged. Since Gal'Blad was a bot native to the virtual environment, she apparently had senses the avatars lacked. It was interesting that the game designer had gone to the trouble to include *odors* in the game. Until somebody invented a virtual digital nosepiece, players would never be able to smell things in the game universe. "What does it smell like?"

Gal'Blad eyed the soaking lumps in the dark pool. "Like rotting meat."

Following Geo's silent gestures, the villagers moved down the ramp and began to fan out around the scary-looking pool at the center.

Trailing the others, Reikan whispered something to Geo. Francis frowned.

"What did she say?" prompted Fiona.

"She said that if we don't find a way up to the citadel and go to Jaspaar's aid, he'll burn their village."

"Of course he will." In the TV episode, Jaspaar had at first seemed friendly. He had quickly revealed his true colors when he'd kidnapped one of the Ranger Cadets and forced him to work in his timedust laboratory, where he was developing a machine to harness the power of timedust for a superweapon. Many of the show's episodes had featured megalomaniacal villains, but few had been as diabolical as Jaspaar.

They reached the bottom of the ramp. Geo shined his flashlight at one of the misshapen lumps in the central pool. "Eew," he said. He'd found the source of the smell: a decomposing human body, savagely crushed and splattered as if it had fallen from a great height. He turned his flashlight straight up at the hole in the ceiling, and then back down at the spike. The spike was streaked with the same dark stains as the disgusting liquid in the pool at its base. There were other shapes in the pool, too, not all of them human, but all in various states of boggy rot.

A watery sound drew Fiona's attention to another corpse, this one wrapped in the tattered blue fabric of a Ranger Cadet uniform from the TV show. A bulge the size of a clenched fist stirred just beneath the uniform jacket, no doubt some hideous cave slug devouring the flesh of the victim.

In "Game Changer," Jaspaar had murdered an unnamed Ranger Cadet by means of a hidden trapdoor in his throne room. Fiona grinned ruefully. The episode hadn't disclosed the murdered cadet's fate, but here in the game, his final resting place was revealed in gruesome detail that would have never been allowed on 1970s television. She relished the little touches of nerdy authenticity from the Gamemaster, details extrapolated from the episode's script, entire settings derived from a passing comment by one of the show's main characters.

Something was in the corpse's pocket. Something she recognized. She moved closer, marveling at the effort that had gone into its appearance. The level of detail was astonishing, from the gaping holes in the flesh and the stringy, maggot-infested viscera within, to the finely woven texture of the uniform fabric.

She removed a blue plastic card from the dead cadet's pocket. It had a magnetic stripe on one side and the planet-and-sword symbol of Jaspaar imprinted on the other.

Next to her, Francis made an appreciative noise. He also recognized the keycard as a security access badge from "Game Changer." It would give them a way to open security doors throughout the citadel complex. "Nice work," he murmured.

Gaia and Geo held their positions at the foot of the entrance ramp while the villagers explored the cavern. She recognized her brother's strategy: if there were any hidden traps, the bots would be the victims, not the avatars. He gestured to the entrance on the opposite wall. "That way? What do you think, Fi?"

Fiona cringed. This bubble cavern was a combat encounter space, she was sure of it. They wouldn't get out of here easily. The first wave of game nastiness would come at any moment. Something would erupt from the pool, or fall from the hole in the ceiling, or maybe the ropey basalt of the cavern walls would turn out to be the tentacles of a horrific beast. Whatever form the dungeon's initial challenge would come in, its arrival was imminent.

The noise came first, a faint echo of running feet. Francis waved to the others. The villagers froze; their murmurs of conversation stopped. The echoing footfalls circulated within the spherical cavern, making it impossible to tell from which direction they came.

Tremendo pointed his shotgun at one entrance, then other. The villagers swung their primitive weapons in wide, unsure arcs.

Something plinked into the dark pool, causing a slow ripple in the thick fluid. A drop of water? A pebble, dislodged from above? All weapons swung in unison to the hole in the ceiling. Murmurs from the villagers. Metallic snicks and clicks of weapons being readied. Silence stretched tightly while they waited for whatever surprise might emerge. Tremendo appeared at her side, crouched low, a savage grin on his face.

"Party time," he whispered.

Most of the villagers were clustered around the pool and its gruesome spike. Everyone stared at the hole in the ceiling, where the beams from their flashlights converged. The rest of the cavern fell into inky darkness.

Silence. The approaching footsteps had stopped. It occurred to Fiona that the footfalls couldn't have come from the hole in the ceiling unless their maker could defy gravity. She looked toward the door on the opposite wall.

There. A flicker. The dim beam of a flashlight, quickly extinguished. A small figure emerged from the doorway. It paused awkwardly at the top of the ramp when it saw the crowd of villagers, then slipped over the ramp's side into the shadows.

"Did you see that?" Fiona asked Francis.

"See what?"

She pointed at the television. "Something came through that doorway. It's hiding down behind the ramp."

"What was it?"

"I couldn't tell."

Francis was already on the move. He raced his avatar around the pool, slowing as he approached the ramp. He swung his weapon over the edge.

Nothing.

"Are you sure you saw something?"

"I'm sure."

Fiona turned her avatar in a slow circle, scanning the cavern for movement.

"Over there," shouted Tremendo. He swung his weapon's attached light toward the rear wall. Defined in the circle of light, a humanoid figure was scrambling along the curved wall, laboring under the weight of a backpack. When it threw a hand up to block the light, Fiona saw that it was a human girl. An oversized Army-style helmet and camo-patterned combat fatigues swallowed her form, as if somebody had stuffed a ballerina into the uniform of a burly commando. After a moment's hesitation, the girl continued climbing along the wall.

Francis frowned. "That's not right."

Before Francis could explain, Tremendo shouted again. "Incoming!"

A pillar of swirling light had formed between Gaia and the pool at the bottom of the cavern. An avatar was spawning, but how? The nearby villagers scrambled away from the solidifying column of sparks.

"That's *definitely* not right," Francis murmured. Avatars couldn't simply spawn into a dungeon. When a player started a new game or reentered a game after a break or after their avatar was killed, their avatar always spawned at a defined start location or the closest save point. This cavern was neither.

The spawn-light faded and resolved into a humanoid figure, but the newcomer was most certainly not human. It was tall and spindly, with a wasp's slender waist, smooth red feathers, and pale flowing hair.

Fiona's headphones crackled. Tremendo whispered, "Oh, fuck."

The villagers turned their weapons on the newly spawned avatar. A dozen red targeting dots danced on its graceful form. The avatar ignored the villagers. Its head moved in jerky circles as it scanned the cavern, like a praying mantis searching for prey. After a moment it locked onto the location of the fleeing human girl. It sprang in her direction.

"Nobody shoot!" shouted Francis. He turned to Fiona. "Is that a Wrathwraith?"

Fiona flicked her trackball toward the waspish figure. As her cursor slid across the avatar, a glowing focus aura outlined its figure and its profile popup flickered on the television screen. It was indeed a Wrathwraith, one of the rarest of all character species, available only to those players willing to fork up a ridiculous premium payment during character creation. It was easily recognizable because a picture of one of the gangly aliens graced the cover of the game's packaging and website. But it wasn't the avatar's species that had prompted Tremendo's curse. "It's an archangel," Fiona breathed. "Francis, look! It's an archangel!"

Suddenly this was no longer just another campaign and certainly not just another dungeon. Francis nodded grimly. "Let's hope she's friendly."

War of the Archangels

The *Longstar* game had ninety-nine regular achievement levels, the lowest of which was Rookie 01 and the highest Galactic Master 99. Fiona, after three months of solid daily play, had earned a level of Initiate 26, while Francis, who'd been playing longer and had much better combat skills, had advanced to Warrior 53. There were only a certain number of slots at each level, so as you advanced, you had to knock somebody out of an existing slot, and the higher you got, the fewer slots there were. By the time you reached the 90s and the Galactic Master levels, there was only one slot per level, so the competition among the very best players was incredibly fierce. The latest Galactic Master 99 was an avatar named Torax who had alternated in and out of the position for several months. Players like Torax had millions of followers on their game-streams and made millions of dollars from product endorsements, just like real-world athletes. They were professional gamers. They competed in gaming tournaments for big prize money. *Longstar* was their day job, and they were its superstars.

As rarified as Torax's position was, there were rumors of another, even higher, achievement level: *Archangel 100*. Nobody knew what it took to gain level 100, and sightings of a level 100 avatar in the game were so rare that most players believed they were a hoax. The archangel level didn't appear on any score leaderboards, nor in any game documentation. And yet, the character profile popup didn't lie. Right there on the TV screen, the proof floated above the approaching avatar's head in unmistakable letters:

AVATAR PROFILE: OAONE
Species: WRATHWRAITH
Level: ARCHANGEL 100
Health: 651/1,000 (YELLOW)

Oaone. A bizarre name. Fiona quickly called up the game's on-screen reference and scrolled down to the "W" section. Wrathwraiths could change color like a chameleon and possessed a vicious sonic-attack feat. A wraith-scream from a low-level avatar could paralyze an attacker, and one from an archangel-level wraith would likely reduce everyone in the cavern to jelly smears on the floor.

Fiona moved the trackball cursor to the archangel's quarry, the fleeing girl in the ill-fitting camo-fatigues. Nothing happened. No glowing focus aura surrounded her to show she was selected as a target, and no profile popup appeared. Fiona jiggled the trackball and moved the cursor over the figure again. Still nothing. She frowned. Even if the character was a computer-generated bot, the on-screen popup should show its character species and health. She tried again. Still nothing. For some reason, the cursor was passing over the girl as if she were a nonselectable game object, like a boulder or a tree. Fiona spun the trackball and pointed at the villager Reikan. The bot's focus aura glowed predictably, and the popup hovered over her head:

NPC PROFILE: **REIKAN**
Species: **HUMAN**
Health: **12/12 (GREEN)**

Francis had noticed the lack of a profile popup too, but he didn't say anything. His avatar, Geo, lowered his weapon and called for everyone to do the same. There was no other option. An archangel could easily kill them all, armed or not. It moved with the suppleness of an avatar whose player was wearing an expensive, full-motion VR rig. Its skin was covered in delicate red feathers that faded to a translucent white on its face and neck, morphing into clear strands of fiber, as light as a spider's web, that streamed from its scalp. Compared to its human prey, it was impossibly thin and gangly, and its neck and limbs were long and deceptively fragile.

The two scrambling figures, tracked by the light from a dozen flashlights, were nearing a narrow ledge halfway up the bowl of the cavern. The girl in the fatigues wasn't going to make it, Fiona realized. With a long, graceful leap, the wraith tackled her prey, pinning her to the cavern wall with thin arms. The girl cried out and tried to fight, but despite the ethereal thinness of the wraith, her struggles made no difference. The wraith spoke to the girl angrily, but Fiona couldn't make out the words.

Shouts from the villagers distracted her from the wraith. Next to the pool, another whirling column of glitter had sprouted from the damp stone.

The Wrathwraith saw it, too. With a sweep of her thin arm she forced her prisoner behind her, shielding the girl from the apparition that was taking shape inside the sparkling cloud.

A second avatar was spawning. Within the mass of sparkles, a shadowy figure resolved into a male human with white skin and shaggy hair. He wore clothes typical of a human rogue avatar: rugged boots, tight pants, and a leather flight jacket covered in faded patches. Fiona rolled her trackball cursor over the new arrival. The avatar lit up, and his profile popup appeared:

AVATAR PROFILE: **ATUM**
Species: **HUMAN**
Level: **ARCHANGEL 100**
Health: **225/1,000 (ORANGE)**

Francis expelled a breath. It was *another* archangel-level avatar.

The Wrathwraith fell into a defensive pose. A gleaming, oversized weapon appeared in her slender hands. Fiona didn't recognize it, but Tremendo jabbered excitedly. "It's a gobsmacker! Jesus, Geo, she's got a goddammed gobsmacker. Now *that'll* even the odds. Woo hoo!"

Next to her, on the couch, Francis leaned toward the television. They'd stumbled into an ongoing battle between two archangel-level players, either of whom could dispatch their entire team with the flick of a fingertip on a game controller.

The new archangel, Atum, didn't hesitate. He leaped toward the Wrathwraith and, in midleap, pulled a silver revolver from a holster at his waist.

The Wrathwraith's gobsmacker detonated with a tremendous *whoop*. Atum flew backward and slammed into the cavern floor. The villagers shrieked and scrambled away, clutching their ears, deafened by the blast. Francis murmured into his headset. "Nobody move. Don't shoot." He turned to Fiona. "Get back. Use your stealthshield."

The gobsmacker blast would have pulped a lower-level avatar, but the archangel Atum sprang up instantly. In the brief moment it took the gobsmacker to recharge, he was on the Wrathwraith, his pistol spitting fire. Several bullets splashed into Oaone's torso, causing her focus aura to flash red. Fiona wondered why she didn't defend herself with her primary feat, the wraith-scream? A sonic attack delivered by an archangel-level wraith would without a doubt kill everybody and everything in the cavern. *Including the girl in the baggy combat fatigues she is obviously trying to capture*, Fiona realized.

Before the injured Wrathwraith could fire again, her target, the archangel Atum, flickered and pixelated, hesitating oddly, his motion stuttering and fitful. Fiona recognized the effect. Whoever was controlling the Atum avatar had a bad wifi connection. She heard his voice cry out, oddly modulated by the poor connection. "Aa nn ah lees," he said. "R u u nn!"

Fiona tried to make sense of the sounds. *Analise, run?*

Several things happened at once. The human girl jumped on the Wrathwraith's slender back, causing it to stumble. The gobsmacker fired but missed, pulverizing a section of the cavern ceiling, which showered down on the villagers, prompting another panicked surge of the crowd.

At the same time, something clattered down the opposite ramp and splashed into the pool at the center of the cavern. "Grenade!" shouted Gal'Blad, but there wasn't time to react. The TV screen went white. A shattering explosion overloaded the speakers in Fiona's headset, far louder than anything else she'd ever heard through the device, loud enough to leave her ears ringing. Francis cursed and yanked off his headset, staring at it in disbelief. When the white glare on the screen began to subside into thick smoke, he quickly put it back on.

On the TV, human-size figures were pouring into the cavern from the opposite entrance. They moved with the coordinated skill and precision of an elite fighting squad. They seemed surprised by the presence of the villagers, whom they quickly surrounded.

Their leader shouted at the villagers, "Weapons down! Lower your weapons, now!"

Confusion and suspicion rippled through the crowd, but most complied with the soldier's order. The man turned to his companions. "Spread out. She's in here somewhere."

The newcomers wore the same style of combat uniform as the girl being pursued by the Wrathwraith, but unlike the petite girl, they were thickly muscular and heavily armed. When Fiona highlighted their leader, a profile popup appeared of a type she'd never before seen:

SOLOMON, COL
SPEC | AR | BRAVO

She didn't have time to consider the meaning of the popup's contents. "There! And there!" cried Solomon, pointing at both Archangel avatars. The newcomers opened fire with what sounded like machine guns. They seemed to be targeting the archangel Atum, carefully avoiding everyone else. Atum staggered back. His health aura flashed red.

He stumbled and fell. The latency of his bad wifi connection meant that he could neither dodge the bullets nor counterattack. His avatar blinked, dissolved into colorful static, and vanished, a sure sign that whoever had been controlling the avatar had lost their internet connection. The roar of the machine guns stopped, revealing the anguished screams of the mysterious girl.

The soldiers quickly attempted to surround the archangel Oaone. They held their fire, perhaps fearing they might hit the girl. Were they trying to rescue her? They were wearing the same style of uniform, after all. Oaone stumbled but continued to drag the girl up the wall toward the ledge.

What was special about the ledge? It was narrow and precarious and provided no protection that Fiona could see. The surrounding cavern walls were identical to the rest of the cavern. Nevertheless, it was clearly the archangel's goal. Was there a weapon or special item up on the ledge, or maybe a hidden exit?

A bright spear of light lit the entire cavern, and a section of the wall behind Gaia blossomed into a meter-wide ball of flame. An energy bolt had come from the opposite doorway.

Another flash, and a second blinding bolt of energy screamed out of the tunnel. It exploded on the wall behind Geo and Gaia, producing a rain of stone shards that peppered their avatars.

"That's a vortex gun," muttered Francis. Yet another competing team had arrived.

A moment of silence, then a furious barrage of vortex bolts. The new team swarmed out of the tunnel and down the ramp in a gray flood. Oaone dropped into an offensive pose and raised her weapon. Freed from her grasp, the girl bolted away from her captor.

Tremendo howled an inarticulate rebel yell and started shooting, at whom Fiona couldn't tell. The din drowned out Francis as he shouted into his headset microphone. "Damn it, Tremendo, hold your fire!"

The breathtaking *whoop* of Oaone's gobsmacker sounded. Several of the gray-caped newcomers exploded into streamers of red mist. The camo-wearing soldiers also turned their weapons on the newcomers. Tremendo discharged his shotgun again, and several of the soldiers returned fire. Gal'Blad leaped away from her overzealous teammate, tackling Fiona's avatar and rolling her away from the hail of bullets. Tremendo went down, his health score dropping far faster than it should have from weapons as primitive as machine guns. His aura flashed red, and his avatar dissolved. He was gone. A line of bullets powdered the volcanic rock just a few feet from Fiona's avatar, and Francis barked, "Stealth, Fi! Do it, now!"

With a clumsy flick of her wrist, Fiona jerked her avatar away from Gal'Blad's protective embrace and back into the shadows behind Geo. She activated her stealthshield. Her ruined hand was no good at aiming, and besides, her primary weapon, the flamethrower, was out of fuel. If she hid in the shadows, maybe nobody would see past the mirrorlike glimmer of her stealthshield.

The soldiers shifted their aim to Geo. Francis cursed. He jerked and twisted as he fought with the game controller. On the TV, his avatar's aura flashed yellow, orange, then red, then dissolved.

He threw his controller on the couch and pounded his fist on the armrest. "That's the *last* time I take Tremendo on my team. He's an idiot!"

There was nothing to do but wait until Francis's avatar respawned at the last save point, which was probably outside the mountain back at the lakeside pier. It would take forever for him to rejoin the fray.

Fiona moved Gaia until she was crouching in the shadow of the ramp. She studied the situation. It looked like a free-for-all, but she knew better. They were in the middle of a multiteam melee, and if they were to survive, she'd need to figure out who was fighting whom, and why. As far as she could tell, there were at least three different groups of combatants. Four, if you counted the archangel Atum, who'd already been killed.

First was the Wrathwraith, Oaone, who was trying to protect her captive, the girl in the baggy combat fatigues. Second were the soldiers in the camo-fatigues, who were obviously trying to capture, or perhaps rescue, the girl. Third were the newcomers pouring in from the rear tunnel. They were attacking the Wrathwraith *and* the soldiers, and they also seemed to be trying to capture the girl.

Unlike the soldiers, who looked like something from real-world TV news, the newest arrivals at least looked like they belonged in the game. They wore 1970s-era science fiction costumes typical for the TV show: brightly colored spandex tights with thick plastic belts, wide shoulder wings, and ashen capes. A quick flick of the trackball confirmed her suspicions. They were all bots, non-player characters generated by the game's AI, which meant they were either adversaries programmed into the dungeon by the Gamemaster or members of a competing team under the control of an avatar who had not yet made an appearance.

One of the bots wore a crimson sash around his waist. He swung a bladed weapon whose shaft trailed a shower of sparks and liquid fire. The blade sliced effortlessly through the torso of a soldier, who fell in two pieces. The intruders must be Mucktu, maybe the same Mucktu they'd seen from the hoverbarge through Geo's electrospecs. It occurred to her that these Mucktu bots had probably been under the control of the slain archangel Atum. That would explain why they were continuing his effort to kill the Wrathwraith. They hadn't arrived in time to save their master, but as his loyal team bots, they were continuing his fight.

So, it was *Wrathwraith* vs. *soldiers* vs. *Mucktu bots*. They were all vying for control of the girl in the baggy clothes and completely ignoring the villagers. None of this made sense; nothing like this had happened in the TV episode on which this game dungeon was based. Fiona searched the smoke-filled cavern for Oaone and her captive, both of whom had vanished in the confusion. She spotted the Wrathwraith retreating into the shadows, her skin-feathers having shifted to match the color of the dark volcanic walls. She was heading for the girl, who had slid down the cavern wall and was kneeling in the spot where the archangel Atum had been killed. The girl was frantically searching for something. She picked up a small item, stuffed it in her pack, then began climbing back up toward the ledge. She wasn't going to make it. The archangel was too fast.

A soldier saw the Wrathwraith and took careful aim. A single burst from his curiously powerful machine gun was enough. Oaone's aura turned solid red. Already injured from her brief battle with Atum, she exploded into a cloud of dust, the contents from her item stash clattering down the rough wall and lodging in cracks and crevices. Fiona looked at the loot and almost laughed. If Tremendo, the idiot, hadn't gotten himself killed, he might have been able to retrieve her gobsmacker.

The soldier lowered his weapon with an expression of great relief, as if he'd just slain a dragon. He had a broad face and a wide, dimpled chin. His popup identified him as Solomon, the same avatar she'd identified earlier as the leader of the soldiers. Solomon looked toward the girl, who had fallen from the blast of the archangel's disintegration. He and another soldier raced toward her. Fiona flicked her cursor over the second soldier's avatar. Nothing happened. No popup appeared. Like the girl in the baggy clothes, this guy didn't seem to have an avatar profile.

The girl glanced toward the approaching soldiers. Instead of rushing to join them as Fiona had expected, she scrambled toward the loot dropped by Oaone. She grabbed a couple of small items and stuffed them in her backpack, then resumed her frantic climb toward the ledge.

The soldier with Solomon, the one with no avatar profile, called out, "Analise! Stop!"

The running girl ignored him. He raised his rifle.

Solomon shouted, "Wolfe, no!" He reached toward his companion, but the gun barked. The girl crumpled to the ground. Solomon tore the gun from Wolfe's hands. "Are you fucking *crazy*?"

Pandemonium erupted. The horde of gray-caped Mucktu bots, still growing as new arrivals streamed in from the tunnel, made a frenzied, hacking charge into the line of soldiers. Another grenade went off. The villagers panicked and the situation dissolved into chaos, bots screaming and darting for protection, but there was none to be had. The combined effects of gravity and the spherical shape of the cavern forced the combatants into a cluster at the bottom, like marbles in a soup bowl, making it impossible to fire their weapons without hitting members of their own team. The roar of gunfire subsided and was replaced by the desperate gasps and grunts of hand-to-hand combat.

The flickerblade-wielding Mucktu had the advantage. Fiona saw the sandy-haired village boy killed in a slash of flame. She watched as his body rolled down the slope and into the foul pool at the center. A pang of regret twisted her heart. He was just a bot, but these upgraded bots were almost like people.

The Mucktu in the red sash shouted and threw something high into the air. The cavern instantly filled with black smoke. In the darkness, the sounds of combat intensified, grew more desperate. Fiona waited and watched as her stealthshield's power bar slowly dropped to zero. She was no longer invisible. Francis was squirming impatiently on the couch. Why hadn't his avatar respawned yet? Without Geo, Gaia was helpless to defend herself.

They both jumped when Francis's phone buzzed on the couch's armrest. He glanced down and canceled the call, instantly returning his attention to the TV screen. Fiona had seen the phone display and did not recognize the number. The caller ID had said it was from Palo Alto. A wrong number, or a spam call.

Something monstrous moved on the dark TV screen. Despite herself, Fiona jerked and almost knocked her controller off the arm of her wheelchair. Even Francis, still fuming next to her on the couch, startled.

Then he laughed. It was Gal'Blad, their team bot. Of all the alien species in the game, the Ghast were the scariest.

Francis choked on his laugh. Gal'Blad was carrying something.

The girl named Analise.

Blood dripped from the gunshot wound in the girl's shoulder. She looked directly at Fiona's avatar, her eyes dull with shock. *She must be some kind of bot*, Fiona realized. *Player avatars don't ever look or act so sluggish, even when they're badly wounded.*

During the melee, Analise had lost her ridiculously oversized combat helmet. Tangled red hair, thick with dust and blood, fell across her face. Despite her small stature, she was older than Fiona had first thought. Not a girl. A woman, maybe in her late twenties.

The girl cried out. Her body spasmed, fell limp.

Francis gasped and Fiona felt her heart clench. They both knew real trauma. They'd both lived through it. This avatar, or bot, or whatever she was, was *hurt*. Badly. The image was far more disturbing than anything either of them had ever seen in the game.

Gal'Blad lowered her eyestalks toward the woman in her arms. "Two archangels were fighting over this person. Obviously, she is important. What do you want to do?"

"Look at her uniform," Francis mumbled. "That can't be right."

Unlike any bot or avatar Fiona had ever seen, there was nothing sci-fi or futuristic about the woman's attire or appearance. In fact, an American flag patch was sewn to her uniform, a clear anachronism. In the game, like the TV show, there was no United States. The nations of Earth had long ago been absorbed into a planetary government. Was the uniform some kind of new costume mod, released as a part of the expansion? Or could it be a clue to the secrets of this campaign?

Francis gestured toward the television. "These guys should be in *Call of Duty*, not *Longstar*. That's a U.S. Marine Corps uniform, and those are M27 rifles the soldiers are using. Maybe they're hackers or something. American marines with M27s don't exist in this game."

Arni

The phone buzzed again. This time it was a video call, from the same California number as before. Francis frowned, picked up the phone, and tapped the answer button. A stranger's face appeared on the screen. Before Francis could say "hello," the man was already talking. No, he was *shouting*. "Please don't hang up!" He was wearing a bulky, expensive-looking VR headset, the visor flipped up to reveal a narrow face, dark eyes, and brown skin. "I'm with Orbital Arena Games. The company that makes the game you're playing right now."

Francis glanced at Fiona. He held the phone so she could better see the caller. The man looked terrified.

"I'm trying to reach Francis Martinez," he said. He looked down at something, probably his computer screen. "Are you Francis? You play the avatar called Geo?"

Francis narrowed his eyes. "Who wants to know?"

The man on the phone sounded exasperated. "Listen to me. I play an avatar named Atum. I'm looking for Fiona Martinez. She doesn't have a phone number on her game account, but I can see that you're both logged on from the same IP address. She's your sister, right?"

Atum? The archangel banished by the bad wifi connection?

Francis's entire left cheek twitched. "How did you get my number?"

The man licked his lips. "I need you to *listen*. I can see that your sister's avatar is still in the boss dungeon on Grone. Gaia, is that right? Her avatar is Gaia. I need to talk to her. It's an emergency."

Fiona reached for the phone, but Francis yanked it back. He scowled at the man on his phone. "What do you want?"

The man glanced away, again referring to an off-screen computer. "You saw a human female in the cavern, right? Before your avatar got killed. She was wearing a military uniform. Big helmet."

"Uh, yeah, maybe." He paused. "Yeah, we saw her."

The man started to speak but his eyes hollowed and the words caught in his throat. He tried again. "Is she still . . . alive?"

Francis looked at the television screen and the image of Gal'Blad holding the girl's limp body. "As far as I know," he said.

The man let out a sharp breath. Fiona put her hand on Francis's arm. He tapped the mute button on his phone. She whispered sharply, "Let me talk to him!"

The man was continuing. "Please, I need your help." When Francis didn't answer, the man's voice cracked. "Please!"

"This is some kind of scam," Francis declared.

Fiona shook her head. "Maybe this is part of the game. Maybe they're doing something new. Maybe it's a special contest or something." When he didn't move, she added, "Look at him! Look at those patches. He's wearing a jacket just like the one the Atum avatar was wearing. He *has* to be from the game company. How else could he know we're playing the Grone campaign? How else could he have gotten your phone number? How else would he know both our *names*?"

"He could be a hacker or something," muttered Francis.

The man on the phone was still talking. "Please! Let me talk to Fiona! There's no time. If we don't get her out of there she'll die!"

Fiona assumed the "her" was the injured girl on the TV screen. She reached again for the phone, and Francis reluctantly handed it to her. She unmuted it, took a deep breath, and stared into the camera.

"I'm Fiona," she said.

The man's jaw fell open. He quickly clamped it shut. She recognized the progression of emotions flashing across his face. She'd seen it a thousand times since she'd received her injuries. On the faces of strangers on the street. On her friends. Even on her own mother.

Astonishment. Involuntary revulsion. Horrified realization. Finally, depending on the person, either ridicule, or pity. With this guy, it was pity.

He stammered. "Uh, *you're* Fiona?"

She glared defiantly into the phone camera. "Yeah. I'm Fiona."

The man appeared to be in his late twenties. He recovered from the initial shock of her appearance more quickly than most. "Uh, I can see that your avatar Gaia is in Jaspaar's death cavern. Do you see a human-looking female at the scene?"

"You mean Analise?" said Fiona.

The man jerked as if she'd touched him with a live electrical wire. "Yes! Analise!"

Fiona flipped the phone's camera so he could see the image on the TV screen. It showed Gaia's view of Gal'Blad. The monstrous Ghast was cradling the limp body of Analise against a background of smoky darkness lit by the flashes of combat. The man made a sound like somebody had punched him in the stomach. "Oh God, are you sure she's alive?"

"She got shot, but yeah. She's alive."

"Can you turn up the volume on your TV?"

Francis picked up the remote and unmuted the television. The sounds of battle, up till now contained in their headset earphones, filled the basement.

"Hold the phone to your headset mic," he said. Fiona pulled off her headset and did what he asked. The man shouted. "Analise! Can you hear me? It's Arni."

On the TV, the image of the girl stirred. She stared numbly at Gaia, Fiona's avatar. From her perspective, the man's words had come out of Gaia's mouth.

"Arni? Where are you?" She sounded confused. "Wolfe shot me."

The man called Arni spat out an anguished hiss. "That *bastard*. Listen, Chun blocked my connection. I can't respawn. I've called a player for help, and she's agreed. This is her avatar. Her name is Gaia." He paused. "Rupe just called. He says Chun is going apeshit. Get out of there before her avatar respawns. I'm trying to block her, but it won't last long. You've got to hurry!"

Chun? Rupe? Fiona didn't recognize "Chun," though something about "Rupe" was vaguely familiar.

On the television, the girl nodded weakly. "I'll make it. We still have time." She coughed violently. "I picked up your holobox when Atum died. I have it and both the emoras with me. Transfer Atum's character stats to Gaia. She can . . . help us. We can . . . still make this work."

"No! Forget the plan," the man pleaded. "Just get out, okay?"

On the TV, a figure appeared out of the smoke. It was a villager bot, running blindly, covered in blood. It stumbled away and vanished into the haze.

The man on the phone shouted. "Analise . . . Analise?" His voice rose in desperation. "Why isn't she answering?"

Without a profile popup, it was impossible to tell whether Analise was unconscious, or dead. Her head rolled limply in the Ghast's arms, but her chest was still moving. "I think she's unconscious," said Francis.

"Fiona, listen to me. Fiona, are you there?" Fiona flipped the camera so the man could see her face. "This is *really* important," he said. "Analise is *not* an avatar. Do you understand? You *cannot* let her die."

"So, she's a bot?" Francis asked.

"She's not a goddamned bot!" the man bellowed. Then, more calmly, "You *have* to keep her safe, at all costs. Get moving. There's a keycard hidden on a dead body in the central pool. Get it, and head toward the exit at the rear of the cavern. You'll need the keycard to open some doors."

"A blue card?" asked Fiona. "With Jaspaar's imperial symbol?"

The man nodded suspiciously.

"I already have it," she said. "It was the first thing I saw."

The man gave her an appraising look. "Rupe was right about you. Hurry, I'll guide you. Don't let any of the soldiers see you. Point the camera back at the television so I can see what's happening."

Rupe? Again, the oddly familiar name. *Rupe.* Something to do with the game, but there was no time to try and figure it out. The man looked off-screen, and Fiona could hear him furiously typing on his keyboard. "Okay, Fiona, I'm tracking your avatar. Get Analise out of there. Move! Be careful! My bots will try to hold them off, but watch out for the marines."

He was silent for a few seconds while he typed. "Okay. I've leveled you up to max and given you Atum's dev-mode permissions, but you're not invulnerable. The marines' weapons deal very high damage. If you get killed, your avatar won't respawn, okay? You'll only get one chance at this. Stay on the phone with me. I'll guide you for as long as I can. And Francis, if you can hear me, please help your sister. Your avatar isn't going to respawn, either. They've closed down the Hero's Gate. Nobody gets in."

"Who's *they*?" Francis demanded. He took the phone from Fiona. "What's going on?"

The man on the phone ignored his question. "Go, now, before Solomon finds you. Hurry."

Francis gave her a look that was equal parts anger, intrigue, and apprehension. He muted his phone. "Fi, I'm not sure this is legit."

She shrugged and returned a nervous grin. "Yeah, but what if it *is*? Even if this Arni guy is some kind of hacker, so what? It's just a video game. It's not like we're breaking the law or anything." As she spoke, she pulled up her avatar's stats:

AVATAR PROFILE: **GAIA**
Species: **DRYAN**
Level: **ARCHANGEL 100**
Health: **1,000/1,000 (GREEN)**

And below, something she'd never seen:

Special: **DEVMODE**

Archangel 100? The man on the phone had said he'd maxed out Fiona's avatar's level. A heated flash of excitement surged through her. Gaia was now an archangel? This proved Arni must work for the game company, right? Who else would have the ability to change her avatar's stats? She paused, her grin widened, and she added, "I like this new game."

Francis frowned. Was it jealousy she saw in his expression? Of course it was. From above, a bright light shot across the basement, and both Fiona and Francis squinted in surprise. At the top of the stairs, Mama peered down from the door, the kitchen light shining from behind into the darkened basement. "La cena estará en cinco minutos," she called in Spanish. "Five minutes till supper. Come wash your hands." The scent of spiced pork drifted down the stairs.

Fiona glanced at Francis. He shouted over his shoulder, "Be there in a minute, Mama. Let us finish our game first."

"Five minutes," Mama said, her voice rising sharply. "Francis, help your sister get washed up."

The door closed and darkness returned to the basement. Francis turned to her. "Go. Hurry!"

On-screen, the newly minted Archangel Gaia turned to Gal'Blad. "Follow me," she said. Francis unmuted the phone while Fiona fumbled nervously at the trackball. The man named Arni called out instructions, guiding them up the steep ramp toward the rear exit. For an instant she wished that Francis could take over her game controller. He had ten working fingers. He was much better in a fight, but he used a standard controller, not a trackball, and if she unplugged so he could control her avatar with his standard controller, it might interrupt play. Then she realized she didn't want him to take over. Gaia was *her* avatar, *her* alter ego.

The sounds of the battle diminished as they ran. The tunnel was long and straight and identical to the one they'd used to enter the cavern. They slowed when a door appeared in the beams of their bobbing flashlights.

"Look for a square area next to the doorframe where the stone wall has been ground smooth. There's an engraved symbol matching the symbol on the keycard." Arni sounded distracted. The loud clattering from his keyboard had increased to an astounding tempo. He was typing faster than seemed possible. What was he doing? Writing programming code? Changing the game in real time?

She studied the TV. *There. Shoulder-high, to the left of the door.* Fiona caused Gaia to withdraw the keycard from her item stash and swipe it through a shallow slot beneath the engraved symbol. The door slid open.

Fiona guided Gaia through the door into a dimly lit passageway. Gal'Blad followed with Analise. The thundering sounds of the battle vanished when the door closed. At last, Fiona recognized an area that looked familiar from the TV episode. In the show, the hero had searched the utility tunnels beneath the citadel, looking for the Ranger Cadet who had been kidnapped by the warlord Jaspaar. Tunnels just like this one.

She paused to examine Analise. Red hair, matted and tangled. Lightly freckled cheeks, smeared with blood and dirt. Green eyes, unfocused and delirious. The entire left shoulder and sleeve of her shirt were black and syrupy. Her left arm hung limply. Heavy drops of blood fell from her fingers.

Wounded avatars sometimes bled, but the way the injuries were rendered by the game didn't look anything like this. When a game character bled, the blood was scarlet red, or whatever color was assigned to the blood of the character's species. This human girl's blood was red enough, but it had quickly turned black as it soaked into the fabric of her clothing. It looked, if anything, too real.

Fiona called up a health-pack from Gaia's item stash and tried to apply it to Analise. A single bullet wound, like the one in the girl's shoulder, would have barely affected an avatar and could be easily healed by applying a health-pack. Likewise, her health-pack would instantly heal even the most mortal of wounds on a bot.

It didn't work. In fact, she couldn't even apply it. When she pressed the appropriate button on her game controller, nothing happened. The health-pack just sat in Gaia's hand, unused, as if she'd tried to heal the air.

That settled it. Analise wasn't an avatar. She wasn't a bot. She was something *different*.

Flight

Francis's phone was propped so that its camera faced the television screen, allowing Arni to guide Fiona's avatar through the dungeon. Next to her, on the couch, Francis unconsciously mimicked Gaia's movements. When Gaia turned left into a side tunnel, Francis leaned left. When she ducked under an obstacle, he ducked, too. Every time Gaia bumped awkwardly into a wall or failed to make a jump over an obstacle, he grimaced and muttered something under his breath. Fiona felt heat rising in her face, but there was no way she was going to let him take over her avatar, no matter how clumsy she was. This was *her* moment. *Gaia's* moment.

Gal'Blad followed obediently, still carrying the wounded Analise. For the next several minutes, the only sounds in the basement were the footsteps from the television and Arni's anxious voice from the phone. He guided Gaia through a series of tunnel junctions and cavernous industrial spaces, crowded with mysterious equipment and machines. This was a maze, Fiona recognized, one that would have taken them hours to complete without his help. As they passed junctions, they occasionally saw figures in the adjacent corridors, but none of them took note of their passage.

When Francis commented on the surprising effortlessness of Gaia's progress, Arni mumbled, "I'm suppressing the dungeon's adversaries and traps as you pass through each area. I'm also routing you around the combat encounter spaces. If we had to fight our way through every level of this place, we'd never make it. As long as we avoid the boss monster, we'll be fine."

They climbed a seemingly endless spiral staircase before Arni directed them through an unmanned security checkpoint and into a warren of low, unlit mining tunnels. Fiona activated Gaia's flashlight. Something glimmered and sparkled in the rough stone walls. Francis said, "Is that timedust?"

"Yeah," replied Arni distractedly. "You're in Jaspaar's mines. You're getting close."

"Close to what?"

"Stop!" At Arni's cry, Fiona jerked her fingers away from her trackball. Gaia froze. Something was in the corridor ahead. Silver tentacles, like a metallic vine, splayed across the floor and walls. "Be careful," Arni said. "That leads to the boss monster's chamber. Don't touch those vines. Take a right at the next junction into the lower tunnel. It goes beneath the boss chamber."

His instructions led Gaia into a square corridor lined with gray metal pipes. After a short distance it ended at a chasm, across which was suspended a cabled steel bridge. Positioning Gaia at the edge, Fiona saw that the chasm was a massive vertical well that led up and down as far as her avatar's flashlight would penetrate. "Wait a sec," Arni warned. "There's a bunch of invisible microflak mines floating above the bridge. Hold on, I'm going to illuminate them for you." After a brief pause, several dozen glowing bubbles, each about the size of a beach ball, appeared above the bridge. "Don't touch the mines," he warned. "And when you get to the halfway point, don't touch any of the silver vines hanging from above. They're a part of the boss, too, and if you touch them, it'll know you're here."

Francis leaned toward the phone. "We're near the boss? Is it the harvester?" In the "Game Changer" episode, the villain Jaspaar's greatest secret had been a million-year-old artifact he'd found buried deep inside the mountain. A long-vanished civilization had designed the alien machine to eat entire worlds in the hope of harvesting a few grains of timedust that might exist in a planet's crust. Jaspaar had managed to reactivate it, only for it to escape and threaten the entire galaxy in subsequent episodes. Every dungeon had one big baddy that had to be defeated. It made sense that the harvester would be the boss of the prime dungeon on Grone.

"Yeah. Doesn't matter, we're going to avoid it." Arni sounded distracted, and she could hear him typing on his keyboard.

Francis raised his hand in a warning motion. Through her headset microphone, Fiona hissed at Gal'Blad, and the Ghast halted.

On the phone, Arni's voice darkened. "What's the matter?"

"I think they're following us," she said. "We hear guns and screams."

"Hold on. I'm checking." There was a long silence. "Go! Run! I can't track the marines, but I can see that Oaone has respawned. She can track you. Hurry!"

"Oaone? The Wrathwraith?"

"Yes! I'll reactivate the dungeon adversaries behind you, but it won't slow her down much. Hurry!"

Fiona spun the trackball, and Gaia raced across the bridge, dodging the floating mines and the silvery tendrils that dangled from the darkness above. Gal'Blad followed, moving with the fluid agility that was the hallmark of her species. They exited the bridge at a full sprint and entered another utility tunnel that climbed sharply upward. Arni blurted directions as they approached each junction. She pictured him hunched desperately over his computer as he whispered into his phone. "Left at the T-junction . . . take the up-ramp, it's a secret shortcut . . . stay to the right, there's a hidden deadfall . . . go through the hole in the wall into the mine tunnel . . . watch out for that pool, it's acid . . . don't touch that boulder . . . *hurry!*"

Several more junctions of dark mining tunnels. They turned a corner. Bodies littered the rough floor, as if they'd all been gunned down trying to flee. Some of the corpses wore the gray capes of the Mucktu; others wore Jaspaar's uniforms she recognized from the TV episode.

"What happened to these guys?"

"Solomon and his marines were here," Arni's voice tightened until he was biting every syllable. "This is where they entered the gamecosm. Hurry! They know this is where you're going. This is the only way out."

They ran past the bodies. The only way out of what? Fiona wondered. What did he mean, "gamecosm"?

"Slow down. Wait, wait. There . . . *stop*. Look right there, on the wall. See it?" As they approached, a portion of the smooth corridor wall began to shimmer, like summertime heat rising from a highway. The area surrounding the shimmer was covered with scorch marks and bullet dings. "That's the Shadow Door. It's still open. Go through it."

Gaia plunged through the shimmer. As she did, the television screen flickered and the speakers issued a screech of static. Fiona pulled her hand away from the game controller. Had the game crashed? Had they lost their connection?

"Oh, shit," said Arni.

The image stabilized.

"No, no, it's okay," he said.

Gaia and Gal'Blad were in a windowless room. It was octagonal, lit by glowing floor panels, ringed by crowded, ornately carved wooden bookshelves and metal cabinets. Many of the cabinets had been ripped open with great force, their mysterious contents strewn across the floor. Behind Gaia, the wall shimmered, marking the location of the Shadow Door through which they'd entered.

A bizarre collection of artifacts covered the tops of the cabinets and the walls, from the stuffed heads of outlandish beasts to a collection of planetary globes and paintings of alien cities and landscapes. At the center of the rear wall and extending floor to ceiling was a magnificent pipe organ with a multitiered keyboard and a dazzling array of bronze pipes.

Above them, a glowing spiral of holographic mist spanned the entire ceiling. It was crisscrossed by hundreds of spiderweb lines and arcs, barely visible, and tiny labels for color-coded regions, lanes, and individual bright points. Hundreds of specks moved slowly along a few of the lanes, and most of them seemed to be converging on a single point near the rim.

"It's a map of the galaxy," said Francis.

The specks were ships, Fiona realized, and the spot they were converging toward was Grone. *They're all coming here*, she realized. Every player in the game galaxy was headed to the newly released planet and its unexplored dungeons.

Beneath the center of the galactic spiral stood a massive and intricate contraption of spinning brass gears, wheels, and orbs. It might have been a machine or maybe just a piece of art. Hundreds of tiny glass spheres rolled on whirling metal channels that weaved like endless Möbius strips around and through the belly of the mechanism.

"What is this place?" Francis said.

Arni answered in a rushed, distracted tone. "It's . . . uh, sort of my virtual workshop inside the gaming system. We don't have much time. Analise, can you hear me?"

Gaia turned to Gal'Blad. Analise hung limply in the Ghast's arms. Her face was slack and frighteningly pale.

"She's breathing, but she doesn't look so good."

Arni cursed. Fiona waited, but he stayed silent.

"What should I do now?" she prompted.

When he didn't answer, Francis turned the phone so they could see Arni's face. It was filled with anguished indecision.

"Can you see a red door?" Arni said.

Fiona looked around the room. Other than the Shadow Door, there was only one exit. "I see it."

"Go through it."

"No," croaked a voice. It was Analise. She was suddenly awake, fighting feebly against Gal'Blad's embrace. "Arni, no. Not yet."

Arni heard her through the TV speakers. He sounded scared. "Fiona, don't listen to her. Get her out of there. Do it now."

"No!" Analise's voice was stronger. "I can still make this work. We're so close. We have time!"

"Chun is almost there, babe! So is Wolfe. He tried to kill you, remember? We can't risk it. We've got to get you out!"

"No." Analise looked directly into Gaia's eyes. *Fiona's* eyes. "Listen to me. Real people will die if you don't do what I say. Real, living, flesh-and-blood people."

"No, no, no!" shouted Arni. "We're out of time."

"Fi, hold on," said Francis hesitantly. "Something's not right here."

He was right. Fiona was still staring into Analise's eyes. They weren't computer-generated eyes. She looked up at Gal'Blad. The Ghast's eyestalks were sluglike and alien, but in them she sensed the same depths.

"What do you think, Gal'Blad?" She'd never asked the opinion of a bot before. Francis raised his eyebrows.

"I don't want to die, but I don't want anybody else to die, either," replied the Ghast. A simple answer, and one that a computer's AI would never have given in a million years.

Gaia turned to face Analise. "What do you want me to do?"

Gal'Blad gently lowered Analise to the floor, placing her in a seated position with her back against one of the wall cabinets.

"Here. Take my things." Analise struggled out of the straps of her backpack and held it out toward Gaia. Normally, when an avatar or a bot offered an item to another avatar, a popup would appear on the screen allowing the receiving avatar to accept the item.

Nothing happened.

"It's not working," Fiona said.

"Shit. There's no code for a capatar to pass an item to an avatar," said Arni. "It won't work. Analise, you need to get *out* of there."

"No. Wait. Let me think."

"Analise—"

"Let me *think!*"

Analise looked as if she might faint at any moment. Finally, she lifted the backpack toward Gal'Blad. "Here. Take this and give it to Gaia."

Gal'Blad took the backpack and held it out to Gaia. A popup appeared on the screen:

```
ACCEPT ITEM AND ADD TO PLAYER INVENTORY?
```

Fiona's mind churned. Why couldn't Analise give the backpack directly to Gaia? Was this a clue to some new mode of gameplay, or could it be a bug in the software? And what was a *capatar?*

There was no time to consider the implications. She selected YES, and the contents of Gaia's item inventory appeared on the screen. She scanned the list. There were several new items at the end:

```
BACKPACK CONTAINING:
-   HOLOBOX #FF0000
-   HERO EMORA
-   SHADOW EMORA
-   UNKNOWN ITEM 1A3326FD-E14E-448F-9151-
    23839606C6ED
```

"Now what?" said Fiona.

The response was the barest whisper. "Take . . . the holobox. There's a holo receptacle on the machine . . ."

Analise fell silent. Her eyes closed.

"Shit," cried Arni. "Get her out of there. Use the red door. Go!"

"No," Analise whispered insistently, eyes still closed. "Tell her what to do, Arni. *Tell her.*"

"Analise!" he shouted.

Analise didn't respond.

"Tell me what to do," said Fiona.

"God damn it," cried Arni. His voice hardened. "God damn it! Hold the item called the Shadow Emora in one of Gaia's hands, then put the holobox into the receptacle of the map generator."

"The what?"

"The brass machine in the center of the room. Hurry! Oaone is already in the approach tunnels. You've got maybe two minutes. I can't track the others. They may be even closer."

Fiona moved Gaia to the machine and examined it. It formed a complex sphere of revolving and counter-rotating parts, maybe six feet in diameter. Dozens of concentric rings and gears turned in a kaleidoscopic pattern within the heart of the machine, driven by a bewildering system of brass gears and shafts. Intricate markings covered each ring. Crystalline marbles roved within channels in the rings, occasionally dropping through holes to land miraculously in the channel of another moving ring. The entire contraption ticked and tocked and tinkled and softly whirred. In any other circumstance, it would have been mesmerizing to watch.

The holobox receptacle was integrated into the thick column that supported the machine. She recognized it easily enough, though like everything in this room, it was heavily decorated with steampunk flourishes.

Fiona used her controller to retrieve the Shadow Emora and the holobox from Gaia's item stash. A smoky, round jewel appeared in one of Gaia's hands, the milky cube of the holobox in the other. She didn't recognize the jewel, but holoboxes were common items in the game, used to store and share virtual data between avatars. Holoboxes could hold pictures, maps, instructions, videos, books. They were the game universe's version of a real-world thumbdrive.

She approached the machine.

PLACE THE HOLOBOX INTO THE REMOTE KERNEL NODE INTERFACE?

Fiona selected YES, and Gaia plugged the fist-size holobox into the receptacle. A red light began pulsing in its translucent depths.

Arni muttered a curse.

"What's wrong? Is it not working?"

"It *is* working," he said. He didn't sound happy about it. "There's no turning back now."

Above Gaia, a hole appeared at the center of the holographic map of the game galaxy. Around the edges of the hole, a host of miniscule sparkles flared and faded, as if the stars were dissolving away. The hole expanded like a ripple from the core of the galactic disk. As it grew, the red glow within the holobox intensified.

Through the phone, Fiona could hear Arni breathing heavily. "Pick up Analise," he said. "When the holobox flashes, grab it and *run*. Fiona, only Gaia can open the red door, okay? Your avatar has to go first through the door, and she has to be holding the Shadow Emora. The Ghast can follow with Analise. It stays open for one minute, then closes. If we're lucky, it'll close before the others get there."

The rotating rings within the machine slowed, and the whirling marbles began to fall into a tray at the bottom.

"What's happening?" said Francis.

The dark hole quickly consumed most of the central disk of the hologram. As it expanded toward the outer rim of the map, Fiona heard a pause in Arni's breathing.

The basement floor rumbled, as if a large truck were passing on the road outside the house. Francis looked up at the basement's sole window. The glass panes were rattling.

"Whoa," said Arni's voice from the phone. "Can you guys feel that?"

On the television screen, the last vestige of the outermost rim of the galactic map disappeared. The red light within the holobox flashed three times, then subsided to a steady glow.

The rumble abruptly stopped.

"Grab the box! Go!"

Fiona spun her trackball. Gaia reached for the cube. Onscreen, a prompt appeared:

```
TAKE THE HOLOBOX?
```

Something burst through the shimmering curtain of the Shadow Door. Fiona spun Gaia in time to see two soldier avatars, the one named Solomon and the one called Wolfe. Both had weapons raised, and they spun toward Gal'Blad. Unseen, Fiona ducked Gaia into a hidden position behind the spherical machine and activated her stealthshield. It had partially recharged since the battle in the bubble cave, but it wouldn't last long.

"Don't move," said Solomon.

Gal'Blad hissed something in an alien language. She lowered Analise's still form to the floor, then stood to face the Solomon avatar. The battle spurs on her chest and shoulders rippled and unfolded, and the toxin sacs on her neck inflated with thick yellow fluid.

"Stand down," warned Solomon.

She leaped. He managed to get off a burst of machine-gun fire before the Ghost toppled him to the ground.

Pinning Solomon to the floor, Gal'Blad looked toward the other avatar, Wolfe. With a gasp of air that inflated a membranous bladder on the back of her head, she spat a bullet of thick yellow mucus directly into his face. His head snapped back with the force of the impact. The toxin's effect was instantaneous. The Wolfe avatar lurched, blinded.

From her hidden position, Fiona tried again to retrieve the holobox.

TAKE THE HOLOBOX?

She selected YES. On the television screen, the holobox appeared in Gaia's hand. Across the room, Gal'Blad was shredding Solomon's chest with her claws. He fired his weapon again, and bullets sprayed wildly in an arc that struck the ceiling and swept down the wall to punch holes in one of the wooden cabinets. As his health points hit zero, his aura flashed, and he vanished in an explosion of dust.

Gal'Blad rolled away and moved quickly toward the flailing Wolfe avatar. She opened her arms and embraced him tightly, impaling him on the battle spurs that had erupted from her chest. He beat blindly against her hold but was unable to break free. Within seconds, like Solomon, he was dead, but unlike Solomon, his body didn't vanish. Not an avatar, then, but some kind of weird bot, like Analise.

Gal'Blad's health points were still at maximum. They hadn't even touched her. In the game, the Ghasts were one of the deadliest adversary character species.

"Holy shitbags," Arni cried. "Hurry. Tell the Ghast to pick up Analise. We've got to *move*. Oaone is almost there."

Hub

Analise groaned as Gal'Blad lifted her. Her eyes were unfocused, dulled by pain. She looked up at the blank ceiling, then at the glowing holobox in Gaia's hand. She made a tight-lipped expression that might have been a grim smile.

"Listen to me," Arni said. "When you go through the red door, things are going to look weird to you. Don't stop. Keep moving, no matter what happens, okay? I'll tell you what to do. Ready?"

Fiona moved Gaia to face the door. Gal'Blad followed with Analise.

"I'm ready."

"Okay, go. Don't stop, no matter what."

Fiona took a breath and moved Gaia through the doorway and . . .

. . . things *changed*.

Gaia was in a corridor, but the resolution of the image on the television had shifted so that her surroundings were almost unrecognizable. The image was blocky and pixelated. The walls, floor, and ceiling were rendered in vivid, primary colors. There was no light source, no shadows, but somehow everything was bright and lurid. She turned to Gal'Blad. The Ghost looked like a blocky 2D monster from a 1990s arcade game. Bizarrely, only the figure of Analise still looked real, like a live-action actor inside a cartoon. Fiona looked down at the hands of her own avatar. They were unarticulated pixels of color.

"Don't stop," came Arni's voice from the phone. "Run as fast as your avatar will go. You're in a network tunnel. You've switched rendering engines. It looks weird. Don't let it throw you."

Using the trackball, Fiona moved Gaia forward. A blocky, red rectangle appeared in the distance.

"Is that another door?"

"Yeah. Use the primary button on your controller to open it."

The door grew quickly as Gaia raced down the corridor. She reached out to the square of color that represented the door handle. As soon as she touched it, the door swung inward.

Beyond was nothing. No color, no image. Just a veil of static, like a television screen with no signal.

"What is that?" Francis asked.

"Technically, it's something like a network bridge," said Arni. "I didn't have time to model it in the rendering engine. Go ahead."

Beyond the screen of static, they entered a small room, also blocky and pixelated. The room was empty save for three doors: the red one they'd just come through and two others equally spaced on the blank walls. One blue, one green.

"The green door," Analise whispered hoarsely. "Take the green door."

Arni hesitated. "Babe, are you sure?"

"I'm not going back," she said. "Not until this is done." She looked to Gaia. "Take the *green* door."

Arni muttered something too softly for them to hear.

Behind the green door was another veil of static, and beyond that, another long corridor rendered in crude primary colors. Another green door lay at the end. They hurried to it, stepped through.

"Whoa," murmured Francis. The blocky pixilation and primary colors were gone. Gaia and Gal'Blad were back in a fully rendered area of the game. It was another octagonal room whose size and shape were identical to the one with the galactic map and the collection of bizarre alien artifacts. Like the previous room, its floor was pale and translucent, glowing softly with a white light. Unlike the other room, this one was empty, save for an identical replica of the brass machine, which sprouted from the same location in the center of the floor. This version of the machine was still and silent. A small globe about the size of a basketball hovered at its center, visible through the many layers of rings and gears. It shimmered like a soap bubble and was filled with tantalizing hints of shape and color.

"Just like before. Take the holobox in one hand, and make sure you're still holding the Shadow Emora in your other hand," said Arni.

Fiona did as instructed. Arni sounded relieved. "Good. Now, while you're holding the emora, put the holobox into....ee....holo recept.... on...th……..chine……..step…………………way read."

Francis picked up the phone. "Say that again. You're breaking up."

Arni cursed and whispered urgently. "They're trying to block my………. Fiona, I have to ………. so please listen carefully…… ru… take the holobox and…into…receptacle………. you'll see……………………. okay? That's all you have to do. Then get Analise back out to the transfer hub, the room with the three doors, and this time take the *blue* door."

Thuds and shouts issued from the phone. It sounded like someone was banging on the door to Arni's room. His words poured out in a frantic tumble, interrupted by bursts of static. "*Shit.* Somebody's here. One more thing…………. the jewel… you took… Shadow…we've got to…. it out of cyberspace and into meatspace." *Meatspace* was the term used by gamers to refer to the real world as opposed to the game's virtual world. "Can you hear me? As soon as you insert the holobox, archive the Shadow Emora to your game account's cloud locker. Do you… me? This is *important.* Once it's archived, move it from your cloud locker to a thumbdrive or data card—*not* to your gaming computer's hard drive. Get it *off* the internet and onto a backup drive…….*not* connected to a computer. You have to *move* the file, *not* copy it, okay? Don't…… a copy or you'll destroy it. Can… hear me?"

"What?" said Francis, suddenly deeply suspicious.

"Go get a thumbdrive," Fiona said. "I think there's one in the drawer beneath the computer. The one I used for school last year."

Francis shook his head. "Fi, this is nuts."

Slam! Whoever had been banging on Arni's door was getting serious about it. Arni gave one last plaintive, "Please, hide the backup until I call!" and the phone went dead.

"I'm turning it off," blurted Francis. He slid off the couch and reached for the game computer's power switch. This was no longer a game, and they both knew it.

"No," Fiona said. "Don't you *dare* turn it off." She could feel tears welling behind her eyes, but she couldn't cry because the accident had stolen her tear ducts along with the rest of her face. For the past year, she'd been entirely at the mercy of others. Doctors. Therapists. The homecare nurses. Mama. Francis. She needed help to eat, to dress, even to go to the bathroom. She'd never walk again, nor breathe freely without supplemental oxygen. The surgeries had been awful enough, and things hadn't improved when she'd finally been allowed to come home. In the past six months, she'd not left the house except for planned doctor visits and a series of terrifying ambulance rides to the emergency room due to bleeding, infections, and once even a collapsed lung.

Worst of all was the ofrenda shrine Mama had constructed in the dining room to celebrate the life of Dad. At the center of the altar, next to the ornately framed picture of Dad, she'd placed a wallet-sized version of Fiona's first-year high-school photo, complete with embarrassing braces and goofy smile. It was nestled innocently amongst the flowers and candles and sugar skulls and perforated tissue paper. When Francis had discovered it, he'd pulled it out of the ofrenda and raged at Mama. Mama had tearfully explained that she wanted Fiona to draw strength from the spirit of Dad, but Fiona knew enough about her mother's Mexican culture to recognize the lie. The ofrenda was an altar to celebrate the lives of dead family members. To Mama, the smiling girl with braces and long dark hair had died along with her father.

Mama wasn't wrong. The girl in the photo *was* dead, to Fiona as much as Mama. She'd become a shrouded ghost who would never walk or run or climb a mountain or kiss a boy. The only way to manifest the life she had lost was through her gaming avatar, Gaia, proud and brave. It was just a stupid video game, yes, but it *mattered*.

"Don't turn it off," she said again.

Francis hesitated, and when he saw her expression, he winced. He pulled his hand away from the computer, then opened the drawer on the television stand. He rummaged through the cables and old game

DVDs until he pulled out a silver USB thumbdrive. He plugged it into one of the ports on the game computer.

"Now what?" he said.

Cataclysm

Fiona worked her trackball, causing Gaia to approach the brass machine. Gaia's left hand held the gray jewel called the Shadow Emora; the right held the glowing red holobox.

"The Immovable Spot."

Both Fiona and Francis jerked upright at the sound of the weak voice. Analise's eyes were open, and she was staring into the heart of the unmoving brass machine. Gal'Blad knelt and gently placed her next to the base of the machine. Both of Gal'Blad's arms were soaked with blood.

"What is this place?" Fiona asked.

Analise pulled herself into a sitting position, wincing sharply and clutching at her injured shoulder. "Arni gave you God Mode, right?"

"My avatar profile says DEVMODE."

"Yeah. Same thing." Analise pointed. "See that blob floating in the middle of the machine? Looks like a soap bubble?"

"Yeah. What is it?"

"Arni calls it the Immovable Spot, but he's a hopeless romantic. The technical name is *remote kernel node interface*. It's sort of like the receptacle on your computer for memory cards and removable drives. We use it to load upgrades and bug fixes to the game's core software." She motioned toward the holobox Gaia still held in her hand, then gestured to the receptacle at the base of the machine. "Plug it in."

Fiona looked at the cube doubtfully. "Is this a game upgrade? Or some kind of bug fix?"

"Or a big fat virus," Francis muttered.

"It's an upgrade." Analise's voice was thin and brittle. "A *big* upgrade. Do it."

Fiona glanced at Francis. He shook his head and mouthed *no*. She understood his concern. This Analise character could be a part of some bizarre game campaign, or she might be something else entirely. Something bad. Something criminal.

Gaia thrust the holobox toward Analise. "You do it."

Analise shook her head. "I *can't*. It will only work for an avatar with archangel privileges. Arni's avatar Atum was supposed to be here with me. He transferred his system administrator privileges to Gaia. Now it's up to you."

Fiona hesitated. "If you're not an avatar, what are you?"

Analise's weak smile faltered. "I'm something new. Hurry. Put the box in the machine."

Francis leaned close and touched Fiona's shoulder. "Fi, wait. Ask her about those guys chasing her."

Analise must have heard his question through Fiona's headset microphone. She winced. "One of them is my boss's avatar. He doesn't understand what I'm trying to do. If he understood, he'd be helping me, not trying to stop me."

Fiona pushed Francis away. "You work for the game company, too? Like Arni?"

"No. Not exactly."

"And who's Oaone? That other archangel?"

"That's Arni's boss. She doesn't understand either. Or maybe she just doesn't care. Look, I don't have time to explain. You've come this far. You've trusted your gut. There's only one more thing to do. Take the holobox and put it in the machine. *Please!*"

Fiona swallowed. "What will happen if I do?"

Analise's weak smile brightened. "Something more wonderful than you can ever imagine."

Fiona slowly twirled the trackball. Gaia approached the machine. She held the holobox toward the receptacle at the base of the machine. A popup appeared on the screen.

PLACE THE HOLOBOX INTO THE REMOTE KERNEL
INTERFACE?

Fiona selected YES. On the television, Gaia reached toward the machine and plugged the cube into the receptacle. The smoky jewel in her opposite hand pulsed with a purple light.

Without hesitation, Fiona selected the SHADOW EMORA from Gaia's items and chose ARCHIVE TO CLOUD LOCKER, just as Arni had instructed. The smoky jewel vanished from Gaia's hand.

She nodded to Francis. "Go."

Francis used the game computer's keyboard to move the archive of Gaia's items to the thumbdrive as Arni had instructed. When he tapped ENTER, the thumbdrive flashed for a moment. He unplugged it, put it in his jeans pocket, and turned his attention back to the television.

On-screen, the great brass machine shuddered. The innermost rings turned first, spinning up to speed, followed by the larger, outer rings. From the floating soap bubble within the machine, crystal marbles materialized and began to drop into the turning complexity. Each marble was caught in a spinning ring and began to whirl within channels cut into the rings' surfaces.

Analise watched intently. Above the heads of their avatars, a mist appeared in the shape of a giant smoke ring that encircled the entire room. At the same time, the red glow within the holobox began to fade, as if whatever energy it contained was being drained into the machine. She smiled.

The smoke ring gradually solidified, and its inner circumference began to shrink toward the center of the room. Fine, spiderwebbed lines began to appear in the mist, along with regions of color labeled with tiny words and symbols.

Francis shifted on the couch and leaned toward the television. "It's the reverse of what happened in the other room. It's rebuilding the map of the galaxy."

The hologram grew more substantial as the void in the center of the smoke ring began to shrink. More details appeared around its innermost edge, including the first hints of a spiral structure. As the size of the map increased, so did the speed and noise of the intricate, whirling rings within the machine. The soap bubble at its core was no longer visible.

Fiona was fascinated, not by the machine or the holographic map, but by Analise's expression. The green-eyed woman watched the expanding torus of stars with a slack jaw, like someone in the throes of religious ecstasy.

Ghostly geometric shapes began to appear along the empty walls of the room. The shapes slowly solidified into the cabinets, bookcases, artwork, and other bizarre paraphernalia that had occupied the previous map room, including the huge brass pipe organ that had dominated the rear wall.

Analise smiled. "It's working."

It only took a few moments for this map room to become an exact duplicate of the previous room. Even the items damaged and displaced during the brief battle with Solomon and Wolfe were similarly scattered here. Wisps of smoke still curled from the bullet holes in the wooden cabinets where Solomon's shots had gone wild.

Something caught Fiona's eye at the edge of the television screen, a movement distinct from all the other odd visual effects happening around Gaia.

Francis saw it too. He tensed.

A shimmer was emerging from the veil of static within the frame of the still-open green door. It slid across the floor like a pale shadow, hugging the wall.

Toward Analise.

Fiona and Francis both shouted a warning. Gal'Blad spun toward the threat.

A shrill pulse poured from the speakers, and the entire television screen flashed red. Fiona's trackball vibrated, and Gaia's health indicator dropped almost instantly from 1,000 to 600. Gaia was thrown from her feet, tumbling several feet away from Analise and the machine.

Francis jumped to his feet. "Something's attacking you!"

Fiona spun the trackball, trying to get Gaia into a defensive stance. She'd never heard of an attack that caused 400 damage points in a single blow. Her avatar responded sluggishly, still dazed from the onslaught.

"It's the Wrathwraith!" yelled Francis, jabbing his finger at the TV. "She hit you with her gobsmacker."

Gaia slowly regained her feet. The Wrathwraith had used her species' chameleon ability to approach unseen. She was just a few paces away. With long, thin fingers, the wraith drew a delicate knife. Fiona put Gaia into a defensive crouch, but the Wrathwraith turned toward Analise, who'd been thrown against the wall by the force of the blast. She wasn't moving. The wraith leaped at her and plunged the knife into her gut. Dark blood blossomed from her belly. The wraith raised the knife for another stab.

Fiona cried out into her headset microphone, which meant Gaia also cried out, and the wraith spun toward her. The wraith sheathed the knife, and the gobsmacker reappeared in her hands. She took aim. Gaia would have no defense. It wasn't even worth trying. Francis was shouting something, but Fiona didn't hear.

Gal'Blad slammed into the archangel Oaone like a freight train, toppling the Wrathwraith and slashing cruelly at her delicate feathered skin. Taken by surprise, the wraith discharged the gobsmacker. The bolt went wild and grazed the spinning machine. With a deafening metallic screech, one of the outermost rings buckled. Several whirling crystalline marbles spilled onto the floor. The damaged ring broke, and for a few moments it whirled crazily around the center of the machine like the blade of a helicopter before flying off and impacting the wall. Above the machine, the galactic map hologram, still only partially complete, wavered and flashed red. A shrill alarm sounded.

Oaone screamed in frustration. It seemed for an instant as though the Ghost might have the upper hand, but she was no match for an archangel-level avatar. Oaone slashed at Gal'Blad with her knife, and the Ghost staggered back with a terrible wound across her thorax.

Preparing to leap toward Gaia, Oaone glanced down. The holobox had been dislodged from the receptacle at the base of the machine. It lay at Gaia's feet, still glowing faintly. The Wrathwraith's eyes widened, and for an instant neither Gaia nor Oaone moved. Above the machine, the smoke ring of stars had almost faded from view.

The basement floor rumbled again.

Fiona manipulated the trackball, causing Gaia to scoop up the holobox and lunge clumsily for the machine. The wraith swung her blade and struck Gaia with a slash, dropping Gaia's health score another 200 points.

Gaia's aura flashed orange. She stumbled but didn't lose her footing. She thrust the box toward the receptacle.

On the TV screen, a popup appeared:

PLACE THE HOLOBOX INTO THE REMOTE KERNEL INTERFACE?

Fiona spun the cursor to the YES command.

Francis slapped his hand over her wrist, preventing her from selecting the command. "Fi, wait!"

The deep rumble grew louder. This was no passing truck, and Fiona knew it wasn't thunder because this was Northern California, where thunderstorms were rarer than unicorns and mermaids.

The archangel Oaone had frozen, was shouting at her, gesturing toward the little box, which Gaia held less than an inch from the receptacle. "Stop! That belongs to *me*. It's *mine*. Give it to me or you'll be in serious trouble. I'll find out who you are, and where you live. Give it to me!"

Something fell off the shelf at the back of the basement where Mama stored her household supplies. Fiona glanced at Francis. Earth tremors here in the valley weren't unusual, but this wasn't like any tremor she'd felt before. Francis's face was drawn into a tight knot.

"I'm going to turn it off, Fi. I don't know what's happening, but this is messed up."

"Let go of me."

"Fi, we could get into—"

"Let *go* of me!" she spat. She jerked her arm free from his grasp. On the television screen, the wraith leaped for Gaia, knife stabbing, but it was too late. Fiona selected YES, and Gaia's hand pressed the holobox back into the receptacle. Just as the holobox clicked into place, a dark cluster of organic tendrils, like questing vines, erupted from its sides and curled away in every direction. One of the tendrils touched the machine's bottommost spinning ring, and the screen went dark. A message appeared:

```
LOST CONNECTION TO SERVER
```

The floor heaved sideways, making Fiona feel as though she were in an accelerating car whose driver had just hit the brakes. Streams of dust cascaded from the ceiling tiles. Fiona instinctively grabbed the arms of her wheelchair, knocking the game controller off the Velcro mount. It fell to the floor. Upstairs, Mama let out a staccato scream. The streak of light beneath the door at the top of the stairs went out, and the television went black. The basement was instantly as dark as a crypt.

The rumbling movement stopped. Silence and utter darkness.

The basement door flew open. Mama's feet pounded down the stairs, illuminating her way with her phone, calling out to her children.

Fiona felt Francis's hand on her shoulder. "Are you okay?"

"Yeah, I think so," she whispered. She could see the fear etched into his face from the sharp light of Mama's phone. "What just happened?"

Francis expelled a hard breath. "I don't know, but it can't be good."

havencosm | CLOUDTOPS

Delicate Things

Kwon Se-Jong's flight arrived a day early, giving him plenty of time to explore Cloudtops Station before his connection home to Askelon. The security lines were short, and he breezed through the immigration portal without incident. His mind was untroubled. His trip had gone well. The interviews with his faculty advisor and the course counselors had been warm and productive. His grandmother would be well pleased.

His ticket included a sleeping pod at the terminal, but to celebrate he splurged on a room in the station's hotel. Soon enough he would be living in a crowded college dormitory, and he felt he owed himself this small luxury.

After checking in, he walked the station's promenade and bought a souvenir T-shirt and a gift for Grandmother, a tube of Bosporan black-chocolate truffles. Later, in his hotel room, he watched a movie on the entertainment screen, took a shower, then lay on top of the bedcovers and stared through the transparent ceiling at the ragged storms of Almost.

Almost was a gas giant, he knew, three times bigger than Jupiter but without Jupiter's deadly radiation fields. Cloudtops Station orbited just a few hundred kilometers from the planet's outer atmosphere, and from this vantage point it seemed to Se-Jong that the station was skimming across the tops of gargantuan storms like a speedboat surfing the wavetops. After a while, he found himself clutching the bed, lost in the giddy sensation of unstoppable speed.

The next morning Se-Jong checked in at the departure terminal only to find that his flight was delayed until the late afternoon. No matter. Time enough for a nap, and later, a meal. He settled into a seat, stretched his legs in front of him, and lowered his eyes. The waiting area was empty, and Se-Jong drifted into a light sleep. Time passed, during which he remained dimly aware of flight announcements from the loudspeakers and hushed voices as the seats around him began to fill with other passengers.

A shouted curse jolted him awake. The woman at the nearby check-in counter was tall and thin, with the corded muscles of a marathon runner. She was arguing fiercely with the counter agent, something to do with the weight of her carry-on bag, and her sharp words cut through the noise of the crowd. She obviously didn't care that she was making a scene or holding up the line. It was clear to Se-Jong that the counter agent wasn't going to budge, but the woman kept arguing anyway.

Eventually, the woman relented and paid the required fee, then huffed and stomped away from the counter, glaring at the people who'd been grumbling impatiently in line behind her. Even though she dressed in a typical fashion, Se-Jong found her appearance to be striking. She was definitely human, but her skin was a deep unnatural gray, like oiled gunmetal, glistening with sweat despite the artificial chill of the air.

She struggled to lift her oversized backpack to her narrow shoulders, ultimately giving up and dragging it across the floor. This seemed odd to Se-Jong, given her athletic appearance. He rose from his seat in the waiting area to offer his help. She studied him suspiciously, her gaze roving from his tight haircut to his crisply pressed clothes to his polished boots. Her eyes were the remorseless blue of a winter sky, a stark contrast to her skin. Eventually, she grimaced and gestured toward the backpack.

Se-Jong discovered that he could barely lift the bag.

"What do you have in here? Rocks?"

Her expression softened and she gave a mischievous laugh. Her name was Nkiru Anaya, which Se-Jong learned over a cup of coffee in the terminal lounge. She was a youth pilgrim, and the bag was indeed full of rocks. Rocks and scraps of metal. Bits and pieces of artifacts from before the Cataclysm.

Nkiru told Se-Jong that she'd begun her pilgrimage from Earth just six weeks earlier. She was traveling alone, an oddity. Pilgrims below the age of twenty-five were almost always part of a group led by a church-sanctioned chaperone. She'd already visited the shrines at Deepstone and Forniculus, she told him, where she'd collected the dubious treasures that now filled her backpack. She spoke breathlessly of her next destination, the massive reliquaries at the Regium Enclave on Assinni.

Even though she wore the customary yellow robes, she didn't look much like a pilgrim. She didn't talk like one, either. She spoke English with an old-fashioned accent, her sentences liberally seasoned with shocking, uncouth words delivered so smoothly it wasn't until after she finished that he realized he should have been offended. Se-Jong knew he should be repelled by her vulgarity, but his harsh judgment evaporated the first instant she smiled at him. Her scowling face split open, and it was instantly obvious that she'd used foul language to see how he would respond. She was judging him! And based on her smile, he'd passed some kind of test.

Apparently, the ramrod boy with the close-cropped haircut and serious expression wasn't as sanctimonious as he looked.

Coffee led to lunch in the terminal's food court, where she spread a few of the artifacts she'd collected on the table and talked about them with fire in her eyes. Lunch led to afternoon drinks at a dim tavern, where she recounted her misadventures on Forniculus. In return, he told her about his campus tour of the War College on the nearby world of Kojax. Compared with her tales of sneaking into a Forniculan shrine or riding a leaky bubble-sub to the watery core of the Deepstone, his accounts of meeting with the faculty and college admissions staff were pretty boring, but somehow she seemed interested. Entry to the War College was a pretty big deal, a fact she acknowledged with teasing scorn. He could tell, though, that beneath her sarcasm was a growing respect, and more than once during lulls in the conversation he caught her glancing at him appraisingly, as if he were being measured for some task.

Se-Jong had never been girl crazy, but he was utterly fascinated by Nkiru. She was smart, that much was obvious from the sharpness of her speech and the light in her pale eyes. She was also clearly fearless, having just traveled alone to Forniculus, the Planet of Righteous Rage, where even the slightest perceived insult to the inhabitants' strict culture—like sneaking into a forbidden shrine—could get you violently dismembered.

By the time they drained their first round of beers, she'd set herself apart from any girl he'd ever known. She was two years older than Se-Jong's nineteen and a half, and though she seemed wiser than her years, she often displayed an alluring immaturity, a hard-edged mischief. She was nothing like the female classmates with whom he'd spent the last four years at Jackill Academy. They'd all been dedicated and ambitious, smart and fearless, but as he listened to Nkiru he began to realize how narrowly focused they'd been. How narrowly focused *he'd* been. Nothing had mattered to any of them except ensuring that their grades were good enough for an appointment to the War College.

Nkiru was different. As the alcohol loosened her tongue, Se-Jong began to glimpse the scope of her passions. She didn't mention her plans for the future, or her friends, or her family, or any of the other typical topics of bar conversation with a young fellow traveler. Instead, with shining eyes, she talked about the endless depths of time and space, about the oldest memories of the galaxy, and occasionally she retrieved some shapeless piece of metal or stone from her backpack and claimed that it was a fragment of an avatar lord's battlepack or the power hilt of a flickerblade or, wonder of wonders, a battered but fully intact scancorder. Se-Jong knew that if it could be authenticated, the scancorder alone might be worth a small fortune.

In the conspiratorial darkness of their private booth, she pulled out her komnic, spent a few moments tapping and swiping on its small screen, and held it out to Se-Jong. He recognized the image, a photo of the famous fresco *Last Refuge of the Avatars* by the artist Leodiva. She zoomed in on a section of the mural, which had been painted on a monastery wall on some faraway world whose name he couldn't remember. In the image, a battleclad avatar was holding something—a scancorder identical to the artifact that lay on the table in front of him!

Se-Jong touched the scancorder, turned it over in his hand. The realness of the cold metal caused something new and frightening to flare in his soul. He'd held relics before, but only in the controlled ceremonial environment of a church reliquary. The Cataclyst scriptures had always been abstract stories, metaphors that provided spiritual guidance but had little bearing on the realities of modern life.

Se-Jong had never been religious, but holding this newly unearthed artifact suddenly made all the outlandish legends of the avatars seem real. He could feel the weight of time in his hands, the endless march of the millennia, and when he looked into the intensity of Nkiru's eyes, he saw the light of ancient suns.

A second and third round of drinks led to both of them losing track of time, intentionally, at least on Se-Jong's part. At one point she removed her rough-fabric head wrap, and when her hair spilled out over her shoulders, he lost his words and simply gaped. She sighed, as if all too accustomed to his startled reaction. In the gloomy bar, her pure-white hair, almost translucent, seemed to glow with its own light.

He wondered if the luminous effect was the result of an artificial treatment. In fact, everything about her appearance—skin the color of graphite dust, eyes of glacier ice, hair as pale as the feathers of a moon-owl—suggested either a truly bizarre genetic heritage or really expensive cosmetic enhancements. It was possible that she wasn't entirely human, though he quickly abandoned the disturbing thought. She would never have been granted pilgrims' credentials nor allowed to visit the holy shrines without having first passed the church's racial purity tests. He felt regretful as she deftly rearranged her hair into a tight twist and replaced the head wrap.

When he finally forced himself to look up at the clock over the bar, he noted with deep and disturbing satisfaction that they'd both missed their flights. She glanced at the clock, too, and gave him a hard, narrow-eyed grin that made his breath catch in his throat.

Se-Jong had never been romantic, but he found himself inviting Nkiru to the station hotel. She was suitably awed by the transparent ceiling in the hotel room and the ever-changing light from the hurricane-shredded planet. They talked late into the night. She spread bits and pieces of broken artifacts across the bedcovers and they took turns making up fantastical and ludicrous purposes for each item. Se-Jong's sides ached from laughing. Eventually he extinguished the room lights, and they lay side by side, watching storms approach and recede as they raced across the nightside of Almost. Shadows from flickers of lightning moved across the room, and when he finally worked up the courage to glance at her, she was staring back.

Despite her fierce looks, she made love hesitantly, as if the activity were new to her. It was new to Se-Jong, too, but their awkwardness was quickly replaced by feverish tumbling that left the bedcovers—and bits of archeological relics—scattered on the floor.

Finally exhausted, they cuddled in silence, her hair forming a halo on the sheets beneath her head.

Her mask of fearlessness dissolved as she drifted into sleep. Her eyes moved fitfully. Her arms and legs twitched. The uneven pace of her breathing and the unexpected way in which she clung to him caused an unfamiliar tightness in his gut. He lay next to her for a long time, not sure what to do. It wasn't until he put both his arms around her that her breathing slowed and she relaxed into deep slumber. Careful not to disturb her, he touched the bedside switch to draw the curtains over the transparent ceiling. In the darkness he discovered her translucent hair did not in fact glow, as he had first suspected, but merely absorbed and reflected the light. He nestled his face into it, discovering its smell, earthy and fresh and enchanting.

He awoke in a tangle of arms and legs, surrounded by broken artifacts and ten thousand years of history. Her eyes were open, and she smiled. His breath seized when she reached toward his face and brushed his cheek with her fingertips.

During the mostly sleepless night, the small flare of awe and wonder in Se-Jong's soul had become a raging pyroclastic eruption. When Nkiru hinted over morning coffee that she would welcome a traveling companion, a whole new possible future revealed itself. His imminent college plans suddenly seemed dreary and petty compared to the beckoning adventure of the Cataclyst pilgrimage, not to mention the tantalizing passions of this peculiar girl. When he'd asked why she was so determined to complete the pilgrimage, she'd told him, "Every minute I'm not living is a minute I'm dying."

Se-Jong had never been impulsive, but after breakfast he dispatched a message to his grandmother and informed her that he would be delaying his return to Askelon for a short side-trip to Assinni. He stopped short of telling her that he was thinking of deferring his War College enrollment by a semester. This, he knew, would not be well received. His grandmother had expressed, in no uncertain terms, the rock-solid expectation that Se-Jong would carry her military tradition into a new generation. Se-Jong had never questioned this expectation. Indeed, he had shared it. It had been comforting, knowing that his path into the future was smooth and clearly marked. He marveled at how such a small thing as a chance meeting with a stranger in a spaceport terminal could have such a profound impact on his long-established life plans. He recalled a line of Cataclyst scripture his grandmother was fond of quoting: *Even the mightiest river can be easily diverted at its source. Beginnings are delicate things.*

Riding a terrifying wave of euphoria, he bought a pilgrim's pass from the station's chaplain, and on the following evening he joined Nkiru on the three-week journey from Almost to Assinni, the homeworld of the Universal Cataclyst Church. By the time his grandmother received his message, he'd be halfway there. He fervently hoped the dozens of light-years of empty space would insulate him from her wrath.

Rose & Chalice

Their transport was the *Rose & Chalice*, one of a dozen church-owned rust buckets that circulated endlessly along the pilgrimage route. It was creaky, slow, and cramped, and they spent most of their time in the small berth they shared. Days passed, during which Se-Jong fell more and more under the thrall of Nkiru Anaya and her obsession with the grand adventures of the distant past. To her, nothing in modern life could compare to the romance of the last days of the Second Epoch, when mighty avatar lords held dominion over galaxy-spanning empires, the praelea angels walked among mortals, and the Oa watched and guided their affairs from their heavenly realm. Her passion was contagious, and he soon found himself glued to the screen of his komnic, searching alongside Nkiru through the *Chronicles of the Second Epoch* for obscure locations mentioned in the scriptures, places they might visit along the pilgrimage route.

It was a frustrating process. Nkiru believed many of the sacred stories of the *Chronicles* to be parables and not accounts of real happenings. Of those she believed were actual, historical events, the accounts were often so vague or brief that it was impossible to tie them to any physical location on a map. Of the small percentage of stories that included hard descriptions of places, such as a landscape, city, or building, most had probably occurred on worlds that had been swallowed by the Devastation during the Cataclysm. Given these grim circumstances, the chance that Nkiru could actually match a setting from a scripture story to an undiscovered site on a known world was vanishingly small.

In fact, Se-Jong would have thought it impossible, but Nkiru seemed to have an uncanny knack for finding references in obscure sacred texts that, upon examination, clearly pointed to locations in the Known Arc, a few even on the pilgrimage worlds they were planning to visit. Had she come up with some brilliant software search algorithm that could scan the ancient texts and identify references that matched a set of criteria? When he asked her secret, she only smiled and said, "It's in my blood."

There was more to it, Se-Jong knew. He quickly learned that Nkiru had the skeptical heart of a scientist. To her, unless a legend could be proven by empirical evidence, it remained myth. She utterly lacked the unquestioning faith demanded by the Cataclyst religion, but that didn't make her a nonbeliever. On the contrary, she fiercely trusted in the divine nature of the Oa, the mythical praelea angels, and the avatars. She had no doubt they'd been supernatural beings from a heavenly realm. In some ways it was this unwavering sense of religious certainty that most intrigued Se-Jong.

As the days passed aboard the transport, Se-Jong began to suspect that her zeal wasn't just scholarly, that there was another reason for her journey beyond earning the coveted youth pilgrim medallion. Every time Se-Jong asked, she laughed and mumbled something vague. "The youth pilgrimage is the cheapest way to see the Known Arc," or "I'll learn more on pilgrimage than I'd ever learn at school." Mostly, she seemed uncomfortable when he got too curious. One night, after too much drink, she assured him, in a tone of mock awe, that she was "searching for the keys to heaven." Though her voice was teasing and flippant, the expression on her face when she took her next sip of wine was anything but.

That night, like most nights, her fearless resolve seemed to melt away when she fell into the cramped bunk they shared. The steel of her posture, her perpetually haughty expression, the purposefulness of her movements: all these things dissolved into something like a desperate vulnerability. She seemed to crave to be held, molding her body against his like molten caramel on a rough pastry. More than once in their first week aboard she had startled him awake with horrific screams, bolting upright in bed, fighting the covers as if they were attacking her, only relaxing back into sleep when he pulled her down into the covers and stroked her remarkable hair.

Purpose

When he'd first stepped aboard the *Rose & Chalice*, the creaking transport ship had seemed like a romantic anachronism, filled with the charm of an earlier, simpler time. Raw aluminum bulkheads. Dripping air-conditioner vents. Tiny berths with thin mattresses. No windows, even in the dining compartment where most of the passengers spent their long days. The company of exotic pilgrims from a dozen worlds.

It hadn't taken long for the romance of the antique vessel to wear thin, and even less time thereafter for him to begin to hate the ship and its passengers. It was overcrowded, and the oxygen reconditioner struggled against the load of almost a hundred souls, dozens more than it was designed to support. The air stank of body odor and machine oil, the food was awful, and because the pilgrim passengers were expected to maintain the shared spaces, the galley tables were rarely clean and the bathrooms were truly vile. There were several Forniculans aboard, as well as a contingent of Betelosians, which, considering the ship had been originally designed for humans, was a big problem. The bathroom facilities were not up to the task of handling the volume and acidity of Forniculan excrement, and the Betelosians simply relieved themselves where they stood, whether it was in a passageway or at a galley dining table. To their credit, they always apologized and swabbed up the gooey mess, but the air filters could never quite overcome the stench of their insectile droppings. He knew that if his grandmother could see his situation, she would be utterly disgusted with him.

Even the company of the exotic pilgrims had turned out to be a massive disappointment. Most were human pensioners fifty years older than he and Nkiru, indulging in a last, great adventure, a last-gasp effort to discover the meaning of life. They clung together at the galley's large central table, a knot of gray hair and sagging flesh, discussing their medical ailments and their grandchildren and drinking Bosporan wine until they retired to their cabins at a ridiculously early hour. The few other youth pilgrims were, well, they were *weird*. Religious fanatics, mostly AON zealots unable to hold a conversation other than to rage about politics. After almost getting in a fistfight the third night out of Cloudtops Station, Se-Jong avoided everyone but Nkiru. She didn't seem to notice the others, or the discomforts of the crowded ship. She spent her days glued to the screen of her komnic, reading about Assinni and the other holy worlds where the final battles of the legendary Avatar Wars had been fought.

On this night, Se-Jong was seriously considering getting into another fight. He and Nkiru were at a fold-down table waiting for the dinner meal, which he knew would consist of bread, cheese, a chunk of greasy protoham, and a slice of dried fruit. He knew this because it was the same meal they served for every dinner. The food wasn't the source of his anger. It was the next table, where four AON punks were whispering and staring. Three were Humanish, but one was a Forniculan, which was the only thing holding Se-Jong back. It muttered something, and they all laughed. The unmistakable odor of jeeb hooch floated from the table, and Se-Jong saw the silver flask in the alien's hand. It was drunk.

Se-Jong winced and ground his teeth. The Forniculan was a juvenile, probably less than fifty Earth years old. It caught Se-Jong's eye. Se-Jong didn't look away. The alien tightened its fore-lips and gave Se-Jong a once-over, taking in his lack of a purity collar, his expensive clothes and shiny military-style boots. "What are ye doing here, bey?" it asked in the heavy brogue of Low Tang, the shared language spoken by most nonhumans. "Yeer nah pilgrim."

Se-Jong didn't answer. He glanced at Nkiru, who was staring into nothingness, absently toying with a pewter ring on the third finger of her right hand. The Forniculan's mouth curled into a sneer, and it turned to its companions. "I dan think our bey here is looking fer enlightenment, um?" They nodded agreement, disgust clear on their faces. The alien turned back to Se-Jong. "Tell me, what are ye doing here, eh, in yeer fancy dods? Dan ye know a pilgrim is supposed te go without wealth or possession? With nau but de grace of de Oa in his heart?" It shook its head. "I dan think it's yeer desire te purify yeer soul, nor te learn de way of de elder heroes." Its eyes moved to Nkiru, then accusingly back to Se-Jong. "I think it's de heat of te flesh dat drives ye. Yeer chasin' dis daerk tasty kitty, aren't ye?"

The crowded main table had fallen silent. The balding and gray-haired pilgrims were watching the interchange, some of them bewildered, some of them obviously sympathetic to the Forniculan.

Se-Jong tried not to react, but his anger must have been obvious from the tremble in his clenched fists. Nkiru put her hand lightly on his arm. "Ignore them," she said, loud enough for the Forniculan and its companions to hear. "They're a bunch of slack-brained fools." When Se-Jong continued to glare at the Forniculan, she moved her restraining hand from his arm to his chin and forcibly rotated it to face her. Her eyes were narrow and demanding. "Ignore them," she repeated.

Se-Jong nodded reluctantly. He let his shoulders fall and unclenched his fists. He could still feel the Forniculan's eyes on him, but he kept his focus on Nkiru. She smiled, and her fingers moved up from his chin to playfully tap the tip of his nose. "It doesn't matter what they think. They have no idea why you're really here. Remember," she quoted one of the lines from the pilgrim's mantra: *"Every pilgrim's purpose is his own."*

He looked around the room, at the array of battered pilgrims' robes, at the staring faces, some kindly, a few uncaring, several suspicious and belligerent. He looked for purpose in their expressions and found only varying states of confusion. It occurred to him that they wouldn't be here on this pilgrimage if they had a life purpose. That was the whole point of the pilgrimage, wasn't it? The pursuit of purpose? Of meaning?

It was suddenly obvious why the other pilgrims seemed resentful. Nkiru had a purpose. It was clear from her confident intensity that she was here for a reason. Unlike them, she wasn't casting about aimlessly in a spiritual haze, searching for some pie-in-the-sky enlightenment. She was on a mission, and her certainty unsettled the others, making their own awkward insecurities glare in contrast.

What was *he* doing here, he suddenly wondered? Had he really allowed his own life purpose to be derailed by a girl he met at a spaceport lounge? From beneath a lowered brow, he studied the occupants of the room. He knew the type. They were like sheep, being led around by an organized religion whose only goal was to suck money and power from the masses. Not one of them could think for themself. This pilgrimage was a perfect example. The church called it the Secta Avataris, which meant the Way of the Avatars, and it supposedly followed the route of the final battles of the Avatar Wars leading up to the Rapture and the Cataclysm.

Se-Jong knew the term Secta Avataris had another, older meaning. The Way of the Avatars wasn't just a pilgrimage route on a star map; it was also a life code—a brutal, militaristic philosophy of a vanished race of conquerors who built galaxy-spanning empires but were destroyed by the Cataclysm at the moment of their highest glory, likely due to their own hubris.

Se-Jong's grandmother, a senior captain in the Solar Guard, had always been his role model, and she'd always scoffed at religion. Unlike most high-ranking military officers, she'd never worn a purity collar, nor had she regularly attended Cataclyst mass. She had, however, kept a small leather-clad book with her at all times, a book that contained an excerpt from the sacred *Chronicles of the Second Epoch*, and across the spine were the words *Secta Avataris*. She'd studied the true Way of the Avatars, and it had nothing to do with visiting a bunch of crumbling shrines on a string of washed-up planets.

His grandmother had always scared him a little. His gaze settled on Nkiru, who was watching him carefully. She scared him a little, too. She was nothing like the other pilgrims. She had a weight to her, a solidness that the others lacked. They were feathers blowing in a breeze. She was the heavy steel shaft of a spear in flight. But what was her target? She dreamed of locating pre-Cataclysm sites mentioned in the sacred texts, but for what reason? Up until now she'd given no hint, other than to satisfy her obviously burning curiosity. She was obviously not just a dungeon diver looking for relics to sell back to the church. No, there was something more.

Had she grown up in the church? Were her parents religious? Did she even *have* parents? She'd once talked vaguely of growing up in California on Earth but had given no details. She'd mentioned a church sponsor for her youth pilgrimage, but she'd resisted Se-Jong when he pressed for details. She talked of ancient scriptural events as if they'd happened last month, but she never spoke about her friends or her school experiences. He had a deep suspicion that something bad might have happened to make her leave home, but his hunch was based on nothing but her regular nightmares and her reluctance to talk about her past.

One thing was quickly becoming obvious to him. Beneath her fiercely confident exterior, Nkiru Anaya was *scared*. She was terrified of facing the future alone. Se-Jong could completely empathize. He'd never admitted it to himself until now, but maybe the War College and a career in the Solar Guard wasn't his true calling. He respected his grandmother, but he suddenly realized he didn't want to *be* like her. Perhaps this explained how he'd allowed his entire life to be sidetracked by a chance meeting with a girl. His future was now a terrifying unknown. If not the military, then what? In any future with Nkiru Anaya, what role would he play?

His face must have betrayed his thoughts, because Nkiru cocked her head and gave him a quirky, questioning smile. Se-Jong felt his anxiety lessen, just a bit, and he returned her smile. It wasn't that he'd gotten sidetracked by a girl, not at all. He'd been sidetracked by a compelling and irresistible enigma in the *shape* of a girl. An enigma he was resolved to unravel.

EASTER EGG

meatspace | FIONA

Suits

The man in the suit tried to smile, but Fiona could tell he had an edge to him, something sharp and unbending that no amount of false kindness could conceal. He and his two companions had come without warning, just a knock on the door and a flash of a government ID that Mama hadn't even seen through her fear. She had ushered them into the kitchen, the only place in the small house with enough seating for everyone. The strangers perched awkwardly on the narrow plastic chairs across the breakfast table from Fiona and Francis.

The man in the suit frowned as Mama swept the half-eaten chilaquiles from the table and dumped the plates noisily in the sink. He cleared his throat. "Ms. Martinez, I'm sorry for interrupting your family's breakfast. This shouldn't take long. I, uh, just need some information from your son Francis."

Fiona's heart thudded so hard she was afraid the others had heard it. She tried to keep her expression neutral and not look at her brother. She knew with stomach-churning certainty why the strangers were here. Francis sat straight, hands folded on the table, but Fiona recognized the telltale signs of anxiety in her twin. He swallowed every few seconds as if his mouth were dry. His knee bobbed up and down under the table in an unconscious rhythm, shaking the kitchen floor. He knew why they had come, too.

The electricity had been restored quickly after the previous night's earth tremor. The only sign that anything was amiss was the cracked glass in the kitchen window and the presence of the strangers at the table: the gray-haired man in the suit; another man in a starched button-down shirt, younger and solidly muscular; and a thick-waisted woman with oversized eyeglasses and a terrible case of adult acne. The two men shifted uneasily in their chairs. The pimpled woman, who had immediately opened and hunched over a battered laptop, glanced furtively at Fiona.

Mama rolled and twirled her necklace between her fingers as if the little silver cross might summon Jesus and he would come and take her away to anywhere but here. She stared at the man with a blank expression. "Is my son in trouble?"

The man raised his hands. "No ma'am, not at all. We just have a few questions for him." He turned to Francis. "You were playing the *Longstar* game last night, correct?"

Francis's knee stopped bobbing. He stared unflinchingly at the surface of the kitchen table, where the crumbs of their breakfast were still scattered.

"Yes, sir." His voice was low and sharp, and Fiona knew the frustration in his tone was directed at her. He'd warned her when things in the game had gotten weird, but she'd begged him to keep playing.

The man in the suit looked down at a tablet he'd placed on the table. "Tell me, Francis, did you get a notification yesterday from Orbital Arena that a game update was being released?"

"Yes, sir."

"What time of day did you receive the notification?"

"Um, I was coming home from school, so it must've been about three o'clock."

The man swiped at his tablet screen, nodded. "It says here you received notification on your phone two hours before the release's general announcement."

"I guess so."

"It also says here that you were the only player out of nine million game subscribers to receive advance notification."

Francis looked up at the man. "Wait. *What?*"

The man raised his eyebrows.

Her brother stuttered. "I . . . um, I had no idea. Why would they do that?"

"I was hoping you could tell me." Francis's look of genuine astonishment seemed to unsettle the man. "Did you notice anything . . . unusual in the game last night?"

"Besides the fact that it crashed?"

"Yes. Before it crashed. Did you notice any unusual behavior from other players? Did any of them ask you to do anything out of the ordinary?"

Francis shifted in his chair. "What do you mean?"

The second man, the big guy in the starched shirt, was watching Francis with the intensity of a lion stalking a lamb. Something was unsettlingly familiar about his square face and deeply cleft chin. The woman with the laptop adjusted her glasses and stared expectantly at Francis. The knuckles of both her hands were crudely tattooed with letters from a language Fiona didn't recognize.

The man in the suit leaned back and crossed his arms. "Did any other player give you anything? Any unusual information, or maybe a virtual item in the game?"

Francis answered without hesitation, "No, sir. Nothing."

Fiona felt a thrill of fear at her brother's lie. He lifted a finger of warning, the tiniest twitch of his hand resting on the table, the subtlest of motions that only a twin sibling would recognize as a signal. Yet somehow, the second man, the one with the dimpled chin, saw it too, and he gave her a piercing look. She had seen the man before. She was sure of it.

The man in the suit hardened his voice. "Francis, I wouldn't be here if this wasn't important. We know you were playing the Grone campaign last night. I need you to describe to me, in detail, exactly what you saw during gameplay."

Everyone focused on Francis. Everyone, that is, but the second man, who continued to stare at Fiona. They locked eyes. One of the corners of his mouth crinkled upward.

Where had she seen him before?

———

The man in the suit eventually introduced himself as Mr. Howe. He'd been spewing rapid-fire questions at Francis for almost thirty minutes, and her brother was showing the strain.

"Other than last night, have you ever encountered the avatars called Atum or Oaone at any other time while you were playing the game?"

Francis shook his head. "No. Last night was the first time I'd ever seen either of them."

Mr. Howe nodded, but his eyes tightened. "And you've never had any prior dealings with any employee of Orbital Arena Games? Either inside the game or in the real world?"

"No, sir."

Mr. Howe tapped his index finger on the kitchen table. "Have you been contacted by anyone at all concerning the events that took place in the game last night? Perhaps on social media?" When Francis again shook his head, Mr. Howe continued. "Have you told anyone about your experience in the game? Talked about it with friends or family? Kids at school?"

"Nobody."

"Did the avatars Atum or Oaone mention any people or places, either in the game or in the real world?"

"I don't think so."

Fear spiked in Fiona's gut. Atum—Arni's avatar—*had* mentioned other names. Somebody named *Chun*. Somebody named *Rupe*. And Analise had named the avatar who'd shot her: *Wolfe*.

Fiona resisted the urge to squirm in her wheelchair. Who *were* these people? Were they FBI? Or worse, ICE? She thought about the backup of her avatar's item stash that they'd made at Arni's request. On it was a copy of the smoky jewel he'd called a Shadow Emora. He'd instructed her to "Get it off the internet and onto a backup drive. Please, hide the backup until I call!"

Francis had done so and had even erased the log of the video chat from his phone, all without understanding the reason for his actions. She was dying to ask who Arni was. Analise had said that he worked for the game company. But who was Analise? Could it be they were both part of some kind of conspiracy? As Arni had requested, they'd moved the backup file of Gaia's item stash off the game computer and onto a removable thumbdrive. Francis had hidden it behind the furnace in the basement. Could it have some illegal stuff on it? She'd seen plenty of movies where the nuclear launch codes or the formula for cold fusion had been hidden on a computer chip. In those movies, the chip had always seemed to fall into the hands of an unwitting civilian who spent the rest of the movie trying to figure out why guys in suits were trying to kill them.

Could this be a similar situation? So far, the strangers hadn't asked any questions that implied they knew about the thumbdrive. Maybe they were here for a completely different reason. No matter; she'd already decided to tell them about it if they asked her. But they weren't asking her. Even when they posed questions seemingly directed at both of them, they always looked at Francis. Maybe it was because she was a girl, but it was more likely they couldn't stomach her appearance. Screw them, anyway. If they couldn't even *look* at her, then she wasn't going to volunteer any information.

Mr. Howe eventually ran out of questions. He sighed and leaned back and nodded to the other man, the guy in the button-down shirt with the chin dimple. He introduced himself: *Jacob Solomon.*

Fiona stifled a gasp. She exchanged a glance with Francis, then looked back at the man named Solomon. *It's definitely him.* The man in the starched shirt had the same chin and the same physique as the soldier avatar whose profile popup had identified it as SOLOMON in the dungeon on Grone.

Just like Mr. Howe, Solomon ignored Fiona and directed his questions to Francis. He seemed friendlier, despite his thick frame and ramrod-straight posture. "You and your teammate Tremendo were the only two players in the caverns on Grone, correct?"

Francis took a moment to answer. She knew what was going through his mind: there had been *three* avatars in the cave on Grone: Geo, Tremendo—and Gaia.

"All the other participants were NPCs, right?" prompted Solomon.

Francis cleared his throat and answered Solomon carefully, not quite lying, but not quite responding to the spirit of the question. "As far as I know, other than my team and the two archangels that showed up, everybody else in the cave was a bot." Fiona remembered that she had been invisible during the battle. Her stealthshield had been active. If this real-world Solomon had been playing the Solomon avatar in the Grone cavern, he wouldn't have seen Gaia. No wonder they hadn't been directing any questions to her. *They don't know I was there.*

"Where did the bots come from?"

"Some were villagers," Francis said. "We used their boat to get across the lake. They followed us into the dungeon. I don't know where the US Marines came from. They just dropped out of the ceiling and started shooting. I've never seen anything like them before in the game."

The corner of Solomon's mouth crinkled again. He'd been in charge of those very same marine avatars. "So as far as you know, other than your avatar Geo, plus Oaone, Atum, and Tremendo, there were no other player avatars in the vicinity."

Without hesitation, Francis said, "Not that I saw."

In the end, Mr. Howe called in agents from SUVs parked on the curb outside. They were apologetic about it, but they didn't ask permission. They simply handed Mama a piece of paper and said it was a warrant to search the location and seize property. They wore navy-blue jackets with *FBI* emblazoned across the back. They went straight to the basement, and while Fiona and Francis and Mama waited silently at the kitchen table, they searched.

It didn't take long. They came back upstairs carrying Francis's game computer. They demanded all their phones. They asked if there were any more internet-connected devices in the house. When they were finished, the man in the suit, Mr. Howe, handed out his business card.

"It may be a while before we can return your property. I'm very sorry. Please get in touch with me *immediately* if you are contacted by anyone concerning the video game. Understood?" Francis and Mama nodded. Finally, Mr. Howe looked straight into Fiona's face. "This is *important*. Call me at once if you think of something you didn't tell us. Okay?"

Fiona didn't reply. The man sighed, nodded, and motioned for his colleagues. Then they were gone, leaving an entire street of neighbors hiding behind blinds and curtains wondering why the FBI had just been at the Martinez house.

Francis grimaced. "How do they expect us to call them, huh? They took our phones." He looked down at the man's business card. Fiona looked down at the business card, too. When she looked up, Francis was staring at her with a disbelieving look.

Reginald Howe
Senior Program Manager
Joint Exercise Environment Battlespace (JEEB)
Initiative
United States Department of Defense

St. Francis

Lights from a passing car shone through the window blinds and sent a geometric cascade of shadows skittering across the ceiling. Next to her bed, the oxygen concentrator hissed, sending life-giving gas through its plastic tubes and into her scarred lungs. Francis was in the cot on the other side of the room, waiting for the 2:00 a.m. alarm that would signal her next dose of medication. Even through the closed bedroom door, Fiona could hear soft sobs from across the hall. Mama was at her breaking point; the day's events had pushed her right to the edge.

Without Dad, Mama had nobody to turn to. Francis did his best to console her, but Mama had grown up in a large, tight-knit Catholic family in a rural Mexican village. More than anything, she needed to be surrounded by the comforting blanket of her kin, but expensive visas and airfare to America were out of their reach. One of her uncles had come for Dad's funeral to represent the family, but her siblings and cousins had been forced to pool their resources to make it happen. She wasn't about to burden them again with her troubles.

Mama was a stranger in a strange land. The only force that could've torn her away from her beloved family in the first place was her passionate love for Dad, a dashing young Silicon Valley hopeful who'd spent a month in her village as part of a team scouting for sites for a lithium battery plant. At the end of that month, to the intense dismay of her parents, brothers, sisters, and vast array of cousins, the handsome mestizo had swept her off to America and into the light of a bright future. But now he was gone, immolated by the same fiery monster that had sealed Fiona's fate, leaving Mama trapped in a nightmare. The very concept of being a single parent was utterly alien to her, but there could be no return to the fold of her Mexican family. Her children were American. Her daughter needed medical care only available in America. There was no going back.

As much as Fiona knew Mama loved her, she also knew that her mother felt only despair when she looked at her. That left Francis as the only thread still connecting Mama to the tapestry of her former dreams. Mama clung to that thread with every ounce of her life force, not realizing that the weight of her desperation was stretching her son to his own breaking point. *Poor Francis*, Fiona thought, listening to the soft cadence of her brother's breathing, fully aware of the irony that *she* was feeling sorry for *him*. *Only fifteen, and he's forced to take care of a broken mother and a dying sister.*

After the government people left, Mama had launched into a shrill tirade in Spanish, unleashing her fears, and her tears, against Francis. Francis had endured silently until Mama's confused fury ran out of steam. Then he'd wrapped Mama in his arms until her sobs had stopped. When he released her, Fiona saw his hands shaking. As much as he tried to seem strong around Mama, Fiona knew the visit from Howe and Solomon had terrified him to the core. She knew exactly how he felt.

Fiona spent the rest of the day parked in front of the basement TV, avoiding Mama. Adding to the general sense of unreality, the television was dominated by news about the previous evening's earth tremor, which had been centered under the Bay Area but felt as far away as Boston and Honolulu. It hadn't been strong enough to cause damage, but the fact that it had rumbled St. Louis and Atlanta and Houston with the same force as at the epicenter in San Francisco seemed to be unprecedented. After a while, Francis joined her and took his customary position on the basement couch. They sat numbly, watching the streamer across the bottom of the news channel:

> *Widespread shock to power grid during nationwide tremor – Almost 4 million homes still without power – Tsunami warning for Hawaii and Aleutians canceled*

Fiona ignored the words. She couldn't get the image of Analise out of her mind, and the memory gave her chills. *"I'm something new,"* Analise had said. Her face had shown real pain when she was injured. She'd bled, not like an avatar, not like a bot, but like a real, flesh-and-blood person. Everyone in the virtual battle in the cavern at Grone had been trying to get their hands on her. Whoever, or whatever, she was, Analise was at the dead center of this whole affair.

Fiona's hand found her brother's. He squeezed gently and didn't let go.

—

At 2:00 a.m., Francis rose, killed the trilling alarm, and sleepily proceeded to give her an injection and apply ointment to the skin grafts on her legs. He didn't speak, but she knew what was on his mind. It was on her mind, too.

The thumbdrive was still hidden in the crack between the furnace and the concrete basement wall. The FBI agents hadn't done a very thorough search. They'd come for the game computer, but they'd apparently had no idea that Arni's avatar Atum had given a mysterious jewel to Fiona's avatar, Gaia. Or that Fiona had, as per Arni's instructions, made a physical backup copy and deleted the file from her profile's cloud account.

It was oddly thrilling to think that a treasure item from the virtual world had made the leap into the real world. The thumbdrive didn't look anything like the little smoky jewel, but its essence was identical. In cyberspace, it had been a shiny, faceted stone. Here in meatspace, it manifested itself as digital data on a little plastic-and-metal stick.

Whatever it was, it had been desperately important to Arni. And now the FBI had shown up here, on their doorstep. And not just the FBI, but also the military. By not revealing the thumbdrive to Howe and Solomon, had they committed a crime?

They hadn't lied about it, exactly. Howe and Solomon simply hadn't asked the right questions. But now, here they were, in possession of something that might be of great interest to the government of the United States. She was beginning to regret the decision not to give it to Howe. Should they turn it in? If they did, could they be arrested for hiding it in the first place? Or should they get rid of it and pretend that nothing ever happened? Who was this Arni guy, anyway? What if he was a terrorist? What if the thumbdrive really *did* contain a stolen copy of America's nuclear codes, or something similarly ominous? If they gave it to Howe or destroyed it, would Arni come after them for revenge?

How had Howe found them? In the game, the Wrathwraith Oaone had threatened Gaia and Geo, saying she knew their real names and where they lived. But Analise had said Oaone was Arni's boss. Arni had also known their names and Francis's phone number and had claimed to work for Orbital Arena. That meant whoever was behind the Oaone avatar must also work for the game company.

She found it interesting that Solomon and his peculiar team of marine avatars had been shooting at both Oaone *and* Atum. Fiona's mind raced. If Solomon worked for the government, why had his team been trying to kill the avatars of the people who worked for Orbital Arena? And how had Solomon identified Francis as the player behind Geo? Had the government somehow hacked into the game? Did it know the private identity of every avatar?

A thought suddenly cut through the worry and made her grin. Francis was putting the cap on a thick tube of antibiotic ointment. He looked at her quizzically. "What's so funny?"

"I wonder if the FBI showed up at Tremendo's house?"

That got a smile from Francis, too. Tremendo's player was a trash-talking middle schooler with overcharged hormones. How had he and his family reacted when the FBI knocked on their door?

A moment passed while they both imagined the encounter. Then Francis's smile faded. "I hope he doesn't tell them that you were there, too." He bit his lip. "What should we do about the thumbdrive?"

She didn't know how to answer. "We need more information."

Research

The library was mostly empty, just a couple of old ladies in the book stacks and a homeless man sleeping at one of the reading tables. The librarian was eyeing the man, obviously trying to decide whether to call the police or let him sleep. She was so focused on him that she barely acknowledged Fiona's motorized wheelchair and portable oxygen tank, a fact for which Fiona was grateful.

They chose two workstations in the rear corner, away from the other desks. Francis slipped the thumbdrive out of his pocket and handed it to Fiona. She made a furtive survey of the other library patrons. Nobody was looking. First, she motioned for Francis to detach the network cable from the back of her computer just in case the files on the thumbdrive might try to automatically connect back to the Orbital Arena servers. She plugged the thumbdrive into the computer. The drive's icon appeared on the screen. She took a deep breath and selected it.

There, amidst the downloaded music and old homework, was a new file:

```
sah_gaia_0401_FFFe5BD.bak
```

She tried selecting the file, but all she got was a message saying *File Type Not Recognized*. She spent several minutes unsuccessfully trying different techniques to open the file, but nothing worked. Finally, she renamed it, replacing the *bak* filename extension with *txt*, hoping to fool the computer into thinking it was a simple text file.

It worked, sort of. A word processor app opened, and the screen filled with pages upon pages of seemingly random gibberish.

```
3zMcxDPNIouwgSLUVB9t
6V5BYn4wuvzxAC4nfitV
tD6f6Cwqu2977L6if7YQ
Yf5UNXhD3QW9IbLlN7Oa
FgGpMOmIQOYZPs4E2vHQ
CJddRj2wLYpzvWBIBjxc
EngG0KB8BZpFY98JuiTN
kxuZ6fiAxhiNzvzLeqeg
Y2rIUtlRtEHPfEJkFghh
6WFY0pwtCn8dhEuJoQUj
zSCIRqG6z6mhKoDMDyNN
qsLtQkpliwT73jEyEnyE
Xo6HXteLz5BItSdFhVbv
sejTqdG7gTm6rwKcGQd0
hDYQCqePmHOfthL4kXSF
```

Francis made a disgusted *pshaw* sound and turned to the other computer. Fiona scrolled slowly through the pages of code, looking for anything recognizable. It took a couple of minutes, but eventually she stumbled across:

```
FAjwbWTn9isS1MkoGosr
tBQ//FLAMETHROWER//
WEAPCLASS:87406//vis
qFx3tW4XvsLWJYp0rB0m
CU9aT456c9TjvKa1SFnS
XAadFW9m0clWptvffh3B
Ayj4MHcXgVpIl1QWKpww
3M4XrdHw6l6suv3b19Vb
```

Flamethrower! That was one of the few weapons she had in her avatar's stash. It made sense for it to appear in the file, as the file was technically a backup copy of her avatar's item inventory. She continued to scroll, occasionally recognizing the names of other items in Gaia's stash:

```
y3SNxuoQ3A75hpiKd6zL
cwT1FRL9UIV80LsvHjOb
ERRibzcRuNtREnJFiZ3X
//STEALTH_SHIELD//
WEAPCLASS:82907//ST
oUF5vfmda6iYNVwH3sqx
```

and

```
oTKxGcqUEbjBQQ6nVEIN
tI6dX//HEALTH_PACK//
ITEMCLASS:22104//VO7
dK9kKC2mT8Wyz25FtNC2
NR1tIy40QYVbQ3ZrBR5X
```

And then, after nearly ten minutes of eye-straining, headache-inducing scrutiny, something she didn't recognize:

```
eF1UObi5m5ISFhQOZ5Im
Yy4dWFupufEQgePaOAg2
//SHADOW_EMORA//
ITEMCLASS:00067//
REQ:ISTARA//Uyh26skK
YCtvur5CwZ0Gbu4XTBxB
ISpsHT53vEGmweC03hhd
```

She stared at a section of the text:

```
SHADOW_EMORA
```

She nudged Francis and pointed at the screen. He looked at it and turned to his computer and typed the words into the search engine.

```
No results found for "shadow emora"
```

He scowled. "That was the gray jewel Analise gave you to open the door, right? Maybe it's some kind of game hack." He scanned the gibberish of numbers and letters surrounding the phrase. "This doesn't tell us anything." He seemed impatient, and he gestured at the screen of his own workstation. "Okay, now check this out." He selected a different tab at the top of his browser. "I looked up Howe and Solomon." His voice dropped to a whisper. "These guys are big leaguers."

Fiona skimmed the article, which had appeared in a magazine called *Silicon Weekly*.

The Joint Exercise Environment Battlespace (JEEB) initiative is the result of a public-private partnership between the Department of Defense and the video-gaming industry. The goal is to enhance the capability of the American warfighter by bringing high-end augmented reality (AR) and virtual reality (VR) technology to real-world battlegrounds. From creating ultrarealistic wargame simulations to developing computer-augmented gear for the foot soldier, the JEEB program leverages cutting-edge technology for combat training, tactical scenario planning, and simplified visualization of complex tactical data.

"Now check this out," Francis said, and he selected another tab. Apparently, while she'd been poring through the gibberish in the thumbdrive backup file, Francis had been busy doing research.

The Defense Department has made the long-awaited award for its $1.2 billion virtual warfare platform, the Joint Exercise Environment Battlespace (JEEB) program. In a statement accompanying the award announcement, program manager Reginald Howe called JEEB "a cutting-edge new approach to technology that will revolutionize how America fights and wins wars."

Air Force Colonel Jacob Solomon, head of the Joint Forces Training Command at Travis Air Force Base, says "building on the success of our partnership with the leaders of the virtual reality industry, we have developed a comprehensive platform to leverage advances in human-machine interfaces that will enable warfighters to better execute the missions of the future—

She hadn't finished reading when Francis suddenly scrolled farther down the page. Before she could object, he pointed to a photograph of a smiling woman in a business suit and square-framed glasses. The caption under her photo read:

> *April Chun, CEO of Orbital Arena Games.*

"Chun!" exclaimed Fiona.

Francis held his index finger to his lips. "*Shhh!* Read this part."

> *Several companies are protesting the decision to award the $1.2 billion JEEB contract to a single vendor. "This acquisition was a sham," says Keith Clarkson, a representative of the National Association of VR Developers (NAVRD). "There was only one company that could meet the requirements, and the government knew it. It wrote the contract specifically for Orbital Arena and its QARMA VR engine. Nobody else had a chance."*

Once again, Francis selected another tab before she could finish reading. This time she saw a strange fire in his eyes. He didn't say anything, just pointed.

On the screen were the results of an image search. The entire screen was filled with thumbnail-size depictions of a thin, wasplike humanoid covered in translucent red feathers.

She looked questioningly at her brother. "A Wrathwraith?"

He nodded and selected one of the images about halfway down the list. A page appeared from a well-known gaming blog:

> There was another sighting yesterday, submitted by a player called YUKON76. Here's a screenshot of the archangel Oaone, showing her profile popup. Unless this is a fake, it proves that archangel-level avatars do exist in the game. The prevailing theory is that the archangel avatars belong to the high-level executives at Orbital Arena, and rumor has it that the archangel Oaone is the avatar for the big kahuna herself, company cofounder and CEO April Chun.

Francis was leaning back in his chair, watching her. She felt a hollow chill sink from her heart into the pit of her stomach. "Colonel Solomon's avatar was fighting Oaone in the cavern on Grone," she whispered, trying to work out the implications in her head. "That means he was fighting the CEO of a company that just won a billion-dollar military contract."

Francis nodded. "There's more," he said, and he selected one of the four remaining tabs on the browser. It was a Wikipedia article:

> Rupert Schroeder (born May 14, 1990) is a German video-game designer, writer, director, and producer. He is known primarily for his groundbreaking work developing the enhanced open-world gaming environment in the Longstar online roleplaying game.
>
> Schroeder is well-known in gaming circles and maintains the immensely popular gaming site Ruperus Bloggus, where he regularly leaves hidden clues for players of Longstar. As gamemaster and chief worldbuilder at Orbital Arena Games, he is responsible for developing the gameplay scenarios and designing the game maps, dungeons, characters, and terrains. His avatar, the mischievous Ruperus, is a common sight at hotspots in the Longstar universe.

A picture of a round-faced man with a scruffy blond beard accompanied the article. Francis gestured toward the photo. "Arni mentioned somebody named Rupe," he said. "He must have been talking about Ruperus." Fiona nodded. *Longstar* was unique among online roleplaying games in that a single, very visible gamemaster guided the game experience of the millions of players. Like a mischievous demigod from Greek mythology, the Ruperus avatar often slipped in and out of the game universe using disguises and aliases to stir up chaos and provoke game rivalries. His always-grinning avatar, devil horned and centaur-like, was the face of the company inside the game, and he ruthlessly enforced game rules—not to ensure fairness, but to ensure the maximum *fun* for the maximum number of players. When players got *ruped*, it meant that they'd received a warning or their avatar had been put in the game's penalty box, where they had to wait in enforced time-out as penance for their misdeeds. Tremendo had once been ruped for an entire day after trash-talking another player.

"Now look at this," Francis whispered, and selected the next tab on his browser. The familiar home page of the Orbital Arena Games website filled the screen. Obscuring the login fields and the colorful ads for avatar upgrades was a square text window with a red background and blocky white letters:

> *Greetings, Rangers! We regret to inform you that the LONGSTAR online game service has been temporarily suspended due to unforeseen technical difficulties. We're working hard to resolve the problem and hope to be back online soon. Watch your notification feeds for updates. We promise to keep you informed, and never fear, we will adjust your billing accounts to compensate you for the downtime. – April Chun, CEO Orbital Arena Games*

Francis leaned back and gave her a sideways look. "I think you crashed the whole game when you put that holobox into that brass machine thing. I *knew* I should've turned the game off, Fi. This is a *big* deal. Orbital Arena is a huge company! What if they sue us? Oh, God, this is going to kill Mama."

Fiona saw the fear in his face and knew she should be feeling the same way. Not only had she crashed one of the most popular online games in the world, but she'd managed to do something that had upset the US government. Why else would the military and the FBI have come to their house and questioned them, taken their phones and their computer?

She knew Francis was right. She should have listened to him, let him turn off the game before she got them into trouble. Strangely, though, no matter how hard she dug into her feelings, she couldn't muster up the dread she saw in her brother. Instead, she felt something that could only be exhilaration, an emotion she hadn't known since before her injuries. Sure, sometimes when she was lost inside the complex puzzles of the *Longstar* game, she could almost forget her situation and let herself experience life through her avatar, Gaia, but even in the most intense in-game moments, she could still feel the cold steel of the wheelchair armrests, feel the constant pressure of the oxygen that was being pumped through a plastic cannula into her scarred nasal passages, sense the discomfort of the urinary catheter and the itch from the latest skin graft. The game was great, but it wasn't *real*. The game's complex mazes and riddles were fabulous fun, but they were manufactured, also not *real*.

This was real. She looked at the open tabs on Francis's web browser and instantly recognized them for what they were—a small number of pieces in a large and complex puzzle. Here was a challenge that hadn't been carefully engineered by a game designer. This was a new game, the game of life, with real consequences for her and her family. Yes, she should be afraid. She should be terrified. But she wasn't. There was something there, lurking below the surface of all the information they'd just discovered. Something important . . .

Analise. Who, or what, was Analise?

She realized Francis was staring at her, probably wondering why she was smiling. She took a deep breath to calm herself. She started to ask Francis to begin a new search, but a loud sniff sounded, and they both spun around. Behind them, leaning over Francis's shoulder and staring intently at the screen, was the homeless man. He saw Fiona and his eyes flew wide open. "Oh, my. What happened to you, dear?"

Fiona hadn't noticed that her face scarf had fallen. She lifted it to cover herself. Francis quickly closed the browser as the librarian hurriedly approached. "Okay, sir, it's time for you to leave," she said, placing a firm hand on the man's shoulder. "You know you're not supposed to be here." She steered him toward the door, flashing Francis an apologetic look.

"Did you see that poor girl?" the man said loudly. "Her face is all burned up!"

The librarian winced. The two old ladies in the book racks both stared. And there, waiting by the front door she'd just entered, stood Mama, come to retrieve her kids. She'd heard the man's loud proclamations, and tears were streaming down her cheeks.

The drive home was silent and somber. Mama cursed at every traffic light, at every crowded turn lane. She'd never been comfortable driving the clumsy minivan needed to transport Fiona's wheelchair. Truth was, she'd never been comfortable behind the wheel of anything. Dad had always done the driving. Fiona ignored her mother's curses. When she looked at Francis, his eyes were on fire.

Visitor

The nurse came three days a week to check Fiona's vitals, deliver her weekly batch of medical supplies, and give her a breathing treatment. Her name was Bianca, and it was very possible that she was the only thing standing between Mama and a total emotional breakdown. By some cosmic miracle, Bianca was from a Guatemalan village just ten kilometers across the border from Mama's ancestral family farm in Chiapas. She even knew some of Mama's kin. As far as Mama was concerned, that made Bianca a treasured member of the family.

While Fiona was in her bedroom sucking medicated air through the breathing-treatment apparatus, Mama and Bianca were speaking raucous, rapid-fire Spanish in the kitchen. The sound of dishes rattling, the teapot whistling. An occasional burst of laughter. Somehow the clatters and clanks were incredibly comforting. They were the sounds of home and family. Of normal life.

Francis was splayed across his cot on the other side of her bedroom, his arm covering his eyes, listening to the hum of her breathing treatment and the voices from the kitchen. Bianca's bright smile and perpetual energy had instantly lifted Mama's spirits, but there was nobody for Francis. Fiona knew she couldn't cheer him up. She was, after all, the biggest part of his problem. All she could do was try to redirect his grief.

She pulled the mouthpiece away from her face and said, "You had two other tabs open on your web browser in the library. What were they? Did you find something else?"

He didn't move the arm that was flopped over his eyes. "I was looking up Arni and Analise."

She waited, but he didn't continue. "And?"

He threw his arm off his face and sat up on the bed. "I was in the middle of my search. I think I found Arni. There's a guy who works at Orbital Arena called Arnold Zaman. Like Arni said, he's a software engineer, but he's also a cofounder of the company. That's about as far as I got."

"What about Analise?"

He shook his head. "I didn't have time to read the results. Damn, I wish they hadn't taken our computer and phones!" Mama had repeatedly ignored their pleas to replace the computer and get them new phones. She claimed they didn't have the money, but Fiona knew that Mama wanted to keep her kids as far away from computers and online games as possible.

She nodded and put the mouthpiece back into her mouth. The medicine-laced vapor of the breathing treatment tasted *awful*, and something in the chemicals always made her jittery. Today she'd started out anxious, so with the addition of the medicine, she was ready to jump out of her skin.

Francis moved to the edge of his cot. His knee began to bobble, and he swallowed dryly. "I think we should call Mr. Howe and tell him about the thumbdrive. We're in over our heads. If we get into trouble, it will kill Mama."

The breathing machine stopped, its cycle complete, and Fiona dropped the foul-tasting mouthpiece into her lap. She nodded at Francis. Heart racing, partly from the medicine and partly from dread, she said, "We'll call Howe in the morning."

—

That night, as Fiona was struggling to brush her teeth, the doorbell rang. Mama was asleep, but Francis was in the living room watching television. She heard his footsteps tromping to the front door. She paused, toothpaste drooling from the side of her mouth onto the armrest of her wheelchair. She heard voices. She couldn't make out the words, but her brother's tone rose in suspicion. A silent pause, then footsteps coming down the hallway toward the bathroom. Francis's face appeared at the door. It was pale and slack. He licked his lips. "There's somebody here for you," he said. "You need to come to the living room."

He waited while she wiped her face and armrest. He handed her a blanket to cover her legs and helped her with her face scarf. She followed him down the hall, the motor on her chair whining softly, and maneuvered through the doorway into the room, expecting to find an FBI agent waiting to take her away to prison.

A man stood at the front door. Pale and heavyset, he wore beach shorts, flip-flops and a sweaty Ms. Pac-Man T-shirt that barely covered his belly. He shuffled his feet. His blond hair and beard were unkempt. He was plainly terrified.

He looked at Fiona and, surprisingly, didn't react to her appearance. He stuck out his hand, ignoring Francis. His words were heavy with a German accent. "You must be Lady Gaia. My name is Rupe Schroeder. We need to talk."

Gamemaster

Fiona looked toward the hallway to the bedrooms, waiting to see if Mama had been awakened by the arrival of the late-night stranger. Rupe's chest was heaving as if he'd been running. A line of sweat ran from his hair and vanished into the unruly mass of his beard. She recognized his face from the Wikipedia article Francis had shown her. It was the creased face of a man who loved to smile and laugh. It wasn't smiling now.

Francis closed the front door after glancing out to see if anyone was watching. "What do you want?" he demanded in a loud whisper.

Rupe's eyes didn't move from Fiona. Clear and blue, they showed none of the usual surprise and aversion of someone seeing her injuries for the first time. Fiona felt the oddly intimate sensation of meeting a long-lost friend, and in a way, she was. Here was the Gamemaster, the man responsible for the fabulous terrains, remarkable characters, and devious plots of the game. She'd been in Rupe's mind, solving his puzzles, every minute she'd ever played *Longstar*.

"I'm really sorry." His voice was low and rushed. "I work for Orbital Arena Games. I'm a—"

"We know who you are," Francis interrupted, "You're the Gamemaster. Your avatar is Ruperus. What do you want?"

Rupe hesitated, taken aback by Francis's hostility. "You met my friend in the Grone boss dungeon. Actually, you met his avatar, Atum. He told me what happened."

Fiona started to speak, but Francis stepped in front of her, placing himself between Rupe and her wheelchair. "We don't want any trouble. The FBI were already here."

"I know. I'm so sorry you got caught up in this mess. It wasn't supposed to go down this way."

Fiona pushed her brother away. "What mess? What's going on?"

Rupe looked around the living room as if expecting a Ghost to jump out of the shadows. Then he glanced at the dark windows, through which the outside streetlights were visible. "Can we talk somewhere away from these windows?"

Francis's jaw tensed. Before he could object, Fiona blurted. "The basement. We don't want to wake up our mother."

Her brother shot her a reproachful glare, and she responded with a sharp shake of her head. Rupe watched the interaction. He turned to Francis, his voice sincere and regretful. "I know this is weird, man. Believe me, I wouldn't be here if it weren't important."

Fiona raised an insistent eyebrow. Francis clenched his fists, but under Fiona's glare his resistance crumbled and his shoulders slumped. They both followed her as she drove her chair through the kitchen, out the back door, and down the ramp to the basement. Rupe's flip-flops smacked nervously on the concrete as he eyed the tall privacy fence that surrounded the yard. Crickets buzzed over the hum of the neighbor's air-conditioning unit. The warm night smelled like jasmine.

Francis pushed ahead of Fiona through the basement door and flipped on the light. Rupe followed, closing the door behind him, and the sweet aroma of the California evening was replaced by the basement smell of mildew, stale popcorn, and sweat. Rupe glanced approvingly at the concrete walls and lack of windows. His eyes roved over Francis's workout bench, then the couch, the television, and the mass of tangled wires where the gaming computer had been located. He flopped down onto the couch and let out a tremendous sigh.

Francis put his fists on his hips and faced Rupe like an Old West gunslinger. "Talk," he said.

Rupe looked hopefully at Fiona. "Please tell me you made a backup of Gaia's item inventory. Like Atum asked."

"Don't you mean Arni?" said Francis.

Rupe's brow furrowed. "Uh, yeah. Arni. Did you make the backup? Did you move it off your computer before the Feds took it?"

Francis shook his head defiantly. "First you tell us what's going on. Why did the FBI show up here? Who is Arni? Who is Analise?"

"And what is a Shadow Emora?" said Fiona.

Rupe started to protest, then stopped. He twisted his cheek into a grimace. "Arni is the cofounder of Orbital Arena. He's the guy who created the rendering software that makes the game look so good. Analise is a scientist from Stanford. She and Arni go way back. They even got engaged once, but that, um, well that's a long story. Suffice to say that she's . . ." he paused, as if searching for an adjective that didn't exist. "She's the single best goddamned human being you will ever meet. She's also the smartest. She works for a government research agency." He paused. "She's got a fucking spectacular theory about how to connect a brain to a computer. She's working on a military combat simulator that—"

"JEEB," said Francis. Rupe gave him an astonished look, and Francis shrugged. "It was on the business card one of the men left here. I googled it. It's a training simulator based on the game."

Rupe nodded, clearly impressed. "Yeah, JEEB. It's basically a copy of the game, but instead of a galaxy full of planets, they created a hyperrealistic clone of modern-day Earth. They call it JEEB Earth. It's incredible. Its full of bots based on real people that run around in exact copies of real meatspace cities . . ." Rupe's voice trailed off. "Um, I'm not sure how much of this I should tell you."

This time it was Fiona who prompted Rupe. "If you want the backup of Gaia's item stash, you need to tell us everything."

Rupe sat silently for a moment, his jaw moving from side to side as though chewing on his options. Finally, he gave a slow nod. "Okay, here's the deal. Arni and Analise stumbled across an unauthorized mod that changes the way the AI system works in the game. It started on the military JEEB servers, so Analise called it the *jeeb virus*. They don't know who put it there, but it's a freaking big deal. Arni and Analise didn't tell anybody about it. They decided to try and figure it out.

They did some things that weren't exactly legal. In the meantime, the jeeb virus started spreading. You remember when the game got an unannounced upgrade a few months back? When the computer-controlled bots all suddenly started acting, um, differently?"

Fiona nodded, and Francis said, "They all became assholes."

"Yeah. That wasn't a planned upgrade, let me tell you. It freaked us all out, too. It was the goddamned jeeb virus. Arni had been experimenting and accidentally managed to infect the game servers in addition to the military system. Anyway, lots of bad stuff happened, and all of a sudden everybody wanted to wipe their systems and destroy the virus. Everybody but Analise. She realized that it was doing something unprecedented and incredible. So, she and Arni did . . ." he paused and sighed, "um, some more illegal things. When you ran into them in the dungeon on Grone, they were trying to set things right. Only, they got caught, and nobody believes that they were trying to do the right thing. They think Arni was trying to steal military secrets, and that Analise is his accomplice. Now Arni is on the run, and Analise is hooked up to a machine fighting for her life."

Rupe shifted on the couch as if the cushions were stuffed with venomous spiders. "I'm not going to lie to you. Arni and Analise are in big-time trouble with the Feds. I'd be in big-time trouble, too, if they knew I was here talking to you tonight." He shook his head. "Analise and Arni were trying to do something incredibly fucking noble, but man, they screwed up. And by screwed up, I mean they screwed the pooch every fucking way possible it is to screw the fucking pooch." He paused and squinted at Fiona with one eye. "Sorry. I get worked up sometimes."

"Are *we* in trouble, too?" said Fiona, pointing to herself and Francis.

"Probably not. All the Feds want is the emora. If you give it to me, then you'll be in the clear. They'll never know you had it."

"Why do they want it?" Francis demanded.

Rupe's pale face darkened. "They want to catch the most talented hacker the world has ever known. They want to recover the most incredible piece of software code that's ever been written in the history of software." He slumped forward, elbows on his knees, and his shrill voice dropped into sorrow. "They also want the emora so they can save Analise's life. Only they'll fuck it up if they try. They'll kill her, trying to save her. They don't know what they're doing, and they won't listen!" He put his face into his hands, and for an instant Fiona thought he was going to cry.

When he raised his head, she expected his face to be filled with the same despair she'd heard in his voice. Instead, it was filled with resignation and hard-jawed determination. "I am *not* going to stand by and watch her die. Please give me your backup of Gaia's stash. *Please.*"

Fiona didn't look at Francis. Instead, she rolled her chair up to Rupe's knees and stared into his face. "You said Analise is hooked up to a machine. What kind of machine?" Rupe flinched, but she didn't see any sign of guile or deceit in his expression. Her mind spun for a moment longer. "Analise's avatar," she continued. "It wasn't a normal avatar, was it?"

For a microsecond Rupe's face went slack, as if his heart had skipped a beat. He glanced down at Fiona's oxygen tank and followed the plastic tube that led up to the scarf that covered most of her face. Something dawned on him, a new expression that gave Fiona a chill, and his panicked breathing slowed. "No," he whispered. "It wasn't a normal avatar."

"Was Analise using some kind of full-immersion VR suit?"

Again, he hesitated for the tiniest moment, but this time the hesitation was followed by the slightest upturn at the corner of his mouth. He shook his head. "No. No suit."

Fiona licked the rough ridges that had once been her lips and tried to hide the detonation of excitement in her gut. She knew Rupe probably couldn't tell her what she wanted to know without breaking the law, but she also knew from the encouraging flicker of a smile on his lips that he would happily guide her to *discovering* the truth.

"So . . . she was controlling her avatar with her *mind?*"

Rupe suddenly leaned forward and reached toward her face. When Francis lurched to stop him, he paused, but Fiona waved her brother away. "It's okay," she said.

Rupe tentatively touched the corner of her face scarf. Her entire body tensed, but his face held no trace of pity, only an intense desire to *understand*. She forced herself to relax and gave Rupe a slight nod.

He lifted the scarf to reveal the full extent of her burns and grafts and surgical scars. He lowered the scarf. "No. Analise wasn't controlling an avatar with her mind. Not exactly."

Fiona felt lightheaded, as she sometimes did when her oxygen was set too high. There was something in her subconscious trying to bubble to the surface. She didn't know what it was, only that it was trying desperately to break free, and that it was *important*. She searched Rupe's face for clues.

"I want to tell you something," he said quietly. "One of the things we score in the game is something called *PPA*. It stands for *player perceptive ability*. It's not something you see on your avatar profile or on the leaderboards. It's an internal score we track at the company. It measures how good a player is at cracking the cyphers and solving the psychological puzzles in the game." His eyes burned into her. "About six months ago I noticed a player whose PPA score was jumping up the charts. I started tracking the progress of the player." Rupe glanced at Francis, who was still tensed at Fiona's side, ready to protect her. "There's a threshold level at the top of the PPA scoring table. Basically, it's a list of the top-ten best problem solvers in the game. This particular player broke into that list faster than I'd ever seen, so I started watching him." Rupe lifted his face to Francis. "It was *you*, Lord Geo."

Francis unballed his fists in surprise. *"Me?"*

Rupe chuckled. "Yes. Or at least that's what I thought at first. But when I started eavesdropping on your headset feed, I realized I'd been duped."

"Wait . . . you *eavesdropped* on my headset?"

"I'm the Gamemaster. I'm an omniscient god. Gods eavesdrop. Get over it, man."

"Dude, that's creepy," frowned Francis.

Rupe shrugged. "The point is, I discovered that Lord Geo was listening to somebody else for advice." He turned to Fiona. "Your avatar, Gaia, seemed to be a low-level underachiever. She was below all my radar screens, but it didn't take me long to realize that she was the brains of the operation." He glanced at Francis. "Sorry man, no offense. You kick ass at combat, but let's face it, your sister is one of the best puzzle solvers and strategists I've ever seen. Her PPA score is as good or better than most top-level Galactic Masters."

Rupe turned back to Fiona. "Sometimes I make special puzzles for the top players on my PPA list. I try to stump them, you know what I mean? I put a few of those special puzzles in the Borwhan dungeon, and at Ghast. I put them there for *you*, Gaia, to see just how good you really were. You breezed right through most of them. It was like you could read my mind. You are the *only* player, to date, to have solved *all* the puzzles in the Ghast expansion. So, with Grone I decided to try something different. I pulled out all the stops."

The persistent fluttering in Fiona's stomach went from butterfly strength to eagle strength. "You designed Grone to stump *me*?"

He nodded sourly. "Some of it, yeah. Why do you think you guys were the first on scene? I sent the early notification of the Grone expansion to Lord Geo *only*. I wanted to see what you two could do before the planet got overrun by the masses. And by damn if I didn't put some of my best puzzles on Grone. Too bad you never got a chance to solve them. In a way it's my fault you got sucked into this mess." He paused, worked his mouth silently. "I was watching you, you know, and would have jumped in to help you, but I got locked out of the game when my boss realized something was up. I'm so sorry. I didn't expect my Grone dungeon to become the site of a corporate battle between my boss and a fucking platoon of US Marines."

"Why are you telling me this?"

He smiled. "Because I'm pretty sure you've already figured out the secret of Analise's avatar."

She shivered at his expression. It was the same look of proud affection that Dad used to give her after she'd accomplished some difficult task. The bubble in her subconscious burst to the surface, and she gasped. "It wasn't Analise's avatar in the game—it was Analise herself! She was physically *in* the game, wasn't she?" She could tell from Rupe's growing smile that she was somewhere near the truth. "She's *still* inside the game, isn't she, and you need this emora thing to get her out."

Rupe made a peculiar sideways motion with his head. "You continue to amaze me, Lady Gaia." His voice rose in a bad imitation of a TV politician. "I can neither confirm nor deny the rumors that Analise's consciousness is trapped inside a malfunctioning video game." His humor faded, and his next words were in a conspiratorial whisper. "But if it were true, and if she were in imminent danger, yes, I would need the emora to get her out safely. It's the key to sorting out this whole mess."

Fiona's eyes narrowed. "But how could she be trapped inside the game? The game crashed, right? Whatever I did killed the game, right? We saw on the Orbital Arena website that the game was shut down." She paused. "It didn't crash, did it? The holobox did something else, didn't it? If the game had crashed, Analise's mind couldn't still be trapped inside, could it? That means the game is still running somewhere, right?"

Rupe winced. "Please, Fiona, will you help me? We need Gaia's backup to save Analise."

Fiona hesitated, backed her chair away from Rupe. His eyes followed her with a furious intensity.

She steeled herself. "I won't give it to you."

Rupe's jaw swiveled open. Francis blurted, "What?"

Fiona nodded defiantly. "You'll *never* see the backup. The FBI couldn't find it, and they searched everywhere. It's *mine*."

"It's *not* yours!" exclaimed Rupe, "That code belongs to—"

Fiona cut him off. "I'll only give it to Arni. In person. On one condition."

Rupe narrowed his eyes. "What condition?"

Fiona couldn't look at Francis, knowing that her resolve would falter if she did. "Show me how Analise got inside the game."

havencosm | ASSINNI

Assinni

After three weeks on the cramped pilgrims' transport, the bright-green skies of Assinni seemed impossibly deep. Behind wispy clouds, the twin crescents of the Angry Moons loomed huge, like two battered faces glaring at each other, mouths snarling in ancient resentment. Se-Jong and Nkiru spent the first few hours after planetfall getting their land legs back, wandering the narrow stone alleys of the Holy City with the other tourists, marveling at the smells of a thousand restaurants and countless street-food vendors.

They'd taken the orbital shuttle to the surface instead of porting down through the ship's t-gate. Nkiru had insisted, claiming that she wanted to see the ancient city and its famous ruins from the air. "Plus," she'd said, "t-gates scare me. When you step through, how do you know it's really *you* who comes out the other end?" Se-Jong had had no argument, though he knew t-gates were perfectly safe. He'd gated dozens of times, and he was pretty sure he was still the same Se-Jong. Regardless, he'd promptly agreed to take the shuttle down, even though it was far more expensive than the t-gate. Nothing got the blood boiling like the fury of a high-speed atmospheric reentry, plus he'd wanted to see the city from the air, too. He'd given Nkiru the window seat, and she'd clutched his hand the entire trip down, both of them craning toward the window to catch a glimpse of the ancient metropolis.

Her excitement was palpable. Through the grip of her warm hand he felt the explosive vitality of life, of a young woman, whole and free, about to visit the landscape of her dreams.

The dense maze of stone buildings and narrow streets they'd seen from the air was even more bewildering on the ground. Cataclyst pilgrims were afforded special status in the Holy City, so the yellow pilgrims' robes they'd been issued prevented them from being accosted by the throngs of child beggars and souvenir touts. Nothing, however, could save them from the press of tourists that surged around them like a sweaty, stinking ocean. The Holy City was the seat of power for both the Universal Cataclyst Church and the SATO Assembly; it was also the most visited museum complex in the Known Arc. Any person they passed on one of the narrow stone streets might be a high church official or a government dignitary or an alien ambassador. Or, more likely, an exhausted and sunburned parent herding a clutch of whining children through the plodding mob of tourists.

Even though the scancorder relic Nkiru kept hidden in her backpack might be worth thousands, she seemed to have little or no money. The free pilgrims' dormitories were rumored to be infested with bedbugs, so Se-Jong used his own money to rent a room in a small boutique hotel just outside the fortresslike walls of the Regium Enclave. Nkiru was delighted. For the first time in two weeks, they shared a real bed instead of a cramped shipboard berth.

When he woke the next morning to birdsong and green sunbeams shining through sheer curtains, Nkiru was already gone.

She'd left him with a carafe of hot coffee and a note encouraging him to explore the city while she visited the Regium library. He couldn't accompany her, she explained, because the library only granted access to church-sponsored pilgrims. The pilgrim's pass he'd bought at Cloudtops Station didn't count.

A true pilgrim, he'd learned, must be granted a sponsorship from a member of the clergy. True pilgrims were supposed to complete the pilgrimage without any money or belongings. True pilgrims paid for nothing: not food, not lodging, not anything. They were supposed to rely entirely on the grace of the church and the kindness of strangers. On the other hand, pass holders like Se-Jong were supposed to pay for *everything*. He'd spent more on their cramped double berth aboard the *Rose & Chalice* than he had for his luxurious first-class compartment on the starliner from Earth to Cloudtops Station. Se-Jong knew a racket when he saw one. His fare was subsidizing the other pilgrims on the transport. He didn't care. He stretched his neck and wondered briefly why it was stiff and sore, but then he remembered his and Nkiru's athletic contortions of the previous evenings. Nope, he didn't care at all.

Se-Jong spent the day sightseeing in the tumbled complex of pre-Cataclysm alleys that surrounded the high walls of the Regium, visiting everything from the Old Souk and the Plaza of Winds to the enigmatic Shrine of the Fat Omne. In the midday heat he ducked into the air-conditioned coolness of a modern centromall, where he browsed the art stalls and bought a small gift for Nkiru, a wrist pendant made of twisted strands of leather and copper wire formed into the fantastical shape of the Seuss trees that lined the streets of the Holy City. The stall keeper looked askance at his pilgrims' robes as he bought the expensive bracelet, obviously judging him. Pilgrims weren't supposed to have money, Se-Jong remembered. After he left the stall, he removed his robes and wadded them into a tight ball that he tucked under his arm. They were scratchy and hot, he told himself, and besides, they made him feel like a fraud, as if he were lying to everyone who saw him. He was no religious pilgrim. Watching the puffed-up priests and the sleazy Olid street vendors selling worthless junk passed off as holy relics, he got the same prickly feeling that he did at the surf casinos back home on Askelon, staring into the eyes of a blackjack dealer.

At the end of the day, when the sun was low and the Angry Moons had already set, he ate alone at a sidewalk café, watching a vagrant jeebie slowly drink himself into oblivion in an alley across the plaza. Nkiru hadn't responded to any of his komnic calls or messages. He was worried, though he could only assume she was busy and distracted, or perhaps the thick stone walls of the Regium blocked the komnic signal. When she finally returned to their room at the pension, it was almost three hours past the bells of midnight. She slid into the bed and her hands teased him awake. He could tell from her fervor that something had happened, but he didn't want to interrupt their lovemaking to find out the details. When they were finished, she fell instantly asleep, her head nestled in the crook of his arm, and when he awoke the next morning, she was gone again. This time there was no coffee, no note.

Her prolonged absences continued for two more days, and on the third night she didn't return until dawn. She wouldn't tell him what she'd been doing, but whatever it was, it had left her both exhilarated and exhausted. She slept until noon, until Se-Jong woke her by waving steaming, freshly baked bread rolls from the corner bakery under her nose. They ate on the bed, her feet tucked under her legs, her dark fingers tearing the bread apart like a hungry lioness ripping open an antelope. She pulled the bedsheet around her waist like a sash, and Se-Jong thought she looked like an avatar princess, proud and breathtaking.

She apologized for abandoning him, but her tone was anything but apologetic. She beamed triumphantly. She'd found something, she informed him, something that her research had predicted. Se-Jong couldn't keep the resentment out of his expression. He didn't like being left in the dark, and he told her so. At his sulky look, she laughed and threw off the sheet and rose to her knees. Facing him, she mimicked his dour expression, comically exaggerating his hunched shoulders and drooping scowl. She barked orders like a company commander at the War College. "At ease, Lieutenant Se-Jong. If you get any more serious, you'll be too boring to stand. Lighten up! Tonight, I'm going to show you something that will blow your mind. But first things first . . ." She leaped at him, and he fell back into the bedcovers, the hungry lioness now tearing at *him*.

Leodiva

That evening as the dusk bells sounded across the Holy City, Nkiru herded Se-Jong beneath the Sunset Gate, through the thick battlements, and into the protected complex of the Regium Enclave. Se-Jong had seen photos and videos, of course, but nothing could have prepared him for the visceral thrill of experiencing the imperial fortress firsthand. The buildings in front of him represented the largest collection of surface structures to have survived the Cataclysm anywhere in the Known Arc. Here and there on other planets, isolated structures had been spared, but only on Assinni had an entire avatar city, complete with the imperial palace of an avatar lord, remained intact.

Nkiru squeezed his hand. Her eyes sparkled like sunlight on ice. She raised her voice over the surrounding crowd of sightseers. "Are you ready?"

Se-Jong scoffed, trying to appear unimpressed and uninterested. He tugged at the stiff collar of the pilgrims' robes she'd forced him to wear. She laughed at him. "Come on, I want to show you something."

She led him down one of the wide streets that radiated like spokes from the domed Avatar Palace at the center of the enclave. At the broad steps in front of the palace, they joined a gathering group of tourists. "I can't get you in without pilgrims' credentials, so we'll have to go in with a tour group."

The tour guide, a Bolo woman with the Linked Trinity symbol as her head tattoo, held up her hand and the crowd quieted. "There's no talking inside the chapel rotunda," she said, "So I'll tell you about it before we enter the palace."

Se-Jong already knew most of what she told the crowd. The Torax Chapel was the centerpiece of the Avatar Palace. In the Age of Avatars, it had been the site of the imperial court and throne room for the Assinni emperors, including, ultimately, Emperor Torax himself. Now it was the seat of the Father Regis, patriarch of the Cataclyst Church and spiritual heir to the long-vanished avatar lords.

Millions of travelers thronged to the Regium each year. Some were drawn by the unique architecture: the vast and mysterious Empty Dome in the bottommost crypt, the living fountains of the Doloro Gardens, the soaring towers and minarets of the Thrim Forum. Others came to see the vast trove of artifacts in the reliquaries and museums, or to guess which of the myriad locked doors and tunnels might lead to the fabled Sanctum Arcanis, the hidden reliquary where the Prophet Kanaan was said to have collected the most dangerous relics of the Avatar Wars. No matter the reason for the visit, the one thing everybody most wanted to experience was the *Reveal of Creation* fresco, the ultimate masterpiece of the artist Leodiva the Blind, which covered the inside of the massive rotunda of the Torax Chapel.

The tour guide instructed her followers to remove their headwear and cover any bare shoulders. "You are entering a most holy place," she said gravely, "and you are about to experience the greatest artistic wonder of the Third Epoch." Nkiru took his hand and squeezed, eliciting a frown from a thick-waisted and ruddy-faced woman in the crowd. Se-Jong gave the prudish woman a challenging glare. The woman looked away.

The guide led them to recite the Avatar's Creed on the steps of the legendary chapel, which the group whispered with far more heartfelt fervor than in any normal weekly mass back in their local parishes.

> *Oh Oa, Lords of the Halo, who*
> *have granted the three mighty*
> *Sacraments of Illusion, Time, and*
> *Destiny, glory to thee and thy Great*
> *Game of nature . . .*

Se-Jong dutifully mumbled the words along with the others. When they were done, the guide herded them up the wide steps and through the doors that led into the antechamber. She motioned for them to gather at the entrance to the chapel rotunda. They surrounded her like eager schoolchildren. "No talking from this point forward," she whispered loudly. The tourists trailed reverently behind as she passed beneath the arched entrance, many of them making the Cataclyst faith-gesture of the Linked Trinity, their fingertips tracing a triangle, circle, and square over their hearts.

Nkiru held Se-Jong back, waiting for the others to pass, giving the two of them the chance to pause alone before entering the cavernous chapel. Se-Jong looked through the arch at the massive rotunda beyond, big enough to be a starship hangar. At the distant center of the chamber, rising above the milling crowds, he could see an empty throne mounted on a high dais. This was the famous Avatar Throne, seat of the final Emperor of Assinni, empty since the Cataclysm.

Nkiru pressed her fingers into his palm. When the bulk of the crowd had passed, she tugged him insistently over the threshold and into the rotunda, neck craned upward. From this initial viewpoint, the smooth, featureless dome was empty. According to the guidebook he'd read the night before, this was intentional: it was the *First Reveal of Creation*, a representation of the Etherium, the timeless infinity of chaos that had existed before the birth of the cosmos, or as one poet had put it, "the silence before the storm."

The hushed gasps from the throng of tourists were the only sounds, save the distant chanting of monks high up on the skywalk that rimmed the base of the dome. He and Nkiru continued slowly across the smooth marbled floor, hand in hand, pressed on all sides by gaping sightseers. As they progressed, the *Reveal of Creation* began to work its enchantment. Through some magic of his artistry, Leodiva had given life to the pigment, so that the painting morphed as they walked beneath it. Some say the artist was divinely enabled; others say he was possessed by a praelea spirit like the avatars of old. Followers of the Mucktu Bloodline cult, who revered his work as much as the Cataclysts, believed that Leodiva had formulated the pigments of his fresco from the forbidden jeeb pollen, and that it was the magical qualities of the pollen that gave life to his art.

However he'd done it, the effect was breathtaking. Se-Jong felt his cynicism slipping away as the painting unfolded above him. He knew that seven different scenes, known as the *Seven Reveals*, were hidden on the ceiling of the rotunda, and as you walked toward the center of the dome, the first six scenes would magically appear, one after the other, each filling the dome and replacing the previous scene, illustrating the story of Creation as told in the opening chapters of *The Chronicles of the First Epoch*.

———

As they followed the tour group, Se-Jong began to see faint but monstrous shapes in the misty gray of the dome. The images faded in and out as they walked, so ephemeral that they might have been tricks of his imagination. From the description in the guidebook, he recognized Leodiva's interpretation of the Infinatis, the disembodied intellects that were said to lurk in the shapeless void beyond time and space, beyond even the realms of the gods.

The Bolo guide herded her flock farther into the rotunda, mindful of the following tour group that was already gathering at the entrance. Se-Jong and Nkiru shuffled along at the trailing edge of the crowd. Directly above the Avatar Throne, at the zenith of the dome, a point of light appeared, a flickering intrusion into the endless gray, a tiny ripple of radiance that solidified into a delicate soap bubble. This was the start of the *Second Reveal: The Birth of the Cosmos*. Another step forward and the interior of the bubble began to fill with kaleidoscopic colors and hard-to-define shapes. This was Leodiva's depiction of the Cosmic Nucleus, the seed kernel of existence, which the Cataclyst scriptures called the Immovable Spot, the fixed anchor point to which all of Creation would be attached. A few more steps forward on the marble floor and the ceiling artwork swelled again, a larger globe materializing around the Nucleus, encompassing it. Se-Jong recognized the globe as the tiny green planetoid that the scripture called the Foundation Core, the workspace of the Archangels of Creation from which they would forge the galaxy.

More steps and another point of light appeared, this time on the surface of the Foundation Core planetoid. It expanded into an open doorway, through which shone the spectral brilliance of the realm of the gods. The crowd surged forward, knowing what was to come next—the *Third Reveal: The Making of Mortals*.

Through the spectral doorway emerged a thin-waisted humanoid with floating, translucent hair. This was Archangel Oaone, highest among the Oa, Lord of Purpose, Rule-Keeper, Master of Souls, and Guardian of the Hero's Gate. She opened her arms to reveal a host of naked, well-muscled figures. These were the soul-patterns, made in the images of heroes from the realm of the Oa, the primal templates on which all mortal beings were based.

A few steps farther led them into the *Fourth Reveal: The Engines of Creation*. In the ever-morphing artwork, two more figures emerged from the spectral door. One was colossal in size but sinister and furtive in appearance. The mood of the crowd tightened deliciously. *Everybody loves it when the villain appears*, Se-Jong thought. The menacing new figure in the painting was the lesser brother of Oaone, Archangel Atum, Lord of Nature, Clock-Keeper, and Guardian of the Elemental Forces. The artist had chosen to portray Atum as an indistinct, shadowy demon. Atum opened his hands to expose three jewels: a yellow sphere, a red pyramid, and a blue cube. These were the Creation Stones, which were also called the Great Emoras.

The other figure to emerge alongside Atum from the spectral door was far smaller in stature than either of the mighty archangels. He was bearded and portly, and wore a cloak of harsh, clashing colors. This was the mysterious Jester, a strange being who, according to myth, was perhaps more powerful than the archangels themselves.

Nkiru tugged Se-Jong forward. Above, from the grassy surface of the Foundation Core sprang the three titanic structures of the Engines of Creation: the iron-plated Hero's Sphere; the crystalline Cosmic Pyramid; and the enigmatic Destiny Cube, made of mountain-size blocks of interlocked stone. All three structures towered so high from the surface of the planetoid that their tops were lost in the haze of the atmosphere.

Se-Jong found himself completely taken by the experience, his earlier indifference forgotten. Suddenly, the voice of his tactics instructor rang in his head. *Don't get swept away by emotion. Never lose track of the objective situation. Pay attention!* For a moment he pulled his eyes away from the seductive images on the dome and scanned his surroundings. They'd passed the halfway point to the Avatar Throne. In front of them, the multitiered throne dais was surrounded by a dozen Dei Militans guards. They wore polished golden helmets and carried ceremonial shields emblazoned with the emblem of their order: the Starry Chalice upon the Altar of Flowers. He recognized them as the elite warrior-priests of the Regia Protectors, the personal bodyguards of the Father Regis. Se-Jong knew from the guidebook that the detail at the Avatar Throne was the highest honor for a militan, but to him it looked like an awful duty. They just stood there, day and night, unmoving like statues, protecting the throne from the greasy fingers of tourists.

Nkiru hissed and yanked at his robes. She gestured upward. Se-Jong turned his attention back to the ceiling. The chanting of the monks was louder now. He felt a chill.

OhhhhhhhhhhAhhhhhhhhh

The *Fifth Reveal* was far more dramatic: *The Making of Worlds*. Above him, the figures of the archangels Oaone, Atum, and the Jester had moved. Each had claimed one of the three titanic Engines of Creation and stood at its base. Each held one of the three Great Emoras. They raised the stones, and the vast machinery within the Engines of Creation thundered to life. From within the emora stones, splashes of vivid color emerged and raced around the periphery of the chapel rotunda. The crowd craned their heads to follow the movement, and gasps erupted as the colors collided and began to form images. Great spinning planets, stars blazing with pure light. Magnificent mountains, emerald forests, azure oceans, and white glaciers. Beasts of every form and function, from gossamer butterflies to massive jakalumphs rumbling over mighty deserts. These were the worlds of the galaxy, where mortals would live and die and play their part in the great game.

At the end, when the worlds were made and the mighty spiral of the galaxy glittered across the entire expanse of the dome, the three emoras fell from the archangels' hands, darkened, their task complete. The mighty energies from the Hero's Sphere, the Cosmic Pyramid, and the Destiny Cube diminished, but did not entirely cease; the Engines of Creation still turned, slowly, maintaining space and time and life within the new galaxy.

The Creation tale was almost finished; only one last great *Reveal* remained. The crowd was anxious, but when it started to surge forward, the guide threw up her arms. She slowly and dramatically pointed to the shadowy figure of Atum. His right hand was open, casting the spent emora into the darkness, but in his other fist he clutched a small clear cube, half-concealed in his robes as if he were hiding it from his mighty sister, Oaone.

Nkiru pulled Se-Jong to a halt, and the crowd streamed around them.

"This is what I wanted to show you," she whispered. "Look, there. Do you see it?"

This had been in the guidebook, so he was prepared. "That clear cube in his hand, it's what he used to ignite the Cataclysm."

Nkiru laughed and pulled him close. "Yeah, but that's not what I want you to see. Don't look at his hands; look at his face."

Se-Jong squinted but could see nothing but shadows. He shook his head. She put her hand on his hip, and as always, her touch thrilled him. "Take a half step this way."

A passing tourist jostled Se-Jong; they were blocking the progression of the crowd. Nkiru ignored the tourist's glare and guided Se-Jong to a spot near the edge of their tour group.

"Now, look."

He tried. "I still can't see anything."

She put her hands on his shoulders and moved him a centimeter to the left. "How about now?"

"What am I supposed to be seeing?" He looked down at her upturned face. She gave him a conspiratorial wink and covertly pushed something into his hand. It felt like a small, polished riverstone, smooth and shaped like a bird's egg. When he raised his palm to examine it, she shoved his hand down. "Keep it hidden," she hissed. "Now look again and tell me what you see."

Se-Jong looked up at the mural, sighed, and was about to protest when he finally did see. Dark eyes and a sneering smile appeared from the shadows. A face, and shoulders. Atum wore a leather coat, crinkled with age. Se-Jong moved his head a millimeter. The face vanished. It took a few moments of repositioning to find it again.

"You see?" she whispered. "It's the face of Atum! You have to be in the exact right spot. Do you recognize him?"

"No. Should I?"

The corner of her mouth twisted, but instead of answering she pointed and spoke. "Now look down."

Se-Jong looked at the floor. Nothing but featureless stone. Nkiru used her sandaled toe to push his boot to the side. A small vein of darker stone ran like a natural swirl in the marbled tile.

"Follow me." She pulled him by the hand through the crowd to a location about ten meters away, next to one of the crowd-control barriers. She pointed down. "Look there!"

Another muted spiral vein in the stone, identical to the pattern in the first tile. "Now look again at Atum," she instructed. He gave her a scowl of disbelief but stood on the mark and looked up. Nothing. He moved his head imperceptibly. Still nothing . . .wait. A ghostly figure took shape out of the background swirls of gray, standing behind Atum, peering over his shoulder.

Se-Jong stood as still as he could, ignoring Nkiru and the shuffling crowd. He moved only his eyes, struggling to focus on the amorphous image. He squeezed the small round object in his palm. A face materialized from the indistinct strokes of the paint.

He instantly looked away. Bile rose in his throat and a sharp prick of heat pulsed outward from the center of his forehead. He'd seen plenty of photos and news footage of Mucktu witches, though he'd never seen one in person before. Or had he? The ghostly face in the fresco seemed intimately and distressingly familiar, arousing the raw, gut-jolting emotion of a recurring childhood nightmare. The boogeyman in the closet. The monster under the bed. Somehow, he *knew* this face. He forced himself to look again, ignoring Nkiru's questioning expression.

High cheekbones. Deep-blue skin. An organic tracery of dark markings at her temples, signifying high eminence in the Mucktu cult. A curling, disturbingly familiar smile at the corner of her lips. The gaping eye sockets, the skin of her cheeks and brow descending smoothly into the deep pits of her skull as if it were completely natural and not a horrific genetic mutation. A Mucktu Eye pressed deeply into the skin of her forehead, the embedded white node gleaming with malevolence. This wasn't just any Daughter of the Bloodline. This was their queen, the mythical First Mother.

Impossibly, the face in the painting *moved*. The Mucktu *smiled* at him, acknowledging his presence, her empty eye pits somehow focusing on him as if he were the most important person in the entire universe.

The air became dense and heavy, hard to breathe. The sounds of the tourist throngs faded to silence. The Mucktu's lips moved.

Who is she, Se-Jong?

Se-Jong squeezed his eyes shut. When he opened them, the face in the painting was gone, the hushed sounds of the rotunda had returned to normal. He looked around; there was no sign that anyone else had heard the voice. He turned to Nkiru. "What the hell? Did you hear that?"

"Hear what?"

A woman next to them hissed, "Shhh!"

Se-Jong shot her a hard glare, and the woman moved on. Nkiru's smile was clenched and excited. "Can you make out the letters? Do you know what they mean?"

Letters? "What are you talking about? What letters?"

She frowned. "In the *holobox*. Look at the cube he's holding in his hand."

Se-Jong steeled himself, and he slowly let his eyes rotate back up to the painting of the archangel Atum. He let out a breath of relief. The image of the Mucktu witch was gone, the memory of her face and the whispering voice quickly fading. He dropped his eyes to the fist-size cube nestled in Atum's fingers. Nothing. He shuffled in place, moving his eyes slowly, carefully. Bright smudges appeared inside the clear cube. He squinted, and moved a tenth of a millimeter, and suddenly he saw it. Engraved at the heart of the cube were four letters: MCTU.

"M-C-T-U . . . What does it mean?"

She was almost shaking with the excitement of sharing her discovery. "Read it out loud," she whispered.

He sounded out the letters. "Mc-too."

"Slower," she prompted.

"Muck-too," he said, and then he felt a shudder pass through him. "Mucktu!"

He stole a glance at Nkiru. Her face was lit by an inner fire, her eyes locked on the dome above. He looked around at the crowd. There were a thousand tourists in the chapel, and none of them, not even the guides, had seen these secrets. In fact, he doubted if any of the millions of people who visited the site every year had ever noticed the tiny, intentionally concealed riddles of the painting.

But Nkiru had. She had a talent for teasing out the deeply hidden patterns of things, in art, in nature, in his soul. She perceived reality through a different lens, one that revealed qualities and imperfections that no one else saw. While everyone else was staring up at the painting, she'd looked down at the floor, searching for the inevitable connections between the ground and the sky. To her, all of Creation seemed to be an intentional mystery, a divine riddle, a game of the gods.

―

She pulled at him. "I've found one more, so far. It's over there."

The chanting was much louder now. Se-Jong couldn't tell whether the monks were cranking up the volume or the effect was caused by the acoustics of the massive dome. Either way, the intensity of the moment put a lump in his throat.

Nkiru led him through the crowd, deftly shouldering her way forward while he stared up at the changing painting, waiting to experience the *Sixth Reveal: The Advent of the Avatars*. On the ceiling, the bearded figure of the Jester raised his arms, and from within the Hero's Sphere poured the multitudes of the praelea angels, each taking the form of an avatar. After the sublime beauty of the other *Reveals*, the appearance of the avatars seemed lurid and cartoonish. The crowd didn't mind. Everyone's face was rapt; everyone wore an expression of intense awe.

As the mob reached the base of the throne dais and crowded around the tour guide, the mural was almost complete. The praelea had merged with their immortal bodies to form the avatars, the masters of the galaxy, and they were scattered across the newly created worlds. The archangels had retreated back through the spectral doorway to their heavenly realm. At the apex of the dome, the Foundation Core and the Engines of Creation finished fading, forever hidden from mortal comprehension. The Creation was complete, and the great game of the Oa had begun.

Se-Jong could tell that everyone wanted to applaud, but the crowd kept a respectful silence. The enormity of Leodiva's masterpiece spanned the dome above. The tour guide smiled and beckoned the gawking horde the last few meters to the security railing at the foot of the Avatar Throne. Nkiru pulled Se-Jong away, toward the edge of the mob. The crowd's collective neck was sore from looking up, but nobody looked away, or even blinked. Everyone was trying to glimpse a hint of the *Seventh Reveal*, the ultimate secret of Leodiva's magnum opus.

The final *Reveal* was designed to be viewed looking up from the ancient glass throne that was perched on the dais at the exact center point of the rotunda. It was rumored to depict Atum's betrayal of the Oa and his secret planting of the Evil Seed, the moment the wicked archangel had set in motion the Cataclysm and the ruination of the cosmos. No one knew for sure, of course. According to the *Chronicles*, any mere mortal who dared plop their mundane buttocks on the Avatar Throne's holy seat would vanish with a cry of pain and a puff of smoke. No one, not even the Father Regis himself, had ever climbed the steps to the throne; it had lain empty since the Cataclysm and the Rapture of the Avatars, covered in dust and rubble, waiting for the return of the avatar lords.

Nkiru ignored the gaping crowd. "There." She pointed at the floor. Another subtle, but identical, swirl in the grain of the marble, next to the security barrier. Se-Jong stood on the mark and turned his eyes to the ceiling.

"Look at the exact center of the highest point of the dome. Do you see it?"

The center of the painting was a featureless, gray mass of clouds that marked the earlier location of the Foundation Core, before it had been hidden by the gods.

Nothing. He shifted again. Nothing.

"I don't see anything."

Her voice was tight and insistent, almost desperate. "It's not easy. This one is a lot harder to find than the others. Keep trying."

She seemed to be filled with an explosive excitement. Se-Jong took a breath and tried to concentrate on the image. Focus. He stood perfectly still and moved his head in the tiniest motions, watching for any change. Still nothing.

"Try to relax," she coaxed, barely whispering. "It's not just the viewing angle that makes it work. I think Leodiva keyed the hidden scenes in the painting to emotional states in the viewer. Your brain filters the image unless you're completely calm." He closed his eyes, held them shut. He felt her fingers searching for his and he took her hand. He inhaled deeply, held the breath. Slowly, he cracked open his eyelids.

There! A new depiction of the Foundation Core appeared like a phantom from within the obscuring clouds. Only now, the image was different. On the surface of the Foundation Core planetoid, something distorted and ugly was growing, a corruption sending groping tendrils across the perfect green surface to curl, like a choking vine, around the mighty structures of the Engines of Creation. The Cosmic Pyramid was almost completely engulfed by the corrupt growth.

"What the hell is that?" he asked.

He felt her excitement through their intertwined hands. "Something is growing inside the Engines of Creation. Something alien." He tore his eyes away from the disturbing image and looked down at her. Her breathing was shallow, rapid, like that of a predator closing in on long-sought prey. "I think it's the product of the Evil Seed planted by the archangel Atum. I think maybe..." Her words trailed off. She looked at him warily, as if suddenly uncertain of his ability to keep a secret.

"Maybe what?" he prompted.

"Maybe we're seeing a part of the *Seventh Reveal*. Look at it! Whatever that tree-thing is, it looks like it's feeding off the Engines of Creation."

He returned his attention to the dome. It took a moment to find the image. The Foundation Core swam into view, along with the Engines of Creation on its green surface. Se-Jong knew this wasn't a depiction of a real place, but of an allegory, a fable, a myth—a metaphor created by a postapocalyptic religion in the aftermath of the Cataclysm, an attempt to explain the unexplainable.

And yet... his pulse quickened as he stared at the hidden painting-within-a-painting. Why had the artist Leodiva gone to the effort of hiding these mirages in his masterpiece? What purpose did they serve?

When Se-Jong started to point, Nkiru jerked his arm down and moved her eyes toward the nearby security railing. One of the Dei Miltans ceremonial guards was watching them. The man cocked his head to the side and mumbled something, as if speaking into a hidden shoulder microphone. Se-Jong felt a queasy twist in his stomach. He felt Nkiru grab for his hand, but instead of grasping it, she pried the small bird's-egg object from his fingers. He'd almost forgotten he'd been holding it. He gave her an inquisitive glance. "Time to go," she muttered. He glanced back up toward the ceiling a final time, but the image of the choking vines had vanished.

Apocrypha

They walked silently back to the hotel, Se-Jong's head swimming with questions. When they arrived, Nkiru sat theatrically on the bed, legs knotted together, shoulders upright, hands in her lap, facing him like some guru preparing to dispense a particularly tasty bit of cosmic wisdom.

Who is she, Se-Jong?

He winced at the memory of the Mucktu witch's voice. It had been his mind playing tricks on him, surely. The artist Leodiva's painting, no matter how magical, couldn't put words into his head, could it?

Nkiru broke the spell by giggling at his confused expression. She patted the bed next to her and leaned forward to give him a quick kiss.

He sat. He asked her how she'd known about the hidden images. He'd never even heard rumors of such things. She told him in a matter-of-fact tone how she'd spent the past few years living in a Cataclyst shelter for at-risk youth in New York City. How one of the monks, a man named Brother Jerome, had taken a liking to her, how he'd recognized her inquisitive nature and asked her to become a research assistant for his scholara studies.

"Scholara?"

"Every monk in his Janga sect has to complete a scholara, a research project on some obscure aspect of the Cataclyst faith. It's sort of like getting a PhD. The sect is very scientific about it. Brother Jerome's scholara was on the art of Leodiva the Blind. He believed that Leodiva left hidden clues in all his frescoes, paintings, and sculptures."

"Clues to what?"

She shrugged. "That's the real mystery, isn't it? Do the hidden images in Leodiva's art point to some greater secret, or are they simply easter eggs?"

"Easter egg?"

She chuckled. "Sorry. Artists sometime hide images or symbols in their work just for fun. Leodiva is famous for it."

He paused, trying to frame his next question so it wouldn't sound judgmental. This was the first time she had volunteered any information about her past, and he didn't want to spoil her sharing mood. "Why were you living in a youth shelter?"

There was a brief silence during which she absently spun her pewter ring around the knuckle of her finger. When she answered, her tone was defiant. "My home life was . . . tough." She made a grim chuckle. "I figured living on the streets of New York would be an improvement."

Se-Jong tried to keep the apprehensiveness out of his voice. He wanted to ask what she meant by "tough," but her expression made it clear he'd better steer away from that particular subject. "So, you finished high school at the youth shelter?"

She nodded. "I went to classes in the mornings and worked with Brother Jerome in the afternoons and evenings. He made sure I always had a room and food at the shelter. He was a good man." Her face clouded. "Not all the monks were so nice to me."

Sensing her discomfort, he changed the subject to the small stone she'd pressed into his hand when she had pointed out the easter eggs in the ceiling artwork. "What was that thing you handed me in the Torax Chapel?"

She gave a dismissive wave. "Just a good-luck charm."

"Let me see it."

"No."

"Why not?"

She grinned. "It might lose its magic."

"So, it's an avatar relic?"

Her grin faded. "No."

"Where'd you get it?"

Now she was frowning. "I didn't steal it, if that's what you're asking. It was a gift." She leaned toward him teasingly. "You're asking the wrong questions, Lieutenant." Several days earlier she'd started calling him Lieutenant because of his stiff posture and shiny boots. She also told him he gave orders like a naval officer directing a deck crew, even while they were making love. He tried to look offended whenever she used the nickname, but he was secretly pleased.

"What questions *should* I be asking?"

"Ask me what *I* saw in the hidden images."

"Okay. What did you see?"

"I saw the face of the archangel Atum. Then I saw the letters M-C-T-U appear in the holobox he was holding." She watched him expectantly.

"Yeah, me too," he said.

"Did you see the symbols on his purity collar? Could you make them out?"

"He wasn't wearing a purity collar."

She hesitated. "Did you see the face behind him, looking over his shoulder? The woman with the green eyes?"

A deep sensation of unease erupted in his belly. "I . . . I'm not sure. I saw . . . a woman. She didn't have . . ." He almost said "eyes" but at the last second changed his mind and said, "green eyes."

She nodded again. "Brother Jerome told me that everyone sees something different in Leodiva's easter eggs." She shifted, uncurled her legs, and leaned closer to him. "Describe what you saw in the last two easter eggs. The Foundation Core."

He told her about the ominous image of the Engines of Creation being choked by a monstrous dark vine, and how the bright skies of the Foundation Core had been darkened.

"I think the vine is what the Mucktu call the Jeeb Tree," Nkiru said. "I read about it in their Apocrypha. It's what grew from the Evil Seed planted by Atum, and it's supposedly . . ."

A chill ran through Se-Jong's heart, and her words blurred into noise. She stopped midsentence. "What?"

He licked his lips. "You read the Mucktu Apocrypha?"

She let out a breath. "Oh, man, I said that out loud, didn't I?"

Se-Jong swallowed the dryness that had suddenly gripped his throat. He knew that the church regularly censored history books to remove any heretical materials, and that over the millennia it had banned innumerable works of writing, music, and art. There was an entire office at the Regium dedicated to enforcing the church's One Voice doctrine, and all published works on every SATO world had to be approved by the office. Of all the banned books, though, one stood out from all the rest: the Mucktu Apocrypha, the ultraheretical sacred text of the Mucktu Bloodline cult, supposedly filled with an arcane evil so dire that reading even a small portion had soul-shattering consequences.

You could be charged with sacrilege, heresy, or even blasphemy by the church Inquisitors for owning any one of the thousands of banned books, but possessing a copy of the Apocrypha was an offense of an entirely different level, sure to attract a midnight visit by a member of the Silent Knife, the clandestine Dei Miltans squad dedicated to wiping out all knowledge of the arcane. Your copy of the Apocrypha would vanish into nothingness, and nobody would ever find your body, or the bodies of your family and friends. Your komnic accounts would vanish along with the contents of your bank accounts and your government records. Even your wiki profiles would be erased. Every trace of your existence would be wiped from the face of whatever planet you lived on. Poof, gone.

Se-Jong cleared his throat and looked around the tiny room, as if somebody might be hiding in the corners. "Where did you get a copy?"

He instantly regretted asking the question. She bit her lip, perhaps also wondering if she should tell him more. If anyone knew about her sacrilege, he'd be suspect. At minimum it might ruin his chance to attend the War College. At worst, he and his family might end up in front of the Inquisitors. If his grandmother was implicated, it could destroy her military career in the Solar Guard.

He knew he should stop Nkiru when she started explaining, but he didn't. She told him how, as part of her research duties for Brother Jerome, she'd made frequent trips to the reliquaries in the crypts beneath Manhattan's enormous Cathedral of the Archangels, studying the Second Epoch artifacts stored there. There was one particular room in which she had not been allowed. One day Brother Jerome had left the door ajar while he was studying a Worm scent-scroll in another crypt. She'd sneaked into the forbidden room. It had been filled with banned books, many of them from the early days of the Third Epoch. One of them had been the Mucktu Apocrypha.

"You read the whole thing? How long were you in there?"

She shook her head. "Not long." She tugged her komnic from the pocket of her coveralls and held it up. "I used a bookscan app to make a copy. I read it later. You want to see it?"

Se-Jong's heart fell. "Is the copy *still on your komnic*?"

She nodded sheepishly, and Se-Jong suddenly remembered the Dei Militans guard who'd been watching them in the chapel. He squeezed his eyes shut and tried to think. If the church suspected the contents of her komnic, both of them would already be in custody, or dead. It was *that* serious. The fact that they were here in their hotel meant they were probably safe, at least for now. Regardless, he threw up his hands. "No, I don't want to read it! What the hell are you thinking?" He realized he was shouting, and he lowered his voice to a furious whisper. "Do you know what would happen to us if they found out you have it?"

She scoffed. "Relax, Lieutenant, it's encrypted. Nobody can find it. I've never told anyone about it."

"You just told *me*," he pointed out.

A twinge of disappointment crossed her face. "Yeah, and I'm starting to see how *that* was a big mistake. I didn't think you'd let yourself get so freaked out. It's just a book."

"A book full of spells and arcanity. It's a manual for death. It's the recipe for a new Cataclysm."

She scoffed and gave him a disbelieving scowl. "Listen to yourself. I read it, remember? It's mostly just myths about the War of the Archangels and stories about the Rapture and the Cataclysm. Honestly, it's not much different from the same stories in the *Chronicles*. A little more detailed, maybe, and definitely from a different point of view, but the same basic stuff. Most of it is garbage, just like the *Chronicles*."

She sniffed at his appalled expression. "The church makes a big deal out of the Apocrypha just to scare people. If people actually read it, they'd see it's nothing to be afraid of. The truth is, as far as I can tell, the Mucktu cult is no worse than the Cataclyst Church. In fact, it seems pretty clear that they're two sides of the same coin."

Se-Jong sullenly shook his head. "The Mucktu don't value life like we do. They're terrorists, plain and simple, and they want to impose their religion on all of us. Look at what they did on Limbaugh and New Britain. And what about Paris? A thousand people died when they bombed the Louvre. Don't you dare make excuses for them."

She raised her shoulders at his accusations. "That's all true, but think about how many more of *their* people died when we tried to kill their Mother Dominus and occupy Caerini Prime. Our hands have just as much blood on them as the Mucktu's. We're just as guilty of fanning the flames of war, of trying to impose our values and our way of life on *them*." She tapped him on the forehead with her index finger. "Open your mind! The politicians and religious leaders on *both sides* use conflict to maintain power. That's why the wars never end. Both sides are awful, and the people are caught in the middle, confused by myths sold to them by the priests and politicians. It's the oldest and most successful con game in the history of the universe!"

Her face was red, and she was breathing hard. He realized he must look the same to her. He tried to settle himself, but he was stunned by her talk. How could she defend the Mucktu cultists and their Caeren puppets? Under the brainwashing of their Mucktu religious masters, the breakaway Earth colony of Caerini Prime had been performing horrendous genetic manipulations on their own children for almost two centuries. The Caerens might still look human, but everyone knew what they'd become: *monsters*. How could she believe differently?

Time to change the subject. He knew from his tenth-grade course in battle tactics that the best way to win an equal contest is to redirect your opponent. He held up his hands. "Listen, I'm not as closed-minded as you think." He tried to keep the desperation out of his voice. "I know the world is screwed up. It's the main reason I want to go to the War College and be a part of the Solar Guard. They have the power to change things for the better."

"With their battleships and fusion bombs? Yep, that'll certainly make things better. A little genocide solves a lot of problems, right?"

He clenched his teeth. "Have you ever read the preamble to the Charter of the Solar Alliance? The Solar Guard's mission is to *prevent* things like genocide and sectarian war. It's the most powerful tool for peace and unity in the Known Arc."

"Keep telling that to yourself, Lieutenant."

He sighed. "I don't want to argue. I'm just worried. One of the guards in the chapel was looking at you."

Her confident smile couldn't quite mask a flash of uncertainty. "Yeah, I saw him."

"And? Are you *sure* they don't know what you've got on your komnic?"

Her forehead crinkled and she looked away. "They don't know who I am," she muttered, almost as if talking to herself. "There's no way they could."

Before he could react, her legs had swept off the bed and she was lacing her boots.

"What are you doing?"

"I'll be back later," she said. "I've got some shopping to do. Don't wait up for me."

"Wait, what?" He jumped to his feet and took her arm. "What are you talking about?"

She shrugged away from his grip. "Stand down, Lieutenant, okay? I don't want to fight with you about politics, so I think I'll go shopping. Get some souvenirs."

Se-Jong's anger evaporated, and he realized that her shocking revelations about the Apocrypha had been another one of her tests, one that he'd obviously failed. How could he have been so stupid? She may have read it, but there was no way she'd keep a copy of the banned scripture on her komnic. She was intense, but she wasn't crazy.

She'd already donned her pilgrims' robes and was pulling her daypack out of the closet. He moved to stand between her and the door. "I'm going with you."

"No, you're *not*," she said firmly. She gave a wry smile and put her hand on his chest. "I'm sorry I lost my temper. I get frustrated sometimes. I always thought that when I left home, things would be different. But they're not. People are the same, everywhere."

He didn't move. "You can't go without me."

Her palm fell away from his breast. Her words were the cold snap of a whip. "Don't you *ever* tell me what I can't do."

All traces of affection were gone from her expression. Se-Jong felt his own anger spike in response. "Fine." He moved to the side, gesturing harshly toward the door. "Go on."

She pulled it open and stepped out. Five minutes ago they'd been laughing, breathlessly discussing their shared adventure in the Torax Chapel.

"I'll be back later," she said, and she closed the door.

He instantly felt more alone than he'd ever felt before. He considered following her, but if she caught him, she would doubtlessly consider it a betrayal. But what if she never came back? What would he do then? The thought of returning home with his tail between his legs disgusted him. The thought of the War College depressed him. In fact, the idea of any future without Nkiru Anaya terrified him. She'd already changed the course of the river of his life, and he doubted there was any way to force it back into its original banks. He remembered her words at the spaceport when they'd first met. *Every minute I'm not living is a minute I'm dying.* He was just beginning to understand what she meant.

He paced their room until the midnight bells, after which he went searching for her. The streets of the Holy City were busy even in the darkest hours. He moved through clutches of drunken revelers, searching for her face. He looked in the bars and the tiny prayer chapels that dotted every block. He went to the gate of the Regium, but it was closed, guarded by a glowering trio of Dei Militans. He waited on the sidewalk in front of the hotel through the early hours, watching the Angry Moons rise above the buildings across the street. As the sky brightened into sunrise, his heart shriveled into a dried husk. When the dawn bells rang, he went inside to gather his things.

As soon as Se-Jong entered the building, the owner of the hotel handed him a note. It was a message from Nkiru. He cursed and rushed to their room, threw his things into his travel bag, and hurried to the shuttleport. She would be in the Guild zone, the message had said, near the gate for a transport called the *Covenant of Andrik*.

When he rushed through the departure terminal to the gate, he found a line of yellow-robed pilgrims waiting to board the shuttle to the orbiting transport. He frowned. Their ship, the *Rose & Chalice*, wasn't scheduled to leave for three more days, though it really didn't matter. A pilgrim could travel on any of the church ships that navigated the pilgrimage route as long as there was room aboard.

He scanned the line but didn't see Nkiru. He found her in a corner of the gate area huddled behind one of the flight status displays. She was bent over a blinking device. For a moment he thought it was the ancient scancorder artifact she'd shown him back when they'd first met at Cloudtops Station, but that was impossible. Avatar technology, no matter how well preserved, simply didn't work in the modern era. Whatever energy had powered the devices' mysterious innards had failed at the moment of the Rapture, ten thousand years ago. When the avatars had died, so had their technology.

Her clothes were filthy, her face bruised. Her pilgrims' robes had a burned streak across one flank just below her left arm, which she seemed to be favoring. The burned streak was pencil-narrow and perfectly straight. *Just like a near miss from a laser rifle*, he thought.

He didn't move. She looked up. When she saw him, she quickly shoved the blinking device into her backpack. He stepped closer and she stood to meet him. Her smile was anxious, vulnerable. Her hands were shaking. She scanned his face, looking for some trace of his mood.

He reached out and touched the bruise on her cheek. "That must have been some shopping trip," he said.

She toppled into his arms, and he had no choice but to hold her. Her face was wet, and he discovered that it wasn't just her hands that shook: it was her entire body. The intensity of her relief at his presence overcame any lingering resistance. He wrapped his arms around her and pulled her into his chest. He held her, listening to the drone of the boarding announcements, measuring the heave of her chest as she was wracked by shuddering sobs. He cursed himself for not going with her, despite her objections. Whatever had happened to her must have been devastating.

When she pulled away and looked up at him, he steeled himself, but when he saw her face, the words of comfort caught in his throat. Beneath the already-yellowing bruises, underneath the tear-stained streaks of dirt, she was smiling. Her bottom lip was split and one of her front teeth was broken, but the wounds only added to the intensity of her expression. What he saw wasn't the tremulous smile of a woman relieved to be in the arms of her protector. It was the jaw-clenching triumph of a warrior queen who'd destroyed her opponents and salted the earth over their graves. He looked at her bruises in a new light. Whatever battle she'd fought the night before, she had *won*.

"We have to go, right now," she hissed urgently, pointing to the boarding line for the *Covenant of Andrik*. She reached down to lift her heavy bag. Se-Jong pushed her hand away and lifted it to his shoulder. Oddly, it seemed lighter than before. No, it was *definitely* lighter than before, as if she'd disposed of most of the ancient trinkets she'd collected. He gave her a sharp, suspicious look.

In response, she grabbed his hand and pulled him toward the gate. "I'm really glad you're here, Lieutenant. Now, let's get the hell off this rock."

GAMEMASTER

meatspace | RUPE

Kindred

Rupe glanced into the rearview mirror at the Martinez twins in the back of the van. The boy was glaring around, disapproving of everything in sight: suspicious, paranoid, protective. The girl sat in her portable wheelchair clutching a small steel oxygen bottle in her lap as if her life depended on it, which it probably did. She met his eyes with a practiced expression of brazen indifference, a skill she'd no doubt developed to ward off the pitying stares of strangers.

He returned his attention to the road. That she was alive at all seemed a miracle. One of her arms was missing up to her elbow. Both her feet were gone, and one leg had been amputated at the knee. Under the niqab-style face scarf, her delicate teenaged skin had been melted by fire, leaving ropey scar tissue to cover her face and scalp. The emotion he felt surprised him. It wasn't pity, it was *anger*. Anger at Fate. Anger at God, though he didn't believe in a god. No human, especially no *kid*, should ever have to endure something like this. He shook his head to clear it.

He glanced into the rearview mirror again. She was still staring at him. And now, so was the boy. He said something that Rupe couldn't hear over the buzz of the engine and the roar of the wind through the open windows.

"What?"

"Where are the seatbelts?" Francis shouted.

"Doesn't have 'em," Rupe shouted back.

"What kind of car doesn't have seatbelts?"

"It's a 1964 VW camper van," yelled Rupe. "Isn't it awesome? I lived in it after my parents kicked me out." After leaving Germany as a teen, he had roved aimlessly through North America's landscapes for almost three years, camping in mountain forests and desert canyons. His travels had inspired many of his landscape designs for the game.

The boy scowled at his sister. "This car is twenty years older than our mother. It can't be safe."

In his mirror, he saw Fiona shrug away her brother's concerns. He recognized a quality in her that transcended her age and situation. He'd seen a similar quality in some of his colleagues, including both Arni and Analise. *Especially* Analise. Rupe had no word to describe this quality. It was far more than simple curiosity: it was the unstoppable urge to look around the corners of the obvious to see what was lurking there.

He'd been following Fiona's progress in the game for months. This girl saw things invisible to normal players. She seemed more interested in figuring out how the game was designed and the intentions of the designer than playing the game itself. Even though it often infuriated her teammates, she delighted in deconstructing the scenes, the actions of the bots, the behavior of the terrain and weather as she looked for clues. The others played the game with religious zeal, to experience the thrill of discovery and danger. Fiona played with the skeptical inquisitiveness of a scientist. She played to *win*.

Whatever her strategy, it worked. She recognized patterns that no one else could. She teased meaning and purpose out of even the frailest circumstance. It was this ability that had caused her PPA score to soar in the game. It was the same ability she'd used the previous evening to work out the fact that Analise's character in the game was so much more than a normal avatar.

He grinned ruefully. *She's one of us*, he thought. *A kindred spirit who knows what it means to escape a shitty reality and find purpose inside a virtual world.* These days he identified far more with his game avatar, the mighty Ruperus, than he did with his meatspace persona of Rupert Schroeder. Rupert Schroeder was an obnoxious college dropout whose entire life had been a perpetual disappointment to his parents. Ruperus was a powerful creature of mischief and mystery, known and feared on a thousand planets as the Gamemaster. The girl in the rearview mirror? She was the survivor of a life-defining accident—but even more so, she was Gaia, a planet-hopping Dryan-scout with a massive talent for sneakiness and puzzle solving.

Havenlab

Rupe drove to the back of the building and parked behind the rusted dumpster. For once, he wished he'd chosen a less conspicuous paint scheme for his van. With its purple-and-yellow tie-dyed swirls, it wasn't exactly a stealth vehicle, but at least it had room for a wheelchair. He helped Francis lift Fiona and the chair to the ground, but when he made a move to push her toward the building, Francis shouldered him away and took control of the chair before he could touch the handles.

Beyond the abandoned loading dock was an unmarked steel door. Rupe stopped and turned to his companions. "Okay, you two: up until now you haven't really done anything illegal. As soon as I open this door, that changes. Think very carefully about that. How will your mother feel if you both get arrested? Seriously, you should just give me the backup file and let me take you home."

Neither of them said anything, but Fiona's determination was obvious. Rupe tried to look stern. "You left your phones at home, like I told you, right? No electronic devices, nothing that can be tracked, right?"

"The FBI took our phones," said Francis.

Rupe sighed. "Another thing. If anybody finds out *anything* about this place, all of us will go to prison. You keep your mouths shut, all right? This isn't a game. Real people will get really hurt if you even hint that you know anything about this place. Got it?"

Again, pursed lips and determined nods.

Arni is going to fucking kill me, Rupe thought as he inserted his key and pushed the door open.

"Whoa," breathed Francis.

Rupe let his hand fall from the bank of light switches. It was hard not to smile. He knew *exactly* what these kids were feeling: the same thing he'd felt when Arni had first brought him here.

The room was as large as a warehouse. There were a few crates along one wall, and much of the floor space was jumbled with oddly familiar furniture and construction debris: chairs, consoles, wall sections. The main attraction crouched in the center of the open space like a fantastic metal bird, its mighty Starlighter engines slung below a gleaming silver fuselage, its vermilion fins emblazoned with a streaking comet insignia.

"It's the *Vigilant*!" Francis's voice echoed in the warehouse as if it were a cathedral.

Fiona's scowl was gone. "That's the movie version, isn't it? It's different than the original ship in the TV show."

Rupe nodded. "Yep. It's the full-size mockup they built for the movie back in the '90s. Arni bought it when he heard the studio was going to scrap it. He bought this building to store it. We were planning to use it to publicize the last major release of the *Longstar* game, but it turned out to be too fragile to move around on a truck. It's been sitting here for two years gathering dust."

"So, this is what a video-game billionaire does with his money," said Francis.

"I didn't like the movie," said Fiona. "The whole storyline about the Algethi was stupid." When they both gave her critical looks, she added, "But I'll admit that the ship is cool."

Rupe chuckled. Fiona pointed to the lowered ladder on the front landing gear. "Can we go inside?"

"It doesn't have an inside. It's just an empty shell. See the rest of this junk?" Rupe pointed to the haphazard collection of furniture and construction debris. "Those are broken-up pieces of the interior sets for the ship. Arni bought those from the movie studio, too. He was hoping to rebuild them here, maybe open a museum."

Francis's eyes roved the space. The front wall was mostly windows, some of which were cracked and most of which were plastered with old newspapers. The sides and rear walls were concrete blocks with peeling paint. Cobwebs swayed from the metal rafters of the high ceiling. "What is this place?"

"Believe it or not, it's an abandoned grocery store," Rupe replied. "It was cheaper than buying a real warehouse."

"It's incredible," whispered Fiona. Rupe knew what she was feeling. The *Starlighter Vigilant* had been the vehicle for the dreams and fantasies of fans of the *Longstar's Rangers* TV show, and this passion had been resurrected in new generations by the popularity of the movie and the video game. Rupe understood perfectly that the needle-nosed rocket was a stage prop made from plywood and sheet metal, but if he squinted his eyes and held his breath, it sometimes *seemed* to be real, as if he could leap aboard like Captain Dek Longstar and rocket off to adventure in the far reaches of the galaxy.

Not today, though. Today, the sad, dusty shape seemed trivially unimportant. He gestured toward a rear door that had once led to the grocery's storage rooms. Francis followed regretfully, pushing his sister, his eyes lingering on the sleek fuselage with its blazing comet insignia, and the three sweeping fins surrounding the mighty rocket engines.

—

Rupe rapped out the drumbeat rhythm from the *Terminator* movie theme, once, twice. He waited. He heard the door being unlocked from the inside. It cracked, and Zia peeked through. When she saw his companions, her eyes narrowed. She made a hissing sound. "*Pizdets!* You brought them *here?*"

"I didn't have a choice," he said, motioning toward Fiona. "The girl wouldn't give me the backup. Said she'd only give it to Arni."

Zia muttered something else in Russian and closed the door.

"What's happening? Who is that woman?" Francis was clutching the handles of his sister's wheelchair, his knuckles white. "She came to our house with the JEEB people and the FBI."

"That's, uh . . ." Rupe paused. He knew better than to reveal Zia's name. He brushed aside the familiar pangs of frustration he always felt whenever he thought of Zia Pyotrovna Volkov. "I think she used to be a famous hacker. She's helping Arni." *Famous* was the wrong word to describe Zia. In fact, nobody at all had known who she was, not even her clients; they'd only known the devastating results of her work. She didn't have many friends. Analise had been one of them. Rupe had tried to become another, but Zia's personality was like a sea urchin. You had to be careful when you approached, or you'd be stabbed by one of her spikes.

Francis looked uncomfortable with Rupe's explanation. "She showed up at our house with the Feds. If she works for the government, why is she helping Arni? Won't she get into trouble?"

Rupe almost chuckled out loud. "She doesn't worry much about trouble. She's helping because . . ." He paused, trying to figure out how to end the sentence. In truth, he wasn't sure why Zia was risking prison to help Arni. He had his suspicions, though, and another pang of frustration whacked his heart. "She wants to save Analise. Just like the rest of us."

They waited. Rupe tried to give Fiona and Francis a confident smile. He knew that Zia and Arni were inside arguing about what to do. Arni wanted to invite them in because they'd helped him and Analise during the fiasco at Grone. Zia, on the other hand, was a secrecy freak, a dark-web hacker who worked as a security specialist for the government's JEEB program. Rupe completely understood her reluctance to admit the teens. She would go to prison if her bosses found out she was here helping Arni.

The door opened, and a stormy-faced Zia glowered at Rupe. "Are you *certain* nobody knows they're here?"

"Their mother works on Saturdays. She thinks they're home."

Zia grunted distrustfully. "No phones, correct?" Rupe nodded, and Zia motioned them inside with a sharp jerk of her arm.

Arni had made some changes since Rupe's last visit to the makeshift computer lab. When this place had been a grocery store, the room had been a locked storage area for beer, wine, and cigarettes. The walls were a grim concrete block, the floor cracked cement. There were no windows, and the only door was the one through which they'd entered. There were more folding tables than last time, and somebody had tried to organize the chaos of wires and cables that connected the various computers, servers, monitors, and keyboards scattered on the tabletops. There were also more whiteboards, already covered by incomprehensible scribbles. They still hadn't been able to fix the air-conditioning. It was oven-hot in the room, which couldn't be good for all the delicate electronics.

Arni stood next to Zia, a head taller and much more gangly, like a beanstalk next to a summer squash. His eyes were red, his face haggard. He was leaning on a thin metal pole mounted on a rolling base. From the top of the pole hung a plastic bag of brown fluid, and from the bottom of the bag draped a thin plastic tube that ended in a needle plugged into his forearm. At the sight of the intravenous fluid dripping into Arni's bloodstream, a knot of tension gripped Rupe's stomach. *Zia has already given him the injection*, he realized. The bag was almost empty. They must've started the process hours ago.

Arni looked at Fiona and winced but held out his hand. "So, you're the famous Lady Gaia who crushes all of Rupe's puzzles. I'm Arnold Zaman," he said. "The archangel Atum. We met at Grone. Sort of."

The girl raised her arm and gripped Arni's outstretched hand as best she could. For the first time, Rupe noticed that one of her fingers was missing, and two of the remaining three were fused together. He wondered briefly how she managed to control her avatar without a functional hand. Or brush her teeth or use a pencil. Arni shook it awkwardly.

Zia didn't introduce herself. Both Fiona and Francis glanced at her but quickly looked away when confronted by her suspicious glare. Arni took a breath. "Do you have the backup of Gaia's item stash?"

Fiona didn't immediately reply. It was hard to gauge her emotions behind her face scarf, but Rupe could tell she was anxious. She cleared her throat. "I, ah, have some questions first." At Arni's fatigued nod, she continued. "Analise wasn't an avatar. I know that. She was inside the game universe somehow. I want to know how."

Zia threw her hands up and slapped them onto her hips. "You *told* her?"

Rupe shook his head. "She sort of figured it out on her own."

Arni's shoulders slumped. He gave Rupe a look of exasperation. His friend's frustration hit Rupe like an arrow to the heart. He was a shitty co-conspirator, and he knew it. He wasn't made for this clandestine cloak-and-dagger bullshit, even though it was his specialty to set up intricately plotted conspiracies inside the game. He was an armchair hero, not a real one. He'd let his friend down and risked everything by bringing these kids here. "I'm sorry," he mumbled.

Arni sighed and turned back to Fiona. He knelt next to her chair, his voice gentle but probing. "On Grone, after my avatar died, did Analise say anything to you? Try to remember exactly what she said. You were the last person to see her."

Fiona nodded. "She told me that if I put the little box—the *holobox*—into the pyramid that something wonderful would happen."

"That's all?"

"Yes. Then the archangel Oaone attacked us." Fiona hesitated nervously, then added, "That was your boss, right? April Chun, the CEO?"

Arni raised an accusing eyebrow at Rupe.

"I swear I didn't tell her that," Rupe protested.

"*I* figured it out," claimed Francis.

Arni winced, still focused on Fiona. "You put the holobox into the kernel interface, right?" Fiona nodded, and Arni continued, his words hesitant and strangled. "What happened to Analise? Was she still alive?"

"I don't know. She was hurt pretty badly. The archangel stabbed her with some kind of knife." Fiona lowered her voice. "Will her avatar respawn if she . . . dies?"

"Maybe. I don't know." The look on Arni's face was heartbreaking. "Something went wrong. We're locked out. We can't see what's happening inside the game."

"I'm so sorry," said Fiona. Her voice was filled with authentic emotion. After a moment, she added, "What exactly happened when I put the holobox into the pyramid? I saw on the news that the entire game crashed, and that the company may never get it running again." She hesitated. "It didn't really crash, did it? The game is still running, at least partially, or you wouldn't be trying to get Analise out."

Rupe felt a lump of terrified admiration in his throat. This wonder girl seemed on the verge of figuring out the entire conspiracy. He held his breath, waiting for Arni to reply. If Arni admitted to Fiona that he, Rupe, and Analise had been conspiring to steal the game environment from the Orbital Arena servers, this innocent girl could conceivably be charged as an accomplice. The last thing Rupe wanted was for Fiona to join the rest of them in the bucketful of felonies in which they were currently drowning.

Arni rose from his kneeling position next to Fiona's chair and pointed toward the jumble of computer equipment scattered across the room. "Yes, we think the game is still running. We're trying to figure out what happened. For some reason, as soon as Gaia activated the holobox, some kind of enhanced firewall went up around the entire game environment. We lost contact with Analise and everything else inside the firewall. I think there may be a way to break through it, but I can't do it without the backup of Gaia's item stash. Will you give it to me?"

Fiona paused, answered nervously. "I'll give it to you if you'll show me how Analise got into the game."

Arni bit his lip and looked toward Zia. She shook her head vigorously. Arni glanced at Rupe. Rupe shrugged. Finally, Arni nodded to Fiona. "Okay. But you *have* to keep every bit of this a secret."

Capatars

Francis pulled the thumbdrive from a zippered pocket of his cargo shorts. Arni took it and rushed to one of the tables, dragging his IV stand behind him. Rupe recognized Arni's workstation by the bank of four large, curved monitors, arranged so that they presented him with a panoramic field of view. Empty protein-bar wrappers and crumpled bags of chips surrounded the keyboard. Arni gently plugged the thumbdrive into the computer, clutched the mouse, and began clicking furiously. He found what he was looking for in seconds. He asked Fiona, "What's your game account password?"

Fiona looked sheepishly at her brother. "It's WonderTwinPowers. No spaces; capital *W*, *T*, and *P*."

Arni's laugh was loud and braying, like a donkey. "Of course it is!" He typed. "Yes! We've got it!" He spun his chair to Fiona, his face plastered with a wide grin. "Thank you, Lady Gaia; you may have just saved everything!"

Even Zia seemed relieved. She closed her eyes and let out a long, sustained breath. When they reopened, they were filled with fire. "Good. We need to get started, now." She checked the IV bag that was dripping into Arni, then looked at her phone. "Everything is ready." She turned to Rupe and gestured at the teens. "Take the Wonder Twins home."

"No," protested Fiona. "You promised!"

It certainly made sense to take the teens away. Arni had what he needed. But it somehow seemed coldhearted to bring them this far and not let them see it play out. It wasn't his call, though. He looked over at Arni.

"Let them stay," said Arni. "They earned it."

Zia scowled. "No. For their own sakes, they need to go."

"If you make us go, I'll call the police," said Fiona.

Francis paled. "Fi, shut up!" From his expression, Rupe could tell the boy was worried that this group of criminals might take them hostage, or do something worse, if they thought Fiona might give away their secrets.

Fiona ignored her brother. "I won't tell a soul, I promise, but you have to show me how Analise got into the game. That was the deal. We stuck to our end of the bargain."

Arni said, "We don't have time to argue, Zia. And really, what does it matter? Let them stay."

Zia grimaced and gave Arni a glare of disbelief. It took Rupe a moment to realize why: he'd just said her name in front of the

Martinez twins. She let out an angry breath. "Fine. We're all fucked anyway."

Rupe started to smile, but then he thought, *what does she mean by that?*

He herded Fiona and Francis to the corner of the room and motioned for them to remain silent. They watched as Arni and Zia proceeded through a brief muttered conversation, both pointing at various displays connected to Arni's computer. Eventually, they both nodded in agreement. Arni wheeled his IV to an overstuffed armchair that looked like it had been dragged out of a dumpster. He lowered himself into the stained cushions. At the same time, Zia fumbled with a set of wires and cables sprouting from a machine next to the armchair.

Rupe pointed and whispered. "See that? That's called an *ESP scanner*. ESP stands for . . ." he paused, trying to remember the technical term. "Oh yeah: *engineered subatomic particles*. ESPs are protons and quarks and shit that they've altered and turned into tiny little radio transmitters. Only it's not actually radio. The particles are *entangled* with the hardware kernel inside the QARMA engine, whatever that means—"

"Kernel?" Fiona interrupted. "Is that the same thing I saw in the game? Analise called the machine thingy a *kernel interface*."

"I'm a game designer, not a programmer. Analise tried to explain it to me once, but it was like trying to explain astrophysics to a monkey. Anyway, they inject you with a dose of this ESP stuff, and the tiny particles float through your bloodstream and embed themselves into your brain. You see that big brown intravenous bag attached to Arni? It's full of those particles. They're coated in some kind of protein that only sticks to the right part of your brain cells. There's like a hundred trillion of them in a single dose. Analise called them *nanospecks*."

"Nanospecks," whispered Fiona. Her eyes were glued to Zia as the woman set up the ESP scanner.

Rupe nodded. "Some folks over at Stanford figured out how to make the nanospecks, but nobody could figure out how to get them into the right parts of the brain. It was Analise who invented the protein glue that targets the right brain cells. Like I said, she was a"—he caught himself—"she *is* a genius."

Arni was talking quietly to Zia as she connected the bundle of wiring to a thickly padded cloth cap. When the bundle was secure, she started typing on a keyboard connected to the ESP scanner. A screen lit up and Rupe heard the whir of a powerful cooling fan. He pointed to the cap. "That's the BCI. Brain-computer interface. Analise invented the cap idea back when she was a doctoral student at the Stanford AI Lab. The cap reads the signals from the nanospecks and sends them to the ESP scanner."

He glanced down at Fiona. She was still watching Zia intently. He continued. "Dr. Chun used to be a physics professor at Stanford. Arni and Analise were both her students. That's how they all met. Dr. Chun saw a connection between Arni's VR work, Analise's AI theories, and her own work in quantum physics. She sponsored a research project. Their goal was to find a way to bypass your eyes and ears and nose and skin and connect the experience centers of your brain directly to an avatar in a virtual environment. Instead of seeing what your avatar sees through a VR headset, you'd experience it in your brain as if it were *real*. If the simulation was good enough, you wouldn't be able to tell it was fake. When your brain signals your arm to move, the avatar's arm would move, and it would feel completely natural. It's the Holy Grail of virtual reality. Since they would be different than regular avatars, they called them *capatars*, because they are controlled by the BCI cap instead of a game controller.

"Capatars," Fiona muttered. She was still engrossed by Zia's slow, deliberate movements as she fitted the cloth cap on Arni's head. Zia began tracing the wires from the ESP scanner to another, smaller device on the same table. Rupe's voice got softer, more reverential. He couldn't help himself. "See that machine she's checking?" The box was featureless metal, except for the softly glowing blue symbols elegantly embossed across the front:

○△□ | H A V E N

Just being near the machine gave Rupe a chill. "That's where the magic happens. That's one of the QARMA engines. There are three of them: Pandora, Sentinel, and Haven. They're the secret to the game's success, and they're *really* hard to build. Pandora was the first one. It's in a secure vault at Orbital Arena, and it's the one that hosts the game universe. Sentinel is the one Dr. Chun sold to the military's JEEB program for a billion dollars. It's at the JEEB Lab over at Stanford while its being tested. This one . . ." his voice trailed off. "This one Arni and Analise borrowed from the company's vault."

Vot Dermo

Rupe winced as Zia disconnected the empty nanospeck fluid bag from the tube in Arni's arm. She started replacing it with a new and smaller IV bag, this one with clear liquid, probably some kind of nutrient to sustain him during the coma phase. She clumsily struggled to attach the plastic tube. "Sorry," she mumbled.

Arni's tall frame was sunk into the cushions of the chair, his forearms stretched along the armrests. His eyes were closed, but Rupe could see the quick rise and fall of his chest. The thick BCI cap made his narrow head look like a mushroom. Zia glanced at Rupe and the teens, scowled, and turned back to her work.

Fiona whispered, "So that's how Analise got in the game? She wore a cap like that?"

Rupe nodded. "She's connected to the Sentinel machine being tested at the JEEB lab over at Stanford University. The cap induces a coma so that your real body's sensations don't interfere with the sensations of your capatar's body inside the simulation. Only problem is, the nanospecks in her brain won't last forever. If Arni can't break her out of the simulation before they fail, her coma may be permanent."

"Why don't they just disconnect her? Wake her up?"

"I thought the same thing, but Arni says it won't work. He says there's a whole process for waking somebody from a capatar coma. It's called *extraction*. He says unplugging Analise without doing an extraction would scramble her brain into pudding."

Francis stared doubtfully at the tangle of wires between the cap on Arni's head and the ESP scanner. "That's insane. What if there's a glitch or a bug in the software? What if somebody tripped over the cord that connects you to the machine?"

"Arni says there's a million fail-safes to keep that from happening. Apparently, that's a part of the problem. When the firewall went up, all those fail-safes got triggered, and until the firewall is lowered, there's no way to start the extraction process. The good news is that he thinks the firewall won't prevent a *new* capatar from being spawned. If he can make it work, then there's a chance his capatar can lower the firewall from the inside and Analise can be saved."

"And if he can't, he'll be stuck inside, too?"

Rupe suddenly realized that he was nervously blabbering all sorts of things that were probably top secret information. But really, what did it matter? Most likely he was already destined for federal prison. He sighed. "Yeah. If he can't lower the firewall, it's a one-way ticket."

It was hard to read Fiona's expression behind her face scarf. "You said Analise is connected to the other machine, the one called Sentinel. How can Arni save Analise from inside *this* machine if she's inside a *different* machine?"

Rupe scratched his beard. This girl was too sharp for her own good. He dared not give any hint that he knew what Arni and Analise had *really* done, and why Arni now needed the Shadow Emora to repair the damage. As it stood, if they got arrested, Rupe could claim some level of ignorance. But if the Feds could prove that he'd known all along what his friends had been trying to accomplish, he'd be put away for life alongside his co-conspirators. He liked this girl Fiona, but he'd already said far too much. He cleared his throat. "Um, I don't know exactly how this all works. I'm not a programmer. I think all three machines are linked somehow."

Fiona's voice shrank to the softest whisper. "If Analise dies in the simulation, does her real body die too?"

Rupe fought down the lump in his throat. "I don't think anybody knows for sure. There are only four BCI caps, and they're all prototypes. This is new to everybody."

—

Eventually they were ready. Zia insisted that Francis and Fiona watch from a distance. Rupe left the twins in a corner and moved to stand next to Arni's chair. His friend's face was pale. Arni looked up. "Thank you," he said. "Thank you for everything." Rupe felt tears forming and dragged the sleeve of his T-shirt across his cheeks. Arni grinned. "For a badass, you're such a softie."

Rupe swallowed. This would be a risky, two-part hack, he knew. First, they had to get Arni's virtual capatar into the game, and second, they had to spawn the Shadow Emora into the game as a virtual object. Without the Shadow Emora, Arni's capatar wouldn't be able to access the critical parts of the system software necessary to bring Analise home. Arni had spent the last three days working on a hack, something he called a *transfer pocket*, which would supposedly get the Shadow Emora through the firewall and back into the game where it belonged, in a secure location easy for Arni's capatar to find.

Standing on the other side of the chair, Zia made a restless show of verifying all the connections between the BCI cap and the ESP scanner. She'd checked them a dozen times already. Rupe wondered if she was worried that she'd missed something, or if she was just stalling. They all knew this whole affair was beyond dangerous. Flipping the switch to activate the BCI cap might send Arni's consciousness into the virtual world, or it might fry his brain. Arni had hacked the stolen JEEB capatar code into the Haven system, but nobody in the room really understood the technology, and the prototype cap Analise had brought there from the JEEB lab had never been tested.

Rupe began to regret allowing the teens to watch. What if, when Zia threw the switch, Arni died in a shuddering, screaming cascade of sparks? If that happened, he and Zia would be guilty of murder, and the two kids would be witnesses to the crime. He looked over into the corner from which they watched with rapt attention. There was no way he would be able to drag them away.

He put his hand on Arni's shoulder. "Bring her home, man. Find a way."

Arni nodded up at Rupe with an expression of savage determination. "I will. I swear." He turned his head to Zia, his motion limited by the thick cables attached to the cap. "Let's do this."

—

Zia's fingers moved warily over the unfamiliar controls of the ESP scanner. "The scanner has a good image of your nanospecks. Resolution accurate to nine sigma. I can see your gross synaptic activity on the monitor. As far as I can tell, everything is working. Are you ready for entanglement?"

Entanglement was the crucial step, Rupe knew. Right now, the nanospecks were inert inside Arni's brain, glued to the trillions of microtubules at the tips of every synapse. The way Analise had explained it, because they were so incredibly tiny, the particles vibrated at the quantum level along with the atoms that made up the synaptic receptors. The artificial particles had become, for all practical purposes, a part of the synapse. When the synapse fired, the energy was felt by the nanospeck. "It's like a wiretap," Analise had explained, "It allows us to eavesdrop on the activity of the synapse."

Zia's scowl was as impenetrable as ever, but Rupe couldn't miss the tremble in her hands. She looked over at the QARMA engine, and he thought he saw her shudder. "Okay, here we go," she said. Her finger paused an inch above the mouse button. She glanced up at Rupe and gave him a questioning, point-of-no-return shake of her head. *Should I do this?* It was the first time she'd ever asked his opinion on anything. He swallowed and nodded.

She tapped the button. Other than a few lights blinking on the ESP scanner, nothing seemed to happen. Zia stared at the monitor, her expression unreadable. Rupe looked down at Arni. His friend's eyes were closed, and he wasn't moving. "You okay, man?" Rupe said.

Arni nodded without opening his eyes. Rupe looked questioningly at Zia. She ignored him, focused entirely on the scanner. He knew she was trying to connect the machine to the capatar code Arni had stolen from the JEEB program and hacked into the Haven machine.

If she was successful, the machine would create his capatar in the Avatar Mall, the weapon-free safe zone where all new avatars first entered the game universe. After his capatar's body was created, his mind would be transferred to the capatar's brain. Arni's meatspace body would fall into an induced coma, and his virtual capatar clone would wake up in the Mall.

In a normal game situation, a new avatar would explore the Mall, buy gear and weapons at the shops, and visit the bars and meeting spaces to find teammates. They'd then use the Hero's Gate portal at the center of the Mall to send themself into the game galaxy, where they would begin their campaign. With the firewall up, though, the Mall would be empty, the stores nonfunctional. Arni's capatar would be naked, and he'd have no way to get clothing or gear. He'd have no choice but to go through the Hero's Gate with nothing but his birthday suit.

"I'm connected to the capatar spawn system," Zia eventually said, but her voice was troubled. "It's building your capatar." She looked down at Arni. "You sure about this?"

He gave a terse nod. Zia took a deep breath. "Here we go."

Supposedly, this was the moment when the magic happened. Through some process Rupe didn't even pretend to understand, the quantum states of each of the individual nanospecks in Arni's brain would be mapped into the virtual brain of his capatar inside the QARMA engine. "It's called *entanglement*," Analise had told him, "but in QARMA physics it works quite differently than in quantum theory. You're entangling a real particle with a virtual particle." He had no idea what she'd meant, but he understood the end result: *Arni's brain was being tricked into thinking it was inside the virtual body of the capatar.*

What was Arni's mind experiencing right now? From the few tests Analise had performed in the jeebcosm, she'd described the sensation as "waking up drunk in a new world." Due to the nature of the technology, the virtual brain of the capatar had to be an *exact* copy of the organic brain of the player, down to the quantum level, which meant that the virtual body of the capatar must also be an exact, DNA-level match of the player's real body. No muscle-bound alien superhero avatars allowed—your capatar was *you*. "It's incredible," Analise had told them with shining eyes. "It feels *completely* real. There was no way whatsoever for us to know we were in virtual bodies in a simulated world. There were smells, tastes, and touch. You could feel sunlight on your skin."

Was Arni's capatar already standing inside the Avatar Mall, staring up at the Hero's Gate? Rupe looked over at Zia. "Is he in the havencosm?"

Zia shrugged.

Fiona was at rapt attention. "What do you mean, *haven cosm*?"

"*Cosm* is short for *cosmos*. It's what they call the simulated universe inside each of the QARMA engines. It's like a blank page you can fill up with virtual stars and planets and trees and people, like we did in the game." He pointed to the Haven machine. "The one hosted on this machine is the havencosm."

Rupe was about to continue when his stomach suddenly twisted into a knot. The ESP scanner began chiming insistently. Zia cursed and her hands flew to the keyboard. The knot in Rupe's stomach twisted again, harder, and he felt bile rising in his throat. He lurched against Arni's chair, grabbing the headrest to keep from falling over. The floor rumbled, and several lazy streams of dust cascaded from the ancient ceiling tiles.

The tremor stopped as quickly as it had started. Arni's eyes popped open. He looked wildly around the room as if expecting a monster to be standing in the corner. "What happened?"

"Vot dermo!" Rupe had been around Zia long enough to know the Russian words for *oh, shit*. "This is all wrong."

"Did you feel the ground shake?" he asked.

Arni, the cables still dangling from his BCI cap, rose from his armchair and peered over Zia's shoulder at the ESP scanner. She pointed at the screen. "Look at this. We managed to activate a capatar spawn point in the Avatar Mall, here, and set up the transfer pocket for the emora here. The connection was open, but . . ."

"But what?"

"Just a minute. Let me check something."

Rupe tried to make sense of the images flashing across the monitor, but they might as well have been hieroglyphs. Arni understood what he was seeing, though, because his finger shot out and tapped the screen. "Holy shitbags! Look at that!" His voice quavered. "Oh, no."

Zia's brows knitted together beneath her oversized glasses. "Your capatar body was created, but . . . ah, look. The transfer pocket for the Shadow Emora was flagged as a security violation and rejected. The firewall completely locked us out."

"No." Arni shook his head. "I mean, yes it did, but look at the timestream index!"

Zia's frown intensified. "I don't understand this. I thought the simulation always ran in real time."

"It does. Or at least, it did. Now it's running too fast. Time in the havencosm has been moving faster than real time. A *lot* faster."

Rupe looked back and forth at the horrified faces of his friends. "What does that mean?"

"No wonder the Haven engine has been acting so weirdly," said Zia. "This explains the excess kernel activity we've seen since we lost Analise." She worked her jaw. "This is not good at all. The simulation clock has been running *a million times too fast*. How could this have happened? Was it part of your migration software?"

Arni shook his head dismissively. "No. No way."

"Did you feel that tremor?" asked Rupe. "That was just a coincidence, right?"

Arni and Zia stared at each other with blank faces. Arni swallowed. "If this started when Gaia put the holobox into the kernel node, then . . ."

Zia paled. "Analise has been inside for almost five days, but from her capatar's perspective, it's been . . ." Her voice trailed off as she brought up the calculator on the computer screen.

"Oh, god," moaned Arni.

"Sixteen hundred years," said Zia. "And for every second, another day and a half pass inside the havencosm."

"Then she's already gone," said Arni.

"You don't know that," retorted Zia. "We don't know if a capatar ages inside a cosm. It's possible she might—"

Arni cut her off. "There's no way the environment sim can be stable at that clock speed. It's technically impossible. The cosm must've crashed the moment the clock got out of sync. The kernel activity we see in the Haven engine must be some kind of by-product of the malfunction."

A long moment passed. Rupe looked over at Francis and Fiona. He shook his head, slowly and sadly. Fiona seemed to be crying, though he could see no tears. He felt water trickle down his own cheek. He put his hand on Arni's shoulder. "I'm sorry, man."

Rupe stopped at a street corner near the Martinez house. The twenty-minute ride from Arni's makeshift lab had been solemn. Francis had asked a few muted questions, but when Rupe hadn't answered, he'd fallen silent. Fiona hadn't said a word. Every time Rupe had risked a glance into the rearview mirror, she'd been slumped in her wheelchair, staring absently out the side window of the van.

Rupe helped Francis lift Fiona's chair from the van to the sidewalk. He shook Francis's hand, then turned to Fiona. "Thank you for all your help. You did everything you could. I'm so sorry it didn't—" His sentence was broken by the sob in his throat. He knelt in front of her chair. "Lady Gaia, you were my favorite player in the whole game. You were the smartest and most adaptable. I know you're in a tough situation. Please don't ever give up hope. You're special, and I'm not talking about"—he waved his hands at the coverings and scarves that hid her injuries— "all *this*. You know it's true."

He waited for a response, but all he got was a slight dip of her head.

"Promise me, both of you, that you'll never, ever tell anybody about what you saw today."

Francis nodded, but Rupe couldn't read Fiona's expression behind her scarf.

"Don't try to contact me. I'll be in touch when it's safe," Rupe said. "Maybe when all this is over, I can get internships for both of you at Orbital Arena. How would you like that?"

Francis smiled, but Fiona didn't react. Rupe sighed. "Auf Wiedersehen, Lord Geo, Lady Gaia. Until we meet again."

Quake

Except for Chun and her small inner circle, nobody in the company knew what had caused the game to irretrievably crash. The company's entire cadre of software, hardware, and network engineers were working around the clock to figure out the source and nature of the impenetrable firewall that had inexplicably popped up around the game environment, obscuring the inner workings of the game servers from their probing. Rupe knew the cause of the disaster, of course, but Chun didn't know he knew. He'd suspected that Arni and Analise had been up to something for months, though it hadn't been until after the crash that he'd learned the true extent of their treachery. By then it was too late. Analise was in trouble and Arni needed help, and he'd joined their conspiracy without hesitation.

Somehow, miraculously, his role in the affair had so far remained undetected. If Chun suspected that he was in league with Arni and Analise, he'd be hanging by his toenails in a jail cell somewhere. As it was, waiting around for his treachery to be discovered was pure hell.

The Orbital Arena corporate campus was in chaos, so Rupe eventually gave up going to the office. After all, without a game, there wasn't much use for a gamemaster. Weeks passed, and the situation did not improve. Chun suspended the accounts of all fourteen million game subscribers, and revenue from the game plunged to zero. A hundred employees were furloughed, and all the others who were not directly involved in supporting the JEEB contract were expected to be dismissed within a week. Rupe was still getting a paycheck, but for how long? The clamor on the game forums, and even in some of the mainstream media outlets, was fiercely critical of Orbital Arena. How could a tech company let its product crash without the possibility of restoration? Didn't it have a backup of the game environment?

Rupe knew that Chun's QARMA engines weren't like regular computers. They didn't manipulate bits and bytes or have things like processors, memory, or hard drives. According to Arni, they were "virtual entropy machines," in which "simulated quantum states decayed just like they did in the real world." You couldn't back up a cosm simulation: it either existed, or it didn't. There could be no copies. Attempting to duplicate the game environment would be, in Arni's words, "like trying to photocopy a summer breeze."

Chun had not given any interviews, and her silence as the founder and CEO hadn't helped calm the uproar. Now rumors were circulating on social media that the company had been brought down by hackers, its exotic technology infected by an equally exotic virus. People were speculating that the hack might have affected the company's billion-dollar government contract. If the game servers could be hacked, why not the military's version too? Rupe had overheard several tense conversations between Chun and Colonel Solomon over at the JEEB lab, and in private, Zia had reported that efforts to revive Analise had stalled. The government contract might be canceled, she'd said. Chun's entire world was collapsing around her, and there was one person upon whom she'd laid all the blame: her partner and cofounder, who had vanished the day the game had crashed:

Arnold Zaman.

—

Rupe knew Arni didn't like him visiting the makeshift lab at the old grocery store. Even though Arni and Zia had gone to great lengths to mask the location from the Feds, nobody knew how long the subterfuge would last. "They're going to find this place sooner or later," Arni had told Rupe. "You don't want to be here when it happens."

Somebody, though, had to keep the conspirators supplied with groceries and coffee and toilet paper. A month had passed since the first attempt with the BCI cap had failed, and since that moment Arni had not left the building. As far as Rupe could tell, Arni was sleeping at his computer workstation. The whiteboards scattered around the room mirrored the decline in his mental state. A month ago, when this odyssey had begun, the whiteboards had been covered in neat but incomprehensible diagrams and technical notes. Now they were smeared with wild scribbles or blank streaks where off-the-wall ideas had been savagely erased. The big board next to his workstation had the word FUCK scrawled across its entire breadth. Rupe put down the bag of groceries. Zia was never here anymore, though she'd kept them posted on Analise's condition and the events at the JEEB lab over at Stanford. Things weren't going much better there.

"Arni?" Rupe called. There was no answer. He walked back into the empty warehouse, where the dusty mockup of the starship *Vigilant* stood guard over ten thousand cobwebs. Rupe looked around, but there was no sign of movement, no sound. "Hello?" Rupe called. "Arni, you out here?"

"Over here," came the reply. Rupe walked toward the voice, ducking under the fuselage of the fake starship. Arni was hidden inside a maze of plywood and plastic, the bits and pieces of the stage sets from the 1990s movie *The Algethi Incident*. Rupe made his way to the center of the pile and found Arni slumped in one of the futuristic flight-deck seats from the cockpit of the *Vigilant*.

"Is that Longstar's chair?"

Arni nodded and ran his hands along the armrests. "Yep." He was wearing a beat-up leather flight jacket he'd bought for an obscene price from a Hollywood collector. Covered with faded patches representing fictional sci-fi military units, it had been worn in the original 1970s TV series by the actor who'd portrayed the show's lead character, Dek Longstar. Rupe knew it was Arni's prized possession, and he rarely wore it except on special occasions.

Rupe handed Arni one of the coffees he'd brought. He found another chair, this one smaller, one of the costar's seats. It swiveled. He spun toward Arni. "How you feeling, man?"

A long moment passed before Arni answered. "I never ran into a technical problem I couldn't solve. Sometimes it would take days, but I *always* found a solution or a workaround. I guess I always believed that any problem could be solved if you worked hard enough. But you know what? I think it's time to give up. Zia and I have tried everything to break the firewall, and I mean *everything*. It's been almost a month. A month!" He made an unpleasant chuckling sound. "You know how long that is inside the havencosm? Guess how long?"

"Arni, I don't want to—"

"Almost ten thousand years! That's right, ten fucking *thousand* years. That's twice as long as recorded human history on Earth, did you know that?" He shook his head, his voice painfully hollow. "Things were already changing fast in the gamecosm because of the virus. Think of what might have happened in ten thousand years if the cosm hasn't collapsed. Entire civilizations might have risen and fallen. Empires built and collapsed. Societies, religions, cultures might all have evolved and then been forgotten." He paused and looked at Rupe. Dark circles ringed his eyes. "What if she *is* still alive, Rupe? What if the simulation is still running? We don't know *anything* about capatars. Do they age? Can they die? *What if she can't die, Rupe?* What would it be like to live ten thousand years trapped on Ghast or one of the Whan planets?"

A blanket of horror fell over Rupe. He'd never considered the possibility that Analise might be stuck on one of the game's virtual worlds, alone and immortal, sentenced to an eternal damnation of fighting off the horrors that he, the Gamemaster, had invented to challenge the players. It had been his job to fill the entire game universe with nasty surprises. He shuddered. What if, during her time in-cosm, she had stumbled across an undefeated boss?

An experienced gamer might have a chance, but Analise? She was a neurophysicist, a hard-driven, real-world achiever with no time for such silly pursuits. She would have no sense of gameplay, how to fight, how to identify and avoid traps. What if she had fallen into one of his snares, and had been trapped there, screaming in pain, for ten millennia? How would that be any different than hell? Even if her capatar had somehow survived, how could she still be sane?

He could see from his friend's expression that Arni had been having similar thoughts. Arni closed his eyes, leaned his head back on the headrest, and whispered. "She's gone, Rupe. I know she is. It's time to call it quits. I'm going to shut Haven down and end this nightmare."

———

They were still sitting silently together when, suddenly and inexplicably, Rupe's skin began to crawl. The tingling sensation was sharp and distinctly uncomfortable, as if pins and needles were lightly pricking the entire envelope of his body. Arni must have felt it too, because he shifted in his chair and began vigorously rubbing his thighs. He looked at Rupe with an expression of puzzlement.

Rupe blinked. Arni's skin had assumed an unhealthy purplish tinge. No, it wasn't just Arni. Everything was slightly discolored, as if a purple filter had been applied to the sunlight coming through the newspaper-covered windows.

The floor dropped several inches. Unlike the string of rumbling tremors that had rattled dishes and roiled stomachs over the past few weeks, this was a sharp and instantaneous booming *crack!* The building groaned, and debris fell from the high ceiling and rained down everywhere. Rupe dove to the hard concrete floor and covered his head. At a metallic crumpling sound, he glanced up to see the nose of the *Vigilant* sinking to the concrete. Its front landing gear had buckled, and the needle nose smacked onto the floor, wrinkling the cheap aluminum fuselage all the way back to the fake gun turrets.

Then it was over, and they were both coughing from old grocery-store dust stirring for the first time in a decade. The tremor had lasted maybe five seconds. The all-over tingling sensation had faded, and the quality of the sunlight had returned to normal. Arni glanced remorsefully at the damaged starship, then at Rupe, then raced back toward the door to his lab.

One of the folding tables had collapsed, but the makeshift lab seemed otherwise untouched by the quake. The power was still on, and the Haven engine still emitted a vaguely threatening blue glow from the embossed symbols on its front panel. Arni swooped into his seat and began flipping through screens of data, probably checking the status of the system. For somebody who had just been planning to shut it down, he seemed awfully worried that it had been damaged by the quake.

"Something's happened inside the Haven machine. The kernel activity has increased by an order of magnitude."

Rupe was picking up the equipment that had spilled off the collapsing table. "What does that mean?"

"I have no idea." A chime sounded from Arni's workstation, and he said, "Uh-oh."

"What?"

"Uh, it's a message from Zia. She's at the JEEB lab. She says something just happened down there, too."

"What?"

"Don't know. Hold on, she's typing."

Rupe hurried to stand behind Arni's chair where he could see the screen. "Man, she's sending you a message *here*? The Feds can't trace it, can they?"

Arni gave him an incredulous glance. "Seriously? This is Zia we're talking about."

The machine chimed again. Rupe could see the message, but Arni read it anyway: *Solomon looking for Rupe, and he's not answering his phone. Is he with you?*

Arni typed: *Yes.*

Another chime: Get him to check his messages: Chun is trying to call him. Send him down to the JEEB lab ASAP. There's a problem with the jeebcosm.

Arni looked uneasy. "Better hurry. Get back here as soon as you can and let me know what's happening."

Rupe licked his lips. Why would Solomon want him? He wasn't a part of Orbital Arena's government contract. Rupe felt a new knot form deep in his bowels. "Arni, what's going on?" He tried to form a sentence around his thoughts. "How come the Haven engine here is acting up at the same time as the Sentinel machine over at the JEEB lab?" Arni didn't reply, just gave him a hollow look. The knot in Rupe's gut tightened. "There was an earth tremor the last time we fooled with the Haven machine."

"I know," said Arni.

Rupe waited for more, but Arni was staring into the nothingness, obviously lost in furious thought. Rupe started to leave but turned back to Arni. "Hey, man, don't turn anything off or shut anything down until you hear from me, okay?"

This broke Arni's concentration. He nodded. "Yeah. But hurry."

Jeebcosm

The VW van could barely do sixty, even on the downhills. Rupe kept the accelerator pedal on the floor, cursing the traffic. He didn't really understand any of this technical bullshit. He wasn't a programmer or a physicist. QARMA, cosms, capatars, brain-computer interfaces, nanospecks . . . Jesus Christ, how had things gotten this far? He was a game designer, probably the best there was. He understood the psychological theories behind thrilling gameplay better than anyone on Earth. He knew he was a genius. It was the fact that his best friends were also geniuses that had caused all this trouble in the first place. You get too many fucking geniuses in a room together, and unpredictable shit happens. All the current chaos had probably been inevitable, foreordained the moment Arnold Zaman had met April

Chun. The addition of Analise Novak had then stirred the genius-pot to boiling. Now the pot was boiling over, and the heat was continuing to rise as he and Zia were being stirred into the mix.

There's a problem with the jeebcosm, Zia had said. No fucking shit! The jeebcosm had been a problem from the beginning. Rupe had never been comfortable selling the game technology to the military. Games were for entertainment, not for training snake-eating SEAL teams. Chun had crossed a line making the sale to the JEEB program.

Rupe vaguely understood how the QARMA engines worked. Each hosted a cosm, which was an artificial universe, a blank canvas of fake space-time in which a game designer could create ultrarealistic environments and situations. The *Longstar* game had been built inside a cosm that Chun and Arni had dubbed the *gamecosm*. It was hosted on the original QARMA engine, the machine called Pandora, located in a secure data center on the Orbital Arena corporate campus. The military had created another cosm for their combat simulator; they called it the *jeebcosm*, and it was hosted on a second QARMA engine, called Sentinel, that Chun had sold them for a billion dollars.

Rupe also knew that the military's jeebcosm had stretched the QARMA technology to its limits. Arni had once tried to explain it over a beer at a Palo Alto brewpub. "The jeebcosm is set up just like our gamecosm. Only instead of all the fictional planets and dungeons you built for our game, they've created a hyperrealistic version of a single planet: *Earth*. They built it with geophysical data from millions of real-time online sources. All the cities, all the buildings, all the roads and lakes and forests. It's even got real-time weather. And not only that, but the AI scans social media profiles and links them to real-time cell-phone locations to make virtual clones for almost every living soul on the planet. They call them *doppelgängers*. I've seen them, and it's unbelievable. They're based on the same technology as the bots in our game, except that instead of using random character class templates, they're built from the data profiles of real-world people. I've seen my JEEB doppelgänger, and it's creepy real."

An asshole in a speeding German sedan almost caused Rupe to miss his exit. Thin tires squealing, Rupe flipped the driver of the sedan the finger as he swerved off the highway. He could see the monochromatic buildings of Stanford University from the exit ramp. He shoved his foot down on the accelerator pedal, but it was already pressed into the floor.

Pandora

April Chun's low-slung Jaguar was parked diagonally across two handicap spaces on the first floor of the parking deck. Rupe bit his lip. He glanced at the license plate just to be sure: *OA One*. Yep, it was Chun's. He took a deep breath. He had no idea why he'd been summoned. He couldn't even go inside the JEEB lab without a government security clearance.

The Computer Science building was a short walk from the parking deck. Clusters of students were milling along the sidewalks surrounding the entrance, waiting for permission to reenter after the earth tremor. An anxious babble of hushed conversations rose from the crowd. Rupe pushed his way through and waved his OA badge at the protesting campus security officer. He pulled open the heavy glass door. Inside the building, except for the lack of students, everything looked normal.

In the lobby he turned beneath a sign that read SAIL: Stanford Artificial Intelligence Laboratory. At the head of the hallway the military had set up a portable security checkpoint consisting of a folding table and a metal detector. A tall soldier with a shaved head watched him put the contents of his pockets into a tray. Rupe presented his Orbital Arena badge. The man examined it suspiciously, then lifted a clipboard on which was hand printed a very short list of names. "Schroeder. Yeah, okay. Go on."

Rupe collected his things. His hands were sweating. He wiped them on his T-shirt. Another guard waited down the hall at the double-door entrance to the JEEB lab. The man checked Rupe's ID again, even though he had just watched his counterpart make the same check at the other end of the hallway. An angry shout emanated from behind the lab doors. The guard lifted an eyebrow and glanced at Rupe as if to wish him luck. Rupe wiped his hands on his shirt one last time, took a deep breath, and pushed the doors open.

Inside was a small suite of six offices along a hallway, with a security door at the far end. Rupe could hear the precise tones of Chun's voice coming from one of the offices. "It was *not* the fault of the OA systems, Colonel. It was clearly some form of sabotage or negligence by one of *your* people."

The name on the plate next to the office door said "Reginald Howe, JEEB Senior Program Manager." Rupe gingerly stepped up to the open door. He recognized all four people inside the cramped office: Zia, who nodded distantly; Colonel Jacob Solomon, the military's project lead; Reggie Howe, Solomon's civilian counterpart; and Rupe's boss, April Chun, CEO and founding partner of Orbital Arena Games. As usual, she reeked of cigarette smoke and poorly repressed irritation. Even though her slight build and gaunt figure were dwarfed by the others, she owned the room. She scowled at him through her eyeglasses. "Good. You're here. Close the door, please." She turned to Solomon like an imperious middle-school teacher preparing to scold a misbehaving student. "Please tell us how you lost an entire planet, Colonel."

There weren't enough chairs in the office, so Rupe leaned against the wall. Colonel Solomon's uniform was rumpled, his face bloated with fatigue. He grimaced and nodded toward the man behind the desk. "Reggie, you're up. Make it fast."

Reginald Howe wore stylish round glasses and a dress shirt that had recently been starched but was now creased by a million wrinkles. A tie hung limply around his neck, like a noose. "It wasn't a security breach. All our protocols were in place. Nobody hacked the system. We have an air gap between us and the internet. Regardless, about forty minutes ago the JEEB Earth sim vanished from the Sentinel server. The QARMA hardware is undamaged, the cosm is still intact and running, but the entire virtual planet is gone."

"Could it have been a malfunction caused by the earthquake?" Solomon asked.

Zia slapped the arm of her chair. "No! That's what I've been trying to tell you. If you look at the error logs, the kernel activity in the Sentinel machine spiked just *before* the quake. It's the same as before. For the past thirty days, every single time we saw one of the weird little activity spikes from the Sentinel engine, there's been a tremor that follows it. The spike that marked the disappearance of the JEEB Earth sim was a lot bigger than any of the others, and so was the tremor."

Chun scoffed. "Do you know how *ridiculous* you sound? You've all seen the news. These earth tremors aren't just local, they're worldwide. It's ludicrous to think that one of our QARMA engines could be causing global earthquakes." She paused and looked around the room at the others. "How could *anything* we do here in a California computer lab cause an earthquake in China or Australia?"

Zia bristled. "The QARMA engines aren't computers, as you yourself have made plain a thousand times. They don't crunch binary data; they sort entropic probability arrays. They don't draw colored pixels on a screen; they render mass and energy particles in a virtual version of space-time. They don't have microprocessor chips; they work with some hocus-pocus bullshit called a QARMA kernel. What *is* a QARMA kernel, anyway, Dr. Chun? Can you actually explain what it *is*, and how it *works*? Because I've read your papers, and I don't get it. It sounds more like metaphysical rubbish than science."

"I wouldn't expect you to comprehend it," sneered Chun. "Besides, it's a trade secret. Even if I could explain it to a nonphysicist, I wouldn't."

Zia curled her lip. "Sometimes I wonder if you really understand your own technology, or how to control it." She turned away from Chun toward Howe and Solomon. "It's not just the earthquakes I'm worried about. Just now, we *all* felt our skin tingle, right? We *all* saw the colors change. And have you seen the news for the past three weeks? What about the sunspots? We've had more solar flares in the past three weeks than in the past five years. What about the GPS satellite failures? They say the atomic clocks on every single satellite all failed at the exact same moment. The Russian and Chinese satellites, too. Too many coincidences begin to stink of causation."

Chun spat out a derisive laugh. She turned to Solomon. "Listen to her. Now she's implying that a video game can cause sunspots."

"It's not a video game," retorted Zia. "Not anymore. It's evolved into something else, Dr. Chun, and you know it."

Chun's tone, always precise, turned razor-sharp. "If so, it's *your* fault. I *never* sanctioned the mods you people made to your Sentinel engine. It was tinkering by your government team that started this nonsense. Analise Novak modified the system kernel, which was expressly forbidden by the terms of your contract. She created the virus that—"

Howe scoffed loudly. "Novak *discovered* the virus, not *created* it. Your business partner Arnold Zaman is also involved in this fiasco. Have you ever considered the possibility that *he* made the virus? Wasn't it Arnold Zaman who *purposely* infected your company's game machine?"

"Under instructions from Analise Novak!"

Howe shouted over her words, "That's a load of bull—"

"Enough!" roared Solomon. "Maybe we should just shut the goddamn thing down!"

To everyone's surprise, both Chun and Zia snapped, "No!"

An awkward moment passed while the two women regarded each other with hostile suspicion. "If we shut down the Sentinel engine, it may kill Analise and Wolfe," said Zia. "None of us understands the capatar interface software that Analise added to the system, or the virus that seems to have altered it. If you break the connection without first untangling their minds from the cosm, it could leave them in a permanently nonresponsive state."

Analise and . . . Wolfe? Who is Wolfe? Rupe wondered. According to Fiona, there had been an avatar named Wolfe at the battle on Grone. It had been Wolfe who'd shot Analise's capatar.

"They're already nonresponsive," Chun said tersely. "They've been in an induced capatar coma for almost a month. That's twenty-eight days longer than the nanospeck particles were rated to operate inside a human brain. They're both dead already."

"They're *not* dead," protested Zia. "Their ESP monitors clearly show that their nanospecks are still entangled with their capatars. If anything, their neural activity has *increased*."

"How?" demanded Chun. "They may still be physically connected to the ESP scanners, but their capatars clearly aren't being hosted on the Sentinel engine anymore. Your ESP scanners are giving you false readings."

From behind his desk Howe let out a theatrically loud sigh. "We're not here to talk about earthquakes or comas or whose PhDs are bigger than whose. We're here to find out what happened to a billion-dollar virtual battlespace that may have been stolen from the United States Department of Defense!"

Chun sniffed loudly, obviously not accustomed to this kind of disrespect. She was many things: a genius physicist who had rocked the scientific world, a woman entrepreneur, and a Silicon Valley billionaire—there was even talk of a Nobel Prize for physics. When it came to dealing with normal human beings, though, she often stumbled over her own greatness. Her face, already hard, became chiseled with repressed fury. "Once again, Mr. Howe, that's *not* possible. There's simply no way that a region within a cosm can be *stolen*. A cosm is not a set of digital data that can be cut and pasted; it's a virtual version of an analog-reality state. What you suggest would be a violation of the laws of physics."

Howe shrugged, clearly peeved by Chun's tone. "So you say, Dr. Chun, but I think that's exactly what happened." He paused and gave Chun a grim smile. "You want to know why?" He spun his computer monitor so that Chun could see the screen. She adjusted her glasses and leaned toward it. Rupe leaned forward and looked over her shoulder.

Howe opened a video player on his screen. It displayed a thin-faced man in a dirty yellow bathrobe raving into the camera in some foreign language. Part of an unpainted concrete ceiling could be seen behind him, festooned with a cluster of thick electrical wires.

"What am I seeing?" demanded Chun.

Howe shrugged. "You tell me. I received a social media message notification on my phone about an hour ago, the same time the JEEB Earth vanished from our Sentinel engine. When I opened it, I found this video waiting for me. I thought it was junk until I realized what he was saying. Listen."

"He sounds like he's hallucinating," Chun said.

Rupe agreed. The man's speech was rapid and fiery; his eyes blazed with fervor. Whatever he was shouting about, he was passionate. At first Rupe thought the man was speaking Arabic, but he quickly realized the language was unfamiliar. Even so, often a word could be recognized, as if the language was sprinkled with heavily accented English.

"He just said 'JEEB Earth!'" Chun exclaimed.

"Yeah, he did. I heard it twice," agreed Rupe. "He said 'JEEB Earth *migration*.'"

"Quiet!" barked Solomon.

"He just said 'easter egg,'" Zia said. "And listen . . . he's saying 'Hero's Gate' over and over."

On the screen, the frantic man looked away from the camera as a loud blast issued from the speakers. A plume of dust obscured him for a moment. The man stumbled, stared in horror at something off camera, and made a hasty series of hand motions over his heart. He blurted something that sounded like "muck two!" An instant later he was brutally cut down by a small, quick figure with a long dagger whose blade dripped liquid sparks. The man in the yellow bathrobe fell hard, knocking the camera askew. For an instant, just as the video ended, the blurred face of his assailant was visible.

"Fuck me," Rupe shouted. He looked around the room at the startled faces. "That thing was using a flickerblade! It's a weapon from the *Longstar* game." He leaned perilously close to Chun to get a closer view of the frozen last frame of the video. Annoyed, Chun slid her chair back to make room. "Sorry," he mumbled. He pointed to the screen, where the final frame of the video was frozen. "What *is* that?"

The creature's face was blurred and mostly hidden beneath a cowl, but what Rupe could make out was feminine and almost human. Deep-blue skin with a blurred tracery of green that curled up its throat, crossed its cheeks, and vanished beneath the cowl at its temples. A milky-white radiance, from a jewel perhaps, shone from the shadows of its cowl where its forehead would be. It had the unreal beauty of concept art from a nightmare-plagued fantasy artist—one who'd set gaping sockets where its eyes should have been. In their stead were two smooth pits: haunting skull holes that made Rupe's skin crawl.

Howe's expression had sharpened during Rupe's outburst. "Mr. Schroeder, this brings me to the reason you are here."

A shiver spilled down the back of Rupe's neck. Did they suspect his involvement with Arni? Every fiber in his gut vibrated with the desire to shout out the truth: that Arni wasn't a traitor, that he was just trying to save Analise from what was, quite literally, a fate worse than death. He bit the end of his tongue. If they knew he was helping Arni, he would leave this room in handcuffs.

Howe indicated the image of the blue-skinned, eyeless creature on his computer monitor. "Dr. Chun informs us that you are the chief designer for the *Longstar* game."

"Chief worldbuilder."

Howe blinked. "What?"

"My official title is chief worldbuilder. I'm not a game designer. I create player experiences, not software."

"Of course. Do you recognize the man in the video or the creature that attacked him?"

Rupe shook his head. "No. I don't recognize either one of them."

"But you said the bladed weapon in the video was from the game, correct?"

Rupe nodded. "Yeah, it's a flickerblade. It's a weapon I made for the game. It's kind of like a cross between a vorpal blade from *Dungeons & Dragons* and a lightsaber from—"

"So, the video was generated in the game environment?"

Rupe shrugged. "It's easy enough for a player to have recorded a scene from the game, though I don't recognize the blue lady as one of our bot classes. She's using a flickerblade so she's a bot for sure, but I've never seen—"

Howe let out a sharp exhale. "Mr. Schroeder, was this video recorded inside the game environment, or not?"

"Um, yeah, probably. Like I said, we make it easy for players to record game action, and even send streaming vid—" He stopped, thinking furiously. The video must have been recorded before the game crashed. Otherwise, how would it have been transmitted through the supposedly impenetrable firewall? "Did you check the timestamp on the video?" he asked.

Howe abruptly turned to the others, effectively dismissing Rupe as if he had pushed a button and sent Rupe plummeting into a hidden trapdoor in the floor. Howe motioned to Zia and Chun. "Thoughts? Impressions?"

Chun gestured toward the image on the monitor. "I thought I heard the man say 'Manhattan,'" she said. "And I distinctly heard him say 'firewall' at least twice."

"He kept saying 'cannon,' too," said Zia. "What does that mean?"

"It sounded more like 'Canaan,'" said Solomon. "Like from the Bible. The Promised Land of the Jews."

Howe frowned. "Wait a minute." He spun his computer monitor toward himself, then typed. When he swung the monitor back around, the video was overlaid by a text window filled with what looked like software code. "This is the metadata that was embedded in the video. It's encoded in a standard format used by social media platforms. Look at the creator ID." He pointed to a section of the code.

```
XKIM_Signature: KANAAN
```

"Is that his name? Kanaan?"

"Could be. The signature in the message header is also Kanaan, not Canaan. Spelled with a *K*." Howe and Solomon exchanged tense glances. Howe placed his fingers in a thoughtful steeple. "The colonel and I have a theory. This Kanaan. It might be Roland Wolfe," he said. "His old hacker name was Kay9. That's phonetically similar to Kanaan.

Rupe said, "Who's Roland Wolfe?"

Zia narrowed her eyes at him, as if to say, *you bonehead, don't ask these people questions.* She answered before anyone else had a chance. "He's a cybersecurity specialist from the Pentagon. He went in-cosm as a capatar with Analise to try to catch Arni."

Rupe felt a spike of anger. Why hadn't Zia told him about this Roland Wolfe, this Kay9?

Zia motioned at the video. "Go back a bit. Pause when you have a good view of the man's face."

Howe did so. Everyone looked at the image.

"Could that be Wolfe's capatar?" asked Zia. "It looks a little like him."

Solomon nodded thoughtfully. "He does look a little like Wolfe. Same nose and eyes. But if that's Wolfe, why does he look so old? He's only been in-cosm for four weeks."

Rupe caught a meaningful glance from Zia, and he suddenly heard Arni's horrified voice echoing in his head: . . . *the simulation clock is running a million times too fast.* If true, Rupe realized, and thousands of years had elapsed inside the firewall, then the man in the image might very well be some version of Wolfe.

"Wolfe's capatar should be identical to his real-world body," Howe said. "Wolfe is what, thirty-five? The man in the video looks to be in his seventies." He paused and frowned. "What is that thing around his neck? A metal dog collar? And why is he speaking that weird language? Anybody recognize it?"

Rupe bit his lip as he considered the implications. Were the capatars of Analise and Wolfe immortal, as Arni had feared? Perhaps they respawned like avatars whenever they perished. If so, Wolfe might have suffered hundreds of horrible deaths through the millennia, only to respawn again and again, doomed to a Sisyphus-like torture of constant life-death-reincarnation. Rupe shuddered. If this man really was Wolfe's capatar, then it was entirely likely that Analise's capatar was suffering a similar fate.

There was a long silence. Howe abruptly rotated his office chair, startling Rupe. "Mr. Schroeder, I want you to look at the video again, and tell me if you recognize anything else."

"What am I looking for?"

"Anything that might point us to the video's origin."

Everyone was staring at him, especially Chun, who was leaning so close he could feel the heat radiating from her forehead. He swallowed and turned to Howe's monitor screen. Howe selected a button, and Rupe watched carefully. "Stop! Back up. Stop! Right there." He scowled at the screen, then leaned back with a grim smile. "See that symbol painted on the wall behind the Kanaan dude? I recognize it. He's inside one of the communications bunkers I designed for the Orbitus campaign last year. I don't know which one. There were four of them, all identical."

"So, in your opinion, this video originated from a virtual location in the OA gamecosm?"

"No doubt about it," said Rupe. "That's one of the comms bunkers on the planet Orbitus. They're a part of the planet's boss dungeon."

Chun lowered her voice and narrowed her eyes. "I need you to be sure, Rupe. Are you *absolutely* certain this a location *inside* the game?"

"One hundred percent," Rupe said. There was no doubt. He'd designed the three-pointed star symbol as an homage to the symbol of the Klingon Empire in *Star Trek*. As he stared at the image, something suddenly tickled the back of his brain, an important and somehow relevant fact that he couldn't quite pin down. Something about the symbol, or the comms bunker.

Chun slapped both her hands on the edge of Howe's desk and leaned back with an expression of triumph. "I *told* you the holobox Analise had at Grone was a migration program," she spat, her voice becoming shrill. "I *told* you we had to stop her at all costs, but you didn't listen."

Solomon's expression didn't change, but Howe winced sullenly. "She's right," Howe said. "The embedded metadata proves the video was transmitted from within the gamecosm *after* the gamecosm disappeared from the Pandora engine at Orbital Arena. The origination key in the transport header matches the Haven engine, which proves the gamecosm has been moved from the company's Pandora machine to the stolen Haven machine, along with the capatars of Roland Wolfe and Analise Novak." Howe sighed and gave Solomon a tight-lipped glance before turning to Chun. "It seems you may have been correct all along, Dr. Chun. There's no longer any doubt that Arnold Zaman and Analise Novak conspired to steal the Orbital Arena gamecosm."

Chun waved off the grudging acknowledgment. "*Both* our calamities are Analise's doing. She and Arni conspired to steal the Haven engine and the gamecosm. Now it seems they've stolen your JEEB Earth, too, needlessly endangering the life of Roland Wolfe. This message, if it is from Wolfe's capatar, is probably a call for help."

Solomon was still sitting stone-faced, staring at the image on the computer monitor. He said, without turning to Chun. "You said it was impossible to move JEEB Earth out of the jeebcosm, that it violated the laws of physics."

Chun's entire face twitched as if somebody had applied a low-voltage shock to the muscles of her cheeks. "I'll admit that it's possible Analise found a loophole in the physics." The bitterness in her response was sharp. Analise had once been Chun's protégé, but that relationship ended badly when Analise published a scientific paper that disproved one of Chun's core QARMA theories. Their longstanding disputes had been followed gleefully within the academic community, especially at Stanford.

Chun pointed her finger at Howe's monitor, from which the frozen image of an elderly Roland Wolfe peered. "Find Arni and the Haven engine, and you'll find our stolen property."

Solomon seemed unconvinced. "Why would Analise do something like this? I know she had concerns about the jeeb virus and the behavior of the doppelgängers on JEEB Earth, but we were putting a study group together to research the effects. Analise was leading the group. She had no reason to steal the simulation."

A dark expression flickered across Chun's face, quickly replaced by a smirk of certainty. "Your people paid a billion dollars for a QARMA engine with a functioning kernel. Now Arni has control of the only functioning QARMA engine on the planet, not to mention the combined intellectual property contained in our respective game simulations. Certainly, the Russians or the Chinese would be very interested."

Solomon still looked doubtful. "You're suggesting this is treason. That doesn't sound like Analise. You seem to be forgetting that her life is in just as much danger as Wolfe's."

Howe made a *don't be so sure* shrug. "We know Arnold Zaman was born and raised in Pakistan, in a region known for extremist tendencies. We also know that Arnold and Analise have an intimate relationship. At one point they were even engaged to be married, am I right?" At Chun's nod, he continued. "Given the national security implications, we must consider the possibility, no matter how unlikely, that Arnold seduced Analise as a part of an espionage plot and recruited her to his cause."

Rupe scoffed loudly. "Arni's the least political person you'll ever meet. The only time I ever saw him support a national cause is when he ran a Facebook poll to convince Netflix to bring back the *Firefly* series."

Zia glared at him, as if to say *keep your mouth shut, fool!* He returned her glare with a sullen frown.

Surprisingly, Chun nodded in agreement. "It's hard to believe Arni could be a terrorist, and the thought that he could seduce anybody is laughable. It's clear to me that Analise seduced *him* to commit these crimes. I've tried to warn you all along: she's delusional, obsessive, and persuasive, and she's infected him with her delusions. Anyway, regardless of who is the mastermind, the two of them robbed my entire company's livelihood, plus your billion-dollar combat simulator." She leaned against the wall and glared at Howe. "The real question is, what are you going to *do* about it?"

"We've got every asset looking for Arni," Howe said. "It won't be long until he makes a mistake, and we catch him."

The thought that was fluttering around in the back of Rupe's head seemed to move closer to clarity, then retreated. *Something to do with the comms bunker on Orbitus, and the video from the jabbering man who might or might not be Roland Wolfe . . . something important . . .*

Zia cleared her throat. "I hate to spoil this party, but this video may be a fake. As far as we can tell, there's no way for anything to penetrate the Haven firewall in either direction. Not a video, not even a short text message."

"The ESP interfaces are still connected to the capatars," pointed out Howe. "And the video seems to suggest that Wolfe's capatar is still functioning inside the Haven engine. That proves that information can pass through the firewall."

Chun shook her head. "No, I'm afraid Zia may be right. The capatar interfaces work via QARMA entanglement that isn't affected by a firewall; otherwise, the capatars of Wolfe and Analise wouldn't still be connected to their physical brains. QARMA entanglement is not the same thing as transmitting or receiving digital data. It's like the difference between receiving a radio signal and experiencing an emotion."

Howe's frustration was plain. "Dr. Chun, what does that even mean?"

Zia interrupted. "It doesn't matter. The point is, you can't send digital videos using QARMA entanglement, and nothing else can pass through the firewall."

The thought that had been eluding him suddenly crystallized in Rupe's head. *Of course!* He blurted it out before thinking, "You say the video came in through a social media app on your phone?"

Everyone turned to face him. Howe was scowling. "Yes. I use it to keep in contact with my daughter at her college. It's configured to notify me when I get a message."

"Let me see the video metadata again," said Rupe.

Howe spun the monitor, and Rupe scanned the dense text.

There!

He turned to Chun, unable to keep the excitement out of his tone. "The video is real. This Wolfe dude, he's using one of the Orbs!"

Orb

The whole thing had been Arni's bright idea. "How much time do players spend in-game, in the personas of their avatars?" he'd argued. "Most of them spend hours every single day! Some of these players identify more with their avatar than they do with their real life—am I right?"

Rupe had been forced to admit that Arni was correct. The virtual life of Rupe's own avatar Ruperus was far more interesting than his meatspace existence.

Arni had been pacing furiously around his office at Orbital Arena, stopping occasionally to scribble something on one of his crowded whiteboards. "What if we partner with the big social media platforms, huh? What if we allow our players' avatars to have their own Instagram accounts?"

Rupe remembered Arni's face, flush with the excitement of creativity. Arni often had jittery episodes in which he'd pace and spout outlandish ideas. Sometimes, the ideas stuck. This one, though, had some issues. Rupe had pointed out that the vast majority of the players already had real-world social media accounts through which they could post screenshots and videos captured from the game.

"No, no, you don't get it," Arni had argued. "This would be different. It would be the *avatar's* account, not the player's. The avatar's life and adventures would be on display, not the player's. It would be from the avatar's perspective. The avatar itself could take a selfie! Think about it, Rupe—we already know that there are lots of interesting relationships between avatars in the game whose players don't know each other in real life. Giving the avatars a medium for sharing their in-game relationships would enhance the sense of reality in the game. Imagine the Instagram feed of Torax and his partner Beejus, or JungleJane and Crakus. Remember, their avatars got *married* inside the game. It was on CNN!"

Rupe had frowned but Arni had ignored him. "We could create a device, like a virtual smartphone, that would let them snap selfies and photos and videos and post them directly from inside the game! Not screenshots of the player's screen. People in the real world could follow the avatars as if they were real people! Don't you get it?"

"I get it," Rupe had said, though he hadn't really gotten it. Sometimes, Arni's wild ideas paid off. Sometimes they didn't. It was Rupe's duty, though, to support his friend, regardless of what he thought. Chun would probably shoot it down anyway. She almost always did.

Thus had been born the *Orb-a-gram*, a working title for an in-game device the avatars could use to make videos and photos and post them to a real-world social media account.

Unfortunately, despite Arni's enthusiasm, the Orb-a-gram prototype had turned out to be a failure, notwithstanding the fact that he'd spent well over a million dollars of Orbital Arena's development money to make it work. "You can't monetize it," Chun had argued. "Avatars don't buy things from the real world. Plus, the security issues alone would cost a fortune to resolve."

―

Chun was explaining the Orb-a-gram concept to Solomon, Howe, and Zia. "It was an experiment Arni started last year. A way for an avatar to post directly to a social media account from inside the game universe. It seems that Wolfe, or whoever that is, may have found one of the Orbs."

Rupe stabbed his finger at Howe's screen, which showed the still image of the man's face from the video. "That dude *definitely* found an Orb. When I was creating the planet and locations for the Orbitus campaign, I created a set of secure bunkers specifically to hold the Orbs. Arni wanted to limit the test to company employees, so I set it up so nobody could get into the bunkers without special privileges. The video was recorded in one of those bunkers."

"How could he have activated an Orb? I thought you said capatars couldn't use avatar devices."

"The Orbs were prototypes, still being tested. They weren't linked to the avatar code yet. Even a bot could use one of the Orbs."

"But what about the firewall?" Zia said. "It would prevent the message from getting out, wouldn't it?"

"That's the thing," Chun replied. "Because it was a limited test, I allowed Arni to jury-rig a message transport system using a public VPN, sort of a tunnel through our normal firewall. Arni's team was still doing testing when all this started, so . . ." Her eyes went vacant for moment. "If Wolfe located one of the Orbs and understood its purpose and technical architecture, then it's entirely possible he could have used the existing VPN to poke a pinprick through the firewall."

"If anybody could do it, it would be Wolfe," said Solomon. "Next to Zia, he is the scariest hacker I've ever met."

Chun's eyes brightened. "If we can find and recover the Haven machine, it may be possible to exploit this firewall breach. We might *both* be able to recover our stolen properties. We need to reestablish contact with this Kanaan character as soon as possible. We should formulate a reply and send it using the same method you received it by."

Zia cleared her throat. "You're forgetting something. We saw Kanaan murdered by the blue skull-faced woman. That sword thing . . ."

"Flickerblade," prompted Rupe.

Zia nodded. "Yeah, that flickerblade practically cut him in half."

There was a long silence. "Do capatars respawn?" asked Solomon.

Chun shrugged. "Possibly. I'd have to see Analise's code to know for sure."

"But there's a chance?" Solomon looked hopeful.

"I don't know." Chun's eyes were flickering around the room, focusing on nothing. When she spoke again, her words frightened Rupe. "We need a contingency plan. What about those player avatars that were involved at Grone? What were the players' names?"

"Francis Martinez and Jackson Jericho," said Solomon. "What about them?"

"Maybe they know something. I'd like to talk to them."

Solomon shook his head. "We interviewed them and searched their homes a few hours after the incident on Grone. We checked their computers and their online histories. The Martinez boy is just a kid. Jericho is a seventy-year-old retired airline mechanic from Atlanta. Both of them thought the events on Grone were part of the game campaign. Neither of them has any connection to Arni or Analise. Their avatars, Geo and Tremendo, appear to have been innocent bystanders."

"What about the other avatar? The female one? The one that was helping Analise in Atum's Lair?"

Rupe swallowed and tried to keep his panic off his face. She was talking about Gaia, Fiona's avatar.

"We haven't been able to identify her yet," said Solomon. "As you know, the profile ID function doesn't work in Atum's Lair, so we're going on your visual description. There are thousands of female avatars that match the one you described. We're still looking."

"It's possible she was an innocent bystander," blurted Rupe. Everyone looked at him. Zia pursed her lips and shot him a frantic warning glare.

"She was *not* a bystander," responded Chun. "Arni used his game administrator's privileges to bump her avatar's level up to Archangel 100. I saw her put the holobox in the kernel to initiate the migration of the gamecosm. She was an accomplice, an insider, surely. Maybe she's one of my employees; maybe she's one of your government people. It's also possible she's a foreign agent. Find her, and we'll find Arni and the stolen Haven engine."

Sentinel

After the meeting broke up, Colonel Solomon pulled Rupe to the side in the short hallway. "I want you to understand that this is a top secret facility, and you do not have a security clearance. As far as you are concerned, this place doesn't exist, and you were never here. You are not to speak of this to *anybody* who was not at this meeting. Am I understood?"

Rupe swallowed. He'd given the same warning speech to Fiona and Francis when they'd visited Arni's Havenlab. For the first time, he felt the crushing weight of an illegal conspiracy settle on his shoulders. A droplet of sweat ran down his neck.

Solomon continued. "We're going to set you up with a limited clearance. I want you to start reporting here every morning. We'll find a desk for you. You're the guy who designed most of the gamecosm, and I need to understand what that message means, and who sent it. Okay?"

Rupe nodded again. "I'll do what I can."

Zia stepped up and thrust out her hand. "Hi, I'm Zia Volkov," she said, as if she'd never met him before. He took her hand and shook it. "I'd like to help you decipher the language in the message, if it's okay with the colonel." She smiled disarmingly at Solomon. He nodded, and Zia took Rupe by the arm and propelled him forcefully toward the double doors at the far end of the hallway.

"What are you doing—" began Rupe.

"Shhh."

He lowered his voice. "Did you hear? They're looking for Fiona!"

Zia's grip on his shoulder squeezed so painfully that he almost yelped. He lowered his voice. "Arni didn't steal JEEB Earth, did he?"

"Of course not," hissed Zia. "I think it was an inside job."

"What do you mean?"

"I mean, Arni can't get through the firewall, either. I think it was Wolfe's doing. Or maybe Analise. They both have the know-how. Their capatars might have done it from inside the firewall using some of Chun's QARMA-tech bullshit."

"But why?"

"How the hell do I know?" She punched a code into a keypad and swiped her security card. The door buzzed. She opened it and pulled Rupe inside.

Unknown to Solomon, Rupe had been in the JEEB lab once before. At the time it had been empty of furniture and full of revelers. There'd been a lone table shoved against the rear wall, adorned with a keg of beer and a dozen boxes of gourmet cupcakes. Somebody, probably Arni, had strung a hand-lettered banner from the high ceiling that read "A Billion Congratulations to OA." Those first few days following the award of the government contract had been incredibly exhilarating. Arni had gone out of his gourd with ecstasy. Rupe knew that Arni considered himself a simple Pakistani kid who'd come to Silicon Valley and hit the ultimate jackpot. Even Chun had let loose at the party. After a few beers she'd sung an off-key version of some Korean pop song on the karaoke machine. Everybody had applauded wildly, and Chun had actually blushed, the first and only time Rupe had ever seen humility peek out from behind her arrogance. Several of her old Stanford colleagues had attended the party, and it had been obvious to Rupe that they were consumed with resentful envy. To them, Chun had once been a noble and righteous scientist, but then she'd sold her soul to Satan for a billion silver pieces.

Now, just over a year later, the JEEB lab was filled with humming and beeping equipment. Rupe followed Zia around a dozen rows of computer racks, each festooned with a chaotic tangle of cables and thousands of anxiously blinking lights. The temperature was very cold and the room smelled of plastic, ozone, and a sharp odor that was familiar, but out of place.

Zia pulled him into a narrow space filled with cables between two of the racks. She didn't release her painful grip on his arm. "Listen to me. Fiona and her brother are not our problem. Do not contact them ever again."

"But if they find Fiona, she won't have any choice but to tell them about Arni's lab."

"They won't find her," she said. "I deleted the phone records of Arni's call to Francis, and I edited the game logs from their confiscated computer to remove any trace of Fiona's avatar. Fiona's not the problem. *You* are. Everybody back in that room knows you and Arni were friends. The government will probably start monitoring you now. It's a miracle they haven't already traced you to Arni's lab. Stay away from now on. Also, if you contact Fiona again, they'll find her for sure."

Her eyes bored into him until he nodded. "Yeah, okay man, I get it. Stay away from the lab. Don't contact Fiona."

She released him and gave him a penetrating stare. "We all knew the risk when we decided to help Analise. We have to stay the course. Right?"

He dipped his head. "Right."

She sighed. "This is important, Rupe. Now I want to show you why. Follow me."

Behind the rows of computers, the rear half of the room looked like the intensive care unit of a hospital. Two nurses in colorful scrubs manned a large desk covered with scattered papers and computer workstations. One of them glanced up and smiled at Rupe. He started to smile back but then noticed the hospital beds. There were four of them. Two had been shoved into a corner and were almost buried under a disarray of cardboard boxes and medical supplies. Two others had been set up next to the nurse's station and were surrounded by a clutter of rolling hospital equipment. Intravenous fluid bags hung from metal poles. Regular rhythmic beeps came from the machines.

He approached the beds. One held an adult-size figure, the other either a small adult or a large child. Each lay on their back beneath layers of blankets. Both were hooked to tubes that led to plastic bags of various sizes. Some of the tubes were pumping fluid into their bodies; others seemed to be extracting waste. Both of the patients wore BCI caps like the one Arni had worn during his failed attempt to enter the havencosm. He followed the cables from the caps across the floor to where they disappeared into a familiar sleek box on the nearest rack of servers. The front of the box was engraved with hair-thin letters that glowed a pale, electrical blue:

○△□ | S E N T I N E L

Here was the billion-dollar QARMA engine that had until an hour ago hosted the military's JEEB Earth simulation. He looked down at the plastic bags collecting bodily fluids beneath the hospital beds and recognized the familiar smell he hadn't been able to place earlier. It was pee. Ozone and urine. The raw smells of machines and biology.

He looked into the face of the larger figure. Gaunt cheeks, thin nose, tight mouth. The man's lips were slack and very chapped. His skin was incredibly pale. Rupe recognized him from the video. *Roland Wolfe. Kay9. Kanaan.* Other than the mechanical rise and fall of his chest, he looked dead. Maybe he *was* dead. His capatar had been murdered in the video. Who knew how that had affected his living mind? Had Analise ever tested that aspect of her capatar technology?

He turned slowly to the other, smaller figure, dreading what he would find. A heart-shaped face. Delicate features. The same white pallor and dry, cracked lips as Wolfe. His heart slammed the inside of his rib cage.

Analise.

"My god," he said.

Zia was staring down at Analise with a forlorn expression. It was the same expression Rupe had seen on Arni's face whenever his friend was talking about Analise. Probably the same expression that was on his *own* face. After all, everybody loved Analise. He had to admit, though, that he had never before seen Zia express any kind of emotion even remotely resembling tender affection. Anger, righteous rage, sharp humor, yes, but never anything that made her look so... vulnerable. Rupe felt an unexpected pang of jealousy. He reached out and put his hand on Zia's shoulder. To his surprise, she didn't shrug it off. He let it drop when he realized the nurses were watching them. Zia took a deep breath, and spoke in a low, urgent whisper.

"Okay. You've seen them. Now get out of here, and don't *ever* come back, no matter what Solomon says. He wants you here so he can keep an eye on you. If you work here officially, and they find out you're helping Arni, you'll be charged with spying. That's *treason*." She glanced around the room, making sure no one could hear. "Listen to me. I need to get back over to the Havenlab and let Arni know what's happening, right *now*." She leaned close, her lips almost touching his ear. "If Roland Wolfe's capatar really did steal JEEB Earth and move it into the havencosm, he may have done us a *huge* favor."

havencosm | ORBITUS

Breakdown

Twelve days had passed since their hasty departure from Assinni. At almost 2,500 light-years, the distance from Assinni to Orbitus was the longest single leg of the entire pilgrimage route. A fast starliner could make the trip in two weeks. The antiquated *Covenant of Andrik* would have normally covered the same distance in a little over a month—that is, if it hadn't broken down in the middle of nowhere, far from the nearest SATO protectorate. They'd been dead in space for almost three days, the hypervee dynamo spun down while the crew attempted to repair the engines. The captain had assured the nervous passengers that the problem would be fixed within twelve hours. That had been two days ago.

Se-Jong knew that duty on old ships like this one didn't attract top-level talent. He'd seen the ship's engineers scurrying around over the past couple of days. They were either young guilders working their apprenticeships or inept rejects from the Olid merchant fleet. It was a little worrying, given that they were stalled on a sparsely traveled and completely unprotected spacelane. Piracy was rare, but it did happen, though he doubted any self-respecting space pirate would waste their time on a church-owned tub filled with destitute religious pilgrims.

If the crew couldn't repair the ship's engines, they would be forced to wait until another ship passed within hypervee radio range and detected their plight. One of two things would then happen: most likely, word would make its way back to Assinni and the church would dispatch a rescue vessel, a lengthy process that could take another month. It was also possible that the Solar Guard would dispatch a fast search-and-rescue cutter, in which case relief might arrive within a week. This was far less likely, however, given that they were in no immediate danger.

—

Se-Jong watched Nkiru study the star map on her komnic. In their dark berth, the light from its screen painted her face with a blue tinge that subtracted the pale blue from her eyes, making them appear completely white except for the round black holes of her pupils. The effect was startling against the deep color of her skin, giving her the otherworldly appearance of an angel. *Or more likely*, he thought with a silent chuckle, *a devil*.

He patted the lump in his pocket, the copper bracelet he'd bought her in the tourist stall on Assinni. He resisted the urge to bring it out, surprise her. Now probably wasn't the best time for such a triviality.

The facial bruises she'd gotten on Assinni had darkened and reformed themselves into ragged crescents below both her eyes. The injuries weren't limited to her face. When she'd peeled off her robes and undergarments, she'd revealed that the entire left side of her abdomen was one large contusion, and from the way she winced when she moved, he suspected she'd bruised, or even broken, a rib or two. She'd refused to go the ship's medic, although she'd agreed to let Se-Jong ask for a bottle of painkillers.

She'd slept for a day and a half as soon as the *Covenant* departed Assinni, after which she'd rebuffed his questions about what had happened in the Holy City. To him, her injuries looked like they'd been sustained from a fall, perhaps down a flight of stairs. He hadn't pressured her to explain. From his military psychology classes at Jackill Academy, he knew that a near-death combat experience could have lingering effects. She would tell him about it when she was ready, after she'd had time to process it.

She'd had a close call with death: of that there was no doubt. It wasn't just the ugly bruises; it was also the small matter of the laser burn on her pilgrims' robes. She'd told him that the burned streak in the fabric had happened when she'd stumbled against a street vendor's cookstove. He wanted to believe her, but the burn mark seemed far too precise to be the result of a clumsy brush against a hot grill.

If his suspicions were correct, somebody had taken a killing shot at her, and barely missed. He'd learned from his range-training instructor at Jackill that laser weapons were never used for warning shots; there was far too much danger of collateral damage. The only time you fired a laser was when the target was a high-enough priority to risk the consequences of beam overpenetration. Lasers were indiscriminate destroyers; if you missed, the beam could continue many kilometers before losing its potency, burning into anything or anyone in its path. Whoever had taken a shot at Nkiru had felt that killing her was worth the risk.

Se-Jong also knew that laser weapons were illegal on Assinni, as on most SATO worlds. Not even the police were allowed to use them. Only the military and the church security forces carried lasers, though it was possible that some criminal had acquired one through nefarious means. Whoever had taken a shot at Nkiru was either a soldier, a militan, or a criminal, and they'd have fired at her only if she'd been involved in something *really* illegal.

Like stealing an artifact from a reliquary.

Se-Jong had seriously considered going through her backpack while she was sleeping. In the end, he'd decided against it. If there was one thing his grandmother had taught him, it was that the highest quality a person could exhibit in life was trustworthiness. That quality, and its close cousin loyalty, represented the root of all ethical decisions, of all morality. You remained true to your family, your team, your tribe, no matter what. You never broke your word. You made commitments sparingly, and unless the commitment turned out to be based on a lie or false information, you never broke trust.

Up till now, as far as he knew, Nkiru hadn't lied to him. She'd kept things from him, but she'd never overtly lied. Until she did, he would respect her wishes for privacy. After all, it was perfectly legal to search for and collect previously undiscovered relics. Every world was littered with crumbling ruins and artifacts from the Age of Avatars. Treasure hunting was encouraged; church doctrine urged its members to look for pre-Cataclysm artifacts and turn them over to their local priest, who would reward the finder with special recognition, status, and sometimes even money. There were individuals who made their living as relic hunters, and some of them had become fabulously wealthy. Perhaps this was Nkiru's goal. He fervently hoped it was, for any alternative he could think of was highly disturbing.

—

Like most children on Cataclyst worlds, Se-Jong had dabbled in artifact hunting as a boy. Growing up on Askelon, when he found a suspected artifact under a stone in one of the dry canyons that surrounded his home, he would excitedly deliver the item to the local priest. Common items like a broken piece of pottery or a rusted fork were called *artifacts*, and they were worth a blessing and a mention of his name in the following week's mass. If by some miracle he'd found a recognizable component of a broken avatar device or a weapon that was in decent condition, it would have been classified as a *lesser relic*, which, in addition to recognition at mass, would have earned him a dispensation that he could redeem for forgiveness from a future sin.

To his great disappointment, Se-Jong's discoveries as a boy had been limited to a couple of shards of metal that might or might not have been actual artifacts. He'd never given up hope, though. Like him, most people hoped to find at least one *greater relic* in their lifetime. A greater relic would be a complete avatar device, like the handheld scancorder that Nkiru had shown him on Cloudtops Station. Depending on the quality of the greater relic, the church might award large sums of money, land rights on a developing world, or even one of the coveted titled positions in the church bureaucracy. Nkiru's scancorder might garner a small fortune, or even the deed to a small farm on one of the colony planets.

An even higher tier of artifact existed as well, though as far as he knew, nobody had found one in the past few centuries. These were the *ur-relics*, items mentioned in the scriptures as having been created for, or used by, the archangels of the Oa themselves. Ur-relics were the holiest of holy items, jealously guarded in the deepest vaults of the Regium. These included the three Creation Stones, also called the Great Emoras, which Leodiva had depicted in multiple frescoes on Assinni. There were also a number of Lesser Emoras, crystal jewels purported by scripture to have been used by the Oa and their archangels for a variety of sacred purposes. If a churchgoer found one of these ur-relics buried in their backyard, it meant instant wealth beyond their wildest dreams.

Equal in value to the avatar relics, but much more disturbing in nature, were the artifacts known as Mucktu Charms. Charms were small, round stones that came in a variety of colors and could easily be mistaken for polished river pebbles. Unlike the avatar relics—which had ceased to function at the Rapture almost ten thousand years ago, and which no modern science could resurrect—the Mucktu Charms could be partially activated under the right circumstances. As with the avatar relics, science was powerless to describe how they functioned; even when broken apart and studied beneath a powerful microscope, a charm was indistinguishable from a naturally occurring pebble. Despite their innocuous nature, though, there was no denying their danger.

According to the *Chronicles*, the archangel Atum created the Mucktu Charms during the Avatar Wars to give his mortal followers the arcane magic they needed to overcome the weapons of the avatars. Bearers of the charms came to be known as the Mucktu, demonic sorcerers bent on overthrowing the avatars through slaughter and mayhem. Each charm gave its bearer some form of control over a fundamental force of nature, enabling the Mucktu to alter the laws of physics and chemistry at a whim. Somehow, the Cataclysm that had wiped out the galaxy and destroyed the avatars and their technology had left the surviving Mucktu Charms with some of their seemingly magical powers.

According to legend, after the Cataclysm, the First Mother of the Mucktu Bloodline and her female descendants found a way to control the charms by eating jeeb pollen. They became sorcerers, magicians and conjurers, always few in number, but greatly feared.

Se-Jong didn't believe in magic. The charms were some form of advanced Second Epoch technology that modern scientists couldn't explain. A person from a pretechnological society would no doubt consider a komnic or a laser rifle to be magic. Whatever the source of their powers, supernatural or physical, in the modern era, members of the Mucktu Bloodline cult hoarded the charms as if they were the ultimate key to life itself. They were said to have recovered many thousands of the magical stones. There were even rumors that they'd dispatched a fleet of ships from their hidden Pollen Planet, sending them around the ring of the Halo for the sole purpose of scouring undiscovered worlds for more of the charms.

In order to deny them to the Mucktu, the Cataclyst Church also greatly desired the charms, though their goal was to eliminate them, not hoard them. When a parishioner found a charm and brought it to a priest, it was immediately shipped off to be destroyed in a ceremony known as a *rectification*, which involved lots of incantations and ended with smashing the stone to powder and then vaporizing that powder in a special kiln that every regional cathedral maintained for that purpose. Se-Jong had seen this happen once when he was a child on Askelon and could still remember the raw fear in the face of the high priest as he'd lifted the iron hammer to crush the charm.

What made the charms so dangerous was that some of them could still be used to summon the remnants of whatever dark energy had given them their original destructive powers. Not every stone could be activated, and not every person could activate a stone. However, enough of the stones remained to make them a problem, and as the Solar Alliance expanded to new colony worlds, more and more of the charms were being unearthed. Every year there were reports of innocents encountering the awful forces lurking in a newly discovered charm. The child who found a charm stone in a recently plowed field and was instantly driven mad, tormented by incurable schizophrenia. The pregnant woman who bent to retrieve a pretty stone from a babbling creek and moments later lost her unborn child to miscarriage. The priest who accidentally touched a charm during a rectification ceremony and, in front of his horrified congregation, exploded into a cloud of bloody pulp.

Se-Jong thought again of the small, egg-shaped stone that Nkiru had placed in his palm while they'd been viewing the dome mural in the Torax Chapel on Assinni. He was fairly sure he knew what kind of stone it had been, and how it had helped him see the hidden easter eggs in the painting. If he was right in his suspicion, and the egg-shaped stone had indeed been a functioning Mucktu Charm, it would explain why the person chasing her on Assinni had been willing to risk the use of a laser rifle to take it from her. It also opened the troubling likelihood that her assailant might not have been a lawful agent of the church or even a criminal relic hunter. It might have been someone who coveted the charm stones far more than anyone else, and who wouldn't have hesitated to kill her if they believed she had one in her possession.

It might have been a Mucktu.

Shiny Things

Nine days after the ship's engines broke down, rescue arrived. A message about their predicament had made it to Assinni, and by some miracle, the local Solar Guard commander had deemed their situation serious enough to dispatch a rescue cutter to tow the *Covenant* to their destination on Orbitus. The passengers rejoiced when the muted roars of the maneuvering thrusters sounded and the distinctive metal clang announced the docking of another ship. Soon after, the hull began to creak and groan from the forces of hypervee acceleration. When the captain came over the intercom to say they were in tow, everyone cheered.

Se-Jong was in high spirits, too. He'd been sleeping on the floor next to Nkiru since they'd left Assinni, but her injuries had mended to the point where she'd invited him back into the bunk. They'd been underway for several hours when he finally snuggled in next to her, allowing her to position herself against him in the least painful manner. They'd just gotten comfortable when somebody knocked on the metal hatch to their berth.

He sighed and swung his legs out of the bunk. He grabbed a towel to cover himself, then padded to the hatch in his bare feet. He unlocked it and cracked it open, expecting to find one of their fellow passengers at the door; they tended to show up at the most inconvenient times demanding that he and Nkiru attend one of the mandated scripture-study sessions. To his great dismay, he found himself staring into the scowling face of an older woman wearing the orange-and-blue uniform of a Solar Guard officer. Not just any officer, either. Her sleeve was crowded with the four braided gold stripes of a *senior* officer. A *captain*. He felt himself involuntarily stiffen into a position of attention.

The woman stared at him through the narrow opening, noting his bleary eyes and unshaven cheeks. "Please come with me."

"Just a minute," he stammered.

"I'll be in the galley," she said as he closed the hatch.

"*Damn, damn, damn,*" he muttered under his breath.

Nkiru was leaning up on one arm, eyebrows raised.

"It's the captain of the Solar Guard ship," he whispered.

A bolt of total panic shot across her face. "Oh, no. What's he doing here? What does he want?"

"It's a *she*," replied Se-Jong, kneeling to retrieve his pants from the pile of clothes on the floor. "Don't worry; she's not here for you."

Nkiru was struggling to sit upright on the bed, wincing in pain and clutching the sheets around her. "How do you know?" she hissed.

Se-Jong sucked in a breath and let it out in a long, slow sigh. "Because she's my grandmother."

—

"Halmeoni," Se-Jong said in Korean, bowing deeply and lowering his head. "Annyeong-hasimnikka." *Grandmother, hello.*

"Sonja," she replied with the slightest dip of her head. *Grandson.* She lifted the mug of coffee and took a sip. She didn't rise from her seat at the galley table, a bad sign indeed.

He sat across from her. The other pilgrims who were crowded into the ship's galley were all pointedly ignoring Se-Jong and his interaction with the Solar Guard captain, and they were all just as obviously trying to listen. Against the rumpled yellow background of their pilgrims' robes, her crisp and brightly colored uniform shone like fireworks in a cloudy sky.

He continued in Korean to thwart their eavesdropping. "It is quite the surprise to see you here, Grandmother."

"Imagine my own surprise," she countered.

Her eyes were as brittle as shards of black coal, expressionless, waiting for an explanation. He tried not to show his anxiety. He suddenly realized why the Solar Guard had rushed to the aid of the *Covenant*: his grandmother had ordered the rescue so she could come here and confront him, a costly diversion of her valuable time to deal with a wayward grandson.

He spread his hands on the table. "I know my message must have been a shock to you. I'm sorry. Don't worry, I still intend to go to the War College. I hope you understand. I just need a few more months. I'll start in the spring semester next year."

If she was listening, she gave no indication. She sipped her coffee again. Se-Jong knew her well enough to see the rage boiling just beneath her disinterest. The angrier she got, the less she showed it. This was a fine quality for a Solar Guard captain. It was less desirable in a grandmother. He knew she would wait patiently until he said what she wanted to hear. If she didn't hear it before her anger exceeded her patience, then she would take forceful action to resolve the situation to her satisfaction. He had no doubt that this action would include dragging him off the *Covenant* and putting him on the next transport to the War College on Kojax. He had a limited window in which to negotiate.

"Halmeoni, I'm an adult. I can make my own decisions." He gestured around at the other pilgrims. "If you're worried that I'm getting sucked into a religious cult, don't. I'm only here because I want to see some of the Known Arc before I start school, and this is a cheap way to do it."

"Who is the girl?" she said unexpectedly.

Se-Jong clenched his teeth. Of course, she would know about Nkiru. The Solar Alliance kept close tabs on its citizenry. Given his grandmother's access to classified government data, she probably knew more about Nkiru than he did.

"She's just a friend."

"Your *friend* has a dubious history. Did you know she was a ward of the church until her eighteenth birthday? That she lived for years in a youth shelter run by Janga monks?"

"I know all that," Se-Jong said with a sigh. "But she's a good person; I swear it." He bit his lip, knowing that if he didn't swiftly stand up for himself, he would crumble against the force of her will. "You always said that hardship builds character." He gestured around the room at the rumpled pilgrims. "She's not like the rest of these people. You'd like her—I swear. She's a scientist at heart, and she has a theory that . . ."

His words trailed off at his grandmother's pointedly disinterested expression. She placed her coffee mug on the table and casually brushed a crumb off the tabletop. She looked up at Se-Jong. "I am not concerned with Nkiru Anaya. I'm concerned about my grandson. I am concerned that his decisions have become clouded." She paused, and her eyes narrowed. "Your father shares my concerns."

"And how is my abuji?" Se-Jong asked halfheartedly. He and his father had rarely spoken since Se-Jong had decided, at Grandmother's urging, to attend the Jackill military academy and the War College. Unlike Se-Jong, his father had rejected the Kwon family's military tradition at an early age, to Grandmother's great disappointment.

"Your father is performing his duty as a businessman. Unlike your companions on this ship, who are sucking at the teat of the church, at least he is actively contributing to the well-being of society."

Se-Jong forced down a chuckle. Grandmother despised the church almost as much as she despised freeloaders. In her mind, becoming a pilgrim was the worst form of freeloading, worse even than that of a street beggar.

"I am proud of my father," he said tightly. "Please give him my regards when you see him."

She studied his face. "So, you intend to continue this nonsense?"

"It's not nonsense, Grandmother." He carefully phrased his words, speaking formally, respectfully. "I've been living in privilege my whole life, thanks to you and my father. I am incredibly grateful for the path that you have prepared for me, and I understand my duty. It's just that once I begin at the War College, I will be entirely committed. This is my last chance to see the Known Arc on my own terms. I believe that this experience will give me perspective that will be valuable to my career."

"Let me give you the benefit of *my* perspective," she said, speaking with equal formality. "Every day I work with great leaders, and I have learned to recognize their qualities. *You* have the same qualities. You have the potential to make a great mark, to live a life of high value. You must not waste that potential." Her eyes flicked toward the nearest table, where a dozen yellow-robed pilgrims sat silently. "Here's the hard truth. People like these *depend* on people like us. Do you understand that? You have an obligation to society *because* you are privileged." She took a deep breath. "This is the time of your life, more than any other, that defines who you will become. It's also the time of life when you will be most distracted by . . . shiny things of little value. You must stay focused on what is important. You are a leader. Any other path would be a fantastic waste. You can't allow yourself to be distracted by anything."

By a girl, you mean. Se-Jong silently finished her sentence. To her, Nkiru was—how had she said it?—a *shiny thing of little value*. His anger flashed, but he didn't allow it to show on his face. He knew that he'd never convince his grandmother that Nkiru was anything more than an inconvenient and possibly dangerous distraction, so he decided to take a different approach. More than anything, his grandmother believed in duty.

"When I started this pilgrimage, I committed to finish it. I am a Kwon, like you, and we Kwons take our commitments seriously. You of all people should understand that." He swallowed and tried to spin his defensive tone into an offensive argument. "Tell me, what project have *you* ever quit before it was completed?"

The corner of her mouth twisted slightly, and he recognized that he'd scored a point with her. "I have never quit something I set out to finish," she admitted. "But neither have I ever dodged my family obligations. It is your obligation to attend the War College. You made this obligation to *me*. You made it to *yourself*. It is not an obligation you can shirk."

He allowed a carefully measured amount of his exasperation to creep into his voice. "I promise you, I'm not going to shirk it! Like I said, right now I'm only planning to defer my enrollment a semester or two. But until then, my time is my own, and I will spend it as I see fit." His guts were trembling as he spoke. This was the first time he'd ever stood up to his grandmother. "Is this acceptable to you?"

A tiny smile bent her lips. "Do I have any choice?"

"No, you really don't." Se-Jong felt a great flood of relief. "I respect you and love you, but in this matter I must follow my own path."

She lifted one hand and stabbed her index finger into his chest, a very non-Korean gesture. "Spring semester," she said in English.

He nodded. "Spring semester, Halmeoni. I promise."

———

Grandmother Kwon's entire visit to the *Covenant* lasted less than fifteen minutes, as if she were loath to spend one unnecessary second among such a useless horde of weak-minded parasites. After their brief confrontation about the War College, she updated Se-Jong on news from home. She spoke in the same tone of voice she might use to brief her officers on the status of an ongoing military exercise. She asked him once more to reconsider the time he was wasting on this ridiculous pilgrimage, then bid him a chilly farewell. He was surprised that she hadn't asked to meet Nkiru, but then realized that such a meeting would have legitimized Nkiru's status as his girlfriend.

She contacted him via komnic one more time the next day, just before her shuttle left for her command station on the border between the SATO and Caeren territories. She admonished him once again to reconsider the foolhardiness of his current situation, reiterated her confusion at his decision to become a pilgrim, and reminded him a final time of his promise to enroll at the War College for spring semester. She gave him a formal head-bow of parting and terminated the call. During the entire conversation he hadn't said one word.

For the rest of the two-week trip to Orbitus, Se-Jong's fellow pilgrims regarded him either with great suspicion or as something of a celebrity. As Se-Jong was the grandson of the regional Solar Guard commander, the captain of the *Covenant* went out of his way to treat him with deference, once even inviting Se-Jong and Nkiru to dine with him in the officers' mess, an affair that turned awkward and regrettable when Nkiru insulted the captain for allowing his ship to fall into such disrepair. Confronted by her insult, the captain had hinted that her bruises must have been the result of a well-deserved beating by Se-Jong, at which point she and Se-Jong had exchanged a glance and both broken out into laughter. The rest of the meal had been eaten in stony silence, and they hadn't been invited back.

Easter Egg

In Se-Jong's dream, something heavy is on his chest, making it hard to breathe. A thudding ache radiates from the center of his forehead. A shadowy face is suspended over him.

Where is Nkiru? He struggles, but something seems to be holding him to the mattress.

The woman's face becomes clearer, and he recoils. It is the Mucktu witch from the Leodiva fresco on Assinni. Her skin is the color of a blue midnight, and the leafy tattoos of the Bloodline crawl up her neck and vanish into her hair.

Instead of eyes, empty pits.

The witch leans close, whispers, repeating the same words as before:

"Who is she, Se-Jong?"

Se-Jong jerked awake. He checked the clock. It was the middle of the night, ship time, eighteen hours before their scheduled arrival at Orbitus.

He steadied his breathing and closed his eyes, but the strange sensation from his dream didn't diminish. He felt Nkiru's warmth next to him, but the normal rhythm of her sleeping breath was missing. He reached over the bedside and touched the light control.

She was staring at him without the slightest trace of sleep in her eyes. He recoiled, startled. "What's wrong?"

She didn't reply. After a moment she turned on her back, eyes toward the ceiling.

"Nkiru, what's wrong?"

"What's wrong with *you*?" she retorted. "You've been acting weird since your grandmother's visit."

Se-Jong let out a groan. He'd given Nkiru a brief summary of his conversations with his grandmother, leaving out her comments about getting distracted by *shiny things*.

Nkiru rolled toward him and placed her hand on his chest. "She said something about me, didn't she?"

"She didn't mention you." *At least, not explicitly*, he added silently.

"Well, she must've said something that upset you. You've been moping around ever since she left."

"I'm sorry. It's just that . . ."

"Just what?" she prompted.

"What am I doing here, Nkiru? What are *we* doing here?"

"We like spending time together. We like exploring new places." Her hand curled down his stomach. "We like sleeping together."

He pushed her hand away. "My grandmother thinks you're a distraction from more important things."

"*Important* things?"

"Things like the War College. Things like career. Things like responsibilities and obligations."

Nkiru's voice was suddenly sharp. "I thought you said she didn't mention me."

Se-Jong sighed. "It wasn't about you. It was about *me*. She just wanted to know I was still on track, that this little vacation wasn't going to derail any of my plans."

"This . . . *little vacation?*" He knew instantly that it had been the wrong choice of words when she rose to a sitting position and glared down at him.

"I'm sorry. You know what I mean."

"So, if this is a *little vacation*, what does that make me? Am I just your little vacation fling? A chance to sow your wild oats before heading off to more *important* things?"

"No, no. That's not what you are."

"Then what am I?"

The misgivings he'd been holding inside for weeks burst out. "You're a damned mystery, that's what you are." His hand flailed in the air as he searched for words. "We're young. We're supposed to be getting drunk and staying up all night listening to loud music and worrying about getting into a good college. Instead, you carry around a backpack you say is full of sacred artifacts and you claim you have a copy of the Mucktu Apocrypha on your komnic. The gods-damned Apocrypha! Then you come back from the Regium after midnight with broken ribs and a laser burn on your clothes. What am I supposed to think?" He paused. "Okay, I'll *tell* you what I think. I think you're *way* more than just a distraction. A distraction is a mosquito buzzing around my ear. You're more like a . . . a giant flaming meteor crashing through the bulkhead of the cabin."

He was afraid to look at her, so he stared at the ceiling. She was quiet for a long time. "This isn't a *little vacation*, Lieutenant, not to me."

"I figured that out already. But I hate lies and secrets, Nkiru, and everything about you is one big secret."

He felt the weight of her palm return to his chest. "I'm sorry," she said. "I know it's been bothering you. I've been trying to decide how to tell you some things, but I don't want you to think I'm delusional." He waited for her to continue. When she did, her voice was halting and uncertain. "When I first saw you back on Cloudtops Station, I thought you were a big goof." She moved her hand from his chest and wiped a few strands of hair from her face. "I was wrong about you. I thought you were just a knucklehead with a great body, but you're not. I mean, not *only* that."

"Thanks, I think."

"We're a good team. It's like, we both love the unknown, but we hate it, too. Nothing turns us on like a mystery, but nothing satisfies us more than solving it." She let out a quiet chuckle. "Brother Jerome was the same way. Maybe that's why he took me under his wing. I was lucky he was the first person I met when I got to New York. If it weren't for him, I would've probably ended up dead in a Manhattan gutter. And if it wasn't for you, my stalwart lieutenant, I'd have never made it off Assinni."

She rolled toward him and kissed his shoulder. "I lied. I'm sorry. You knew I was lying, and I thank you for not calling me out. You were right about the laser burn. I went somewhere I shouldn't have, and somebody shot at me." She shuddered. "It was a close thing. It sounds ridiculous, but I think the only reason I made it out was because I was worried what you would think if I got myself killed." She pulled away and leaned on her elbow, facing him. "If I tell you what happened, do you swear on the Flowery Altar and the Starry Chalice that you'll never tell another soul?"

Se-Jong suddenly wondered if he actually *did* want to know Nkiru's secrets. What if she confirmed some of his darkest suspicions, the ones that had flashed through his mind a million times late at night as he'd lain awake listening to her breathe next to him. What if she was involved with the Mucktu cult, or the Splinter, or worse?

He pushed his reservations out of his mind and nodded. She searched his expression and found something that satisfied her. "Okay. I had a meeting on Assinni with a friend of Brother Jerome's, a Janga monk who works in the Regium. He's the one who told me about the easter eggs hidden in the ceiling fresco. He gave me something that would help me see the hidden images." She bit her upper lip. "It was a—"

"A Mucktu Charm."

"Yeah, a charm," she admitted, nodding. "I thought you might have suspected. Anyway, when I saw the hidden images, I had to show you too. It was too amazing to keep to myself. It was also incredibly stupid of me. I could've gotten you arrested. You could *still* get arrested, if they ever figure out who I am and realize you were with me on Assinni."

"You need to get rid of it," he blurted. "We can give it to the ship's chaplain; he should be ordained to receive a holy relic. You can tell him you found it on Assinni and you didn't know what it was . . ." He paused at her growing scowl. "What are you not telling me?"

Instead of replying, she turned away from him, leaned over the edge of the mattress, and dragged her heavy backpack onto the bed. He sat upright as she unzipped it. "Swear again to never tell a soul."

"Nkiru, I—"

"Swear!" she demanded. His protest died on his lips at the intensity of her expression. Her painful secrets, until now buried beneath layers of flippant misdirection, were emerging. Only a thin veil of mistrust remained to separate him from the truth.

"I swear."

She lifted something from her backpack that looked like two metal saucers and an oddly shaped plate held together by a fabric-and-leather harness. She carefully untangled it, rose to her knees, and slid it over her head, shivering as the metal plate slid over her bare skin. As soon as it was in place, it seemed to change shape, molding itself to the curves of her narrow chest. At first he thought it was an illusion, but then the two saucer-shaped attachments fell into place on either shoulder, also seeming to re-form themselves to fit her frame. The fabric web that held it together was richly embroidered silk, a series of intertwined abstract shapes in a rainbow of shimmering colors.

"What the hell is that?" he whispered. His voice sounded raw in his own ears.

In response, she gave a wan smile and—
vanished.

He fell off the bed. "Damn, damn, damn!" he screamed far too loudly, stumbling away on hands and knees, banging his shoulder painfully against the far bulkhead. He looked frantically around the tiny room, heart racing. "Nkiru? What just happened? *Nkiru!*"

"It's okay," she said calmly. She was back on the bed, her smile unchanged.

Se-Jong caught his breath and stared at her.

She reached up to touch the copper breastplate. "It's a stealthshield," she said. "It can make you invisible."

"But . . . but . . ." Se-Jong clamped his teeth together to stop stammering. He knew what a stealthshield was. It was a mythical device from the Second Epoch. "That's an avatar relic," he finally managed.

She nodded.

"But nobody has ever found a way to activate avatar relics," he said.

She shrugged. "Until now."

"Upon the fucking bleeding heart of Andrik," he cursed. Maybe this trip had begun as a fun little vacation with a pretty girl, but if so, the pretty girl had just transformed it into something he couldn't begin to understand. *Shiny things, indeed.* He remembered something that had been bothering him. "At the shuttleport on Assinni, I thought I saw you using the scancorder you showed me when we first met at Cloudtops Station."

She reached into her backpack and pulled out the ancient scanner. She touched a button.

It beeped and lit up.

His thoughts crashed together into a desperate wreckage of confusion. Only the avatars could use their devices. They'd all stopped working at the Rapture, ten thousand years ago when the avatars vanished. He looked at her and whispered. "You're . . . an *avatar?*"

She reached out for his hand. He recoiled without thinking, and a sudden hurt flashed across her face. "No. I'm flesh and blood, just like you."

He waved at the stealthshield and the softly beeping scancorder. "Then . . . *how?*" He paused, thinking furiously. "Is it the Mucktu Charm? Does it let you activate these relics?"

She shook her head. "The charm has nothing to do with it."

"Then how are you doing it?"

"To be honest, I'm not sure. There's something in my blood. Brother Jerome called it a *terrible gift*. He kept the church from finding out about me. I was pretty stupid at first, but he saved me from the Inquisitors."

Se-Jong reached out tremulously. "Can I see it?"

She handed him the scancorder. He held it for a moment, but as soon as he touched one of the controls it went dark and the beeping stopped. "I found it on the Deepstone," she said. She reached up and hooked her thumb into the stealthshield's harness. "And I got this on Forniculus."

"You stole them from the reliquary shrines, didn't you?"

She didn't answer, but it had to be true. Greater relics like these weren't just lying around under rocks to be found by a casual pilgrim, but it also seemed impossible for her to have stolen them from a secure reliquary. Had she gotten herself mixed up in some kind of Janga cult conspiracy? He looked up at her with an entirely new perspective.

"Nkiru, what's going on? This is . . . this is . . . *unbelievable.*"

She nodded as if in total agreement. "Yeah, I know. Maybe this is a bad idea, but I had to show *somebody.*" Her eyes hardened as she looked at him. "You're the only person I can trust." From the tone of her voice, he knew it was a question, not a statement. *Can I trust you?* He handed her back the scanner. She tucked it into her backpack.

"What else do you have in there?" he asked, truly afraid of what she might pull out next.

She shrugged out of the stealthshield harness and stuffed it into the backpack alongside the scancorder. Her reckless handling of a beyond-priceless avatar relic caused him to shudder. She zipped the backpack shut. "Nothing else, really. Some pajamas I never wear and some toothpaste. A few rocks and things. A couple of cheap souvenirs."

"And a gods-damned Mucktu Charm."

"Yeah. One of those, too."

She was obviously still waiting for his answer to her implied question: *Can I trust you?* He felt like a man who'd walked onto a lake he'd thought was solidly frozen, only to hear the ominous cracks of thin ice beneath his feet. How could he answer her question if he didn't even know if he could trust himself? This girl could *activate avatar tech*!

When he didn't reply, she slid away from him across the mattress until she was leaning against the cold metal bulkhead, her knees drawn up to her chest, arms wrapped protectively around her sides. Her sudden childlike vulnerability made it seem as if *she* were afraid of *him*.

He tried to relax his posture, but he made no move to sit next to her on the bed. Stealing relics from the church was a violation of sacred law, not just civil law, and the church's Inquisitors were far more unforgiving and brutal than the civilian court system. If she'd stolen these artifacts, as he suspected, and she got caught, the police would turn her over to the church. Given her special talent to activate the avatar tech, the Inquisitors probably wouldn't send her to the gallows, but they might very well torture her to uncover her secrets.

And her accomplices.

The cramped cabin suddenly seemed smaller, darker. "Who else knows about this?" he asked. "What about this Brother Jerome and his friend on Assinni? What's their deal?"

She bit her bottom lip. "They both know I can activate some of the avatar relics. Janga monks on the Deepstone and Forniculus helped me get the scancorder and the stealthshield."

"Why those items?"

She didn't answer, but he could easily guess the purpose for an invisibility shield and a scanner that could see through stone walls. "The monks wanted you to steal something from the Regium on Assinni. That's how you got hurt, isn't it? You almost got caught, didn't you?"

Her eyes flickered briefly to the backpack, and she reflexively rubbed the fading bruise on the left side of her rib cage. When she didn't answer, he reached for the backpack. She grabbed it and yanked it away. He cursed and backed across the small cabin until his shoulders hit the bulkhead. "Damn, damn, damn," he muttered. "You stole something from the gods-damned Regium."

She was rocking slightly, side to side, searching his face. He watched as the last remnant of her composure crumpled like the roof of a collapsing building. For the first time since he'd met her at the spaceport terminal on Cloudtops Station, he glimpsed the true magnitude of her unspoken fears.

"I can't do this by myself anymore," she blurted. "None of this is fair. I didn't ask for this, okay? I didn't cause *any* of this. Fuck it all to hell!" She shoved the backpack toward him. It flew off the bed and clattered heavily to the floor at his feet. "I get it, okay? I've put you in a terrible situation. How was I supposed to know your grandmother was a Solar Guard captain? You kept secrets from me too, Lieutenant! If you're smart, you'll turn me in, right now! Go to the captain, or better yet, the chaplain. Tell them what you saw here. Do it! You'll be a hero. Otherwise, you'll be an accomplice, right?" She pointed at the backpack. "Go ahead. Show it to them."

He pushed her backpack away with his foot, carefully, as if it might contain a nest of vipers. She was right. If she got caught with stolen avatar relics, especially relics from the Regium, of all places, the Inquisitors would go after everybody she'd ever known. Especially the guy who'd been sleeping with her. He was fucked. Even if he didn't get the gallows, the fallout would ruin his future. But it wouldn't stop there. He had a sudden vision of his grandmother, Captain Kwon Ophelia Namjoo, standing stoically beneath the masked faces of a Panel of Inquisitors while a black-robed death monk ripped the military insignia from the shoulders of her uniform. The only way to save himself and his family would be to turn Nkiru in, right now, and claim that he'd just learned of her heresies.

"I need some air," he said, and without looking at her, he turned and left the cabin.

Kanaan

Under tow from the Solar Guard rescue cutter, the *Covenant* was bizarrely silent. Se-Jong walked the length of the ship from bow to stern, cutting through the galley and several narrow access corridors, avoiding the eyes and ignoring the greetings of pilgrims along the way. He ended up in the only place on the entire ship with a window: the cargo airlock at the ship's stern, which sported a small, round porthole of thick glass. It was a crew-only area, so it was one of the few places on the crowded transport where none of the pilgrims ever went. If one of the crew caught him there, he'd get thrown out, but a scolding from a crew member seemed ridiculously unimportant considering his current situation. He stared through the porthole at the featureless gray mist of the hypervee cloud.

Nkiru had stolen a relic from the Regium. He was sure of it. To make matters worse, she seemed to have gotten herself involved in some kind of treacherous conspiracy with the Janga monk Jerome and his associates. Se-Jong knew there were many monastic orders in the Cataclyst Church, and that they all had differing agendas. The Jangas rejected the literal interpretation of the scriptures in favor of a metaphorical interpretation. Where church doctrine emphasized the worship of the mystical archangels and avatars, the Jangas revered nature and the sacred cosmos. This often put them at odds with the Regium, who saw the Janga insistence on using science as an affront to their official dogmas.

Nkiru had lived in a Janga-run youth shelter. Maybe they'd brainwashed her. Maybe she was just a pawn in some grand plan of theirs. No, not a pawn. With her ability to wield avatar tech, she was far more powerful than a pawn. She was a *queen*. He tried to imagine the moment when some monk had first seen her activate an avatar relic. It would have shaken the monk to the core of his pious soul. Jangas were well-known as skeptics, doubters. Although there was ample physical evidence that avatars had indeed existed in the Second Epoch, their true nature was widely disputed. The prevailing doctrine taught that the avatars had been physical manifestations of the praelea, who were angels from the realm of the Oa. Even the Mucktu cult believed the same, except instead of angels, in their view the praelea spirits had been demons from hell. Nonbelievers and even some Janga speculated that the avatars might have been a noncorporeal alien race that had possessed the bodies of unsuspecting mortals, or perhaps a mutation plague that had swept through the galaxy giving the infected special powers.

Whatever their origin and nature, avatars had indeed existed: of that there was no doubt. Every world was littered with ruins and relics of the avatar empires. Even on Earth, where avatar relics were oddly absent, the precontact religions had been replete with legends of avatars. The word itself, *avatar*, was from the Hindi language and described the physical bodies of the supernatural Hindu deities. The Greek gods had regularly walked among humans disguised in mortal forms. The very basis of the entire Christian religion had been built upon the concept of a single avatar: Jesus, the Earthly embodiment of the One God, Yahweh.

Avatar or not, there was no backing away from the fact of Nkiru's talent. If word got out, it would rock the pillars of the church and all of modern civilization. It would be the most important discovery of the Third Epoch. She'd denied being an avatar, but what other explanation could there be? If she was an avatar, maybe the praelea angel that possessed her body was simply lying about its true nature. Or maybe it had lost all reason and forgotten its origins. It was possible, he speculated, that she might actually be an avatar and not realize it. The realization fell on him like a massive weight: the scared girl back in their cabin might just be the most important person alive.

Her face was drained and slack, and her eyes didn't move away from their blank stare when he entered the cabin and quietly closed the door. Over the past hour while he'd been searching his soul, she hadn't budged from her position on the bed, still curled into herself. The backpack hadn't moved, either. It remained where he'd pushed it with his foot.

He spoke softly. "You're right. We *are* alike, me and you."

She looked up at him. Her cheeks were dry, her eyes empty. She was a deflated balloon, a dead battery, a wild animal lying in the desert sun, shriveled and dying from thirst. He suddenly realized that he was afraid of her.

"There's a First Epoch dungeon on Grone," she announced absently, in the same unconcerned tone she might use to reveal the ingredient of a soup.

His breath caught in his throat. "What?"

"There's a dungeon on Grone. A really big one. Nobody knows it's there. I think I know how to find it."

He stared at her uncomprehendingly. Grone was the next pilgrimage stop after Orbitus, their current destination. It was a minor planet, the location of a cathedral that enshrined an important event in ancient church history. Like most habitable worlds, it probably had a few avatar ruins, but he'd never heard even the slightest rumor of the existence of a dungeon on the planet.

Her words remained flat, emotionless. "It might have been destroyed by the Cataclysm, like most of the others. But if not . . ." She shrugged.

Se-Jong could only stare at her slack expression. No wonder she'd been so secretive. Since antiquity, locations had been known for only four dungeons, and all four were mentioned in the *Chronicles*: the Memory Tombs on Ghast, the Deepstone, the Borwhan Enigma, and the Spire of Jeru. All four of them had been at least partially leveled by the Cataclysm, and all of them long ago looted of their treasures, their secrets ravaged by time, war, and greed. Other dungeons were mentioned in the scripture, but in ten thousand years of searching, no one had ever unearthed another, probably because they'd been in the area of the galaxy that now lay within the Devastation. An undiscovered dungeon on Grone wasn't just unlikely: it was unthinkable.

"Why do you think there's a dungeon on Grone?"

A glint of her customary fire returned to her eyes. "I *know* there's a dungeon on Grone."

"How?"

She hesitated. "Research. Putting two and two together. Plus, I know somebody who went there once."

"Who?" he demanded.

"A friend. She's dead now."

"You have a dead friend who went to a dungeon on Grone."

Nkiru nodded. "She told me how to find it."

"Your friend?"

"Yes."

Se-Jong's train of thought derailed in a crashing screech of confusion. He stared at her. She didn't exactly flinch, but he could see fear behind her steady gaze.

"It's going to be dangerous," she said.

"No shit," he retorted. Even the avatars had been terrified of dungeons. Dungeons were the physical remnants of the primordial war between the Gurothim and the Predecessors, two long-vanished alien species who'd been among the first civilizations to explore and colonize the galaxy. Their dungeons—and nobody knew why they were called *dungeons*, other than the fact that they were usually underground—had been filled with enigmatic and vastly powerful ancient technology that was protected by equally powerful defensive systems, bizarre mazes, and traps. Sometimes, this tech was infested with monstrous alien creatures. The Avatar Wars of the Second Epoch had been fought to control the dungeons and their fabulous treasures. An avatar lord who controlled a dungeon and its secrets had the power to wield an empire.

The Rapture and the Cataclysm had put an end to the galaxy-spanning empires of the avatars, but plenty of competing political powers had arisen from their ashes. The Regium. Ghast. The Olids. The Whan worlds. More recently, the Solar Alliance and its troublesome offshoot, the Caerens. Any of which would see an undiscovered, unlooted dungeon filled with First Epoch wonders as the pathway to domination of the Known Arc.

If his grandmother believed a new dungeon lay undiscovered on Grone, she'd be ordering a Solar Guard warfleet to the planet, for sure. Assuming, that is, that Nkiru was telling the truth, though after the demonstration he'd just witnessed with the avatar stealthshield and scancorder, he was inclined to believe anything she told him.

She gestured toward her backpack. "The relics. You asked me why I have those particular items. I'll need them on Grone; that's why."

"When were you going to tell me all this?"

"I wasn't going to tell you. I didn't think you'd last this long. I didn't expect to . . ."

He felt a sudden, hard shaft of anger . . . and something else. "Expect to *what*?"

She turned away, but he knew what she'd almost said. The rush of emotion hit him so hard he almost staggered. Adrenalin, terror at the enormity of the situation, all with a topping of sweet triumph.

"If I'm going to risk . . ."

"Everything," she said.

He nodded slowly. "Yeah. If I'm going to risk *everything*, you have to tell me the truth. *All* the truth."

She didn't hesitate. "I'm looking for someone."

"In a dungeon on Grone?"

"Maybe. I hope so."

A moment passed. "Who?"

"The Prophet Kanaan."

Se-Jong hadn't expected that. "Uh, what?" He blinked. "I'm afraid you're about eight thousand years too late."

"I think he's still alive. In fact, I *know* he is." A hint of defiance had crept back into her face.

Se-Jong stifled a scoff. "I don't get it."

"You know the legend of the Lost Avatar, how Kanaan was the only surviving praelea angel who avoided the Rapture?" She paused, toying absently with the pewter ring on her right hand. "It's true. Kanaan really was a kind of avatar, and he really did get trapped here during the Rapture."

"Kanaan wasn't real. He's just a character from a scripture parable."

"No, he *was* real, and I think he *wrote* those scriptures. Avatars are immortal, remember? He's still around, and I'm going to find him."

"Why?"

"Brother Jerome believes Kanaan knows what caused the Cataclysm." She extended her arms widely, as if trying to encompass the entire cosmos, "I've seen his scholara research, and I think Brother Jerome is right. If I can find Kanaan, maybe I can use my talent with the avatar relics to help him fix the damage. Maybe restore the worlds eaten by the Cataclysm. Maybe bring the galaxy back to life."

The yawning gulf between what he'd expected her to say and what she'd actually said caused his brain to stutter. Not only was it supremely blasphemous, but it was also patently ridiculous. "That's impossible."

"Isn't it also impossible for a girl from a New York homeless shelter to activate an avatar stealthshield?"

He sighed heavily. "Yeah, that's impossible, too." He thought for a moment. "Okay, I want to believe you. Why do you think the Prophet is still alive after thousands of years?"

"Brother Jerome has found clues in dozens of Leodiva's paintings. Kanaan left his tracks across the centuries."

"How would a painter from the Middle Ages know details about Kanaan's life? Leodiva lived five thousand years *after* Kanaan."

She raised her eyebrows. "What if Leodiva *was* Kanaan, just in a different guise? After all, if you're immortal, every century or so you'd have to change your identity or people would get suspicious."

"That's . . . nuts."

"Clues from Leodiva's paintings guided me to the relics in my backpack," she offered as proof. "You can't deny that Leodiva's easter eggs are intentional hints leading to something. I just have to figure out the pattern."

"You think the easter eggs will lead you to Kanaan?"

"Maybe. It's not just the easter eggs. There are other clues, too."

"I'm afraid to ask."

"Do you know who established the pilgrimage? Who laid down the route of the Secta Avataris?"

Se-Jong thought back to the orientation literature he'd read back on their first transport ship, the *Rose & Chalice*. There'd been a lot about the history of the pilgrimage; most of it he'd promptly forgotten. He did remember that the first pilgrim had traced the route back in the third millennium, and—

He suddenly remembered. "The Prophet Kanaan."

She nodded, her eyes bright. "Yup. Brother Jerome thinks that the pilgrimage route itself is a big, stinking clue. After all, it's supposedly the route Kanaan took after the Cataclysm to establish the church. The scriptures say he was searching for the three Great Emoras, among other things. Think about it; maybe he wasn't just trying to bring religion to the surviving worlds of the Halo. If he really was an angel stranded here after the Rapture, maybe he was looking for something that would help him get back *home*."

Se-Jong held his hands up as if to ward off any more words. In any other context, and coming from anyone else, he would have said these theories were ridiculous. "It doesn't add up. Why is Brother Jerome keeping your talent a secret from the church? It seems to me that if the church knew you could use avatar tech, they'd make you a gods-damned saint, and Brother Jerome would be promoted to a consenti at minimum. With the resources of the church behind you, you'd find this Kanaan for sure."

That got a reaction, though not one he'd expected. Her face hardened and she spoke bitterly through clenched teeth. "One of the monks eventually *did* go to the church. They arrested him, and then they came after his chaptermates. Luckily, he hadn't implicated Brother Jerome, but three of the other monks who were helping me were charged with capital heresy and executed. They almost found me, but Jerome helped me get off Earth."

Se-Jong didn't even try to keep the shocked expression off his face. "You're a fugitive from the church?"

She bit her lip and nodded. "The Father Regis wants to control me. The Dei Militans are looking for me. But don't worry. I don't think they can find me." She paused and worked her jaw indecisively, as if trying to decide how many more of her secrets she should reveal. She waved her hand in front of her face. "They never really knew what I looked like. Plus, I'm . . . changing."

"What?"

She bit her top lip. "I didn't always look like this. Whatever is in my blood is changing me. It started a couple of years ago, but it's speeding up. Nobody recognizes me anymore."

The sinking feeling in Se-Jong's gut hit rock bottom. He'd always assumed that Nkiru's striking appearance was due to some unusual ancestry, the result of her parents being of different Humanish lineages. Had the Janga monks done something to her? He'd heard of appearance-altering treatments based on black-market Caeren genetic technology. They violated the very core of the church's racial purity commandment. Modifying your genes was a crime almost as bad as stealing avatar tech. He pushed down a feeling of hysteria. *Possession of a copy of the Mucktu Apocrypha . . . Possession of stolen avatar relics . . . Possible recipient of banned genetic treatments . . .*

She gave him an apologetic look. "You asked me to tell you everything."

"I guess I did. I just wasn't expecting . . ." He swallowed and studied her face. "What . . . what do you normally look like?"

She made a harsh, barking laugh. "Don't worry, I'm not a Forniculan or a Ghost or anything. My skin's getting darker and my hair and eyes lighter. I think my, uh, cheekbones may be narrowing a little. Other than that, I'm still me."

A suspicion hit him, hard. "Is that how you . . . did the Janga . . . put something in your blood? Is that how you can use avatar tech?"

She shook her head. "No. I could always do that."

"Is . . . is Nkiru even your real name?"

She didn't answer. His head felt hollow, empty, like his brain had seized. Her revelations had blasted so far beyond his suspicions that he had no idea where to go from here. "So . . . the Dei Miltans really are looking for you."

"I'm sorry," she finally said. "I know I shouldn't have gotten you involved. I didn't mean to, at first. I just wanted somebody to keep me company. I was scared. I should've never let it get this far. I seriously won't blame you if you walk out that door and I never see you again."

He stood for another long few moments. He cleared his throat. "We can get off at the next station. You can leave the relics in a trash bin at the spaceport. I have enough to buy you a cash ticket to one of the far colony planets, maybe Mogul or Libertaria. They'd have a tough time finding you way out there."

Tears formed in the corners of her eyes. "I have to try to find Kanaan," she said. "I have to try. I'm sorry."

Se-Jong bent down and picked up her backpack. He tossed it next to her on the bed. He considered his next words carefully. "I can get off at the next stop and fly home. It's not too late for me to get into the War College this semester and put my life back on track." He threw out his hand to preempt her reply. His stomach churned the way it had in his first zero-G experience. Freefall. He closed his eyes and tried to steady himself. "Or, I'll risk ruining my life to hang out with a very pretty but mind-fucked fugitive girl who wears an avatar stealthshield and steals sacred relics so she can search a dungeon for some guy from a ten-thousand-year-old myth."

He opened his eyes. She was staring at him. The thing that was roiling in his gut gained substance. It crawled slowly up through his stomach and into his throat. He thought he was going to throw up, but when the knot of tension reached his mouth, he realized it was an idiotic smile. He tried to swallow it, but it persisted, and forced its way out onto his face. Then the gods-damned thing jumped across the room to Nkiru, where it had the same effect. It was ridiculous, and totally unstoppable.

They both laughed, hard, hysterically. He dropped on the bed next to her. They laughed until both their faces were bloated from the exertion. When the laugh had exhausted itself, they stared at each other with hollow and terrified eyes.

"Fuck," muttered Se-Jong.

"Fuck," Nkiru agreed.

Skybridge

Nkiru's body continued to mend. Her facial bruises faded. The pain in her ribs slowly subsided, but by the time they reached the next pilgrimage stop at the legendary Skybridge of Orbitus and Ragnu, their mutual anxieties had grown to thermonuclear proportions.

There was one bright side: the knowledge that they might be arrested for grand heresy as soon as they stepped off the ship had led to an unprecedented level of ferocity in their lovemaking. When the captain called for the passengers to secure their belongings and strap in for the docking maneuvers at Centerpoint Station, they were already so engaged in their own maneuvers that they didn't even hear the warning. As the ship's motion surged with the firing of its thrusters, the inertia sent their entwined bodies sliding back and forth across the floor of their tiny cabin, tumbling against the bulkheads, laughing and clutching each other in a desperate embrace. Finally, in a ship-shuddering series of loud metallic clangs, the *Covenant* locked itself into the receiving port of the spacedock. At the same moment, Nkiru cried out and pressed herself into him with an intensity he'd never known, her body quivering, her eyes locked on his.

"You're the best team bot, ever," she murmured.

"What?"

She answered with a quick laugh, and by smothering his mouth in a wet kiss.

Se-Jong had always been fascinated by the Skybridge, ever since visiting it as a child on one of his family's rare vacations. Stretching between the worlds of Orbitus and Ragnu, the Skybridge was the most titanic accomplishment of planetary engineering in the Known Arc. He remembered holding his father's hand at the window of the hyperliner as it had approached the Centerpoint of the Skybridge, where the spaceport was located. From his child's perspective, the structure had looked like a short thread connecting two brightly colored bowling balls, with a glistening drop of water suspended from the center of the thread like a raindrop on a spider's web.

At some point in the lost ages of the First Epoch, the red desert world of Orbitus had been towed from its original location by the mysterious race known only as the Predecessors, and carefully positioned five thousand kilometers above the north pole of Ragnu, a blue-marble water world. The engineers had leveraged some complicated gravitational effect to hold the planets in positions relative to each other, like two aircraft flying in tight formation, and had exploited a further loophole in the laws of physics to keep the gravitational pull of the two worlds from tearing each other apart.

The ancient engineers had then pivoted Orbitus so that its rotational axis was locked in a straight line that extended through both planets' poles. It was along this axial line that the Skybridge had been constructed. Rising from the north pole of Ragnu, it crossed the intervening space to descend to the south pole of Orbitus. Each end was anchored to a city-sized turntable that canceled the motion of its planet's rotation, allowing the Skybridge to remain stationary even though the two planets were spinning at different rates in opposite directions.

The two worlds connected by the Skybridge were different in every way. Red Orbitus was a stark desert world of stone plateaus, vast canyons, and a small but lovely artificial sea in its northern hemisphere. Blue Ragnu was a water world, the only dry land being the artificial island at its south pole, constructed as the anchor-point foundation for the Skybridge. In eons past, some ambitious avatar lord had installed vast pumps along the length of the Skybridge that had begun to move water from Ragnu to Orbitus in what had probably been a terraforming project interrupted by the Cataclysm. Like all avatar technology, the pumps were now inert, though some ambitious politicians on Earth had proposed replacing them and resurrecting the terraforming project to turn both worlds into livable colonies.

—

The trip down the Skybridge elevator from Centerpoint to the surface of Orbitus took eleven hours, during which Se-Jong and Nkiru huddled together in the windowless car, hands intertwined as they dozed or listened to the aimless chats of the other passengers.

The car was crowded with disgruntled pilgrims from the *Covenant*. The captain had announced after docking that due to the engine breakdown, the ship would be out of commission for the foreseeable future. If they wished to continue their pilgrimage, they'd be forced to take the next scheduled pilgrims' transport, which would leave in just thirty-six hours; otherwise, they'd be forced to wait almost two months for the next scheduled ship. This didn't give the disappointed pilgrims much time to explore the many religious sites on both planets and on the Skybridge itself, so the entire lot was frantically visiting the few shrines they could reach in the allotted time.

More than half of the pilgrims had chosen to stay at Centerpoint and attend mass at the Skybridge Cathedral, from which the close view of the great red and blue globes was considered the most awe-inspiring astronomical vista in the Known Arc. Most of the rest had chosen to descend to watery Ragnu to visit the Anchorpoint Catacombs, a series of tomb-like warrens dug into the bedrock of the artificial island by ancient Worm monks. The Worms had eventually vanished en masse as Worms are known to do, but not before leaving behind a spectacular series of cave sculptures purported to tell the story of Andrik the Redeemer.

The rest of the pilgrims, a scraggly dozen, were on the elevator car with Se-Jong and Nkiru, along with a bored-looking Ghast whose responsibility it was to operate the elevator. The Ghast sat on one side of the car, and everyone else crowded into the seats on the opposite side, eying it warily. Nkiru wrinkled her nose and whispered in Se-Jong's ear delightedly, "I've never seen one in real life! They're a lot bigger and scarier than I imagined. I also never realized they *smelled* so bad!" Se-Jong shushed her. Ghasts had extrasensitive hearing, and the last thing they needed was an offended Ghast in a small elevator car. Luckily, if the alien heard her comments, it ignored them. The Ghast kept its arms crossed and its eyestalks retracted. Maybe it was asleep, Se-Jong thought.

Nkiru and Se-Jong were headed to see the Jebil Syrioc, the holy mountain on Orbitus where the Prophet Kanaan was said to have attempted communion with the gods. This site was arguably far more important than any of the others on either Orbitus or Ragnu, but the blistering heat, the difficult nature of the terrain, and the fact that the atmosphere on Orbitus was barely breathable had discouraged all but the hardiest pilgrims.

As the elevator car approached the terminal at the base of the Skybridge, Nkiru's grip on Se-Jong's hand hardened and his own excitement intensified. Somewhere down there, she'd told him the night before, another fabulous avatar relic was waiting to be discovered.

—

Se-Jong adjusted his filter mask and tried to smile at Nkiru, who ignored him. Their guide was giving instructions to the group of a dozen pilgrims. "The atmosphere is mostly breathable, but the winds kick up dust from the dry seabed that's toxic and slightly radioactive. Be sure to keep the seals on your facemasks tight, no matter how gritty they may feel. Believe me, it's better to have a few raw spots on your neck than it is to spend a week at the Centerpoint hospital attached to a lung machine." He carefully helped a young Forniculan adjust their mask. "If you get a runny nose, start to cough, or experience shortness of breath, let me know immediately, okay?"

Everyone nodded. The guide gave them an encouraging grin before donning his own mask. "Oh, and be sure to stay on the trail, and watch where you step. There are some nasty little beasties that live in the desert." He adjusted the mask radio. "Okay. Can everyone hear me? Raise your hand if you can." He counted the hands, then pointed to the timer above the airlock door. "We've got two minutes, folks. Everybody get ready. When the door opens, we'll be stepping off the rotating anchor point onto the surface of Orbitus. Once every 26.2 hours—the length of the day on Orbitus—the airlock lines up with the exit platform near the trailhead to Jebil Syrioc. When the door opens, don't hesitate. Step quickly over the threshold and grab the handrails on the platform. This close to the pole, the rotational speed of Orbitus is only about five kilometers per hour, so the platform will seem to be moving at a quick walking pace. It's still fast enough to trip you up if you're not careful. Pretend like you're stepping off a sideways-moving escalator." The guide gestured to the airlock. "Okay, folks, this way. Form a single-file line, please. As soon as the airlock opens, exit quickly, one at a time, and step onto the platform. Do not hesitate. Use the handrail; the wind can knock you over, even though the exit platform is in a canyon. If the person in front of you trips, please help them." On the wall above the line of nervous pilgrims, the timer diminished to the final few seconds. "Ready? Ready? Okay, here we go!"

The hike to the base of Jebil Syrioc wound through a series of slot canyons, some of which were so narrow in spots that Se-Jong had to turn sideways in order to squeeze through the gap. He tried to imagine some of the portlier pilgrims attempting this path and laughed. Nkiru had an easier time with her slight frame, though she had to remove her bulky backpack more than once.

The wind was weaker in the canyons, but it was still strong enough to occasionally form a river of blown sand that whirled beneath their footsteps. The effect of the seemingly fluid ground made Se-Jong dizzy, so he kept his eyes locked on Nkiru's back. She moved easily through the narrow, winding passages, hopping from rock to rock like a gazelle, her feet barely brushing the ground.

The guide was talking about the geology of the surrounding desert as they emerged from the canyon onto a wind-scoured stone plateau, and all eyes were on him or on the treacherous footing. Suddenly he paused, and Se-Jong could see his wide grin even through his dust-frosted faceplate. When he spoke again, the guide's voice was mockingly serious, filled with theatrical bravado. "While I've been yammering," he said, "you've been missing something. Everyone, please turn around."

Gasps filled the earphones of Se-Jong's facemask. He glanced at Nkiru, and they turned together.

"Behold, Orbitus Anchorpoint," said the guide.

A small city lay before them, set out in a perfectly circular plan. At its center rose something that reminded Se-Jong of photos he'd seen of the original Eiffel Tower before it was redesigned following the Mucktu bombing, but on a scale a thousand, a million times larger, and infinitely tall. Even from here he could tell that the entire anchor-point city, including the tower, was slowly rotating. Se-Jong's eyes climbed the colossal silver scaffolding of the Skybridge until he was leaning so far he almost toppled backward.

Even more impressive than the Skybridge was the sky itself. Inexplicably, exactly half the sky was a dark blue that faded to inky black at the horizon, and half was a bright-blue haze, as if some divine razor had sliced the heavens into dark and light halves. The blue haze of the bright part of the sky was smeared with delicate, feathery shapes arranged in broad streaks and spirals. The shapes were also present in the dark half, but they were much harder to see.

His overwhelmed mind was trying to make sense of the vista when he realized the true nature of the view. Instead of sky, he was looking straight up at the ocean surface of Ragnu, almost close enough to touch! The face of the planet filled the entire celestial dome, the blue half lit by the daylight sun, the dark half in the gloom of night. The feathery twirling shapes were clouds, but clouds on Ragnu, not here on Orbitus. The *nearness* of another full-sized world in the sky almost caused him to stagger. Indeed, several of the other pilgrims had fallen to their knees, hands clasped, mouthing silent prayers.

Nkiru let out a barely audible mumble. "Wow. This is way more impressive in person."

He turned to her. "What do you mean?"

The guide's voice interrupted her reply. He pointed straight up. "If you look closely, you can see the lights of the floating colony cities on the night side. They're populated mostly by humans from the Pacific Islands on Earth. They're hoping to expand their cities and increase their population to the point that they can claim the planet as an Earth colony and apply for SATO protectorate status. One of those tiny little points of light is my own home village where my parents live."

Appreciative mumbles rose from the other pilgrims, then changed to startled gasps as a powerful gust of wind hit the group. Se-Jong lurched against Nkiru for support. The guide motioned them forward. "Yep, it gets pretty breezy out here sometimes. Everybody okay? Come on, let's go see the main attraction."

―

The hike to the summit of Jebil Syrioc was steep and treacherous, made more difficult by the gusting wind. The seal of Se-Jong's mask was already compromised by grit, but he resisted the temptation to reseat it. About halfway up, the guide called for a rest in a sheltered, boulder-strewn cove. As the pilgrims gawked at the surrounding landscape, the guide pointed out the shallow sea off in the distance and explained how it was all that was left of the artificial ocean the avatars had begun flooding with seawater pumped down from Ragnu. "Another few hundred years and it'll be gone completely, unless they find a way to restart the Skybridge pumps." He went on to indicate the remnants of a crater near the circular city where some forgotten avatar lord had tried to nuke the Skybridge anchor point. "They missed, thank goodness. If they'd hit the anchor point, there's a good chance it would've destabilized the entire system and the two planets might have crashed into each other. The dust of the dry seabed is still radioactive even after ten thousand years."

Nkiru wasn't listening. She led Se-Jong to a stone shelf away from the others, where she dropped her backpack and sat heavily. Se-Jong sucked at the water straw in his facemask and watched her scan the horizon. "I remember the sea," she said absently. "The mountains look different, too."

Se-Jong looked around at the stark desert ridges. "You've been here before?"

She made a dismissive shake of her head. "No. Not like this."

"What does that mean?"

She motioned for him to take a seat by her side, and she made a show of switching off the radio in her facemask. He did the same, and they leaned together so that their masks touched and sound could travel without being overheard by the others. She pointed toward a distant bluff that was capped with massive piles of stony rubble. "That's the ruins of an avatar citadel. It was built above the entrance to the Orbitus dungeon." Her voice was wistful, as if she were reliving a fond memory. "It was guarded by a sand boss you couldn't kill with regular weapons. The only way to beat it was to flood the citadel with water from the Skybridge pumps."

"There's a dungeon over there? I don't remember that from the *Chronicles*," Se-Jong said.

She made a one-shoulder shrug. "It's long gone. The citadel and the dungeon were bombed into pebbles during the Avatar Wars." She swiped at her komnic. He recognized an overhead map view of the mountain they were climbing. She tapped the screen and enlarged a section of the map for an area about halfway between their current position and the summit. "That's where we'll slip away from the tour group." On the map, four small icons, placed equidistantly around the periphery of the mountain, marked the locations of small ruins. She pointed to the one nearest their location. "We'll try this one first." She put a hand on his knee and lowered her voice. "The *Chronicles* say the Prophet Kanaan tried to contact the gods from the summit of this mountain. They're wrong. He went to one of these communications bunkers instead."

He studied her scowling face as she scrutinized the map on her komnic. Despite his scratchy facemask, despite the biting wind and the heat and the glaring sun, it dawned on him that there was no place in the Known Arc of the Halo where he'd rather be than right here with this extraordinary woman. "Who *are* you, Nkiru Anaya?"

She grinned at him through the hazed plastic of the facemask. "Just a girl on a mission, Lieutenant."

Jebil Syrioc

It was easy to break away from the tour group. Se-Jong and Nkiru were last in line, and when Nkiru gave the signal, they ducked behind a rock. It would take the group another thirty minutes to reach the summit. If they spent thirty minutes at the top praying or chanting or doing whatever pilgrims did up there, it would be ninety minutes before they returned. He pressed his facemask against hers. "We have an hour and a half," he said, noting the time on his komnic. "Let's go."

His anxiety spiked as she pulled out the scancorder relic and brought it to life. It beeped and flashed and made noises similar to those of a modern scanner, but this one could see through a hundred feet of solid stone like it was an ultrasheer silk curtain. He peered over her shoulder at the display. It showed a directional indicator and a flashing red crosshair. She moved the scanner until the two lined up. "That way," she pointed.

When she'd briefed him back on the ship the previous day, she hadn't told him what kind of relic they were looking for, only that it was probably small enough to carry. "It should be round, fist size, or maybe a bit bigger."

They made their way sideways across the dry, broken shale of the mountainside, occasionally stopping for cover when hit by a particularly strong sandblasting, courtesy of the erratic wind. The windblown grit was working its way deeper into the crevices between his facemask seal and his skin, and it was starting to hurt, especially at the tight neck seal. After a while he stopped turning his head to minimize the scrubbing action, which made the climbing even more precarious.

This particular flank of the mountain was steep, and although there were plenty of handholds and ledges, the stone was of poor quality and often crumbled beneath their fingers and boots. Eventually Nkiru stopped to consult the scanner. Once again, she waved it around until the icons lined up on the screen. She leaned into his faceplate. "There it is."

What the map had labeled *ruins* was a hump of crumbling sand and rock jutting from the side of the mountain, identical to a dozen other natural protrusions. Thousands of years of constant exposure had either buried the original structure or, more likely, worn it down to gravel. They scrambled toward it on all fours, creating a series of tiny, dusty landslides that marked their passage.

When they reached it, Nkiru once again pulled out the scanner. The screen was hard to read in the direct sunlight, so Se-Jong moved behind her to supply shade. They leaned together, faceplates touching. Her voice trembled with keen expectancy. "Se-Jong, it's *here*. Look at that red blob. It's putting out power!"

Se-Jong smiled so widely inside the facemask that it hurt the raw skin of his neck and cheeks. He was excited that they'd found something, but he was more struck by the fact that she'd called him by his name. *Se-Jong.*

"It's about four meters over there and three down below the soil." She pointed at one corner of the mound of rubble. "We need to dig right *there*."

Working diligently with the folding shovels he'd brought in his pack, it took almost twenty minutes to burrow deep enough to find the original concrete outline of the structure, and another twenty to find the opening that might once have been a door. Half their time was gone, Se-Jong realized, and they hadn't even gotten inside yet.

He fervently hoped the interior of the bunker hadn't collapsed or filled with rubble. They didn't have time for a major excavation.

The material in the opening was mostly fine powder, and they discovered they could move it faster by scooping it away with their bare hands. It took another five minutes to uncover the empty doorway, but when Se-Jong tried to scoop sand away from the opening, he met a hard, invisible surface, as if a pane of the purest glass stretched across the opening. The structure was full of sand, and when he threw sand into the opening, it moved freely through it. When he tried to push his hand through, it met the hard barrier. He turned questioningly to Nkiru.

She was smiling. "We're at the right place." She reached out and put her flat palm on the barrier. "Han shot first," she said, and her hand fell into the opening. She gestured for him to continue digging. He moved his hand through the opening. The barrier was gone. Nkiru laughed and shrugged. He started to grimace, but it occurred to him that having a girlfriend who was an avatar was a pretty cool thing.

The inside of the bunker was almost completely filled with dry, fine-grained sand above which an airspace extended into the darkness. Nkiru started to crawl inside, but Se-Jong held out a hand. "Let me go first," he said. He regretted his words at once, as this was her discovery, not his, but she only shrugged and gave him a *be my guest* motion with her hands.

It was tight inside, nothing but a sloping floor of sand and the pitted concrete of the ceiling barely a meter above. The light suddenly dimmed, and he realized that Nkiru had crawled in behind him, blocking the sunlight from the opening. He clicked on his facemask radio and motioned for Nkiru to do the same. There was no way the weak signal would penetrate the thick walls, and he wanted to be able to talk freely. "What does the scanner say?"

"Two more meters, straight ahead, and one meter down."

He was close. He crawled two meters. Nothing, just more sand. "Dig here?"

She nodded, and he began scooping away handfuls of loose sand, half of which tumbled back into the hole he was making. There wasn't much room to work, and he kept bumping his head on the low ceiling. If the scanner was correct, the relic should be just a few more centimeters down—

A sharp pain tore into his thigh. He cried out and jerked backward. Something skittered away into the darkness. He shined his light in the direction of the motion to find a small crater of sand had formed and was quickly refilling. Something had just buried itself. He looked down at his leg. A coin-size spot of blood was spreading into the fabric of his pants. "Something bit me," he shouted. He tried to twist around to examine the bite, but the space was too tight and he knocked his head against the ceiling. Something else moved in his peripheral vision—something with far too many legs. Sudden panic welled up. "Back up! Get out!"

They both scrambled out of the tight space and back into the glaring sun. Se-Jong crouched and examined his wound. The bite mark was a couple of centimeters wide and penetrated the skin into the muscle beneath. It bled freely but, surprisingly, no longer hurt. In fact, it felt numb. Nkiru looked at the wound, frowned, then swung her light back into the dark opening. He saw her twitch and jerk back. "It's a nest of rockspides." She looked around the mountainside as if searching for something she didn't want to find. "These are babies. I don't see the mother anywhere. She must be out hunting."

"These are *babies*?" The crablike shape he'd glimpsed skittering away had been the size of a dinner plate. "How big is the mother?"

"Big," said Nkiru. "And dangerous. If I remember, rockspides swim under the sand and pop up when you least expect them. Take your whole leg off in one snap."

Se-Jong thought again of the guide's warning to stay on the trail.

Nkiru gave him a serious look. "She could be back at any moment. We need to hurry."

"You can't be serious. You want to go back in there?"

"The babies aren't too bad. Their bite isn't all that poisonous."

"How do you know?"

"The dungeon on Orbitus was notorious for rockspide swarms. You could kill one or two of them pretty easily with a shotgun, but there were a lot of them, and when they swarmed, they could be really dangerous." He glanced up the slope at a sound that might have been the wind but, for all he knew, might instead have been a horde of pissed-off sand-swimming crab-spiders. "We need to hurry," she said. "Move out of the way; I'm going back inside."

He blocked the opening. "No way you're going back in. What if the mother is in there?"

She scoffed. "If she were inside then we'd already be dead." She made this pronouncement in the same tone of voice she might have used to discuss the weather. The fact that, moments earlier, they might have been killed and eaten by an alien monster didn't seem to bother her at all. Se-Jong had done some stupid things as a teen back on Askelon, but he'd never come even remotely close to anything this risky. He looked at the bite on his leg and gave an involuntary shudder. She saw it and winced. "Look, Lieutenant: you're okay. It's just a little bite. Now let me inside. I'm smaller than you and can move around better. It'll only take a second. I'll be fine."

She'd gone back to calling him Lieutenant, he noted. Conflicting emotions erupted in his gut. He couldn't let this skinny girl's bravery outshine his own, could he? But then again, it was sheer madness to crawl into a nest of biting alien spiders. An image flashed unbidden into his head of Nkiru writhing in agony, covered by a dozen of the many-legged horrors.

Nkiru's expression hardened. "Move. We're running out of time."

She shoved him to the side, and before he could say "Be careful," she'd scrambled into the dark hole. He knelt and shined his light into the opening, illuminating the soles of her boots and the smooth skin of her dust-covered legs. Heart pounding, he flicked the light around the opening, watching for movement. When he saw one of the little beasts emerge a couple of meters to her left, he grabbed a stone and flung it at it. The creature vanished in a spray of sand. "Hurry," he said.

"Okay, I'm digging," she called out. Another creature, or maybe the same one, popped up next to one of her feet. It sprang on her boot, engulfing it in its multisegmented legs, and drove its fangs into the tough leather.

"Damn, damn, damn," muttered Se-Jong, and he lunged inside, one of the folding shovels clenched in his hand like an axe.

Their fellow passengers stared at them during the ride back up the Skybridge elevator to Centerpoint. It was no wonder. Se-Jong had crude bandages on his arms and one leg, raw-skinned facemask abrasions on his face and neck, and a torn shirt that revealed the pale skin of his shoulder. Nkiru was missing one of her boots, and her foot was wrapped in another hastily applied bandage. Se-Jong couldn't keep the grin off his face, and every time he looked over at Nkiru, she was grinning, too. She winked at him and glanced down at the floor between them where his now-heavy backpack rested. He leaned close and whispered, "Every minute I'm not living is a minute I'm dying." They both laughed, and the watching pilgrims scowled, confused.

When the group returning from the summit of Jebil Syrioc had found them by the side of the trail, pandemonium had ensued. Nkiru had told the guide that they'd encountered a clutch of baby rockspides that had attacked them on the trail, causing them to become separated from the others. The guide had been mortified and had rushed the group back down to the anchor-point airlock, where he'd torn open a first aid kit and clumsily applied bandages to their wounds, all the while muttering things like "I'm so sorry," and "I told you to stay together on the trail," and "Please don't lodge a complaint."

Nobody, not the frantic guide or the bewildered pilgrims, had paid any attention to the heavy, round bulge in Se-Jong's backpack.

Centerpoint

The small window of their room in the pilgrims' hostel faced outward from the system's sun, which meant that only the nighttime sides of the planets Orbitus and Ragnu were visible. From Se-Jong's vantage point at Centerpoint Station, strung like a city-size pearl in the middle of the Skybridge that connected the two worlds, each planet took up opposing halves of the sky, separated only by a narrow band of stars. Even knowing the details of the extraordinary astronomical configuration, Se-Jong found it hard to understand what he was seeing. Neither world was completely dark, as their proximity to each other meant that sunlight from the daytime side of one planet reflected onto the night side of the other. The dark surface of blue Ragnu had a reddish tint from the reflected light of Orbitus, while the midnight sky of Orbitus was bathed in a soft blue radiance reflected from the sunlit ocean of Ragnu. Tiny flashes in the darkness caught his eye, and he realized he was watching a thunderstorm over the midlatitudes of Ragnu.

He turned away from the window. Nkiru was still at it, sitting cross-legged on the bed, the new relic cradled in her lap like a crystal ball. The air in the room smelled like garlic and rosemary. The remains of their dinner were messily spread on the floor where they'd eaten: an empty platter that had been heaped with pasta, the remains of a block of hard cheese, a torn loaf of freshly baked bread, two empty bottles of Italian wine imported from Earth. Se-Jong had spared no expense on the meal. Centerpoint was a popular tourist destination with restaurants that catered to the wealthy. After weeks of eating greasy protoham and drinking ship's water recycled from liquid waste, a room-service meal from a fancy restaurant had been a fabulous treat, just what they'd deserved. After all, they were celebrating.

He'd never seen Nkiru so excited, or so uneasy. Like the scancorder and the stealthshield, the thing he'd dubbed the *snowglobe* had glimmered to life as soon as she'd touched it. She'd actually gasped when it had lit up, her face flooded with desperate relief. Whatever this thing was, she was *really* glad it was working.

It was the size of a softball and seemed to be made of glass or some other transparent crystalline material. A subdued red glow, much weaker than the light of a candle, formed an indeterminate haze at its core, while dispersed throughout its crystal structure danced minuscule particles of light that flickered like dust motes in the beam of a flashlight. He briefly wondered if the floating particles would spin and swarm if you shook it like a real snowglobe. He didn't think so. As far as he could tell, the globe wasn't filled with liquid: it was solid crystal.

She asked Se-Jong to turn off the room lights. As she tucked the snowglobe between her knees, sparkle from the flickering motes made static dots on the dark skin of her inner thighs, little constellations of stars. Just above, her tight jaw and deeply furrowed brow were bottom lit by the blue glow of her komnic. Dressed in slight panties and a green camisole, she looked entirely magical, some long-limbed forest sprite who'd just unearthed a dangerous secret from beneath the roots of an ancient tree. The shape formed by her white hair as it arced around her dark face reminded Se-Jong of a yin-yang symbol, the dualities of light and dark, fire and water.

Maybe she *was* magical, he thought. Somehow, she'd cracked a code that scientists and clerics had been searching for since the Rapture. As far as he knew, nobody, not the mightiest Cataclyst priest or the most powerful Mucktu sorcerer, had ever been able to activate an avatar relic. Se-Jong keenly felt the importance of this moment, even though he didn't quite understand it. Sitting in front of him was a girl not yet twenty-two years of age who'd just made one of the most important archeological discoveries of the Third Epoch and was poised to make even more.

He gently cleared his throat. "Hey."

"Hmm?" She didn't turn her attention from the screen of her komnic.

"I'm definitely falling in love with you."

The words had spilled out without him realizing he was about to say them.

She didn't move, but her gaze flicked away from her komnic toward him. Her face remained neutral, and her voice held the distracted tone of a person abruptly disconnected from a deep thought. She blinked. "What?"

"You heard me."

Her mouth fell open as if she were about to respond, but then it just hung there. She stared at him, unmoving.

Someone out in the hallway shouted and laughed. Nkiru still didn't move. Time seemed to stretch out. Se-Jong didn't know how long he waited. It felt like years. An intense calm flooded his soul, like a deep, cool river, washing away all his worries and fears. She closed her mouth and shifted uncomfortably, as if the weight of the magical snowglobe in her lap had just increased tenfold.

"That . . . might not be a good idea," she finally said.

"I don't care." He felt like a puppet, with somebody else controlling his voice. Somebody who wasn't afraid to say exactly what he felt. He was in good hands. He waited to see what his puppeteer would say next.

Nkiru licked her lips. "Se-Jong, I—"

"I like it when you call me Se-Jong," he said.

Confusion flashed across her face. "I don't think . . . I mean, now isn't a good time—"

"Now is a perfect time," came his smooth, confident words. He smiled. All was right with the world. He felt the warm glow of love all around and—

"Would you *please* stop interrupting me," she demanded sharply.

The bubble of tender confidence that had surrounded Se-Jong popped and vanished. He swallowed. "Sorry," he mumbled. "I just—"

"You're just drunk," she said, pointing at the bottles of wine. "I only had a sip; you drank the rest."

"So what if I'm drunk?" he said, and for the first time he heard the slur in his own words. "Doesn't matter. I meant what I said." He turned his attention back to the window and the majestic view of Ragnu and Orbitus. The equatorial lightning storm had intensified down on the surface of the ocean world, a cascading ripple of light revealing the billowing tops of a sprawling thundercloud.

A moving point of light caught his eye. A ship was transiting above the planet, heading for the Centerpoint spaceport. He leaned closer to the window glass, stopping when his forehead bumped the cool, smooth surface. The ship was barely more than a tiny splinter of light, but it glinted oddly, for an instant reflecting sunlight like a mirror. He squinted. Silver-metallic, long and thin . . . like a needle.

He'd never seen the *Navis Sacris* before, but everyone knew what the flagship of the church's Holy Navy looked like. A slender silver needle, mirrored hull, pointed at both ends, two hundred meters long. Unknown propulsion system—it didn't have accelerator wings like every other interstellar ship in the Known Arc. And it was *fast*, far faster than even the Solar Guard's fleetest starcutters. It was the personal transport of the church elite, including the Father Regis himself.

Se-Jong cursed under his breath and glanced surreptitiously back at Nkiru. She was still sitting cross-legged on the bed, her attention back on her komnic. Her expression was different, though. Something glimmered on her cheek. She reached up to wipe it off with the back of her hand. He'd been an idiot. He'd upset her by mentioning love. Stupid, stupid, stupid.

He looked away, back toward the window. The tiny, slender shape had vanished, lost against the massive cloud banks of the planet below. Maybe he'd imagined it. He stared for a long time, searching the dark thunderclouds, but saw nothing but sparkles of lightning.

"Damn, damn, damn," he muttered. Seeing Nkiru's tears had caused something new to bloom in his gut. Unlike the chaos that had surrounded him from the moment he'd first seen her, this new emotion was something familiar, something he could understand. If he had any role in Nkiru's story, it was as her protector, and it was high time for him to take action to secure her safety. The Dei Militans would no doubt be searching for the phantom thief who'd taken an artifact from the Regium's sacred reliquaries. He leaned his head against the cool glass of the window and watched the thunderstorm grow on the surface of the planet below, a germ of a plan sprouting in his mind.

———

To Se-Jong's great relief, they boarded their transport without incident early the following morning. The *Legacy Sky* was newer and larger than either the *Covenant of Andrik* or the cramped *Rose & Chalice*. Where the first two vessels had been converted from long-retired Guild transports, the *Legacy Sky* had once served as a luxury hyperliner, which meant the berths were larger and had private bathrooms. Best of all, the ship featured a massive observation lounge with dozens of tables and an expansive glass window from which the passengers could behold the wonders of the cosmos. True, the bulkhead paint was peeling, and the chairs and tables were stained and battered, but this ship was a vast improvement over their previous transports. As they boarded alongside almost two hundred others, jostling for position in the crowded line, Se-Jong joked to Nkiru that the upcoming leg of the pilgrimage would be wonderful if it weren't for all the pilgrims.

———

The entire ship's complement crowded into the observation deck for the departure from Centerpoint. He and Nkiru snared a table near the base of the big window. Despite the truly mind-jacking view, she seemed troubled. He worried that she might be upset by the things he'd said the previous evening. She seemed to be pretending that his drunken profession of love had never happened, which suited Se-Jong just fine.

The maneuvering siren sounded. Conversations became subdued as everyone in the lounge rotated their seats to face the window and buckled their seatbelts. The captain's voice came over the speaker. "Attention. Attention. This is your captain. Prepare for close maneuvers. Anticipate lateral inertial surges beyond the limits of the artificial gravity. In other words, ladies and gentlemen and trins and quads, buckle up, hold on tight, and enjoy the view!"

A series of staccato clangs sounded through the bulkheads, and with stomach-twirling suddenness, the ship began to move. Through the soaring glass window, the docking port rotated smoothly out of view. A sheet of sunlight poured around the edge of the window and crossed the observation deck like an opening curtain of light.

Appreciative gasps and murmurs filled the air as the fully sunlit surfaces of Orbitus and Ragnu hove into sight. Beyond the shiny metallic sphere of Centerpoint, the Skybridge fell away in both directions like a lesson in perspective, its two ends dwindling in opposite directions to the anchor points on both worlds.

As the ship spun into the direction of its travel, the spectacle of the Skybridge rotated away to be replaced by a sparse field of stars. They were headed coreward, toward the massive region of broken space-time known as the Devastation. Se-Jong felt a hollow regret when confronted by the morosely vacant skies. Before the Cataclysm, the same view would have been crowded by the blazing star fields at the heart of the Milky Way. Now, just a few stragglers twinkled between their location and the edge of the Devastation. One of those forlorn pinpricks of light was their destination.

Grone.

The name made him shiver, and his spirits lifted with excitement. Could there really be an entire, unspoiled First Epoch dungeon waiting there, as Nkiru claimed? If so, the two of them were about to make history. He tried to imagine his grandmother's face as he told her he'd helped to discover a new dungeon. She wouldn't have any choice but to admit that his decision to accompany Nkiru had been a brilliant stroke of fortune.

Soon enough, Se-Jong could hear and feel the rumble of the hypervee dynamos spinning up. The passengers watched and chattered excitedly as the ship's accelerator wings began to unfurl like the sails of an ancient wooden ship. Once they were fully extended, the energy from the hypervee dynamos surged through the sails, outlining their shapes with tiny bolts of blue lightning. Without any change of sensation, the star-speckled blackness of space vanished into the swirling colorless mist of hypervee. They were on their way.

Almost everyone clapped. For many of the passengers, Se-Jong knew, the pilgrimage was probably the first and only time in their entire life they'd ever leave their homeworld or experience space travel. He scanned the upturned faces. Most were filled with wonder and joy. He recognized many of the individuals from the earlier legs of the pilgrimage route, but there were also many new faces, including, astonishingly, a group of three Ghasts who were alone at a table that would otherwise seat a dozen. Some of the passengers were praying, a few loudly reciting the Avatar's Creed, thanking the Oa for the miracle of their creation. He'd never seen such a serene crowd, not even after the Mass Chant ceremony of a particularly uplifting church service.

Suddenly Se-Jong locked eyes with one of the unfamiliar newcomers, a bearded and shaggy-headed human standing against a far bulkhead near one of the exit hatches. The man was dressed in unusually ragged pilgrims' robes but was otherwise unremarkable except for his brash stare. He'd obviously been studying Se-Jong for some time, ignoring the vista unfolding through the window.

Se-Jong's smile faded. He gave the man a hostile glare. The man looked away, fumbled at something inside the waist of his robe, and slipped out through the exit hatch. Se-Jong felt a tightness grip his chest. He glanced over at Nkiru. She was also looking in the direction of the shaggy-haired man, frowning suspiciously. She'd seen him, too. Her lips formed a silent curse.

HACKER

meatspace | ZIA

Crazy Shit

Arni didn't greet Zia when she arrived, just unlocked the door and dropped despondently into Havenlab's weather-beaten armchair. Zia hurriedly unpacked her laptop and set it up on the adjacent table. He listened without reaction as she explained that the JEEB Earth sim had been taken from the military's Sentinel engine, and that he was the prime suspect for the theft. She logged into her laptop and brought up a copy of the video from the JEEB lab, turning the screen toward Arni. He watched it intently, but without expression. When it was over, he turned his bloodshot eyes in her direction. "What the hell?"

"Howe and Solomon believe the man in the video is Roland Wolfe's capatar. Chun thinks he found an Orb and a way to transmit through the firewall."

Arni squinted at the screen. "*Was* Roland Wolfe's capatar, you mean. That blue woman cut him in half."

"Arni, this proves that capatars do respawn! How else could Wolfe have survived for thousands of years in the accelerated timestream? If Wolfe is still alive, then so is Analise!"

Arni looked unusually sluggish. "Yeah, but did you see him? He looked like shit. Like a madman. Maybe his capatar survived, but people weren't built to live forever. He's not Wolfe anymore." He expelled a breath, and Zia knew what he must be thinking. *If ten thousand years of enforced immortality has turned Wolfe into a raving lunatic, what has it done to Analise?*

She raised her voice. "Did you *hear* me? Wolfe and Analise are *alive*. This message is proof the gamecosm is still running on the Haven engine." She tried to slow the excited rush of words. "Wolfe migrated the JEEB sim to the Haven machine for a reason. He knows the JEEB environment has a more advanced version of the capatar code than the early version you and Analise copied to the Haven engine. He probably detected our failed attempt to spawn your capatar. Maybe by stealing the government's more advanced code, he's sending us a message."

The poorly ventilated air in the grocery-store lab was stale and hot. Arni shrugged wearily. "There's no way Wolfe could've migrated JEEB Earth to Haven." His voice was slow and slurred. "Even without the firewall, you can't move a part of one cosm into another cosm on a different machine. It violates the laws of—"

"Yeah, yeah, it violates the laws of physics," she scoffed. "That's what Chun kept saying, over and over. Trouble is, it *happened*, laws of physics be damned. You know what it means? *With the more advanced capatar software, we can try again!* Your nanospecks are still active. There's nothing stopping us from sending you into the cosm *right now*." She paused. "What the hell is wrong with you?"

Arni's eyelids had closed, and his jaw hung stupidly open. She looked around the lab and saw the beer cans tumbled across the floor beneath his workstation. A stab of fury shot through her chest, and she kicked Arni's extended leg, hard. "Are you kidding me? You're *drunk*?"

He yelped. His eyes flew open. "Holy shitbags, Zia. She can't still be alive. The machine's kernel activity is unstable as hell. I doubt the rendering engine is even working, and even if it is, the sim clock is out of control. It's been ten thousand years inside the havencosm. She's *dead*. Or *worse*. It's too *late*. Analise is gone, and we're all going to prison."

She felt the muscles of her face twisting into a snarl. "Ty che, suka, o'khuel blya? You will *not* give up on her; suka, blyad! Get your ass up out of that chair." When he didn't move, she slammed her fist into his armchair's headrest. "Rupe and I have risked *everything* to help you, you ungracious ass. Either you're going in-cosm, or I'll put on the goddamned cap and rescue Analise myself!"

"You can't," he reminded her. He tapped the side of his skull. "No nanospecks."

"There's a spare dose," she pointed out.

Arni rose unsteadily from the chair. "Nope. It's formulated for my blood type. Did you know Thomas Edison had AB-negative blood, too? It's the blood type of creative geniuses." He lurched and she reached out to steady him. He patted her on the shoulder and leaned close enough for her to smell the reek of beer on his breath. "Thanks, my friend," he said. For the first time since she'd arrived, his eyes focused on her. He looked over toward the table where the Haven engine hummed quietly "So Wolfe is alive and kicking inside that little silver box. Huh. Interesting."

"He's alive," she said. "And so is Analise."

"And he found a way to move JEEB Earth into the havencosm? He could do that?"

"Yes. Solomon said Wolfe was the second-best hacker in the world."

"After you, of course."

"Of course. And who knows? Maybe Analise helped Wolfe migrate JEEB Earth. It was part of her plan all along, if you remember." She paused. "Here's what I think. In order for Wolfe to escape back to his meatspace body, he has to trigger the capatar extraction system, right?"

"Yeah."

"But he *can't*, because the interface for the extraction code can only be accessed inside the Foundation Core, and there's no way for a game character to enter the Core without one of the emoras."

Arni shook his head. "Even if Wolfe managed to find one of the emoras, it wouldn't work for him. The system only recognizes avatars with archangel-level clearance, *period*. And a capatar is *not* an avatar. Even if I could take the Shadow Emora with me, which I can't, I couldn't use it because it only works for an avatar. Without a way into the Foundation Core, my capatar will be just as trapped as Wolfe's."

She scoffed. "You *designed* the Foundation Core. You coded most of it. If anybody can figure out a way to hack into it, you can. With the time dilation effect, your capatar will have plenty of time to figure it out." She put as much emotion as she could muster into her voice. "Arni, we *have* to try. Analise will die if we don't."

He reached out to squeeze her shoulder. He seemed to understand that her feelings for Analise went beyond simple friendship. In this they were kindred spirits. "I'll make some coffee, and we can get started." He released her shoulder. "This is some crazy shit, isn't it?"

She nodded. "*Crazy Shit* will be the title of my memoir."

Zia Pyotrovna Volkov was no stranger to crazy shit. Crazy shit didn't scare her. In fact, she *thrived* on it. Truth was, she'd changed the course of world history more than once, and nobody had any inkling. Had Zia's victims realized that they had been attacked and defeated, then her life's work would have been a failure.

Before her work with the US government, Zia had been a freelancer, working out of coffee shops and public libraries, anywhere with free and anonymous wifi. Her specialty had been a sort of undetectable computer virus that was designed to prowl the deep connections and interfaces within the bowels of the world's digital networks, looking for specific traces of activity or certain code signatures. When the virus found such a trigger, it would secretly and subtly insinuate itself into the target codebase like a tiny, invisible spore, where it would sit silently, waiting for a certain state or condition, sometimes for years.

When the trigger condition was met, the spore-virus would begin to ever-so-elusively alter the operation of the software in a way that was entirely undetectable. Most of Zia's spores were designed to affect the deepest kernels of embedded systems, the kind of software that humans never see, the kind that is buried deep inside a machine's guts. This type of software, called an embedded controller, runs everyday machines like refrigerators and ATMs and automobile engines. More relevant to Zia's clients, embedded controllers also run traffic signals and jet engines and dam floodgates and guidance systems for nuclear missiles.

Zia's spores were like little covert operatives, sabotaging the enemy's operations from behind their lines. In a way, her spores were far more sinister than any bomb or missile. One of her tiniest little spores, uploaded from a Starbucks in Atlanta, had been used to prevent a power plant in Syria from providing peak load at a specific time on a specific day, resulting in a blackout that had foiled a planned government operation against rebel forces. One of her spores, written at a beachside bar on Ibiza, had diverted the aim of an American cruise-missile test so that its targeting system seemed to be at fault, causing over a year of delay in deploying the missile. Another spore, created in a studio apartment over a bakery in Seoul, had caused the introduction of a specific chemical into the water supply of a military base in Iran, giving three entire divisions of the Islamic Revolutionary Guard a bad case of the shits, resulting in the cancelation of a major training exercise. A simple little spore, written propped up in bed with a purring cat in her lap, had targeted an Emirates airliner and caused it to inexplicably lose cabin pressure, forcing an emergency landing in Tel Aviv where Israeli police were able to detain a Frenchman with known ties to ISIS. Yet another of her spores had caused the oxygen levels on a particular Russian submarine to read normally even though the crew was suffering from a continual state of mild hypoxia that eventually led them to make a series of bad decisions, resulting in the court-martial of the captain. She was particularly proud of this one, written in a Portland kombucha bar and uploaded while watching a pirated copy of *Hunt for Red October*.

Thanks to the subtle genius of Zia's spores, in all these cases nobody would ever suspect malicious intent, and nobody would ever know why things had gone so terribly wrong. Zia was a superstar of darkness, a warrior princess of smoke and illusion. Her work for governments ranging from Israel to the UK to China had always been arranged through a dazzlingly complex array of intermediaries. She was a specter, supremely confident that she'd completely shielded herself from discovery.

That is, until the day when a covert American agent had plopped down across from her at a coffee shop in Montreal wearing jeans and a Black Sabbath T-shirt. With a vicious smile, he'd pushed an envelope across the table at her—an envelope that contained a threat, and an offer she literally could not refuse.

Polumrak

"I've got a good image," Zia reported. The ESP scanner showed a rotating 3D image of Arni's thoughts. More accurately, the image depicted the quantum vibrational activity of the engineered subatomic particles—the ESPs—embedded in Arni's brain. It had been twenty-four days since the particles had been injected in their first failed attempt at projecting a capatar into the havencosm, and nobody knew how long the ESPs would remain viable. At some point the natural cleansing action of the brain would purge the cells in which the particles were embedded. Hopefully, enough remained in his system for the capatar link to work.

Arni squinted up at her from his overstuffed armchair. The BCI cap looked ridiculous on him. Its fabric covering had been hand sewn by Analise, and though she might be an expert physicist, she was no seamstress. Zia wiped the cold sweat from her neck and nodded at him.

"It looks good. Are you ready to lose your mind?"

"I am so *very* ready." His nervous smile exposed his anxiety. Despite the chill, he was sweating, too. They'd spent the last three hours fine-tuning their plan. He would spawn into the havencosm's Avatar Mall as a capatar and use his prodigious software skills to hack into the Foundation Core, a secure location in the cosm restricted to programmers. Using the virtual tools available at the Foundation Core, he would fix the racing system clock and resynchronize it to the timestream of the real world. Then he would lower the mysterious firewall that the system had apparently erected automatically, and that had prevented them from rescuing Analise before now. The moment the firewall fell, Zia would gain visibility into the cosm and be able to instantly locate the capatars of Analise and Wolfe. She would then trigger the extraction process to bring all three capatars home.

After that, the plan was a little hazy. It probably involved a substantial jail sentence unless Analise could prove her theory to the authorities and justify the extraordinary lengths they had gone to in order to protect her world-changing breakthroughs.

Zia handed Arni a small coin. "It's a shekel," she said. "It's old, from the time of the Roman Empire. It has always brought me luck." She watched as Arni tucked it in the pocket of his leather flight jacket.

"You know it won't go in-cosm with me," he said. "My capatar will be naked as a baby."

"It's not for your capatar. It's for *you*." She sniffed to cover up the choking feeling in her throat. "Get it done and get out, okay? Don't waste time being a tourist. I don't want to have to change your nappies." Arni's smile widened, and he nodded reassuringly. In preparation for an induced capatar coma that might last many long hours, Arni had donned a pair of adult diapers.

Arni took a deep breath, then suddenly reached out with both hands. Zia took them and squeezed. She was almost crying, though she would never let Arni see tears. Strength seemed to flow into Arni, and he held her grip for a long moment. "Okay, let's go."

Zia had met Dr. Analise Novak for the first time at the JEEB office kickoff meeting. From the moment Analise had entered the conference room, Zia couldn't stop looking at her. On the surface, she was the classic example of everything Zia hated in modern society—a privileged little white girl from a wealthy American family with a perfect little body and a perfect little life. She was tiny, probably forty-five kilos soaking wet, but there was no denying that her presence had lit the room like a thousand-watt bulb. Analise had seduced the entire assemblage with her easy smile, her confident expression, and a crackling spark of intelligence that energized the collective mood. Everyone wanted to be near her, talk to her. Even Reggie Howe, the unflappable project manager, had cracked a furtive smile whenever he looked at Analise.

Despite herself, Zia was dazzled. It was surprising, really. Analise was most certainly *not* her type. After her first high-school crush (an image of the rock star P!nk on the cover of *Cosmopolitan*), Zia had dated a few times, but only once seriously: an aspiring singer-songwriter named Noemi whose melancholy songs and haunting voice might have propelled her to stardom had it not been for her self-destructive behaviors. Noemi had been deeply exotic. Moody, passionate and artistic, deeply intelligent but unable to control the substance-abuse demons that eventually ate her soul.

Analise, on the other hand, was a textbook American-girl success story, daughter of a surgeon and a pharmaceutical executive, poised and graceful, with green eyes and lightly freckled skin that lacked a single piercing or stroke of tattoo ink. She was undeniably brilliant, one of the youngest PhDs ever produced from Stanford University's neurophysics program. Unlike Noemi, who had spent her days fighting a long and inexorable slide into tragedy, Analise was one of those enviable people for whom the universe seemed to bend its ways to make life easy.

Analise, along with Arni, had been on the team under the mentorship of Dr. Chun that had developed the world's first operational QARMA kernel. It had been Analise who had created the breakthrough method of linking entangled subatomic nanospecks to the synaptic junctions of the human brain. In fact, Analise had been Chun's star protégé, right up until she wrote a paper titled "The Probabilistic Nature of the QARMA Effect in Synaptic Entropy States." Zia had read it and found it incomprehensible. It had disputed one of Dr. Chun's most cherished theories, and when the consensus of the scientific community had shifted toward Analise's competing views, Chun had attempted to blackball Analise from the world of academic research. This nasty breakup had forced Analise out of the world of academia and into the welcoming arms of the military-industrial complex. Within a month of her dismissal by Chun, Analise had been working for a consulting firm with ties to DARPA, the military's advanced research program, where she continued her work exploring the mind-machine boundary. Ironically, when she was assigned to the JEEB project, she and Chun had been forced to work together again. Only now, to Chun's great dismay, Analise was on the power side of the equation.

The genuine kindness that Analise had shown Zia on their first meeting had completely upended Zia's preconceived notions. Analise had walked up to Zia, taken her hand, and looked right into her soul with those electrifying green eyes. She'd not noticed the lip ring or the acne scars or the regrettable knuckle tattoos that spelled П О Л У М Р А К. She'd simply squeezed Zia's hand and, with totally authentic delight, had said, "I am *so* excited to finally meet you. You and I are going to do great things together!"

And *boom*, just like everyone else, Zia Pyotrovna had fallen under the thrall of Analise Novak.

Infection

Arni closed his eyes and leaned back into the overstuffed chair. From her location at the ESP scanner, Zia smiled. The machine had successfully interfaced with the JEEB capatar spawn system. This confirmed the theory that JEEB Earth, along with its underlying enhancements to the capatar software, had been migrated into the havencosm.

"We're linked to the spawn platform in the Avatar Mall. Beginning the render."

The cooling fan on the ESP scanner whined as the machine strained to detect the trillions of nanospecks embedded in Arni's skull. Zia hovered the mouse pointer over the START command but hesitated. Despite Arni's bravado, they both knew there were too many unknowns, too many risks. The accelerated passage of virtual time inside the havencosm was especially worrying. The hope was that Arni's capatar would spawn into a fully functional virtual sim, but it was a real possibility that he would materialize into a completely broken virtual reality where time and space were twisted beyond recognition. It might instantly kill his capatar and leave him permanently comatose in the lab's armchair. Or, his mind might be trapped in a vortex of virtual delirium, unable to escape. Even if he succeeded, from the instant he went in-cosm, for every second that passed in the lab, a day and a half would pass for Arni's capatar. For every hour that she and Rupe anxiously waited, fourteen *years* would pass in the havencosm. If Arni's body remained in the armchair for a full day, over *three centuries* would pass for his capatar.

Any of these fates might already have befallen Analise. Even if her capatar was still alive after ten thousand virtual years trapped inside a universe built for a video game, how would Arni find her? After all, there were thousands of planets in the game simulation. Even if by some miracle of miracles her capatar had managed to survive the millennia inside the havencosm, would she even remember who she'd been?

It didn't matter. They had no choice. Zia's finger descended on the mouse button. *Click.*

―

In the beginning days of the JEEB project, Zia had tried to ignore Analise's presence in the JEEB lab. Analise had made it impossible. She'd obviously made it a point to befriend every single member of the JEEB team, including the reclusive Russian-Israeli hacker responsible for digital security. She'd kept coming by Zia's desk, ostensibly just to chat, or to drop off one of the homemade baked treats she was always distributing to her coworkers. If it had been anyone else, Zia would have put an immediate stop to it. She'd never been good at social interactions, especially not with the popular girls and their disingenuous personalities. Zia had initially convinced herself that Analise's overt kindness was a sham, a cover for some hidden agenda, and it had taken months for Zia to realize that the behavior was completely genuine. She'd never before met anyone like Analise. It had been utterly impossible *not* to fall in love with her.

The only person who didn't love Analise was Dr. Chun. Zia had gotten a firsthand taste of their relationship at one of the rare meetings where they were both present. Analise and Chun had argued about some obscure technical artifact of the QARMA engine. Analise criticized Chun's approach, and Chun exploded in front of the entire JEEB team, accusing Analise and her boyfriend, Arni, of conspiring to wreck Orbital Arena's business. She charged them with making unauthorized modifications to the software that had affected the entire game environment. Analise denied the accusations, and her response convinced everyone in the room that Chun had held an academic grudge for far too long. Everyone, that is, but Zia, who'd glimpsed an instantaneous but undeniable flicker of hidden purpose in Analise's green eyes. It was that moment when Zia began to suspect that she'd been deceived by Analise's demeanor. Perhaps Analise had a hidden agenda after all.

That very evening, from a laptop in a Palo Alto coffee shop, Zia did what she did best: *hacked*. Arni and Analise had been careful, but their security precautions fell like bowling pins to Zia's cypher-breaking babies. What she discovered in a hidden and encrypted folder on Arni's workstation twisted her intellect to the breaking point. She spent the next two hours examining the files, drinking cup after cup of Turkish mud coffee, growing more and more confused and excited. It took less than thirty minutes to pinpoint the location of the makeshift lab where Arni and Analise were planning their covert action against both Orbital Arena and the JEEB program. After that, it took only ten minutes to drive from the coffee shop to their secret lair in the abandoned grocery store. When she banged on the door, Analise answered. Upon seeing Zia, Analise had hesitated, then smiled ruefully and opened the door wider, inviting Zia into an irresistible conspiracy that would forever change the course of human history.

Analise had called it the *jeeb virus*, because she'd first detected it on the JEEB program's Sentinel engine. At first, she hadn't recognized that it was a foreign intrusion. After all, QARMA engines were based on an entirely new computing paradigm and were therefore completely invulnerable to classic viruses. After studying the virus's odd behavior for over a month, she'd shown it to Zia, who was mortified that it had slipped through all the intrusion detection routines. After all, it was Zia's job to make sure that nobody could hack the Sentinel engine. Yet there on Analise's screen was proof that somebody had done the impossible. The hack was subtle, discreet, and completely untraceable. It affected the deep-core routines of the QARMA kernel in such a way that none of the kernel's external interfaces showed any sign of manipulation. She felt an intense stab of jealousy. Zia was a virtuoso in the world of ultra-elite hacking, and in this mysterious virus she recognized the work of a true master.

She'd been furious. By keeping the viral intrusion a secret, Analise had exposed a top secret US military program to potential foreign interference. "Why didn't you tell me about this?" Zia protested. "Why didn't you tell *anybody*?"

Analise had smiled, and the electric sparkle in those incredible green eyes ramped up to lightning voltage. She opened a video chat window on her computer and gestured at the woman on the screen. "Because of *her*."

At first, Zia had thought it was a selfie image from Analise's own webcam, because it showed Analise's face staring into the camera. But when Analise moved out of her chair and motioned Zia to take her place, the image on the screen didn't move correspondingly.

Analise motioned toward the screen. "Zia, meet Analise."

On the screen, the image of Analise had peered back suspiciously. "Hello, Zia," it said.

Malfunction

SPAWNING... PLEASE WAIT

The status bar crawled across the screen of the ESP scanner. Zia looked down at Arni, who hadn't moved since the spawn sequence had begun.

On the screen below the status bar, line after line of text flashed up the screen. It was scrolling too fast for her to read, though occasionally she could make out a specific line when the list paused during the execution of a particularly complex command.

```
Resolving etherium pathway... 100%
Activating spawn platform 19E0AF... 100%
Establishing platform exclusion zone... 100%
Gene scan complete... 100%
Starting capatar render engine
Rendering capatar... 0%
```

At this point a secondary status bar appeared, and her heart leapt into her throat. The machine had established a connection to the spawn area, and the virtual body of Arni's capatar was in the process of being created.

```
Rendering capatar... 100%
```

Her hand was shaking. She lifted it from the mouse, rubbed it. "Your clone awaits," she announced.

Arni smiled without opening his eyes. "Okay. I'm ready. Do it."

She clicked BEGIN ENTANGLEMENT.

```
Starting entanglement...
ESP scanner: Kaiser-Salim test... PASSED
Stimulating ventrolateral preoptic
nucleus of subject hypothalamus
Subject unconscious: CONFIRMED
Scanning for nanospecks... 100%
Source nanospecks density... MARGINAL
```

At this point the display froze, and she let out an involuntary "Oh, no." She glanced down at Arni, but the system had already induced unconsciousness.

On the screen, a message appeared:

```
Nanospeck resolution in player's brain is
at minimum threshold levels.
Continue with spawn process?
WARNING: Process is irreversible from
this point.

Y/N
```

In the weeks since Arni had injected himself with the first batch of nanospecks, many of the particles had already been cleansed from their correct positions in his brain. Were there enough left? She could stop the process now and they could try again later. The problem was, they couldn't give Arni another dose of nanospecks without deactivating the ones already in his brain. That took a special machine they didn't have.

If she chose to continue, the ESP scanner would attempt to link the remaining nanospecks in Arni's organic brain with the virtual neurons in his capatar's brain. She didn't know what would happen if the density was too low for the link to be successful. Most likely, the spawn process would fail. If it did, would the failure harm Arni? He was already in the capatar coma, so she couldn't ask him what he wanted to do. And for every second she hesitated, a day and a half was passing in the accelerated timestream of the havencosm.

She knew without a doubt what *she* would want if she were in his situation. On the keyboard, she pressed *Y*.

```
Starting entanglement...
```

The percentage rose slowly. At 93% it froze, and the machine chimed.

```
Link to capatar... malfunction detected.
Attempting capatar extraction... failed.
```

"Wait. No. This can't be right," she muttered. A sinking feeling like she'd never felt before began in her gut. She lurched toward the armchair and grabbed Arni's shoulders. "Wake up! Wake up!"

```
WARNING: Carrier detected, but link
incomplete.
ENTERING SAFE MODE
```

Arni's body moved like a rag doll under her hands. His head lolled to the side, stretching the cables that connected his BCI cap to the machine. The sinking feeling intensified, and a powerful wave of vertigo caused her to grab the solid bulk of the ESP scanner. She wondered if she was having a panic attack. She'd never had one before, but then again, she'd never murdered a friend before.

```
WARNING: QARMA field instability
detected; recommend shutdown.
SHUT DOWN?

Y/N
```

A pale fog of purple light filled the room. It was everywhere, all at once, with no apparent source. She barely noticed when she fell, cracking her head on the concrete floor. Her eyeglasses skittered away. She reached for them, but a broad crack appeared in the concrete and she jerked back. She clutched the base of the ESP scanner, trying to fight the intense nausea that had gripped her like a vise.

She waited for the earth tremor to subside, but it only grew stronger. The ceiling tiles began falling like leaves in a windstorm, crashing in clouds of dust onto the delicate equipment of Arni's lab.

This was not just another tremor. The floor juddered with increasing savagery, breaking into a jigsaw puzzle of little concrete islands. Jagged cracks tore through the walls as the concrete blocks shifted and jostled and sprayed broken mortar into the room. The lights flickered, then went out, and were replaced by the dim glow of emergency lighting. She screamed but couldn't hear herself. There was no way she could dodge the heavy ESP scanner as it teetered and toppled toward her.

―

After her first visit to Arni's makeshift lab, Zia had had a million questions about what she had seen, especially concerning the behavior of the bot with Analise's face. Analise had promised to answer them all. She'd invited Zia to the apartment she shared with Arni for "wine and enlightenment," and even though every paranoid fiber of Zia's being had screamed *NO!*, she'd instantly accepted the invitation. To a hacker like Zia whose life was based on utter secrecy and anonymity, Analise's openness, especially as she was casually admitting to the felonies she and Arni were in the process of committing, was astonishing. To someone like Analise who peered into the infinite swirling cauldron of QARMA physics on a daily basis, petty little things like rules and laws just didn't seem to apply.

Analise had sunk tiredly onto the couch next to Zia, tucking her legs beneath her, nursing her own wineglass. It had been a remarkable day, a day of surprises that had rocked Zia's notions about the JEEB program. Arni and Analise were collaborating on a secret project that neither Orbital Arena nor the military knew about. They had set up their own lab in an abandoned grocery store, complete with an ESP scanner and a QARMA engine that were both probably stolen. Whatever they were doing, they were willing to risk prison to pull it off.

They drank together in silence, Analise staring blankly into nowhere, Zia casting surreptitious glances at Analise's bare legs. Just like Analise, the wineglass was delicate and slender, and Zia's stubby fingers had felt clumsy as she'd tried to grasp it by the stem. She felt like a scraggly crow perched unsteadily on a branch next to a small but beautiful tropical bird. Zia knew that her presence here could get her arrested. She didn't care. She'd always been seduced by the power of technology, and what she'd glimpsed in the Havenlab had completely overwhelmed her reluctance to break the law.

Zia finished her wine and carefully placed the glass on the coffee table. It was strewn with books and papers and crumbs from meals eaten on the couch. Like the coffee table, the entire apartment was surprisingly sloppy. Zia had assumed that Analise's apartment would be as elegant as its occupant, but it was obvious that she was a slob.

They were alone. Arni had remained back at the Havenlab muttering about an "unsolvable" technical problem. Zia could sense a raw excitement just under Analise's skin. Zia knew the feeling; the self-imposed guardianship of extraordinary secrets was an occupational hazard of a hacker. Zia had many of her own stories of triumph that she'd have loved to share with someone who could appreciate them. Maybe, someday, she'd share them with Analise.

"Enlighten me," Zia prompted. The bot on the video chat screen had looked like Analise. It had spoken in Analise's voice with identical speech mannerisms and physical idiosyncrasies. It *wasn't* Analise, though: that much had been clear when Zia had questioned it and its responses had shown little understanding of its own past or its current situation. It had seemed confused, unsure. It had behaved like a version of Analise stricken by amnesia. "That was your doppelgänger, wasn't it?"

Zia's role in the JEEB project was to safeguard the traditional digital networks and systems that surrounded and interfaced with the QARMA tech. She'd never been allowed to interact with the QARMA engine or its operating software directly; that part of the project was above her security clearance. She did know the basics: that the JEEB Earth sim combined billions of sources of personal and census data with cell-phone locations and social media profiles to create a virtual copy of every individual on Earth. Technically, these virtual replicas of real people were manifested by the same AI software as the bots in the game, but the JEEB programmers had dubbed them *doppelgängers*.

Their role was to make combat scenarios more authentic by providing a realistic civilian background population.

Analise sipped her wine. "What did you think of her?"

"It's amazing. She looked and sounded *exactly* like you."

"What about her behavior? Notice anything strange?"

"She seemed a little . . . simple," Zia had replied. When Analise frowned, she added: "But I guess that's all that's needed for a background actor in a combat simulator."

"What about her emotions?"

"She seemed confused. A little scared."

"Why do you think she was scared? Didn't you think that was odd? What programming trigger caused her to be frightened? She wasn't being threatened by an attacker or a dangerous situation. Programmatically, she had no reason to be afraid or confused."

Zia chuckled. "Most people are scared all the time, aren't they? Life is scary, after all . . ." Her grin faded at Analise's critical stare.

"You're anthropomorphizing. Remember, it's not a person: it's computer software."

"Um, yeah, I guess it doesn't make sense for software to be afraid. What's causing it, some kind of bug?"

Analise nodded with reserved approval, as if Zia had come close to the truth but hadn't quite nailed it. "From the beginning, something was wrong with the doppelgängers. They were behaving badly. And by badly, I mean their emotional responses were outside the boundaries of the AI behavior templates. As soon as we first booted the JEEB Earth sim, the doppelgängers started to fight among themselves and attack the soldier avatars without provocation. Like you said, at first our engineers thought it was a bug. So, of course, Colonel Solomon blamed Chun and Orbital Arena. And Chun ordered Arni to figure out what was wrong."

Analise chuckled grimly. "Clearance was necessary to work at the JEEB lab, so Solomon made Arni apply for a top-secret security clearance. During the background check, they discovered that one of Arni's brothers back in Pakistan had some shady friends. They denied

Arni's security clearance, which meant he couldn't get anywhere near the JEEB system, even though it was an identical copy of the original QARMA engine he and Chun had created."

"That's ridiculous."

She scoffed. "Yeah. He's the biggest nerd you'll ever meet and the farthest thing from a political zealot you can imagine, but the government didn't see it that way."

"So, what happened?"

"I was on the hook. I eventually traced the weird behavior of the JEEB Earth doppelgängers to a single QARMA filament buried in the Sentinel engine."

"The jeeb virus you told me about?"

"Yes. And it was *tiny*, just a single filament."

Zia knew that the architecture of the QARMA engine was based on a hierarchy of programming structures with names like *forests*, *groves*, *roots*, *trunks*, *branches*, *twigs*, *veins*, and *filaments*. Programming in the native language of QARMA was nothing like building code in a traditional digital computer. Chun had once described it as "weaving a tapestry." In the virtual tapestry of QARMA, a *filament* was the tiniest component, like a single whisker of cotton that, when entwined with innumerable other whiskers, made up a strand of thread.

"No matter how hard I tried, I couldn't figure out the purpose of the filament. I couldn't remove it, either. Somehow, it had *spread* to infect the entire system architecture. In the QARMA engine, all filaments are linked to the QARMA kernel itself, and nobody really understands what that means. The filaments somehow draw their functionality directly from the kernel. My best guess was that the jeeb virus had somehow changed the nature of the kernel."

"That can't be good," Zia said. If the Sentinel machine's kernel was infected, that could mean the loss of the entire JEEB program. QARMA kernels were irreplaceable. Nobody but Chun knew how they were manufactured; their origin was the most closely held trade secret of the Orbital Arena corporate empire. Whatever the process, it was monumentally difficult. In over a decade of constant attempts,

Chun had only managed to generate three working kernels. If the Sentinel kernel had been ruined by the jeeb virus, a billion dollars of taxpayers' money had gone up in smoke.

"I was out of my depth. I needed help. I couldn't ask Chun for help—she hates me—but I could ask Arni, her partner."

"But he wasn't allowed to work at the JEEB lab."

"Nope, he wasn't, not without a security clearance. That should've stopped me, but it didn't. I knew Arni from when we'd worked together as part of Chun's postgraduate team at Stanford, and I knew that he understood more about the QARMA engines than Chun herself."

Zia knew that Analise was greatly simplifying the story. She had neglected to mention that during the two years she and Arni had spent together on Chun's team, they had fallen in love, and their relationship had progressed to the point where Arni had asked her to marry him. Zia knew this not from her research, but from the prodigious amount of office gossip on the JEEB team. She also knew that something along the way had come between Arni and Analise just after Analise published her paper disproving Chun's pet QARMA theory. Zia suspected that Chun had offered Arni a position as a founding partner at Orbital Arena Games but had shunned Analise. Chun would never have allowed her upstart rival to have a position at the new company. Arni had obviously accepted Chun's offer, alienating Analise. Or at least that was the prevailing theory in the office gossip. Whatever had caused the breakup, it had apparently been a bitter affair.

Analise was still explaining. "I invited Arni to meet me at a coffee shop. I showed him the weird filament of code. He told me it didn't appear in the original Orbital Arena version of the software; he thought somebody from the military must have put it there. I told him no way. We argued, a lot, but in the end, I convinced him to help me." She grinned. "I can be very convincing."

Yes, you can, thought Zia with a sting of jealousy.

"We spent weeks together here in this apartment trying to decipher the virus, to trace its origin and purpose. There were none of the typical fingerprints of a hacker. The viral filament seemed to have sprouted from *inside* the kernel. Eventually, Arni decided to try to duplicate its functionality on the company's backup QARMA engine: the Haven machine, which was kept in a vault at Orbital Arena. He knew the risk: if we couldn't figure out how to remove the virus from the Haven machine, he would be ruining the last remaining QARMA kernel. He was confident, though. As far as I know, Arni has never encountered a technical problem he couldn't solve. He didn't tell me or Chun or anybody about it; he just did it. I think he was trying to impress me."

At this revelation, Zia swallowed, hard. Arni had risked a billion-dollar prize to regain her affection.

"He set up a lab in the back of the old grocery store. We lived off of coffee and junk food. It took a sleepless month, but we eventually created a test population of bots on the Haven machine. Without the filament of the jeeb virus, the bots acted normally, exactly as they did in the game. Which is to say, exactly as the AI programming dictated they should act. But when we inserted a copy of the jeeb virus filament, things changed dramatically. The bots began behaving erratically, just like the doppelgängers in the JEEB Earth sim. I ran a battery of controlled psychological tests on the bots and couldn't believe what I saw.

"Nothing in the AI code could have produced those results. The jeeb virus had tapped into something in the kernel that couldn't be explained. From the moment they spawned, the bots exhibited completely unexpected behaviors in response to the stimuli dictated by my test plan. When we presented the jeeb-infected bots with situations outside their preprogrammed responses, their actions seemed to indicate a high level of self-awareness and knowledge of cause and effect. In a combat situation, instead of dodging incoming fire and hiding behind obstacles to avoid injury, one test subject showed panic and ran away from the scene, while another became enraged and blindly charged into battle.

"Here's the thing: neither fear nor anger were preprogrammed behaviors for the test scenario. The test subjects' behaviors were in direct conflict with their programmed combat goals. Simply put, the bots were acting exactly like inconsistent, emotional *people*. Whatever the weird code filament was doing, the result was indisputable: the bots in our cosm were *self-aware*."

Zia shifted on her cushion, feeling like a fish speared by Analise's penetrating gaze. "You're fucking with me."

Analise leaned uncomfortably close. "That's what you saw in the eyes of my doppelgänger. She was frightened because she was *sentient*. She could sense that something was wrong with her. She was spawned as an adult, with a fully functioning virtual brain that replicates the functions of the human mind down to the quantum level, and yet she has no idea of her purpose, or the purpose of the world around her. The AI programming gives her instructions for behavior she doesn't really understand. She feels compelled to do certain things, but she doesn't know why. She has a simple set of false memories based on my social media activity, but she has trouble reconciling them with what she sees around her. Basically, she's a person. Not an artificial person: a *real* person. And she's *scared*." Analise peered at Zia over the rim of her glass. "Just let that sink in for a minute."

—

Ferocious pain woke Zia. Her chest was on fire, every breath agony; her mouth was coppery with blood and bitter dust. Everything was darkness.

Where am I?

No, not quite darkness. The mysterious purple fog had vanished, leaving a faint blue glow in the dust-laden air. She turned her head toward the glow, forcing her eyes to focus through the haze.

○△□ | HAVEN

She knew the symbols and the word meant something important, but she couldn't recall what or why. There was something both reassuring and terrifying about the fact that they were still glowing, even though the power was obviously out.

There'd been an earthquake, she remembered. The ceiling had fallen.

Arni! She tried to find him, but the debris limited her view.

She might, or might not, have been moving in and out of consciousness. *What is consciousness, anyway?* Something heavy was on her chest and she could not push it away. It was stealing her breath. A hollow space inside her was filling up with liquid, but she couldn't cough. The darkness rumbled again and again, to the sound of groaning metal and breaking concrete. Time seemed to be passing, but it moved in hesitant, surging waves.

She was swimming upward toward the light, but there was no light.

But there was a voice.

"Zia! Oh, man . . . Where are you?"

It was a familiar voice. She opened her eyes and tried to speak but only managed a hideous bubbling cough. Spears of light were stabbing through the thick, dusty air like inverted searchlights. One of them found her, blinded her.

"Oh, man, here she is!"

Behind the light, a face. Round, with a bushy blond beard and bright-blue eyes. She knew the face.

Rupe. *Wait, he isn't supposed to be here.*

"Don't try to move," he said, and there were tears spilling down his cheeks.

"It's okay," she said, but her words wouldn't form.

He was shouting. "Over here! She's here!"

Then there were many faces, and a crowded babble of voices as somebody lifted the heavy thing away from her and a whole new version of pain flooded her chest. Along with the faces were uniforms: police, fire, EMT. And one she recognized.

Colonel Solomon.

She knew vaguely that some sacred trust had been broken. Solomon should most certainly *not* be here in Arni's grocery-store lab. There were others here from the JEEB lab, too, and they were crowding around the Haven engine, talking in low, earnest voices.

"What happened?" she tried to say, but then they were lifting her, and then she was outside amidst the sound of sirens. She smelled smoke. In the distance across the abandoned parking lot of the old grocery store, she could see the blocky skyline of San Jose. Without her glasses, it was blurry, but it was obvious that it had *changed*. The shapes were ragged, and there were fires and smoke. She looked up. An EMT was kneeling over her, doing something to her chest. Behind his head were Rupe and Solomon, both staring down at her.

Rupe must have gone for help, she realized. Damn him! Then suddenly, *Where's Arni?*

Something caught her eye, something glowing indistinctly in the dusky sky above the heads of Rupe and Solomon. Rupe kept glancing up at it, too.

The shape was hazy and unclear, and it wasn't because Zia had lost her glasses. It was hard to look at, as if it offended her brain. There was something about it that was simply *wrong*. Curled into an impossible ontological bundle, like a slithering knot of Gordian snakes, the shape was vaguely spherical. To her brain it seemed to be twisting and writhing, though to her eyes it was obviously stable and unmoving. It was much bigger than the full moon, but it had a moonlike quality that she suddenly realized was due to its distance. Whatever this thing was, it was big, bigger than the moon, and far outside the Earth's atmosphere.

Zia and Analise had emptied the wine bottle and opened another. Curled at opposite ends of the couch in Analise's apartment, both a little tipsy, Zia had listened while Analise revealed her dangerous secrets. The jeeb virus and the doppelgängers of JEEB Earth had been only the beginning.

After purposely infecting the Haven machine with the jeeb virus and creating a small test population of bots who were, to all appearances, self-aware, sapient beings, Analise and Arni had been confronted by a staggering ethical dilemma. If they were successful in their efforts to destroy the jeeb virus on the Haven engine, it would kill the bots they had created, or at least turn them back into the senseless automatons they were originally intended to be. Furthermore, if they applied the fix to the military's Sentinel server and cleansed the virus from the JEEB Earth sim, they would essentially be murdering the billions of doppelgängers that populated the virtual Earth. How was it any different, Analise argued, than killing the entire population of the *real* Earth?

At first Arni had scoffed. It took almost two months to convince him, during which he and Analise conducted hundreds of experiments with the test population of bots to determine their levels of awareness. It was a difficult task, as the newly-sapient bots differed from real-world humans in that they lacked the life-long memories of a real person. While they had been created with a minimal set of machine-generated memories, the bot's behaviors were oddly divergent, highly neurotic, and often psychotic to the extreme. *You'd be a bit crazy too if you suddenly woke up one morning and realized that you, and everyone else on Earth, had amnesia*, Analise had explained to Arni. *Imagine coming into a world where you can't remember who your parents are. You can drive a car and operate a computer and speak the language, but you don't remember learning any of it—and everyone around you is in the same boat. Just imagine what kind of society might arise from that kind of beginning?*

Eventually, Arni came to realize that Analise was right. Despite the bizarre behaviors, by every clinical and psychological definition the bots were living, thinking beings. To kill a bot in the virtual world would be no different than murdering a person in the real world.

Analise told Zia how she and Arni had furiously debated whether they should tell Chun or Colonel Solomon about their discovery. Arni argued that the government had spent a billion dollars on the Sentinel machine and wouldn't care if the removal of the jeeb virus restored the doppelgängers to their original state of robotic senselessness. "That's exactly what they want," he'd proclaimed. "They see the doppelgängers' behavior as a bug, a flaw."

Chun, he believed, would be even less inclined to accept that the jeeb virus had somehow created a new world of sentient beings. "Orbital Arena needs the money from the government contract," he'd confided in Analise. "We're stretched pretty thin. If we lose the contract because the virus is causing the JEEB Earth sim to malfunction, the company is in big trouble."

Analise had argued that a truly sentient AI would be worth far more than the government contract. She'd said the discovery would revolutionize human society. For the first time in the history of the human species, we *Homo sapiens* were no longer alone. There was another intelligent species in the universe: *Homo synthetica*.

Arni had argued that there was no accurate test for consciousness. Nobody really knew what consciousness was, much less how to test for it. "They'll just insist the bots' behavior is false sentience, an artificial by-product of the AI malfunction. There's no way for us to *prove* the bots are alive. This goes way beyond a Turing test."

In the end they decided that Arni should take the discovery to Chun, who they felt would be easier to convince of their theory than the US government. Surely Chun would see the importance of the need to protect the new species of beings, whom Arni had dubbed *the Awakened*. The JEEB Earth sim held almost eight billion of the Awakened, and Arni and Analise were determined to find a way to save them all. They made the decision not to reveal Analise's role in the deception, as it would likely rile Chun's competitive nature.

It hadn't gone well. In fact, right in front of Arni's eyes, Chun had panicked, furiously demanding that he immediately cease any further experiments with the Haven server. She'd castigated Arni for ruining the Haven engine. Despite the fact that he hadn't mentioned Analise, Chun had blamed Analise for fabricating the jeeb virus for her own personal gain. She'd accused Analise of intentionally ruining the JEEB project in order to exact revenge on Chun. She told him that it was total nonsense to claim that the bots were sentient. She ordered him out of the building, saying that she would take this treachery immediately to the board of directors with the recommendation that Arni be terminated.

Badly shaken, Arni and Analise had realized that they needed to act quickly to prevent Chun from taking control of the Haven engine. After the meeting, Arni rushed down into the vaults of the Orbital Arena corporate headquarters, where he removed the Haven machine from its storage bay. He took it to his lair in the old grocery store. Nobody knew about the building, which he had purchased with the intent to someday turn it into a science fiction museum, and it was deeded to a company that didn't really exist except on paper and had no obvious ties to Arni. He would be safe there, he believed, until he and Analise could find a way to save the sentient bots and reconcile with Chun.

Over the next few weeks, Analise and Arni had struggled to understand the nature of the jeeb virus and its link to the sentience of the Awakened. The problem was suddenly compounded when the jeeb virus, inexplicably, infected the Pandora machine at Orbital Arena, which powered the *Longstar* video game. Overnight, all of the billions of gamebots rejected their programming and started acting in their own self-interest. Both Arni and Analise had been flabbergasted. How had the jeeb virus made the leap to the Pandora machine? It had no physical or digital connection to either the Sentinel machine or the Haven machine.

Arni had speculated that the virus had somehow propagated across an unknown medium that existed outside the digital networks of the modern internet infrastructure. It was a closely held company secret, but Chun had long suspected that the QARMA kernels in the three machines might have some sort of bizarre link to each other. She'd seen hints that the state of all three kernels changed when certain conditions were met in a single kernel. She'd called it the QARMA echo, and she'd insisted it was evidence of a theoretical field through which these signals were transmitted: the *etherium*. So far, despite multiple attempts to pin it down, there had been no other empirical evidence that the etherium actually existed, though if it did, it would provide a convenient explanation for the mysterious propagation of the jeeb virus.

Regardless of the method of transmission, the fact remained that all three of the QARMA engines had become infected with the jeeb virus. Players of the video game had suddenly noticed a marked change in the behavior of the game's bots and assumed that Orbital Arena had made an unannounced upgrade to the game's AI. Chun was mortified, but the new bot behavior was applauded by the millions of players, resulting in a major jump in game subscription revenue.

This had presented a huge new problem. Unlike the Haven machine or JEEB Earth, where the Awakened were relatively safe in their virtual environments, in the gamecosm they were being actively slaughtered by the millions. Players had no qualms about killing bots in the game; in fact, it was encouraged. Combat was an integral part of gameplay. Without realizing it, millions of teenage players had become mass murderers overnight.

"That's when Rupe got involved," Analise told Zia. "He and Arni had been best friends ever since Arni hired him a few years ago. Arni explained that the malicious designs of Rupe's dungeons and campaigns were causing the wholesale slaughter of the Awakened.

"Rupe almost collapsed from grief, God bless him," Analise said. "He didn't question the science; he just believed Arni was telling the truth and that the Awakened were living beings with souls. He instantly promised to do whatever it took to help stop the killing."

So, the conspiracy was formed and the plot hatched: Arni, Analise, and Rupe would work together to find a way to save the Awakened, starting in the Orbital Arena gamecosm where they were most at jeopardy, but also on JEEB Earth, where their future fate was at the whim of the US military.

Analise told Zia how, over the past few months, the three of them had brainstormed a daring plan: they would steal the worlds of the gamecosm, removing the entire population of the Awakened from the murderous game environment of the Pandora machine at Orbital Arena to the Haven server in Arni's lab, where they would be safe. Afterward, the three would find a way to save the doppelgängers of JEEB Earth, too.

Zia stared across the couch at Analise. Analise stared back, her expression grave. Zia had long expected that the brilliant but seemingly innocent Analise Novak possessed a hidden agenda. And it was a real doozy, as Rupe might say. Analise took a deep breath, and, with a thrill, Zia knew what she was going to say next.

"Help us. With your hacking skills, we might be able to get it done without anybody going to jail."

Zia felt her natural caution slipping away. She'd been dazzled by Analise since the day they'd met. Now that this new, dangerous side of Analise's personality was revealed, Zia found herself more dazzled than ever. Analise wasn't a naive innocent, as her pleasant girl-next-door facade implied. Like Zia, she was a *hacker*. Still, Zia forced herself to analyze the situation rationally.

"How? How will it work? Look, even if you succeed in migrating the gamecosm to the Haven server, how long can you keep it a secret? Sooner or later, somebody will trace your actions and discover your plot, and you'll be right back where you started, except that you'll all be in prison." She paused, remembering the day at the café in Montreal when her freelance career had ended. "I know. I'm the best in the world, and *I* got caught."

"So we'll learn from your mistake. It's a huge risk, yeah, but think about it: *what risk isn't worth taking to save billions of innocent lives?* Zia, the Awakened aren't just unlucky bits of software code. They're *people*, just like you and me, with cares and desires and fears and dreams. I challenge you: go into the game with your avatar and walk among the Awakened. You'll see what I mean."

As compelling as Analise had been, especially given the fact that she'd been leaning so close that her perfume filled Zia's world, her argument was impossible to accept. Bots weren't people. They couldn't be. Arni and Analise had deceived themselves. They'd fallen into the anthropomorphic trap. She shook her head. "I can't help you. I won't stop you, but I won't help. It doesn't make sense. Bots aren't worth risking everything for. Even if you do manage to get them onto the Haven server, the first glitch or power outage will wipe them out. It just isn't worth it. Computers don't last forever. Eventually, they will all die anyway."

She'd expected Analise to be disappointed or angry. Instead, Analise smiled mysteriously. "It won't matter. I've discovered something about the true nature of the QARMA kernels. I think I know how to make the gamecosm *permanent*. I know where to put it where nobody can ever touch it again." At Zia's confused silence, she continued. "Haven't you noticed that the QARMA engines aren't plugged into an electrical outlet? Not Sentinel. Not Haven. Not Pandora. They don't draw their power from the grid."

At that point, before Zia could dispute her unlikely claim, Analise had reached out and touched Zia's shoulder, sending a jolt through her endocrine system. Even though they were completely alone in the apartment, Analise's voice dropped to the softest of whispers. "This thing is bigger than you can imagine, Zia. Way, *way* bigger. Here's the thing: The QARMA machines aren't computers. Not even close."

"What are they?"

"They're bridges. Bridges between our reality and what's inside the QARMA kernels. And the kernels aren't what Chun has made them out to be. She has lied to us all. She didn't create the three kernels. She *stole* them."

"Okay, I'll bite. Who did she steal them from?"

"As far as we can tell, she stole them from God."

havencosm | GRONE

Guardian

"I can't get it to work," Nkiru admitted three days into the trip from Orbitus to Grone. The *Legacy Sky* had far more powerful engines than the rusty old *Rose & Chalice* or the broken-down *Covenant of Andrik*, making better than twice their speed with significantly more comfort. Instead of a month, the entire journey would take only ten days. Nkiru was sitting upright in bed next to him, the snowglobe cradled in her lap. It was midnight, ship time, and she'd been at it almost every waking moment since they'd departed Centerpoint Station. She was convinced that the device was some sort of communications transceiver, but up till now it had done nothing but blink and sparkle.

Se-Jong yawned, almost asleep. "So, the Prophet Kanaan isn't answering his phone, eh?"

"Screw you," she replied crossly. She turned back to the orb.

He let out a silent sigh. Her growing frustration had set him on edge. It was becoming obvious that she was in a dangerous situation in which she had no real control or understanding. This Brother Jerome and the so-called Janga monks had sent a young woman on a solo secret mission that even she couldn't explain.

He didn't buy the story that the Prophet Kanaan might still be alive and that he might hold the key to restoring the galaxy to its pre-Cataclysmic glory. Nkiru believed it, obviously, but perhaps she'd been purposefully misguided by Jerome and his cultists. Church politics and the spider's web of relationships between the different orders, cults, and factions had been a labyrinthine maze of shifting alliances for thousands of years. Widespread knowledge of Nkiru and her avatar abilities would crash the old system of coalitions and rivalries. The monk Jerome would know this. There was a very good chance that he was exploiting Nkiru as a weapon to catapult the Janga Order to the forefront of the church, and to put a Janga, perhaps Jerome himself, in the seat of the Father Regis.

When he'd raised his suspicions with Nkiru, she'd scoffed. "The last thing Brother Jerome wants is to be the Father Regis. He's a good man. A spiritual man. He's not using me: he's *helping* me."

"Helping you what?" he'd demanded.

"Find Kanaan," she'd replied defensively.

"And you really think the Prophet Kanaan is hiding in an undiscovered dungeon on Grone?"

"Maybe," she'd said. "Hopefully."

Perhaps they'd brainwashed her. That seemed more likely than the existence of an immortal prophet on some backwater planet near the edge of the Devastation. Then again, the very existence of her avatar abilities was just as improbable. Se-Jong's mind spun. He knew himself to be a pragmatist, like his grandmother, but the variables in Nkiru's bizarre situation fell outside the realm of pragmatism. They required something with which he was distinctly uncomfortable.

Faith.

But faith in Nkiru was different than faith in Jerome and his henchmen. If the Janga were using her as he suspected, she needed to be protected from them just as much as she needed protection from the Dei Militans. Whatever Jerome's secret agenda, it was serious enough to warrant a charge of capital heresy. Nkiru had said that Jerome had gone before the Inquisitors. Considering their infamous interrogation methods, it was likely only a matter of time before they would learn of Nkiru and her pilgrimage. Maybe they already knew, in which case their reception on icy Grone might be warmer than they'd hoped.

Making matters worse was the fact that Grone lay in an area of space claimed by the breakaway Earth colony of Caerini Prime. The Caerens belonged to the Mucktu cult and, in general, were much more rabid about their faith than the Cataclyst worlds. Pilgrim transports were exempt from regular border checks, but if the Caerens got even the faintest hint that Nkiru had avatar powers, the ship would be boarded and the pilgrims would likely all vanish into Caeren prisons. Being captured and interrogated by the Caerens or, worse, their Mucktu masters, would make torture at the hands of the Cataclyst Inquisitors look like a day at the beach.

It was time he acted. Nkiru was too important to become a naive victim of a Janga conspiracy. If she ended up in an Inquisition torture cell or a Caeren prison, he would never forgive himself. The fallout from her arrest might also consume him and his family, and he might end up in the same cell.

For the first time in his life, Se-Jong glimpsed the usefulness of power. The Kwon family had been a force in the Solar Alliance for generations. His great-grandfather had been a signatory to the Solar Alliance Treaty Organization, SATO, the closest thing to a rebirth of one of the old avatar empires as had happened in the past ten millennia. His grandmother was on the fast track to become a fleet captain. His father was a respected civil engineer and businessman on Askelon. The Kwon family had real clout, and by extension, so did he. It was time to flex some of his clan's muscle to protect Nkiru from the forces that threatened her.

Breakfast, and another slab of greasy protoham. Nkiru picked at the meal absently. His stupid and drunken profession of love at Centerpoint Station had caused a definite change in her behavior. He'd avoided bringing up the subject, but the closer they got to Grone, the more distant she became and the more his worry grew. He was almost certain of her feelings for him, but so far, she'd not vocalized any of them. It seemed silly. They were sleeping together every night, and they spent almost every hour of every day together. Putting their relationship into words should be easy and natural, but Nkiru seemed to think that calling it "love" might trap her into something permanent and unbreakable.

Maybe, hopefully, her change in attitude was just nerves about what might be waiting for them on Grone. He was nervous about that, too, but also hopeful. If she could find the undiscovered First Epoch dungeon she believed to exist, then in addition to being the greatest archeological discovery of their time, it might give them the leverage they needed to avoid prosecution by the church. Knowing the location of a boss dungeon and its fabulous treasures would be quite the bargaining chip.

Se-Jong was deeply engaged in extracting a piece of protoham gristle from the back of his teeth when he noticed that Nkiru was peeking furtively over his shoulder. "That weird guy is staring at me again," she said in a low voice. "No, don't turn around."

Se-Jong turned anyway. He glared across the dining tables at the shaggy-haired man. The man flinched and looked away. Se-Jong started to rise, but Nkiru put her hand on his arm. "No. Don't."

"That guy is definitely stalking you," Se-Jong growled. "Are you sure you don't know who he is?"

"He was in the terminal lounge at Centerpoint while we were waiting to board the ship. That was the first time I noticed him. I've seen him a few times on the ship, but he always runs away when he sees that I've noticed him."

"He looks like a jeebie to me." Se-Jong said.

"All the more reason to stay away from him," muttered Nkiru.

Unbeknownst to Nkiru, Se-Jong had already confronted the shaggy-haired man. On their fourth day out of Skybridge, on his way back from a workout in the ship's gym, Se-Jong had caught the man in the corridor outside Nkiru's cabin, obviously trying to listen through the cabin door. A spike of sheer terror had gripped Se-Jong's heart. Was he an agent of the church? A covert Dei Militans spy? Some kind of bounty hunter?

Without thinking, Se-Jong had shoved the man against the opposite corridor wall and demanded that he explain himself. The man's dark eyes had the wild and unfocused look of a jeebie, and sure enough, his pilgrims' robes reeked of jeeb hooch and body odor. Beneath his shaggy hair, a deep growth of unkempt beard covered his gaunt and deeply wrinkled face. Something about the face caused Se-Jong to hesitate. Had he seen him someplace before?

The man had giggled and gone completely limp beneath Se-Jong's rough handling. When Se-Jong again demanded to know why he was eavesdropping, the man became silent, his manic giggles instantaneously replaced by a somber, glassy-eyed expression.

"I know who she is," the man had stated with absolute certainty.

"You don't know shit," Se-Jong had countered angrily. He'd pressed his forearm into the man's thin throat, forcing his head against the wall. The man made a sharp choking sound, but Se-Jong didn't relent. He'd been in plenty of hand-to-hand matches in his Physical Combat course at Jackill, but this was the first time he'd ever attacked someone in anger. He was more than a little embarrassed by how good it felt. For the briefest instant he thought about tightening his grip until the man stopped breathing. The murderous impulse only lasted a second, but in that second Se-Jong realized that he was more than willing to take someone's life to protect Nkiru. The realization calmed him, as if it had given him a great power over his destiny.

"Stay away from her. You hear me? If you touch her, I'll break you in half." Se-Jong had surprised himself with the unexpected ferocity of his threat. The man made a half-giggle, half-choking sound, and Se-Jong released him. He crumpled to the corridor floor like a rag doll, holding his throat. Se-Jong backed away. "Get away from here, and don't ever get near her again."

The man had spit on the floor at Se-Jong's feet, made a hoarse wail of misery. "I'm not going to hurt her, but *you* will," he cried.

Se-Jong had lifted his fist and the man scrambled away, at first on all fours, then rising and staggering against the corridor walls. Se-Jong relaxed a little. There was no way this weirdo could be a Dei Militans agent.

Arrival

Everyone crowded the observation lounge as the *Legacy Sky* glided into orbit. While not quite matching the spectacle of the Skybridge, Grone was undoubtedly prettier than either the ocean world of Ragnu or the desert planet of Orbitus. According to scripture, way back in the First Epoch, millions of years before the days of the avatars, Grone had been a barely habitable ball of ice. That is, until a Gurothim attack had broken the planet's moon into chunks and sent them descending in a fiery Armageddon into the planet's crust. In addition to exterminating the inhabitants of the world, the fiery impacts had also thrown up some of the highest and craggiest mountains in the Known Arc, and the circular seas that now filled the impact scars were the deepest and bluest anywhere. The pilgrims' guidebook called Grone "the beautiful gemstone in the ring of the Halo."

They'd approached from the night side. On most coreward worlds near the empty void of the Devastation, the nighttime starscape was skimpy at best. Grone was an exception to this rule. The Grone system was located on the outskirts of the Great Nebula, giving it a spectacular view of a tight cluster of stars that had coalesced out of the nebula's gases just a few million years ago. The dimly glowing clouds of the nebula were visible to the naked eye, like gossamer wings abandoned by a fallen angel, a backdrop for the piercing blue pinpricks of the star nursery. From their vantage point, the nighttime side of Grone was a black circle at the exact center of the angel's wings, creating a striking astronomical alignment. Se-Jong suspected that the captain had arranged the ship's course to set up the view for the passengers.

Minutes after the thrusters had fallen silent and the captain announced that orbit had been achieved, a rapid sunrise began to reveal Grone's famous beauty. The growing sunlit crescent tugged at Se-Jong's soul. Here was a battered planet that had come through the forge of hell to become one of the most beautiful worlds in the Known Arc. There was a lesson to be learned here; he was sure of it.

Nkiru stood at his side, clutching his hand in a grip that was unusually tight. She hadn't said a word for almost an hour, ever since Grone had first appeared as a tiny smudge of light in the massive windows. She'd reached a whole new level of anxiety, or maybe excitement, but he couldn't read her expression. He decided not to say anything, just to stand and hold her hand and watch the planet rotate majestically beneath them.

The evenly spaced climate zones of Grone reminded Se-Jong of the cloud belts that encircled gas-giant planets like Jupiter and Almost, but instead of the yellows and reds of ammonia and hydrocarbons, Grone's belts were shades of green and white, of plant life and water ice. Gleaming ice caps extended from the poles to the midlatitudes of both the northern and southern hemispheres, where they broke against vast, featureless plains of pale-green tundra. The pilgrims' guide said the plains had once been the seafloor of an ocean that had frozen when the planet's orbit had shifted away from its sun. Separating the northern and southern plains was a thick, sharp-edged belt of arboreal forest that circled the equator.

He felt Nkiru's fingers tense against his palm when the first of the blue crater seas rotated into view. Her eyes were scanning the surface terrain, looking for a landmark, perhaps the location of the dungeon she insisted lay beneath one of Grone's high mountains. He let out a silent sigh. Even though she'd promised not to keep secrets from him, it was obvious that there were many, many things in her mind to которой he was not privy. Dangerous things.

———

They lingered in the observation lounge after the crowd had dissipated. Nkiru seemed hypnotized by the planet as it moved below them, the broad arch of night darkening half the globe. Without thinking, Se-Jong shoved his hand in his pocket and brought out a small object wrapped in thin paper. He held it out to her. "This is for you."

She looked down at the stained, clumsily wrapped package, then back up to Se-Jong. He saw her hesitation, and he immediately regretted his impulsiveness. He'd been carrying around the bracelet since Assinni, hoping to find the right moment to give it to her. Why this moment was different than any of a thousand others, he had no clue. Obviously, it was a mistake. He wished he could shove it back in his pocket.

She took it from him, holding it gingerly. "Is this . . . blood?" She held up the wrapping paper, looked at him questioningly.

He shrugged. "I was carrying it in my pocket when I got bit by the rockspides back on Orbitus. I meant to rewrap it, but . . ."

She raised an eyebrow, and one corner of her lip quirked upward. He watched as she slowly unwrapped it. It was such a silly little thing. A stupid little copper bracelet bought at a stupid little souvenir stand. To a woman who collected priceless avatar relics, such a worthless trinket might simply be insulting.

She held up the bracelet, examined it. The workmanship that had seemed so charming back in the store now looked crude. "It's supposed to be the Seuss trees back on Assinni," he said dully.

"I can see that." She slipped it on her wrist. Against her deep skin, the copper strands gleamed. She jangled it. The beads woven into the copper tinkled.

"It's stupid, I know," he said.

"It's *not* stupid," she replied. She reached up, took his cheeks in her palms, and forced him to look directly at her. "It's beautiful."

—

Like Assinni, Grone was a tourist planet. Adventure seekers from across the SATO worlds descended by shuttle or t-gate to the largest city, Andriksburg, to enjoy the clean air, healthy food, and mountain views. Grone had the tallest waterfalls and the highest peaks of any world in the Known Arc, two of which climbed completely out of the atmosphere and could only be summited in a space suit. Grone had the wildest rivers, the most impressive glaciers, and an immense network of volcanic caves whose extent had never been fully determined. Forests blanketed the planet's temperate belt, and the equatorial crater seas provided endless opportunities for sailing and aquatic sports. However, despite the fact that the entire planet was a wonderland of outdoor-adventure fantasy, only a few tourists ever left the capital city of Andriksburg. The vast majority came to experience one thing: the Mass of the Starry Chalice, which was held daily in the Ice Cathedral carved into the glacier that spilled down from the crater walls above the city.

For thousands of years after the chaos of the Rapture and the Cataclysm, the planet Grone had concealed a secret in the unexplored mountains of its equatorial crater belt. It wasn't until a local hunter followed a river into an ice cave that the planet's significance came to light. Grone was the location of two particularly sacred events in the Cataclyst scriptures: the redemption of the Prophet Andrik and the origin of the Cataclyst Covenant. By some miracle, the obsidian chalice into which Andrik had spilled his blood was still on the altar, and the altar's central spike was wreathed by yellow flowers that had somehow survived being frozen inside a glacier for thousands of years.

The newborn cult of Andrik the Redeemer had preserved the ice cave containing the altar and the chalice, and as the cult grew into the mighty, world-spanning Universal Cataclyst Church, its people carved a spectacular cathedral into the surrounding glacier. On holy days in the modern era, thousands of worshippers, many of them devout pilgrims from faraway worlds, performed the First Rite of the Covenant. They formed a long queue and, one by one, approached the spike of the Flowery Altar, where they each pricked their palm and added a drop of blood to the Starry Chalice, thus upholding the Covenant of Andrik.

For almost everyone aboard the *Legacy Sky*, the First Rite was the entire reason for their pilgrimage. Grone would be their last stop before returning home. Only the most devout or the most thrill seeking would apply for permission to continue onward, and only a few of these applicants would be eligible. It took special permission from the Regium and a hard-to-get medical certificate to qualify for the grueling, months-long Outer Pilgrimage. For this reason, Se-Jong fervently hoped that Nkiru would also end her quest at Grone. If she wanted to continue on the Outer Pilgrimage, he'd have to make the most difficult choice of his life: accompany her and lose any chance of ever attending the War College, or abandon her to face the journey alone—and likely never see her again.

To Se-Jong's great relief, at Grone's orbital spaceport they were not met by a squad of Dei Militans or a detachment of Caeren troopers or a shrouded Mucktu witch. Instead, they stood in line at the reception area and were confronted by a bored Caeren border-control officer, who stamped their documents without as much as a glance at their faces.

Once again Nkiru refused to use the station's t-gate to port to the surface. She patted her backpack with a nervous look and told him it might not be a good idea to carry its contents through a t-gate. At her anxious expression, he agreed and shelled out the fare for two shuttle tickets to the surface.

They landed at the Andriksburg shuttleport in late afternoon and were once again hustled through the arrival process without the slightest hint of suspicion. By dinnertime Se-Jong had booked them a three-room luxury suite in the city's grandest hotel, the Triple Peaks. When Nkiru had objected, Se-Jong had chided her. "I can afford it," he'd said. "Plus, I think it's time we splurged a little." Privately, he felt much safer in the secure hotel, away from the prying eyes of the other pilgrims. He desperately wanted to make their stay in Andriksburg special, as one way or another, it was likely to be their last stop on the pilgrimage.

After a late meal delivered by room service, they took a hot bath and lay together between crisp sheets among a mountain of pillows, a real treat after the narrow bunks and thin mattresses of the pilgrims' transports. Throughout the entire evening nobody knocked on the door and invited them for scripture study, and not a single call to prayer blared out of the intercom, as would have happened at a pilgrims' hostel. "Ah, civilization," Nkiru sighed, stretching on the luxurious bedding and staring out the floor-to-ceiling windows at the trio of high peaks that had given the hotel its name. Contrasted against the brilliant white of the sheets, she looked like a flowing sculpture of obsidian, rare and incredibly fragile.

They cuddled, and he did his best to hide his restlessness. He waited until he was sure she was asleep, then quietly dressed and slipped out of the room. He made his way to the ground floor, where he used a government postal booth to compose a message to his grandmother, informing her of his plans. It was not an easy message to compose, and he could only imagine the extent of her alarm when she received it. He sent it high priority, spending a small fortune to have it delivered by the fastest method possible to her command base at Trumbull Station. It would take several days to get there, and several days for her reply to arrive at Grone. In the meantime, he would enjoy his time with Nkiru and refrain from worrying what the future might hold.

Train

The next morning Nkiru flitted out of the hotel early, before breakfast, leaving him to spend his day wandering alone and aimlessly through the city. She'd told him she was going to the monastery at the city wall to talk to the Janga monks. They wouldn't let him in without church-issued pilgrims' documents, she'd said, so he might as well relax and enjoy a day alone. "I'll be back by dinner," she'd proclaimed, and before he'd had time to object, she was gone.

She was looking for clues to the location of the dungeon, he knew. She'd shown him a photo on her komnic the night before, a fuzzy image of a mountainous crater that looked to him exactly like the hundreds of other mountainous craters he'd seen from orbit. "Is that it?" he'd asked.

"I'm not sure," she answered.

He resented the maddeningly vague answer, but he didn't press her for details. No matter what her plans, he would keep her safe. No matter what.

—

As the days passed on Grone and her search for the crater in the photo dragged on without results, her anxiety increased. Despite his delicate probing, she continued to refuse to talk about it. In fact, after the first three days, she pretty much refused to talk at all. Every morning she left early, before breakfast, and when she finally returned to the hotel, she immediately curled up with her komnic, donned her earphones, and lost herself in whatever it was that she was always doing on the device. When he tried to peek over her shoulder, she would spin away and glare at him as if he'd invaded her most personal space. At bedtime she assumed a fetal position on one corner of the giant mattress, facing the window, and when he touched her, she shrugged away. Several times when he woke in the middle of the night, he found her awake, the snowglobe relic cradled in her lap, her face lit by the glow of her komnic, her brow furrowed, her eyes bleary. His only comfort was that she was still wearing the bracelet he'd given her.

———

On the evening of the sixth day she returned just before midnight, sweeping in the door in a burst of cold air, the hood of her coat pulled tight around her face. Her coverall was streaked and stained with what looked like oil, and the fabric over one knee was torn. She told him that she'd tripped and fallen on the street, but later, after her shower, when they were in bed, he could feel her entire body trembling. When he tried to gently pry the day's events from her, she redirected him by telling him that they were going to see the Starry Chalice in the morning. He couldn't decipher the tone in her voice. It sounded both terrified and exhilarated. She'd found something, he guessed, and tomorrow she would lift the curtain and reveal her secrets.

———

During the night he felt her leave the bed. He watched groggily through slit eyelids as she went to the wide, curtained window and pulled the shades back a few centimeters. She sank into the cushions of an armchair beneath the windowsill, legs crossed beneath her, and spent a long time staring through the glass, her eyes downward as if searching the city streets below. Her insomnia was an almost nightly occurrence, so when she didn't move for several minutes, Se-Jong drifted back to sleep.

He woke again to soft murmuring. The hotel room was lit with an almost imperceptible blue glow. He sat up in bed and looked over to the armchair. Nkiru was gone. The blue glow came from beneath the closed door that connected the suite's bedroom to an expansive sitting room. He tossed the covers aside and padded to the door, pressing his ear against the richly patterned wood grain. Silence. He reached down to the handle and quietly opened the door.

Nkiru was standing at the opposite side of the room before the wide glass window, through which a nighttime panorama of the Three Peaks and the glacier-hewn Ice Cathedral was lit by hundreds of spotlights shining up from the city. In the extended fingers of her right hand, she held the snowglobe up to her face. The tiny red flickers in its depths were gone. They'd been replaced by a steady blue glow, the source of the radiance he'd seen shining beneath the door. Se-Jong quietly retreated a step, closed the door to a tiny crack, and peered through.

Nkiru had donned one of the hotel's linen bathrobes, but her hair was still mussed from sleep. Her fingers were moving across the surface of the globe in a purposeful pattern. The steady blue glow flickered and died. She cursed. She shook the globe, once, twice, then again with both hands. She muttered another curse.

He pushed open the door. She saw the movement and looked at him. She didn't seem startled or surprised. She gestured at the snowglobe, her voice barely above a whisper. "I got it working for a minute."

Se-Jong swallowed. "Did it . . . say anything?"

She shook her head. Her eyes were very wide, and very pale. By chance, her silhouette against the floor-to-ceiling window was positioned so that the angel wings of the Great Nebula spread behind her shoulders into the night sky. He shivered.

"I found a way to make it take a photograph," she whispered. "I tried sending it."

"Still trying to reach the Prophet Kanaan?" he scoffed playfully. When she winced, he realized that he shouldn't have tried to joke. He kept his voice neutral. "Who did you send it to?"

She turned to stare out the window. "To anybody who is listening."

"Was that a good idea, you think?"

"I sure hope so."

———

They dressed before dawn and ate a quick, silent breakfast at a corner café, surrounded by a sparse collection of other early risers, most of them happy and babbling. After a few minutes of picking at her food and ignoring her coffee, Nkiru shouldered her backpack and stood. Se-Jong tossed back the last of his coffee and hurried to follow her. Outside the café, she donned her sunglasses even though the sun had not yet fully risen, pulled up her hood, and looked around furtively. Se-Jong looked around, too. Other than a few shopkeepers opening their stores, nobody else was on the street.

"Let's go," she said. She turned east, toward the dawn.

Se-Jong hurried after her, frowning. "We're going to see the Starry Chalice today, right?"

"Uh-huh," she replied.

"We're going the wrong way. The cathedral is the other direction."

"Yep."

Se-Jong was confused. "Wait. We're not going to the Ice Cathedral?"

"Nope."

"But the Starry Chalice is in the cathedral."

She shrugged. "Maybe."

"Am I only going to get mysterious, one-word answers from you all day?"

"Probably," she said, but to his relief she smiled, the first smile he'd seen from her in a week.

It turned out she was headed for the transport station at the city center, where she bought tickets on a backpackers' train heading east, into the dense forests that lay beyond the Triple Peaks. The train was clean and modern, and as they passed what seemed like endless vistas of snow-streaked peaks and heavy blue glaciers, Nkiru's mood lightened. When a herd of ungainly, three-legged herbivores galumphed alongside the train, pacing them for several astonishing moments, Nkiru's hand found Se-Jong's, and they watched and laughed together.

Every few minutes Nkiru pulled out her komnic and compared the view out the window to the image on her screen. Se-Jong peered over her shoulder at the image, the same blurry, pixelated crater scene that she'd shown him when they'd first arrived.

Today, he realized, they'd be looking for the mountain that held the Grone dungeon.

The train stopped at every major trailhead along the way, and at each stop a trickle of adventure seekers seeped off the carriages, most carrying backpacks and camping gear, some hauling skis or snowboards, others shouldering hunting rifles or fishing gear. Every time the doors opened, the carriage filled with the crisp scent of pine and snow. Each time the air was a little colder, a little thinner. The rail line climbed into the mountains, gaining altitude, and as one hour turned to two the trees thinned and eventually vanished, leaving them in a monochromatic world of dark granite and white snow and blue glacier ice. Still they trundled forward, losing passengers at every stop until Se-Jong and Nkiru were the only ones left in the carriage.

Ten minutes after the last passenger left the train car, Nkiru once again pulled out her komnic. This time, instead of pocketing it with a sigh, her eyes narrowed and she leaned toward the window, her face raised toward a rounded peak that was just coming into view.

"Is that it?" Se-Jong asked. It did sort of look like one of the mountains in the grainy crater photo.

"Maybe," she muttered. "Just maybe."

"Why do I get the feeling that you're about to blow my mind again?"

She shrugged and bit her top lip. "Don't get your hopes up."

―

The now-empty train followed the outer arc of one of the moonfall crater walls, eventually coming to a point where the crater intersected a second, larger crater like two parts of a Venn diagram. At the junction of the two rims lay a massive, U-shaped valley flanked by rounded peaks that had been ground down by thick glaciers. Overflow from the overlapping crater lakes spilled across the ridge at the head of the valley in a series of spectacular waterfalls. From their base, a river cut its way through the valley basin and vanished into the thick forest beyond.

They disembarked at the river station near the lowest set of waterfalls. The train platform was surrounded by a handful of picturesque stone buildings: a wilderness outpost that catered to adventure-seeking tourists. There, at a mountain outfitter, they rented coldsuits and camping gear, a food pack, and a heavy inflatable pack-raft, "For the lake," Nkiru explained cryptically. To Se-Jong's dismay, the merchant, a shiny-headed, thick-eared Olid, also insisted that they rent two orange cylinders of Yok-Stop, which he claimed would stop a charging yok-beast at a distance of fifteen meters. The Olid's English was so burdened by a Tang accent that Se-Jong had to concentrate to understand his words.

"Make noise along trail so dey hear ye come, yae. Never surprise dem. If one charge ye, don't run. Dey catch ye every time, yan dey climb trees. Pull out Yok-Stop, aim, cover eyes, squeeze trigger. Don't let get on skin. It nerve agent. It burn like hell. Ye be blinded for hours." It grinned toothily at Se-Jong's concern. "Donna worry, it been nearly two months since we lost city boy like ye to yok attack."

The trail began behind the cluster of stone buildings and climbed alongside the river toward the base of the waterfall. The air was cold, the sun shockingly bright, and the scenery breathtaking. For the first time since they'd arrived on Grone, Nkiru's mysterious dark mood lifted completely, and despite the fact that she'd barely slept in over a week, her pace was quick along the bouldered trail. She sprang lightly from stone to stone, the toes of her boots barely brushing the trail's surface. Se-Jong, who'd always prided himself on his fitness, struggled to keep up, bent under the weight of the heavy pack-raft she'd insisted they bring along. "It's the altitude," he mumbled to himself, but it was obvious that Nkiru's slim physique was far more practical for mountaineering than his own thickly muscled frame. He felt like a warthog stumbling after a gazelle.

Their path followed the river through groves of the biggest trees Se-Jong had ever seen, climbing gently until it reached the base of the lowest waterfall. There, in the rainbow mist of the cascade, the path narrowed and began to rise sharply along a series of tight switchbacks. The valley opened out beneath them as they climbed. From this vantage point, the rail station and attending cluster of buildings looked like toys someone had left in the scattered tumble of boulders. Se-Jong's eyes were drawn to the straight, thin line of the railroad as it pierced the glacial moraine and vanished into the thick forest of the lower elevations. They'd been hiking for less than an hour, but it already felt like they were a thousand years from civilization.

Soon they were both sweating from exertion. Nkiru pulled off her coat and peeled her coldsuit down to her waist. Beneath she wore an athletic halter that highlighted the strength of her shoulders. Se-Jong couldn't stop staring. When she turned and smiled at him, even the blinding reflection from the nearby ice paled in brightness. Se-Jong sucked in a deep, searingly cold breath and grinned up at the surrounding mountains.

The switchbacks were endless. By noon they'd reached the altitude of the second waterfall halfway up the crater wall. The wide valley spread out beneath them, the looping blue thread of the river contrasting with the laser-straight silver filament of the railroad. The trail had become surrounded by snow and ice, though the footpath remained clear. Along the way they'd passed continual geological evidence of the catastrophic birth of these mountains: city-size blocks of terrain torn from the planet's crust and upended by the forces of impact; ridged lava tubes as big as train tunnels through which the molten landscape had drained; wide areas of mountainside swept clean by landslides, some of them apparently quite recent.

Even in the harsh, treeless landscape there was life. Here and there, peeking up through stony cracks and between ice-tumbled boulders, were densely mounded clumps of green and yellow foliage about the size of a soccer ball. Nkiru stopped at one and knelt, and when she touched it, she looked up at Se-Jong with a surprised smile. "It's warm!" she exclaimed. "They're little furnace-weeds." Se-Jong stooped at her side and put his hand next to hers. The tufted mass of tiny yellow blooms was cottony soft and deliciously warm to his frozen fingers. He'd never heard of a plant that generated its own heat. He leaned toward Nkiru's smiling face, but she rebuffed his advance. "Not now," she said, rising to her feet. "We need to get to the top by noon."

The final two hours of the climb were brutal. Se-Jong completely forgot the view of the valley, ignored even the magnificent cascade of the upper falls that roared beside the trail like the bellow of an angry water god. The universe constricted to one thing: the simple task of putting one foot in front of the other.

Climb. Climb. Up, always up. The cold air scorched his lungs like an icy blowtorch. The muscles of his calves screamed for relief. His fingers were completely numb, despite the gloves. Sweat trickled inside his coldsuit, wicked away to drain out the little tubes on the heels of his boots. Behind him the light was softening as the sun descended toward the horizon, but he barely noticed. *Climb. Climb.*

About three-quarters of the way to the top, Nkiru stopped at the edge of a cataclysmic landslide. A sizable portion of the mountainside had been scooped out by gravity and now lay a thousand meters below, parting the dense forest with a broad tongue of tumbled white boulders and scree. A horizontal stone ledge, big enough to land a ship on, had been torn in half by the slide. Nkiru moved slowly onto the remains of the ledge. She knelt and placed her palm on the smooth stone, then shaded her eyes to examine the long view over the valley. She nodded. Her smile, when it came, was wistful, full of memory and emotion. "This is the right place." She pointed up the slope. "That way."

"The trail goes the other direction," Se-Jong said.

Her smile widened, and she replied as if reciting scripture. "We will choose our own paths, while we are young and our light is at its brightest."

The last time they'd ventured off-trail, back on Orbitus, they'd been attacked by a swarm of rockspides. There were no rockspides here on Grone, but there were yoks, which were by all accounts just as deadly. He loosened the buckle securing the can of Yok-Stop to his waist, patted it reassuringly, and with a groan followed Nkiru as she blazed a new path up the mountainside.

Her way eventually led into a gap between two sharp, talus-covered peaks. By this time, she was a hundred meters ahead of him, and when she vanished into the gap, he cursed and forced his screaming muscles into a fast scramble to the top. When he caught up, his chest heaving and his heart ready to explode, she was standing at the base of a thirty-meter-high cliff that spanned the entire gap, seemingly blocking the way. He pulled up next to her, huffing and wheezing. She was staring up at the cliff face with an expression of satisfaction and awe.

"This is *definitely* the right place," she said. Before he could gather enough breath to respond, she was on the move. The loose scree beneath her feet clacked hollowly as she angled to the left side of the cliff. He muttered a curse and followed.

The first hint of an opening was the blast of frigid air through a tall crevice of stone, so narrow that they had to slide through sideways. The vertical slot extended a hundred meters into the rock, and he picked his way laboriously through a long array of boulders wedged at its bottom. As he was slowed by his complaining muscles, Nkiru got ahead of him. At first Se-Jong thought something was wrong when he heard her cry out. Had she gotten stuck in the constricted stone passage? He pushed through, faster, and as he came to the exit, he saw the reason for her cry.

Crater

A sapphire sea spread before them, deeply cradled in a surrounding bowl of sun-fired cliffs. Dark forest ringed the bottom third of the crater down to the shoreline. Above the forest, slopes of broken scree and talus extended up to the raw stone of the peaks. Several milky-blue glaciers spilled down the inner slopes of the crater at irregular intervals, cutting through stone, talus, and forest like the icy finger-swipes of a titanic sculptor. A few of the larger icefalls extended all the way down to the water, where small bergs could be seen floating around their broken bases. Others culminated in waterfalls that spilled over forested cliffs into the sea. He pulled in a purposeful breath, filling his lungs with the pine-scented air of an alpine wilderness.

Views like this one were the specialty of Grone, advertised by tour operators all over the Known Arc. He had difficulty processing the immensity of what he was seeing. The tallest mountains on the far side of the crater were more than fifty kilometers distant, but the frigid air magnified them so that even the tiniest details were crystal clear, and their aspect was mirrored so perfectly in the surface of the water that Se-Jong felt a twirling vertigo. This was a *small* crater, he reminded himself. He tried to imagine the view inside one of the dozen or so major craters, some of which were *thousands* of kilometers wide.

In the bull's-eye of the circular lake, the crustal rebound from the impact had thrust up a mountainous island like the tombstone of a god. It had once been flawlessly conical, but at some point in the past, the summit and one entire side had collapsed into the lake, forming a wide, slumping fan of jumbled alluvia. The island peak was of a yellow stone completely unlike that of the encircling mountains.

Next to him, Nkiru's face was shining. She held her hands above her head and screamed out at the vista, as if challenging it to reply. The howl dissolved into laughter. She squatted and picked up a shard of the purple-gray scree that blanketed the slopes above the tree line. For a moment he thought she might bring it to her lips and kiss it, but instead she rose and flung it down the slope, screaming once again. She waited for an echo, but the vastness swallowed her jubilation.

Was this the dungeon she'd been searching for? He looked around for anything dungeon-like, then realized he had no idea what the entrance to a First Epoch dungeon would look like.

Seeing his confusion, she grabbed him by both hands and they danced in a circle, stumbling on the steep slope and sliding in the loose talus. Even though he had no idea of the cause for her joy, he was happy to participate in it. When she flung herself into his chest and hugged him so hard it hurt, he returned the embrace, though carefully, mindful of her bruised ribs. She said something, her voice muffled into the fabric of his coldsuit.

"What?"

She tilted her head up from his chest. "I never thought I'd actually be here in person," she repeated.

He made a show of looking around. "Um, where, exactly, is here?"

Nkiru released her grip, backed away, and pointed toward central island peak. She said, breathlessly, "That's the Citadel of Jaspaar. Or what's left of it."

He stared dubiously across the lake toward the crumbling ruins. "Who's Jaspaar?"

"He was a timedust hoarder back in the Second Epoch. A villain. He built his citadel on that mountain, but when he dug too deep, he found something he hadn't counted on."

Se-Jong stared across the water. "The dungeon? It's inside that mountain?"

For a moment her face clouded with worry, but then she was tugging him urgently toward the downward slope in the direction of the lake. "Let's go! We're almost there."

If she shared his aches from the arduous climb, she showed no sign. He took a deep breath and adjusted the straps of his heavy pack. "Okay. Lead on."

Crossing

They descended through the band of forest toward the water's edge, Se-Jong stumbling under the heavy weight of the pack, both of them talking loudly so as not to surprise a sleeping yok. They passed through several small meadows carpeted by low mounds of the heat-producing flowers Nkiru dubbed *furnace-weed*, and in each meadow the air was fragrant and surprisingly warm, so much so that Se-Jong began to sweat in earnest.

He'd never seen Nkiru so nervous, or so excited. Her giddiness emboldened him, and when the conversation lulled, he risked embarrassment by breaking into a song he'd learned from one of his instructors at Jackill.

> *"As I walked 'long the star-docks far above Jove*
> *Parading the star-ships I did so love*
> *I heard an old guildee singing a song*
> *Won't you take me away boys, me time is not long*
>
> *"Wrap me up in me smock and me jumper*
> *For no more on the star-docks I'll be*
> *Just tell me old shipmates, I'm taking a trip mates*
> *And I'll see you some day at the Hero's Gates"*

Se-Jong paused and glanced at Nkiru. She'd stopped, her thumbs hitched at her waist, staring at him with an expression of surprise. She cocked her head to the side. "And he sings, too."

Se-Jong grinned and kept walking.

> *"Now the Hero's Gates is a place I heard tell*
> *Where the guildies go if they don't go to hell*
> *Where skies are all clear and the star sprites do play*
> *And the cold of the vacuum is far, far away*
>
> *"Wrap me up in me smock and me jumper*
> *For no more on the star-docks I'll be*
> *Just tell me old shipmates, I'm taking a trip mates*
> *And I'll see you some day at the Hero's Gates"*

This time he didn't pause between verses, just kept walking and increased his volume. If there were any yoks lurking about, they would want nothing to do with this loud, brash pair of intruders.

> *"When you get to the Gates and the long trip is through*
> *There's grub and there's clubs and there's pubs in there too*
> *Where there's nary a harsh word and the beer it is free*
> *And the golden dust flows from the tree"*

Se-Jong didn't expect Nkiru to join in on the chorus, but when she did her singing was unhesitant, unapologetic, and utterly off-key. He nodded encouragingly. She grinned and they sang together.

> *"Wrap me up in me smock and me jumper*
> *For no more on the star-docks I'll be*
> *Just tell me old shipmates, I'm taking a trip mates*
> *And I'll see you some day at the Hero's Gates"*

Se-Jong lowered his voice and slowed the tempo for the final verse, singing it like a soft dirge.

> *"Now, I don't want a harp nor a halo, not I*
> *Just give me some wings and a clear piece of sky*
> *I'll play me a ballad and sing me a song*
> *With the angels behind me to push me along"*

Spinning toward Nkiru he sang the chorus at the top of his lungs. She laughed and joined in, also shouting.

> *"Wrap me up in me smock and me jumper!*
> *For no more on the star-docks I'll be!*
> *Just tell me old shipmates, I'm taking a trip mates!*
> *And I'll see you some day at the Hero's Gates!"*

By the time they arrived at a high bluff just above the lakeshore, the sun had passed its zenith and had begun to sink toward the craggy rim of the far crater wall. Nkiru insisted they stop while she dug something out of her backpack. It was the snowglobe relic.

"Come here," she ordered. She positioned Se-Jong next to her, facing away from the lake. She held the snowglobe at arm's length, high above their heads, so that their faces and the background vista were reflected on its curved surface. "Watch this," she said mysteriously, and swiped her thumb across the smooth glass. When she dropped her hand and brought the snowglobe closer, the reflected image on its surface didn't change. It still showed their two faces framed by the crater walls with the island in the background, her beaming with joy, a goofy grin plastered across his own unshaven face.

"I figured out how to use it to take a selfie," she proclaimed proudly.

"Well, I guess that's pretty cool," he said, but he felt a hesitant dismay. He didn't know what a "selfie" was, but it seemed unlikely that the snowglobe relic was simply some kind of camera. She'd said it was a communications device. Who might be receiving a copy of their "selfie" photo, he wondered?

They continued along the bluffs until a path to the shore revealed itself. The terrain at the edge of the lake was flat, and there were signs of past campsites. Trash littered an area around a stale fire ring, and the nearby tufts of furnace-weed were trampled and dead. Nkiru looked at the scene with distaste. "Filthy bastards," she murmured.

Eyeing the position of the sun, Se-Jong suggested they set up camp, but she shook her head. She pointed across the water to the central island, shielding her eyes from the sun's reflected glare. "We need to get across. We'll camp on the island."

It took longer than Nkiru wanted to inflate the heavy pack-raft and get it into the water. Se-Jong insisted that they read and follow the directions in the included instruction manual. He gestured to the lake. The island mountain was backlit by the setting sun and cast a long shadow across the water that seemed to be pointed directly at their position on the shoreline. "That looks really deep, and it's a long way across."

She paced while he fought to unpack and inflate the raft. "Hurry," she said. Se-Jong was dismayed by its small size, but eventually even he had to admit it was ready, and they piled in. He activated the small expeller jet, and they began the journey across the still lake. The raft was surprisingly fast, and their smooth passage left a marring, V-shaped wake in the water's mirrored surface.

Halfway to the island, Se-Jong realized that the central mountain's strange composition stemmed from the fact that the entire peak, from shoreline to summit, was completely and uniformly blanketed by furnace-weed. The peculiar golden color was a combination of the yellow flowers and tiny green leaves, blended by distance.

"The *real* Flowery Altar," Nkiru said suddenly. She grabbed his hand. Her eyes were watery from the cold wind of their passage across the water, and they shone with excitement.

"What do you mean?" The Flowery Altar, where Andrik the Redeemer was said to have sworn the Cataclyst Covenant, was in the Ice Cathedral back in Andriksburg.

She gave him a *you'll see* grin and returned her attention to the vista. The mountain's flanks slid steeply into the water, giving boaters no place to land the raft, and the jumbled collapse of the landslide was far too treacherous to climb. They circled its base, eventually coming to a large and decaying concrete landing at the water level. Se-Jong tied the raft to one of the piers and they scrambled ashore. Warmth from the countless furnace-weeds caused the air around the flanks of the mountain to rise, drawing in a cold breeze from the lake's surface.

They quickly found they were not the first explorers to visit the island. Far from it, if the amount of trash on the concrete landing was any indication. The spell of wonder that had enthralled them both as they approached the island was instantly spoiled by the childish graffiti spray-painted on the crumbling concrete.

KILL THE JANGA BUMBLEBEES

Nkiru kicked a beer can into the water. "Assholes," she muttered.

Dreams

As the sun sank in the west, the long shadow cast by the central island slowly climbed the distant ramparts of the eastern rim wall. Daylight dimmed into dusk as they explored the island's landing. The concrete structure, which consisted of several broken piers jutting from a fifty-meter-wide central platform, had been crudely poured a very long time ago atop a much older stone foundation. Several pits had been recently bored into the mountainside by an enterprising miner, but none went very deep. Nkiru seemed perplexed and anxious, pacing the base of the mountainside, where several small landslides had spilled house-size hillocks of soil and pebbles onto the landing. She'd retrieved the scancorder relic from her pack and was pointing it at one of the mounds of dirt and stone debris. "There should be an entrance right there," she said. "It's gone."

He gestured toward the graffiti, the trash, the mine shafts dug into the rocky soil of the mountainside. "We aren't the first people here, not by a long shot. If there's a dungeon inside the mountain, why hasn't somebody found it already?"

While Nkiru searched for the missing entrance, Se-Jong used the last of the daylight to make camp atop the largest of the debris mounds. The rocky soil was carpeted by the golden flowers of the furnace-weed, creating a bubble of comfort that kept the icy cold at bay. As he worked, he watched her pace the length of the pier, waving her scancorder at the mountainside. He was in no position to dispute her theory that the mountain held an undiscovered avatar fortress. If she said it was here, it was probably here.

He'd never considered himself an explorer, a discoverer of lost things, but here he was, in the middle of nowhere on a remote pilgrimage world, setting up a tent on an island inside a giant impact crater. This was *way* more exciting than anything the War College could offer. Even if Nkiru turned out to be wrong, and the mountain was just a mountain, he would have no regrets. Just being here with her was enough.

Eventually, darkness forced Nkiru to give up her search, and she joined Se-Jong at the campsite. They ate a self-warming meal and drank equally warming whiskey from a flask that Se-Jong had purchased from the outfitter. Afterward, neither spoke as they sipped and watched the last sunlight slip off the highest points of the eastern crater wall. The huge bowl of air beneath the rim was completely still, and they endured an arctic silence that neither of them had ever experienced. There was no twilight; as soon as the sun set, the bright-blue stars of the Oorik Cluster and the angel wings of the Great Nebula revealed themselves with no warm-up or introduction, like a cloud of unexpected fireworks frozen in place an instant after detonation.

It wasn't the spangled sky that held Se-Jong's attention, however; it was the circular sea. In the absence of even the slightest breeze, the surface of the water had settled into a geometric plane of unimaginable flatness. It had, in essence, become a fifty-kilometer-wide optically perfect mirror in which every single photon from the night sky was reflected with perfect clarity.

The psychological effect was disconcerting. To Se-Jong it seemed like he and Nkiru were trapped in some intermediate dimension between two different starry universes, one above, one below, identical in every respect. At one point, when he'd stared too long into the reflection, he felt a sudden giddiness, a sense of falling, and he grabbed at the tufts of furnace-weed to keep himself from tumbling into the abyss of the below-sky. "Which one is real?" he whispered, and Nkiru answered, "Both of them."

The whiskey and the warm flowers and the alien skies and the total, absolute solitude made them lightheaded. They were alone. They were the only two conscious beings in either cosmos, above or below, two tiny specks of determination floating between two opposite and uncaring heavens. He could feel the tension in her muscles as she leaned into his warmth. She waved her arm out over the immense bowl-shaped crater filled with the bright, reflected sparks of the star cluster. Se-Jong could barely make out the motion in the darkness, but her words were clear:

"Behold, the *real* Starry Chalice."

He looked out over the lake. How had he not noticed before? The bowl-shaped crater with its conical central peak was exactly the same shape and proportions as the bowl-and-spike of a Cataclyst Church altar, just on a much larger geological scale.

Her breathing quickened. "You know the Leodiva painting of the *War of the Archangels*?" Se-Jong didn't reply, didn't move, afraid he would clumsily break the magic of the moment. After a while, she continued, as if she were talking to herself. "The setting for that painting is inside this mountain."

Se-Jong kept perfectly still and waited. Next to him, Nkiru reached down and picked one of the blossoms from a furnace-weed, which had opened with the setting sun. "This wasn't just any dungeon. This place was ground zero for the Rapture of the Avatars and the Cataclysm." She crushed the petals of the flower and rolled them between her fingertips, releasing a strong peppery scent. She dropped the crushed petals. "The Second Epoch ended right here."

Se-Jong thought of the cracked concrete, the trash and graffiti, the piles of stone rubble. Compared to the unparalleled majesty of the glacier-hewn Ice Cathedral, this place was a shithole. "What about the cathedral in Andriksburg? What about the caves beneath the glacier? That's where it supposedly all happened."

"Ten thousand years is a long time. They forgot what really happened. The church rewrote history. Who knows?" She sighed, and the glimpse of worry he'd seen in her face when they'd first entered the crater was again evident in her voice. "Maybe I'm wrong. Tomorrow, we'll find out."

—

They huddled together atop their sleeping bags in the bed of warm furnace-weed, the thin air crisping their skin, the stars above close enough to touch, the reflected stars in the lake even closer. She pointed to the brightest star. "I think that must be Horu. There's a tiny little shrine on the fifth planet called the Temple of Gaia." She lowered her arm and snuggled closer to his warmth. "After we're done here, I'd really like to go. It's not on the pilgrimage, so we'd have to buy transport tickets."

"Horu is a Caeren world," he reminded her. "It's not on the pilgrimage. They wouldn't give us a visa."

He felt her shrug. "We'll find a way."

She was right, he knew, thrilled that she'd said *We'll find a way*, instead of *I'll find a way*. They *would* find a way. Se-Jong suddenly realized that he'd follow her anywhere. Together, they were invincible. He pulled away from her and rose to his knees. Craning his head high, he howled at the top of his lungs, just as Nkiru had done earlier. Nkiru laughed, and she too rose and howled. Vapor from their breath sprayed outward into the cold air like a dragon's fire, making them both marvel.

"Just tell me old shipmates, I'm taking a trip mates!" sang Se-Jong.

"And I'll see you some day at the Hero's Gates!" responded Nkiru.

They continued until they were both hoarse, waiting for an echo or an answering call that never came. Then they collapsed in laughter, and when that was done, she slid quietly back into his arms, watching the stars, while his heartbeat slowed and his skin prickled from evaporating perspiration. Exhaustion and a deep satisfaction dragged him toward sleep.

A faint, almost subsonic moan rumbled across the far lake. The sound was like nothing he'd ever experienced, an eerie thrumming interspersed with low-frequency crackling booms that were felt rather than heard. Nkiru tensed in his arms. For an instant he wondered if the spirits of some forlorn god might be replying to their shouts, but Nkiru whispered in his ear: "A glacier is moving." He tried to imagine one of the gargantuan rivers of ice in motion, creeping down the crater wall toward the starry hole in infinity. The grinding moan persisted for many long seconds, and was followed by an echoing, watery thunder as a colossal iceberg collapsed into the lake.

He felt something touch his lips and he opened his eyes. He could barely see her face just centimeters away, but he could sense that her eyes were open. She moved her fingertips from his lips across his nose and cheeks, lightly brushing his skin like someone without sight reading a story in Braille. He didn't move, and all his senses shut down until his entire universe constricted into the moving spot of nerve endings where her fingertips touched his skin. She continued exploring his features, grazing his eyes, hair, chin, and neck. Eventually, her hand came to rest, palm down on his chest, like a small bird alighting on a branch. He closed his eyes.

―

The Mucktu witch is standing over him, a dark silhouette against the sky. She doesn't speak, but he can feel the intensity of her attention like heat radiating from a nuclear furnace. She's staring at him with eyeless sockets. The stone embedded in her forehead gleams in the starlight; the dark leafy tattoos climbing her neck to her temples are in writhing motion.

He can't move, can't cover his nakedness, but after an eternity he realizes that the witch isn't staring at him.

She was never *staring at him.*

She is staring at Nkiru, with an expression of dawning recognition.

She smiles, and something dark moves in the recesses of her empty eye pits.

"Of course. You're at Grone, aren't you?"

―

Se-Jong's eyes flew open, but the nightmare was gone, replaced by a black sky and a sparse patch of stars. The Oorik Cluster had set, leaving in its wake the empty skies of the Devastation. His breath fogged in the frigid air. Deep in the sleeping bag they shared, Nkiru stirred in his arms and mumbled something indistinct. He kissed her gently on the top of her head. Her night terrors had gradually faded since they'd started sleeping together, but his own bad dreams had blossomed into an almost nightly affair. Maybe he'd absorbed whatever anguish had originally caused her nightmares. If so, he had no regrets.

―

As he was drifting back into sleep, something caught his eye: a brief shimmer in the sky no larger than a coin held at arm's length. It quickly shrank to a dot that crawled slowly across the background stars. Se-Jong recognized the shimmering phenomena as a hypervee splash; a starship had just arrived above Grone and was maneuvering into orbit. A surge of adrenalin brought him fully alert; only a big military starcutter had engines powerful enough to create a splash that could be seen from the surface.

A tiny buzzing sound, like an insect in the furnace-weed, sounded next to his head. It took him a moment to recognize the muted alert of his komnic. Moving very slowly, he reached into their haphazard pile of clothes and extracted the buzzing device. He touched the screen. A message appeared:

SET YOUR KOMNIC TO TRANSMIT LOCATION

He listened for Nkiru's breath to make sure she was still sleeping, then looked up at the moving dot in the sky. A flood of ice-cold indecision froze his hand above the komnic screen. Once he sent their location, it would be less than an hour before all this would end, and Nkiru would be safe. On the other hand, once he touched the screen, this mystical journey they were sharing would also end, maybe forever. He suddenly regretted the message he'd sent to his grandmother. Even more, he regretted not telling Nkiru what he'd done. He was suddenly convinced that she would see his well-intentioned actions as a betrayal, and whatever this thing was that had developed between them, this magical bond, would be irreparably shattered.

Nkiru moved against him, as if in her sleep she could sense his turmoil. A few stray strands of her hair tickled his nose, and he smiled bitterly. He slowly lowered the komnic and deactivated its transceiver.

Not yet, he said silently to the bright dot in the sky.

He cradled her for the rest of the night, watching the sparse star field wheel above the crater, a growing emptiness gnawing at his guts. Twice during his vigil the bright point of light traversed the sky, and he watched it with morbid dread until it dropped below the horizon. There would be no easy way out of this situation he'd caused.

Archangel

An arc of blue above the crater rim announced the dawn. As the skies grew lighter, the constricting knot of nerves in Se-Jong's gut slowly began to loosen. Whatever the coming day held, there was nothing he could do but let it play out. He drew in a deep breath of the cold air, careful so that the motion wouldn't wake Nkiru. She was a warm weight glued to his side, her head completely buried inside the sleeping bag. Her presence felt completely natural, like a part of his own body. He stretched, slowly, carefully. His head hurt from the whiskey, but that ache was nothing compared to the burning in his legs from the previous day's climb. He swallowed, and realized his throat hurt, too, hoarse from their nocturnal howling match.

"You shouldn't have been so loud last night," a man's voice announced.

Se-Jong exploded into full wakefulness, struggling in the tight sleeping bag to extricate himself from the tangle of Nkiru's legs. Stirred awake by his struggles, she muttered something sleepily, angrily.

Se-Jong cursed. He'd made a huge mistake by assuming they'd been alone. He was naked, tangled in a sleeping bag with an equally naked girl, with nothing he could use to defend himself. He grabbed the nearest weapon he could find, a fist-size rock, and spun toward the voice.

The shaggy-haired pilgrim from the *Legacy Sky* squatted on his haunches a few feet away, bundled and hooded in multiple layers of pilgrims' robes. He flinched as Se-Jong raised the rock. There was enough light to see that the man's hands were empty, but Se-Jong knew he could have a weapon concealed in his ragged robes.

Nkiru jerked into a sitting position and let out a yelp of surprise. By this time, Se-Jong had managed to extricate himself from the sleeping bag. He wobbled upright on the loose talus, barefoot and naked, trying not to drop the heavy rock. Nkiru instinctively clutched the edge of the sleeping bag and held it up like a protective shield.

"I knew you would come back here," the man said, matter-of-factly.

"What do you mean?" Se-Jong demanded. "Who are you?"

The man's dark eyes glittered, his gaze directed at Nkiru. She was blinking rapidly, fighting the collision of sleep and adrenaline.

Se-Jong brandished the rock. "Answer me! Who *are* you?"

"She knows." The man pointed a knobby finger toward Nkiru.

She stared at the man without any hint of recognition. She looked up at Se-Jong, shook her head. Se-Jong glared at the man. "Tell me what you're doing here or I'll . . ." His words trailed off. He wasn't sure what he would do. The man hadn't made any threatening moves and seemed to be unarmed. Se-Jong's pounding heart slowed a bit as his initial burst of panic subsided. "Or I'll . . ." He tightened his grip on the rock and made a throwing motion.

The man cried out and drew back. "No, please!"

Nkiru struggled into her coverall, her skin covered in goose-pimples from the cold. She stood next to Se-Jong, who was acutely aware of his own awkward nudity. He lowered the rock, but kept it clenched in his fist. "Don't you move," he told the man. He kneeled and found his undershorts draped over a mound of furnace-weed. Using one hand and hopping briefly on one foot, he struggled into them. The fabric was warm from the plant's heat. He stumbled, almost toppling into Nkiru, who reached out to steady him.

Watching their clumsy antics, the man broke into loud, braying laughter. He sounded like a donkey, Se-Jong thought.

Nkiru made a sharp intake of breath. The fright dissolved from her face, replaced by a wide-eyed expression of dawning comprehension. After a moment's hesitation, she crept toward the squatting man.

"Nkiru, wait," Se-Jong warned, but she held up a hand. She knelt in front of the stranger. He shrank back a few inches and then froze like a statue, as if suddenly hypnotized by her gaze. She reached out and delicately pushed the hood away from his face. When she spoke, her voice was a trembling hush.

"Arni? Is that you?"

The shaggy-haired man looked up at Se-Jong with a glare of righteous triumph. "See? I *told* you she knew!"

Needle

Se-Jong watched as Nkiru made breakfast for the man, cutting up one of the apples they'd bought at the outfitter and combining it with a packet of self-heating porridge. She fawned over him like he was a long-lost lover, repeatedly touching him on the shoulder as if convincing herself he was real. In return, he giggled and spouted nonsense, basking in her warmth. Once he even burst into some kind of childhood song. Nkiru clapped delightedly, but when she turned away her eyes were deeply troubled.

The man was broken. Twitchy and wild eyed, he jumped at every sudden movement, and every so often, with no provocation Se-Jong could see, he would jerk upright and look around frantically as if he expected to find a fearsome yok leaping at him. When he spilled his coffee, Nkiru clucked and helped him squeeze it from the hem of his filthy robe. She spoke to him earnestly in a low voice. Occasionally he would nod or laugh.

When she had him settled with his breakfast, she came to Se-Jong, who'd been watching from the edge of the campsite, sipping coffee. He had a million questions, all of which died in his throat when he saw the tears streaming down her cheeks. She wiped them away with the back of her hand and sat on the rock next to him.

The sun was cresting the eastern rim wall, bathing their ridgetop campsite with warmth. He noticed that the tiny yellow flowers of the furnace-weed clamped shut into hard yellow shells wherever the sun's rays touched. He unzipped his coldsuit and waited for her to explain. She squinted up at the light and brushed a strand of hair out of her face. She glanced at the man, who was wiping ineffectually at a clump of porridge dribbled in his beard, and let out a long breath between pursed lips, as if gathering herself for a strenuous physical effort. "He was a . . ." She paused and her brow crinkled. "I'm not sure how to explain what he was. I knew him before I moved to New York. I guess you'd say he was an engineer, but mostly he was a dreamer."

"What's he doing here? Is he following us?"

"I think he *lives* here," she whispered, glancing across the water to the ruins of the citadel. "He must have recognized me on the transport ship."

"How did he recognize you? I thought you'd changed your appearance."

"I did. I don't know how he knew it was me."

Se-Jong looked over at the man, who had managed to deposit even more porridge into his beard. "What's wrong with him?"

"I'd heard he was . . . injured. I didn't know how badly. He's lost his memories. He remembers my face, but not my name. I'm not sure he even knows who *he* really is."

"What's he want?"

She made an anxious face. "I'm not sure of that, either. This isn't how I remember him. I didn't even recognize him back on the ship, not with the beard and the hair. He's older than I remember."

The man was mumbling into his bowl as he scraped out the last bit of porridge. He licked his fingertips and smiled broadly at Nkiru. "Most delicious," he said brightly. He squinted up at the morning sun. "Time's a-wasting."

Se-Jong thought he recognized hints of Nkiru's strange accent in his voice. He remembered the odd sense of familiarity he'd felt when he'd first encountered the man. "He's from California, like you? What kind of engineer did you say he was?"

Nkiru's mouth opened, froze, and then hung that way for a few seconds. She made a humorless chuckle and gestured around at the crater-and-sea vista. "I guess you'd say he was a landscape engineer."

Her vague answer caused a flare of heat in his chest. "Did you come here looking for him?" Her hesitation provided the answer. "So *he's* the guy you've been looking for? You think this whack job is the Prophet Kanaan?"

"No, no. Not him." She glanced at the man, who was picking ineffectually at a clump of dried food stuck to his robes. "That's not Kanaan."

He slammed his fist into his thigh. "Damn, damn, *damn!* You told me *no more secrets!*" He immediately regretted his outburst. After all, he was concealing one whopper of a secret himself.

Her hand flew to his shoulder. "No! It's not like that! I didn't expect him to be here, I swear!" She paused. "Though I guess I'm not too surprised." She tightened her grip. "He's important, Se-Jong. *Very* important. I didn't know he would be here, but I'm really happy to have found him. He's like . . . *me*. He can help us!"

A thunderous *crack-crack!*, and they all looked up as the sound echoed and bounced off the mountainside and reflected into the lake. *A sonic boom*, Se-Jong realized.

The thread of a bright, high-altitude contrail caught the morning light. It began scribing a long, gradual arc across the sky as the reentering ship decelerated and maneuvered. His heart jumped into his throat. From the direction of travel, it was obvious that the ship was *not* in the approach pattern for the Andriksburg shuttleport.

They've found us.

He looked over at Nkiru. She was frowning, watching the thin white streak grow longer. The arc of its path tightened just as it disappeared over the edge of the crater rim. She turned to him, her expression uneasy. Her eyes moved to the bearded man.

"Arni, do you know the way into the mountain? The old entrance is buried."

"It's a secret," he said, eyeing Se-Jong with suspicion.

Nkiru squeezed Se-Jong's shoulder. "This is my friend. I trust him. You can trust him, too."

"He was going to hit me with a rock," Arni said accusingly. "I don't like him."

Nkiru dropped her hand from Se-Jong's shoulder. "You scared him when you woke him up. He won't hurt you. He's our friend, I promise."

Arni shook his head. "I still don't like him. I'm a good judge of people, you know." He eyed Nkiru critically. "You had sex with him, didn't you? You shouldn't have had sex with him. That was a really bad idea."

Nkiru bristled. "That's none of your business. I'm old enough to do what I want."

Arni shook his head furiously. "A capatar must *not* have sex with a bot. It's *dangerous*."

Se-Jong felt heat rising in his cheeks. The words *capatar* and *bot* meant nothing to him. He shot a questioning look at Nkiru, but she was focused on Arni. "What are you talking about?"

"You're not based on a bot template, you know. Your code doesn't work like his. You're catastrophically incompatible. It breaks the law of Conservation of Consciousness and all that, don't you know? Do-do-do-don't you know?" He dropped his voice to a whisper. "The Infinatis are watching and listening." Arni made another braying laugh, and the fleeting moment of lucidity was gone.

"What's a bot?" Se-Jong blurted.

Arni spun to him with an angry shushing sound, pressing his index finger against his lip. "Didn't you hear what I just said?" he hissed. "They're *listening*."

Nkiru gave Arni a bewildered look. "Arni, this isn't important. Right now, I need your help to get into the mountain." She glanced up at the sky, where the contrail was already dissipating. "We need to hurry."

Arni nodded slowly, then shot a distrustful glance toward Se-Jong. "Stay away from her."

A low, thrumming rumble interrupted Se-Jong's response. At first it sounded like it was coming from everywhere, and Se-Jong thought it was the sound of another glacier moving as they'd heard the previous night. As it persisted and grew louder, he realized it was no glacier.

"It's a ship," he said with a frown. But that didn't make sense. It had been less than a minute since they'd heard the sonic boom and seen the contrail in the sky. If a reentering ship had been heading here, as he had suspected, there was no way it could've descended so quickly.

The rumble grew abruptly louder and they turned toward its direction. A bizarre sight greeted them. Floating serenely into view above the crater's rim was a towering silver shape, pointed straight into the sky, two hundred meters high but needle thin. Its mirror-finish hull was smooth and unmarked and came to a symmetrical point at both top and bottom. It moved smoothly as if it were suspended from an invisible thread. There were no visible thrusters, and no smoke or flames. Even the rumble sounded nothing like any ship's jets Se-Jong had ever heard.

Nkiru gaped. "What the hell is that?"

Se-Jong let out a slow exhale. They were well and truly and utterly fucked. "It's called the *Navis Sacris*. It's the flagship of the church's Holy Navy." He turned to Nkiru. "All that stuff in your backpack? I think the Father Regis wants it back."

Betrayal

He'd waited too long, and now it was too late. He'd wanted one more night with Nkiru, just the two of them, and his desire had led to disaster. He frantically dug his komnic out of the pocket of his coldsuit. He turned it on and waited anxiously for it to boot up, staring at the *Navis Sacris*. The ship had paused above the eastern rim of the crater, bizarrely surreal, its outline ultrasharp in the frigid morning air despite the distance of many kilometers. The thrumming roar of its mysterious motive power echoed around the crater until it seemed to be emanating from the water and the stone instead of the sky. He shook his komnic, waiting for it to light up. "Damn, damn, *damn*. Hurry *up!*"

Nkiru was hurriedly sealing her coldsuit. She grabbed her backpack. Her eyes flitted between the titanic silver needle in the sky and Se-Jong's komnic. "What are you doing?"

The device lit up, and he swiped to the settings app and activated the transceiver. He found the message he'd received during the night and turned on location sharing with the sender. His komnic was now a secure homing beacon. He tapped a response to the message, his cold fingers stumbling numbly on the tiny keyboard.

NAVIS SACRIS HERE. HURRY.

He tapped Send, turned to Nkiru. "I'm calling for help."

Her skin paled. "Calling *who* for help?"

The sudden mistrust on her face caused his heart to skip. He gestured up at the *Navis Sacris*. "There's a company of Dei Militans on that ship. Probably the Regia Protectors, and maybe even the Silent Knife." She was blinking rapidly, and he worried she wasn't even listening to him. "Nkiru, *they know you can use avatar relics!* They *know* you stole relics from the shrine worlds. They probably think you're some kind of Mucktu superwitch. If they get you, they'll *torture* you. They'll try to *rectify* you."

In his hand, the komnic chimed. Nkiru's gaze darted toward it. Se-Jong raised the device to read the message.

ALREADY EN ROUTE. HOLD YOUR POSITION. IN CONTACT WITH NAVIS SACRIS. STAND BY.

The contrail they'd seen had been the cavalry coming to rescue them, not the *Navis Sacris*. It wouldn't be long, now. He had a sudden flare of hope. He smiled reassuringly at Nkiru.

Her expression was guarded. "Answer me. Who are you talking to?"

"My grandmother."

"Your grandmother . . . the Solar Guard captain?"

He winced at her confusion. "Her cutter arrived last night. I was going to tell you but—"

She pulled away from him. "What is your grandmother doing here? I don't understand!"

"I'm trying to help you. To keep you safe." He gestured up at the *Navis Sacris*. "I *knew* something like this would eventually happen. I sent a message to my grandmother as soon as we got to Grone. I asked her to give you her protection from the church. Asylum."

"You did . . . *what?*"

This was going to be far worse than he'd expected. "I'm sorry I didn't tell you. I wanted to but . . ." He spread his arms placatingly.

She stared at him. "You said I could *trust* you. You *promised*."

A numbness spread from the center of his chest. She was right to feel betrayed. He'd been a fool. *Damn, damn, damn*, he muttered silently. There was nothing he could say to defend his actions. Everything he'd done had been her best interest, but as his tactics instructor at Jackill would've said, he'd "dicked up the comms during execution."

All emotion vanished from Nkiru's face as if some internal switch had been flipped. She spun to Arni. "Can you get me into the mountain?"

Arni looked confused. He addressed Nkiru while frowning at Se-Jong. "I think your friend may be a bad man. Is he a bad man?"

"Let's ask him." She fumbled angrily at her backpack straps, raising it to her shoulders. "Tell us, Lieutenant, are you a bad man?"

"Nkiru, I—" He stopped, realizing he didn't know what to say. He gestured toward the unmoving ship. "My grandmother says she's talking to the *Navis Sacris*. I'm sure she's telling them to stand down. See? They're not moving. She told us to wait here until she arrives." When Nkiru's hard expression didn't change, he added. "It's going to be okay. I promise."

"You *promise*," she scoffed, shaking her head in disbelief. "Come on, Arni." She pulled the shaggy-haired man to his feet. "We need to hurry. Get me into the mountain, now."

"You'll have to swim," Arni said.

She nodded and cinched her backpack straps. "Let's go."

Se-Jong stepped into her path, tried to take her shoulders. Desperation caused his words to be sharper than intended. "Please, Nkiru. You've lied to me too, kept secrets from me, too. We both knew we'd eventually need help. I didn't have a choice!"

She recoiled. Her hand plunged to her waist and pulled something away from her belt. She thrust it toward him. It took a second for him to recognize the small orange cylinder: Yok-Stop, the chemical defense spray they'd bought at the outfitters. He threw up his hands, palms out. "Whoa!"

The hand brandishing the Yok-Stop was rock steady. Her voice was equally hard. "I only lied about one thing, Lieutenant. Truth is, I did fall a little bit in love with you. My mistake."

He blinked. For a moment, neither of them moved. He slowly lowered his hands. "I'm sorry I lied to you. I messed up. I was afraid the church would come for you." He gestured toward the *Navis Sacris*. "And I was right. You're *too important*. They'll never stop until they catch you."

As if on cue there was a change in the eerie roar from the *Navis Sacris*. They both looked up, but the titanic silver needle hadn't moved. The new sound became the whistling scream of jet turbines as a delta wing aircraft darted over the rim wall a few kilometers from the church ship. Se-Jong shaded his eyes. The orange and blue stripes on the ship's nose identified it as a Solar Guard craft, but it wasn't his grandmother's shuttle, as he'd expected. It was a tactical dropship, a high-speed troop carrier. He frowned. It dropped smoothly over the edge of the crater rim and sped along the descending terrain toward the lake.

Words spilled out of his mouth. "That's her! See, I told you she was coming."

The dropship reached the lake and rocketed toward them, so low the force of its wake caused a rooster tail of water a dozen meters high. It was moving fast. *Too* fast. Another motion drew his eye. The *Navis Sacris* had also begun to move, effortlessly gliding in their direction.

Something was wrong. The armored dropship wasn't slowing as it neared the island. Nkiru lurched toward the water, pulling Arni behind her. Without thinking, he moved to block them. "Wait! My grandmother says to stay here!"

Nkiru paused for the slightest, regretful instant. Before he could react, she squeezed the trigger of the Yok-Stop. He spun away, but a milky stream of ice-cold liquid bathed his face and neck. He squeezed his eyes shut, wiping frantically at them.

Nothing happened. He opened his eyes.

Nkiru was staring at him. "Crap," she said.

Arni jerked her arm and they splashed into the water. Se-Jong sputtered the foul-tasting fluid out of his mouth. He'd expected it to be some kind of liquid fire, like the pepper spray he'd been forced to endure during his combat training in his senior year, but despite the warnings of the Olid shopkeeper, apparently what worked to stop a yok didn't stop a man.

Arni vanished beneath the surface of the lake. Nkiru took a deep breath and followed him under, kicking strongly to propel herself into the depths. The sun's glare on the water prevented Se-Jong from seeing the direction they were swimming.

The dropship's turbines suddenly changed pitch. It was decelerating hard, flaring almost vertically for a full-on tactical landing at the concrete pier. The jets were earsplitting, spraying lake water that pelleted his skin like bullet-rain. Se-Jong knew they wouldn't be risking such a dangerous maneuver unless they needed to get in and get out, fast. Behind them in the sky, the mighty bulk of the *Navis Sacris* was descending like the silvery awl of a god. He spun back toward the water. "Damn, damn, damn," he said. He took a deep, lung-filling breath and dove off the pier.

The shock of the freezing water caused him to completely expel the breath he'd taken. No matter. He'd always been a strong swimmer, courtesy of the uncounted hours he'd spent as a child on the shores and warm green seas of Askelon. The orange of Nkiru's coldsuit was clearly visible two meters beneath him, following Arni downward along the curve of the pier's stone foundation to where a darkness between two huge stones indicated an opening.

He increased the strength of his strokes as she vanished into the opening and was puzzled when one of his arms went numb, sending him into an awkward spin. Then his face was numb, and suddenly he could no longer hold his breath. Water flooded his throat. Panic gripped him: the Yok-Stop must have a delayed effect on humans! Without warning, a trillion volts of pain struck every nerve ending in his body. He spasmed violently, once, twice, then could no longer move at all. His lungs relaxed, his throat opened, and he sank into the blackness.

Someone floats above him in the cold water. He looks up into the empty eye sockets of the Mucktu witch from his dreams.

"Help me," he whispers.

The witch smiles sadly. "I can't help you. What's done is done."

This isn't a dream: Se-Jong is sure of it. This is real. But how can it be real? He is in the water at Grone. That is reality. He is drowning. There is no question about it. His lungs have filled with frigid water. He is dying.

But . . . he won't drown. He'll be pulled from the water, won't he? He'll survive! He will go inside the mountain with Nkiru and Arni, into the heart of their dark secrets. He feels a strange, excited flutter of his heart muscle as the past and future crash together. Something happened inside the mountain / has yet to happen inside the mountain.

He looks up at the witch, gripped by an awful certainty.

"She's going to die!"

The witch reaches out with both hands and gently cradles Se-Jong's face. Her hands are warm against the icy cold of the lake water. "Stay with me, just a little longer. You can't save her, but you may redeem her death."

LOADOUT

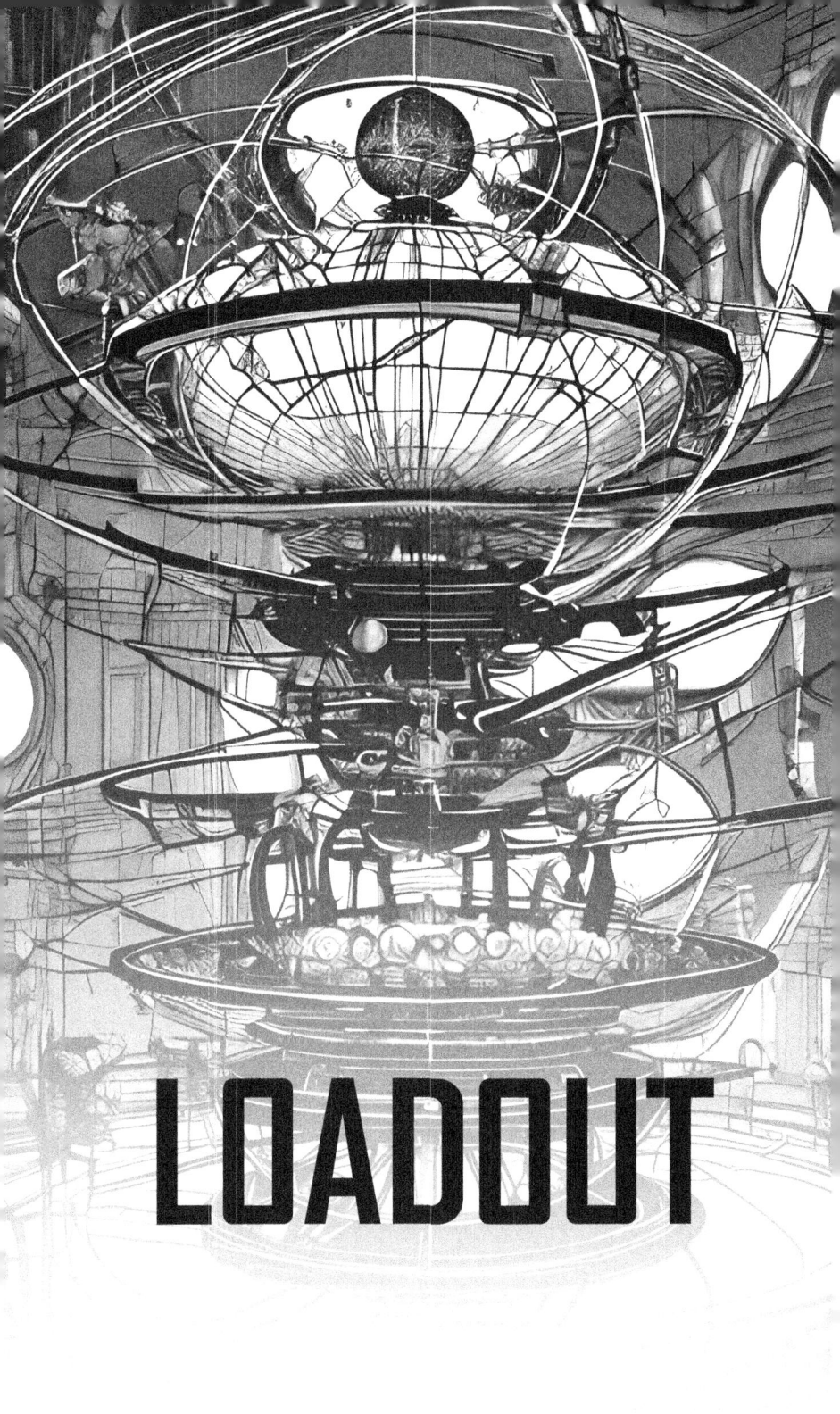

meatspace | CHUN

Horsemen

She scratched at her forearms. The tickling sensations were getting worse, distracting her at a time when distractions could be disastrous. April Chun stubbed out her cigarette and reached for the can of Coke on her desk. Spread across her computer monitors were the published works of Kaiser and Salim, the two physicists who'd uncovered the original QARMA theory upon which her own breakthroughs were based. They'd developed three supremely elegant equations that encapsulated the theory and described the QARMA effect. One of the three equations held the solution to her current dilemma. She was sure of it. The answer was buried in the math. The answer was *always* buried in the math. The trick would be finding it before they were all dead.

Since the demise of Dr. Reichard Kaiser, the theoretician whose work had first hinted at the QARMA effect, there were only two living souls—and one ghost—who really understood QARMA theory. Chun herself was the first and foremost living expert. The second was Dr. Imani Salim, the physicist who had coined the term QARMA: Quantum Recurrent Macrocosmic Anomaly. Salim was the first to observe the QARMA effect during a botched supercomputer simulation of a nuclear fusion reaction, and the first to describe the bizarre but undeniably real phenomenon of a microcosm singularity. Despite the keen interest of her peers, three years after publishing her groundbreaking work, Salim had suddenly and completely withdrawn from the world of high-energy particle physics, left her tenured chair at Stanford, and resigned her fellowship at the Lawrence Livermore National Laboratory. Rumor had it she was now living in a Jain farming community somewhere in western India, surrounded by pacifists and goats.

The third person who deeply understood QARMA theory was Analise Novak, Chun's former protégé and now her bitterest rival. Analise was now a ghost in the QARMA machine. There was, of course, no way to contact her, either.

That meant it was up to Chun, and Chun alone, which was surprisingly comforting. Chun had never liked working with others. Really, they just slowed her down. Or they betrayed her, as her colleagues Arni and Analise had done—and now Rupe and Zia had also been revealed as traitors and co-conspirators!

She sighed bitterly. At least the secret was out. Rupe had led Solomon's team to the wreckage of Arni's lab. Arni's comatose body had been brought to the JEEB lab at Stanford, still attached to the recovered Haven engine. Rupe and Zia were in Solomon's custody.

Based on her questioning of Zia, it was clear that Arni's tampering with the Haven engine had somehow caused an instability in the QARMA kernel, an instability that was somehow affecting the real world. The earthquakes, the sunspots and solar storms, the bizarre weather—all appeared to be somehow linked to the timestream discontinuity inside the havencosm.

Here, alone in her small, darkened office, she would save the world. She just had to focus. Break down the problem. Deconstruct it into discrete issues, then resolve each issue. Just her and the math. She took a deep, fizzing drink from the can of Coke, emptied it, and placed it on her desk with all the other cans.

The entropic timestream inside the Haven microcosm was running six orders of magnitude faster than the same measure in the real world. The QARMA equations suggested that this was impossible, as the rate of time and entropy were metacosmic constants. Either the equations were wrong, or she wasn't interpreting them correctly. She had a sneaking suspicion that the timestream discontinuity was at the root of the entire problem, that the physical universe simply couldn't contain two different entropic rates, even if one of them was entirely virtual.

When she raised the Coke, nothing came out, and she remembered the can was empty. She put it back down and retrieved the can next to it, heavy with liquid. What had caused time to speed up inside the havencosm? The acceleration had begun a few nanoseconds after Analise's holobox code had been injected into the havencosm kernel, meaning it was likely a result of the code's manipulation of the kernel, perhaps combined with the unknown effects of the mysterious jeeb virus.

She sipped the second can of Coke and realized her mistake when something soggy bumped her lips and the taste of stale ashes washed into her mouth. She spat the liquid back into the can. When she looked at it, she saw the cigarette ashes on the top and the old butts floating in the dark liquid. She made a spitting noise and wiped her lips on her sleeve. Her concentration broken, she threw the half-empty can, which she'd been using to dispose of her cigarette butts, into the recycling bin, along with the other empties. From the fridge next to her desk she pulled a fresh can, and the magic of Coca Cola flooded the taste of the ashes down her throat.

Smoking wasn't allowed in the building, but as CEO she'd made herself an exception to the rule. She never smoked in her expansive public office, located on the corner of the building's top floor overlooking the corporate campus, but the adjacent private office in which she spent the vast majority of her productive time had an air-exchange system to whisk away the smoke. Caffeine, sugar, and nicotine had fueled some of the mightiest creative moments of her life, moments that had changed her destiny and perhaps that of the world. She saw no reason to stop now. *Especially* not now.

If there were any limits to the processing power and data management capabilities of a QARMA engine, they'd yet to discover them. No one, not even Chun, had plumbed the technical depths of a QARMA simulation. Nobody really knew how much data a QARMA engine could store and crunch. So far, it seemed limitless. The JEEB Earth sim manifested over eight billion complex non-player characters, plus an ultra-realistic model of earth's geology and ecosystems. The Orbital Arena gamecosm hosted an entire galaxy of equally-detailed worlds and bot characters.

This inconceivable computing power did have bizarre inconsistencies: due to the nature of the beast you couldn't run a spreadsheet or word processor using a QARMA engine, but you could create a simulation of an oak tree, or an elephant, or indeed an entire world's population of plants and animals down to the subatomic level. Hell, an entire *galaxy's* worth of worlds, all dynamically generated from a simple set of input parameters.

There was no way of knowing what was happening inside the stolen Haven engine, or what might be done to resynchronize the accelerated timestream. The problem was the firewall, which prevented any exchange of data between the Haven microcosm and the real-world macrocosm. Unlike a typical security firewall, it wasn't designed to protect the system from outside intrusions or hacks; it was meant as a shield to protect the sensitive electronics inside a QARMA engine's hardware from a local increase in the QARMA effect, which tended to fry the delicate circuitry of the quantum processors. She had designed and coded the firewall to automatically reconfigure itself based on the threat, but she'd never envisioned a situation like this one where it would block *all* access, even hers. There was no way in heaven or Earth, in-cosm or from the outside, to lower it without first resolving the issue that had prompted its automatic activation: the acceleration of the Haven timestream. It was a classic Catch-22 situation: the only way to repair the kernel was to lower the firewall, but the only way to lower the firewall was to repair the kernel.

She lit another cigarette. Colonel Solomon's team was trying to find a way to exploit the single known interface through the firewall—Arni's Orb code—to send instructions to the kernel node, but given the architecture of the system, that was about as likely as hitting the moon with a bullet fired from a hunting rifle. They'd also been sending text and video messages through the Orb interface, trying to contact Wolfe's capatar in the hope they could pass along instructions he could use to repair the malfunction from inside the firewall, but there was no indication that any of them had been received. The timestream differential might make it impossible for the virtual devices in-cosm to receive the transmissions. Or perhaps all the Orbs had been lost. Or perhaps Wolfe's capatar hadn't respawned after his brutal murder by the blue-skinned woman.

Other than the single message from Wolfe's capatar, there had been no other contact. They still didn't understand the message's cryptic contents. Solomon had a team trying to decipher it, to translate the bizarre language, but so far, no real progress had been made.

In the meantime, the world was coming apart at the seams. Despite the firewall, the instability within the Haven microcosm was somehow leaking, or perhaps *echoing*, into the real-world macrocosm. Until Analise's hack, the QARMA effect had only been observable in the immediate vicinity of the QARMA engine, within a couple of centimeters of the CPU at most. The effect was barely measurable even with the most sensitive scientific instruments: just the tiniest microscopic changes in the mass and energy of the physical machine and the surrounding air molecules. Bizarre and intriguing, but harmless.

After Analise's hack, the QARMA effect had gone macroscopic in a big way, amplified by a trillion-trillion magnitudes. Instead of heating the air molecules around the hardware enclosure by a few nanodegrees Celsius, or mysteriously increasing the mass of the hardware by a nanogram or two, it was affecting the fundamental forces of nature on a scale that was easy to detect.

Really easy, like solar storms, earthquakes, and tsunamis. And this Christ-forsaken skin prickle that every human on Earth seemed to be feeling. Social media had been lit up all morning. The Tingle, they were calling it. She scratched her arms again, but it didn't help. Nothing did. It was barely perceivable, just enough of a sensation to set her on edge.

She took a long drag on her cigarette that ended in a dry, burning cough. She'd set a new record for cigarettes in the past few hours, maybe one too many. She dropped the butt into the Coke can. It made a brief fizzling sound.

Analise had caused the entire crisis. The rumblings had begun the instant she, via her capatar, had stolen the gamecosm and migrated it to the Haven machine. The situation had grown worse when she'd subsequently stolen the jeebcosm from the military's Sentinel engine, a feat that Chun still couldn't explain. Then, last night's amateurish attempt by Arni to rescue Analise by spawning his capatar into the havencosm had caused a full-scale cosmic rupture of some kind. In an instant, the thing Rupe was calling the *bugaboo* had appeared in the sky and the situation had gone from moderately bad to apocalyptically desperate. Chun had insulated herself from the news trickling in from Asia, but she'd heard enough to know that the quakes and flooding were unprecedented. The loss of the world's network of communications and navigation satellites made it hard to get any word at all, but what had managed to trickle in was all bad. Worse than bad. She pushed the thoughts of the devastation from her mind. She had relatives in Korea, but that was just a distraction. Until the roof of the building fell on her head, she must focus on nothing but identifying and reversing the damage Analise and Arni had done.

Some of the people at the JEEB lab, especially the Russian hacker-bitch Zia, had blamed the past month's tremors on the malfunctioning QARMA engines. Chun now had to admit that Zia had been correct.

The bugaboo was clearly a real-world manifestation of a raw, unconstrained QARMA singularity, though it was unlikely that anyone else had yet recognized it as such. It had all the same basic observable properties of a virtual QARMA singularity, except that instead of being smaller than a proton and existing only in the qubits of a quantum processor, it was *real*, and it was the size of the *moon*.

The very thought of it made the Tingle worse, and she lit another cigarette. Somehow, a virtual construct from a computer simulation had materialized in Earth's orbit. This was no different than a fictional character from a favorite novel suddenly appearing in the flesh in Times Square. It was *impossible*. Objects from imaginary virtual worlds simply weren't . . . *real*.

For the moment, she decided to set aside the impossibility and simply accept it as a fact. Denying physical evidence was foolish and unscientific. Instead, she tried to frame the situation in terms of something she could understand: physics. The amount of energy required to manifest a QARMA singularity the size of the bugaboo was inconceivable. How much power was required to chime the entire Earth, from crust to core, like a gong? How much energy was required to stretch the fundamental space-time constant so that atomic clocks no longer functioned and ocean tides tripled in intensity? Christ, how much energy was required to generate *sunspots* on the freaking *sun*?

She didn't know, but it was a *lot*. Last night's Bay Area earthquake, occurring at the same instant as the appearance of the bugaboo, had measured 8.1 on the Richter scale. It had released at least sixty petajoules of energy, more than a dozen hydrogen bombs. The microtremors that had been rattling the entire planet ever since required a continuous release of energy in the yotta range, sextillions of joules every *instant*. Where was this energy coming from? It had to come from *somewhere*.

Despite the firewall, all three of the QARMA engines—Pandora, Sentinel and Haven—were showing signs of coordinated activity in their kernels, as if their singularities were somehow connected to each other, and the activity seemed to directly correlate with the increasing frequency and strength of the global earth tremors. She hadn't been able to confirm it yet, but she suspected that the activity of the bugaboo was similarly coordinated. The end result was that the physical structure of space-time in the vicinity of Earth was being stretched, just as the virtual singularities in each of the QARMA machines altered the space-time within the machine enclosures.

All this was scary enough, but the entropy-dilation effects that Dr. Salim had noticed at the subatomic level were now happening on a planetary scale, and they might soon result in a disaster that would make the author of the book of Revelation blush with envy. With her unauthorized hack of the Haven machine, Analise Novak had singlehandedly summoned the Four Horsemen of the Apocalypse, only instead of Conquest, War, Famine, and Death, she'd called forth Gravity, Electromagnetism, Weak Nuclear Force, and Strong Nuclear Force.

The four fundamental forces of nature were being twisted out of balance by the runaway QARMA effect, and unless the situation could be brought back under control, the end results would be unthinkable. John the Apostle could never have imagined the moment the entire solar system, and possibly even a good-size chunk of the surrounding galaxy, might explode into fermionic dust. Or collapse into a massive black hole. Or simply cease to exist.

Chun grimaced. If there was any way to stop the bugaboo from tearing the Earth to shreds—and she admitted to herself that it might already be too late—then she *must* find a way to penetrate the Haven machine's firewall and restore the Haven kernel to its original configuration. Put it back to the way it had been before Analise screwed it up.

Chun had opened another Coke and lit another Marlboro when the door to her office flew open and banged against the wall. She spun toward the intrusion, a blistering curse forming on her lips. It died in its first syllable. It was Geoffrey Mozingo, Orbital Arena's business manager and her closest confidant. Moz knew better than anyone not to interrupt her in her inner sanctum. For him to have barged in without even knocking meant that something truly extraordinary must have occurred.

"They want you over at the JEEB lab, right now! Howe says they're planning to send another capatar inside."

"Christ," Chun muttered, and she dropped her cigarette into her can of Coke.

Meatspace Avatar

"What is *she* doing here?" Chun demanded. The collapse of Arni's so-called Havenlab during the quake should have killed the hacker-bitch, but here she was, bruised, bandaged, and splinted, looking like the smug, punk-ass schemer she was. Zia should be in prison on charges of treason, not sitting at the right hand of Colonel Solomon in the JEEB lab conference room.

"Good to see you too, Dr. Chun," Zia said quietly. Her injuries had not diluted her insolence.

"She's under arrest, in my custody," snapped Solomon. "We need her, for now."

Rupe was also present. She glared at him, but he avoided eye contact, fumbling instead with something in his lap. Analise had seduced him into treason, too, with that false charisma she'd always used like a weapon. Guys like Rupe were particularly susceptible to the attentions of a pretty girl, especially if the girl was smart. Analise had been both. Pretty, smart, and *cunning*. Chun felt a small amount of pity for Rupe. He'd always been shackled by his emotions, over which he had no control. He was like a child, and his childlike naivete had led him into a criminal conspiracy.

There were others in the room, too, but a quick scan showed them to be unimportant. Reggie Howe, the JEEB program manager; a half dozen of the JEEB engineers; one of the BCI techs; a couple of terrified flunkies taking notes; and a dull-looking man with tufts of frizzled hair and a vaguely familiar corporate logo embroidered on his polo shirt. Without exception, every face was hollow and tense, every expression haunted by the knowledge that they'd had a role in the unfolding global disaster.

Howe, who always considered himself to be in charge, stood. He had dark circles under his eyes, but there was a crackling energy in his voice that she hadn't heard since all this began. "Thank you for coming, Dr. Chun. I think you know everyone here except Dr. Lieberman."

Lieberman. Of course. The guy with the polo shirt and frizzled hair. Now she recognized the corporate logo as that of ZavosGenomica. A spike of resentment stabbed her gut. Dr. Jakob Lieberman was the geneticist who had collaborated with Analise to develop the gene-scanning and editing components of the capatar technology. She'd read of his work on epigenetic enhancement. It wasn't her field, but she had recognized why it was so controversial. Changing the physical characteristics of an adult human, making them more attractive or smarter by injecting customized, gene-altering compounds, was sensational stuff.

"Dr. Chun," he said, without standing or offering his hand. "Jakob Lieberman. It's my pleasure."

She gave Lieberman a noncommittal nod. Ignoring Howe, she turned to Solomon, whom she knew was the real power in the room. "Why am I here?"

Solomon gestured to the whiteboards that covered every wall. "The team has come up with an idea. We want to run it past you."

She pushed down her anger. "Colonel, I'm incredibly busy. Nothing matters but finding a way to lower the firewall, and I'm the only person who can do it. Every minute I spend in useless meetings is worse than a complete waste of time. It's literally a crime against humanity."

"We *know* you're the only person who can fix the problem, Doctor. That's the reason you're here. We'll make it fast. Reggie?"

Howe moved to one of the whiteboards, where someone had hastily drawn a rectangle with the word HAVEN scrawled inside. A dotted red oval surrounded it. "The firewall is an automated security measure that was thrown up when the havencosm's internal timestream was accelerated. As long as the timestream remains accelerated, the firewall cannot be lowered. However, it is possible to resynchronize the timestreams if we can apply a software patch directly to the machine's operating system kernel. Isn't that correct, Dr. Chun?"

She let her annoyance pour through her words. "Of course. I've already written the patch. But unless I can find a way to lower the firewall, there's no way to access the kernel."

Howe took a deep breath. "That's not entirely correct, Doctor. There's no *direct* way to access the kernel, true . . . but a *capatar* might be able to reach the kernel node inside the cosm. The capatar interface is the only interface not affected by the firewall. With the video from Roland Wolfe's capatar, we also now know that a capatar can survive in the modified havencosm environment."

"I saw that video. There's no way to prove the man was Wolfe. Also, whoever it was, I also saw what happened to him. Brutally gutted by a blue-skinned assassin, if I remember correctly."

"We've analyzed the video. We're certain the man is Wolfe's capatar. His facial structure and physical marks are identical to Wolfe's. As for the attack . . ." Howe paused. "It's highly likely that he respawned. In fact, if capatars have a normal human lifespan, he has probably respawned more than a hundred times over the course of the extended timespan."

"So what? It doesn't matter. Look what happened last night when Arni tried to insert another capatar into the cosm." She motioned up to the ceiling, where many of the acoustical tiles were missing from the recent quake. "Half of San Francisco is on fire. The Bay Bridge is in the water. And you've all seen the pictures from Taiwan and Korea. I've warned you all along—the system architecture was never designed for anything like capatars."

Howe's face turned ashen. There was no denying that he and his JEEB team had played a role in the deaths of thousands—maybe millions—over the past twenty-four hours. The bulk of the blame lay with Analise and her conspirators, Arni, Rupe, and Zia, but Howe's team had been complicit by supporting Analise's dangerous software mods to the QARMA kernel.

He cleared his throat. "Arni's attempt was misguided and foolhardy. He was using prototype capatar hardware that had never been fully tested. We have one remaining capatar system here. It *has* been fully tested, and in fact it has been used more than twenty times to insert capatars into our test environment on JEEB Earth. We are confident that we can send a fully functional capatar into the havencosm using the JEEB spawn point. *Without* causing more instability in the QARMA environment."

Chun let out a frustrated breath. "It *still* doesn't matter. Okay, let's say you do send some patsy into the havencosm as a capatar. What good would it do? Capatars aren't like avatars: they don't spawn with their gear or have access to an inventory of weapons and supplies. They don't have superhuman strength or resilience like avatars. A capatar is an in-game clone of a normal, everyday organic human. They're *naked* when they spawn. Whoever goes inside as a capatar can't take anything with them but their wits. They certainly can't take a laptop loaded with the software patches required to repair the kernel."

Howe glanced at Solomon. Solomon nodded, and Howe took a shallow breath. "We've thought of one item that can be carried in-cosm by a capatar. Something that contains all the necessary materials to repair the kernel."

He paused and looked around the room, as if drawing emotional support from the others. Chun followed his gaze. They were all looking expectantly at her. She'd never been good at reading people's expressions but guessed that they were waiting for the great intellect of the renowned Dr. April Chun to dawn with comprehension, to understand where Howe was leading her with his vague riddle. To them, the answer should be obvious. Whatever Howe was referring to was the product of hours of brainstorming to which she had not been privy. Her eyes met Zia's, and Zia made a sneering smile.

Her temper flared. "A capatar can't carry *anything* from meatspace into the cosm. It's impossible."

Howe smiled. "It's not impossible. A capatar can carry *your brain*, Dr. Chun. And your brain contains all the knowledge required to fix the problem. If we send *you* in-cosm as a capatar, you can use your knowledge to directly reprogram the Haven kernel."

The faces on the hospital beds were terrifying. Especially Analise and Wolfe, though Chun drew a certain amount of cold satisfaction from the ridges of tight muscles that had stretched Analise's expression into a rictus of fear. Both Analise and Wolfe looked like zombies, with pallid, dry flesh and sunken features. The nurses had applied balm to their hollow eyes and cracked lips to treat the dry skin, which further enhanced the appearance of the undead. There was no motion beneath their eyelids. They weren't dreaming. If it weren't for the mechanical rise and fall of their chests, she would have assumed they were corpses.

Arni looked a little better, though he'd sustained some facial cuts when the ceiling of his grocery-store lab had collapsed on top of him and Zia during last night's quake. It had been a miracle that the BCI cap had remained in place and the ESP hardware had remained connected and powered. Solomon had insisted that they bring Arni and the Haven engine here, instead of returning them to the OA campus as Chun had wanted. "National security," he'd said abruptly, his only explanation.

Unlike Wolfe's and Analise's, Arni's eyes were moving under his lids, darting frantically as if he were in the midst of an intense nightmare. His breathing was also irregular, punctuated by occasional sharp gasps. Zia had told them that the capatar insertion had been incomplete, that Arni's mind had not fully transferred into the havencosm. Whatever was left of his consciousness in his meatspace body was obviously tormented. Perhaps he was stuck half-in and half-out of the cosm, straddling two completely different realities.

"Ouch," said Chun. She was in a chair next to the nurses' station, and a medical tech was drawing blood from her arm. She watched the vial fill with dark liquid. The tech pressed a cotton ball over the insertion point and withdrew the needle. At the nurse's instruction, Chun pressed the cotton ball over the tiny wound and flexed her arm.

Howe was gesturing at the empty fourth hospital bed and the adjacent machinery. "This is the unused capatar rig. Like Reggie said, it's been successfully tested more than twenty times. We'll start brewing a new batch of nanospecks tailored to your blood sample. It should be ready in about twelve hours, after which we can immediately perform the capatar insertion. Assuming you agree."

Chun glanced at the empty hospital bed, the BCI cap, and ESP scanner. Her eyes wandered briefly to the Haven engine, which had been placed on a table adjacent to the now-useless Sentinel engine. The machine's titanium enclosure had a few scratches but seemed otherwise undamaged from the chaos at Arni's lab. All the lab techs had moved aside and were standing silently at a respectful distance, watching Chun. The only sounds were the beeps and whirs of the medical equipment and the adjacent server racks. Her skin tingle seemed worse when she looked at it, so she looked away.

Her eyes returned to the corpse-like figures of Analise and Wolfe, and the tortured un-sleep of Arni. All three of them were ghastly testaments to the consequences of becoming a capatar. She'd *never* been comfortable with Analise's capatar project, even after all the early rounds of human trials had indicated it was safe. For her to become a capatar herself was unthinkable. The look on Analise's face made her shudder. No matter what the medical experts said, Analise was gone. Her body was in a comatose state, presumably permanently. She was *dead*. So was Wolfe. She wasn't sure what Arni was—some sort of half ghost. Chances were, he was dead, too.

But what was the alternative? She knew more than anyone else that unless something was done about the runaway QARMA effect, and *soon*, the entire real-world planet might die. Worst of all, Howe was right: she was the only living person with the technical knowledge to reprogram the kernel from inside the firewall.

Without any warning, she felt a laugh erupt from her lips. This entire situation was so surreal, so *absurd*. She was a born physicist. She'd grown up watching *Star Trek*, enthralled by the technology but peeved by the show's obvious scientific inaccuracies. She'd advanced through graduate and postgraduate studies disgruntled by the obvious limitations of the current theories of physics. She'd begun her career building supercomputer simulations of atomic nuclei but had quickly become disillusioned by the constraints of the computing technology. All along, the thought had been poking at her from the back of her mind: *We've had thousands of years to figure this shit out; why haven't we yet?* And another, even deeper conviction: *We've been searching down the wrong path from the very beginning . . .*

Then, out of the blue, a new path had revealed itself, and in an instant the universe had opened its cloak to reveal a surprising and unexpected secret. She discovered, hiding in the millions of gigabytes of data from her nuclear simulations, a single, bizarre statistical artifact, a mathematical impossibility that she recognized from the theoretical model developed by Kaiser and Salim in their obscure papers: a QARMA microcosm singularity. The discovery and capture of the singularity led to the kind of breakthrough that most scientists can only dream about: an entirely new method for building self-sustaining, quantum-level simulations of nature. With her new discovery she could replicate any natural system—from a single atomic nucleus to an entire galaxy—as a virtual reality model of incomprehensible fidelity, without the need for a gymnasium-size data center filled with servers. Had she followed her initial impulse and published her discovery instead of keeping it a secret, by now she might have rewritten the story of physics.

But she'd gotten sidetracked. Her graduate assistant, a Pakistani-born VR genius named Arnold Zaman, along with his entrepreneurial friend Geoff Mozingo, had convinced her to monetize her discovery by pivoting into business mode. The level of fidelity offered by her crude prototype QARMA engine far outstripped any commercial VR platform in existence. *If you built a video game based on the QARMA engine*, Arni had told her, *it would be so far ahead of the curve it would totally crush the competition. The gaming market is huge, bigger than every other form of entertainment combined. You could fund your own physics lab, maybe even your own particle accelerator. You could make* billions, *and not have to rely on grants to continue your work.*

And thus, Orbital Arena Games had been born, with Chun as senior partner and majority shareholder, and Arni and Moz as her junior partners. Moz had gone to work raising investment capital and Chun had built the hardware and coded the kernel and operating systems, while Arni, an avid gamer and science fiction fanatic, had devised the game concept and coded the VR engine. It had been Arni who had later brought Rupe into the company to design the game settings and scenarios. Arni had begged Chun to hire Analise to work the new AI system, but Chun had categorically refused.

From the beginning, she had recognized Analise's brilliance. She'd brought the young neurophysicist under her wing and mentored her, eventually revealing to her some of the deep secrets of the QARMA technology. Secrets that Analise had later used to betray Chun when she'd published a paper disputing key aspects of Chun's own published works. Instead of working together, coauthoring the paper as Chun had insisted, Analise had taken her findings and gone behind Chun's back. Her charm and fake humility had completely fooled Chun. She'd stabbed Chun in the back, ruined her academic reputation. Loyalty had meant *nothing* to Analise. Her off-the-wall theory that the QARMA effect represented the interface between physics and consciousness was based on an unquantifiable variable in a hypothesis that was utterly untestable.

Despite Chun's efforts to keep Analise away from the work of Orbital Arena, Analise had managed to weasel her way back in. As a key member of the JEEB project team, Analise had gained unprecedented access to the QARMA technology. And once again, she'd screwed Chun.

Just look at the results of her arrogance, Chun thought. The condition of the three capatar subjects in the hospital beds proved that the capatar project was a total failure. Worse, the unintended consequences of Analise's modifications to the QARMA kernels had caused their current predicament. And now the US government was asking Chun, who'd warned them from the beginning that building Analise's capatar machines was a mistake, to don one of the things and become a capatar herself!

"Christ," she muttered. It seemed that Analise had found yet another way to screw her.

DNA

"There are so many problems with this plan that I don't know where to begin." Chun glared at the others around the conference room table. "In order to apply the software patch to the kernel, once my capatar spawns, I'll have to find a way to transcribe it out of my head into a digital format that the kernel interface will accept."

"What about the VIDAs in the Foundation Core?" said Rupe. "Isn't that what they were made for?"

Howe gave a questioning look. "VIDA?"

Chun grimaced. "Virtual Integrated Development Appliance. In-game they appear like a tablet device, designed to be used by a coder's avatar to make in situ changes to the game. I *could* use a VIDA, except for one thing: I'll be a *capatar*, not an *avatar*."

Howe nodded, but Solomon looked confused. "What do you mean?"

"There's a big difference between a capatar and an avatar. Capatars are made of virtual flesh and blood, like bots. They are fully realized simulated biological organisms, right down to their DNA. Avatars are empty remote-controlled shells that are designed for one purpose: as a platform to allow the player to manage and operate an inventory of weapons and devices. There's an algorithm built into the avatar's profile that determines which devices it can use based on factors like skills and achievement level. A level 01 avatar can only use the simplest weapons and devices, while a level 50 avatar can use many different and more powerful devices.

"Bots, and capatars by extension, weren't designed to work with avatar devices. In the game, a bot can pick up a laser rifle, but it can't use it. Bots don't have quantifiable traits, skills, and achievement scores like avatars. Bots don't have invisible item stashes, like avatars. They can use a certain limited number of weapons and technology in the game, but not the items built specifically for avatars. Remember, bots were originally designed to be background characters in the game, with limited interaction in the game's plot."

"So, your capatar won't be able to use the VIDA," Solomon said.

"Only as a doorstop," she said. "There are other problems, too. The kernel node is in the Foundation Core, and Arni had all the blockchain keys to the Core gateways."

"In the game they're called *emoras*," said Rupe. "The keys... they're called emoras. But they're more than just keys. They're like super-VIDAs. They can also—"

Chun cut him off. "Even if my capatar could find one of the emoras, it couldn't use it."

"Because the emoras were designed for avatars," Solomon said.

Chun nodded, glaring at Rupe. He winced.

Solomon leaned back in his chair and put his hands behind his head. "It seems that we have a big hole in our strategy."

A long silence ensued, during which a subsonic rumble caused ripples in the coffee mugs scattered on the table. Since Arni's and Zia's ill-conceived capatar attempt last night, the tremors had become almost constant, punctuated every few hours by an alarming shudder that brought down ceiling tiles and cracked windows. And with each tremor, the Tingle seemed to get a little bit stronger, though maybe that was just her anxiety. Everyone tensed. They all knew that a city destroyer, or even a world ender, could strike at any time.

At the far end of the table, Jakob Lieberman cleared his throat imperiously, like a Caesar preparing to proclaim an edict to the citizens of Rome. "I have a question. How does a device meant for an avatar know it's in the hands of an avatar? What's the technical property that signals to the device that it's in the hands of an avatar and not a bot?"

Eyes furrowed as everyone considered the question and its implications. Lieberman leaned forward theatrically in his conference room chair and folded his arms on the table, waiting for the answer.

Rupe spoke first. "Mostly it's the avatar's achievement level. The higher the level of an avatar, the better the gear it can use. Better ships, better guns, better armor."

"I understand that, but what, specifically, is in the avatar's software coding that triggers the activation of a device?"

"It's a set of properties in the avatar's profile definition," said Chun. "They're called *traits*. Each device is programmed to work based on certain traits in the avatar's profile. Like level, character species, skills, et cetera."

"But bots have profile definitions, too, if I recall," Lieberman said.

Chun snorted. The pompous ass had been instrumental in helping Analise create the code for the bots. He knew full well that bots also had a character data profile, though they were much simpler than those of avatars. Where was he going with this?

He continued. "If I recall correctly, bot traits are decentralized, encoded into each individual bot instead of into the central avatar database. What if it was possible to recode a bot's profile so that it included all the traits of an avatar? Wouldn't it then be able to activate avatar devices?"

"The profile data of a bot is encoded into its DNA," Chun said. "It would be impossible to change it."

Lieberman smiled smugly and said, "Impossible? Really, Dr. Chun?"

Lieberman's argument went thusly: since bots were quantum-fidelity reproductions of organic life, what worked for organic beings in the real world should also work for bots in the virtual world. Since it was possible to edit the genes of an organism in the real world, why couldn't the virtual genes of a capatar be similarly edited to add the traits necessary for it to use devices meant for avatars?

Coming from him, it wasn't idle speculation. Lieberman had spent decades and made fortunes showing the world it was possible to reprogram a section of an organism's DNA and change the organism's physiological structure. He'd patented techniques to change an adult human's eye color, hair density, even skin color. He was working on patents of epigenetic techniques that would, among other things, improve a student's ability to concentrate on abstract math problems, improve an athlete's stamina, or regrow a missing limb.

Of course, Lieberman's work was highly controversial. Even the world's most progressive thinkers took pause at the consequences of the ultrarich improving their DNA when the rest of society couldn't afford it. Chun didn't really care one way or another, but since Lieberman had been a colleague of Analise, she completely mistrusted his motives.

"How would it work? How would you alter the capatar's DNA?" Chun argued. "The capatar's body doesn't even exist until it spawns into the cosm. Then it's behind the firewall where you can't touch it. Last time I checked, there aren't any gene-editing labs in the video game."

"Maybe we could edit the capatar template in the ESP scanner as it's scanning the subject's DNA," suggested Howe. "When the capatar clone spawns, it would incorporate the modified DNA."

"The ESP scan is an analog process," said one of the techs at the back of the room. "You can't edit the image. We don't really even understand what the image *is*."

Another long silence, during which Chun noticed that Lieberman was still smiling. The smug bastard was going to wait until the rest of the room showed their ignorance before he presented what would no doubt be a brilliant solution. Chun refused to let that happen. "Why don't you enlighten us, *Doctor* Lieberman," Chun said. "You seem to have all the answers."

Lieberman released a condescending sigh that he'd obviously been holding just for this moment. "Okay, but you may not like it, *Doctor* Chun. The solution is simple, and quite obvious. I'm surprised you didn't think of it yourself, actually."

Christ, Chun almost said aloud. *You're such a dick.*

Lieberman continued. "Of course you can't edit the genes of a capatar once it has spawned into the havencosm. That's not what I'm proposing at all. I mean to modify the DNA of the human subject *before* she ever dons the BCI cap or attaches herself to the ESP scanner." He paused, his grin widening. "I mean to edit *your* DNA, Dr. Chun, and turn you into Earth's first meatspace avatar. When your capatar spawns inside the havencosm, it'll carry your newly implanted avatar DNA with it."

Relics

Liberman, thankfully, had taken his techs and left the conference room, no doubt to stir more DNA madness into the broth of his ridiculous genetic stew. Rupe was at the whiteboard listing the game items Chun's capatar would need to collect inside the havencosm. Zia, Howe and Solomon watched intently.

Chun had an overwhelming urge for a smoke. Things were moving too fast, out of control. Their strategy was born of desperation and impulse. The others had simply accepted it without discussion or argument. There had to be another way. There were always options if you looked hard enough.

Rupe was pointing to his whiteboard list. "So, let's see, you'll need a VIDA, which will be easy to find because there are a bunch of them in the Foundation Core. You'll also need a scancorder and a holobox to transfer the software patch from the VIDA to the kernel interface node. Every avatar had a scancorder and at least one holobox in their item stash, so they should be pretty easy to come across. Remember, when the game crashed, the contents of every avatar's stash got left behind at the avatar's last location. The game map should be littered with millions of piles of avatar inventory, especially around the major dungeon sites."

Chun was barely listening. *Lieberman wants to inject me with DNA-altering soup, for Christ's sake, and Solomon is insisting that I subject myself to the capatar process that made the last three subjects comatose—probably permanently. Why am I even remotely considering going along with them?*

Rupe was still droning. "You might be able to find the stuff you need on Grone, but since it was a new release and so few avatars made it there before the crash, you'd be better off looking on one of the older campaign worlds where millions of avatars went. I'd head to one of the empire planets like Bhahir or Krepula or Assinni if I were you."

"I wish you *were* me," she muttered. Rupe sounded genuinely excited, like he'd been in the old days in design meetings back at Orbital Arena. The more he talked, the bigger the hollow void in her gut grew. She tried to imagine herself inside the havencosm, just as she was inside this conference room right now. She put her hand on the table, felt its cold solidity. Would a similar table in the cosm feel just as solid to her capatar? If the reports from Analise's early capatar experiments were true, then yes. The fidelity of the simulation inside the QARMA microcosm was, from a sensory perspective, identical to the fidelity of the macrocosm. The world around her capatar would feel just as real as the real world.

"I'd try to find an Orb, too." Rupe was still writing on the whiteboard. "Just in case you ever want to phone home. There were four of them on Orbitus. We know Wolfe found one of them, but the others may still be there. They're stored in concrete bunkers protected by a force field. There's a password you'll need to access the bunker. Just say, 'Han shot first.'" His smile turned limp when he looked at her. "Um, they're sort of in a desert, so the sand might have covered them up by now. You might have to dig them out."

"Dig for an Orb," she repeated. "Christ almighty. This is a nightmare. You need Lara Croft, not me." She was a physicist-turned-businesswoman. She'd never been a gamer and had never been good at playing any of Rupe's campaigns, even when Arni and Rupe had coached her. She had no delusions—this plan to send her into the gameverse as a capatar was a suicide mission.

When her avatar died in the game, it was no big deal. She'd curse and wait for it to respawn, after which she'd rejoin the action. With a capatar, it would be different. She wouldn't be sitting in her office maneuvering an avatar with a game controller or VR rig. Her capatar would be *her*. She'd be *in* the game, and everything inside the gameverse was designed to *kill* you. If she got shot, the bullet would tear into her flesh and organs, and she would experience the excruciating pain. If she got stabbed, she'd feel every inch of the blade as it scraped her ribs and pierced her heart. If she got eaten by a Jagnuckle or a Ghast, how would it feel as their claws tore her open? If she died, she'd experience whatever horrifying sensations came with death. Yes, maybe she would respawn, but she'd still have gone through the agony of *dying*.

In the video from Wolfe, his capatar had been disemboweled by the blue woman's blade. His shiny, gooey intestines had ruptured out onto the table and he'd gaped down at his own guts. How had that *felt*, she wondered.

This whole scheme was the worst idea ever. She needed to be back at her inner sanctum, smoking a Marlboro and sipping a Coke, searching through the QARMA equations for a mathematical solution to the apocalypse they were facing. Instead, she was in a war room with a soldier, a foulmouthed Russian hacker, and a video-game geek plotting a poorly conceived strategy in which she would arrive naked and alone in an unknown, hostile territory populated with flesh-eating monsters. She'd seen some of the awful creatures Rupe and Arni had invented: Creenors. Ghasts. Grews. Forniculans. Jagnuckles. Rupe could be a twisted fuck when it came to game design.

Rupe was smiling at her, but his smile was strained. "Here's the deal, boss. Normally, you'd spawn your avatar into the havencosm and then immediately use your Great Emora to open a portable gateway to the Foundation Core. Then you'd apply your software patch to the QARMA kernel, and that would fix everything." Rupe's smile faded. "Only problem is, with the firewall up and Arni's system lockouts in place, even your master emora won't give you full access to the Core."

"So . . . how do I get there?"

"It's not going to be easy. Um, here's the deal." Rupe cleared his throat. "Arni built a system of secret interfaces between the three QARMA engines so that he and Analise could sneak their avatars between the cosms without anyone noticing. He called the main interface the Cosmic Hub. It links the Cores of all three QARMA engines."

Chun's breath caught in her throat. *So that's how he did it.* The implications were staggering. She wouldn't have thought it possible to link the kernels of the three QARMA machines. Arni had been keeping more from her than she'd thought.

Rupe continued. "In the havencosm, there's a gateway to the Cosmic Hub on Grone. It's hidden inside the prime dungeon, in a passageway near the final boss chamber. Arni called it the Shadow Door. It leads to a place inside the Foundation Core called Atum's Lair."

Solomon frowned. "Atum's Lair?"

Rupe chuckled grimly. "Arni's avatar was named Atum. He built himself a secret virtual workspace inside the Foundation Core where he and Analise could try out game modifications without anybody noticing. He called it his lair."

Zia spoke to Solomon. "Colonel, you and your marines passed through the Shadow Door into his lair when your avatars were chasing Analise's capatar from JEEB Earth. That's how your avatars ended up in a cave on Grone. Without even realizing it, you'd gone through the Cosmic Hub from the jeebcosm on the Sentinel engine into the gamecosm on the Pandora engine."

Chun's hands were shaking. Arni's betrayal was far more extensive than she'd realized. He'd been tinkering with the core system software beneath her very nose. No wonder the Haven engine was malfunctioning so badly. Who knew what untested modifications he and Analise had cooked up in his secret lair?

Solomon and Howe exchanged tired glances. "Atum's Lair? Cosmic Hub? God save us from the nerds," Solomon muttered.

"Um, yeah." Rupe cleared his throat. "There's one more thing . . . Zia?"

Chun turned to the bruised and bandaged hacker. Zia stared defiantly at Chun. "In Atum's Lair, there's a remote node interface that links directly to the QARMA kernel."

"That's not possible." She realized the moment the words left her lips that she was only displaying her ignorance. Arni and Analise had obviously discovered something about the QARMA engines that they'd chosen not to share.

Zia shrugged insolently. "Arni figured it out. It works in your favor, Dr. Chun. If your capatar can make it to Atum's Lair, you can use the remote node to upload the software fix directly to the system kernel."

"Christ."

"One last thing. When Roland Wolfe moved the JEEB Earth sim into the havencosm, he included the JEEB version of the capatar spawn code. It's different than the version Arni and Analise were using. There's still a Hero's Gate, but it only links to spawn points on JEEB

Earth. This means you can't spawn anywhere else in the game galaxy other than JEEB Earth."

"So what?"

"Isn't it obvious?" Zia said. "We know JEEB Earth was migrated into the havencosm, but we don't know *where* it ended up on the game map. Did it replace the game's version of Earth, or did it pop into some empty corner of the galaxy? No matter what, you'll have to get off-planet and make your way to Grone."

"So how will I get to Grone? Call a space taxi?"

Rupe cursed beneath his breath.

"What's wrong?" prompted Zia.

Rupe's excitement had vanished. He spoke slowly. "Oh, man, it just occurred to me that JEEB Earth won't have starships or beamriders. You guys designed it based on twenty-first-century Earth. Unless the doppelgänger version of Elon Musk or Richard Branson invented warp drive, there may not be any way for her to get from JEEB Earth to Grone."

"Christ."

"It's probably okay," Rupe said unconvincingly. "Even if they don't have their own starships, by now one of the game's other sentient species has probably discovered JEEB Earth. The psychological drive for exploration and empire building was programmed into their behavior templates." He took a deep breath, his eyes avoiding her. "We'll just have to assume that there's a way off-planet."

"What if there's not? What if I get to JEEB Earth and it's full of talking apes?"

Rupe cleared his throat. "Honestly boss, I have no idea what things will be like in the havencosm. Based on Wolfe's video, it's safe to assume that things may have, um, changed. I mean, ten thousand years is a *long* time. The cultures we designed for each of the bot species may have evolved. They may not even speak English anymore, except maybe on JEEB Earth, which has only been in the cosm for about two hundred subjective years." He paused and gave a bleary grimace. "The good news is that with the time acceleration, your capatar will have years and years to figure it out."

Years? Chun looked around the table at the worried faces. She pointed at Rupe's scrawls on the whiteboard. "This plan has zero chance of success. Even if I can find any of these items, they'll be thousands of years old. What are the chances they'll still work? Entropy in the cosm is exactly the same as entropy here, you know. All these things will have rotted into dust."

Rupe glanced at Solomon, who sighed. "Dr. Chun, we have seven hours until your nanospecks are fully cooked. Let's stay focused and not give up just yet, please."

"You should send me," said Zia. "I won't whine about it."

"You don't know the first thing about reprogramming the kernel," Chun shot back.

"You might be surprised what I know," Zia retorted.

Solomon slapped the tabletop with an open palm. "Continue, Rupe."

"Um, yeah. So, when you get to Grone and find Atum's Lair, there's a small chance the gateway to the Cosmic Hub may still be open. When the game crashed, there was nobody there to close it, but it probably closed when the firewall went up."

"And if it's closed?"

"Then you'll need the key to open it."

"And where do I find the key?"

Rupe looked at Howe. Howe pulled a thumbdrive out of his shirt pocket. "This is the blockchain encryption key that Arni made. He called it the Shadow Emora. It's like the other three Great Emoras, except that it works in all three of the cosms. It's a master key to the entire QARMA metaverse, if I understand correctly."

"Like the One Ring," said Rupe. "One emora to rule them all . . ."

A flash of heat rose into her cheeks. She couldn't conceive how Arni had interfaced the three cosms. She took a deep breath to calm the roiling in her gut. There was still a fatal flaw in this plan. The encryption key was here, in the macrocosm. "How do you plan to get the key through the firewall?"

From the way Howe grimaced, she knew she wasn't going to like his answer. Everyone in the room turned their eyes to the figure sitting at the other end of the table.

Jakob Lieberman, who'd been silently watching the proceedings, smiled and leaned forward in his chair. "I guess this is where I come in."

Blood

Chun knew that Lieberman's company, ZavosGenomica, had been contracted by Analise to help devise and build the experimental capatar system for the JEEB project. It was a diverse firm that included disciplines ranging from cloning to gene editing to epigenetics. It had built much of the hardware and software for the capatar systems, including the BCI caps and ESP scanners based on Analise's prototypes. It had also been instrumental in designing the virtual cloning process that enabled the game's spawn engine to fabricate a bot's body that was a DNA duplicate of a human subject. Lieberman himself had been the project manager and chief scientist for the project and had been deeply engaged with Analise throughout the entire effort.

As far as Chun was concerned, there was no way Lieberman could have *not* known about Analise's plans to steal the gamecosm. As prime contractor for the capatar project, he'd worked hand in hand with Analise on a daily basis for over two years. She'd probably recruited him in the same way she'd seduced Arni, Rupe, and the other conspirators. Looking around the table, Chun suddenly realized that everyone in this room had been pawns in Analise's plans. They had *all* betrayed Chun in one way or another.

Lieberman was jabbering about something, but the words were lost inside Chun's red fog of anger. She had brought these people the greatest scientific discovery in a century, a whole new branch of physics, and they'd turned it into a circus of corruption and deceit. They had *all* betrayed her, and now that their scheme had gotten out of hand, they were turning to her to risk *her* life to save *them*.

"I need a cigarette," she announced to the startled room, and she rose and stormed out.

—

It had been a mistake to come outdoors for a smoke, she realized. The bugaboo hung above the southern horizon, visible through the occasional breaks in the pall of smoke that hung over the valley. The sounds of distant sirens echoed across the Stanford campus. She lit a cigarette with shaking hands and avoided looking up at the accusing shape in the sky.

An armored personnel carrier squatted in the street in front of the Computer Science building, surrounded by a hundred scared-looking soldiers. Several of them watched her warily, wondering who she was, and what she'd been doing in this building they'd been ordered to protect with their lives. A small tremor rumbled across the campus, sending waves of frightened murmurs through the lines of soldiers. Had they all felt the momentary surge in the Tingle? From their expressions, they had. The Tingle was setting the whole world on edge, almost more than the quakes.

Most of them were just kids, younger even than the undergraduate students here at the university. They had no idea what was happening to the world, or why they were here protecting a building full of hackers instead of at home with their families. A sudden irony forced a sigh through her lips. These kids were probably gamers, and most of them had probably played the *Longstar* video game. Even though she was the CEO of the game company, any one of these raw-faced kids would be better suited than her to go inside the gamecosm as a capatar. Any one of them might survive where she was sure to perish.

She squashed the half-burned cigarette under her heel and turned back into the building.

Lieberman was at the whiteboard. He stopped talking as she reentered the conference room. She took a chair and tried to keep her emotion off her face. Lieberman gave her a concerned look, then glanced at Howe. Howe nodded for him to continue. He turned back to the whiteboard and pointed to a crude sketch of a DNA helix.

"There are big slices of human DNA that are filled with junk data, old evolutionary adaptations that aren't useful anymore. That's the part we modify. It turns out that DNA is a fabulous storage medium for digital data. It's self-replicating and has built-in error correction. We've gotten pretty good in the past decade at editing genes, using special enzymes and proteins that are programmed to target a junk section of DNA and replace it with custom data. This is how we'll edit the subject's genes so that the avatar devices will recognize her capatar as an avatar and not as a bot."

Everyone turned to look at Chun. She tried her best to keep her face neutral. She felt like a bug pinned to a slide under a microscope. A month ago, she'd been highly regarded as a wealthy CEO of a Silicon Valley giant. Now, she was nothing but "the subject" of a desperate DNA experiment.

Lieberman continued. "Here's the cool part. We can code *any* digital information into a strand of the subject's DNA. It can be simple data, or a complex software program. To encode the encryption key from the—what did you call it?"

"The Shadow Emora," said Rupe.

"Yes, the Shadow Emora. The encryption key is just a string of digital data, so it's a simple process to encode it into the subject's DNA, and even target a specific type of cell—say, red blood cells or skin cells." He paused for effect and tapped the whiteboard marker against the sketch on the board. "*That's* how we get the Shadow Emora into the havencosm. We code it into the subject's blood. When we spawn her capatar, the code will be replicated in her capatar's blood."

Murmurs cascaded around the table. Some were nodding; others were shaking their heads. Lieberman continued, obviously pleased by his own brilliance. "We're also looking at including the patch for the malfunctioning kernel in the edited gene. It's quite likely that we can load all the software she'll need to repair the timestream and lower the firewall, meaning she wouldn't have to re-create it from scratch when she arrives in-cosm."

"What if the subject doesn't want you tampering with her genes?" Chun blurted. "Wouldn't you normally do months of testing and clinical trials before you'd perform this kind of treatment? What if you make a mistake?"

Lieberman paused, and for the first time his veil of confidence wavered. "There's always the chance of unintended side effects, but in light of the pending apocalypse, in my opinion the risk to the subject is acceptable."

"In your opinion? What if the subject doesn't find the risk acceptable?" She turned to Solomon. "What then, Colonel? Are you willing to strap the subject down and force your treatment down her throat?"

Solomon, always the peacekeeper, fixed his gaze on her. She didn't expect the hardness in his eyes or the sharpness of his retort. "Only if it's necessary, Dr. Chun."

"Christ," she muttered.

"Fucking hell, *I'll* do it," Zia said. "If you can code the software patch into anybody's DNA, then we don't need *her*." She gestured toward Chun. "Anybody can do it."

Rupe brightened. "No, it should be *me*. Nobody knows the game better than me. It'd be crazy to send anyone else."

The room erupted into a mass of overlapping conversations. Suddenly, Chun had gone from the center of attention, the potential savior of the world, to being completely irrelevant. Her humiliation was complete.

Howe raised his hand. The room went mute. He turned to Lieberman. "What about it, Dr. Lieberman? Could we send one of the others instead of Chun?"

Lieberman stared into empty space for a moment. "There's no reason I couldn't implant the software package into anyone's genes, so in that respect we could send Rupe or Zia."

Chun broke in. "I'd like to remind everyone here that Rupe and Zia are both under arrest. We wouldn't be in this situation if they hadn't already betrayed us."

"Fuck you, Chun," sneered Zia, and once again the room erupted into a mass of voices.

"Enough!" bellowed Solomon.

Lieberman raised his voice above the din. "We may not have a choice who goes. The problem is the time frame. If we dispense with quality testing, it'll take a couple of hours to encode the software fixes and the encryption key into a DNA template. Then we'll have to insert the modified DNA template into the carrier viruses, which will take another hour. Once we inject the subject, it'll take some time for the virus to infect the target cells and the epigenetic process to begin. So, let's say six hours before the subject will be ready."

"Let's get started," said Zia. "I'm ready right now."

Lieberman was shaking his head. "The problem isn't the DNA treatment; it's the nanospecks. They take a lot longer to brew. We started making a new batch this morning based on Dr. Chun's blood sample, but it'll be several more hours before it's ready. Unless Rupe or Zia has the same blood chemistry as Chun, which is doubtful, we'd have to make a new batch starting from scratch. That would mean at least another fourteen hours before we could start the nanospeck transfusion and then another hour or two before we could send either of them into the cosm." He looked around the table. "Does anybody know how much time we have left?"

The room went silent. Everyone knew another massive quake, or something worse, could strike at any moment and destroy the lab and its unique equipment. Lieberman sighed. "Okay. As it stands, it's only six hours before we can spawn Dr. Chun's capatar. That's still our best bet. If we choose somebody else, it'll be a minimum of *sixteen* hours before the nanospecks will be ready."

Solomon rubbed his eyes. "We need contingencies. Get started on the DNA treatment now. In the meantime, get blood samples from everyone in this room and begin processing nanospecks for all of us, just in case. Start with Zia and Rupe." He turned to Chun. "For now, Doctor, I'm afraid you're still our best hope. I'm sorry, but we're counting on you."

Boss Dungeon

Chun was Colonel Solomon's prisoner. He'd informed her that the entire JEEB lab was on lockdown, that she wouldn't be allowed to leave. He'd stationed guards at every exit. A few minutes earlier, a helicopter had landed in the street and vomited out a bunch of high-ranking soldiers and officials in suits. Solomon was with them now, in another part of the building. There'd been another earthquake, too, this one not as bad as last night's but strong enough to send everyone diving under the nearest table.

The lab was a whirlwind of activity in which she was forbidden to take part. Instead, they made her endure the two thirty-minute episodes of the *Longstar's Rangers* TV series upon which the Grone campaign had been based. Such silliness, but she watched intently, warned by Rupe that her capatar's life might depend on some plot detail or device shown in the episode. In the episodes, the characters had been pitted against a series of increasing dangers, from the diabolical warlord Jaspaar to an ancient and impossibly powerful entity called a Gurothim harvester. Afterward they'd scheduled two hours for Rupe to brief her in detail on what her capatar might encounter in the gamecosm. As if that would be enough time.

She and Rupe were alone in an empty office. He was standing uncomfortably close to her, drawing frantically on the small whiteboard. Since they'd started ninety minutes earlier, he'd yet to meet her eyes.

He cleared his throat. "To open the gateway to the Cosmic Hub at Atum's Lair, you'll need to find one of the three Great Emoras, either yours, Arni's, or Rupe's. *Any* of them will work. All your avatar's inventory items, including your emora, should still be at the location of your avatar when the game crashed. The bad news is that *your* emora, the one Arni created specifically for your avatar Oaone, is stuck inside the Foundation Core where your avatar died. The good news is that Ruperus's emora should still be on my avatar's spaceship, which was in orbit around Jagnuckle when the game crashed." He took a hopeful breath. "The even better news is that Arni's avatar died in the dungeon at Grone. Unless some curious bot picked it up as a souvenir, his Great Emora should still be there in the cave where the two of you fought. Once you find one of the emoras and activate your DNA modifications, you can reprogram it to think it's the Shadow Emora with a drop of your blood. Just prick your finger and touch the emora."

He waited for her to acknowledge his instructions. When she didn't, he plowed ahead anyway. "There's just one problem. Last time you were at Grone you were playing an archangel-level avatar, and you took a shortcut through the Cosmic Hub and the Shadow Door. You bypassed most of the dungeon's mazes and combat areas. It'll be different this time because you'll have to go in like a player and find your way through the dungeon to Atum's Lair. You'll have to solve some of the game puzzles and maybe even fight some of the adversary bots, assuming they're still around after ten thousand years. Thankfully, there's a secret shortcut so you can avoid the worst of it."

Rupe was facing the whiteboard, gesturing at the crude diagram he'd drawn. "You'll probably get to Grone by a spaceship or maybe a beamrider, so you'll have to locate Jaspaar's citadel, or what's left of it, and find a way inside. You can go in through the citadel on top of the mountain, but that's the most dangerous way. It's a rule of thumb: anytime something seems obvious, it probably means it's a trap. Once you get inside, follow the path I told you about. Under no circumstances should you get anywhere near the dungeon's final boss. If you wake up the Gurothim harvester, you're doomed." He'd been talking nonstop for an eternity, spouting locations she should visit or avoid, important devices and weapons she would need to find, dangerous traps that could electrocute or eviscerate or burn her capatar to death, monsters that could eat her or dissolve her or trap her for eternity.

Now he was talking about what would happen if she got injured, or killed, telling her that there was no guarantee that her capatar would respawn like a regular avatar. "You should avoid combat at all costs. You can't let yourself get into a hopeless situation where there's no escape. Keep in mind that the suicide express probably won't work for a capatar."

Chun knew that *suicide express* was a phrase from a sci-fi writer named Philip José Farmer, one of Rupe's favorite authors and a major source of inspiration for the game settings. The characters in Farmer's story were famous but deceased historical figures brought together in the afterlife, forever cursed to travel down an endless river. If they died along the river, they respawned back at the headwaters and had to start the journey all over again. One of the characters regularly used suicide as a means to deliberately escape back to the start of the river.

The suicide express was a popular tactic with the players of *Longstar*, who sometimes used it to respawn their avatars in order to escape from an unwinnable situation. When a player purposely killed their own avatar, or allowed it to be killed, it would typically respawn at the last save point, enabling the avatar to retreat to a safe location before reentering the dangerous situation to try again, this time armed with foreknowledge.

"I hate you," Chun said, and she meant it.

Rupe flinched. He waited for her to say something else. When she didn't, he cleared his throat. "Um, the best way inside is through this service tunnel at the base of the mountain, right on the lake." He pointed to a spot on the whiteboard diagram. "There aren't any hidden pitfalls or traps in the tunnel, although once you get to Jaspaar's death cavern, there are some things you need to be careful of."

"You know you're going to spend the rest of your life in prison, don't you?" she said. "Why didn't you tell me what Arni and Analise were planning?"

Rupe's mouth fell open. He slowly put the cap on the whiteboard marker. His shoulders slumped and he sagged into a chair. "I'm sorry. It wasn't ever supposed to happen like this."

"What did you *think* would happen?" she snapped. "You stole a billion dollars of intellectual property and destroyed a company with three billion a year in revenue. You betrayed me, Rupe. Deliberately."

"We . . . we weren't thinking like that." Rupe's eyes had filled with tears. "Arni and Analise tried to talk to you. They tried to explain. You wouldn't listen."

"Of course I listened! They just didn't make any sense. Analise was psychotic, Rupe. Remember her mood swings? How she used to pace in circles for hours, lost in thought? She had every symptom of delusional schizophrenia. She was obsessed by her conviction that the bots had come to life. Christ, Rupe, she believed that every time a kid killed a bot in the game, they were committing murder! You and Arni allowed yourselves to get sucked into her delusion."

"The bots changed after the jeeb virus got into the system—"

"*The bots aren't alive, Rupe!* They were *never* alive, and they sure as hell didn't suddenly come alive because of some computer virus. They only seemed self-aware because we *programmed that behavior into their templates*. I shouldn't have to keep saying it. Bots are *not* alive."

A voice came from the doorway. Lieberman was leaning against the doorframe and had obviously been listening. "Your man Rupe has a point, Doctor," he said. "If I woke up in the cosm and didn't realize where I was, and I dissected a bot, how would I know it was a bot and not a human? Thanks to the magic of your QARMA engine, bots have virtual biological bodies with organic, biological brains, identical to our own."

"Which is all rendered by software based on templates defined by a database. They're not *real*, Jakob. They're just qubits flying around in a quantum processor. They're no more alive than a spreadsheet or a phone app. You know this."

"Do I? Aren't you and I rendered by the machine of nature, and our templates programmed by evolution?" He raised his eyebrows. "I tell you, Chun, I've seen your gamebots and the JEEB Earth doppelgängers, and if I didn't know they were virtual simulations, I would have never guessed. In my opinion, they pass the Turing test with flying colors."

"Passing the Turing test doesn't make them alive or self-aware, and it certainly doesn't give them legal rights. That was Analise's argument and look where it's gotten us. To the verge of Armageddon."

He shrugged again and pushed himself away from the doorframe. "I can't argue with that, I guess. I came to tell you that the DNA treatment is almost ready. Can you come with me?"

She rose and followed Lieberman and didn't look back at Rupe.

Lieberman had commandeered one of the offices in the hallway leading to the JEEB lab. He motioned for Chun to sit in a chair in front of the desk. A man wearing medical scrubs was waiting. He placed a metal tray on the desk next to Lieberman. Lieberman inspected the tray's contents, nodded to the man in scrubs, then squeezed his oversized hands into a pair of too-small latex gloves. He turned to Chun. "The epigene treatments will take time to mature and make their way to all the target cells in your body. It'll take some time for the genetic code to be firmly established in your capatar."

"How long?"

Lieberman lifted a computer printout and examined it. He spoke absently while he read. "There may be some slight changes to your physical appearance as the treatment modifies your DNA. It's possible you may notice a darkening of your skin, a subtle lightening of your eye and hair color. It will take a few months for the changes to start to show up in your capatar, and a year, or maybe two, for the transformation to be complete." He paused, considering. "To be safe, I'd give it at least three years."

Chun felt her mouth fall open. "Three *years?*"

"Remember, that's only a few minutes here in meatspace."

"And what about my real body?"

Lieberman lowered the printout and picked up a syringe. He squinted at the syringe, then consulted the printout. He nodded. "Your body here will go through the same changes. Only it will happen in meatspace time."

"Can the changes be reversed? Once I get back, can I go back to normal?"

"We'll do our best to treat any adverse side effects. I won't lie, though; there may be no way to completely reverse the process." He moved to her side, motioned for her to roll up the sleeve of her blouse.

"When it's time to come home, how do I get extracted back into my real body?"

"If the firewall is down, we should be able to track you and bring you home from this end. If that doesn't work, you'll have to find a way back to the Avatar Mall and start the recall process yourself. If the firewall doesn't come down, then I guess it won't make much of a difference." He paused. "In a way I'm jealous. We may have only a few more hours here in meatspace. You'll have decades in the cosm."

"Decades in Rupe's freakshow doesn't sound like much fun to me." She hesitated. "What happens to my capatar after my consciousness gets recalled?"

Lieberman answered distractedly, his hands busily preparing the needle. "Your capatar body will collapse into a comatose state. The autonomic bodily functions like heartbeat and respiration will continue for a short time. Without medical assistance, it dies in a few minutes."

She scowled. "Christ."

In a fluid series of motions, he swabbed her arm with alcohol. "Even more interesting is what might happen to your capatar if your *real* body dies here in meatspace. What would happen, hypothetically speaking, if I murdered you while you were in the capatar coma?"

She sneered at his bad humor, but something in his expression gave her pause. She thought about his question, but the answer was simple: the entanglement between the nanospecks in the host brain and the brain of the capatar was absolute. "The capatar would die."

He examined the syringe, lowered it to her arm. When it was an inch away from her skin, he paused. "Are you sure about that? During entanglement, your entire brain function is essentially transferred to the capatar's virtual mind. In this state, your capatar has a fully operating human consciousness. A soul. *Your* soul. If your meatspace brain dies, why wouldn't your capatar keep living?"

"That's not the way the QARMA effect works. The capatar isn't alive. It's not real."

"But isn't its virtual brain doing all the processing? Aren't the virtual synapses of your capatar's mind interpreting the sensory input from your virtual eyes and ears? In the coma, your meatspace mind is mostly inert. Your awareness, your consciousness, has been transferred into the virtual world, which it perceives as reality. That means your capatar is *self-conscious*, doesn't it? And isn't self-consciousness the definition of sentience?"

She felt nothing as he pushed the syringe into her skin and depressed the plunger. When he spoke, his tone bordered on mocking. "Like you were telling Rupe, there's no law against killing a virtual being in a computer simulation, right? If there were, every teenage gamer in America would be guilty of mass murder. That was Analise's entire justification for stealing the gamecosm, wasn't it? To protect the bots from indiscriminate slaughter by the avatars." She flinched away when Lieberman suddenly leaned close, his face inches from hers, his voice low and accusing. "How many bots were killed by players in an average day of gameplay? Huh? How many? Hundreds? Thousands? *Tens of thousands?*" He cocked his head to the side as he applied a bandage to the injection site. "What if she was right? What if they were sentient? If the QARMA engine can host the sentience of your capatar, what technical reason would prevent it from hosting other sentient beings?"

He placed the syringe in a trash can next to the desk. "That would make *you* the psychopath, not Analise. In fact, it would make you the worst genocidal maniac in history. Hitler killed six million Jews in just under a decade. Your avatars killed that many every single weekend."

Christ, she thought, *Analise brainwashed him, too.*

He saw the scorn in her expression and sighed. "Who knows for sure? Although, come to think of it, I guess you're about to find out, one way or another. I can't wait to hear your story when you get back." He sighed again. "We're done here. They need your help in the lab to get the equipment set up."

They told her to sit on the hospital bed next to the three horror stories of Wolfe, Analise, and Arni.

The Tingle had worsened from an annoyance to a major distraction that was beginning to affect everyone's work. Nerves were frayed, tempers flaring. *How ironic*, she thought, *that the world might end not by fiery apocalypse, but by an Armageddon of itching.*

When the soldiers arrived with the Pandora engine, she pushed away the tech who was test-fitting the BCI cap. "What in Christ's name are you doing?" she demanded. "How did you get my machine?"

The Pandora engine had been secured in a vault on the Orbital Arena campus under secure lock and key, guarded by an armed private contractor. The only reason it could be here was if Colonel Solomon had ordered it to be confiscated. She lurched to her feet and rushed toward the soldiers. "You can't do this! That's my property. You don't have the right!"

Solomon, who had been directing the soldiers, moved to intercept her. "The governor of California has declared martial law, so I *do* have the right. I'm sorry, Dr. Chun. These machines represent a clear and immediate danger to the United States of America. I'm impounding all three of them."

The nurses were pulling at her shoulders trying to restrain her. She shoved one of them away, prompting Solomon to step in and push Chun forcibly back into the concrete block wall.

"Let go of me," she growled.

Solomon didn't relent. She struggled to look over his shoulder. There were six soldiers, and they appeared to be taking measurements of the three QARMA engines.

"What are they doing?" she cried.

Solomon's voice was quick and low. "They're an Army EOD team from Fort Irwin. They're coming up with a safe way to destroy the QARMA engines in case everything else fails."

"Christ almighty, Colonel! I've told you a thousand times that you can't just destroy them."

"I know what you told me. But for every minute that passes, those machines are killing more people. It's my job to stop them, one way or another. If your capatar can't fix the problem, we're going to blow them up."

She reached out and grabbed his wrist. "Listen to me, and really *listen* this time. There's something called a raw microcosm singularity at the heart of each of those machines. You can blow up the hardware, but you *can't* destroy the singularities. Right now, the singularities are constrained. If you destroy the hardware, you'll release them into the environment. All the bad stuff that's happening now could get a whole lot worse."

Solomon paused, worked his mouth like he was chewing a rotten piece of meat. "God damn it, Chun. Have you always known how dangerous these machines you built are?"

"Of course not! They were perfectly safe until Analise Novak got her hands on them."

"I wonder if that's true. I guess it doesn't matter now. Regardless, if this doesn't work, I'm going to blow up all three of these fuckers."

—

Two hours later, thirty people or more were crowded into the lab, arranged in a rough semicircle around her hospital bed. Rupe, Zia, Solomon, the JEEB technicians, and Lieberman and his gene demons, along with three older men she didn't recognize in starched military uniforms with stars on their shoulders. Her head was heavy with the bulk of the BCI cap and the thick cable connecting it to the ESP scanner. The machine's display showed a three-dimensional view of the nanospeck activity in her brain. Everything was ready. Everything except *her*.

Solomon stepped forward. His face was a mask of military precision. "You have four hours. If the firewall isn't down, we're going to destroy the QARMA engines." He held up his hand with four fingers raised. "Four hours, Doctor. Good luck and Godspeed."

Rupe's face was soaked with tears. He tried to smile at her. "See, boss, you have plenty of time. Four hours. Decades!"

She did the math. "That's fifty-seven years, one month, and six days in the havencosm. In four hours, I'll be ninety-seven years old."

Rupe gave a lopsided grin and wiped his nose. "Go slow and be careful. Remember, all you have to do is find a way from JEEB Earth to Grone and collect the gear along the way that you'll need to reprogram the kernel. When you get to Grone, go to Jaspaar's citadel and find the Shadow Door. Use the emora to open the Shadow Door and pass through the Cosmic Hub to Atum's Lair. Activate your DNA enhancements, then apply your fix to the remote kernel node in the lair. Boom! You're done." He sounded breathless. "At that point, the timestream will resync, the firewall will come down, and we'll all zoom in as avatars with big guns and escort you back to the Avatar Mall. Easy-peasy."

"If I get eaten by a Ghast or fall into one of your bungie pits, I'm going to rip your heart out with my bare hands when I get back."

His grin only widened. He didn't realize she was being serious. "Good luck, boss. Remember what I told you about the dungeon on Grone. Watch out for the microflak mines and stay the hell away from the boss."

The ESP tech sounded nervous. "Okay, we've got a good link to the spawn platform in the Avatar Mall. The exclusion zone is in place. The gene scan is working . . . still working . . ."

A low-pitched alarm sounded. The tech frowned. Howe looked over the tech's shoulder at the machine's screen.

A spike of fear caused Chun's rapid breathing to pause. "That didn't sound so good."

The tech pushed a series of buttons and her frown intensified.

"What is it?" Chun insisted.

The tech avoided looking at her and instead turned to Lieberman. She pointed at something on the machine's display. Lieberman studied it for a moment, and his expression of tense expectation dissolved into confusion. "Should we proceed?" the tech asked.

Chun tried to twist in the bed to see the display on the ESP scanner, but the wires and restraints on her BCI cap prevented her from turning her head. "Good Christ, what's happening?"

Maddeningly, Lieberman ignored her and motioned for Solomon. The colonel joined him at her bedside. Lieberman indicated the display. "Some of the nanospecks don't seem to be correctly bonding to the granules in her cerebellum. We were in a rush." He shrugged apologetically. "There wasn't time for proper testing."

Solomon considered this. "What's the chance it'll cause a problem?"

Lieberman shrugged again. "No way to know. It's a tiny, tiny fraction of the 'specks. Most likely it won't be a problem at all." He hesitated. "Or maybe it'll cause irreparable brain damage."

His fake-casual tone was infuriating. "Excuse me," Chun said. "I'm right here."

Solomon looked down at her. "Sorry, Doctor." They'd taken her glasses, so his face was fuzzy, but it was clear Lieberman's cavalier tone had angered him, too. He turned to the geneticist. "You're not being helpful. We're out of time. I need a recommendation. Do we proceed, or not?"

Lieberman seemed unfazed by the colonel's hostile tone. "We don't have time to make another batch of nanospecks for Chun. The other batches we've started won't be ready in time, either. It might work. It might not. I can't give you a probability. We were rushed, and nobody but Analise Novak really understands how the capatar tech works. If I were you, I'd do it. It's a big risk, but what alternative do we have?"

Chun swallowed, looked toward the Haven machine. It glowed impassively. A strong wave of the Tingles caused her to shudder. The others felt it too. Solomon grimaced. "We're running out of time."

Zia slapped the bed rail with the ball of her fist. "She's *afraid*. Get her unplugged. Even if my nanospecks aren't fully cooked, maybe it's enough. *I'll* do it."

Solomon expelled a sharp, frustrated sigh. He looked down at her. "It's your call, Dr. Chun."

"Christ on a stick," she muttered.

havencosm | ATUM'S LAIR

Resuscitation

Se-Jong flailed out and jolted to full consciousness when his fist unexpectedly struck something soft. Somebody made an *Oof!* sound, and the painful pressure on his ribs vanished. He gagged, vomited bile-tinged lake water, took a juddering breath, and vomited again. There were hands on him, turning him on his side, and someone was pounding at his back. He fought to regain his breath, coughing furiously, fighting panic. Where was he? Flashes of imagery, of the titanic silver needle of the *Navis Sacris*, the shrieking jets of the Solar Guard dropship, Nkiru's distraught face. She'd sprayed him with Yok-Stop. Why had she done that? Then, he'd been drowning in the lake. The Yok-Stop must have paralyzed him. He'd passed out . . .

More coughing. Eventually he managed to suck in enough oxygen to fill his lungs. The pain lessened by a magnitude. He opened his eyes.

The shaggy-haired man was straddling him, hand raised to deliver another blow. When he saw that Se-Jong was conscious, he grimaced. Another coughing spree caused Se-Jong to ball into a tight fetal position, and the shaggy-haired man—*Arni?*—moved away. When the coughing fit finished, Se-Jong tried to sit up. Again, he felt hands on his back, roughly supporting him.

He turned. The hands belonged to Nkiru, her waterlogged hair plastered to her shoulders, her face twisted in anger and desperation. She and Arni must have saved him from drowning, pulled him into the underwater opening beneath the lakeside pier.

Her hands released him. He looked around. He was in a dark tunnel next to a pool of frigid lake water. The floor was covered in pasty mud. Nkiru's coldsuit was smeared with the same mud. So was his own. The only light was from a battered flashlight held by Arni.

Nkiru's expression was as brittle as a shard of flint. "I should've let you drown, you son of a bitch."

"I'm sorry," he huffed hoarsely. "I'm so sorry." In the cold air, mist from his breath formed little clouds in front of his face.

"You're an idiot."

The water in the pool from which they'd dragged him began to roil. She glanced at it, gave him a fierce glare. She rose to her feet and turned to Arni. "They're coming. He's okay. Let's go."

They hurried away, the beam from Arni's flashlight dancing on the tunnel walls, leaving Se-Jong enveloped in a terrifying darkness. He tried to climb to his feet but discovered his legs were still paralyzed, courtesy of the Yok-Stop. He called after the retreating pair. "Wait!"

Nkiru paused and looked over her shoulder, but only for an instant. Then she was running, and the jostling, diminishing light outlined their silhouettes, and then they were gone.

Se-Jong fought panic. His lungs were on fire. Even the slightest breath triggered a hacking cough, the burning stench of the Yok-

Stop still covering him despite his brief swim in the lake. His arms and legs tingled furiously, and the areas of exposed skin on his face and neck that had taken the brunt of the spray were completely numb. The coldsuit had protected him from the assault of the frigid lake water, but he was still shivering uncontrollably.

Think. Don't lose it.

How much time had passed since he'd leaped into the lake? Probably only a minute or two. A Solar Guard dropship had been screaming toward him; certainly it had already landed up on the pier. At this moment it was probably disgorging a contingent of Solar Marines. They'd surely seen him jump into the water. It wouldn't take long for them to follow him into the underwater entrance.

A sound. He held his rasping breath and sat for a moment in total silence. *There it was again.* The water in the pool was slapping against the rock. A dim, flickering radiance appeared deep in the pool. Someone with a light was swimming up from the depths. No, several lights, several someones.

There was another sound, too. A faint but unmistakable thrumming that came from the floor and walls—the sound of the needle ship's mysterious antigravity drive, rumbling down through the rocks. Worst case, the someones rising from the depths were the Dei Militans, come to arrest him and Nkiru. Only slightly better, they were Solar Marines from the dropship, dispatched by his grandmother to rescue him from his folly. He didn't think Grandmother would let him be taken by the militans, but given the nature of his situation, he wasn't sure who had the higher authority.

He managed to pull himself to his knees by grasping at rough, ropey protrusions along the tunnel walls. *Solidified lava?* It felt like it. The tingling in his legs had blossomed into a searing pain, but along with the pain came new strength. He gained his feet, steadying himself against the wall, and fumbled at his waist for the coldsuit's emergency kit. It took a moment for his numb fingers to locate the kit's flashlight. The pitiful beam barely lit the opposite wall only a couple of meters away, pale compared to the growing brightness emanating from the pool. He pointed it down the corridor in the direction Nkiru had gone. The narrow beam was absorbed by the darkness.

"Damn, damn, damn," he muttered, and hurried after her.

—

The fire in his muscles intensified as he rushed through the tunnel, weaving drunkenly as he fought to maintain balance and avoid tripping over the stones and boulders that littered the path. He cursed every time he stumbled, and when he finally toppled, his rubbery arms couldn't protect his face from the jagged basalt. The impact thudded through his skull. It stunned him but, oddly, didn't hurt. He put his hand to his left cheek to find a flap of loose skin hanging below his cheekbone. His hand came away dripping with blood. Something was wrong with his nose, too. It felt odd and squishy. He lay on his side, closed his eyes. A sudden, bone-chilling cold radiated outward from his gut.

I'm going into shock.

—

A moving light penetrated his closed eyelids. There were voices, just a few quiet, clipped words. He tried to open his eyes, but they wouldn't cooperate. Someone was here.

Solar Guard? Dei Militans?

The whispers grew more urgent. Suddenly rough hands were on him, exploring his body. He opened his eyes. A thick-necked woman in a Solar Marines tacsuit was holding his shoulder like a vise. She had a pharmaneedle that she'd apparently just removed from his arm. "Can you see me?"

Se-Jong managed a nod. The medic looked up at someone standing nearby. "He's conscious."

Another face moved into his field of view, round and severe, bracketed by the padding of a tacsuit helmet onto which was embossed a silver eagle, wings spread.

"Halmeoni," Se-Jong gasped.

"Sonja," his grandmother replied without the slightest trace of affection.

The medic held her hand up. "How many fingers?"

"Three," croaked Se-Jong. Water from his matted hair ran into his eyes, and he wiped it away. When he looked at his hand, he saw it wasn't water, but blood. He shivered despite his coldsuit.

"What happened to you? What's that chemical smell?"

"I got Yok-Stopped."

The marine's eyes narrowed. "Can you tell me what day it is?"

"I'm starting to think it's judgment day," said Se-Jong.

Grandmother made an angry snort and nodded curtly at the medic. "Get him on his feet."

The medic backed away. Two marines hauled him to a standing position. He looked around. There were twelve of them: his grandmother, ten marines, and an awkward young Solar Guard ensign who seemed completely out of place in a combat unit. All were wearing full tacsuits, dripping with lake water, their boots smudged with mud from the tunnel floor.

Se-Jong gulped down astonishment. Grandmother had led an entire squad into the tunnel. That meant there was probably another squad back up on the pier with the dropship. He'd known his plea for help would be answered, but he'd expected her to show in a courier shuttle, not a starcutter brimming with weapons and a platoon of Solar Marines.

From his position tucked between two marines' shoulders, Se-Jong met her eyes. He waited for her to speak, his reeling head beginning to clear, either from fear or from whatever drug the medic had given him.

"You have cracked open a nest of hornets," she said. "The Dei Miltans are here."

"I know. I'm sorry."

She took quick stock of his injuries and permitted herself a small, regretful sigh. She took Se-Jong's shoulder and motioned for the marines to release him. Her grip was strong. She beckoned the awkward-looking ensign to join her. The young officer took his other arm. They both leaned close. Grandmother whispered, "Your message said that Nkiru Anaya can activate avatar technology. Is this true?"

He nodded.

"We saw her attack you, then flee into the water with another man. Who is the man?"

"His name is Arni. I think he lives here in these tunnels."

"Is he the Janga monk you mentioned in your message? The one helping Anaya?"

"I don't think so. He's some kind of hermit."

The young ensign interrupted her captain's response. "How did Anaya learn to use avatar relics?" The ensign's shoulder badge identified her as a reliquist, an expert on avatars and their artifacts. His grandmother had brought a scholar.

Se-Jong tried to shrug, but his shoulders were held tightly by Grandmother and the reliquist. "I don't know. She knows about avatar history. She's taken me to places where we've found undiscovered greater relics."

"What relics did you find? Can she activate all of them?" Framed by the padding of her tacsuit helmet, the reliquist's face shone with giddy curiosity.

Before he could answer, the medic approached. She opened her medical field kit and extracted a swath of gauze. "Don't move," she ordered, making a gruesome flinch as she dabbed at his face. "You've got a broken cheekbone and a nasty gash filled with dirt, and you've done a real number on your nose. Hold still; this will hurt." He felt the rough pressure of her resetting the position of his nose, heard the cartilage crackle, but felt no pain.

Grandmother's voice hardened. "Anaya did this to you?"

"I did this to myself, Halmeoni. I fell and hit my face. It's not Nkiru's fault. She and Arni saved me when I was drowning."

"And then she left you here to bleed to death?"

"She didn't have any choice but to leave me. She was afraid the militans would get here first."

Grandmother inhaled deeply. She leaned close and whispered rapidly into his ear. "She was right to be afraid. These aren't Dei Militans regulars. They are the Regia Protectors, the personal guard of the Father Regis. They have a consenti with them, and likely an Inquisitor, too. Legally, they have the authority to arrest you. This is an extremely dangerous situation. Do you understand?"

His head was still ringing from the Yok-Stop and the near-drowning, but he was coherent enough to know that if the militans arrested him, his life would be over. He started to speak, but the medic barked, "Don't move. I'm going to irrigate your wound." The pressure on his cheek increased, and when she pulled the gauze away, it was drenched in gooey, bloody mud. She muttered something, reached into the first aid kit, and pulled out a spray cannister. "Close your eyes," she ordered.

He did as he was told. He heard the hiss of the spray but felt nothing. A moment later came the sound of a plastic packet being torn open, then more nudges and pressure on his cheek. The medic sighed. "That's as good as I can do for him, Captain. The triage glue will numb the pain and help the bleeding. He's going to need more irrigation, debridement, and a lot of stitches."

Grandmother grunted a dismissal to the medic. Se-Jong opened his eyes to her cold stare. "I've instructed the marines at the dropship to delay the militans, but not to engage in combat," she said. "They won't hold them off for long. Tell me why the Anaya woman brought you here, to this place." When he hesitated, her eyes narrowed. "Sonja, you have put me in a most difficult position. Anaya is accused of stealing relics from the Regium, and they think you're an accomplice. Grone is a pilgrimage world. The church has jurisdiction here, not SATO, which means I don't have any legal basis to keep the militans from arresting you. I don't want that to happen, but I also won't order my marines to confront the militans without a very good reason." She paused, her eyes as dark as coal. "Now tell me, why did she bring you here, to this mountain. What is this place?"

It would be no use trying to hide the truth. "Nkiru believes this place is a major undiscovered First Epoch dungeon. She thinks the War of the Archangels was fought here."

The young reliquist let out sharp gasp. Grandmother gave her a withering glare before turning back to Se-Jong. "And you believe her?"

"I do. I've seen her activate avatar tech. Like I said before, she's taken me to other places where we've found undiscovered greater relics."

She stared at him as if measuring his sanity. "I would say her claims are ridiculous, and yet the Father Regis has sent the *Navis Sacris* here, and there are indications of panic within the walls of the Regium." She hesitated. "How can I be sure she isn't just a clever charlatan? Why should I endanger my marines and risk starting a religious war for something I have always known to be a myth?"

"I guess you'll just have to trust me."

"Not good enough."

Her cold rebuke slashed like a razor. To his grandmother, he was a wayward kid who had shirked his family duty and allowed himself to be seduced by . . . what had she called it? . . . *Shiny things of little value.* "You can't let them take her," he demanded, his voice rising to an angry shout. "I called you because I trusted you. If you're not going to help me, then get the fuck out. I'll find a way to save her myself."

"He's right," blurted the reliquist. "If there's even the slightest chance Anaya can activate avatar tech, we can't let the church have her. They've been collecting avatar weapons in their reliquaries for thousands of years. What do you think the Father Regis will do if he gets his hands on Anaya?"

It was reckless for a subordinate to lecture a senior commander, but Grandmother didn't admonish the ensign. Her reply was flat, emotionless. "It will push him over the edge. He'll withdraw from the SATO Charter. He'll claim the Avatar Throne and try to disband the civilian government."

The reliquist nodded in sharp agreement. "There'll be a war for sure. The Father Regis knows Earth and the Solar Alliance have no defense against avatar weapons."

Se-Jong noted the reliquist's name from the tag on her tacsuit: *Littlefeather*. She was hardly older than Se-Jong, yet she seemed to have his grandmother's ear. She continued breathlessly. "The risk is much higher if you let the church take her. They won't dare take action against us if Anaya is in our custody."

One of the marines stiffened, then spoke softly into the microphone of his tacsuit helmet. He called to Grandmother. "The dropship reports that a party of ten Regia Protectors has entered the lake and is following our trace. We have two minutes before they get here."

Grandmother pursed her lips. It never took more than a second or two for her to make a decision. Five seconds passed.

Ten.

Fifteen.

Se-Jong could feel the throb of his heartbeat in the swollen wounds on his face.

Grandmother's eyes passed over Littlefeather, who nodded. She turned to Se-Jong. "You'd better be right about the girl, Sonja." Her voice rose as she addressed the marine squad leader. "We will take the girl and her companion into custody. We must avoid the militans at all costs. Let's move."

Cathedral

The tunnel went on endlessly. Se-Jong ran, supported by two marines, lurching through the debris that littered the tunnel floor. The only sounds were the rustling of tacsuit fabric and the occasional soft clatter of a dislodged stone. The marines used no lights, and he could only see a meter or two with his tiny flashlight. The cold moisture in the air had coated the rough basalt walls, and the tiny droplets glistened like a field of stars in the flashlight's dim beam.

Here and there parts of the ceiling had collapsed, but in every case, someone had cleared a narrow passage through the debris. Often the passage was so small they had to wriggle through like worms, and he scraped and tore the tough fabric of his coldsuit against the abrasive igneous rock. The numbness in his joints and face was lessening, replaced with a furious ache that felt like he'd been pummeled by a prizefighter. The front of his coldsuit was streaked with the blood from his cheek. He was starting to feel that pain, too.

By the time they approached a dark void that signaled the end of the tunnel, his lungs had become watery pits of agony and his legs were stilts of fire. "Stop, stop," he hissed. He covered the lens of his flashlight with his palm and leaned against the wall. "If Nkiru hears us coming, we'll never catch up. She has an avatar relic called a stealthshield. It makes her invisible. If she uses it, we'll never find her." He fought to catch his breath. "Let me go first. If she knows you're here, it'll scare her."

The marine squad leader looked to Se-Jong's grandmother. She nodded reluctantly. Without a word, the squad leader unclipped the night-vision monocle from the visor of his tacsuit and handed it to Se-Jong. "You know how to use these?"

In fact, he did, courtesy of his tactical classes at Jackill. He pocketed his flashlight and nodded. "Wait out of sight. I'll signal when it's okay."

"You have two minutes," Grandmother said.

Se-Jong started to object, realized it would be fruitless. He nodded. "Okay. Two minutes."

Nkiru's voice sounded faintly in the void. From the hollow echoes he judged that the cavern was very large. He couldn't smell through his swollen nose, but the moist, frigid air tasted like old mud. He peeked around the threshold, holding the night-vision monocle to his right eye.

The cavern had once been almost perfectly spherical, about eighty meters in diameter, but part of the ceiling had long since collapsed into a jagged tumble of boulders. The walls were the same rough black volcanic rock as the tunnel. It was a natural cavern with no signs of artificial construction other than a crumbling concrete ramp that led from the tunnel mouth down into the basin and a second, identical ramp that led to another tunnel on the opposite wall.

There! Below him, about thirty meters away, at the very bottom of the spherical basin, was a moving circle of light. Two recognizable silhouettes were kneeling next to something that looked like a pit-altar from a Cataclyst cathedral. The dish-shaped depression was about four meters in diameter, and the central spike rose about two meters. Nkiru and Arni were staring into the water that partly filled the depression. Arni pointed upward, to a circular hole at the highest point of the cavern, directly above the pit-altar's spike. He waved his hands and whispered something urgent to Nkiru.

Se-Jong crept down the ancient ramp. At the bottom, he stumbled over a stone. It clattered down to the two shadowed figures.

Nkiru's light jerked toward him. She raised her arm and pointed something at him.

He stopped and threw up his hands. "Don't shoot. It's me!" He was surprised to hear the drunken slur in his words. "It's Se-Jong."

Nkiru didn't lower her arm. There wasn't enough light to see her expression, but there was enough to recognize the orange canister of Yok-Stop in her hand. He waited.

She cursed softly and dropped her arm. Before she could speak, he rushed clumsily to her side. "They're behind me, in the tunnel."

"Who?" He was close enough now to see the glint of fear in her pale eyes. Fear, but also fury. At him.

"My grandmother." He tried to speak around the numbness in his lips to minimize the slur. "And behind her, a squad of Dei Militans."

A cascade of twitches and winces tumbled across her face: indecision mixed with near-panic. Also, a sorrowful loathing. For an instant he thought she would slap him. Or maybe give him another dose of Yok-Stop.

He grabbed her arm. She tried to wrench away, but he yanked her closer. "Damn it, Nkiru. *None of this is my fault.* The militans are chasing *you*, not me. They would've come for you whether I called my grandmother or not. Don't you understand? I'm trying to *save* you!"

She turned her flashlight into his eyes, made an involuntary gasp when she saw the condition of his bandaged face and the wet stains on his coldsuit. Shock and concern overwhelmed her anger. "Oh my god. What happened? You're covered in blood!"

"I fell and hit my face. I think I broke something. It doesn't hurt. My whole head is numb from the Yok-Stop." He released her arm. "Doesn't matter. The cavalry is here to help you. You have to trust me. I know my grandmother. She won't let the militans take us. She's waiting for my signal, but she won't wait much longer."

Her eyes narrowed and she rubbed her arm where he'd grabbed her. She glanced at Arni, who was staring into the pit-altar. Se-Jong looked at the circular pool, saw nothing but stagnant water crusted by floating cave scum. Arni made the sign of the Linked Trinity over his breast, stood, scowled at Se-Jong.

Nkiru was scowling too, staring up into the darkness toward the tunnel entrance. "Who's up there with your grandmother?"

"A squad of Solar Marines in battle gear."

"What is your grandmother going to do?"

"Honestly? She wants to keep me from getting arrested by the militans. But she's also very interested in you, and what you can do."

"What did you tell her?"

"I told her everything. I don't know if she believes me, but for now she's willing to give you the benefit of doubt. She certainly doesn't want the militans to get you."

The angry flare of betrayal he'd seen in her eyes just before she'd Yok-Stopped him shone again from her face. "So, I'll be *her* prisoner instead of the church's? No thanks."

"*You don't have a choice*," said a new voice.

Nkiru looked over Se-Jong's shoulder and recoiled. Se-Jong spun toward the voice. A few meters away, a human-shaped figure was rising from the darkness, brandishing a rifle. Next to it another figure rose. Then another, and another. Se-Jong turned in a complete circle. They were surrounded.

One of the figures, smaller than the others, stepped forward. He let out a breath when he recognized his grandmother. Somehow, the marines had crept into the cavern and encircled them in the few seconds he'd been talking. This was absolutely not the way he'd imagined Nkiru would be introduced to his grandmother.

"I told you to wait!" he hissed.

"Yes, you did," she said. "But there is no time for waiting and you are not in charge." She looked at Nkiru dispassionately. "Nkiru Anaya, I am Captain Kwon Ophelia Namjoo, commander of Trumbull Station. I am here to retrieve my grandson from whatever trouble you have gotten him into." She hesitated, giving Se-Jong a sideways glare. "If what he says about you is true, I am also willing to grant you provisional asylum and the protection of the Solar Guard. If you don't agree to come with me and accept asylum, I will arrest you. Decide, now. The militans are almost here."

Nkiru looked around at the encircling marines, then sharply back at Se-Jong. The frightened loathing had returned to her expression. "Like you said, I don't have a choice."

Something made a low beep. The marine squad leader checked a device attached to the wrist of his tacsuit, raised a hand, and made a fist. "Here they come," he announced in a low voice. "One-fifty meters and closing fast." The others tensed, and several of the marines turned and raised their rifles toward the tunnel opening.

Grandmother grimaced. "Is there another way out?"

"Ask him," Se-Jong said, pointing to Arni. "He lives here."

She turned to Arni. "You. Can you get us outside using a different route?"

Facing the barrels of ten laser rifles, Arni had curled into his pilgrims' robes like a turtle trying to withdraw into a too-small shell. Grandmother raised her voice. "You! Is there another way out?"

"You're scaring him," Se-Jong advised. "Tell the marines to stand down."

With a nod from his grandmother, the marines lowered their rifles in unison. Se-Jong pushed past the medic and went to Arni's side. "Arni, we can't get out the same way we came in. There are bad guys following us, and we have to get Nkiru to safety."

Arni clenched his eyes shut and promptly began to hyperventilate. Se-Jong put a hand on his shoulder. Even through the thick robes he could feel Arni's thin, undernourished sinews.

"Arni, we have to keep Nkiru safe. Help us get out of here."

Arni opened his eyes. "Since the mountain fell, there's only one other way out." He glanced up toward a narrow stone ledge on the cavern wall. "Through the dungeon. But it's bad, bad, bad."

"Why is it bad?"

Arni cringed. "That's where the boss is."

Boss? Se-Jong had studied enough scripture to know that the mythical creatures known as *bosses* had been the guardians of the treasures of the ancient dungeons. "I'd rather take my chances with a myth than be caught by the Dei Militans," he said. He looked to Nkiru for support. Her face was tight with anger, fear . . . and hard resolution. She nodded curtly.

Everyone turned to Arni. His eyes flicked back and forth between Nkiru and the marines. He was breathing fast and hard, puffing streams of mist into the cold air. Suddenly, he blinked and gave a short, hysterical giggle. "Okay okay okay. Gear up, everybody—here we go."

Grandmother spun to the marine squad leader, a sergeant with a square face and flattened nose. "When the militans arrive, misdirect them," she ordered. "Delay them as much as possible. Do whatever you can to keep them from following us, but do not—do *not*—get into a shooting fight."

"Aye, Captain." The man had the marks of the Sacraments on his forehead. He looked unnerved, Se-Jong thought. For a pious fellow like him to stand up to the Dei Militans would be like a loyal son defying a domineering father. Se-Jong suspected it was the reason Grandmother had chosen the man to stay behind. He'd be the least likely to start shooting.

Grandmother wasn't finished. "Give me your two best riflemen to accompany us."

The squad leader pointed at a young, stern-faced marine. "Sergeant Toroni, you and Private McCloud go with the captain."

―

The bottom of the cavern was shaped like a bowl. From the lowest point of the cave at the edge of the water-filled depression, Arni led them up an ever-steepening climb toward the ledge he'd indicated earlier. He was as surefooted as a mountain goat, occasionally pausing to wait as they scrambled behind him. Nkiru followed close behind, then Se-Jong, then Grandmother and the two marines and the reliquist. As they approached the ledge, Se-Jong stopped and looked back over his shoulder. The marines they'd left behind had moved to flanking positions on either side of the original ramp and the entrance tunnel. In the darkness, they were ghosts.

"What is this place?" Se-Jong panted.

"It's the very first Cataclyst church," Nkiru replied, also out of breath.

"What does that mean?"

"It means you both need to shut up and climb," growled Sergeant Toroni.

Without warning, a hard-edged spotlight blazed from the entrance tunnel. Somebody behind him, probably the reliquist, gasped loudly. The spotlight shifted across the floor and walls, searching. It paused on the pool and spike at the bottom, then moved up to reveal a circular hole in the ceiling directly above the pool.

Nkiru and Arni had frozen the instant the light had appeared, but now they were moving, fast and frantic. Se-Jong hurried behind them, but the blinding spotlight hit him like a blast of searing air, pinning his shadow against the basalt wall in stark relief. He threw his hand over his eyes.

Across the cavern, somebody shouted. A stern male voice with a strong High Tang accent.

The militans had found them.

Arni reached the ledge, motioned desperately for them to follow.

From the cavern floor, the Solar Marine squad leader shouted a challenge at the militans.

The spotlight swung away from Se-Jong and toward the marines. Se-Jong's head twirled with an overwhelming dizziness. The marine called Toroni caught his flailing hand and tugged him along, hard.

Nkiru climbed onto the ledge alongside Arni. Grandmother, the reliquist, and the marines hurried behind, with Se-Jong in tow.

The ledge was narrow, less than a meter across, and barely big enough for their entire party. Heated words between the marines and the militans echoed below them.

"Now what?" Se-Jong whispered. There was nothing here, and they were sitting ducks, clearly visible from below. Arni pulled a blue, metallic card from his filthy robe and used it to make a slashing motion against a section of the cavern wall. He nodded toward Nkiru. She stepped toward the wall and was gone.

Vanished.

Se-Jong was struck by a sudden vertigo. He gave Arni a panicked glare.

Shouts from below. A bright light shone upon them. A voice rang out.

"Stop there! Don't move!"

Arni clutched the blue card and fell into the volcanic rock wall. He vanished, just like Nkiru.

More angry shouts. Se-Jong's head twirled with an overwhelming dizziness. He teetered, reached for the rough rock to steady himself. His left hand grabbed a shard of crusty basalt, but inches away, his right hand passed through an adjacent area of the black stone, disappearing up to his elbow. He flailed, but there was nothing but air. Before he could react, somebody grabbed his submerged wrist and tugged, hard.

He fell sideways, twisting. He screamed. He was being dragged against the jagged volcanic rock. Then he was tumbling, falling into heap of sweat-stained and smelly robes. He opened his eyes. Arni was dragging him across a smooth floor, away from a series of grunts and thuds as more bodies tumbled behind him.

They were no longer in the cavern. The beam of Arni's flashlight revealed a square room expertly carved from native rock. Small and crowded, it appeared to be a junction of three dark corridors. Behind them, a rectangle of gray mist was set into the polished stone wall. He'd just fallen through the vaporous opening. His grandmother and the two marines were climbing to their feet, sweeping the room with their rifles. The reliquist was staring anxiously at the mist-filled doorway.

Nkiru had the expression of a wild animal cornered by poachers. She pulled him, wobbling, to his feet. He looked at her.

"What just happened?"

"Secret door," she said distractedly, looking around as if seeking a familiar landmark.

"Close it," Grandmother ordered.

"*Shhh!*" hissed Arni. "They can still hear us. Can't close it. It stays open for hours."

"A secret door," whispered the reliquist. "That settles it. This really is a dungeon."

Nkiru was staring into the mist of the secret door with a mixture of hard-jawed regret and pure adrenaline. She gave Se-Jong an *I-told-you-so* smirk. Se-Jong felt a deep ache in his chest. A *dungeon!* Placed here, the church claimed, by the gods, to test the mettle of the elder heroes. He swallowed and looked around. A cheap sleeping mat on the floor, a large water can, and a pile of boxes and supplies. He turned to Arni. "Is this where you live?"

Grandmother interrupted Arni's reply. "The militans saw us come through the wall. We need to move, *now*. How do we get out of here?"

Nkiru gestured toward the tunnel to the right of the secret door. "That way?"

"*Not* that way," said Arni.

"But that's the direction I went last time—"

"No," Arni insisted. "That was a shortcut. During the Cataclysm the mountain fell down and the lake rose up. You can't go that way anymore."

Nkiru stared at Arni disbelievingly. "Then how do we get there?"

"I tried to tell you," he whispered hollowly. "We have to get past the boss."

Nkiru's words set off alarm bells among Se-Jong's racing thoughts. "You've been here *before?*" he blurted.

A string of muffled shouts and curses issued from beyond the opaque mist of the secret door. Quarreling voices. The marine squad leader. The stern voice with the High Tang accent.

Grandmother stiffened. "No more arguing. We need the fastest route out of this mountain to a place where I can call the dropship." She snapped at Arni. "Which is the way out?"

Arni put both hands on his face and filled his lungs with air. When he dropped his hands, Se-Jong saw a deep desolation in his eyes, a complete absence of hope. Arni lurched toward the right-hand tunnel. Nkiru hesitated, then followed.

Grandmother gave Se-Jong a questioning glance. He shrugged and followed Arni and Nkiru.

Dungeon

Arni rushed them through a confusing maze of passageways carved from the black basalt. He moved with a breathless purpose, never hesitating when he approached a junction or a side tunnel.

Rusted fasteners lined the smooth walls and ceilings, along with the long-rotted remnants of pipes and wiring. Buoyed by the stimulant given by the marine medic, along with a heavy dose of painkillers, Se-Jong felt almost normal. He could even see a bit through his left eye, although the ugly swelling in his cheek allowed only a narrow squint.

They moved silently: Arni first, then Sergeant Toroni, who used the situational display on his wrist scanner to peer ahead in the dark corridors. Nkiru and Littlefeather followed a few paces behind, Littlefeather peering at the screen of her komnic, recording their surroundings and tracing their route through the maze. Se-Jong was last, helped along by Private McCloud. McCloud's smooth face showed a disturbing lack of emotion, as if fleeing the Regia Protectors through a ten-thousand-year-old dungeon were no more troubling than mowing the lawn.

Grandmother took position at the rear, pointing a red-hued headlamp in their direction of travel. She studied the floor, grimacing at the trail of footprints they were leaving in the grimy debris. If the militans found the secret door, they would have no trouble tracing their path.

The corridor didn't seem like something from a mythical avatar dungeon. He'd expected walls of gold, piles of treasure, and devious traps. Instead, this place looked like a run-of-the-mill utility hallway one might find beneath a factory. He stole a furtive glance at Nkiru. She was clutching the straps of her backpack with tight gloves.

Se-Jong shrugged away from McCloud's grip. He moved to Nkiru's side.

"Back there at the secret door, you told Arni you went 'that direction' last time. What did you mean, *last time*?"

She acted as if she hadn't heard him. Her attention was locked on Arni and the passageway ahead. They almost plowed into him when Arni suddenly stopped at the base of a staircase set into the wall. He licked his lips, stared nervously up the dark stairs.

Nkiru followed his gaze. "Arni, what is it?"

"I just realized . . . there may be . . . another way."

"A way around the boss?"

Arni nodded thoughtfully.

She pointed up the stairs. "That way? Where does it go?"

"To the bridge across the seeker pit."

"The bridge with the microflak mines?"

He nodded again. "The bridge is broken. I fixed it once, but it broke again, and I fell and died." He pointed to the two marines and the array of utility gear strapped to their tacsuits. "But they might be able to get us across."

The marines looked at each other. Sergeant Toroni said, "You died?"

Arni nodded. "But you probably wouldn't."

The marine rolled his eyes. Grandmother gestured toward the stairs. "Are you saying this is the best way out?"

Nkiru shrugged. "Maybe. It's better than trying to get past the boss."

"What is this . . . boss?" Se-Jong could tell from Grandmother's skeptical tone that she was beginning to regret her decision to trust him.

"It's a harvester," Arni whispered. Everyone turned toward him. He shrank back into his robes. "The boss . . . it's a Gurothim harvester."

Nkiru nodded in grim confirmation. The temperature in the corridor seemed to drop. Se-Jong was suddenly and very acutely aware of even the tiniest scents and sounds surrounding him. The puffs of mist before each face dissipated. Nobody was breathing.

"Ah, murd," muttered Sergeant Toroni. Private McCloud traced the sign of the Linked Trinity over his tacsuit's breastplate. The reliquist's entire face twitched.

Grandmother opened her mouth. She snapped it shut without speaking. She gave Se-Jong an accusing stare, but he was too dumbfounded to care. *A Gurothim harvester?*

Nkiru continued. "This harvester malfunctioned millions of years ago during the First Epoch while it was pulverizing Grone's moon looking for timedust. When the moon's debris fell to the planet, the harvester fell with it. It's why a warlord named Jaspaar built a citadel here during the days of the avatars. It was one of the few pieces of Gurothim technology ever discovered during the Age of Avatars. Jaspaar thought he could control it, turn it into a weapon."

"And you know this how?" asked Grandmother. At Nkiru's silence, she waved her hand. "Never mind. Continue."

"The harvester was badly damaged. Jaspaar managed to partially repair it. He was still working on it when the Rapture and the Cataclysm happened. It's been trapped in this dungeon ever since."

"Eating timedust," said Arni. "And getting fat."

Grandmother made a dismissive motion at Nkiru. "I don't know what this place is, and I don't know who *you* are. My grandson says you can activate avatar devices. I can see that he believes in you, but he is young and guileless. I, on the other hand, am old and skeptical. I need *proof*." She swung her arm to point up the dark staircase. "If I'm going to jeopardize my life and the lives of my marines, I need to know without a doubt that you are worth the risk."

A barely audible beep. Toroni had raised the display on the wrist of his tacsuit. He gestured urgently back in the direction they'd come from. "Contacts. Two hundred meters and closing."

"The militans?" said Grandmother.

He gave an uncertain shake of his head. "Probably. They're too far to tell for sure."

Everyone stared at Grandmother. She was glaring at Nkiru. "Show me proof, right now." At her nod, Private McCloud raised his rifle toward Nkiru.

"Grandmother, please," said Se-Jong.

She ignored him, her eyes still fixed on Nkiru. "Show me. Quickly!"

Nkiru unslung her backpack and gently removed the scancorder. She tapped a control. Nothing happened. She tapped it again. Nothing. A note of frantic desperation entered her voice. "This happens sometimes. Hold on a second."

She shook the scancorder and jabbed forcefully at the controls.

Still nothing.

Grandmother's expression, always neutral, didn't change, but Se-Jong could see the seething fury. She was about to issue an order that, once uttered, would seal Nkiru's fate. "I swear to you, she can do it," he blurted. "I've seen it with my own eyes. You have to believe me!"

Grandmother didn't react, didn't turn away from Nkiru.

"Halmeoni, *please!*"

"A hundred fifty meters," reported Toroni. "It's the militans. Twelve signatures, moving fast."

Se-Jong held his breath. One second passed.

Two seconds.

Grandmother made a guttural growl, looked in Se-Jong's direction, then turned to Arni. She motioned toward the stairs.

"Go!"

The stairs were endless. Nobody spoke. The higher they climbed, the warmer and drier the air became. Soon Se-Jong was sweating in his coldsuit, and when he stumbled, he realized that the stimulants were being cleansed from his bloodstream by the exertion of the climb. So were the painkillers. The medic had stayed behind at the bubble cavern, so there would be no more military-strength drugs. Se-Jong gritted his teeth and climbed.

Their path became increasingly littered with stones and rubble. Arni picked his way through the debris, eventually coming to a ragged, meter-wide hole in the wall that looked like it had been recently blasted open. He gestured proudly, pointing into the dark hole. "It's through there. I tried to make a shortcut around the boss."

Nkiru knelt next to Arni and stared into the hole. After a moment she glanced back at the others. When her eyes swept over Se-Jong, she winced. He felt a sting of regret. For the past two months she'd been his constant companion. His lover. His best friend. Now he was nothing but the guy who'd betrayed her. She'd been anticipating a moment of glory here at Grone, but he'd ruined everything.

Behind him, he heard his grandmother say to Toroni, "Status?"

The marine tapped the screen on his wrist, scowled. "I can't tell if the militans are following or not. All I'm getting is static."

"It's the harvester," said Arni knowingly. "We're getting close." He ducked into the tunnel, crawling on all fours. Nkiru followed. Grandmother nodded at the marines. Se-Jong cursed softly. He dropped to his knees and crawled into the dark hole.

Crawling, it turned out, was far more difficult than walking, especially with his injuries. After an endless period that might have been only a few minutes, Se-Jong faltered and signaled that he needed to stop. He sagged against the tunnel wall. The others waited, his grandmother engaging in an urgent conversation with the two marines and the reliquist.

In front of him, Nkiru had turned and was squatting. He tried to read her expression. She pulled off her gloves and retrieved her water bottle. She drank deeply, hesitated, then offered it to Se-Jong. He took it and pulled a long stream of water into his parched throat. He handed the bottle back to her. She replaced it at her hip.

"You should have talked to me before you called your grandmother," she said in a low voice. "You should've told me."

"If I'd told you, you would've said no. I was afraid you might . . . leave me."

"You're damn right I would've said no, but I wouldn't have left you." She took a deep breath and expelled it. "Your cut is bleeding again." When he raised his hand to touch his face, she grabbed his wrist. "Let me do it."

Grimacing, she adjusted the loose bandage on his cheek. Her fingers were cold against his swollen skin. She pulled a roll of tape from her coldsuit's emergency kit, tore off several short lengths, and used them to secure the bandage. She sighed. "That's as good as I can do. You're going to need a lot of stitches."

She pulled her gloves back on. He glanced at her wrist. She was still wearing the copper bracelet he'd given her.

"You're right, you know," she said. "The militans are after me, not you. I got you into this mess. I guess I shouldn't be surprised you called for help." She shook her head, made a sad smirk. "You remind me of my brother. You think you need to protect me, when it's actually the other way around."

Nkiru had never mentioned her family. "You have a brother?"

"Yeah. He thinks he's a badass, just like you do, Lieutenant."

Lieutenant. She'd called him Lieutenant. A tight knot in his gut loosened. Se-Jong gestured theatrically at his torn, bloody coldsuit. "I *am* a badass. After all, I smashed a boulder with nothing but my face."

The tickle of a smile passed across her lips, then disappeared into a frown. She looked at the rough-hewn walls. "To answer your question, I haven't been here before, not exactly. I know some people who were here, though. One of them told me about it."

"Who?"

She sighed. "His name was Rupert. He was an expert on places like this."

At the mention of the name, Arni's face popped up over her shoulder. "Rupe," he mumbled.

"Was he a Janga monk?" Se-Jong asked.

"No." Nkiru's frown faded. "Though he would make a perfect monk." She touched the rough stone of the tunnel wall. "I wish he could see this. Look here." Her fingers traced a delicate row of specks in the rock, like a sprinkling of salt crystals. They sparkled in the dim light. "You know what this is?"

He shook his head.

"It's timedust. This whole mountain is full of it. It's from Grone's moon, you know. It's why the Gurothim blew it up a million years ago—to harvest the timedust at its core! When a piece of the moon fell and made this crater, it brought the timedust with it."

"That's . . . *timedust?*"

When Nkiru nodded, he pulled off his coldsuit gloves and brushed his fingertips across the embedded crystals. Timedust was rumored to be older than time, the only remnant of a cosmos that had existed before the Big Bang, a substance from a previous reality that had somehow survived the explosive birth of the universe.

In the mythical wars of the First Epoch, a million years before the coming of the avatars, the ancient Gurothim had ravaged the galaxy in search of timedust. To harvest a single teaspoon, they would shatter a planet to its core, regardless of whether it was inhabited, and their harvesters would sweep through the trillions of gigatons of debris in search of the few, precious grains. The Gurothim had vanished at the end of the First Epoch, only to inexplicably reappear a million years later at the end of the Second

Epoch, at the height of the Age of Avatars, to resume their destruction. The avatars had fought the Gurothim Scourge—and each other—until their war was interrupted by the Rapture and the Cataclysm, vanquishing them all. Whether the myths were true or not, the legends surrounding timedust made it incredibly valuable, even though no one had yet figured out a use for it other than as a historical novelty.

He felt an urge to laugh out loud at the absurdity of his current situation. If he'd never met Nkiru, he'd be starting classes at the War College instead of sitting inside a mountain beneath an avatar's citadel staring at an exposed vein of timedust. He looked at Nkiru. From the moment he'd met her at the spaceport terminal at Cloudtops Station, his journey with her had consisted of one unlikely and extraordinary revelation after another. She'd denied it, but he was now convinced that she was some kind of avatar. Even if she wasn't a true avatar, there could be no doubt she was something special. A lightning rod for events of scriptural proportions. She had a destiny, this girl. A *mission*. She'd hinted that she might know the cause of the Cataclysm, and how to reverse its effects. If true, that made her . . .

A messiah.

And he was a part of it all somehow. He only wished he understood his role. Right now, he was useless. Worse than useless, he was a burden.

He used his fingernail to flake a few dozen grains of timedust out of the rock. He placed them in a shallow utility pocket at the waist of his coldsuit, then pulled his gloves back on. Behind him, his grandmother and the marines were anxiously waiting for him to gather his strength to continue. He gestured down the tunnel.

"Lead on."

———

The crude tunnel eventually opened into a much larger passageway. From there, Arni led them through a maze of unmarked corridors and stairways. Along the way he occasionally warned them to avoid a particular section of the floor or refrain from touching what seemed to be a perfectly safe handhold. Once, he rushed them through a section of passageway where the walls were covered with intricate, geometrical carvings of alluring beauty. "Don't look at them," he warned. "Those are nightmare hieroglyphs. They'll erase your brain."

At one junction, Littlefeather tapped Se-Jong's shoulder and pointed at a large alcove embedded in a side wall. Within the alcove stood an egg-shaped, human-sized booth made of thick glass. "Gods, I think that's a beamrider."

Se-Jong's heart jumped. In the stories of the avatars, beamriders had been used to travel instantaneously across galactic distances. He'd seen pictures of the beamrider the church kept in a reliquary on Bosporan, the only example of the legendary device ever discovered.

The door to the oval pod hung limply open, and the glass had been shattered since antiquity. Littlefeather looked to Arni, who shook his head. "It's busted," he said glumly. "Plus, they only worked for avatars."

The air had become thick, dead, almost unbreathable. It felt dry in his mouth, tasted old. Se-Jong wondered if he was inhaling the same air as the ancient avatars. As the painkillers wore off, the pressure and the searing flare from his swollen cheek and nose were almost unbearable. He could see his cheek ballooning out below his left eye. He was afraid to touch it lest it burst like an overripe tomato. Nkiru kept glancing at it anxiously, and Arni refused to look at him at all.

Worse than the pain was the nausea. It took every ounce of his concentration to keep from throwing up. Every few minutes he was forced to stop; lean forward, hands on his knees; and take a series of deep breaths, trying to ignore the repulsive odor of the Yok-Stop that still saturated his coldsuit. Grandmother moved to his side and took his arm. When he stumbled again, he felt another set of hands on his other arm. It was Nkiru. She and Grandmother exchanged an awkward glance, then propelled him forward.

—

"Whoa, what's that?"

They'd gone a hundred meters when Toroni called out. The entire party stopped, looked at the patch of floor where both marines were pointing their rifles. Threads of silvery metal lay along the base of the corridor wall. The tips of a few of the thin tendrils waved in the air a few centimeters off the floor, like the raised heads of tiny mercurial snakes. The intertwined threads disappeared into the darkness ahead of them.

Littlefeather took a step back. "It looks like slime mold."

Arni made a maniacal, braying laugh before stifling it with his palm. "Don't touch it. Don't even get near it."

—

They hugged the wall away from the bundle of thin metallic vines. As they hurried along, Se-Jong began to see sparkles on the periphery of his vision, tiny flashes of light. When he turned his head, they moved along with his vision. Had his head injury damaged his eyesight? Were the flashes a symptom of a concussion? Or were the drugs affecting him?

The odd flashes intensified and soon were accompanied by a prickling sensation on the exposed skin of his face. He wasn't alone, either. The two marines murmured as crackling sparks popped between their fingers and the clasps of their armor or the battery housings of their rifles. When Se-Jong reached up to investigate a strange sensation on his scalp, he discovered that his entire head was a porcupine of static-energized hair follicles.

The marines moved to the front of their party, where they led slowly, rifles ready. With every step forward, the creepy-crawly feeling grew, eventually reaching the point that it felt like electrified ants were crawling on every inch of Se-Jong's body. The tangy smell of ozone began to overwhelm the stale cave odor of rock and mud. Nkiru was silent, craning to see over the shoulders of the advance marines. When Toroni suddenly stopped, held up a fist, and knelt, they all followed suit. He silently indicated something on the ceiling, just a few meters ahead of their position.

Grandmother flicked her headlamp upward. More rippling threads of silvery tendrils grew across the stone ceiling, terminating in a dinner-plate-size crater of pitted stone.

Nkiru looked to Arni. "Are those seekers?"

Arni nodded, his voice completely lucid. "The harvester has been sending out these seekers to find timedust grains for more than a million years. The whole mountain is riddled with them. Don't touch them; they'll kill you."

As the party continued, the seeker vines grew heavier and more abundant, finally consolidating in a root as thick as a human thigh. It lay on the tunnel floor, extending into the darkness ahead, pulsing slowly like a grotesque artery of liquid mercury.

Toroni frowned at his wrist display. He pounded it into his palm, checked it, and his frown intensified. At Grandmother's questioning look, he said, "It's not working."

"It's the seeker," murmured Nkiru. She touched the zipper of her coldsuit. A tiny burst of static electricity popped between her fingertip and the metal zipper. She raised her komnic, but even after repeated shakes, it didn't respond to her activation. "I forgot about the seeker's powerfield effect. It screws with our electronics." She gestured at the silver trunk. "We need to stay as far away from that thing as we can."

Bridge

The corridor ended at the verge of an abyss. Nkiru pushed her way past the two marines and stood at the opening. Se-Jong followed her. At Grandmother's order, Toroni swept the emptiness with a floodlight. He muttered a curse. The walls were sheer vertical faces, smooth and artificial. There was no floor or ceiling, just dark voids extending above and below. Even at full intensity, the marine's light was swallowed by the yawning throat of the mountain. Toroni raised his spotlight to illuminate the far wall. Another opening was dimly visible, more than fifty meters away across the abyss.

There had once been a bridge across to the opening, but it had long since collapsed. Someone had recently attempted a repair. Partially spanning the chasm was a haphazard arrangement of mismatched scaffolding. The entire whack-jawed contraption hung together by a clumsy spiderweb of ropes and cables.

"Looks like something my six-year-old would build," said Toroni.

Arni made a miffed sound. Nkiru frowned. "You made this?"

"I tried. I thought I could follow the cables left from the old bridge, but it was too hard to get past *that*." He pointed to a massive vertical tube in the center of the void that hung from the darkness above and disappeared into the emptiness below. "That's the main seeker trunk from the harvester. We're directly below the boss chamber."

The tube reflected the light from Toroni's floodlight like a curved mirror. The vine they'd been following through the corridor extended pendulously out over the abyss, where it was absorbed into the side of the tube.

"This seeker pit goes all the way to the planet's core," Arni said. "Believe me, it's a long, long fall. But if we can get across down here, we won't have to face the harvester."

The reliquist peered into the yawning space. "Enclosed spaces. Traps, mazes, bottomless pitfalls, hazard fields. It has all the markers of a dungeon, just like the scriptures say."

Nkiru scoffed at the reliquist's wide-eyed wonder. She looked around, eyes searching for something. Se-Jong watched as she moved to the side of the corridor, kneeled, and scooped up a handful of grimy dust. She returned to the opening and flung it into the chasm.

The cloud of dust expanded into the air of the opening. They all jumped when it suddenly crackled and hissed like a strand of children's firecrackers, outlining an invisible sphere the size of a large beach ball floating in the air about two meters from where they stood.

Nkiru exhaled. "That's a microflak cloud mine. It's an invisible field of charged particles. The seeker pit is filled with them. If you touch one, you die."

"*Definitely* a dungeon," the reliquist whispered.

Next to her, Arni stroked his beard, and for a moment he looked like a wise and ancient prophet, especially given his grimy and disheveled robes. The illusion vanished the instant he spoke.

"I fucking hate this goddamned place."

Toroni gave Arni a crooked grin. "Preach it, brother," he said. He turned to Grandmother. "Orders, Captain?"

———

They followed Nkiru onto the convoluted bridge. Each consecutive platform rattled and shifted with the weight of their passage, and there were no railings or safety lines. The dark abyss was plainly visible through the wide grating, so Se-Jong kept his eyes affixed to Nkiru's back.

Every few meters she pulled a handful of dust from her pocket and tossed it into the empty air. More often than not, the dust particles hissed and spat as they encountered a floating microflak mine, outlining its size and shape. The density and frequency of the invisible obstacles meant that they often had to wait until a mine floated lazily out of their path.

As they approached the massive tube of the seeker trunk, the sensation of electrical static grew far more intense. The random, tiny flashes of light expanded to fill Se-Jong's entire field of vision, even with his eyes closed. He guessed that the powerfield generated by the seeker was strong enough to interfere with his optic nerves. He sincerely hoped his entire nervous system wasn't getting permanently cooked.

He looked up and tried to follow the path of the seeker trunk as it vanished into the empty darkness above. It was hard to see beyond the visual interference, but there was definitely a distant hint of motion, a slowly writhing coil of . . . something.

His grandmother was looking up, too. She caught his eye, and in that brief instant he suspected that in some way she was *enjoying* herself. For a moment the years fell away, and he saw the excitement, the adventurousness, of a smooth-skinned young woman confronting the unknown. He stared into the face of the audacious girl, and she smiled at him. How had he never seen it before? Grandmother hadn't always been the hard-nosed administrator; once she had been a bold explorer, a warrior.

Grandmother looked away, and Se-Jong realized that she'd given him a rare gift. She'd *meant* for him to see the crack in her callous demeanor. She'd known it would cause his own courage to surge. *Her blood is in my veins.* She'd always been a hard woman to love, but suddenly he loved her more than ever before.

The chaotic bridge ended prematurely on a final, wobbling platform, not even halfway across the abyss. They stared across the intervening space toward the tunnel opening, still more than two dozen meters away. Here, near the middle of the abyss, they were perilously close to the seeker tube. The electrified ants on his skin had multiplied and become supercharged. It took all his willpower to keep from slapping hysterically at his coldsuit.

He sank to his haunches, sweating, thankful for the chance to rest. The pain in his face had returned in full force, and the lasting aftereffects of the Yok-Stop had drained his energy reserves. He was stupendously tired, enough so that he knew his judgment and physical abilities were seriously impaired. He was becoming, he realized shamefully, a dangerous liability to the others.

Grandmother called a hasty confab to discuss options. She crowded onto the final platform alongside Se-Jong, Nkiru, and the reliquist. Arni and Private McCloud crouched outside the huddle, Arni staring nervously down through the platform's steel grating into the abyss, McCloud coldly regarding Arni as if he were some kind of unwelcome stray animal. The private's utter lack of fear gave Se-Jong the creeps.

Toroni pointed at the trunk of the seeker. "Can we attach a line to that thing?"

Nkiru shook her head. "No. We can't touch it, or even get too close. If we do, the harvester will know we're here. It'll blast a thousand new tentacles out from that root that will fry us all on contact. We wouldn't last ten seconds."

Toroni curled his lip. "You obviously have never seen what a pissed-off Solar Marine can do to alien slime."

Nkiru scoffed. "The harvester is a legendary class monster. Even a high level avatar would've been deathly afraid."

Two cables, probably from the original bridge, narrowly passed on either side of the seeker trunk and led to the other wall. Grandmother tapped her chin thoughtfully. "Sergeant, can you rig up a line across the remaining gap without getting too close to the seeker?"

Toroni shone his spotlight at the far tunnel opening and moved it in a slow circle across the surrounding wall. "Maybe. It's too far to throw a grapple, though we might be able to shoot a tethered spike deep enough into the rock to support a single climber. If we could get somebody across, they might be able secure a stronger line that would hold the rest of us." He chewed his top lip. "They'd still have to get pretty close to that seeker trunk. And see those offshoots that have buried into the wall around the tunnel opening? If the line gave out and the climber fell, they'd swing right into one of them, or even the main trunk."

Grandmother grunted. She turned her eyes to the others. "Ideas, anyone? We're running out of time. We can't stay here, and we can't go back without running into the militans."

Se-Jong turned to Nkiru. "You don't have anything else hiding in your magic backpack, do you? An avatar jetpack, maybe?"

Nkiru shook her head. There was a long silence. Finally, the young reliquist nervously cleared her throat. They all looked at her. Her eyes widened and she flinched, shriveling like a flower caught in a blast of heat.

"Speak up, ensign," Grandmother barked. "At this point there are no bad ideas."

The reliquist's mouth moved for a moment without sound. She cleared her throat again. "I'm the smallest and lightest person here. If anybody should try to climb across, it should be me."

Littlefeather

The reliquist's name matched her appearance. Littlefeather was even shorter than Se-Jong's grandmother. Her spare frame and wide, dark eyes gave her a childlike appearance, especially when she stood next to the brawny marines. Se-Jong watched as she removed her pack and the outer armor of her tacsuit to shed weight, the hanging platform on which they stood wobbling with her every move. She shivered in the tight webbing of her undergear, though it was hard to tell if it was caused by the chill of the subterranean air or her obvious anxiety. When she pulled off her helmet, the raw marks of the Sacraments shone redly on her forehead. Not only was she an officer of the Guard, but she was also a fully adorned member of the Cataclyst faithful. By remaining loyal to his grandmother and defying the Dei Militans, she was risking excommunication. Or worse.

Toroni cinched her into a climbing harness while McCloud prepared to fire a tethered spike across the chasm, into a bare patch of stone above the tunnel opening. After a final check, Toroni nodded to Grandmother. She turned to Littlefeather. "Are you ready?"

The ensign nodded, but her clenched teeth and rapid breathing betrayed her fear. Reliquists were glorified librarians who spent their days with noses buried in ancient texts, not dangling from threads above bottomless pits. Grandmother squeezed the young woman's shoulder. Littlefeather winced. Grandmother gave her a hard smile. "Didn't think you'd be doing the job of a Solar Marine today, did you, Ensign?"

Toroni chuckled and put his massive gloved hand on Littlefeather's other shoulder. "It's true: you'd make a fine marine. But I think you're an even better Guard officer. Oorah."

"Oorah," repeated McCloud.

"Oorah," Littlefeather said, though without much gusto. She made the sign of the Linked Trinity and smiled weakly. "I suppose I'm ready."

They gathered behind the ramrod-straight figure of McCloud. He calmly raised his rifle and tucked the stock into his shoulder. He pressed his eye against the gunsight. He'd attached a chunky, spooled device to the bottom of the barrel.

"If he misses and hits one of the seeker tentacles, we're all dead, dead, dead," warned Arni.

Toroni chuckled darkly and clapped the private on the back of his shoulder. "McCloud never misses—do you, Private?"

McCloud didn't react at all. Se-Jong held his breath as the young marine squinted through the gunsight. The weapon's report was louder than he had expected, and he jumped. A shrill whine as the tether unspooled, then an almost immediate *plink!* as the spike embedded itself into the far wall, a meter above and to the side of the tunnel opening. Toroni was alert, rifle at ready for any reaction from the seeker. As the echoes from the gunshot died without response, everyone relaxed. Everyone, that is, but Ensign Littlefeather. She blew a lungful of air through pursed lips and waited silently as Toroni and McCloud secured the near end of the tether to the sturdiest-looking section of scaffolding. As they ratcheted it tight, it thrummed softly, like the lowest note of a piano plucked by ghostly fingers.

The tether was ridiculously thin, like the string of a kite. It seemed impossible that it would bear her weight, and it sagged alarmingly when she attached her harness and tested it by raising her feet off the platform. Toroni used a carabiner to clip the end of a strong climbing rope to her harness. The plan was to pull it behind her, and when she reached the other side, she would secure it to one of the rusted attachment points for the original bridge that were embedded in the stone around the opening. Once it was secure, the others would use the sturdier rope to cross with all their heavy gear.

Toroni lifted a double handful of dirt he'd collected from the tunnel and heaved it out over the chasm. A cluster of popping sparkles outlined three microflak mines floating in the intervening space. He motioned toward them. "Go now, before one of them moves into your path."

Littlefeather took a series of rapid breaths, grasped the thin tether with gloved hands, and swung her feet up and over the line. She dangled upside down for a moment like a tree sloth, then began tugging herself along the line, staring resolutely up into the darkness. The marines were silent. When she reached the edge of the platform and slid out over the abyss, nobody moved. She took a raw, shuddering breath. Slowly, she inched her way along the line, half a meter at a time, dimly lit by his grandmother's headlamp. Next to Se-Jong, McCloud played out the climbing rope Littlefeather was towing, careful not to let it sag and touch the seeker.

Toroni launched another handful of dirt into the air. It rained down on Littlefeather but also revealed that the three microflak mines had moved no closer to her path. The admiration of both marines was palpable. Here was a desk jockey, a history geek, putting herself in harm's way to accomplish the mission objective. Toroni was scowling forcefully, willing the ensign across the line, obviously trying to reinforce her courage with his own.

Grandmother watched impassively, though Se-Jong knew her well enough to see the tension in the set of her jaw. He glanced at Nkiru. She wasn't watching the reliquist. Her attention was focused on the silvery trunk of the harvester and its pulsing malevolence. When she saw him watching her, she gave him a tight grimace.

The only sound was the huff of breath from the ensign each time she slid herself forward on the line. Her swaying motion was transmitted back through the tether to the attachment point on their platform, so that with her every move, the platform swayed and creaked. It seemed to take forever for her to reach the halfway point, but Se-Jong knew it had probably been less than a minute.

Littlefeather paused and looked around, noting the position of the massive tube that was now just a few meters away. "Uh, uunh. Feels like I'm being electrocuted. All I can see are sparkles."

"She's too close," murmured Grandmother. "The seeker is overloading her nervous system."

"You're right next to it," called Toroni. "Don't swing side to side, and don't stop. You're doing great. Just keep going no matter what."

"I can't do it," came the sobbing reply. "My skin is on fire. Ah, it *hurts!*"

"Keep moving," barked Toroni.

Nkiru suddenly clutched Se-Jong's hand in her own. She was watching the reliquist with open-faced horror, as if she could feel Littlefeather's pain.

"I'm burning all over!" Littlefeather cried.

Nkiru squeezed so hard the bones of his knuckles made a crackling sound. He'd never seen her react with such intensity to *anything*. He tightened his grip. "You okay? What's wrong?"

She released his hand. "It's nothing. I'm sorry."

Littlefeather moaned, but she pulled herself farther along the line. The chasm beyond the seeker trunk was outside Toroni's throwing range, so she was risking contact with an unseen microflak mine. As she approached the far wall and the tunnel opening, Toroni called out softly, "Watch yourself, ensign. Open your eyes. Only a couple of meters to go. Don't touch any of the seeker tendrils."

She pulled herself until she was suspended just outside the tunnel opening. Dozens of seeker tendrils surrounded her like a silvery forest, the closest just centimeters away.

"I'll talk you through it," called Toroni. "You're directly over the old bridge cable. Drop your feet straight down, slowly." His voice was strong and soothing. "You can do it, marine. Just lower your feet slowly. Hang from the harness, easy as pie. Let your feet dangle."

With a moan of sheer terror, Littlefeather slowly unwrapped her feet from the tether and let them fall, one at a time, until she was hanging vertically.

"I can't see," she cried.

"You're almost there. Raise your left foot, then move it forward a few centimeters. Lower it. Feel that? That's a little ledge sticking out from the tunnel floor. All you have to do is pull yourself forward half a meter and you'll be standing on it."

The reliquist did as she was told. She missed her first attempt and gasped when her foot met nothing but empty air. She tried again without prompting, this time finding purchase. One foot, then another, and she was standing on the tunnel floor.

"Lean forward slightly and detach the harness," said Toroni. "Don't let it go. Take a few steps forward away from the edge. Then move to your right to get away from the seeker."

The reliquist shuffled forward a step, struggled to unclip the harness, then fell to the right, clutching the harness to her stomach as she stumbled to her knees. She paused for a moment, panting. "I'm feeling better," she announced.

"That's because you are a gods-damned steel-spined warrior, Ensign Littlefeather," called Toroni. "Oorah."

"Oorah," repeated McCloud.

"Now, see if one of those metal hoops on the side of the tunnel is strong enough to secure the climbing rope."

Nkiru let out a long sigh and released his hand. The warmth from her palm lingered.

It took forever. Pulling himself across a bottomless pit on a thin rope was truly terrifying, and Se-Jong fought to keep his panic from rocketing out of control. He could tell by the bob and jerk of the rope that Nkiru was still in front of him, hauling herself across. Then there were more jerks and tugs, and he could hear Arni complaining behind him as Toroni prodded him off the platform.

He cursed. Hanging upside down and pulling with all his might had caused the blood to rush to his head. The pressure made the swollen wound on his cheek bloat in almost unbearable agony. He turned his head to the side and vomited, the thick fluid falling soundlessly into the abyss. Far below, his vomit hit a microflak mine with a burst of noise and light.

There were voices ahead of him, from silhouettes in the dim light, one of them the shape of Nkiru. She was being hauled into the tunnel by Littlefeather's extended arm. "I made it," she called softly. "Hurry up, Lieutenant. You're almost halfway across. Get ready; it hurts."

Se-Jong's breathing became a series of short, rapid puffs as he fought the spread of pain from his cheek into his forehead. If he passed out, he would dangle from his harness, a dead weight that would be difficult for the others to drag to safety, and a target for any microflak mine that might float his way. He focused on the motion of his hands and legs, wrapped around the rope, heaving himself forward.

His entire field of vision, eyes open or not, was a field of sparklers, and his flesh felt like he was standing in the path of a blowtorch. The stinging electrocution of the seeker's powerfield was unbearable. A new and vicious surge of nausea brought him to a sudden stop. His hands were slipping, and he suddenly realized that he wasn't going to make it. Waves of darkness erupted inside his head.

Then a voice, soft and encouraging. He wasn't sure if it was real or his imagination.

"Come on, Lieutenant. Every minute you're not living . . ."

". . . is a minute I'm dying," he said, his voice a dry croak. He felt his arms moving. Pull.

Pull.

Pull.

Hands were on him, tugging, yanking. A thudding impact on his side, and movement, a scraping of skin across grimy concrete. The nerve pain lessened, then mostly disappeared. The throbbing in his cheek and head did not diminish, and he heard himself moan loudly. He clamped his teeth together.

Somebody was stroking his hair. He managed to crack open his right eye. All was dark, except . . . except a barely perceptible pattern of tiny lights in the shape of a Seuss tree. It was Nkiru's copper bracelet, sparkling with flashes of static from the seeker's powerfield.

"You with me, Lieutenant?"

His reply was cracked. "I'm okay. Just . . . give me a second."

Another meaty thud landed next to him. He recognized Arni's voice. "Holy shitbags, that kind of sucked."

A flurry of raised voices echoed, and a dim light flared from the platform on the other side of the abyss. Through his cracked eyelid Se-Jong saw his grandmother bobbing from the rope, moving fast, almost across. Nkiru and Littlefeather guided her onto the ledge and helped her out of her harness.

The line behind Grandmother jerked and sang from tension as the two marines sped across almost effortlessly. After they'd both tumbled into the tunnel, Toroni dropped to his knees and pulled something from his tacsuit belt. A knife. He used it to saw through the tether. It dropped into the darkness, away from the seeker tendrils. "That'll slow the militans down, but it might not stop them. Let's go. Move out."

And just like that, they were past the menace of the harvester. Se-Jong felt a new glimmer of hope. Arni had said the harvester was the only major obstacle to their escape. Arni's face, though, was not triumphant. If anything, he seemed even more scared than before.

"How much farther?" Toroni asked.

Arni stared into the darkness of the tunnel ahead. "We're close, but we need to keep watching for the microflak mines." He stooped and gathered a handful of grime from the floor and tossed it into the air. "The air currents sometimes cause a stray mine to float into the tunnels in this direction."

Se-Jong rose, stumbled weakly, and lurched into the wall. Littlefeather and Nkiru took up positions on either side of him, draped his arms over their shoulders, and hustled him along the passageway. The marines led the way with bright flashlights, occasionally tossing a handful of dust in front of them. Grandmother followed a few paces back.

Nkiru kept casting worried glances back at Arni, who trailed behind them all, his eyes darting around the dark tunnel as if expecting a Ghost to pop out of the nothingness.

"Seriously, who *is* that guy," Se-Jong whispered.

She shifted her grip, helping to steady him. "He had . . . a girlfriend, a scientist who studied avatars. She came here to Grone and went missing. He came later, to look for her. Something happened to him along the way." Sensing his frustration, she continued. "I promise to explain everything. Let's just get there, first."

"Get where?"

She glanced at him, as if gauging his ability to handle yet another revelation. "Atum's Lair."

At his other shoulder, Littlefeather frowned. "Atum?"

Se-Jong was too out of breath to protest. Nkiru seemed relieved by his silence.

—

The tunnel climbed sharply upward. Eventually Arni led them through a series of junctions until they emerged into a finely constructed corridor of polished stone. To their left the corridor continued into the blackness, but to their right, revealed by the beam of Toroni's flashlight, the wall of the corridor was covered in deep pits and scars. Crisply delineated at the center of the damaged area was a door-shaped rectangle. Within the rectangle, the wall surface was smooth, undamaged.

"Wait," Toroni ordered. He swept his light across the floor to reveal a figure lying at the foot of the wall. He approached it cautiously, prodded it with the barrel of his rifle. A puff of dust rose from what was obviously a long-mummified corpse. He swept his light around to reveal several more crumbling shapes. "All dead," he reported. "For a very long time."

Arni knelt next to one of the shapes. He reached out tentatively, touched the papery skin on the face of the mummy with his fingertips. "Our team bots. They died in the Rapture," he said matter-of-factly. "Some of them were my friends. This was Daquan. He had a bad temper, but he loved Analise. They all did."

Everyone turned to stare at him. He shrugged defensively, gestured toward the other bodies. "Not all of them were my friends. Some of these were bad guys."

Grandmother gestured toward the oddly undamaged door shape and the blasted and pitted wall that surrounded it. "What happened here?"

Arni shrugged. "That's the Shadow Door. I've been trying to get it open for a really long time."

Nkiru was holding Se-Jong's arm. He felt her grip grow tighter. "I can't believe I made it back here."

"I *told* you I knew the way," said Arni.

"Is that the way out?" demanded Grandmother.

Instead of answering, Nkiru unslung her pack and retrieved the small wooden box that held the Great Emora. Se-Jong glanced at Littlefeather, then his grandmother, wondering how they would react when they saw the box's contents. He didn't get a chance to find out. Nkiru palmed the stone from the box without revealing it to the others. She moved to stand in front of the smooth, door-shaped section of the corridor wall.

Nothing happened. She turned to Arni. "How is this supposed to work? Do I touch it to the wall, or just hold it or—?"

In front of her, the solid surface of the door began to ripple like cascading water. The marines trained their weapons on the movement.

Arni's face broke into a dazzling smile. He beckoned her forward. She placed the stone back in its case, then turned and tugged at Se-Jong's arm. Se-Jong took a deep breath, and they both stepped into the wall together.

Atum's Lair

The large windowless space was octagonal, lit by a colorless glow that emanated, oddly, from the floor. The air was stale and smelled strongly of oiled brass and ozone. Se-Jong felt the hairs on his arms stand up, as if he was enveloped in a field of static current. It was a different sensation from the painful electric field of the seeker. It felt like excitement.

Nkiru led Se-Jong to a dusty ledge next to the door. He sagged onto it and closed his eyes, no longer fighting the exhaustion. His face throbbed horribly. The inflammation in his cheek had swollen his left eye shut.

Nkiru patted him on the shoulder and went to join Arni. Se-Jong forced his uninjured eye open and looked around the strange room. The octagon was about a dozen meters across. Not huge, even though it felt that way after the cramped tunnels of the previous couple of hours. Grandmother and the marines were at the doorway, scanning the room for threats. Littlefeather was turning in circles, jaw open. Nkiru was hugging Arni. Was she crying? He squinted his good eye. They were *both* crying, as if they'd reached an impossible goal.

The central floor space was dominated by a bizarre brass-and-steel machine. It consisted of an open spherical framework of concentric brass rings—all oriented at different angles and taller than Se-Jong—mounted on a sturdy pedestal of iron. It resembled a massive armillary sphere, one of those mechanical devices from Earth's Victorian era that reproduced the astrological movements of the planets and stars. Somehow it looked both archaic and supremely advanced at the same time. It was obviously broken. One hemisphere was smashed and bent, as if someone had taken a sledgehammer to it.

Below the bewildering array of rings and gears, mounted into an ornate receptacle, was a clear, fist-size cube. Se-Jong recognized it as a holobox like the one he'd seen in Leodiva's mural on Assinni. His town's local chapel back on Askelon had possessed a similar cube in its reliquary, and he'd seen others in various churches and cathedrals. It was a common-enough relic, though this one looked singed at its corners and had an obvious crack along one face.

The room's walls were covered by an array of corroded metal cabinets and lockers, many of which had been torn apart. A dense row of bullet holes punctured one entire section of cabinets. Thousands of old-style paper books crowded the shelves, though they looked like they would crumble to dust at the lightest touch. Shrunken husks of various creatures lined the tops of the shelves, mummified by the extreme passage of time. A curious assemblage of rusted metal pipes and tubes had once occupied the rear wall. A few were still vertical, but most had collapsed into a heap. The floor was littered with debris, mostly items pulled in haste from the shelves, plus hundreds of clear, pebble-size marbles. When Toroni knelt to pick up one of the marbles, Arni blurted shrilly, "Don't touch those!" Toroni jerked his hand away and stood up sheepishly.

There were two exits: a nondescript green door at the opposite end of the room, and the still-open portal through which they'd entered, which Arni had called the Shadow Door. The dark corridor and two of the mummified bodies could be seen through its translucent curtain of falling mist.

Grandmother hurried across the room to the green door. She rapped its surface with her knuckles. *Thuck.* It sounded entirely solid, like a thick slab of lead. "Where does this go?"

Arni shook his head. "Please, don't touch it."

"Is it the way out?"

He made a shrill giggle. "Way, *way* out." He clamped his hand over his mouth and burst into tears. The lucidity he'd shown while leading them on their chaotic dash through the dungeon was quickly fading.

Se-Jong saw explosive frustration building in his grandmother's posture. He expected her to demand an explanation, but instead something caught her eye, and she looked up. Everyone else followed her gaze.

Se-Jong had been dimly aware that the ceiling was colorful, and when he looked up, he saw why. A three-dimensional hologram of a spiral galaxy turned lazily, breathtaking in its complexity, covering the entire ceiling. Thousands of sparks glimmered inside the wispy arms of the spiral, as did long strands of colorful spider silk that connected most of the sparks in an irregular grid pattern. Each spark was labeled and color coded, each strand of the spider's web identified by a coordinate number.

It was obviously a star map. Not of the Known Arc, or even the Halo, but of the entire Milky Way galaxy, as it had existed before the Cataclysm.

On every modern map of the Milky Way that Se-Jong had ever seen, the inner ninety percent was always a black circular void marked by the region's common name: The Devastation of the Cataclysm. Everyone knew that hundreds of billions of stars; thousands, maybe millions, of inhabited worlds; entire star-empires had been consumed by the Devastation, but their natures and locations, and the lost cultures that had inhabited them, were nothing but rumors and mystery.

This star map was different. It was *complete*. A blinking red overlay delineated the extent of the Devastation, but the vast central region was anything but empty. The seven legendary spiral arms were clearly visible, swirling down into the glowing bulge of the central core.

At the outer rim of the map, a meter-wide ring of stars encircled the blinking red disk of the Devastation. This was the Halo, Se-Jong realized, the outermost rim of the galaxy that had survived the Cataclysm. He searched for the Known Arc, that part of the Halo that had been explored by the Olids and other sentient species since the beginning of the Third Epoch.

There! *Assinni. Ghast. Forniculus. Askelon. Orbitus. Grone.* The worlds he knew were a pitiful few, a tiny cluster of labels on the margin of the vast spiral wilderness of stars. He could cover them all with his palm at arm's length.

He dropped his hand to his lap and squinted. One of the worlds was blinking. Unlike the others, its label was red like the disk of the Devastation, and it was blinking at the same rate.

JEEB Earth.

It was in the right location for Earth, tucked between Ghast and Forniculus, but why was it blinking? And why was it labeled JEEB Earth? Jeeb was the name of the mystical tree that the Mucktu worshipped, the source of the pollen they ate. It had nothing to do with Earth.

He turned his attention to the blinking red disk of the Devastation. Between blinks, he tried to make out some of the tiny labels and markings. *Janrus. Kroll. Klethyn. Xankisia. V'kwoir, Rottergall, Vulcanus. Roc.* He didn't recognize any of them. A dozen or more large areas were marked by colorful, sometimes overlapping borders. These labels were larger, easier to read.

The Keppan Empire. Falus & Crome. The Gretanis. Meier's Empire. The Keppan Annex. He recognized some of these names from the *Chronicles of the Second Epoch.* These were avatar empires.

By now everyone was staring up at the ceiling. Seeing the full, primal shape of the unspoiled galaxy only reinforced the unimaginable scale of the destruction that had occurred in the Cataclysm. A fluttery, hollow feeling grew in Se-Jong's gut, the same feeling he sometimes got when he was confronted by an idea so vast in scope that it overwhelmed his rational mind. Like when he thought about the gods. Or lately, when he thought about Nkiru and her abilities. He was young and inexperienced, but he completely understood the immensity of this moment.

Littlefeather's face was lit with blinding excitement as she exuberantly snapped photos with her komnic. She pointed upward and silently mouthed the words, *Can you believe this?*

She was feeling the moment, just like everyone else in the room. If this was an accurate representation of the galaxy prior to the Cataclysm, it would rewrite the history books and shake the Cataclyst Church to its foundation.

Something was wrong with Arni. He stood in the center of the room next to the spherical machine and wrung his hands. He seemed to be desperately trying to remember something, something on the tip of his tongue but maddeningly elusive. Nkiru was whispering earnestly to Arni, but he kept shaking his head.

Grandmother moved to Se-Jong's side, watching them suspiciously. "What is this place?" she demanded. "Where have they brought us? They were supposed to lead us *out* of the mountain."

"I have no idea. Nkiru called it Atum's Lair."

"As in the Archangel Atum?"

He shrugged.

Grandmother made a grunting sound. She lowered her voice so only he could hear. "Listen to me. It is a mistake to trust these people. The Father Regis thinks the Janga Order may be planning a coup. He wonders if Anaya may be a part of their plot, given her past association with their monastery on Earth. He thinks the Janga have made some kind of discovery, and that her powers may be the result of that discovery."

"Nkiru doesn't care about politics, Halmeoni. She's not trying to overthrow the church."

"But she is a zealot: that much is plain. She has a goal, some sense of purpose driving her to do the things she has done."

"She won't talk about it. I think . . ." he paused. "I think she's trying to protect me."

It was obvious from her pitying look that his grandmother believed his feelings for Nkiru had blinded him. His anger flared, but he knew she was right. His feelings *had* blinded him. And they were stronger than ever. "Halmeoni, I trust her."

Grandmother considered him for a moment. "Until her motives become clear, I do *not*, and neither should you."

They were interrupted by a gasp from Littlefeather. She was kneeling at one of the cabinets, lifting something. She raised it cautiously, blowing the dust off the chrome surface. For its size, it seemed surprisingly light. Toroni looked at her. "Good gods, Ensign, what have you found?"

The tubular device looked like the offspring of a shoulder-fired missile launcher and a trombone. Littlefeather's eyes were on fire. "I think it's an avatar weapon."

Nkiru spun to Arni. "Is that . . .?"

Arni nodded ruefully. "It was Chun's."

Nkiru reached for the device. Littlefeather took a step back.

"You can't use it," Nkiru urged. "Give it to me."

The reliquist grudgingly handed the object to Nkiru. She hefted it with what seemed to be a hint of sentimentality. The two marines stirred, watching intently, not quite raising their rifles.

"What does it do?" Littlefeather said.

Nkiru paused, then gave a grim smile. "It evens the odds."

She took a deep breath, touched a control on the side of the device. There were several gasps when it beeped and lit up. Nkiru looked relieved that it had worked. Se-Jong saw a twitch on Grandmother's cheek.

Nkiru held it out for Littlefeather to inspect. The reliquist approached cautiously. She waved her military komnic a few inches from its barrel. "My gods," she muttered. "My gods. It's giving off varichromatic radiation. It's a real relic, and it's definitely powered up."

Toroni eyed Nkiru with a mixture of amazement and troubled suspicion. McCloud made the sign of the Linked Trinity. Littlefeather gaped at Nkiru with the awestruck expression of somebody who's just seen an angel. Which, Se-Jong admitted, might not be too far from the truth.

Nkiru lifted the weapon, turned to Grandmother. "You wanted proof?" She leveled the barrel of the tube so that it was pointed out the misty Shadow Door, into the darkened corridor.

Grandmother waved to the marines, who were guarding the open doorway. "Stand clear." They hastily retreated. She motioned to Nkiru. "Show me."

Nkiru held the weapon up to her shoulder and sighted it. She licked her lips, tightened her grip, and pulled the trigger.

WHOOP!

The detonation staggered the two marines. A translucent ripple of energy rocketed from the weapon and flickered through the doorway and down the long corridor, igniting a sensational blast of rock shrapnel at the far end. Dust filled the corridor. Nkiru lowered the weapon. She was breathing rapidly.

Se-Jong couldn't look away from her. Deep gray skin, flowing snow-white hair, eyes like lake mist, standing beneath the rotating map of the galaxy holding a smoking chrome megagun.

"My gods," muttered the reliquist. "My gods."

Grandmother had remained impassive for the demonstration, but Se-Jong noticed yet another twitch in her cheek. A double twitch, actually. For Grandmother, this was the equivalent of a volcanic emotional eruption.

Se-Jong pointed at the expanding cloud of dust. "See? You *cannot* let the church get their hands on her. They'll use her abilities as a weapon. Remember, the avatars had planetkiller bombs! What if the Father Regis has one of those hidden in a vault beneath the Regium? With an avatar at his disposal, he could do anything he wants."

Grandmother pursed her lips. Se-Jong waited, counting silently.

One second.

Two seconds.

Three seconds.

He glanced at Nkiru. She was cradling the ridiculous gun, watching his grandmother. It was still powered, he noticed. He met her eyes. They were cold. Cold, and just below their surface, very, very frightened. Se-Jong swallowed involuntarily.

"What is that thing?" said Littlefeather.

"It's a goddamned gobsmacker, that's what it is," Nkiru replied.

Grandmother shook her head as if waking from a daydream. "Well then, that settles that, doesn't it?" She turned to Nkiru. "I grant you full asylum under the Charter of the Solar Alliance. Consider yourself under the protection of the Solar Guard. Under *my* protection."

"Oorah," muttered Toroni.

"Oorah," echoed Private McCloud.

Oorah, said Se-Jong silently.

There was a long silence. Grandmother cleared her throat, "Now, how do we get out of here?"

Arni and Nkiru exchanged a glance, turned their eyes to the armillary sphere at the center of the room. Everyone followed their gaze.

Arni shook his head sadly. "No, no, no. It's locked, and the activation key is stuck in meatspace."

Very gently, Nkiru took Arni's hand. "Believe it or not, I think I have everything I need to fix it." She squeezed his wrists. "It's almost over, Arni. Just a few more minutes and you can go home. We all can."

SPAWN

meatspace | FIONA

Aftermath

They slept outdoors beneath the bizarre new thing in the sky, Fiona in her motorized chair, Francis and Mama huddled on blankets in the grass. Their house was still standing, one of the few on the block without cracked walls or shattered windows, but with the continuing aftershocks, some as strong as the initial earthquake, they knew it could come crashing down at any moment. It was safer to sleep in the yard, under a dark night sky crowded with the unfamiliar stars revealed by the citywide power outage. The view would have been breathtaking under different circumstances.

    The earthquakes were bad enough, but the Tingles were something altogether worse. Everybody was feeling them, all over the world, or at least that's what was being reported on social media. Everyone here felt them for sure. They came in waves every few minutes, each wave a little stronger than the last, like an ocean tide slowly building on a beach. Mama couldn't stop shuddering, even between the waves. She'd spent the last couple of hours with her eyes closed, praying. Francis was praying, too. He was holding Mama's hands, their heads bent together.

Even without the Tingles, the thing in the sky would have made the experience entirely surreal. Fiona stared up at the apparition. As the hours had passed, the moon and stars had wheeled behind it, but it had remained fixed in place in the same spot above the southern horizon. She knew the word: *geostationary*. Like a communications satellite, the thing must be orbiting at a precise altitude so that it matched the rotational speed of the planet, always remaining directly above a specific geographical point on the equator. Its apparent size against the background stars was several times larger than the full moon, but she knew that could also be an illusion. Maybe it was simply *closer* than the moon. That didn't mean it wasn't big. She didn't know the exact math, but she knew that geostationary satellites orbited tens of thousands of miles above the Earth. If the thing was that far away, it must be gigantic. Maybe hundreds of miles in diameter. If it really was that big and that close, then it could easily be the cause of the earthquakes. Its gravity would be tugging at the Earth's crust, wobbling the tectonic plates like they were a rippling mat of leaves floating on the surface of a disturbed pond.

Alternatively, it might be something much less apocalyptic, like a cloud of something hanging in the upper atmosphere. She'd seen the aftereffects of rocket launches from Vandenberg Space Force Base, and sometimes the rocket trails lingered for hours in the night sky as glowing clouds of colorful gas. But they'd looked nothing like this . . . thing.

What was it? As far as she knew, it had appeared moments before the earthquake, like a gargantuan soap bubble materializing in the blue sky, at first pale and wispy but quickly solidifying into something massive and undeniably substantial. Fiona hadn't seen it happen, but she'd seen the videos posted to social media. The entire afternoon sky had shifted from blue to purple, and the thing had bubbled into existence seemingly out of nowhere.

On the phone videos it had looked like an out-of-focus blob of purple light, but when she and Francis had rushed outdoors to see it with their own eyes, it had been instantly obvious that something was clearly *wrong* with it. The object seemed to be covered with intricate details, but her brain couldn't process the markings. What at first glance had looked like mountain ranges and seas had suddenly become the dense scribblings of some unintelligible alphabet, then a writhing ball of tightly entwined worms, then a hazy, indistinct cloud through which the background sky was plainly visible. It wasn't that the surface of the thing was changing; it was as if her mind simply couldn't interpret the thing's true nature. Its appearance whirled and stumbled as her brain frantically searched for a metaphor for what her eyes were seeing, unable to settle on a concrete representation. Oddly, it reminded her of the little floating ball of haze that Gaia had seen inside the brass sphere at Atum's Lair, back in the final moments of the Grone campaign. Just before the lights went out and all the trouble started.

It had appeared eight hours and just as many aftershocks ago, at the same time as the first noticeable wave of the Tingles. She'd been staring at the thing in the sky for most of the time since, trying to make sense of it, but it was like looking at a TV that was flipping so rapidly through different channels that the only pictures you could grasp were tenuous blurs and afterimages. She and Francis had compared what they each saw, and it was clear that neither of them had the right words to convey their impressions. To Francis, it looked more like "the open end of a deep tunnel," or "fizzy soda bubbles being stirred in a glass."

Mama refused even to look at it. She huddled on the blankets next to Francis, clutching her rosary, mumbling prayers in Spanish. She'd spoken with one of the police officers who'd come through the neighborhood hours earlier, just before sunset. She'd begged the policeman to take Fiona to the hospital, but the man and his partner had told her that the hospitals were overflowing and that unless she were in immediate danger, Fiona would be better staying put. The man had told them that the city would be setting up disaster relief stations as soon as the aftershocks subsided. He hadn't been very convincing or reassuring.

The helicopter came just before sunrise. They watched it approach low over the hills to the east of San Ramon, assuming it was another news copter taking pictures of the earthquake damage. It wasn't until it was directly overhead that it became obvious it was a big military aircraft shaped like a monstrous snub-nosed porpoise. The roar was world-shattering. It flew in a series of tightening circles low above the neighborhood, its beaming searchlight moving up and down the streets. It eventually passed directly overhead, and the searchlight swept over their small yard, blinding them.

Then, astonishingly, the searchlight beam jerked back toward them, pinning them in a raging circle of blistering white light. Mama cried out and Francis cursed, shielding his eyes from the glare. The *whop-whop-whop* of the rotor blades intensified, and they were suddenly in a hurricane of grit as the rotor wash sandblasted the street in front of their house.

The helicopter was *landing*, Fiona realized, right in front of them. It completely filled the narrow street, its spinning blades extending over the yards and driveways on both sides like the sword of a furious Valkyrie, the blast ripping and tearing at the manicured shrubbery that delineated the small residential lots. As soon as the aircraft's fat tires touched the street, two figures leaped from the open side door. One of them wore a dark flight suit and bulbous helmet; the other was dressed in wrinkled shorts, a Pikachu T-shirt, and flip-flops. Fiona glanced at Francis, who had jumped to his feet. His jaw was hanging open. Mama simply looked terrified.

"Rupe?" she said.

Rupe skidded to a stop in front of her chair, his beard twisting from side to side in the gale. "Oh man, Fiona, thank God you're okay." He gestured to the man in the flight suit and helmet. "She's okay!" he shouted.

The man tugged off his helmet. It was Colonel Solomon, one of the men who, a month earlier, had come to their house and taken their game computer. He knelt next to Mama, who was curled into a horrified ball of fright. "Ms. Martinez, I need you and your family to come with us right now."

Fiona had no time to react. Francis stepped between Solomon and Mama. "What's happening? What do you want?" he shouted.

Rupe said, "We need your help. It's important."

Francis didn't budge, but Fiona could tell he was terrified. She felt no fear, only a vast astonishment.

Rupe glanced at Solomon, who nodded curtly. Rupe turned back to Francis. "It's about the *Longstar* game. It turns out the game machine fucks around with particle physics, or some shit like that. When the game crashed, we think it broke something in the real world, too." At Francis's confusion, Rupe stabbed his finger toward the new thing in the sky. "Meatspace is crashing, dude, okay? We don't have much time, and we need you and Fiona."

Flight

The helicopter rose with stomach-puckering swiftness, lowering its nose so dramatically that Mama let out a scream and Fiona grabbed for her seat restraints. In moments it had clawed its way into the sky above the Coast Range that separated their home in San Ramon from the urban strip of Silicon Valley.

As they crossed the mountains in the early dawn light, the earthquake damage became much more obvious. Solomon had given them all heavy headphones with swiveling mouthpieces so they could talk to each other over the roar of the engine. "Where are we going?" Francis demanded, his voice tinny in the headphones.

"Stanford University," Rupe replied. Francis started to say something else, but Rupe began narrating the flight like an overexcited tour guide. "Look, there, you can see the San Mateo Bridge. One of the suspension towers is down. It's horrible. And over there to the north, that's the fire at the San Francisco airport. An aviation fuel tank ruptured and poured into the bay. Power is out everywhere. They've shut down the Rancho Seco nuclear plant. Oakland and Alameda have been hit by something like a tsunami. The airport at Oakland is underwater."

Fiona could see very little. With her permission, they'd lifted her from her wheelchair and strapped her into the seat in the center of the fuselage. Mama had her eyes closed, but Francis was glued to one of the large windows in the sliding door, with Rupe staring over his shoulder and pointing at the various aspects of the earthquake devastation. "They say the big quake yesterday was a 7.9, and some of the aftershocks have been over 7.5. It's the worst ever. Multiple faults broke all at once up and down the coast. But this is nothing compared to what happened in Japan. The news is saying the city of Kobe was completely swallowed up. A million dead, maybe more. Bad quakes in Italy and Turkey, too. The bugaboo is screwing with the tides, causing earthquakes everywhere."

"Bugaboo?" Francis struggled over the clumsy word.

"The thing in the sky. It's trouble, man, real big trouble." Rupe's voice trembled. "I think it's causing the Tingle, too. For all I know, it's giving everybody on the planet a dose of radiation poisoning. I sure hope not."

"Do you know what it is?" Fiona asked.

Rupe bit his lip. He pulled out his smartphone and flipped through his photos. He held it up to show a photo of a purplish sphere covered with strange dark markings against a solid black background. It was the clearest picture Fiona had seen yet of the sky apparition, though it didn't really capture its unearthly character. She studied the image, then looked questioningly at Rupe.

"This is a screenshot captured last year by a player and posted to my blog. The player wanted to know what it was. I told him it must have been a bug in the game's rendering system." Rupe flipped to another photo. It showed a similar purple sphere, this one hanging in the sky above a stark mountain range. "This was another screenshot posted six months ago. The player was in the middle of the Varwhan campaign." Another swipe of his thumb brought up another picture. "This one was last month, just as the Grone expansion was released."

Francis's voice was incredulous. "Wait. You're telling me that these are screenshots from the *game*?"

Rupe nodded vigorously. "Yep. Fucked up, ain't it? We called them *bugaboos*. Never did figure out what caused them. They didn't show up on the logs as errors. Could've been a bug, or maybe an intrusion by a hacker."

"It can't be the same thing. It's a coincidence, right? How could something from a video game show up for real?"

"The bugaboo appeared a few seconds after Arni's capatar spawned inside the havencosm. The earthquake hit at the same time. It can't be a coincidence." Rupe's expression soured. "Zia thinks the QARMA engines are screwing around with the laws of physics. I don't really understand it." He pointed out the window at the strange object in the sky. "All I know is that the thing up there looks exactly like the unexplained visual artifacts we've been seeing in the game for over a year."

The flight lasted only about ten minutes and ended with a breathtaking vertical drop that made Fiona feel like she was trapped in a falling elevator. When Solomon slid open the door, Fiona found herself looking out over a manicured lawn with an ornate central island of flowers.

"Where are we?" said Mama, silent up till now.

"This is the Oval at Stanford University, ma'am. We need your kids to help us . . . um . . . solve a problem in . . . a video game. It's very important. National security."

Mama eyed the colonel and the surrounding soldiers and the still-turning blades of the military helicopter. She turned to Fiona. "This is about the game you played on the TV in the basement?"

Fiona shrugged and shot Rupe a questioning glare. He grimaced in return. "We're headed for the JEEB lab. Arni's here too, along with the Haven engine."

Apocalypse

The university campus looked more like a military base than an institution of higher learning. Solomon hustled them into a waiting Humvee, and the vehicle raced a couple of blocks before screeching to a halt in front of a large building. Like all the other structures on campus, this one was made from yellow sandstone blocks. Above the door and below a great, arched window was engraved WILLIAM GATES COMPUTER SCIENCE. Several panes in the arched window were broken, the glass shards snarling like jagged teeth.

At least a hundred soldiers surrounded the building, along with a dozen more Humvees, several of which sprouted big machine guns from their roofs. At Fiona's direction, Solomon and one of the drivers helped Francis set up her folding wheelchair and get her placed on the seat. Mama clutched Fiona's functioning hand and stared with an open jaw as the cordon of guards at the entrance opened like a magic curtain as they approached. Solomon hurried them through the wide doors into the building.

Fiona had expected a fancy briefing room with a big gleaming table, lots of high-backed leather chairs, and large-screen video monitors on the walls. Instead, Solomon rushed them into a cramped office with scuffed walls and folding chairs brought in hastily from adjacent rooms. He asked Mama and Francis to sit. Rupe hurried in as Solomon was unfolding more chairs. With him was Zia, the Russian-Israeli hacker Fiona and Francis had met at Arni's grocery-store lab. Zia's left arm was in a cast that was strapped to her side by a sling, and thick tape was wrapped around her chest from her armpits to her navel. She hobbled slowly around the desk and painfully lowered herself into a folding chair. "Hi, Fiona," she said, "Hi, Ms. Martinez."

Fiona nodded. Just as before when Zia had sat at her kitchen table, Mama was staring at Zia like she was a roach that had crawled out of the kitchen cupboard. Tattoos, piercings, terrible acne scars, a giant bruise on her cheek that was rapidly turning into a black eye, Zia was completely unlike anyone else in the room. Mama didn't have a chance to respond before another woman stormed into the office, thin with East Asian features and square eyeglasses. Fiona recognized the woman from Francis's web searches.

The woman glared at everyone, especially Solomon, then gestured down at Fiona. "That's the girl?" Her voice was as shrill and sharp as a razor. At Solomon's uncertain nod, she spun to Rupe. "Are you completely sure about this? She's just a kid."

"A kid with the highest PPA score of all fourteen million players," Rupe said. "And according to her medical records, the right blood type."

Francis gave Fiona a sharp glance. His jaw hardened. The butterflies in her stomach suddenly multiplied by a factor of a thousand as she realized that *she* was the reason they'd been brought here.

The woman made a dismissive sigh. Solomon awkwardly cleared his throat and completed the introductions for Mama. "This is Dr. April Chun. She runs the company that makes the computer game your children played. This is Rupert Schroeder; he works for Dr. Chun. He designed the video game. This is Zia Volkov. She works for me here at this government lab."

Fiona's cold excitement intensified. Most of the key avatars from the battle at Grone were here in the flesh. She and her brother, Gaia and Geo, but also Colonel Solomon, the leader of the squad of doomed U.S. Marine avatars. April Chun had appeared at Grone as the archangel Oaone. Analise had been there, as had Wolfe, and of course Arni as the archangel Atum. The virtual battle in the game was being continued here, in the real world.

In a rush of words, Solomon explained to Mama that the military had licensed Dr. Chun's game for use as a high-tech training simulator. He explained how Arnold Zaman and Analise Novak, two disgruntled employees, had tried to steal the game software. He told Mama how Arni and Analise had gone into the game as player avatars and had encountered the avatars of Francis and Fiona there. "That's why we came to your house and questioned your children," he said. "We were trying to find out what had happened in the game."

Mama turned to Fiona and gave her a wide-eyed stare of disbelief. "Is he telling the truth?" Fiona swallowed and nodded.

Solomon continued. "This is going to be difficult to understand, Ms. Martinez, but you must believe me. The computers we built for the game and our military simulators are *very* special machines. There are no other devices like them anywhere else in the world. In fact, they aren't really computers at all. We call them QARMA engines, because they're based on a branch of physics called QARMA theory . . ." His voice trailed off at Mama's blank stare. He licked his lips. "So, here's the deal. Remember the first earthquake about a month ago? The one that started all the tremors?"

Mama nodded suspiciously, and he continued. "That earthquake happened the same night your son and daughter encountered Analise Novak in the game. I was playing the game too, as was Dr. Chun. We were trying to stop Arni and Analise from stealing our technology. Analise convinced your daughter to help her. I want to be clear: we know Fiona didn't realize what was happening. None of this was her fault. She assumed the events were all part of the game's plot. Analise asked her to take an object and deliver it to a certain place inside the game. Fiona followed her instructions and became an unwitting accomplice.

"This would have been bad enough, but Analise and Arni had made a major miscalculation. Neither of them really understood the way the special computers actually worked. When Fiona followed Analise's instructions, it caused a major breakdown inside the computer's guts. Nobody could have predicted what happened next. When the computer crashed, it sent shock waves into the real world. I don't have a physics degree, so I can't explain how it happened, but the experts," he gestured at Chun and Zia, "assure me that it's true. That first earthquake and all the ones since, including the big one last night, were caused by the computer malfunction. The power-grid failures, the crash of the GPS system, the sky anomaly—"

"The bugaboo," corrected Rupe.

Solomon gave Rupe a pained look. "Okay, fine, the *bugaboo*. We have reason to believe that all these events are related, and the malfunction is getting worse by the minute. We're all feeling the Tingles. Even the sun is affected. I know you've seen the news about the sunspots? We're pretty sure they're also caused by—"

"Why don't you turn the bad computers off?" Mama demanded, interrupting the colonel. "Turn them off so they won't keep causing these problems?"

Solomon's lips formed a thin line. He shook his head regretfully. "That is a very good idea, ma'am, but it isn't that simple. These computers don't have a regular power switch. They are powered by a special thing called a QARMA kernel. We can destroy the machines, but we're not sure if it's possible to destroy the kernels they contain. In the end we may try anyway, but I'm told it should be our very last resort." He kneeled in front of Mama so that his eyes were level with hers. "Ms. Martinez, I cannot overstress the urgency of our predicament. The situation is deteriorating. If we can't fix the malfunction, there will be more global earthquakes, and they'll just keep getting stronger. Do you understand what I'm telling you? We've created something that can destroy us all, and we don't have much time left."

Mama's face was very pale. Her grip on Fiona's hand was cold and clammy. She stared at Solomon blankly.

He took a deep breath. "The good news is that we think we can fix the computer malfunction that's causing this nightmare." He paused and turned to Fiona. The purposeful intensity of his gaze caused a shift of energy in the entire room. Suddenly, everyone—Zia, Rupe, Solomon, Francis, and Mama—was looking at her. "Here's the thing: the problem can only be fixed by *playing the game*. Believe me, we've looked at every other option. We've agonized over this decision. Time is running out, and we have no other choices. *None.* You, Fiona Martinez, are our last, best hope to make things right. If we don't try, there's a good chance we'll all be dead before this day is over."

Mama sprang to her feet, releasing her hold on Fiona's hand. "No, no, no! Absolutely not. Not my daughter. This is crazy!" She motioned to Francis, indicating that he should take control of Fiona's wheelchair. "Let's go. We're leaving right now."

Francis was also on his feet, shouting at Solomon. "Are you kidding me? This is some kind of *Ender's Game* bullshit? She's a terrible fighter in the game! She's never even made the leaderboard. It's ridiculous to think—"

"Enough." Solomon clenched his jaw and exchanged a grave look with Zia and Chun. His eyes were bloodshot, his voice grim. "I need to show you something. All of you, come with me."

Talent

Solomon led them to a set of double doors at the end of the main hallway and motioned them inside. Strong smells of ozone and chlorine disinfectant caused Fiona to twist her nose. Mama followed Solomon; Francis pushed Fiona's wheelchair across the raised threshold. Rupe, Chun, and Zia followed.

The JEEB lab was busy and crowded, forcing Francis to carefully guide her chair through a maze of cubicles and between racks of computers as they followed Solomon. The chaos seemed oddly familiar, and then she realized why: she'd seen this exact scene in dozens of disaster movies. This was the command center where distraught scientists would be trying to save the world from a looming apocalypse. If her theory held, there would be a big digital clock on the wall somewhere, counting down to Armageddon. She looked for it, but the walls were covered with whiteboards and a couple of large posters she recognized as photos of Albert Einstein and Alan Turing.

As they emerged from the racks of computers that filled the front half of the room, Mama suddenly stopped. "What?" Fiona said. Mama moved to the side. The rear half of the room was set up like a hospital emergency room. There, four medical beds were surrounded by a bewildering variety of rolling trays, medical monitors, wires, tubes, and lights. Three of the beds were occupied. Each of the three patients wore one of the bulky white caps she recognized as brain-computer interface devices, just like the one Arni had donned back in his makeshift grocery-store lab before his unsuccessful first attempt at entering the havencosm. In fact, one of the patients was definitely Arni.

Rupe saw her staring. "The quake trashed Arni's lab at the grocery store. Zia was hurt, and it was a miracle that Arni's BCI cap didn't get disconnected. We didn't have a choice but to call the colonel. He brought Arni here after the earthquake, along with the Haven machine." He pointed to the nearest computer rack, where the three gleaming QARMA engines—Pandora, Haven, and Sentinel—nestled side by side.

The two beds next to Arni were also occupied. The first held a long, thin man, the second a petite woman. Arni still had color in his cheeks, but the other two looked like corpses: faces shrunken and gaunt, skin a pallid bluish-gray. They were hooked up to beeping machines, so they were alive, but they certainly weren't healthy. Was the woman Analise? And who was the other man? She looked questioningly at Rupe. He nodded. "Yeah, that's Analise Novak. The other guy is Roland Wolfe. He's the Army cyberexpert from the Defense Department." He paused, his voice tinged with fury. "It was his capatar who shot Analise at Grone. What a fucking hero."

"Wolfe was doing his job," snapped Solomon. "Let's not forget that Arni and Analise were trying to steal a billion dollars' worth of top secret military technology."

"Let's not forget that Wolfe might have *killed* her," shot back Rupe, pointing at Analise's gaunt body on the hospital bed.

Solomon made a guttural growling noise. "We all made mistakes that day. Including *you*, if you remember."

Rupe bristled. "We were trying to save lives."

"And how has that worked out for you? You tried to save the 'lives' of a bunch of computer-generated virtual bots, but you may have ended up killing *real* people in the *real* world. There are a million dead in Kobe alone. If Wolfe had stopped Analise, those people might still be alive."

Rupe's jaw trembled. "We don't know for sure if the QARMA machines are causing the Tingles or the earthquakes."

"No, we don't, and that's why you and Zia are here instead of in a military prison."

A feeling of abject horror opened like a deep pit in Fiona's soul. She'd been with Analise at Grone. She'd *helped* Analise. It had been Gaia who had placed the holobox on the machine in Atum's Lair. She'd seen the effects of the earthquakes firsthand, and now Rupe was saying a million people were dead in Japan. Had she played a role in their deaths?

She realized Colonel Solomon was talking to her. He was gesturing toward the figures in the hospital beds. "We believe that all three of them are still active as functional capatars inside the Haven machine, though we can't be completely sure." He shook his head regretfully. "With the firewall in place, there's no way to contact them or monitor their condition."

Mama seemed entranced by the gaunt figures in the hospital beds. "Who are these people? This isn't about a video game. What is this place?"

Fiona barely heard her. She was staring at the fourth, unoccupied hospital bed. An ESP scanner like the one in Arni's lab stood next to it, and a lumpy BCI cap like the one Arni had donned lay empty on the sheets, its sheath of wires coiled neatly next to it. The butterflies in her stomach burst into a rocket-fueled flutter-frenzy.

Solomon saw her looking at the empty bed. He started to speak but Zia interrupted him. "It's your blood," she said. "We've got one remaining BCI cap and one remaining dose of nanospecks." She gestured toward Dr. Chun. "She was our first choice, but when we tried to make a new batch of 'specks for her, they malfunctioned, and there's no time to try again." Fiona glanced at Chun and saw a flicker of relief on her tight face. Zia continued. "All we have left is the original dose made for Arni, which is keyed to his blood type: AB-negative. The same as yours, if your medical records are correct."

"You want me to go into the game and fix what Analise did."

Solomon nodded gravely. "Miss Martinez, I like this less than anybody. The thought of sending a fifteen-year-old into an unknown situation of awesome responsibility turns my stomach. But there's no time to find or train somebody else. Less than four percent of the population has the right blood type. None of our JEEB special-ops instructors or soldiers has it. We tried contacting other high-scoring civilian game players, but the internet is out and the phone systems are overloaded with traffic. Of those players we managed to reach, none have AB-negative blood. I'm afraid *you* are our only feasible candidate. You can refuse, but if you do, we will be forced to destroy the QARMA engines. Both Zia and Dr. Chun think that will only make things worse. Even in the best case, it will kill Arni, Analise, and Wolfe, whose capatars are all trapped behind the firewall."

He took a deep breath. "If you agree, then you'll be fitted with the last remaining BCI cap, injected with nanospecks, and spawned into the havencosm as a capatar. Once in-cosm, you'll have to find a way to return to Grone and—"

Francis broke in angrily. "No, no, *no!* They can't make you do this, Fi." He gestured wildly toward the comatose figures. "Look at them. Are they even still alive?" He spun to Solomon. "My sister can't handle another medical procedure. She's been through more than you can imagine. There has to be another—"

"I'll do it," Fiona said.

Francis stopped, his mouth still open. Mama gave her a disbelieving stare. Fiona squared her shoulders. They needed her to play the game, not as an avatar, but as a capatar, like Analise. The butterflies in her stomach were gone. "I'll do it," she repeated into the silence.

Francis spun to Solomon. "If this is about blood types, I'm her twin brother. I have the same blood. If you choose somebody, it should be me. My avatar had *twice* the achievement level of hers. I'm a much better player!"

Rupe shook his head sorrowfully. "You're decent at game combat, Francis. That's not what we need. You know better than anyone else that Fiona has a special knack for the game. Her perceptive score is off the charts, and that's what—"

Zia stepped in front of Rupe, facing Francis. "This isn't about fighting or physical ability, kid. This is about adaptability and resourcefulness."

Fiona looked up at her brother. The agony in his eyes stabbed her like a dagger. She reached out and gently touched his arm. "Please don't try to stop me. I *want* this." Tears ran down his cheeks, and she knew exactly what was racing through his thoughts. The same memory that had replayed in both their minds a million, million times. They were twins, after all. Nobody understood her pain more deeply than her beloved brother.

Fire

Francis pinched her ear. "Ow!" she cried, and he laughed. She leaned against the car's seatbelt and slapped back at him, almost dropping her phone. He fended off her blows, still laughing. "You're so intense," he said. "Where do you go when you're reading like that?"

"Leave me alone," she protested. "It's a good book. I'm into it, that's all."

"But I'm bored. What are you reading, anyway?" He grabbed for her phone, and she jerked away.

"None of your business."

"It's one of those girly love-bug books, isn't it? A city girl goes off to summer camp and meets a country boy. But then the city girl finds out that the country boy already has a girlfriend. And then she—" Francis dodged away under a renewed set of blows. "—and then she finds out that both of them are vampires, and she has to save the camp—ow!"

One of her slaps had finally found its mark. Francis held up his hands in defense and cried out in mock pain. "Dad, she hit me!"

"You deserved it," said Dad calmly from the front seat. "Don't worry, Fi, I like vampire stories, too."

"It's not a vampire book," she protested. In fact, she'd been reading *Dreams of Elephants*, but she wouldn't admit it to either Francis or Dad. They'd just make fun of her for rereading it for the umpteenth time. She was at her favorite scene, where Princess Nkiru had ridden her mighty war elephant, Anaya, to face the Scythe King—the part where she pulls off her bronze helmet and lets her long black hair spill out, revealing her true identity to the demon lord. She mouthed Nkiru's words silently:

"We know your lies! My people will no longer waste a single precious moment in dull toil, hoping for a promised destiny that will never come. We will choose our own paths, while we are young and our light is at its

brightest. For every moment we aren't living," Nkiru cried, *"is a moment we are dying!"*

Fiona hadn't completely understood the words, but every time she read them, they stirred a bubbling excitement in her soul. She'd refused to let her own hair be cut ever since she'd first read this scene more than a year ago. Nkiru was such a badass.

Francis had already lost interest in pestering her. "Dad, how long till we get there?"

Dad lifted his phone from among the bags of groceries and vacation gear on the passenger seat and consulted the GPS. "It's another twenty minutes to the beach house. Mama might beat us there. She's riding with Julie and Damien." He frowned. "Wait a minute. I've got a text message from her . . ."

Fiona swiped to relaunch her e-reader, preparing to rejoin Nkiru as she sat atop her warrior elephant at the gates of the Scythe King's fortress. But then Dad yelped, and Fiona lurched hard against her seatbelt. Cold window glass pressed against her face. The fruit and vegetables and meats from the grocery bags flew everywhere. A cluster of purple grapes migrated to the top of the windshield and across the car's roof, then dropped into Francis's lap. Something bit painfully into her shoulder, then her hip, and her long hair twisted itself around her face. Dad was screaming something incoherent and the car's windows were shattering as the roof suddenly buckled and crunched down toward them.

Then it was over, and the world of the back seat had been suddenly transformed into a cramped and silent coffin. The headrest in front of her was bent obscenely backward. Something was caught between the crumpled upholstery and the crushed roof, something dark and wet. A biting, eye-watering smell filled the air.

She was still staring at the wet mass pressed between the driver's seat and the roof when she realized Francis was shouting. He was kneeling next to her, struggling with her seatbelt. She looked at him drunkenly. His forehead was cut, and a thin line of blood ran down to the tip of his nose. She reached out toward him, but her arms were pinned by something. She heard the nearby screech of tires and the panicked, shouting voices of approaching strangers.

A loud *whoomp!*, and a blast of heat scorched the back of her head. Francis screamed, and his efforts to pull her out of her seatbelt became frantic. The awful smell, which she began to recognize as gasoline, suddenly jolted her to full awareness. Her feet were ankle-deep in a growing pool of fuel.

"Help me, Fi!" cried Francis. His voice was oddly shrill. "Can you reach your buckle? I can't reach it!"

A searing pain on the back of her head prevented her from answering. The smell of gasoline merged with the odor of burning hair. *Her* hair. Panic found her, and she tried to beat the fire away. It hurt.

Suddenly orange flame was all around her, and it formed into a tunnel, through which she could see the horrified face of her brother as he was wrenched away, falling (or being pulled?) out of the car door. The pain bit her everywhere, all at once, and no amount of struggling or screaming could make a difference.

Colonel Solomon made Mama and Francis wait in the meeting room, promising he would bring them back soon. Zia and Chun escorted Fiona to an adjacent office that had been hastily converted into a medical room. They waited outside while a nurse helped her get undressed and put on a hospital gown. Once she was dressed, Solomon and Rupe joined them, along with a frizzy-haired doctor who hurriedly asked her a bunch of questions about her injuries and her medications. About halfway through the interview, the floor trembled, and everybody in the room stared at the ceiling and walls, bracing themselves for the worst.

When it came, the wave of Tingles almost made Fiona want to crawl out of his skin. This time it wasn't just a prickling sensation: it was real pain, covering every inch of her, a million needles all at once. As always, it didn't subside completely, but the new background level of tingling seemed to have increased. Someone made a shuddering sob. When the wave subsided along with the tremor, the sense of urgency in the room had tripled.

The doctor hurried away. Solomon, Chun, Rupe, and Zia clustered around her bedside. She felt naked. The nurse had removed her prosthetics, her cap, and her face scarf. The flimsy gown did nothing to conceal her injuries. Solomon, Rupe, and Zia did their best not to show their dismay, but the Chun woman stared at her clinically. "It's terrible what happened to you," she said. Fiona nodded and felt no insult. Chun was right. It had *been* terrible. It *was* terrible. It would *always be* terrible. She tried to control her breathing. It wouldn't do for them to see just how scared she really was.

Chun was still staring. "This is your chance to fix what you did at Grone."

Fiona flinched. Back in the game, Chun's avatar, Oaone, hadn't been able to stop Gaia from putting the holobox into the kernel node. If she had, none of this would be happening, and all those people dead from earthquakes and tidal waves might still be alive. Even if her capatar succeeded in lowering the firewall and they could stop the earthquakes, all those real-world people would still be dead. "I'll try," she said. Chun pursed her lips and nodded. "We're going to give you the nanospecks now. It won't hurt, and you won't feel anything. It'll take a few minutes. While that's happening, we'll bring you up to speed."

Nobody would tell her the truth when she finally awoke after the car accident. Mama was there, as was Francis, but Dad was inexplicably missing. Her entire body was immobile. As far as she could tell, she was wrapped in loose plastic like a mummy from head to toe. Her face was oddly stiff, and it took an effort to force her mouth to make words. Even with her best efforts, her speech was incoherently slurred. Something was wrong with her lips. She tried to lick them, but her tongue met a crusted, scabby ridge. Days passed while she drifted in and out of consciousness. It was almost a week later before Mama and Francis told her what had happened. "There was a terrible wreck," Mama said. "You got hurt. Your papa was . . ." Her voice broke, and Fiona waited for Mama to reveal what she'd already guessed. "He was killed."

The day they took the face bandages off was the worst. The room was crowded: Mama, Francis, Aunt Julie, and Uncle Damien, but also the doctor, two nurses, and the hospital's chaplain. Mama held her remaining hand as the doctor slowly unpeeled the bandages from her head. When he was finished, her worst nightmare stared back at her from the mirror. Its lips and nose were gone, giving it the appearance of a gaping skull. Its eyebrows and hair were gone, too, except for a patch over its right ear. Oddly normal eyes peered out of narrow slits of scar tissue. The rest was an abomination, the stitched results of a dozen graft surgeries. The pebbled and ridged dragon skin that stretched across the monster's face glistened in the light, thickly swabbed with salves and medicinal creams.

Francis smiled at her, but she could feel Mama's shuddering sobs through her grip on her hand. The doctor told her that the angry red swelling of the skin would subside, and that with further plastic surgery and a few custom prosthetics, her appearance would eventually improve.

Fiona stared at the last remaining wisp of her hair, which jutted from a patch of undamaged scalp above her left ear. Her dream of growing a savage mane of hair like Princess Nkiru was gone. The patch of hair was no larger than a quarter, and it was all that was left of the pre-accident Fiona. The rest belonged to this new thing she'd become.

While Solomon fumed and Rupe fidgeted, the nurse plugged an IV needle into her wrist and hung a bag of brown fluid on a pole next to her chair. Fiona was no stranger to needles and IV fluids; the nurse's actions seemed to bother everyone else far more than her. Only Chun watched dispassionately. Once the brown fluid began flowing through the tube into her arm, Chun made a heavy sigh. "Rupe says you are an exceptionally good player. Is that right?"

"I guess so. My brother and I make a good team."

Chun's voice sharpened. "Your brother won't be with you. You'll be alone. How do you feel about that?"

Fiona ignored her question and turned to Zia. "What will happen when they spawn my avatar?"

"Your *capatar*," Zia corrected gently. "It's not an avatar, remember." She paused. "Analise told me it was like waking up drunk. You'll feel normal, but you'll have a little trouble at first learning to control your capatar's muscles. It's a DNA match to your real body, but it's *not* your real body. It's sort of like a virtual reality clone. Any injuries or surgeries you've had won't be—" Zia stopped, a trace of a smile worked across her lips. She stared at Fiona for a long moment before continuing. "Because it's a virtual clone of your body's natural state, your injuries won't appear on your capatar. You'll be able to walk and run and do everything you did before you got hurt."

Fiona's heart made a single, savage *thunk* that felt almost like a punch to the ribs. She sucked in a deep breath. Rupe leaned close. "You gotta remember, though, that you're *not* an avatar. You'll be *yourself* in the cosm. You won't be superstrong or superfast like Gaia. Like Zia said, your capatar is a virtual genetic match to *you*. You'll have the body of fifteen-year-old Fiona Martinez, with all its physical limitations. Also, keep in mind that we don't know what will happen to your capatar if it gets hurt. The respawn code in the game was built for avatars and never tested with capatars. You might not respawn. If your capatar dies, *you* might die. That means you can't depend on game tactics like the suicide express, okay? Treat your situation as if your life depends on it, because it does. *All* our lives depend on it. Be *careful!*"

The doctor with the frizzy hair spent several minutes in the corner with Chun and Zia discussing something in hushed tones, occasionally glancing over at Fiona. Rupe remained at her bedside, holding her hand. His smile was genuine, his anxiety palpable. "Bet you never expected to save the world before you graduated from high school, did you?"

The nervous giggle that erupted from her throat felt completely alien, and she stifled it. Rupe squeezed her hand. "If anybody can do this, Gaia can. I've seen her at work."

Referring to her as Gaia, not Fiona, somehow calmed her. Rupe nodded toward the frizzy-haired doctor. "That's Dr. Lieberman. He's going to give you a series of shots. Listen to me very, very carefully. These shots are going to give your capatar some special abilities that you'll need to fix the malfunction of the QARMA kernel. They may also make Gaia look a little different than Fiona, with darker skin and lighter hair. Don't be freaked out."

For the next half hour, while Dr. Lieberman worked with Zia, Chun, and a series of technicians to prepare Fiona's shots, Rupe gave her a detailed overview of her in-game campaign. He explained how her DNA-enhanced capatar would be able to use most avatar devices, how she would need to make her way to Grone and along the way collect several crucial items, especially one of the Great Emoras. He warned her about the traps and pitfalls of the Grone dungeon and told her the secret ways to avoid the horrific boss monster. He told her how to find the Shadow Door, how to make her way through the Cosmic Hub to Atum's Lair, how to activate the enhancements to her DNA, and how to use the emora to repair the system software and lower the firewall. He explained the timestream discontinuity, how it meant that for every year she spent inside the game, less than five minutes would pass in the real world. He told her to take her time, to be careful. Inside the game, she had five *decades* before the deadline. A whole *lifetime*.

"Now listen to me: this is really important. Don't tell anybody but Wolfe, Arni, or Analise who you really are, and don't *ever* let anybody know you have the blood of an avatar. And most importantly, *don't let anybody know about the dungeon on Grone or the Shadow Door to Atum's Lair*. Keep it *all* a secret. Promise me."

She nodded. He lowered his voice. "There are also a few unauthorized easter eggs I've hidden inside the game that nobody knows about." In hushed tones he told her where to find them. It was a lot to remember, but her mind was as clear as it had ever been.

He glanced up as Lieberman and the others approached. Rupe squeezed her hand. "I really wish I was going with Gaia. I've always wanted to see the gameverse from the inside. It's going to be spectacular!" He gave her hand a final squeeze and moved aside for the doctor and the technicians.

Dr. Lieberman looked down at her and smiled. "Hello Fiona. I want to thank you for agreeing to help us. You are a very brave girl."

After the injections from Dr. Lieberman, they wheeled her to the fourth hospital bed in the lab, next to the comatose figure of Arni. His face seemed peaceful enough, which gave her a small measure of comfort. She glanced over at the rack that held the three QARMA engines: Pandora, Sentinel, and Haven. It was hard to believe that something so small could hold an entire virtual universe. The Haven machine was scuffed and slightly dented, most likely from the earthquake damage it had sustained at Arni's makeshift lab, but the blue glow from the symbols on the front panel seemed unaffected.

While the nurses and technicians connected and prepared the ESP scanner and the BCI cap, Solomon, Chun, and Zia continued Rupe's hurried briefing. Zia explained how Fiona would be spawning into the havencosm, which was hosted on the Haven machine. Because Analise had stolen the game universe and migrated it to the Haven machine, all the locations from the game probably still existed in the havencosm in some form. Additionally, the JEEB Earth sim had also been migrated to the havencosm by a mysterious character called Kanaan, who was probably the capatar of Roland Wolfe.

"You'll wake up in the JEEB version of the Avatar Mall. You're going to feel disoriented, and it may take a while for your mind to become comfortable in your virtual body." She coughed lightly. "Here's the hard part: When your capatar spawns, it'll be naked. You won't have an initial item stash like a new avatar. You'll have nothing, and the stores in the Avatar Mall will all be empty." Zia paused while one of the nurses hooked a urine collection bag to the catheter that they'd inserted in the prep room. When she was finished, Zia continued. "As soon as you can walk, go straight to the Hero's Gate. Because this is the JEEB version of the Gate, you can only use it to spawn to a single place: JEEB Earth. It's a virtual copy of the real Earth, so you should at least have an initial frame of reference. The spawn location will be a random outdoor spot somewhere in our virtual version of Manhattan. We can't know exactly where you'll appear, just the general vicinity. The area was chosen for a planned military training sim that never happened. Since the firewall went up, we don't have any way to change it."

"I'll spawn into the middle of New York . . . without any *clothes*?" The idea that she might appear naked on a crowded street should have been cause for great alarm, but instead she only felt a mild regret that she wouldn't be able to use the Avatar Mall to design a cool costume, one of her favorite activities in the game. Nakedness didn't bother her. Embarrassment was an emotion she no longer felt, not after a year of thoroughly humiliating medical procedures. She'd find clothes, somehow.

After all, it was just a game.

The floor rumbled, and the sensation of the Tingles made her wince. The others grabbed her bed rail to steady themselves. She glanced at the Haven machine. Was it her imagination, or had the lights on the front of the machine dimmed during the tremor?

Zia gathered herself. "Be ready for anything, Fiona. When you exit the Hero's Gate, there's no telling what you might encounter. I recommend finding a hidey-hole, waiting until dark, and then peeking outside to see what the world looks like. Things, uh, might not be what you expect." Her eyes flickered to Rupe. "Did you explain the timestream discontinuity?"

"Yeah. Solomon is going to blow up the Haven engine exactly four hours from the time Gaia spawns. Four hours here is fifty-six years in the game. She'll have plenty of time."

Chun grimaced like she'd eaten a sour grape. "We may not have four hours. If there's another big earthquake, it could bring down the lab and kill us all, or the Tingle could get so bad we won't be able to function. Don't waste any time. And one more thing. We don't know what to expect when you spawn on JEEB Earth. Even though it happened only a few days ago, in the accelerated timestream, it's been almost 250 years since JEEB Earth was migrated from the Sentinel machine into the havencosm. That means it may seem like you've jumped 250 years into the virtual future. JEEB Earth might not have changed, or it might have changed dramatically. There's no way to know." Chun's scowl deepened, and Fiona wondered if she ever smiled. "The problem is compounded when we also consider the larger game universe was migrated almost a month ago. On the worlds of the game, almost ten thousand years have passed. Things may have changed dramatically from what you remember when you and your brother last played."

Rupe piped up, interrupting Chun and earning a glower, which he ignored. "Don't freak out, Fiona. It may or may not mean anything. The game wasn't designed for the characters and places to age, so things may be just as you remember them from the game. However, nobody really understands the jeeb virus that infected the system. It changed the behaviors of the bots, and it may have caused other changes as well." He paused and tried to sound reassuring. "It's nothing Gaia can't handle. Arni deactivated the random adversaries in the Grone dungeon, so you won't have monsters jumping out of the shadows, but you'll still have to be careful of the usual tricks, traps, and red herrings."

Tricks, traps, and red herrings, she thought. *Gaia's specialties.*

There was a long silence. Something occurred to Francis. "Um, so how does she get back?"

Uncomfortable silence. It was Solomon who finally answered. "Once you complete your mission and the timestream has been resynchronized, we should be able to lower the firewall. When that happens, we'll come find you and escort you back to Jeeb Earth. We can extract you there."

"Fuck that," Rupe blurted. "When the firewall goes down, I'll come get you with a whole army of avatars! No, a whole goddamned imperial warfleet! A thousand ships for the empress Gaia!"

Brainstorm

The lab was solidly packed with people, many of them in uniform, here to witness one of the most unlikely events in human history: the United States military was preparing to transfer the mind of a disabled teenager into the body of a virtual character in an out-of-control video game in order to stop a real-world apocalypse. She almost giggled out loud.

Of course, there was every likelihood that the attempt would fail and her capatar would be killed either during the spawn process or as soon as it emerged into whatever world lay on the other side of the virtual reality membrane. If that happened, she might never wake up, but the prospect of imminent death didn't bother her, not one bit. It was hard to imagine anything on the other side that could possibly be more difficult than her current reality. If she died during the spawn process, at least she would die trying to save Francis and Mama and the rest of the world.

On the other hand, if everything went to plan, she would emerge into the virtual world of the havencosm whole and healthy. She would be able to walk and run and breathe without pain. Not only would she be freed from her injuries, but she would also be living in a fantasy world where it was possible to fly on spaceships and visit thousands of worlds filled with bizarre aliens and exotic locales. She would become Gaia.

But . . . she wouldn't be Gaia, would she? Not exactly. Gaia was an avatar, an empty shell, a marionette operated by a girl with a video-game controller. She wouldn't be Fiona either. This new being, her capatar, would be an opportunity for a complete reinvention of her life. Her new self would be *bold*. She would be *fearless*. As soon as they flipped the switch on the ESP scanner, she would become an entirely new woman. She would have a new name, a new purpose, a new life in a new world.

She would do everything she could to fix the kernel malfunction, but when the task was complete, whether she succeeded or not, *there was no way in heaven or hell she'd return to the real world.*

The intensity of her resolve scared her, but she'd been thinking of nothing else since they'd asked her to volunteer. It would mean that she might never see Francis or Mama again. The thought caused her heart to squeeze tightly into itself. Mama would be devastated, but Francis, she knew, would celebrate her freedom. More than anyone else, he understood her. They'd shared the entire awful experience; every minute, every second of it. *Together.* It had trapped them both in lives neither of them wanted. This way, they'd both be free. Mama, too, though it would be hard for her to understand.

I will choose my own path, she mouthed silently.

They crowded around her bedside as the nurse checked the fit and connections on the BCI cap. Colonel Solomon straightened, his voice having returned to his normal commanding tone. "Don't be a hero.

Be *extremely* cautious. If something happens to your capatar, all is lost, so take *zero* unnecessary risks." He gestured toward the three adjacent beds and the comatose figures they held. "Try to find Roland Wolfe's capatar. Explain what you're doing, and why. Get him to help you. He knows the technology best." He hesitated, wincing slightly, "If for some reason you can't get to Wolfe, then try to find Arni or Analise. But be aware that their time in the cosm may have changed them. Don't tell them, or anybody else, who you are or what you're doing until you're sure they're willing to do what it takes."

"Okay. I understand."

Solomon nodded and looked to the others.

Zia stepped up to the bedside. She smiled coyly. "Don't fuck up."

Rupe joined Zia and tried to grin. It wasn't at all convincing given the volume of tears streaming down his cheeks. His beard was soaking wet. "I actually feel pretty good about this whole thing," he announced loudly. "Honestly, dude, with your PPA scores you're going to crush it. Wish I could come with you. Between Ruperus and Gaia, we'd have a great time saving the world."

"It's not a game," said Chun dourly.

Rupe sniffed. "Everything is a game, boss."

———

When she was fully wired to the ESP scanner and all the connections had been tested, they ushered Mama and Francis into the lab. The nurses and technicians stood back at a respectful distance, as did Solomon, Chun, Rupe, and Zia. Mama and Francis leaned over the bed. Mama kissed her forehead, and a tear dripped onto Fiona's cheek. Mama regarded the bewildering array of wires and tubes connected to Fiona with dismay. "You can still say no. They can't make you do this. Please, don't do this!"

Fiona smiled at her and replied just as softly. "Mama, I *want* to do this. Don't you understand? When I'm inside the game, I will be whole again. Don't you want that for me?"

Francis put his hand on her shoulder. "I'm only sorry I can't be there too." He squeezed. "Stay in the shadows. Keep out of fights. Do what you do best. Just . . . be *careful*." He leaned forward and kissed her forehead, just as Mama had. "See you soon, Sis. Kick some serious ass in there, you hear me? I'm counting on you."

"Don't worry. I promise, one way or another, I'll be okay. I *promise*, okay, Mama?"

Mama nodded and leaned down to kiss her forehead again just as Solomon appeared at the bedside and apologetically hustled them away to a far corner of the lab, where they stood forlornly, hand in hand. Francis gave her a stiff salute.

———

She was ready. Her head was tightly ensconced in the BCI cap. On the ESP scanner next to her bed, she could see the 3D image of the nanospecks firing in her brain. She was wired to monitors of every kind: heart, lungs, renal, liver, gastric, endocrine, and brain activity. She was plugged into supplemental oxygen and tubes that would collect her urine and waste. She was connected to several IV bags, and there was a feeding tube on a table next to her bed they would insert once she slipped into the induced capatar coma.

"Nanospeck resolution accurate to nine sigma," said the female tech next to the bed. She glanced away from the ESP scanner toward Solomon. "We're ready to begin."

Solomon smiled at Fiona, then nodded to the tech, who nodded back. "Okay. Starting the spawn process."

The tech looked down at Fiona. "Here we go, sweetie. You shouldn't feel a thing, okay?" She paused, and a nervous frown tickled the edge of her lips. "Good luck in there."

Fiona tried to control her rapid breathing. "Thanks."

The tech turned back to the machine. "Spawning now," she said, and her hands moved across its controls. It began to whir as the cooling fans kicked in.

Fiona looked beyond the technician at the computer rack that held the QARMA engines. The Haven machine, no bigger than a breadbox, was inscribed with block letters that glowed back at her in a pale, electric blue.

"Resolving spawn platform in the Avatar Mall," the tech announced. "We've got a lock on platform One-Niner-Echo-Zero-Alfa-Foxtrot. Exclusion zone established."

Everyone shifted, and an appreciative murmur went through the room like a breeze. Fiona felt a thrill slip from her gut into her throat. She'd never been to New York before.

"Starting capatar render engine," the tech announced. "Rendering. Rendering. Fifty percent. Seventy-five percent. Stand by..." She looked up from the machine with a broad smile. "Rendering complete!"

Her new body was waiting for her. Everyone in the room clapped, and many shouted. The tech looked down at Fiona and said in a quiet voice, "Ready, sweetie? This next part will put you to sleep. You won't feel a thing."

"Ready," she replied.

"Starting entanglement," the tech announced.

Fiona sucked in a deep breath of the last meatspace air she would ever breathe. She closed her eyes and silently recited: *Back into the darkness, I command you, for fear is your abode, not mine. Life is more than just waiting to die. I will choose my own path, while I am young and my light is at its brightest. Every moment I'm not living is a moment I am dying.*

havencosm | STARCHILD

Thief

Despite the chill, Nkiru peeled back the top half of her coldsuit and draped it around her waist, then tugged the long-sleeved sweater over her head to reveal the gray tank top beneath. To her it was a casual, thoughtless motion. To Se-Jong it was a sudden and unexpected distraction, a momentary forgetting of their dire situation. Toroni and McCloud noticed, too, casting furtive glances as they worked. Even filthy and sweat stained, there was something otherworldly about Nkiru Anaya. In this subterranean chamber surrounded by pre-Cataclysm enigmas, she was the most tantalizing mystery of all.

After her astonishing demonstration with the avatar weapon she'd called a *gobsmacker*, she'd been walking slowly around the armillary sphere, examining its intricacies in exhaustive detail. She seemed both awestruck and worried, taking note of the damage to its outermost components. Arni followed her, agitated, his hands fluttering at his sides like two birds trapped in a net. The sour scent of his filthy robes mixed with the pervasive odor of oiled brass from the machine.

Across the room, Littlefeather supervised the marines as they tore open the locked cabinets and removed their enigmatic contents. They arrayed the items across the floor while the reliquist photographed them and whispered notes into her komnic.

Se-Jong watched them work while his grandmother examined his wounds. She adjusted the bloody dressings on his face and clucked angrily. He couldn't tell her thoughts from her expression, but he guessed her anger was directed at him for causing this whole misadventure.

Everyone worked quickly, knowing the Dei Militans might still be in pursuit. While Littlefeather and the marines hurriedly cataloged the last of the relics removed from the cabinets, Nkiru dragged a table across the room to the base of the armillary sphere. She opened her backpack and began removing the contents, one by one, placing them carefully on the table's surface. Se-Jong rose unsteadily and moved to her side.

He recognized the snowglobe, the stealthshield, and the scancorder, plus the polished, white Mucktu Charm she'd shown him at Assinni. Next was some kind of brown organic shell, about the size of a small lemon. It was dry and seemed hollow, like a desiccated seed husk. The last object was a small, ornately decorated wooden box, like a jewelry container.

Someone behind him said, "What's that?"

He turned to find Littlefeather, who had abandoned her cataloging to see what mysterics Nkiru's pack contained. The others crowded around. Grandmother watched intently, though she seemed more interested in the emotions on Nkiru's face than in the artifacts in her pack.

Nkiru lifted the wooden box and, to Se-Jong's surprise, handed it to the reliquist. "Open it. Just *don't* touch what's inside."

Littlefeather twisted the clasp and very carefully opened the lid. Inside was an innocuous yellow jewel about the size of a peach pit. She looked up questioningly.

"An emora," said Nkiru. "A Great Emora, actually."

"Hey, that's *mine*," exclaimed Arni. He reached out for the box, but Nkiru slapped his hand away.

Littlefeather looked at Arni, then at Nkiru. "I . . . I . . . I don't . . ." She clamped her mouth shut.

Se-Jong felt a laugh of ridicule rising in his throat. It died before it reached his lips as he remembered the night on Assinni when Nkiru had returned to their rented room, breathless and bruised, with laser burns on her pilgrim's cloak. *Damn, damn, damn. She's been carrying that thing in her backpack ever since.*

Everyone stared at the jewel. Se-Jong tried to remember Leodiva's depiction of the three Creation Stones in his *Reveal of Creation* mural at the Regium. One had been amber yellow, just like this one.

He felt a strange reluctance to look at Nkiru. He turned to his grandmother instead. Her eyes were locked on the stone, her lips pressed tightly together. Se-Jong knew exactly what she was thinking: if this was a Great Emora, then the crime committed by Nkiru, to which Se-Jong was a likely accomplice, went far beyond the highest of felonies. There would be no escaping the wrath of the Father Regis. Se-Jong's involvement would likely cause the utter ruination of the entire Kwon family, and everyone in their sphere of influence. At minimum it meant the end of the military career of Captain Kwon Ophelia Namjoo. The knot of nerves in Se-Jong's stomach, already painful, constricted even more.

Littlefeather's voice was hollow. "There were rumors that someone broke into the Sanctum Arcanis. It's no wonder the Dei Miltans brought their fastest ship here to find you."

Nkiru reached out to Littlefeather. "Close the box, carefully, and hand it back to me."

Littlefeather hesitated, glancing down at the beyond-priceless relic. Se-Jong expected that she would look to Grandmother for guidance, but after a moment she handed the box back to Nkiru.

Nkiru placed the box—far too casually, Se-Jong thought—back on the table.

Grandmother's expression was darker than he'd ever seen it. "You admit you stole these items from the church?"

Nkiru bit her lip, didn't answer.

Grandmother set her jaw. "Answer me, Anaya. This isn't some kind of game."

"Actually, it is," muttered Nkiru.

Arni blurted a braying laugh. Nkiru glanced at him with a grim smile. Se-Jong watched the exchange. Were they mocking Grandmother? The situation was out of Grandmother's control, a condition he knew she would not tolerate. Arni and Nkiru had led them here to this strange octagonal room filled with relics, promising escape. Had they been deceived? If so, this room was a terrible place to be trapped. Se-Jong knew the militans hadn't given up their pursuit. They were rabid fanatics, after all. His heart sank as he watched Nkiru and Arni. *Never underestimate a fanatic.* He glanced over at the gobsmacker, which Nkiru had leaned against the table. If the militans did show up, they were in for a nasty surprise.

"Where did you learn the ability to activate avatar technology?" Grandmother demanded.

"It's in my blood."

"Your blood? You were born with it?"

"You could say that." Nkiru's tone was both defensive and defiant.

"Where were you born?"

"I was born in meatspace."

Meatspace. Arni had used the word earlier.

"Where is meatspace?"

Nkiru seemed unsure how to answer. "It's not a . . . It's . . . on Earth."

"You're from Earth?"

"Yes."

Grandmother's eyes narrowed to slits. "You're not involved with the Mucktu Bloodline, are you?"

"Of course not."

"Are you working for the Janga cult?"

Nkiru winced. "No. They're helping *me*, not the other way around."

"What are you trying to accomplish?"

"The world is about to end. I'm trying to stop it."

Grandmother's eyebrows shot up. Coming from anyone else, Nkiru's response would have brought ridicule. Coming from a young woman with the powers of an avatar who'd stolen the Cataclyst Church's most sacred relic from the deepest crypts of the Regium Fortress, it sent a chill through the room.

"How is the world ending?"

"I don't know," Nkiru said. "I don't really understand how any of this works. I'm doing my best. I never expected it to be this hard."

This was not the answer Grandmother was expecting. She turned to Arni. "It's obvious you two are in this together. What's going on? Explain it, now."

Arni whimpered and squeezed his eyes shut. He said something unintelligible.

"What?"

Arni strained to get the words out. "The Cataclysm . . . was . . ." He faltered, took a deep breath, and tried again. "Time is . . . broken. There's a . . . virus . . . and a firewall . . ." He was gasping now, forcing the words out as if squeezing each syllable through a meat grinder.

Grandmother interrupted, clearly exasperated. "You told me you would lead us out of this mountain. What are we doing here?"

A sudden certainty settled over Se-Jong. This room was not an escape route. It was something else. The damaged armillary sphere was the goal Nkiru had been seeking all along, the reason for her entire unlikely journey across the Known Arc. The reason she'd come to Grone. It was the reason they were *all* here: the mysterious Arni, the Solar Guard, the Dei Militans. Nkiru had risked her life—*all* their lives—to find it.

Arni quickly wilted under the heat of Grandmother's glare. Nkiru stepped forward and put her hand on his shoulder. "It's really hard to explain. It will be better if you let me show you."

"Show me what?"

"The only way any of us is going to get out alive."

Holobox

Nkiru approached the magnificent armillary sphere. Carefully, like she was defusing a bomb, she applied gentle pressure to the outermost of the concentric brass rings.

Littlefeather inhaled sharply. Se-Jong had seen it too. As Nkiru moved the ring, above their heads the holographic map of the galaxy rotated correspondingly.

Some of the tension drained from Nkiru's shoulders, as if she'd avoided a trap. Proceeding toward the center, she rotated the next ring, then the next. At each movement, the map responded, each ring apparently controlling a different aspect of the display. One seemed to control the axial rotation, another the zoom, another the level of detail.

Littlefeather watched raptly, moving to Nkiru's side. "What are you doing?"

"I need that holobox," she replied tersely.

Se-Jong's eyes fell on the clear cube mounted within the first set of rings near the base of the sphere. Nkiru was arranging the rings so that she could reach inside the machine and remove it. When one of the rings slipped, Littlefeather reached out to secure it. Nkiru gave her a sharp, suspicious glance.

"Let me help," Littlefeather said.

Nkiru hesitated, then nodded.

Arni mumbled something. He was watching them with bright, expectant eyes.

Nkiru continued to gingerly rearrange the orientation of the rings, Littlefeather holding them in place as Nkiru moved farther inward. As she worked, Se-Jong studied the changing map. Moving one of the smaller rings deep inside the machine decreased the number of labels on the map, until only about a dozen were highlighted. Had these been the most important worlds during the Age of Avatars? His eyes flitted over the names, and he recognized many of them from legend.

Raolix. Uchisar. Duga Resa. Rakonen. Orcani. Earth. Olymkos. Asos...

Wait a minute.

Earth?

The label for Earth was embedded in one of the thicker spiral arms of the galaxy, about two-thirds of the distance from the core to the outer rim, in a part of the galaxy that was now deep inside the Devastation. His eyes flicked across the map to the region of the Known Arc, and the flashing label "JEEB Earth." He was about to point out this odd discrepancy when Nkiru moved another ring and all the labels vanished.

Nkiru had cleared a path through the metal rings to the holobox. She took a deep breath, then leaned inside on her tiptoes and strained to reach it. She fumbled with the mount, and the cube popped free into her hand.

Se-Jong half expected the galactic hologram to vanish, but its appearance didn't change with the removal of the holobox. Nkiru extricated herself from the machine and nodded to Littlefeather, who released her hold on the rings. Freed, the rings moved slowly back to their former positions and the map returned to its original state. Se-Jong scanned the area where he'd seen the label for Earth.

It was still there, among thousands of others, absolutely in the wrong place. *Maybe there had once been another world called Earth?* Just another mystery to be added to the lengthy list of enigmas contained in the map.

Nkiru held up the holobox, examining it wistfully while Littlefeather peered over her shoulder. She seemed both relieved and keenly apprehensive, as if she'd cleared a hurdle she'd been dreading but had reached a final, far more terrifying obstacle. She placed the holobox on the table alongside the other relics.

"Now what?" demanded Grandmother.

Tears

Nkiru drew her shoulders upward, placed her palms together in a gesture of prayer, and pressed them to her lips. She took several deep breaths, holding this pose for a long moment while everyone watched. Then, oddly, she looked down at her outstretched arms and ran her fingertips lightly along the ridge of her forearms, wiggling her fingers, touching her face, and finally, collecting her long hair into a bundle and draping it over her shoulder. She stroked it softly, her eyes distant, wistful. Something in her expression, a bleak sadness that he'd never glimpsed before, caused a part of Se-Jong's heart to break. All of his awe, all of his excitement about their wondrous surroundings suddenly vanished, and was replaced by a simple, profound dread. She mumbled something that he couldn't hear clearly.

"Wait a minute," he said.

Nkiru overrode his objection with a wave of her hand. "It'll be okay. This will either work, or it won't." She gave him a smile, then clenched her jaw and turned to Arni. "I need your help."

Nkiru turned to the relics on the table. She lifted the scancorder. With trembling hands, she snapped the holobox into a receptacle on the back of the device. It made a *snick!* sound like a power magazine being pushed into a laser pistol. She checked that the cube was correctly seated, then tapped at the scancorder's controls. Nothing happened. She cursed, rapped it sharply on the side of its casing. It beeped and lit up.

She presented the scancorder to Arni. "Take it. Go stand over there, and when I tell you, point the scanner at me until I tell you to stop. Don't touch any of the controls or it'll stop working."

Arni looked confused and terrified. She reached out and squeezed his shoulder. "Don't worry. It'll be okay." To Se-Jong it sounded as if she were reassuring herself, not Arni. The marines shifted uncomfortably. Littlefeather watched the exchange breathlessly. His grandmother stood silently, unmoving.

Arni moved to Se-Jong's side, gingerly clutching the scancorder like it was a sleeping animal that would bite his arm off if awakened. Nkiru remained at the table, gathering herself for some difficult task. He wanted to go to her, but from her posture and attitude it was obvious that whatever was about to happen, it was hers alone to endure.

"Arni, can you turn off the lights?" she said.

Arni nodded. He moved to a panel of switches and touched something. The illuminated floor went dark. The galaxy hologram above them loomed large, suddenly the only thing visible. For a moment Se-Jong felt as if he were in intergalactic space, looking up at the pale glow of the distant Milky Way.

As his eyes adjusted to the dim radiance of the hologram, he could see Nkiru's silhouette moving slowly at the table. From the movement of her shape, she seemed to be lifting something over her head. She placed it on the table, then knelt and did something to the boots of her coldsuit. She rose, then bent, pushed her heavy coldsuit down her legs, kicked it away.

She's undressing, he realized with a shock. He scanned the faces of the others. Everyone, including Grandmother, was watching intently.

It only took a few more seconds for her to remove her base layers and undergarments. She reached down and selected something from the table. The wooden box that held the emora. She removed the jewel from the box and lifted it to her mouth.

Everyone gasped when she spat on the emora, then enclosed it tightly in her fist. Even Grandmother, who rejected all religion as hogwash, seemed appalled by Nkiru's blatant sacrilege. They waited, their eyes locked on her shadowy silhouette as the holographic galaxy rotated silently above.

Littlefeather muttered something. Both marines whispered excitedly. Se-Jong struggled to see the cause of their reactions. His left eye was still swollen shut, and his right eye was watering fiercely. He wiped it with his wrist and squinted. As far as he could tell, nothing had changed.

He blinked, and blinked again. *There!*

Tiny specks of white light had appeared on Nkiru's skin. Just a few, randomly placed at first, but more were flickering to life.

The tiny, starlike specks were multiplying rapidly, so numerous that the shape of her shoulders, waist, and hips were defined by their soft glow. The pinpricks extended down her legs and arms, crawled up her neck to fill her face with light. A pattern began to appear in their placement, as if an entire encyclopedia of some complex alien script were being written in light across the curves and hollows of her body. Every scintilla of doubt about Nkiru and her intentions vanished from his mind.

She was not of this world.

When she moved, it was the most beautiful thing he'd ever seen, a cascade of thousands of symbols of light in the shape of a woman, as if she'd eaten the galaxy, and the multitudes of constellations were visible through her skin.

When she spoke, everyone jumped.

"Point the scancorder at me until I tell you to stop."

Next to him, the shadow of Arni raised the scancorder. It cast a faint blue light on his shaggy beard.

Nkiru snaked her arms above her head and placed her hands together, cradling the emora between her open palms. She began a slow, surreal pirouette in concert with the rotating galaxy above her head. They were dancing like daughter and mother, Nkiru and the Milky Way, both creatures of starlight.

She made a complete turn, the scancorder reading the patterns on her skin. It beeped, and the light bathing Arni's face turned green. Nkiru dropped her arms. A new voice broke the silence. It was Private McCloud, and they were the first words he'd uttered in Se-Jong's presence. "What the fuck just happened?"

"They turned her skin into a QR code," whispered Arni. He looked down at the scancorder. "Fucking brilliant."

The relief and excitement in Nkiru's voice was evident. "Turn on the lights."

She was struggling back into her coldsuit when Arni hit the light switch. Se-Jong released the breath he'd been holding when he saw her vast, jubilant smile. The glowing symbols on her skin were drowned out by the light of the room. He wondered if they would fade over time, or if she would go through the rest of her life as a walking star child.

She pulled on her gloves, shivering. "Nobody told me it would be so cold in here." Her tone was eager, not dismayed. She reached out and took the scancorder from Arni. She examined its display screen.

"It worked," she breathed.

"What worked?" Littlefeather asked, dumbfounded. Se-Jong knew just how she felt. The image of Nkiru spinning like a woman-shaped galaxy would stay with him forever.

"The scancorder had to be configured for what comes next," Nkiru explained.

"You configured it by spitting on that rock and taking your clothes off?" asked Toroni.

Nkiru laughed nervously, but the overwhelming dread was gone from her expression. She began squinting and working the muscles of her cheeks. She paused, head down, and held the pose. When she raised her face, her eyes were full of tears. She harvested a teardrop with her fingertip.

She gave him a look that said, *okay, here goes nothing*.

She carefully deposited the droplet on the scancorder's sensor array, then tapped the controls. The scancorder beeped and the attached holobox began to pulse with a dim yellow light. After a few seconds, it made a single white pulse and then darkened. She waited for more, holding her breath. When nothing else happened, she exhaled. "I guess it finished. The indicators are all green. *Something* got transferred to the holobox."

She rotated the scancorder and ejected the holobox. Se-Jong didn't think it looked any different than before, but Nkiru was smiling. When she looked at him, her smile collapsed. She put the holobox on the table and returned the emora to its wooden case, then took his shoulder and guided him back to the ledge. "Sit down; you're bleeding again."

She helped him sit, grimacing at his wound. She gently adjusted the soggy bandage, then leaned close and kissed his forehead. She whispered, "Thank you, Lieutenant. For everything. I wouldn't have made it here without you."

"What did you just do?" he asked.

She held up the holobox. "I mixed up the ingredients of the recipe that's supposed to save the world." She kissed his forehead again. "Sit tight. It's almost over, I promise."

Blood

Nkiru dug into her coldsuit's utility pouch and pulled out the emergency kit, the same one she'd used to treat Se-Jong's injuries after he'd first fallen on his face. She extracted a small pair of miniature scissors. She gave him a smile. He tried to smile back, but the triage glue and gooey bandages prevented him from moving his cheeks.

"Hold this," she said to Littlefeather, offering the reliquist the open emora case. "Don't touch the stone, no matter what happens." When Littlefeather eagerly reached out, Nkiru jerked the case away. "I'm serious. No matter what, from this point forward, *none of you can touch it*. Understood?"

The marines stiffened. Littlefeather nodded solemnly. She took the case and held it with straight arms, as far from her body as possible. For such a small thing, it seemed quite heavy.

Nkiru swallowed and gathered herself. She took the scissors in one hand and extended her other hand so that it hovered above the emora. She bit her lip, looked at Se-Jong for support. Since he had no idea what she was about to do, he kept his face neutral. She nodded to herself, lifted the scissors, pressed them into the pad of her middle finger.

Grandmother's arm shot out and grabbed Nkiru's wrist. "What are you doing?"

Nkiru winced. "I'm trying to save us all."

"By *bleeding* on a Great Emora?"

Nkiru glared defiantly. Grandmother tightened her grip.

Littlefeather cleared her throat. "Captain, remember the Cataclyst Covenant requires a sacrifice of blood. On holy days, the faithful prick their finger on the altar and let a drop of blood fall into the chalice."

"What's that got to do with the emora?"

Littlefeather hesitated, suddenly sheepish. "I have no idea, but it seems relevant."

Grandmother sighed and released Nkiru.

Once again Nkiru extended her hand, palm down, over the emora. She pushed the pointed tip of the scissors into her finger, inhaling sharply. A droplet of blood formed at the wound. She squeezed the finger, carefully holding it a few centimeters directly above the emora. The droplet of blood swelled, distended into a teardrop shape, and fell from her fingertip.

Almost instantly, the hard, jewellike stone absorbed the blood. Arni gasped as its color began to fade, and once more his words became lucid. "Saliva. Tears. Blood. They coded an avatar profile and the emora's blockchain encryption into your body chemistry, didn't they? Same with your little QR code lightshow. That's how you managed to get the software fix through the firewall. I can't believe it! Whose idea was it?"

She didn't reply. Arni turned to Se-Jong, visibly excited. "It was in her blood all along! We're saved by the blood of the lamb!" He tittered loudly, dancing in a circle and tugging his beard. He suddenly stopped, pointed at the holobox. "What's that? What did they put in your tears?"

"A fix for the timestream bug," she said distractedly. "If I can get this holobox to the kernel node, it's supposed to resynchronize the timeline and bring down the firewall."

Arni's eyes widened. Without warning, he grabbed her face with both hands and planted a kiss on her forehead.

Nkiru pulled away from him, intent on the transformation of the stone. Its color had shifted from golden amber to clear and then to a pale lavender, like an amethyst. She waited, staring.

"Something's wrong. It's supposed to turn black."

Arni glanced down at the stone, then back up at Nkiru.

"Maybe you didn't give it enough blood," suggested Toroni, caught up in the excitement. "Maybe it's still thirsty."

Nkiru repeated the exercise, drawing another pearl of blood from her fingertip and dripping it onto the emora. This time, the droplet simply rolled off the hard surface of the jewel. The color remained purple.

Something dawned in Arni's eyes. He recoiled in horror. "Don't touch it!" he warned.

"What's wrong?" Nkiru yelped.

"It's *ruined*," he said, his voice growing shrill.

Nkiru looked at Arni with dismay. "What do you mean, ruined?"

"Bad blood!" Arni whispered something to himself and shot a glare of pure malice at Se-Jong. "This is *your* fault," he spat.

Everyone was staring at him. "What did *I* do?"

Arni resumed the nervous tugging at his beard. "I told you! I warned you," he screeched.

"Warned me about *what?*"

"You ruined everything. *Everything!*"

Based on Arni's reaction, something had obviously gone horribly wrong. Was the stone about to explode and kill them all? Littlefeather quickly placed the emora's wooden case on the table and backed away.

Arni turned his glare toward Nkiru. "I told you not to let him touch you," he shouted. "He's ruined your blood chemistry, ruined *everything!*"

Se-Jong stood, reeling from dizziness, then steadied himself by leaning on the wall. "Arni, what the hell are you talking about?"

"You made her pregnant, you idiot."

Grandmother gave him a sharp glare. The room erupted into shouts and arguments. Se-Jong leaned against the wall and tried to ignore the stench of the Yok-Stop that still clung to his skin and clothes. His dulled senses were suddenly clear and painfully crisp. They'd been careful, hadn't they? From the beginning she'd assured him that she was protected. He'd shrugged off Arni's concerns as delusional ravings, but . . . he'd had sex with a gods-damned *avatar*. *Many* times. Something inside him stirred, a dark and cold phantom from a previously unknown corner of his soul. *What if she really is pregnant? With* my *child?*

Nkiru was chasing Arni as he paced in a tight circle. "I'm not pregnant. I can't be. I took the pharma treatment. It's one hundred percent foolproof."

"Foolproof? Ha! You're not a bot. Capatars are *different!*"

"Arni, I'm *not pregnant!*" Nkiru shouted. "All I have to do is activate the holobox! After that we don't need the emora."

"It won't work it won't work it won't work," chanted Arni as he continued to speed in circles around the room.

Nkiru stopped chasing him. Her arms hung limply at her side. "Then what should I *do?*"

It took a moment for Se-Jong to realize that the question was not directed at Arni, but at him. It jolted him. Since the moment he'd met her, he'd been following her lead. She'd never asked him for advice of any kind. The desperation in her expression forced him to clear his mind.

He searched his memories for everything he knew about the emoras. The only places in scripture where they were described in any detail were the opening chapters of the *Chronicles of the First Epoch*. They were the keys to heaven, used by the Archangels of Creation to cross between the mortal worlds and the ethereal realm of the Foundation Core. The stones harnessed the unfathomable energies of the Engines of Creation, giving the archangels ultimate control over matter, space, and time. If emoras were real and not simply the imaginary products of a colorful myth, an emora would be *incredibly* dangerous. *Especially* an emora that might be malfunctioning.

He cleared his throat, unable to suppress a shiver. "You think the Foundation Core is behind the door."

She nodded. "Brother Jerome once told me it's a real place, but it's hidden. He called it the basement of the cosmos." She pointed. "That's the basement door." She turned to the amethyst-colored emora on the table. "And *that* is supposed to be the key." She shrugged helplessly. "All I know is that I'm not supposed to touch the emora until it turns solid black. It turned *purple* instead." She paused, searched his face. "What do you think? Should I try it anyway?"

"Don't touch it don't touch it don't touch it," chanted Arni.

"What happens if she does?" said Littlefeather.

Arni abruptly stopped pacing. He tugged at his beard. After a moment, his eyes widened. "If she touches it, everyone will know."

"Who's everyone?"

Arni looked haunted. "*Everyone*," he repeated dramatically, his eyes roving around the room as if searching for lurking spirits. "Every*where*."

Se-Jong looked at Nkiru. "That doesn't sound so bad."

"Oh, it's bad." He glared at Se-Jong. "I told you not to have sex with her."

"You were a little too late, buddy," Se-Jong retorted.

Nkiru turned toward the table. She picked up the emora case. "I'm going to try it. I don't have a choice."

With an inarticulate howl, Arni rushed her. Se-Jong bounded toward him, punched him, hard. Arni staggered into the table. Several of Nkiru's priceless relics clattered to the floor.

Arni pressed his palm to his jaw where Se-Jong had punched him. Blood from a split in his lip trickled into his beard.

"Enough," roared Grandmother. The two marines rushed to break them apart.

At a strangled noise from Littlefeather, they all stopped and turned.

Nkiru had removed the emora from its case and was holding it in her bare hand.

Glitch

She raised the purple stone up to her eyes, examining it closely. Se-Jong climbed to his feet, supporting himself on the edge of the table. He couldn't control the shaking in his hands.

Nkiru licked her lips, looked toward the mechanical sphere. Inside the brass rings, the holobox had begun to glow.

Arni moaned softly. Nobody else moved.

An edgy smile appeared at the corners of Nkiru's mouth.

With a creaking, clanking shudder, the concentric rings of the damaged mechanism began to rotate around the central axis.

"What's it doing?" asked Toroni.

The two outermost coils of the device, bent and warped from ancient damage, clanged into each other with a screech. The sound of stuttering metal gears filled the room. One of the coils broke away from the machine and fell noisily to the floor. The inner rings began to spin faster, each layer turning in opposing directions.

Littlefeather gasped. She was staring up at the ceiling.

Se-Jong looked up.

From the center of the majestic holographic map, a pattern of illumination was radiating outward from the galaxy's core. A wave of incredibly tiny sparkles—thousands, millions of them—spread slowly outward like a pond ripple of microscopic embers, leaving behind only darkness at the center.

"What's happening?" asked Toroni, alarmed.

Nobody answered. The ripple continued to spread from the center of the galactic map in a silent torus of cascading light.

There had been nearly five hundred billion stars in the galaxy before the Cataclysm. Above him, in the galactic hologram, every one of the billions of missing stars were being counted. Almost as if an inventory were being taken.

An inventory of stars.

And as soon as each star flickered, it went dark.

Already the innermost half of the galaxy was a blank disk. Labeled systems vanished, one after the other. *Janrus. Fortrani. Greebus. Vulcanus. Klethyn. Rottergall.*

"No no no no no," cried Arni. He leaped toward the rotating sphere and grabbed the outermost ring, trying to stop its motion. It lifted him from the floor. He lost his grasp, fell. The ring he'd been holding slammed into one of its bent neighbors, snapped with the force of a compressed spring, and exploded outward with the crack of a whip. It struck Toroni in the wrist, smashing the scanner built into the marine's tacsuit gauntlet. Toroni grunted and dropped into a defensive position, shielding his face.

The machine was shredding itself.

Nkiru looked down in confused alarm at the hand holding the emora. It had drawn itself into a tight fist. She shook it. She didn't seem to be able to open her fingers.

Within seconds, the ring of sparkles had grown to span two-thirds of the galactic map, leaving a yawning void in the center. More systems were swept into darkness. *Raolix. Krang. Duga Resa. Arcani. Corella.*

The oddly misplaced label for Earth went dark.

Another loud report as a second overstressed metal coil broke from the sphere and fired itself into the wall like a missile. The rotating assembly had become badly unbalanced, and as the spinning coils picked up speed, the machine began violently wobbling against its iron mount. Arni threw himself against the mount in a vain attempt to steady it.

The sparkles were approaching the edge of the red disk that delineated the Devastation. A wave of uneasiness washed over Se-Jong. His eyes moved to the outer perimeter of the map, looking for a particular label he'd seen earlier.

There it was.

Grone.

"Um, guys, I don't like the looks of this," he heard himself saying.

The leading edge of the ripple approached the tiny label for Grone.

Something else broke away from the sphere. Arni staggered back. The entire room rumbled.

Nkiru gave a single, violent convulsion and toppled to the floor, still clutching the emora. He launched himself away from the table and slid to her side. Her eyes were open but rotated so that only the whites were visible. A spiderweb of red lines shot through them. The red lines grew thicker as he watched. Her body was gripped by deep, ruthless spasms.

The rumble grew louder. Things began to fall off the ancient shelves.

A dim purple light shone through Nkiru's clenched fingers. Se-Jong grabbed her wrist and shook, but the emora was buried inside her fist. He heard Littlefeather scream. One of the marines shouted something.

Se-Jong pried open her fingers, one by one, then slammed her hand against the floor. He slammed it again.

Again.

The emora rolled out of her hand and skittered away, the purple radiance gone. In the center of the room, the spinning rings of the great machine shuddered to a standstill.

The rumbling faded, replaced with curses, dust, and coughing.

Se-Jong looked up at the map. The sparkling ripple had vanished. The entire center of the galaxy was a featureless disk, extending almost to the location of Grone.

Almost.

Se-Jong closed his eyes, rolled onto his back, and gasped for air.

It took him a moment to realize that Grandmother was at his side, lifting him, cradling his shoulders.

"Sonja. Sonja!" she shouted. When he didn't reply, she barked "Kwon Se-Jong!" in her most imperious tone.

He opened his good eye. She was staring desperately, inches away. Was that the trace of a tear at the corner of her eye?

Not a chance, he decided.

"Halmeoni," he croaked.

"You appear to have cracked open *another* nest of hornets," she said.

"Yeah."

A guttural moan drew their attention toward the center of the room. Arni stood next to the wreckage of the armillary sphere, curiously studying the meter-long shard of brass coil that protruded from his chest. He crumbled to the floor next to Nkiru, who lay motionless, staring sightlessly up into the holographic ruin of the galactic map.

Lockout

Se-Jong rushed to Nkiru's side. Her eyes were crimson with burst capillaries. They didn't move, didn't register his presence. He grabbed her hand. The fingers were stiff and rigid, feverishly hot. The knuckles were starting to swell. Oh, gods, had he broken her hand when he'd slammed it into the floor?

"Nkiru?"

No response. Her chest rose and fell in a rapid panting motion.

"Nkiru!"

Her hair was plastered to her forehead, its ethereal translucence dimmed by filth. He brushed it away, terrified by the heat radiating from her skin.

Something moved next to him, and he felt hands on his shoulders. He jerked away, a numbing panic expanding in his chest.

"Nkiru!"

Not even a flicker of reaction. Clear droplets appeared on her face, his own tears raining down. If Arni were right, and by making love to her he'd unwittingly altered her blood chemistry, then all this really was his fault. He'd endangered her, endangered them *all*, and he was pretty certain that he'd endangered something even larger. *Much* larger. The galaxy hologram above their heads was clearly reflected in her vacant eyes, an empty void surrounded by a thin halo of stars.

The hands on his shoulders tightened, pulling him away. He fought back, striking out with both fists.

"Kwon!" Toroni was shouting. "Pull yourself together!"

The marine's face was earnest, urgent. Se-Jong slumped and allowed himself to be pushed to the side. He watched helplessly as Toroni examined Nkiru, his fingers prodding her body.

"No visible injuries," said Toroni. "She's nonresponsive, though. Stiff as a plank. That thing gave her a nasty shock." He glanced at the emora on the floor a couple of meters away, still the pale amethyst color it had turned when Nkiru had offered it her blood.

On the floor nearby, McCloud had wrenched Arni's robes open to reveal gaunt ribs, a sunken stomach, and a sea of smeared blood. Se-Jong looked away, reminded of the wound triage sims he'd hated back at Jackill. He'd never had the stomach for blood. And there was a *lot* of blood. Real blood, from a real man.

"Oh, gods," said Littlefeather.

A brutal gash extended across the bottom of Arni's rib cage, where the broken coil had entered his body. Deeply embedded, the shard of brass was as long as Arni's arm and stuck out from his abdomen in a dramatic curve. The wound bubbled and gushed with every shallow breath.

Se-Jong forced himself to watch as McCloud pulled his emergency kit from his pack, retrieved a cylinder of triage glue, and waved it over the wound. A foam spray covered the bubbling mess and began to harden. Hands steady, he selected a pharmaneedle from the kit and injected something into Arni's sternum above the protruding brass spear.

Arni convulsed in a series of wracking coughs. Thick clots of blood sprayed into the air, and his eyes flew open, full of wild terror. "Can't . . . breathe," he gasped. More blood ran from his mouth into his beard. Toroni and McCloud exchanged grim looks.

Littlefeather knelt next to McCloud at Arni's side. Arni gulped for air. "Help me sit up."

She sat on the floor and propped Arni's head in the crook of her shoulder. This seemed to ease his labored breathing. He flinched and shuddered as he examined the brass shard embedded in his rib cage. Se-Jong wondered if they should try to pull it out, then realized removing the shard would probably only make matters worse.

Arni looked at Nkiru's still form, noticed Se-Jong was clutching her hand. "She shouldn't have touched the emora," he wheezed. "I told her. You heard me. She did it anyway."

Littlefeather stroked his arm reassuringly, as if comforting a child. She kept her voice neutral. "What happened when she touched it?"

"I made the emoras, you know. I coded their security countermeasures. She just triggered them."

Toroni scoffed. Littlefeather gave him a sharp glare. She turned back to Arni. "What does that mean? What happened to her?"

"The emora didn't recognize her as a valid user. When she tried to access its encryption key, it triggered a lockout. It lasts thirty minutes, meatspace time. Thirty minutes . . . that's seven *years*. Until then, none of us can touch it."

Meatspace time?

"What happens if we touch it?" Toroni asked.

"If anybody touches that emora while it's in lockout mode, it'll erase this entire planet."

Toroni rolled his eyes, but his mocking expression vanished when he turned to Grandmother and saw her serious intensity.

"So now what?" Littlefeather prompted.

"Seven years." Arni whispered, tried to catch his breath. "Actually . . . it'll probably . . . *never* work. The emora is ruined. It's his fault." He pointed at Se-Jong.

"Fuck you," said Se-Jong.

Arni's response was lost in a fit of coughing. Littlefeather held him tightly until the coughs subsided. He dragged his sleeve across his bloody mouth.

"Shit. I hate this part."

"What part?"

"The dying part."

"You're not going to die," said Littlefeather. "We're all getting out of here."

In response he spat up a terrifying amount of bright-red blood. He threw off Littlefeather's enfolding arm, began fumbling for something deep in the tattered remains of his robe. He coughed again, waved urgently for Se-Jong's attention.

Se-Jong leaned close. Arni pressed something hard-edged and sticky into his palm. It was a memory card from a komnic, covered in blood.

"What is this?"

More coughing. Arni's breath stank of copper. "Algethi."

The word meant nothing. "Algethi?"

Arni nodded fiercely. "Give the chip to Gaia if she survives."

"Who?"

Arni pointed to Nkiru. "Her! Give it to *her!*"

Another spate of violent coughs, each weaker than the last, until they became a series of watery gasps. "Tell her to find me . . . on Earth. Manhattan." He pulled Se-Jong close, his eyes haunted. "Tell her *not* to look for Analise, and pray that Analise doesn't find me first."

"Analise?" Se-Jong glanced questioningly at Littlefeather, but the reliquist was focused entirely on Arni.

Arni blinked several times. His lips moved. The fact that no words came out seemed to make him panic. He tried again, gulping air between each word, eyes clenched shut. "I had a child here, once, you know. If your baby . . . is born . . ." his voice drained into silence, and he slumped into Littlefeather's shoulder.

A thrill of fear stabbed Se-Jong's heart. He shook Arni. When there was no response, he shouted, "Arni! What if my baby is born?"

Arni's eyes flickered but didn't open. "Don't let her find it. If she does, there's no hope at all."

Se-Jong recoiled. "Don't let *who* find it? Arni? What are you talking about?"

Arni's mouth gaped open. He let out a watery sigh. They waited, but the breath was his last.

Littlefeather shot Se-Jong a look of astonishment. Nobody spoke. Everyone's eyes turned to the emora. Covered in dust, no bigger than a fat purple grape, it was an innocuous piece of glass, a colorful stone, far too small and mundane to be something so consequential.

Another broken coil fell from the brass machine and clattered loudly to the floor, causing everyone to jump.

"We're done here," announced Grandmother. She nodded toward Arni's body. "Search him. Canvas this entire room and bag up anything that looks like a relic. The Dei Militans will find this place, and we need to be elsewhere when they do. Get moving."

Flight

Toroni unfolded a field litter and placed it on the floor next to Nkiru, carefully avoiding the emora, which lay nearby. Littlefeather put her hand on Se-Jong's arm.

"You need to let her go."

Nkiru's chest was moving, but each gasping breath was forced, as if she were fighting against the contracting muscles of her chest wall. Her eyes were red, unblinking, and empty. He released her hand and backed away.

Toroni moved close, reached toward her face, used his fingertips to gently close her eyelids as if she were a corpse. He and McCloud lifted her into the webbing of the field litter. In their rough hands

Nkiru seemed infinitely fragile, a crystalline figurine that was already cracked and on the verge of shattering completely. Toroni wrapped her in the webbing, securing her for transit.

Next, they lifted Arni to the table. Toroni placed a small device on his forehead. When it beeped, he turned to Grandmother and confirmed what they already knew. "He's dead."

Se-Jong stayed at Nkiru's side as the others scurried about in preparation for a hasty departure. Toroni and McCloud swept through the debris in the cabinets and shelves, bagging anything that might be an avatar relic. Grandmother circled the room, using her komnic to record every detail.

Littlefeather located a pair of long metal tongs, which she used with utmost care to scoop up the emora and put it back into its wooden box. She returned it to Nkiru's backpack along with the other relics. With trembling hands, she slung the backpack over one shoulder, the gobsmacker over the other. This entire affair was a reliquist's dream, Se-Jong realized. It would make her famous. Assuming, of course, that they made it out of the dungeon without being killed, and that afterward she wasn't excommunicated and imprisoned for her role in defying the Dei Militans.

"Ready, Captain," reported Toroni. "We found a few things. Don't know what they are." He patted a bulging sack under his arm. "It might all be garbage."

Grandmother turned to Se-Jong. "Can you walk?"

He nodded. "Where are we going?"

"Back the way we came."

"What about the militans?"

"We'll avoid them."

"How?"

She looked anything but certain. "We'll find a way."

They left Arni's body on the table, wrapped tightly in the thin metal foil of McCloud's emergency blanket. Surprisingly, it had been McCloud who had insisted on performing an abbreviated version of the Cataclyst death rites. The young private had rushed through the litany, made the required Gestures over the body, and taken a hair clipping, which he placed in a clear packet and handed to Littlefeather. "So he can rest in a proper Cataclyst crypt," he told her earnestly.

Grandmother designated Littlefeather as best qualified to guide their escape back through the dungeon. The reliquist led them into the corridor, her dimmed headlamp lingering for a long, morbid moment on the mummified corpses outside the vault door. The marines carrying Nkiru's litter followed. Se-Jong stayed by Nkiru, leaning on Grandmother for support, listening for any changes in the rhythm of Nkiru's labored breathing. His fist was pressed deeply into the pocket of his coldsuit, Arni's blood-soaked komnic card clutched tightly in his fingers. He couldn't get the whispering voice out of his head: *If your baby is born . . . don't let her find it.*

They hurried down the corridor to the rough-hewn tunnel entrance from which they'd come, pausing briefly to give Se-Jong a chance to catch his breath. The throbbing in his head had reached epic proportions, and his right eye was showing signs of sympathy swelling with his left. He tried to apologize to the others, but their anxious expressions drove him back to his feet after only a few seconds of rest.

Littlefeather glanced at the route trace on her komnic, then peered nervously into the tunnel.

"Go on," prompted Grandmother.

The reliquist raised a fist of caution. "I hear something."

The marines placed Nkiru's litter on the floor and unlimbered their rifles.

"Someone's coming," Littlefeather whispered. "The militans."

Grandmother muttered a curse and scanned their surroundings. The corridor they'd been following continued past the tunnel entrance, vanishing into the darkness outside the range of Littlefeather's headlamp. "That way. Hurry."

Littlefeather grimaced but didn't question Grandmother's orders. Their party was outnumbered by the militans and hobbled with two seriously injured members. Their only choice was to flee into the unexplored depths of the ancient dungeon and hope that some means of escape would present itself.

GAMECHANGER

meatspace | RUPE

Resynchronization

Four beds. Four still figures. Four souls, trapped in a malfunctioning video game in which time was speeding so recklessly that for every hour in the real world, their capatars experienced almost fifteen *years*. Analise, Wolfe, Arni, and Fiona were true pioneers, the first humans to ever leave the shells of their physical bodies to explore an entirely new world beyond time and space.

Rupe bit his lip. The four of them were victims of the world that he'd designed, a world that he'd filled with deadly traps and vicious evil, a world created to exploit the craven desires of a society bored by its own tedious existence. Four souls. Three jaded warriors, and one innocent teen sent into harm's way to repair the damage the warriors had caused.

He glanced up at the wall clock. Fiona had been inside the havencosm for almost fifteen minutes. That left three hours and forty-five minutes before Solomon's goons would blow up the QARMA engines. Given the timestream discontinuity, Gaia had about fifty more years to lower the firewall. Surely, plenty of time.

A thought struck him. Inside the havencosm, nearly three and a half years had already elapsed for Fiona's capatar. She'd already celebrated her eighteenth birthday, and her capatar would have a new birthday every four minutes and eighteen seconds. *Even if she doesn't succeed in her mission and Solomon destroys the QARMA engines, she'll end up living to almost the age of 70 in the havencosm.* A full life. For some reason, this realization made Rupe very happy.

Francis was by Fiona's side, watching her chest rise and fall. Mrs. Martinez stroked her daughter's open palm gently with her thumb. She seemed to be reciting a prayer beneath her breath. Rupe suddenly wished he knew a prayer.

The technicians moved around them like a blur, their soft conversations nothing but dim background noise. Rupe stood at the foot of Fiona's bed, watching as Dr. Lieberman checked yet another reading on the ESP scanner. Lieberman scowled and made a note on his tablet.

Fiona's spawning had been accompanied by the worst wave of the Tingles yet, and they'd had to remove and sedate one of the medical techs who'd succumbed to the awful sensations. Painkillers seemed to help a bit, but it wouldn't be long before the creepy-crawlies got so bad that none of them could function. He knew that if the Tingles got that bad, Solomon would destroy the QARMA engines before the deadline.

His mind was racing, despairing. There was so much he should have told Fiona about the challenges she would encounter. There simply hadn't been time. He'd neglected to mention that she could nullify the entire microflak minefield by shorting out its controller with water from the lake. He hadn't told her about the disorienting effect of the boss monster, how getting too close could disable her eyesight and cause uncontrollable spasms. He'd forgotten about the secret back door to the boss chamber, and the hidden elevator from the citadel to the death cavern. So many things he had forgotten. But really, she'd be okay, he told himself. She'd seen the TV episode on which the dungeon was based probably a dozen times. She knew Rupe's signature tricks. She'd be okay.

She had to be.

He felt useless. The lab was full of experts deeply engaged in complex tasks. A trio of JEEB techs circulated among the equipment racks. A handful of uniformed military staff sat in low cubicles, occupied by their workstations. Medical techs in blue scrubs kept careful watch over the four comatose subjects. No one spoke. The rhythmic pulsing of the medical equipment and the cooling fans in the computer racks provided a lulling background to the furious keyboard clacking coming from Zia's cubicle.

The floor rumbled, and everyone paused, waiting for the tremor to subside. They were coming once every two or three minutes now. His hands shook. He tried to ignore the urge to scratch every inch of his skin. He wove his fingers together. The Tingles were irrelevant. The only thing that mattered was happening right in front of him.

Francis and his mother clutched each other in the background as a nurse fussed over Fiona. Dr. Lieberman muttered something, frowning at the ESP scanner, rubbing his chin. He watched closely as the nurse checked and rechecked the forest of wires and tubes that connected Fiona to a half dozen medical monitors. Chun was across the room, huddled over the Haven engine. She'd opened the machine's case, which Rupe hadn't known was possible, and was tinkering with something inside with the delicate intensity of a neurosurgeon probing a human brain. Solomon stood watchfully at her side, his anxiety and mistrust obvious. He seemed poised to tackle her at any moment, shove her away from the machine.

Despite the silence, despite the seeming calm, Rupe was very aware that the two smartest people in a building full of geniuses, Chun and Lieberman, were both freaking out. Lieberman had begun actively punching the touchscreen of Fiona's ESP scanner, disturbed at whatever he was seeing. Across the room, Chun was mumbling loudly about runaway entropic states and engorged Planck values, whatever that meant. The floor rumbled again, as if the planet itself was reminding them of their folly.

He felt an incapacitating surge of guilt. He'd built Grone with the sole intent of stumping Fiona Martinez, a fifteen-year-old girl with the highest PPA score in the history of the game. If she failed and the world ended, it would be his fault.

Fiona's eyelids were sunken and unmoving, her cheeks flooded with color. She was wrapped tightly in blankets, only a sliver of her face visible between the bulge of the BCI cap and the rim of her ventilator mask. Rupe couldn't stop staring at her wounds. Such strength. Such awful beauty. An astounding girl like no other, forged in fire.

He felt a tiny, white-hot spark of hope. If anyone could see beyond his traps and mazes and puzzles, it would be Fiona. It might take time, but she had all the time she needed. A whole lifetime.

Her eyes darted rapidly beneath her eyelids, and every so often she made a tiny, almost imperceptible wince. He leaned over the bed, placed his palm on her exposed wrist. Through the medical tape, her skin was warm, and he could distinctly feel the living throb of her pulse. He leaned close and whispered so only she could hear.

"Go, Gaia, go."

Ten minutes passed. Fifteen. Rupe's heart sank deeper into despair with every second that elapsed on the wall clock. He wasn't good at math, but she'd already spent an hour in the havencosm, so assuming Fiona's capatar was still alive, she would be almost twenty-two years old.

He glanced down at Francis. The boy's eyes were red. He looked fifty, not fifteen. His breathing was irregular and made a dry, rasping sound.

"I need some fresh air," Rupe announced to nobody in particular. "Come with me," he said to Francis. "We won't take long."

Francis didn't look up, but he nodded.

The air outside wasn't fresh. It was heavy with the smoke of the burning city. The impossibly twisted shape of the bugaboo glared at them through a smoldering orange pall. Francis stood quietly, staring up at the apparition, hands pushed deeply into the pockets of his jeans.

"Is the world going to end tonight?" he asked quietly.

"I don't know. I hope not."

Francis continued to stare into the orange sky. "I wish I was with Fiona."

"Me too," Rupe said. "This world sucks."

"Yeah."

A military Humvee rumbled by the front of the building. The driver looked scared. Rupe put his hand on Francis's shoulder. The boy was trembling.

"I'm sorry I got you and Fiona into this. It's my fault."

Francis was silent for a moment. When he spoke, his voice was hollow. "She was a different person, you know, before the accident." Rupe looked down at him, but Francis kept staring at the bugaboo. "Dad called her his apple blossom. She was always his favorite. It made me jealous."

The boy lapsed into silence. "You're a good brother," Rupe said. "Your sister loves you more than anything."

"That's the thing. She shouldn't love me. She should hate me."

Rupe was taken aback by the venom in his tone. He let his hand fall away from the boy's shoulder. "That's a stupid thing to say."

Francis pulled his sleeve across his cheeks. "I could've saved her, you know. I tried, but when the car caught fire, I got scared. All I had to do was unfasten her safety belt. Just click the little red button. Instead, I panicked."

Rupe felt his own tears drip into his beard, but when he glanced down, he saw that Francis's face was dry, solemn. "It's not fair what happened to you or your sister or your dad," he said. "No kid should go through something like that. As far as I'm concerned, both of you are superheroes."

They returned to the building past the nervous guards. Rupe knew something was wrong the instant they pushed through the lab's double doors. Lieberman, Solomon, and Zia were clustered around Fiona's bedside, surrounded by a cadre of anxious medical techs. The normal hisses and droning beeps of the machines had been replaced by the shrill dissonance of multiple overlapping alarms.

Solomon saw them coming. He waved Rupe away. "We put the mother in the conference room. Take the boy to her and get back here."

"What's wrong?"

"Take the boy to the conference room!"

"No way," muttered Francis. He moved to the foot of Fiona's bed.

Solomon grimaced but was distracted when a medical tech gestured frantically at Lieberman. Lieberman shouldered the tech aside and studied the display on the bedside ESP scanner. He typed furiously on the keyboard, his keystrokes powerful enough to cause the entire machine to shudder, pausing occasionally to read the information on the screen.

"What's happening?" Rupe whispered to Zia.

"A bunch of her alarms went off, all at once."

Lieberman had begun tracing each of the wires and tubes that connected Fiona to the life-support equipment, his fingers sliding down each line to its connection point on her body. He scowled, turned back to the ESP scanner, and resumed pounding the keyboard.

Francis's voice was shaking. "Is she okay?"

"Mmm," Lieberman mumbled. "Just checking some things." He stared at the screen for a moment, then turned to the tech. "Go get Chun. Hurry."

Fright flared in Rupe's chest. "What's the matter?"

Lieberman didn't turn away from the machine's display. "Some changes. Probably nothing to worry about."

Rupe glanced at Francis, saw the panic in the boy's eyes. "What kind of changes?"

Lieberman turned his attention away from the ESP scanner to a digital tablet mounted on a stand next to Fiona. He pulled the tablet off the stand and studied its screen, a colorful display of dense graphical squares, like the world's largest, most complicated crossword puzzle. His voice was distracted. "You should all go wait in the conference room until we get this sorted out."

Francis glared at Lieberman. "I'm not going anywhere."

The tech arrived with Chun in tow. Lieberman pointed at the tablet's screen, handed it to her. She peered through her glasses. "What am I looking at?"

Lieberman tapped the screen. "Take a look at the phenotype markers, there and there. And see the Miescher array? There's been a whole series of exogenous nucleotide insertions."

Chun's brow furrowed and she unconsciously clacked her teeth. "I take it these aren't part of the DNA edits you made?"

Lieberman shook his head. "No, no. My edits were in a different locus entirely. You can see them, there. This is something different. It's not a somatic mutation. It's affecting the operational segments of her germline." He studied Chun's reaction to make sure she recognized the significance of his revelation. Rupe didn't understand a word of it, but Chun's expression caused his gut to twist into a knot. Lieberman's next words crackled with electrified apprehension. "I don't think this is something we caused. This just started . . . look, my god; it's changing as we speak!"

Chun adjusted her glasses. "I don't understand. You haven't seen this in the other capatars?"

"No, never. It's almost like . . ." He winced, then pounded his forehead with ball of his palm. "God, I can't think straight with these fucking Tingles!"

"Steady, Dr. Lieberman," said Solomon. "Take a moment if you need."

Lieberman shook his head, pointed at the tablet's screen. "Look at the base-pair architecture of the new sequence. Just *look* at it . . . those are the frameworks that Analise and I designed for the gamebot templates!"

"That's absurd," said Chun. "How can that be?"

Lieberman didn't answer. The color drained from his face. He spun to one of the nurses. "Where are her blood chemistry readings?"

The nurse held out a sheet of paper covered with dense columns of text.

Rupe took a deep breath and put his hand on Francis's shoulder. "She'll be okay. Don't worry."

Lieberman yanked the sheet of paper from the nurse's hand. He studied the printout, mumbling something rapidly beneath his breath. Solomon and Chun, both haggard and bleary, looked on as he gestured toward the rows of figures printed on the paper. He said something to Solomon in a low voice. Chun scoffed sharply. Rupe moved closer to hear the whispered argument. ". . . completely atypical, which probably means it's an error in the data."

"How can it be an error? It's right there on the page. Use your eyes, Dr. Chun."

Solomon rubbed his face. "Tell me again, the third-grade version, please."

Lieberman's voice resonated with the troubled excitement of a scientist confronted by impossible experimental results. He pointed at the screen of his tablet. "Look here, and here. See the repeating sequences? These are gene segments from the genetic template we designed for the game's non-player characters. They're tagged and coded into every bot's genes so specific instructions can be triggered by the game's event handlers."

"Why are you showing me this?"

"Colonel, this is *Fiona's* DNA. It's like a gamebot's virtual DNA is being spliced into her real-world genes."

Solomon stopped rubbing his face. He looked up sharply. "A *gamebot's* DNA?"

Lieberman nodded, unable to keep the amazement out of his voice. Rupe suddenly realized that to Lieberman, Fiona wasn't a person, but simply a misbehaving experiment.

Lieberman nodded. "The bots in the game are based on genetic templates I helped Analise design. They're virtual copies of human DNA, with modifications so that they can interface with the game's QARMA kernel and the underlying operating system. What we're seeing in Fiona are some of those artificial gene segments replacing her native genes."

"How can that be?"

"I have *no* idea." Lieberman's chest was so tight that his words were breathless. He looked down at Fiona, then reached out hesitantly and placed his hand, palm down, gently on her belly. He studied her face, then the BCI cap that enclosed her head, then the wires that connected it to the ESP scanner. His eyes continued up the thick cable that rose from the scanner and ran through a conduit to the ceiling and across the room, then descended to the table at the base of the equipment racks. Everyone else followed his gaze to the terminus of the cable.

On the table, the Haven engine stared back at them. As they watched, the lights across its face slowly shifted from blue to a pure, crystalline purple. Rupe cleared his throat. "Um . . . Dr. Chun, is it a good thing or a bad thing when the little lights change color?" Chun didn't answer. She was staring at the machine in astonishment.

An unfamiliar *ping-a-ling*, and Francis stiffened. It repeated: *ping-a-ling*. Rupe watched the color drain completely out of the boy's face. Francis pulled his phone out of his jeans pocket. He held it delicately, fingertips only, as if it might shatter at the slightest pressure. He studied the device, made a tentative swiping motion across the screen. When he raised his eyes to meet Rupe's, they blazed with astonishment.

"What is it?"

Francis turned the phone so that Rupe could see the screen. Rupe leaned close, surprised that the cellular data service was still working after the quakes.

The scene in the photo was instantly familiar. A vast, circular lake. A central island peak. Glaciers and forests. Thunderclouds in the distance. Even though he knew every intimate detail, it took him a minute to realize what he was seeing.

Grone. The Citadel of Jaspaar.

From the center of the photo beamed two smiling faces, selfie-style, cheek to cheek. A serious-looking young man with dark eyes, straight black hair, and a broad face. An athletic young woman with a bizarre gray skin color and silver hair pulled tightly into a ponytail that draped over her shoulder. From their easy expressions, the connection between the pair was obvious: they were lovers. He didn't recognize her male companion, but there was something eerily familiar about the woman's smile.

He looked up at Francis. "You just got this?"

The boy's eyes were haunted. "It just posted to Fiona's Instagram account."

Without warning, the four comatose figures on the beds spasmed. Fiona's back arched away from the mattress as she convulsed. Arni and Analise both cried out, and Wolfe twisted so violently that his bedcovers were thrown to the side, revealing his thin, pasty limbs. Everyone recoiled away from the animated bodies. At the same time, a resounding boom thundered through the earth beneath the building, and everyone grabbed for something to hold as the floor moved like an ocean wave.

Rupe grabbed Fiona's bedrail, steeling himself for the surge of Tingles that always came after a tremor. The lights flickered; the tremor faded. The bodies of the four capatars suddenly fell back into stillness.

Silence, and the rapid breathing of the room's occupants. The drone of the computer racks, the rhythms of the medical equipment. Whatever had happened, it had only lasted for a split second. Rupe's heart pounded as he waited for something else. As the moments ticked by without further incident, there was a mass release of held breaths. The attendants, technicians, and nurses moved to the four beds, replacing the disturbed covers and checking the displays of the medical monitors.

Something had changed. Something fundamental, significant. It took Rupe a few breathless seconds to realize what it was.

The Tingles were gone. The awful creepy-crawly sensation that had plagued his days and kept him awake at night for the past four weeks was gone. He gasped air into his lungs.

"You feel that?" he said.

Zia nodded frantically. Her face held relief, like that of everyone in the room.

"What just happened?" Solomon said. When there was no answer, he shouted across the room. "Check the firewall!"

Rupe held his breath. The tech took an eternity to answer.

"The firewall is still holding, Colonel. No change."

Rupe looked at Francis. The boy's eyes were darting between Fiona and the photo he'd just received on his phone, and he was whispering beneath his breath. His love for her was obvious and fierce. He believed in her with all his heart. Rupe suddenly realized that he felt the same.

He grabbed Francis's hand, phone and all, and studied the photo on the phone's screen with a new intensity. The woman in the picture Francis had just received—her eyes, her facial structure, her intense expression—despite her gray skin, silver hair, and pale eyes, it was Fiona. There were no traces of her awful meatspace injuries, but it was definitely her.

No, it's her capatar, he corrected himself. It was Gaia, smiling triumphantly.

"She made it," he whispered. Still grasping Francis by the wrist, he thrust the boy's hand into the air like he was announcing the winner of a prizefighting match. He gestured toward the phone and shouted into the room, "Look at this! She made it! Gaia made it to Grone!"

Startled, Solomon gestured for the phone. Francis held it up so he could see the screen. The colonel examined the photo, turned to look down at Fiona's still form. A confused recognition spread across his face. Chun peered over his shoulder, as did Lieberman. Zia pressed into the group, demanding that Francis lower the phone so she could see the screen.

"Christ," muttered Chun.

"She's older," Zia said. "Early twenties. Capatars *do* age."

Lieberman made a self-satisfied nod. "See her skin and hair? Those are side effects of the epigene treatments. I told you it would affect her capatar's pigmentation."

"Who's the guy?" said Zia. "That's not Arni or Wolfe with her. Anybody recognize him?"

Nobody had an answer. The colonel looked at Francis, incredulous. "This just came through on your phone?" Francis nodded. Solomon turned to Rupe. "How is this possible?"

Rupe could barely speak through his excitement. "I told her to look for an Orb, like the one Wolfe used to send us the video. Remember, the Orbs were designed so an avatar could post to social media from inside the game. She must have found one, then somehow figured out how to use it to access a social media account. It's fucking genius."

"Uh, Colonel, sir?" It was the technician again, calling loudly from his workstation across the lab. He sounded puzzled and was squinting and frowning at something on his computer monitor. "The firewall is still up, but there's something else. Maybe you should all look at this."

They hurried from Fiona's bedside to stand behind the tech's chair. He cleared his throat, pointed at something on his screen. "It just happened, when the subjects spasmed. See these two markers? They were erratic before; now they're parallel and perfectly flat."

"They measure the Salim-Kaiser entropy inside the QARMA environment," said Chun. She stared at the screen, her lips moving silently as she worked through the implications. Suddenly, she grabbed the back of the tech's rolling office chair and pulled him away from his desk. He cursed, but she ignored him. She grabbed his mouse and began clicking rapidly. Rupe watched with dreadful fascination.

Chun's index finger stabbed at a new image on the screen. "There! Look at the timestream differential."

To Rupe, it was gibberish. Solomon knit his brow. Lieberman also seemed confused, but Zia's tense expression melted into incredulity. "The Zakai signal durations are inflated, but the time-frequency waveforms are . . . they're . . . *identical*."

Chun nodded. Her voice held an odd mix of disbelief and hope. "The firewall is still up, and the kernel clock speed is still a bit unstable, but for now, the time discontinuity is gone. Whatever the girl did, it seems to have resynchronized the timestream. The havencosm is once again running in real time. A minute here is a minute inside the machine."

All of them turned to look at Fiona. Francis blinked, then blinked again.

The silent room erupted into an explosion of cheers and clapping. Rupe put his hand on Francis's shoulder and squeezed. The boy looked stunned.

The doors to the lab burst open. A soldier entered, gestured to Solomon. "Sir, you'd better come see this."

Bugaboo

Rupe, Francis, Zia, and Chun followed Solomon as he sprinted outside the building, close on the heels of the soldier. The pall of smoke had grown thicker, and the soldiers guarding the entrance looked even more nervous than before. The soldier pointed up into the hazy sky.

"Good Christ," said Chun.

The bugaboo had changed. It had grown in size, or perhaps moved closer to the Earth. Rupe wasn't sure which possibility was more frightening. The brain-twisting convolutions of its surface were more energetic than before. Its color had shifted to a deep amethyst, and the increased violence of its writhing swirls gave it a newfound malevolence. Before, it had seemed to Rupe to be a baleful, godlike eye staring down from the heavens. Now it was pulsing in a regular rhythm, like something was battering at the other side of reality, trying to break through.

Without looking away from the apparition, Zia addressed Chun. "I thought you said the bugaboo was caused by the differential in the timestreams. That it would go away when the timestreams were resynchronized."

Chun's voice was steady. "I said it *might* be caused by the discontinuity. I *hoped* it was caused by the discontinuity."

"Apparently not," accused Zia. "It's *bigger*. And *closer*."

"And *scarier*," whispered Francis. The boy glanced down at his phone, where the photo of Gaia and the dark-haired boy was still shining from the screen.

"Why didn't the firewall come down?" said Zia to Chun. "You said it was triggered by the time discontinuity."

"Christ, how should I know what the girl's capatar did inside? If she did what we told her to do, the firewall *would* be down. She must've done something wrong."

"She did something *right*," Francis retorted. "The Tingles have stopped, haven't they? The earthquakes, too, in case you haven't noticed."

Francis was right. Rupe hadn't felt a tremor since the one that had accompanied the capatar's spasms.

Chun glared up at the bugaboo. "Whatever the girl did, something is still wrong with the Foundation Core on the Haven engine. Even though she managed to resync the timestreams, the firewall won't drop until we fix the Core."

Something tickled Rupe at the back of his thoughts. He closed his eyes, blocking out the bugaboo and the arguments of the others, and let the tickling sensation move closer to the center of his attention. It approached his awareness like an arrow in flight, straight and unwavering, and he knew it was important. Not just an idea, nor a simple revelation, but a full-blown epiphany. He waited for it to arrive, and when it struck the target, it was a bull's-eye.

"Hey," he said to the others. When no one listened, he shouted, "Hey!"

The argument between Chun and Zia stopped, and they looked at him angrily. Solomon raised an eyebrow.

The words poured out in a stumbling stutter. "Okay, so like, Wolfe used an Orb to send us a video message, right? But the timestreams were running at different speeds, so we couldn't reply, right? And just now, Francis got a message from Gaia on his phone, right? Just as the capatars spasmed and we felt the earthquake and the timestreams resynchronized, right?"

They were all watching him impatiently. He continued. "Don't you get it? The only place Gaia could have resynchronized the timestreams was in Atum's Lair on Grone, right? She must have just delivered the software patch to the kernel node."

He glared at the blank faces of the others. "Come on, you guys! The photo was taken on Grone. Francis got the photo an instant before the resync. That was what, about five minutes ago? You know what that means, right?"

Nothing but more confused stares. He felt himself smile. He'd stumped the geniuses. "Time on Grone is running at the same speed as here. It means that if Gaia was in Atum's Lair five minutes ago, *she's probably still there!*"

Chun's eyes narrowed. Zia smiled. Solomon hardened his jaw. Nevertheless, Rupe knew that none of them had yet grasped the implications of his epiphany. He pointed to Francis and the phone clutched in the boy's hand. "The timestreams are synced. We have a working link through the firewall to Gaia's Orb using Francis's phone. Don't you get it? We can *call* Gaia."

havencosm | CONTACT

Shaft

The corridor sloped downward. Se-Jong got the sense that they were heading toward the mountain's core, exactly the wrong direction for an exit leading to the outside. Toroni and McCloud struggled beneath the weight of Nkiru's litter. Littlefeather's flashlight was in constant motion as she scanned the dark walls of the passageway. She whispered to Toroni whenever they passed an adjacent corridor or an entrance into one of the mine tunnels, seeking his advice on their route. Only Grandmother, who hurried next to Se-Jong with a firm hand on his waist, seemed as calm as ever, though her eyes never left Nkiru.

Nkiru was still alive. Her chest rose and fell beneath the tight webbing that secured her to the litter. Her cheek was still hot with fever. Whatever shock she'd received when she'd activated the emora relic was still coursing through her system.

There'd been no other sign of the Dei Militans since they'd fled from the disaster in Atum's Lair, but they all knew that their pursuers couldn't be far behind. The proximity scanner on Toroni's wrist had been damaged so they couldn't know for sure, but the militans had thus far shown an uncanny ability to track them through the mazes of this awful place.

They came to a major junction with another corridor. Littlefeather brightened her headlamp to illuminate her options and, after a whispered discussion with Toroni, chose to turn left into an identical corridor that seemed to lead them nowhere.

The burst of adrenaline that had been holding back Se-Jong's exhaustion was wearing off. The pain and nausea from his swollen face was vengeful. He leaned into Grandmother's shoulder to keep from stumbling.

She tightened her grip on his waist. Her voice was low, troubled. "Did you understand what the crazy man was saying to you before he died?"

"Not really," he said.

"He called the girl Gaia. Is that her name?"

"I don't think so. Maybe he was delirious."

"What is Algethi?"

"No idea."

"Who is Analise?"

"Don't know. Nkiru never mentioned anybody named Analise."

They hurried for a few steps in silence.

"He gave you something. What was it?"

Se-Jong tightened his grip on the object in his pocket. "A memory chip from a komnic."

"Any idea what it contains?"

"He said something that sounded like 'Algethi.' Do you recognize it?"

"No."

"He told me to give the chip to Nkiru."

"I'll want a peek at it first," she said. "He whispered something else to you at the end. What did he say?"

Se-Jong shuddered, remembering Arni's gasping whisper: *If your baby is born . . . don't let her find it.*

"I . . . uh, I couldn't understand him."

They were discovered less than a minute later, when the corridor ended at a T-junction. Littlefeather peeked left, then right, then risked another bright beam from her headlamp.

A commanding shout sounded from behind them.

"Stop! Stop or we'll shoot!"

Toroni spun toward the voice, rifle ready.

"Go, go," hissed Grandmother. "They won't fire. They won't risk hitting Anaya."

Littlefeather ducked into the left-hand corridor. The others rushed behind her. She and McCloud lowered Nkiru to the floor. Toroni gestured to McCloud, who took position at the junction corner.

"Slow 'em down," ordered Toroni.

McCloud nodded, his eyes clear and determined. He aimed into the darkness and loosed a laser bolt back down the tunnel toward their pursuers. Se-Jong winced at the flash.

Toroni motioned down the corridor. "Get going. We'll stay here and hold them off."

Grandmother shook her head, gesturing at Nkiru's heavy litter. Toroni grimaced. Some kind of silent agreement passed between them. Toroni looked down at his younger subordinate. He took a deep breath, started to kneel next to McCloud, but Grandmother stopped him.

She knelt instead. She put her hand on the younger marine's back. "Private McCloud, do you understand what's at stake here?"

"Aye, sir. The girl is an avatar."

Grandmother nodded. "We need Sergeant Toroni to help us carry her litter, and to protect her. That means I need *you* to stay here and hold this position as long as you can. Cover our retreat. Do you understand?"

McCloud tensed, his shoulders stiffening. The seriousness of their situation hit Se-Jong like never before, not even at the death of Arni. The ethics of ordering a subordinate to sacrifice themself in combat had been a frequent topic at the Jackill Academy, but in the confines of a classroom it had been nothing more than an abstract concept, a game. Here it was *real*. McCloud was younger than Se-Jong. The top entry in his komnic contacts was probably his mother. Se-Jong exchanged a glance with Littlefeather, who seemed equally aghast.

McCloud looked to Toroni as if for confirmation of his captain's orders. Toroni nodded solemnly. "Do not let them get past you, marine. If we make it out, I'll personally lead a rescue team back for you. Understood?"

McCloud took a deep breath. "Aye, aye." With a quick motion he closed the faceplate of his tacsuit helmet and sighted back down the corridor with his rifle. The rigid lines of his posture made it clear that he no longer wanted to discuss the matter.

Grandmother's face was clouded, her expression darker than Se-Jong had ever seen. He knew her thoughts from the anguished lines of her face: *It would be better for the avatar girl to die, for all of us to die, than to let her fall into the hands of the church.*

Damn, damn, damn, cursed Se-Jong silently.

They hurried away. He looked back when another flash lit the corridor. The distant figure of McCloud was on one knee, aiming carefully around the corner. Another flash. So far, the militans hadn't returned fire.

Toroni directed Littlefeather to take McCloud's place carrying Nkiru's litter, but when she struggled with the weight, Grandmother relieved her. Littlefeather offered to assist Se-Jong, but he waved her off. Everyone was exhausted; his bashed-up face and queasy stomach didn't qualify him for special treatment.

Besides, the reliquist was carrying Nkiru's heavy avatar devices, including the ridiculous avatar gun.

If only they could wake Nkiru, everything would change. She could use the scancorder to locate their pursuers. She could use the gobsmacker to 'even the odds' against the militans. She was still burning with fever and breathing in staccato gasps. He prayed that she wasn't dying from whatever awful shock the emora had given her.

He pulled out his komnic and squinted at the time. The swelling around his right eye was becoming almost as bad as his left. If it continued, he'd soon be blind.

Unbelievably, it was only early afternoon, local Grone time. They'd been inside the mountain for less than four hours.

The sound of a far-off explosion echoed from the darkness behind them. "Grenade," said Toroni, his voice bitter. He motioned for the party to stop. They waited, listening, but the steady rhythm of McCloud's laser fire had stopped.

They weren't going to make it, Se-Jong suddenly realized. All this effort, all this pain, for nothing. They were lost in an avatar dungeon. Nkiru might never wake.

—

The passageway ended at a set of elevator doors that had been torn from their tracks, exposing the shaft within. There was no elevator car, just a precipitous circular shaft three meters across that extended vertically up and down for as far as Littlefeather's headlamp could reach. Another door lay across the shaft, also jammed open, beyond which the passageway seemed to continue.

"We might be able to jump across," she said doubtfully.

Toroni and Grandmother lowered Nkiru's litter to the floor, grateful for the respite. Grandmother rubbed her arms. She had the stamina of a woman half her age, but the effort was taking its toll on her.

Toroni pushed his head into the shaft, looking up and down. "Something feels weird." He pulled a meal bar from his utility pouch and held it, arm extended, into the shaft. When he let go, the bar remained floating. He tapped it, and it drifted across the shaft and through the opposite door, where it promptly fell to the floor.

"It's a zero-G transit shaft." The marine pushed off through the door and sailed across the emptiness, grabbing the frame of the opposing door to steady himself. "There's a breeze coming up the shaft. What does it smell like to you?"

Se-Jong leaned into the doorway. "Fresh air?"

Toroni nodded. "*Outside* air. I can smell the lake, and those little yellow flowers that grow on the island." He fired a laser bolt straight down the shaft. The bright flash vanished. If it struck bottom, it was too deep for them to see.

A quick discussion settled it. They could continue running blindly through the endless maze of corridors and passageways, or they could follow the fresh breeze to its source. All of them had completed zero-G training, Se-Jong at Jackill and the others as part of their Solar Guard drills. They secured their pouches and pockets, then connected themselves to each other using carabiners and thin strands of climbing rope. One by one, they kicked off from the elevator doorframe and went sailing downward through the shaft, the fresh breeze gentle on their faces.

Rails along the walls provided handholds, and the weightlessness seemed to ease the painful pressure in Se-Jong's swollen face. One hand sliding along the rail, he reached out to grip the corner of Nkiru's litter. "I'll take her," he said to his grandmother. Nkiru was *his* responsibility. Grandmother glanced doubtfully at his injuries, but when he gave her a defiant glare she relinquished the litter.

Se-Jong focused on keeping Nkiru's litter centered in the tunnel as they moved, away from the walls. His mind filled with images of their time together: the captivating angle of her shoulders when she stretched after awakening, the way she always hiccupped after drinking her first sip of beer, the tender smiles she'd given him when she thought he wasn't looking. *Love flourishes best under the shadow of a sword*, a prophet once said. In this dark place, surrounded by death and mystery, his feelings for Nkiru were living proof of the prophet's wisdom.

—

With no sense of up or down in zero-G, Se-Jong felt as if he were moving horizontally in a tunnel, instead of downward in an elevator shaft. They floated at a rate of a couple meters per second, the same pace as a slow jog on solid ground. At regular intervals they moved past doors, some closed, but most torn open by violence in the distant past. At each opening they paused to determine if it was the source of the breeze. No one spoke. Everyone focused on the faint scent of sunshine and flowers. All their eyes were locked on the darkness of the tunnel ahead, their hope growing by the moment. Even Nkiru's labored gasps seemed to be slowing, each subsequent breath deeper and less forced.

The air had warmed, the stale dryness of the ancient dungeon replaced by a sweet, welcome moistness, presumably carried from the lake by the breeze. Se-Jong released his hold on the guide rail and allowed himself to float for a moment in the lazy air current. The fresh air smelled like hope, and he closed his eyes for just a moment of rest. They would soon find the source of the breeze. They would emerge from beneath some cave-in, or some hidden entrance built by the avatars. It was still daylight outside, and they would summon the dropship. Soon after, they would be in total comfort and safety aboard a well-armed Solar Guard starcutter.

He cracked open his less-swollen eye to orient himself. He'd fallen slightly behind the others and had begun a slow rotation. He reached out to the rail to steady himself. Unbalanced by the mass of the litter, he lost his center of gravity. He flailed in the empty air, his free arm windmilling as he fought to keep hold of Nkiru.

He forced himself to relax. Thrashing in zero-G would only make matters worse. He waited, hoping to grab the rail as he turned a complete circle in the air. If he missed, he would call for help. The others were only a couple of meters ahead, facing in the direction of their travel, their backs thankfully turned so they weren't witnessing his embarrassing awkwardness.

He heard a crackling noise, then a male voice.

"Hello? Can you hear me?"

The others heard it too. From his lead position, Toroni spun and looked back. The voice was muffled. It sounded tinny and electronic, like an undersized speaker from a cheap komnic.

Toroni held up a fist with one hand, put his finger up to his lips with the other. *Shhh.*

The voice came again. *"Um, can anybody hear me? Is anybody there?"*

A pause, then another person's voice, a woman's, sounded faintly. *"Why isn't the video working?"*

Everyone turned toward Littlefeather. The voices were coming from inside the backpack she carried.

Nkiru's backpack.

Littlefeather's eyes went wide. She looked toward Nkiru's unconscious form, then to Se-Jong, then to Grandmother.

Grandmother grasped for the handrail and stopped her downward motion through the zero-G shaft. Everyone else did the same. They floated motionlessly in a tight group, one hand on the handrail, all lights focused on Littlefeather.

"Hello?" A pause. *"Hello, hello? Gaia, can you hear me?"*

The voice spoke with a thick accent. Something about the tone and phrasing was archaic, like the centuries-old recordings from just after Earth's First Contact. It reminded him of Nkiru.

Grandmother gestured toward the pack and silently mouthed the words *Open it.*

Littlefeather lifted the pack from her shoulders and fumbled with the clasp. A faint and flickering blue glow appeared from the opening. She peered inside.

She gasped.

"What?" demanded Toroni.

The voice sounded again from inside the pack, louder and less muffled. *"Wait. Something is happening. I see light."* A pause. *"Hello? Gaia, are you there? It's me, Rupe."*

Rupe? Nkiru and Arni had mentioned somebody named Rupe back in Atum's Lair.

Littlefeather reached gingerly into the pack and pulled out a glass sphere that Se-Jong recognized as Nkiru's snowglobe. He'd seen it dark and featureless, he'd seen it animated with tiny red fireflies, he'd seen it filled with blue glowing sparkles. He'd never seen it like this before. Held delicately by the tips of Littlefeather's fingers, it contained a face. Round, bushy blond beard and hair, red-rimmed eyes, consumed with desperate concern.

The bearded face spoke. *"Oh, thank god."*

The sound of cheers and clapping erupted from the snowglobe.

BOSS

meatspace

"That's not her, is it?"

They were back in the lab. Chun was pressed against Rupe's back, peering over his shoulder at the phone screen. He tried to push her away. She cursed.

"Transfer it to the big screen," she barked, pointing at the large monitor used for teleconferences. "We all need to see this."

Rupe flicked and swiped his phone and activated the screen mirroring function. The wall screen lit up with the strange woman's face peering out. He tried to keep his dismay out of his expression. Like the others, he'd expected Fiona to answer the video call he'd made to the Orb.

No, he corrected himself, *not Fiona but Gaia, the older, gray-skinned, silver-haired Gaia from the photo she'd sent to Francis.*

Instead, the screen held a stranger. A bot.

"Hello. To whom am I speaking?" he said politely.

The young bot was in a dark room, her face lit by what looked like multiple flashlights. She wore a tight-fitting helmet and a tactical military uniform. Her skin was dirty and scratched. She was sweating. Rupe didn't recognize her uniform, which wasn't surprising given that ten thousand years had passed inside the Haven machine. The sentient bots would have had plenty of time to reinvent themselves, their clothing, their entire cultures. Did they even still speak English? He and Arni had invented rudimentary languages for the alien species in the game, but most of the bots had spoken English by default as their primary language.

He tried again. "Um, what's your name? Do you speak English?"

The woman on the screen looked away as if getting permission to reply. She nodded, then looked back at Rupe. Her voice quavered, her accent strange.

"I speak English. Who are you? What do you want?"

To Rupe's left, Solomon gave a sharp, negative shake of his head. Rupe ignored him. "I'm Rupert Schroeder. I'm trying to reach a friend of mine. Her name is Gaia. Dark skin, long silver hair. Do you know her?"

The woman looked confused, indecisive. She glanced off-screen. When her attention returned to Rupe, her eyes had hardened. *"Where are you, and why are you looking for this person you call Gaia?"*

"I'm in California. Um, that's on Earth."

"I know where California is."

"Are you on Grone?"

"Why are you looking for Gaia?"

"Like I said, she's my friend. I'm trying to help her."

"Help her do what?"

"Help her survive the dungeon on Grone."

The woman paused. Rupe could hear other voices whispering urgently. An older woman. A man. No, two men, arguing. He couldn't make out the words.

The woman returned her attention to the screen. *"You're lying. It's impossible I could be speaking to someone on Earth."*

"Why?"

Her lips curled. *"Physics."*

He considered her reaction. If she was on Grone, then perhaps she couldn't understand how someone on Earth could be talking to her. In the game, it was possible for avatars to communicate across interstellar distances using a device called an *ansible*, a term he and Arni had borrowed from one of Arni's favorite science fiction authors. Ansibles had been rare and expensive, even for avatars, and they couldn't be activated by bots. In a world populated only by bots, there would be no means of instantaneous communications between worlds.

"I'm not lying. Have you ever heard of an ansible?"

She hesitated. *"The avatar device?"*

Another hasty background conference, during which he overheard the woman on the screen say, *"But they* do *exist. There is an ansible in the reliquary on Bosporan."* A hushed and indistinct argument ensued, after which she returned. *"Prove to me that you're not a Dei Militans, or an officer of the church."*

"Or a Caeren," added an unseen male voice.

"I don't know what you mean. I'm none of those things. I'm, uh," he paused, thinking furiously. "Please, if you're in the dungeon on Grone, you probably need my help. I know my way around. I'm not a *day-militans* or a *karen* or whatever you said. I definitely don't go to church. I'm a friend of Gaia's and I really, really need to talk to her."

The woman bit her lip. Rupe was trying to think of a way to reassure her when he saw movement behind her head. In the darkness, several meters behind her, a figure swam into the dim light, moving fast, floating as if weightless and holding what was unmistakably a weapon.

"Watch out," he blurted. "There's somebody behind you!"

havencosm

At the bearded man's warning, Se-Jong spun to face the threat. There were four, no, six of them, gliding silently and rapidly along the tunnel's centerline, all wearing the dusky golden tacsuits of the Dei Militans. The closest man was near enough for Se-Jong to make out his expression through the faceplate of his tacsuit helmet. The militan grimaced and raised a handgun. With his other hand, he grabbed for Nkiru's litter.

Se-Jong recoiled, flailing for a handhold. Something hit him in the side, knocking him away from the attacker. It was Toroni, who flipped like a high diver in midplunge to bring his rifle to bear on the newcomers. The marine's first shot went wild, striking the wall of the shaft in an explosion of sparks and concrete shards. His second shot struck the militan in the center of his faceplate. Less than a meter from Se-Jong, the man's head exploded inside his helmet, spraying superheated gore from the pierced faceplate in a stream that painted the tunnel wall with a gruesome splash of color.

Se-Jong screamed as the man's body collided with him. He fought with thrashing arms, kicking and spasming until he was free. Nkiru's litter had floated away, and he pulled the climbing rope that connected them, yanking her closer until he could grab the litter's webbing.

Toroni fired again. One of the pursuers veered into the wall of the shaft, his chest armor smoking and flaring. Grandmother was shouting, but Se-Jong couldn't make out her words. He was spinning out of control, desperately holding onto Nkiru's litter. It struck the wall and rebounded violently.

A set of hands grabbed for him. He spun toward their owner, fists raised. "Let go," Littlefeather cried.

He let go. Littlefeather disconnected him from Nkiru's litter and kicked hard at one of the guide rails. Dragging Nkiru, she raced away from the attackers.

They seemed to fill the shaft. One stretched toward him, then twirled away with a sharp cry as his ablative armor was struck by another of Toroni's laser bursts. Se-Jong grabbed for the nearest handrail, directly across the shaft from Grandmother and Toroni. Maneuvering in zero-G was always difficult; it was doubly so when your brain was addled by Yok-Stop and your face was a swollen pizza of goo.

Had the militans grabbed Nkiru as they'd planned, he and the rest of his party would already be captured, or dead. As it was, the militans' failed attack had created a difficult tactical situation. In the narrow tunnel, Toroni could shoot at them, but they couldn't shoot back without the risk of hitting Nkiru.

He heard the voice of the bearded man cry out from the snowglobe, *"What's happening?"*

Littlefeather had lost the relic in the melee. It was floating away, casting a dim glow on the walls of the tunnel as it moved into the empty space between the two groups. For a moment the two parties drifted silently through the shaft, warily facing each other, everyone watching the glowing Orb. The closest of the militans turned his rifle on it. Se-Jong's head throbbed wickedly, but he forced his injured eye fully open. Before the militan could act, Se-Jong launched himself toward the Orb and curled his arm around it like he was catching a football in one of his zero-G games back at Jackill Academy. He tucked it into his chest and kicked off the handrail on the other side of the tunnel, propelling himself toward Toroni.

Toroni used one hand to grab Se-Jong's collar without losing his aim on the militan. He pulled Se-Jong close and pointed to one of the openings that punctuated the shaft every few meters.

"That's your target," he hissed. "Get inside. I'll help the reliquist get the girl's litter through the door. We'll have to make a stand."

Se-Jong glanced over his shoulder. Their drifting motion meant the doorway was coming up fast.

"Now," said Toroni. Without losing his aim, the marine kicked against the rail to propel himself toward Littlefeather and Nkiru.

The tunnel handrail split into two parallel bars at the doorway, providing a convenient anchor for those wishing to use the door. Se-Jong grabbed it and swung himself clumsily into the opening.

The sudden return of gravity took him by surprise. He lurched and fell to his hands and knees, dropping the snowglobe, which rolled away to clank loudly against the corridor wall. He scrambled toward it as Littlefeather shoved Nkiru's litter through the opening and onto the floor. Grabbing the snowglobe with one hand, he reached for the litter with the other, pulling it as hard as he could. Grandmother and Littlefeather fell into the opening. They dragged Nkiru's litter farther into the corridor. The bearded man in the snowglobe was shouting something. Se-Jong glared into the Orb and whispered. "Shut up!"

Toroni managed the transition from the tunnel with ease, positioning himself half-in, half-out of the elevator shaft, his rifle still trained on the militans.

"They're holding their position in the tunnel," Toroni whispered from the doorway. "About ten meters away. I count six of them." He spat on the floor. "How did they make it through the microflak minefield? The seekers? Over that damned bridge? How did they track us?"

"There are only six of them," Grandmother pointed out. "There were twelve before. Not all of them made it."

"Even so, they must have somebody with them who knows how to navigate this dungeon," Littlefeather said darkly. "We wouldn't have made it at all without Arni." She paused, her tone shifting from anger to dismay. "What *is* this place?"

"Arni?" It was the voice from the snowglobe. *"Did you say Arni?"*

"Quiet!" snapped Se-Jong. The snowglobe went silent.

They were in a short corridor with an open doorway at its far end. The floor and walls were scorched and pitted, indicating an explosion and fire in the distant past. The ceiling sagged perilously through a spiderweb of cracks, cratered where basketball-size chunks of concrete had fallen to the floor. Beyond the open door at the far end was a room lit by artificial lights. It was not the source of the fresh air, he noted glumly. If anything, the odor coming from the doorway was bafflingly alien.

A loud crack and a spray of shrapnel erupted from the elevator shaft. Toroni jerked away, then leaned into the shaft to return fire. A fusillade of laser bolts was the response, deafening Se-Jong and filling the short corridor with smoke and more shrapnel. Toroni rolled away from the elevator opening and sprang to his feet. "Go," he cried. "I can't hold them."

Se-Jong wedged the snowglobe into a too-small utility pocket at the waist of his coldsuit. He grabbed Nkiru's litter and, along with Littlefeather and Grandmother, ran toward the doorway at the opposite end of the corridor. Toroni followed them, covering their retreat. Skidding inside, Se-Jong helped Toroni shove the door closed. The ancient hinges groaned in protest, but the door closed with a reassuring slam.

Se-Jong looked around the room for anything to blockade the door. Moldy, mummified lumps of humanoid size and shape were scattered everywhere. The center of the room held a security barrier and an arched walk-through scanner. Beyond the barrier, the far wall was dominated by a heavy blast door marked with alternating yellow and red stripes. They'd found a security checkpoint, designed to prevent access to whatever lay beyond the blast door.

Or to prevent whatever was behind the door from escaping, he thought.

Like the approach corridor, this room showed signs of fire. Two of the many light fixtures were still working, the first sign of electrical power they'd seen in this ancient place. There was nothing in the room that could be used as a barricade. Something moved in Se-Jong's peripheral vision, and he swung his head toward it. Nothing.

No, there it was again. A small, sparkling flash. He felt the hint of a familiar skin tingle and recognized the sensation. The others felt it too, based on their startled expressions. Grandmother scowled. They must be near a timedust seeker, though it wasn't visible.

Toroni pulled a tactical knife from his waist, tried frantically to lodge its thin blade under the entrance door. Littlefeather rushed to the opposite wall to check the blast door. As she passed beneath the arched scanner with the gobsmacker slung beneath her shoulder, a siren briefly sounded. She paused, panicked, but when nothing else happened, she continued to the blast door.

The entrance door buckled with a loud thump. Toroni cried out and pushed against it with his shoulder, barely holding it shut. The militans hit it again. This time it opened several centimeters before Toroni shoved it closed. The knife he'd tried to use as a doorstop skittered across the floor.

Se-Jong and Grandmother abandoned Nkiru's litter beneath the scanner arch and rushed to the marine's side. Together they leaned heavily against the entrance door. If the militans chose to shoot through the door, they were doomed.

Thud! The door shuddered painfully against his shoulder.

Across the room at the colorful blast door, Littlefeather cried, "It's locked!"

"Use the key," shouted Se-Jong.

"What key?"

A muffled voice from the snowglobe. Se-Jong looked down. It barely fit in his utility pocket, and part of it peeked out the top. Within the sphere, the bearded man seemed to be gesturing wildly.

Thud! The militans hit again, harder. The door hinges made a cracking sound.

Se-Jong dug his feet into a crack in the floor and leaned into the door with all his might. "The card key. The blue one that Arni used!" He'd seen a planet-and-sword symbol on a panel next to the blast door, the same symbol that had been on the other doors the key had opened.

Thud! The top half of the door buckled inward and didn't spring back into shape.

Littlefeather muttered angrily as she fumbled through Nkiru's backpack. "Here it is!"

Thud! The top of the door buckled more. Gloved fingers curled through the opening. Toroni headbutted them with his helmet. They jerked back.

"It worked!" Littlefeather cried.

Beyond the security checkpoint, the heavy blast door was rolling open on metal tracks. The alien smell he'd noticed before immediately grew stronger. A new alert siren sounded, deeper in tone and echoing in whatever space lay beyond the blast door. Toroni nodded curtly, his voice strained with effort. "Go! I've got this!"

Se-Jong and Grandmother scrambled to lift Nkiru's litter. The blast door was moving slowly, too slowly. Littlefeather pushed ineffectively against the smooth metal, trying to speed its opening.

A rumbling sound came from beyond the blast door. It sounded like the watery, mechanical heartbeat of a giant steam engine:

Whoom, whoom.

The alert siren stopped. Voices from the snowglobe in his utility pocket were shouting indistinctly, but suddenly the words were lost in a swell of crackling static.

The entrance door was grinding open despite Toroni's efforts. A boot shoved its way into the gap. Toroni stomped it. It withdrew.

Something else fell into the opening, something the size of a chicken egg.

"Stun grenade!" shouted Toroni. He leaped away.

An incredibly loud, incredibly bright detonation struck Se-Jong in the back like a shove from the hand of a god.

—

Whoom, whoom.

Sparkles and tingles all over his body. A man's smooth voice sounded in his head, echoing from the bottom of a well. "Captain Kwon Namjoo, isn't it? I am Captain-Brother Obraheem Kaiin of the Ordum Regia Proctoris Dei Militans."

"I know who you are," Grandmother's gravelly voice replied.

Se-Jong opened his good eye as much as he could, blinking to clear the thick fluid that coated his vision. He was lying face down on a hard concrete floor next to one of the moldy corpses. From where he lay, Nkiru's litter was just a meter away. She seemed unharmed. Littlefeather was also on the ground, leaning groggily against the base of the open blast door. Toroni had taken the brunt of the stun-grenade blast and lay unmoving on the floor.

Se-Jong turned his head. Grandmother was the only one of their party still standing. Her muddy boots were close enough to touch, and from her wide stance he could tell she was unsteady from the blast of the grenade. She faced a Dei Militans officer, presumably the man with the smooth voice. He wore the same style of tacsuit as the other militans, except that his shoulder guards and breastplate were polished gold instead of dusky yellow. He had removed his helmet to reveal tightly cropped black hair, thin features, and a narrow nose. The other five militans had crowded into the room behind the officer. They stood in an arc, weapons raised.

Grandmother's sharp voice cut through the whine of his grenade-stunned ears. "Your assault was unprovoked. You've broken the SATO treaty, Captain-Brother Kaiin."

"As have you, Captain Kwon. I shouldn't have to remind you that Grone is a sacred pilgrimage world, under the juris of the Cataclyst Church." The man paused. "Clearly, this place is an undiscovered avatar dungeon that belongs to the church, as specified by the treaty. We are within our rights to protect our sacred heritage."

Whoom, whoom.

With a jolt, Se-Jong realized his grandmother was holding her sidearm, and she was pointing it at the officer's face. "This is a Solar Alliance protectorate world, Captain-Brother Kaiin, as *you* well know. This place may indeed be an undiscovered avatar dungeon, but it has not yet been sanctified by the church nor recognized by the government. We have every legal right to be here. You have no authority to interfere with us, and you certainly had no authority to fire on my marines. There will be consequences."

The man's voice hardened. "A matter for the courts and the politicians, Captain."

Whoom, whoom.

Se-Jong glanced toward the open blast door, but the source of the deep rumble was hidden by the darkness.

The man named Kaiin took a step toward Nkiru's litter.

"That's close enough," warned Grandmother.

Kaiin gestured to Nkiru. "What's her condition?"

"She received an electrical shock. She's unconscious."

Whoom, whoom.

Kaiin's gaze drifted to Littlefeather and the gobsmacker strapped to her shoulder. His eyes brushed over Toroni's still form and settled on Se-Jong, noting that he was awake. His face was neutral, cold, expressionless. He turned his attention to Grandmother. "Nkiru Anaya is a known accomplice of Janga extremists. She has desecrated multiple sacred shrines and stolen relics from pilgrimage worlds, including ur-relics. She has violated multiple sanctums within the walls of the Regium. As you know, these are all capital heresies under the Cataclyst Covenant." He waited for a response. When none came, he continued. "The SATO treaty recognizes the religious laws of the Covenant. By protecting this criminal, you aren't just risking excommunication from the church: you are breaking the civil laws you are sworn to uphold. You know this."

"I know that if the Father Regis gets his hands on Nkiru Anaya, the SATO treaties will be meaningless."

Kaiin took in a deep breath. "This situation need not escalate further, Captain. We are here to arrest Anaya and her accomplices and recover our property. Once this is done, you and your marines are free to go."

"Unacceptable." Grandmother smiled coldly at Kaiin. "If you withdraw from this place and allow us passage back to my ship, I will agree to present the matter to the Religious Affairs Council for their deliberation."

Whoom, whoom.

Kaiin scowled. "In the name of the Father Regis of the Universal Cataclyst Church and the offices of the Trinity Curia and the Holy Inquisitors, I hereby take custody of the heretic Nkiru Anaya. I also charge her accomplices with—"

Grandmother took a step forward and thrust the barrel of her sidearm to within a meter of the forehead of Captain-Brother Obraheem Kaiin. "You're not charging *anybody* with *anything*."

Any of the militans could shoot her where she stood, Se-Jong realized. At best, holding a gun on Kaiin was a futile gesture. At worst, it was suicide.

Kaiin shrugged. "I'm unclear how you're going to stop me, Captain Kwon." He took a step closer until his forehead was almost touching the barrel of Grandmother's gun. "Surrender Anaya and I can guarantee—"

A new voice, cracked and hoarse, sounded weakly. *"Wolfe?"*

Kaiin stopped in midsentence. Se-Jong rolled on his side to face Nkiru. Her bloodshot eyes were open, and she was staring at Kaiin.

"Wolfe?" she repeated, her voice gaining strength. "Roland Wolfe?" She gaped disbelievingly at the Rose & Chalice sigil emblazoned on Kaiin's tacsuit. "You're a . . . *Dei Militans?*"

Kaiin turned away from Grandmother. His mouth opened, and stayed open, but he didn't speak.

Whoom, whoom.

At the rumbling sound, Nkiru looked around in bewilderment. Se-Jong pulled himself to Nkiru's side, ignoring the militans' rifles, which followed his movement. He touched her face. "I thought I'd lost you!"

She gave him a dark, frightened scowl, struggling against the webbing that bound her tightly to the litter. "Get me *out* of this thing!"

Se-Jong untangled Nkiru from the litter's webbing, and together they climbed to their feet. She braced against his unsteady shoulder, looking around wildly, taking in Kaiin and the five armed militans at his side; Toroni's supine form on the floor; Grandmother with her sidearm pointed at Kaiin's face; and finally, the dark, yawning space behind the open blast door, upon whose threshold Littlefeather was leaning.

"Where are we? What happened?" Her voice was groggy, weak.

He didn't want to mention the emora in front of Kaiin. "You got a bad shock. You've been unconscious. We were trying to get you out of here when this guy showed up."

Nkiru turned to Kaiin. Her words poured out, tumbling over each other. "Mr. Wolfe, I'm from the JEEB team. Colonel Solomon sent me here to find you and Analise Novak!"

Se-Jong felt a stab of confused dismay. He glanced at Grandmother. Her eyes hadn't wavered from Kaiin, her aim hadn't budged, but Nkiru's apparent recognition of Kaiin had rattled her, too.

Nkiru nervously licked her lips. "You *are* Roland Wolfe, aren't you? You work for the JEEB program at Stanford University. Don't you remember?"

The momentary crack in Kaiin's composure vanished as quickly as it had appeared. He cleared his throat and said, "We've been looking for you since you were seen at the shrine on Forniculus. I must congratulate you. Did you know you were the first person to discover the location of the Sanctum Arcanis in five thousand years? And the first person *ever* to steal artifacts from its vaults? Quite the feat for a young woman with no public wiki profile and no church dossier, wouldn't you say?"

Nkiru pulled away from Se-Jong. She took a wobbling step toward Kaiin. "It's been a long time, I know. I need you to *remember!* We've tried to reset the timestream and lower the firewall, but something went wrong. Colonel Solomon gave me the tools we need. If you help me, Mr. Wolfe, maybe we can fix it, and *you can go home.*"

Whoom, whoom.

Kaiin's expression was unreadable. He spoke suddenly. "Come with me voluntarily, and I'll release the others."

Nkiru narrowed her eyes. "Where is Analise? Is she with you?"

Something flickered across Kaiin's expression. Recognition? Confusion? Loathing? Arni had warned against Nkiru trying to find somebody named Analise. He'd been pretty insistent about it, too.

Nkiru's whole body was trembling. She was looking at Kaiin with an expression that alternated between dismay and unbridled hope.

Hope? Was it possible she was *considering* Kaiin's offer?

Grandmother must have been thinking in similar terms. She shifted her stance, pressed her gun closer until it was a centimeter from Kaiin's skull. "This negotiation is over."

Kaiin ignored her, still focused keenly on Nkiru. "You have the emora?"

Nkiru's bloodshot eyes widened until they settled on her backpack, slung across the reliquist's shoulder. Littlefeather flinched, pulled the backpack straps closer into her chest.

Se-Jong took Nkiru's arm. "Arni said it was ruined. Nobody can touch it. It almost killed you."

Nkiru shook off his grip and faced Littlefeather. "Give me my pack."

"Do *not* give her the pack," barked Grandmother.

Kaiin's eyes flicked to Littlefeather.

Whoom, whoom.

Littlefeather took a step away.

"Please," implored Nkiru.

Littlefeather gave her a regretful look.

Nkiru's anguish was clear. "I *have* to try again. I don't know what happened when I touched the emora. Arni said that it . . ." She suddenly seemed to recall the events in Atum's Lair, including Arni's accusation that she was carrying a child. *Se-Jong's* child. Her hands flew to her belly and she gave him a look of sheer, heartbreaking panic. "Where is Arni? And the other marine?"

"When you touched the emora, the machine with all the brass rings exploded. Arni's gone."

A look of incomprehension fell over her face. "Arni . . . died?"

He nodded. "You almost died, too."

"And the machine exploded?"

"Yeah."

"Oh, *fuck*." She hesitated. A tear streaked through the grime on her cheek. Her voice was small, hollow. "And the marine? McCloud?"

Se-Jong jerked his head toward Kaiin. "He murdered him."

Kaiin pursed his lips. "Come with me, and I give you my word that the Regium will not bring charges against—"

Kaiin winced, his words caught in his throat.

Se-Jong felt it, too, a familiar sensation of skin prickles and visual static in the back of his eyes.

"Oh, *no*," said Littlefeather.

Everyone turned toward the reliquist. Still at the threshold of the open blast door, still clutching Nkiru's backpack, she was looking down at her feet. Near them were slithering tendrils that had crept into the room from the darkness beyond the blast door. Littlefeather recoiled from the closest strands. *Seekers.* The painful, skin-crawling static intensified as the tendrils crossed the blast-door threshold.

Whoom, whoom.

Grandmother was briefly distracted. Kaiin surged forward, his fist slashing down on her outstretched arm, knocking her aim to the side. Her gun flashed, and the bolt hit the floor near Toroni with a loud *crack!*

Se-Jong lunged for Kaiin. He heard a laser discharge but managed to get both arms around Kaiin's waist. They both tumbled to the ground.

Nkiru shouted something unintelligible.

Another laser discharge, and the bolt vanished into the darkness beyond the blast door, briefly illuminating something huge in its depths.

Littlefeather shrieked, "Stop!"

Se-Jong struggled, but the militan officer was far stronger. Kaiin slammed Se-Jong's swollen face with the side of his pistol.

Se-Jong felt the purest agony he'd ever experienced as the makeshift bandages and adhesives burst. Somehow, he managed to keep his grip, preventing Kaiin from regaining his feet.

Littlefeather shouted again, her voice choked with primal horror. "Stop! Oh, gods, stop! *Look!*"

Kaiin pulled away.

Se-Jong wedged open an eye. Kaiin was frozen, half standing.

Grandmother had pinned Nkiru in a brutal chokehold. Her handgun was pressed against Nkiru's temple. Nkiru's face was bright with fear.

Se-Jong's heart faltered. Grandmother wouldn't hesitate to execute Nkiru if it meant keeping her from Kaiin. "Halmeoni, *no!*"

She wasn't listening. Like the others, she was staring through the blast door, beyond which the vast chamber was slowly lighting up.

Whoom, whoom.

One of the militans gasped. Another muttered, in High Tang, "Ajae nora traxus, apocolyptica!"

Se-Jong recognized the famous final words of Andrik the Redeemer from the scriptural *Chronicles of the Second Epoch*:

"And thus, from the darkness will arise the end to all things."

meatspace

Rupe huddled with the others beneath the wall screen, watching the image, listening to the muffled sounds, trying to make out what was happening. The brief battle had ended and a male bot had picked up the Orb, but when Rupe had shouted to get his attention, the bot had ordered him to be silent. Zia cursed loudly when the bot shoved the Orb into a pocket, giving them only a blurry slit through which they could see nothing but the ceiling and occasionally the bot's flailing arm.

There'd been a melee fight; that much was for sure. From the muffled sounds, it seemed as if the fight was over, but the voices were still tense. Snippets of conversation could be heard, but without context they were meaningless. They were speaking in thickly accented English infused with unrecognizable words, but he was certain he'd heard one of them mention Arni's name.

Then, another sound, still muted, but recognizable. Rupe threw up his hand, silencing the whispers around him.

"What?" said Zia.

The others looked at him. A cloud of static was beginning to obscure the image on the screen.

"Oh, no, no, no."

"What?" Zia demanded.

"Hear that sound? That siren?"

Rupe picked up the conference microphone from the center of the table and shouted directly into it. "Hello? Hello? Can you hear me? Can anybody hear me? You've got to get out the way you came, or you'll be trapped there! Can you hear me? Anybody?"

A loud but indistinct shout from the speakers, then a staccato blast. On the screen, a flash through the narrow pocket slit, then the image tumbled. The static obscuring the image was getting worse. If Gaia didn't retreat, he realized, they'd soon lose the Orb's signal completely.

He cried, "Gaia! Gaia! Listen to me. You've got to get out of there, right now! Can you hear me? God damn it, Gaia, can you hear me? *Get out of there!*"

havencosm

The cavern beyond the blast door was the size of a football stadium, rectangular with a high ceiling that was arched along the room's long axis. Several metal catwalks had once extended completely around the chamber about halfway up the high walls, providing access to the bays and workshops that overlooked the cavern floor.

All but one of the catwalks had been torn from their moorings and lay in wreckage below. The cause of the destruction was obvious.

A gray colossus hovered weightlessly between the floor and ceiling of the cavern like a starship-size sea anemone. It had no definable shape. Whatever body it possessed was hidden beneath a thick mass of gelatinous tubes and protrusions that sagged under their weight. Where they draped and touched the floor, each trunk divided into hundreds of pulsing seeker tubes, each further subdividing until the cavern was carpeted by a mat of overlapping tendrils identical to the ones they'd been avoiding in the tunnels. Some were thin and almost transparent, but most were heavy and robust, extending into the walls, floor, and ceiling of the chamber, surging into wide cracks and deep pits excavated in its endless craving.

Se-Jong swallowed a surge of horror. Of all the routes they could have taken in this underground maze, somehow they'd stumbled upon the worst possible path. The *very* worst.

The Gurothim harvester was a million years older than the Cataclysm, a weapon from the legendary First Epoch wars between the Predecessors and the Gurothim. In Tang, Gurothim literally meant "the primordial enemy." Who knew how many worlds this very harvester had pulverized in the distant past in its ravenous quest for timedust? How many billions of innocents it had killed?

A particularly massive seeker tube, much larger than all the others, extended from its swollen belly into a hole in the floor. It was, Se-Jong realized, the seeker trunk that they'd had to avoid when they'd crossed the crude bridge an hour earlier. Arni had said that the bridge was directly below the boss chamber.

Splotches of radiant color began to erupt from deep inside the central mass of gelatinous tubes. Some of the tubes were hardening into black metal spines, like those of a sea urchin, while others were distending into flexible trunks that were spouting even more seeker tendrils like those creeping through the blast door. Encircling the monster's base where the main seeker trunk fell away into the bottomless pit, a rim of hardened nodules was sprouting. They pulsed with the red-orange glow of fiery heat.

Whoom, whoom.

It's waking up, he realized.

Kaiin climbed to his feet, staring in disbelief. His militans stirred, not sure where to aim their weapons. Littlefeather retreated from the blast door as more seeker tendrils moved inexorably into the room.

Nkiru tugged weakly against Grandmother's iron grip. She was eyeing the harvester, trying to speak, but her words were choked. Se-Jong crawled to his feet, fighting the pain from his fractured cheek.

"Halmeoni, please. Let her speak!"

Grandmother hesitated, then loosened her grip without releasing Nkiru or removing the gun pressed to her temple.

Nkiru filled her lungs in a great, wheezing gasp. She coughed, looked in the direction of the colossus beyond the blast door. "Why in fuck's sake did you come *here?*"

"We didn't mean to," Littlefeather retorted, stabbing a finger at the militans. "They were chasing us. Chasing *you*."

A man's voice sounded, thin and reedy, almost lost in a crackling electronic hiss. *"Get out of there!"*

Everyone turned to Se-Jong. He looked down to his waist, where part of the hemisphere of the snowglobe protruded from the utility pocket. From his perspective looking down, the frantic face of the bearded man glared up at him, veiled by a thin skein of white static. *"Hey, you! Yeah, you! Can you hear me?"*

Nkiru, gasping and grimacing from the pressure of Grandmother's headlock, gave Se-Jong a disbelieving look. Her eyes moved down to the visible hemisphere of the snowglobe protruding the waist of his coldsuit.

"Rupe?" she croaked.

The image of the bearded man flickered as the static increased. The powerfield from the approaching seekers was interfering with it, Se-Jong realized.

"*Gaia? Is that you? Get out of there, go back the way you came right now, or you won't be able to get out at all... guidance algorithm will trap you in... you've triggered th—*" The bearded man's voice dissolved into a thick foam of white noise.

Whoom WHOOM!

Only partially visible through the blast door, the harvester's body shuddered in great waves that encircled its grotesque form. The seeker tubes draping from its belly pulsed as if they were being pumped full of fluid. In the guardroom, the tendrils at their feet suddenly doubled their rate of growth. A crescendo of loud static issued from the snowglobe. Surging electrical pain from the seekers' powerfield flared through every nerve ending in Se-Jong's body. From their winces, the others felt it, too.

Behind Kaiin, outside the door to the entrance corridor, debris clattered down from the sagging ceiling.

"Ah, shit," said Nkiru.

The clatter became a thundering cascade. A spray of dust and a mound of stony debris poured through the entrance doorway into the room, causing the militans to scramble for safety. One of them dragged Toroni's inert body away from the calamity, leaving him at Grandmother's feet.

The dust cleared quickly, drawn through the blast door into the troubled air currents of the chamber beyond. The entrance corridor leading back to the elevator shaft had collapsed, blocking any retreat.

Kaiin considered the cave-in, turned accusingly to Se-Jong. He looked down at the snowglobe. "Bring it out so we can all see it."

Two of the militans shifted their rifles to Se-Jong. He tried to keep his hands from trembling as he extricated the globe from the tight utility pocket. He held it up. As he watched, the bearded man's face slowly began to resolve from within the blank field of static. He was saying something.

"*... hear me ... please ... timestream ... you're at ... can track the Orb ... avoid ...*"

Nkiru's eyes were wider than Se-Jong had ever seen them, and behind her panicked grimace he thought he saw the trace of a fierce smile.

Kaiin saw it, too. He glanced at the cave-in that blocked their exit. "You knew that was going to happen."

Nkiru scoffed. "Mr. Wolfe, this is the prime dungeon of Grone. All pathways eventually lead to the final boss. It's a *game*, don't you remember?" At his look of confusion, she shouted, "Jesus, if we all just *stand* here, we're going to die! *Let me go!*"

Grandmother's eyes gleamed through narrow slits. Se-Jong saw her intent in the tight set of her jaw, the tension in the hand holding the gun to Nkiru's forehead. If she released Nkiru, the militans would take her and kill the rest of them, Kaiin's promises notwithstanding. The only sure way to keep the girl out of the church's hands would be to burn her brains out.

Kaiin saw it too. He waved his hands in placation. "No. Wait. Stop." He turned to his subordinates. "Lower your weapons. Stand down."

He glanced at the snowglobe in Se-Jong's hand, from which spasms of syllables could be heard between periods of dense static. Turning back to Grandmother, he drew the ceremonial black-bladed dagger every Dei Militans carried, pulled off his tacsuit glove, and lightly drew the tip of the dagger across his palm. "By the covenant of Andrik, I offer a blood truce." He stretched the hand, palm up, toward Grandmother.

Grandmother stared coldly at the thin line of blood welling up in Kaiin's palm. A blood truce was supposedly unbreakable, but for something as important as a girl with the powers of an avatar, would Kaiin really respect the ancient military tradition?

A renewed burst of noise flared from the snowglobe, and the bearded man's face was once again completely swallowed by static.

Whoom, whoom.

In the harvester chamber, another pulse of light and chaos, along with a new sound: a deep, resonant whirring, as if some enormous mechanism within the great beast's gut was starting to spin. The glowing red nodes beneath the skirt at the base of the harvester began to shimmer with a heat he could feel through the blast-door opening.

Nkiru pulled at Grandmother's choke hold, tried to keep the panic from her voice. "Listen to me, all of you. The boss is powering up its flight systems. We're out of time."

Whoom, whoom.

More of the harvester's anemone tubes had hardened into black spikes. With a loud suction sound, the massive seeker trunk that hung from its base suddenly detached and fell into the depths of the bottomless well, pulling thousands of seeker tubes with it. The mass of remaining seekers continued to swell as the harvester diverted its energies to their growth.

Nkiru's voice grew even more frantic. "See that? That's a Gurothim harvester."

Even the stoic militans reacted to this pronouncement. They glanced at each other, their fear mixed with disbelief. Nkiru continued. "It was damaged and captured by a warlord named Jaspaar back in the Age of Avatars. It's been in semistasis since the Cataclysm, but we just woke it up when we opened the blast door. Right now, it's looking for its *motive core*, a device it needs to escape. Jaspaar removed its motive core to try and find a way to control it, to turn it into a weapon. It can sense that the core is nearby, and it won't be long before it finds it." She jerked against Grandmother's tightening grip. "When it does, it'll light its engines, and that will bring down this whole mountain on our heads."

Kaiin grimaced, thrust his outstretched hand closer to Grandmother. "I swear to abide by the blood truce. In the name of Andrik the Redeemer, as long as you hold my blood in your palm, I am not your opponent."

Whoom, whoom.

"Halmeoni, *please*," Se-Jong said.

Grandmother whipped her gun from Nkiru toward Kaiin. To his credit, the militans didn't flinch. Without releasing Nkiru, she lowered the gun and holstered it, pulled off her glove, took Kaiin's hand. "While I hold your blood in my palm, I am not your opponent. I accept your blood truce."

She freed Nkiru. Se-Jong rushed to her. Nkiru was breathing hard, shaking from weakness. She rubbed her neck, gave Grandmother a vicious glare, then reached out to pluck the snowglobe from his hand. She looked into the static, gave it a shake. The bearded man's face was barely visible. "Rupe? Can you hear me?"

"*Gaia! Thank god! We're . . . interference . . . move away from the boss . . . seekers . . .*"

Nkiru glanced wistfully at the cave-in blocking the entrance door. "Rupe, we're trapped in a security guardpost outside the boss chamber. Is there another way out?"

Whoom, whoom.

The bearded man's face dissolved into static as the harvester's energies pulsed again. She shook the snowglobe, then cursed.

Grandmother looked at the globe, then at Nkiru. "Who was that?"

"A friend. He knows this place. He can help us stop the harvester, but his signal is too weak."

"Where is he?"

"He's calling from meatspace. It's a long way from Grone."

Se-Jong looked at Littlefeather, mouthed the word: *meatspace?* Littlefeather shook her head. *Never heard of it.*

Grandmother turned to Kaiin. "If Anaya is right, and this harvester launches itself into space, we have to warn our ships at all costs."

Nkiru scoffed. "Your ships won't be able to stop it. Your whole *fleet* won't be able to stop it." She clutched the snowglobe in both hands, shook it. The static particles within whirled and spun but did not clear. "Rupe? Rupe? Can you hear me?" The hint of newfound hope Se-Jong had seen in her face vanished. "We're too close to the harvester, and the powerfield is only going to get stronger."

Whoom, whoom.

She looked through the blast door at the awakening monster. "We're on our own. There's no way out, except to try to get past it."

meatspace

"I'm getting a signal from the Orb, but it's just noise," reported Zia.

Solomon turned to Chun, who was pecking furiously at her laptop. "Are the timelines still synchronized?"

She nodded. "The Kaiser-Salim values are . . . wobbling a bit, but the synchronization is holding for now."

"It looks like the transmission is being blocked on their end," said Zia.

"It's the boss." Rupe lowered Francis's phone and looked up at the others. "Gaia and her team bots activated the Gurothim harvester when they opened the blast door into its chamber. It's ramping up its powerfield. That's what's blocking the signal from the Orb."

"Can't we do something?"

"Their only chance is to run back the way they came. It's too late to do anything else. They can't kill the boss. They can't even hurt it much. They're *supposed* to lose, by design. It's a *Kobayashi Maru* scenario." Rupe gritted his teeth at the blank stares of the others. "The harvester will find the motive core and escape into the galaxy, just like it did in the TV episode. It'll start eating planets again. We designed the entirety of next year's gaming campaign around the effort to find and kill the harvester as it rampages through the galaxy. There's *nothing* they can do to stop it. The tools and weapons they need aren't on Grone."

Zia and Chun exchanged bleak glances with Solomon. Solomon gestured toward Francis's phone. "How did she get herself into so much trouble? When you briefed her, didn't you tell her to avoid the final boss?"

Rupe nodded miserably. "Yeah, but it's not that easy. The game's dungeons are designed to funnel players into the key conflict areas. We put subliminal psychological cues everywhere, in the design of the rooms and corridors, in the placements of objects and furniture, in the scene lighting and color schemes—we even use subtle textures on the floors. In the heat of the game, the vast majority of players don't even notice they're being shepherded toward danger. What made Fiona so special was that she could instinctively spot my subliminal tricks." He looked over at her hospital bed, where Ms. Martinez was adjusting Fiona's blankets. "Early on, she figured out that I always programmed an avoidance route around every combat scenario. The avoidance routes are always hidden and require a great deal of strategic thinking and puzzle-solving ability. They're more difficult than the combat option. Gaia's superpower, the reason she has such a spectacularly high PPA score, is that she is really, really good at finding the avoidance routes and working out the puzzles."

Chun scowled. "If she's so good, how'd she end up in the final boss chamber?"

"Either she wasn't paying attention, or somebody else was calling the shots."

"So, she *can* escape?" asked Zia hopefully. "You put an avoidance route in the boss dungeon, right? She can go around the boss without having to fight?"

He could feel the wetness on his cheeks and in his beard. It was impossible to stop the tears, so he didn't even try. "Yeah. But remember, I designed this boss monster with Fiona in mind. I put in false clues to throw her off track. I tried to use her superpower against her, to trick her."

Zia grabbed his arm. "Rupe, she *has* to escape. If her capatar is killed, even if she respawns she'll lose all the items she needs to lower the firewall."

Rupe shrugged despondently. "She'll be killed for sure if she stays where she is. She knows that. She's studied the television episode this dungeon is based on. She'll *think* she knows the escape route, but she won't. I added things that weren't in the TV show. I didn't go over any of those changes when I briefed her. I barely mentioned the final boss at all, other than to describe its basic attack modes. There wasn't time. She wasn't supposed to go anywhere near it."

Solomon looked at the faces clustered around Rupe. His eyes settled on Chun. "Can *you* do anything?"

Chun's face darkened. "Like what? The girl failed to lower the firewall. Until it comes down, I can't access the kernel, the operating system, the application modules, or the game databases. It's a lucky miracle that the Orb works, but that pinhole through the firewall is too limited for me to do anything useful."

A long silence. "I heard somebody mention Arni's name," Rupe said.

Zia nodded. "I heard it too. They said he was killed."

Everyone looked at Arni's hospital bed. His eyes were still moving beneath his eyelids.

"Arni's capatar will respawn, though, right?" asked Francis. "I mean, the Wolfe guy is still alive after ten thousand years of Haven time, so he must've respawned dozens of times."

Zia shook her head. "Doesn't matter. Even if Arni does respawn, he won't be able to help. His capatar will spawn into the Avatar Mall, and the only portal out of the Mall is to Manhattan on JEEB Earth. Gaia failed to find some way to lower the firewall, so . . ."

Her voice trailed off.

Solomon looked over to the Haven engine. "We could destroy the machine, right now. It might save us."

"It *won't*," Chun countered. "I keep telling you. If you destroy the machine, we lose any chance of *ever* controlling what's going on."

"Much as I hate to admit it, she's right," said Zia. "We don't really understand anything about it, except that it seems to be wrecking the laws of physics. If you kill the machine, the bugaboo might go away, or we might just piss it off so much it eats the Earth. At minimum, if you shut down the machine it'll kill the capatars, and who knows what *that* will do to their meatspace bodies."

Chun's voice dripped fury and disbelief, all directed at Rupe. "You designed the dungeon to beat her, eh? So really, this girl you urged us to put into the game *turns out to be the worst possible choice you could have made!* She's useless, worse than useless, and it's *your* fault."

"What's wrong with you people?"

It was Fiona's mother, who must have escaped her confinement in the conference room during the chaos. No longer quiet and subdued, Ms. Martinez glared at each of them in turn. "That's my daughter inside that machine. My *daughter!*" Her face was swollen from hours of exhaustion and anxiety. "You think any of this is *her* fault? *You* people put a teen girl into that awful place. *You* did this. Not just him"—she pointed at Rupe—"but *all* of you."

Solomon reached out to placate her. She recoiled. "*You* put Fiona into danger. *You're* the only ones who can help her. You *created* this machine and this awful game. My daughter is a child. *You're* the adults. *You're* responsible for this mess, *not her*. So *do* something! *Fix* this! *Save my girl!*"

Francis gripped his mother's hand with white-clenched knuckles. His face echoed her helpless rage. He was glaring at Rupe. He was *blaming* Rupe. After all, it had been Rupe who had suggested that they send Fiona into the game. It had been Rupe who had convinced the skeptical JEEB team that a teen was their best chance at fixing the awful mistakes they'd all made in their vain attempts at glory and profit. A hard fist clenched Rupe's heart, and he thought for a moment that it had stopped beating.

He turned away from Francis and Ms. Martinez. Chun was nothing but cold despair. Zia was staring at her feet. The technician, who had silently witnessed the entire terrifying exchange, turned to his superior officer for guidance. All the others, including the boy and his mother, joined his gaze. Across the room, conversation faded.

Colonel Solomon set his jaw and mouthed a silent curse at the supreme misfortune of being the officer in charge during an apocalypse. With a deep, galvanizing breath, he spoke loudly for the room to hear. "Ms. Martinez is right. None of this is Fiona's fault. We caused this disaster, and it's ours to fix." He turned to Zia. "I've seen you punch through the military's most hardened security systems like they were tissue paper. I need you to forget everything we've tried up until now. You're the hacker. It's time for you to *hack*." He swiveled to Chun. "You created this machine. You know the principles of its operation better than anyone alive. I need you to stop telling us what we *can't* do, and instead tell us what we *can* do. You're the inventor: it's time for you to *invent*." Finally, he turned to Rupe, sending a shiver down Rupe's spine. "You're the Gamemaster. You know what Fiona is up against better than anyone else alive, and you understand her style of play. It's up to you to figure out a way for her to beat this boss you invented."

He waved his hand, encompassing the group. "Up until now, we've been bickering and fighting. No more. We're hackers, inventors, coders, and expert gamers—the very best in the world. It's up to us, and nobody else. We have to come together right *now*, not to save the planet, but to save one person only. We must save Fiona Martinez and her capatar, Gaia, so that she can save *us*."

He lowered his voice to a cold and unforgiving whisper, directed only at the core group surrounding him. "Figure it out. Find a way to get usable instructions to Fiona's capatar using any means possible. Our job is to get her *out* of that game-dungeon in one piece. We have minutes, at most." He pointed to the doors leading out of the lab. "Conference room. Now."

havencosm

The Dei Militans medic patched Se-Jong's face, hurriedly applying adhesive strips and more triage glue to the cut reopened by the blow from Kaiin's handgun. She had a dispassionate military demeanor, but when she inadvertently made eye contact, Se-Jong also saw a burning curiosity and a grudging respect. She applied a final spray of sealant to Se-Jong's burst cheek, nodded curtly, and turned her attention to Toroni, still unconscious on the floor.

Grandmother retrieved Toroni's rifle and moved aside for the militan medic. The medic placed a scanner on Toroni's forehead, examined it, and then selected a pharmaneedle, which she injected into the treatment port on his tacsuit. Almost instantly he gave a great, heaping gasp and arched his back. His eyes fluttered open, and he recoiled from the militan.

"Stand down, Sergeant," said Grandmother. "Can you hear me? We're under a temporary blood truce with the militans."

Toroni nodded dully and pulled himself into a sitting position, waving off the medic's offer of aid. His eyes scanned the room, taking in the new tactical situation. The seeker's tendrils were climbing the walls around the blast door and had progressed across the floor to the scanner arch in the middle of the room. He rose to his feet and took his rifle from Grandmother.

Se-Jong followed Grandmother and Toroni to the blast-door opening, carefully avoiding the tendrils spreading across the floor. Nkiru was with Littlefeather, surveying the immense chamber beyond. Se-Jong started to speak, but Littlefeather raised a finger to her lips. Nkiru had entered her familiar trance of deep concentration, intensely scrutinizing every aspect of the boss monster and its surroundings. Traces of a troubled frown flickered across her expression, as if she was looking for something and not finding it. Every few seconds, she glanced down at the snowglobe in her hand but found no solace or inspiration in its static-filled depths. She looked up at Se-Jong, pointed through the doorway into the boss chamber. "Over there, beneath the harvester. See that freestanding console? See how it's attached to those big cables that lead up into the belly of the monster? That looks important. There's a clear path to it, no seekers."

"What does it do?"

She shrugged. "I don't know. But by the way it's placed, I can tell that we're meant to see it." Before Se-Jong could react, she pointed in a different direction. "Now look over there, at that tall gantry frame that goes from the floor to the ceiling. Doesn't that look like some kind of giant blast cannon about halfway up? See those enormous power cables that lead to it? That looks important, too, and it looks like we can get to it by climbing up that ladder over there, scaling the exposed rock wall, and then jumping across those balance posts. We're meant to see that, too, which scares me. It seems too easy."

Se-Jong considered the torturous route they'd have to navigate to reach the blast cannon. "Too easy? Are you kidding me? What are you, a gymnast?"

She bit her bottom lip, her eyes still scanning the chamber. "Tricks, traps, and red herrings," she muttered. She seemed uncomfortably aware that everyone was watching her. She sighed and nodded to herself. "I can't see any option but to fight our way through."

She pointed at the elevated catwalk that ran along all four walls of the monstrous chamber. "See up there, near the top of those catwalk stairs? That's another blast door just like this one. It leads to Jaspaar's timedust lab, where he kept the motive core. If we can make it to the lab before the harvester, we might be able to escape. There's an emergency exit that goes to a flitter pad on the side of the mountain. If we get out in time, we can call the dropship." She paused, chewing her bottom lip. "Problem is, as soon as we step into the boss chamber, the harvester is going to attack us."

Whoom, whoom.

The floor-rumbling heartbeat had grown strong enough to rattle Se-Jong's teeth. Nkiru handed him the snowglobe. "Watch it. If something changes, no matter what, let me know."

He nodded. She turned away from the blast door and began inspecting the mossy humanoid shapes that littered the floor of the guardroom. Numbering more than a dozen, they were likely the remains of the security force that had crewed this guard station. From their contorted positions, he guessed they'd been struck down in combat. Nkiru kneeled, grimaced, and plunged her hands into one of the ancient corpses, sifting through the mossy remains. She retrieved something the size of a deck of cards, brushed it off, and lifted it so the others could see.

"Everybody needs one of these. Remember how awful the seeker powerfield was back when we crossed the bridge?" She gestured into the boss chamber. "It'll be *much* worse in there. As soon as we cross the threshold we'll be blinded, and we'll start taking damage." She stuffed the device into the pocket of her coldsuit. "These are called *inhibitors*. They're like little personal shields that filter out the worst of the harvester's powerfield. Everybody find one and carry it with you. They're not avatar devices, so they'll work for everyone. They're energized by the seeker powerfield."

The militans all looked at Kaiin. He nodded.

Grandmother and Littlefeather bent to the gruesome task, moving quickly between the corpses, recovering their inhibitor devices. As soon as Littlefeather handed one to Se-Jong, his vision cleared and the pain from the seeker powerfield vanished.

While the others stowed their inhibitors, Nkiru repeated their escape plan to Toroni. The entire group gathered around her at the blast door. "We don't have much time, so listen up. The boss won't notice us unless we touch one of its seekers. Problem is, it's impossible to get to the catwalk *without* touching a seeker. You'll have to hop and jump between the clear spots on the chamber floor. As soon as one of us steps on a seeker, the fun begins.

"The boss has three attacks." She pointed to the tendrils. "First is the *seeker sting*. If you touch one of the seekers, or allow one to touch you, it'll electrocute you, and all the other nearby tendrils will go into a frenzy and electrocute everything around you. Your inhibitor won't protect you.

"Second"—she pointed at the thick mat of seeker tubes that covered most of the boss chamber's floor—"is the *seeker slam*. The boss can pulse all of its seekers at once. It causes global damage to everything and everyone in the chamber. It has to recharge between slams, and that's when it's vulnerable.

Whoom, whoom.

"Right now, your rifles are jammed by the powerfield. They'll only work in the few seconds after a slam attack, while its recharging. Okay, now see those glowing nubby things around the bottom of the harvester? Those are called thruster nodes. If you shoot them while it's recharging, it slows down the recharge. The only problem is that if you cause too much damage to the harvester, or get too close to it, it'll activate its third attack, a *powerfield blast*. You'll know it's coming when all the seeker tendrils start glowing blue. If that happens, you've got about ninety seconds to kiss your asses goodbye. The powerfield blast uses a *lot* of energy, so it can only do it once every few minutes, but that doesn't matter, because the blast will *definitely* kill everyone in the boss chamber." She looked at the others. The militans had raised their faceplates, and their solemn expressions were filled with both mistrust and awe. Even the stoic Kaiin seemed taken aback by her knowledge of this place.

Nkiru gestured to Littlefeather. "I'll take my things." At Grandmother's nod, the reliquist reluctantly unslung the gobsmacker and the backpack. Kaiin watched intently as Nkiru took the items. She turned to Se-Jong and handed him the snowglobe. "Keep a constant eye on it. I don't think it'll work until we're far away from the harvester, but just in case, let me know if the static clears."

Turning back to the others, she pointed through the doorway. "We're heading for those stairs up to that one remaining catwalk. The floor along the way is covered with seekers. Remember, if you step on one, it'll discharge a hundred tentacles that will attack you and anyone near you. Keep a safe distance from each other. If we bunch together, a single seeker sting can get all of us. When it does a seeker-slam attack, and it will, don't lose your balance and stumble onto a seeker. Everybody got it?"

She licked her lips. The shifting light of the harvester played across her pale hair and gave the bloody crimson of her eyes the appearance of fire. "You all know the legends about avatar dungeons and how dangerous they were, but really, you don't know *anything*. We would have never made it here if Arni hadn't deactivated the random adversaries and bypassed most of the dungeon with his tunnels. Without those tunnels, even the greatest avatars would've taken weeks of fighting and exploring to get to the place we're standing right now. Weeks that were all just a warm-up to the boss monster we're about to face.

"For us to survive, you all need to do *exactly* what I say. *Don't* touch a seeker, not even the tiniest tendril. *Don't* shoot at the thruster nodes until *after* it does a seeker slam." She turned to Littlefeather. "You have the security access card from Arni? If we make it to the catwalk, we'll need it to open the blast door to Jaspaar's timedust lab."

Littlefeather tapped a pocket on the front of her tacsuit and nodded.

Nkiru gripped the gobsmacker and activated it. It lit up with a soft whir.

"So it is true," Kaiin whispered. He made the sign of the Linked Trinity. The other militans repeated the gesture over their golden flak vests. Grandmother frowned at their reactions to Nkiru's display of avatar powers.

Whoom, whoom.

Se-Jong stowed the snowglobe in his utility pocket so that it protruded just enough to keep an eye on it. "Still nothing but static," he reported.

Nkiru gave him a look that was intended to be encouraging, but he saw only fear in her eyes. "Move fast," she said to the group. "Stay at least three meters apart. Ready?"

Grandmother, Toroni, and the militans all closed the faceplates of their tacsuit helmets and powered up their weapons. Nkiru smiled at Se-Jong. "Lieutenant, you ready for this?" At his nod, she inhaled deeply and lifted the gobsmacker to her shoulder. "All right. Let's go."

―

In the living room of his childhood home on Askelon, there'd been a wall-to-wall rug imported from Earth. The rug had been embroidered in a random pattern of circles and squares of assorted colors. It had been a favorite game of Se-Jong's on rainy days to pretend that the circles on the rug were land mines and the squares were safe areas. Jumping from square to square, avoiding the furniture, balancing on one foot, then the other, it had been almost impossible to make it all the way across the room without blowing himself up.

This was worse. He eyed the mat of seeker tendrils. He'd made it less than ten of the forty meters to the base of the catwalk stairs, and he was already in trouble. There were occasional clear patches of floor, but they were irregularly spaced and required perfect balance and precise foot placement to move through. Wobbly from his injuries and the lingering effects of the Yok-Stop, he suddenly realized he'd never make it.

Whoom, whoom.

He took a step, teetered, windmilling his arms to keep his balance.

"Give me your hand." Grandmother had moved to his side.

"Nkiru said to keep our distance from each other."

"You're weaving all over the place. I'm staying with you." When he started to protest, she barked, "Shut up and *hold my hand.*"

Five minutes earlier she'd been a finger-twitch away from blowing Nkiru's brains out. He understood her reasoning, but it didn't diminish the fury he felt toward her. He stifled his anger, took her hand, pausing for only a fraction of a second to regain his balance.

The first seeker slam came with no warning.

In concert with the roaring heartbeat, the entire collection of seeker tendrils, many metric tons in all, lifted off the floor, rising as high as Se-Jong's knees before dropping with a resounding crash.

Whoom, whoom.

A searing burst of nerve pain and visual static swept over him as the powerfield briefly overwhelmed his inhibitor device. It caught him midstep, and it took everything he had to keep his balance. Only a well-timed jerk on his hand by Grandmother kept him from falling.

From high above, chunks of loose concrete tumbled from the ceiling and impacted all around them, setting off scattered explosions of seeker stings as the tendrils attacked the debris.

One of the militans screamed. Writhing, he vanished into a heap of seething tendrils, his body sparking and smoking.

"That was a seeker-slam attack," shouted Nkiru. "Now, shoot at the thruster nodes! Don't let up, and keep moving!" She raised the gobsmacker and sent a blast of shimmering energy toward the boss.

The militans, Littlefeather, and Toroni all opened fire. Where their shots found their marks, the thruster nodes shuddered and imploded, releasing gouts of fluid that instantly ignited and rose in a cloud of fire to blacken the sides of the harvester.

He and Grandmother hurried along, hopping and stretching between clear spots, sometimes forced to balance on one foot while searching for a place where the other foot might land. Se-Jong glanced ahead. Still twenty meters to the catwalk stairs.

Whoom, whoom.

Again, the entire corpus of seekers lifted off the floor and slammed down with an explosive concussion, rearranging themselves into a new tangle. Again, debris fell from high above, causing outbreaks of seeker activity all around him. Toroni cursed and sprang away from a blossom of tendrils, hopping like a dancer until he found a clear spot large enough for both boots.

"Shoot!" cried Nkiru.

More laser fire. More ruptured nodes and fireballs that scorched the sides of the harvester. But there were *hundreds* of nodes. And were some of the nodes they'd already hit starting to heal?

Next to him, Grandmother huffed loudly. They lurched forward another few meters, but they'd fallen far behind the others.

Whoom, whoom.

This time he was ready. As soon as the heartbeat commenced, he stiffened and found his center, steeling himself for the disorienting nerve pain and momentary blindness. The seekers rose and fell, rearranging into yet another pattern. Debris splashed around him. Two more militans died in a conflagration of sparks and smoke. Not Kaiin; his shining gold tacsuit was still standing, just behind Nkiru.

Grandmother cursed. "Truce or no truce, if he gets to the catwalk first with the girl, he'll take her and kill the rest of us." She made a sharp hand gesture to Toroni, who'd been holding back to protect his commander. She pointed at Kaiin. The marine nodded and began hopping recklessly toward the militan officer. Behind and above them, the great roaring whir from the harvester was rising in tone and volume.

"Oh, no," said Nkiru. "Rupe, you *hijo de puta!*"

Se-Jong didn't recognize Nkiru's words, but her frustration was clear. In front of her, the mat of seekers was now unbroken. There were no more clear spaces into which she could step, and she was still ten meters away from the catwalk stairs.

meatspace

Zia's lime-green marker flew across the conference room whiteboard, drawing boxes and connecting lines to hastily scribbled labels. Everyone in the crowded conference room watched anxiously. Lieberman had stayed behind with the unconscious patients, and Ms. Martinez had refused to leave Fiona's side. Chun, Solomon, Rupe, and Francis, plus two of the scientists from the lab, were watching anxiously as Zia tried to depict the situation. The faint smell of smoke from the fires in the surrounding city had infiltrated the building's air-conditioning system. Mixed with the fruit stench of Zia's scented dry-erase marker and the odor of too many people in need of a shower and fresh clothes, the room simply stank.

Zia pointed at a section of the incomprehensible diagram and turned to Rupe. "This is a rough overview of the game's external communications interfaces. See that? That's the tunnel through the firewall that Arni used to test the Orb. It's how Gaia sent us the photo, and how we called her using Francis's phone. And these parts here, and here, are the transmission protocols, and this other part over here is where it links to the various social media platforms."

"If you say so," he replied.

She snorted with frustration. "The point is, it's all *outside* the gaming codebase, and outside the firewall. I can hack these code modules."

"What good is that?" asked Solomon.

"I have no idea," she admitted. "But it's the only bit of code in the entire multimillion-line codebase we can control. Now that the game is running in real time, there might be something we can do."

"We've looked at the Orb software before," said Chun. "I had a dozen people working on it. We couldn't find a way to exploit it."

"That was before the timestream resynchronized."

"I don't see how that changes anything," argued Chun. "The code *works*. We've proven we can establish two-way video with the Orb. The real problem is that the boss monster is jamming the signal."

Rupe chewed his lip. "The boss monster's powerfield fluctuates on a cycle. The jamming effect gets weaker for a few seconds after each cycle. If we time it right, we might be able to get something through in those moments."

"How will we know when the timing is right?"

He shook his head. "There's no way to know. The cycles last about thirty seconds."

After a short silence, Zia said, "What if we transmit a continuous message? A repeating loop, or a still image. It'd have to be short, something that they could receive and understand during the moments between cycles."

"Not good enough" Chun said. "This Orb technology was never really playtested in the game. We don't know if the signal will be strong enough to penetrate the boss monster's jamming field, even at its weakest. And even if we can figure out a way to send a message, what do we send? What advice can we give Fiona that will help, especially given that she may only see it for a second or two?"

Everyone turned to look at Rupe. It was the biggest question of all, one that only he could answer. He stared at the diagram Zia had drawn, looking for inspiration. Nothing came to him. "Give me a minute to think."

Solomon started to object but turned away when Rupe cried, "Give me a fucking minute, *please!*"

The awful truth was that no player, no matter how skilled, could defeat a dungeon boss without dying and respawning many times. Boss encounters were intentionally engineered so that each time a player's avatar was killed, the player learned a valuable strategy needed for the next attempt.

Gaia knows this, he thought. She knows the only way to learn to defeat a boss is to die and be respawned a dozen times. But she isn't an avatar. She knows this, too. She knows she won't respawn on the scene.

She knows she has only one chance. How will that knowledge affect her decisions?

He closed his eyes and tried to envision what she was seeing. Before the Orb had gone blank, she'd been in the security guardroom, and the blast door had already been opened. That meant the encounter timer had started, and the boss would be waking up. He wondered how ten thousand years of accelerated time had affected the boss. Had it evolved, and if so, how it had changed over the millennia?

He shoved the thought to the side. Keep it simple, he told himself. She'll know that the only possible escape path is through the boss chamber. Taking the catwalk to Jaspaar's Motive Core lab is the most obvious route. It's what the characters in the TV show had done. It's the route that promises the most loot, the most glory. She knows this. She'll suspect it's a trap. She'll be looking for the avoidance route, instead. It's what she always does, and she's good at it.

His gut clenched with guilt, and sorrow. What she doesn't know is that there is no avoidance route. There are tantalizing clues that point to three different potential escapes, but all of them lead to certain death. The only way out is the obvious way, through the Motive Core lab. Hard combat, then an escape room with a ticking time bomb and a bizarre puzzle with no time to solve it.

He glanced up toward the whiteboard, where Zia and Chun were in a competition to cover Zia's initial crude diagram with more indecipherable software gibberish. It was the first time he'd ever seen the two women work together. They'd given up on him and had turned to their own schemes.

It didn't matter. Several minutes had already elapsed since they'd lost the signal from the Orb. It was probably too late. It was *certainly* too late if Gaia had already chosen one of the three red-herring routes. Even if she chose the catwalk path, the chance of her surviving the combat phase was almost nil.

Rupe closed his eyes and tried to relax. He pushed the awful imagery out of his head. *Don't think. Just relax.* Inspiration wasn't an on-demand resource. Epiphanies couldn't be made-to-order. He waited.

Nothing.

After a while he opened his eyes. The two women were still at the whiteboard. Tall and severe Chun and short and round Zia. The Inventor and the Hacker. They seemed to be excited about something. Chun waved to Solomon, pointed at something on the board.

Watching the earnest faces of the two adversaries as they worked together prompted a flash at the back of his mind. Something was missing. He waited for the thought to harden, knowing that if he tried to rush it, it would crumble and dissipate.

Zia whirled to her laptop, which lay open on the conference room table. She typed furiously while Chun looked over her shoulder. Chun pointed at something on the laptop and Zia nodded. She tapped a key, stared intently for a moment at the screen. She pounded her fist on the conference table and her face broke into the biggest smile Rupe had ever seen. Even Chun seemed impressed.

Zia tapped another key. The conference room's video screen flickered to life with a video of frantic motion and chaos. The video's perspective seemed to be from someone's waist pocket, looking up at the person's torso toward the ceiling. Whoever was carrying the Orb was running and jumping, making the image so jerky it was impossible to make out the situation. Indistinct shouts overlain by a continuous roar sounded from the wall screen's speakers.

"It's the video feed from the Orb," Zia announced. "We found a way to filter out the boss's interference. They still can't receive our transmission, but we can see and hear what's happening in real time."

Francis went pale. "Is that the boss chamber?"

"Yeah. Yeah, it is," murmured Rupe.

Francis's finger stabbed toward the jostling image. "See, there! Was that the Gurothim harvester? It's not supposed to look like that, is it?"

"No," said Rupe. "It's . . . grown."

havencosm

Se-Jong clutched his grandmother's arm as they teetered on a shrinking island of bare floor. The sea of seekers surged around them. Toroni and Littlefeather were still making slow progress ahead of them, but at the front of the procession, Nkiru and Kaiin had stopped. They'd almost reached the catwalk stairs, but the final few meters were blocked.

Nkiru spun in a complete circle, frantically searching for a way forward. She raised the gobsmacker, aimed it at a section of floor at the base of the stairs. A gout of energy detonated from the barrel and blasted the seeker mat, causing an eruption of activity from the impacted area.

"Oh, shit!" she cried, stumbling backward to avoid the radiating wave of tendrils. She fell into Kaiin's arms and almost dropped the gobsmacker.

Whoom, wha-whoom.

The harvester's heartbeat stuttered. Instead of rising and falling as before, the seeker tendrils began tossing and thrashing as if whipped by a storm. The area cleared by the gobsmacker blast instantly refilled. Se-Jong looked down. The bare patch in which he and Grandmother stood was closing up. They jumped to a nearby patch, but it, too, was shrinking. Nkiru's gobsmacker attack had prompted a murderous counterattack.

Se-Jong realized with surprising calm that he was entering the last few seconds of his life. He felt the pressure of his grandmother's grip on his arm, and along with it a wave of remorse. She was here because of him. He would be the cause of her death.

She said something. The grip on his arm increased painfully.

"I'm sorry," he whispered.

Grandmother shouted again, directly into his ear. "Give me the timedust!"

"What?"

"I saw you collect grains of timedust in the mine tunnels. Give them to me!"

Startled into action, with his free hand Se-Jong dug out the pouch of timedust from the pocket of his coldsuit and handed it to her.

She released her grip. "Get to the girl. Hurry!"

"What? No!"

Her face, always grim, had hardened into a mask of carbon steel. "Go!"

He suddenly realized what she was thinking. The seekers *ate* timedust. They *craved* it.

"Go, Sonja. *Please*."

He'd never before heard her utter the word *please*. When he didn't move, she hissed, "Remember *who you are*."

He glanced toward Nkiru. Kaiin had a hand on her elbow, pointing, suggesting a path forward. Littlefeather was just ahead of Se-Jong, staring uncertainly at Kaiin. Toroni was stranded in a rapidly diminishing island of floor, as was the only other surviving militan, the medic who'd treated his face. The marine raised his rifle toward Kaiin, sighting carefully though its scope. Realizing this, the militan medic swung her weapon toward Toroni.

The cold phantom that had been hiding in the corner of Se-Jong's soul stirred and began to move into the light. An unexpected resolve flooded him. He pushed the pain and nausea into a mental container and thrust it aside. The chaos surrounding him slowed, brightened, becoming crystal clear in every detail, as if a lens he'd never known existed had fallen into place over his eyes.

"I'm a Kwon, just like you," he said to Grandmother.

She nodded, her eyes bright. He released her hand and sprinted toward Nkiru.

———

For an instant he thought he'd misread Grandmother's intentions. One heartbeat, two . . . leaping from one tiny, moving patch of floor to the next, forcing both eyes open despite the swelling.

Nothing . . . nothing . . . nothing.

He was almost upon Nkiru and Kaiin when the timedust crystals she'd flung toward the female militan began to pepper down. The reaction from the harvester was instantaneous and overwhelming.

With a thunderous roar from the body of the beast, pseudopods erupted from the nearby seekers with ludicrous speed, striking everywhere a grain of timedust lay, each impacting the floor with the explosive force of a grenade and sending shards of stone ricocheting in all directions. The militan was impaled a dozen times, juddering soundlessly as the seeker tentacles pumped their deadly energies directly into her body. She screamed, but the continuous roar of the Gurothim harvester filled the universe.

Like a receding ocean tide filmed in fast motion, the great mass of seeker tentacles around Se-Jong withdrew, flowing in a wave toward the timedust crystals. He leaned forward, shoulder first, and plowed into Kaiin just below the waist.

They fell together, and a part of his mind noted that the retreating seekers had begun to shine with the same bright bioluminescent blue as the oceans of his homeworld, Askelon. Nkiru screamed something, but Se-Jong was occupied with Kaiin, kicking and pounding ineffectually at the militan's armored tacsuit, knowing that all Kaiin had to do was draw his sidearm and the fistfight would be over.

With one hand, Se-Jong clawed at the militan's faceplate and wrenched it open. His other hand shot to his waist and wrapped around a metal cylinder attached to the belt of his coldsuit. He raised the cylinder, aimed it into the open faceplate, and pulled the trigger.

The unexpected stream of Yok-Stop caused Kaiin to flinch and sputter. The momentary hesitation was all Se-Jong needed. He punched Kaiin's nose, hard.

The militan's head snapped back, and he stumbled. Se-Jong moved in again and grabbed the wrist holding the gun. He tried to wrest it away, but Kaiin's grip was too strong.

How long had it taken for the Yok-Stop to work when he'd been sprayed by Nkiru? Ten, twenty seconds? He held Kaiin's wrist with all his might, summoning energy he hadn't known he possessed.

Shouts and screams howled around him, but he ignored them all, focused instead on the task of not getting shot.

Despite his best effort, Kaiin pulled away and lurched to a standing position. With a growl, he wiped the Yok-Stop from his eyes and swung the pistol toward Se-Jong. Se-Jong tried not to flinch.

Kaiin didn't fire. Instead, he blinked, then blinked again. He let out a horrifying screech and dropped his handgun. He stumbled and fell. He curled into a fetal position and began convulsing, clawing at his eyes.

Littlefeather rushed to Se-Jong's side and helped him to his feet. He looked back at the snakelike mass of seeker tubes, all intertwined and moving with terrifying speed, thickly centered on the area where Grandmother had thrown the timedust.

Of Grandmother, there was no trace.

meatspace

"Shit," cried Rupe. "*Shit!* Look!"

Zia and Chun were huddled over Chun's laptop, heads almost touching, arguing over software code. They swiveled toward the wall screen. The image being transmitted from the Orb jostled and shuddered, but it was possible to make out several figures leaping and jumping through a jungle of thrashing boss tentacles.

"Did you see what that old woman just did?"

They stared blankly.

"She fucking used *timedust* to distract the boss," he shouted. "That was *never* in the game script. Fucking brilliant. That old woman sacrificed herself to save the others. Watch them. See, they're *helping* Gaia!"

Chun frowned. Zia looked startled, confused. Rupe tried to keep his voice steady. "I designed the dungeon to be solved by *players*. I never counted on the bots to have minds of their own. Gaia has friends with her. They're working together, and they're *smart*."

havencosm

A tornadic wind filled the chamber. Nkiru shouted over the roar of the harvester, gesturing toward the now-clear path to the catwalk stairs. The entire raging sea of seeker tentacles was glowing a bright blue. Was the gods-damned thing ramping up to a powerfield blast?

Se-Jong looked frantically for Toroni. The marine had been near the epicenter of the seeker reaction and was stranded on a rapidly shrinking island of floor.

How long did they have before the blast? Nkiru had said ninety seconds, but how much time had already elapsed? He screamed into Littlefeather's ear, "You and Nkiru go! I'll get Toroni!"

She nodded and raced toward Nkiru. Without looking back, Se-Jong stooped to grab Kaiin's fallen pistol.

A two-meter-wide river of glowing tentacles separated Toroni from escape, too far to jump. Se-Jong fired into the seekers, surprised by the noise and recoil of Kaiin's unfamiliar handgun.

No effect.

He sprayed Yok-Stop into the tentacles. Nothing happened. He flung the cannister into their midst.

Arching and leaping, they attacked it. He watched in astonishment as the stream of seekers redirected itself toward the orange can, blasting it with arcing voltage enough to liquify the metal. Within seconds the river had thinned to the point Toroni could leap across. He slapped Se-Jong's shoulder, and they both ran for the catwalk stairs, fighting the howling wind. They shot past Kaiin, who was still writhing on the floor. Se-Jong had a momentary thought to help him, but there was no time.

They leaped onto the stairs, raced up to the catwalk, then bolted toward the figures of Littlefeather and Nkiru, who had reached the blast door to Jaspaar's timedust lab.

The escalating roar of the harvester threatened to crush his eardrums. Se-Jong hadn't been counting the seconds, but he knew there weren't many left. Ahead, Littlefeather waved Arni's access card against the wall and the blast door began to slide open. She ducked inside. Nkiru hesitated, turned to Se-Jong. She beckoned, her hair flying around her head like a white halo.

Suddenly, silence, and the expression on Nkiru's face went from alarm to horror. He and Toroni were just a few meters away when the blue radiance from the seekers detonated into a silent flash of room-filling brilliance. It felt like all the air was being sucked from Se-Jong's lungs. He stumbled.

Hands, pulling, tugging. He leaped through the narrow opening, Toroni beside him, and collapsed to the floor. Behind him, the blast door slammed shut.

meatspace

The wall screen showed a low view across a debris-littered floor, hazy as if the lens were smeared with grime. The bot carrying the Orb had fallen, but the glassy sphere was protruding far enough from his pocket for much of the scene to be visible. Rupe pointed to an indistinct figure on the screen. It approached the Orb, dropped to its knees. Even through the grime obscuring the lens, he saw dark skin and silver hair.

"She made it to Jaspaar's lab. That's Gaia, right there! Do you understand? She made it through the boss chamber on her *first attempt!*"

Francis let out a shuddering exhale. On the screen, Gaia was shouting at her team bots. The roar of the harvester had diminished but was still too loud for them to make out her words. The view shifted as the bot carrying the Orb rolled onto its side.

Rupe turned to the others. "We don't have much time. Pay attention. Things in Jaspaar's lab are about to get really, really tricky for Gaia. Combat with the boss was bad enough, but what happens in the lab will be a real test for Gaia's wits. To get out alive, she needs to make directly for the rear exit, which leads to a flitter pad on the side of the mountain. If she hurries, there's just enough time to take a flitter and get far enough away from the harvester before it launches and destroys the mountain." He paused and took a breath. "I'm afraid that instead of going for the exit, she'll waste time looking for the treasure that she knows is hidden in the lab."

"The controller for the motive core?" said Francis.

Rupe nodded. The boy knew the plot of the "Game Changer" episode as well as his sister. He knew that the device Jaspaar had been building to control the harvester was somewhere in the lab, and that if Gaia could secure it, she would have one of the crucial components that Dek Longstar had used to confront the harvester in the final episode of *Longstar's Rangers*.

"She'll absolutely try to find it," said Francis.

"I know," agreed Rupe. "And she'll run out of time."

"Why?"

"There's a puzzle she has to solve to get the controller. It's an easy puzzle if you know it's there, but it's not in the Gamechanger TV episode and I didn't brief her on this part of the dungeon. The hard part for Gaia will be realizing that the puzzle even exists."

havencosm

Se-Jong and Toroni lay side by side on the metal floor, both panting deeply. The marine swallowed, tried to catch his breath. His eyes fell on Se-Jong's battered face. "That must really hurt."

"Yeah."

Toroni scrambled to his feet, offered a hand. Se-Jong took it, and the marine hauled him upright. "That was some badass shit back there, kid."

High praise coming from a sergeant of the Solar Marines, Se-Jong realized. Toroni pulled off his helmet and wiped the sweat from his face. He gave Se-Jong a somber look. "Captain Kwon saved all of us."

Se-Jong nodded. He didn't have time to release the unexploded bomb of emotions surrounding Grandmother's death. The pulsing roar of the harvester's powerfield shook the floor.

Whoom, whoom.

Se-Jong almost toppled when Nkiru flew into him, wrapping her arms around him and squeezing painfully. Her filthy and matted hair smelled like smoke and lavender. He tried to return the embrace, but she pulled away, shouting over the roar. "We've got a minute, maybe two, before the harvester comes through that blast door." She grabbed his arm and tugged him toward the center of the room.

Jaspaar's timedust lab was a perfect cube, ten meters to a side and ten high. Unlike all the other settings they'd visited in this ancient dungeon, it looked as if it had been in use yesterday. There was no dust, no corrosion, no rot from ten thousand years of history.

The walls were lined with shelves, storage lockers, lab workspaces, and gleaming consoles, all lighted, all blinking and displaying dazzling images on overhead glass screens.

At the center of the floor was a device that could only be the motive core. It was smaller and less impressive than he'd imagined: a white, basketball-size sphere impaled by a metal tube that passed through its axis and protruded a few centimeters on either side. Both ends of the tube were packed with wires and connection points. Thick bundles of cables led from the device to the consoles along the room's periphery. The whole assembly sat on a pedestal situated inside a large metal cage. Se-Jong, Nkiru, and Toroni joined Littlefeather, who was peering through the bars of the cage.

"That's the motivator thingie?" Se-Jong shouted.

"That's it," said Nkiru. "The motive core."

As far as he could see, there wasn't a door into the metal cage. He reached out to test the strength of the bars. Nkiru grabbed his hand. "Don't touch it. It's energized. It's a shield Jaspaar hoped would keep the harvester from detecting it."

"It'll keep the harvester away?"

She shook her head. "Not a chance. The harvester has been biding its time since the Cataclysm, dreaming of this moment, getting stronger and stronger. It *knows* the core is nearby."

Whoom, whoom.

A flicker caught Se-Jong's eye. Visible through the top of the utility pouch, the snowglobe had changed its appearance. The static had partially cleared, and he thought he could see moving shapes. He dug it out of the pocket, squinted. Sure enough, there were people in the Orb, though there was too much static to see anything but their shapes.

He held it up. "Look at this!"

Nkiru grabbed the sphere and cradled it in her palm. "Rupe! Rupe, can you hear me?" The blurry shapes in the snowglobe reacted, and clustered close to their camera. One of them had a shaggy beard and lots of hair. He was saying something, but his words were lost in the static. Nkiru shook the snowglobe. "Rupe, we're in Jaspaar's lab. What do I do next?"

The shape in the snowglobe grew animated, but the interference made it impossible to tell what it meant. Nkiru growled in frustration.

"Is that the way out?" said Toroni, gesturing toward the door on the rear wall.

Nkiru nodded. "Probably."

"What are we waiting for?"

Nkiru was staring at the motive core.

Toroni looked at Littlefeather, then at Se-Jong. "Let's go!"

Nkiru expelled a hard breath. She handed the snowglobe to Se-Jong. "There's something I have to do. Go ahead with the others. I'll be right behind you."

His heart fell. "That's nuts. The harvester is coming through that blast door at any second."

She hesitated.

"Damn it, Nkiru. We're not leaving you here. What's so important?"

"Remember I said Jaspaar was working on a way to control the harvester? To use it as a weapon?"

He nodded.

"That's what he was doing in this lab. He put something inside the motive core. It's connected to a controller device."

"A controller? To control the *harvester?*" He looked at the consoles on the surrounding walls. "Where is it?"

She grimaced. "The controller is small, portable. It's hidden somewhere in this lab."

"Hidden?"

She nodded.

"If we can find it, can you stop the harvester?"

"I don't know. Maybe." She inhaled deeply. "Jaspaar was still working on it when the Cataclysm hit. He hadn't perfected it."

"So it might not even work?" Toroni gave Littlefeather an incredulous glare. In the absence of the captain, she was the senior officer present. She squared her shoulders, took a deep breath, and turned to Se-Jong. With a shock, he realized that she was looking to him for guidance.

He spun to Nkiru. "How much time do we have?"

"A minute, max."

There was no time to sort it out. He knew what his grandmother would have done. If the harvester escaped, no planet in the Known Arc would ever be safe again.

"Let's find the gods-damned thing," he said.

meatspace

"No, no, no," Rupe shouted at the video screen. "She's going for the controller."

"How much time does she have?" asked Solomon.

"Not enough. Not nearly enough."

"She saw you," Francis shouted. "She saw you and recognized you. We all heard her. At least some of our signal must be getting through to the Orb."

Rupe tried to calm himself. "Maybe the blast door is blocking some of the harvester's powerfield. She couldn't hear me, though, and the picture on her end must be bad, because she wasn't sure it was me."

Francis broke in, his voice trembling. "If she can see *anything* in the Orb, that's a start, right?" He looked around at the faces of the scientists and military. "We should be able to signal her somehow, right?"

Around Rupe, nothing but blank faces. Finally, Zia said, "If the image quality is bad on her end, maybe we can transmit a simple text image instead of video? She moved to the whiteboard, grabbed a whiteboard marker, and wrote in six-inch block letters:

NO TIME! GO <u>NOW</u> TO FLITTER PAD!

Chun nodded. "It might work. A simple two-color, high-contrast image like text on a white background might be visible through the interference. Take a photo of what Zia wrote on the whiteboard and send it."

Everyone around Rupe was nodding. Everyone except Francis. The boy started to speak but hesitated.

It suddenly hit Rupe: out of everyone present, among all the PhDs and high-ranking officers and certified geniuses, only he and Francis were gamers, and between himself and Francis, only the boy really knew his sister. It hadn't been just Fiona's perceptive ability that had led to their mutual success in the game before the crash. They worked as a team. A team of twins.

"What is it?" he prompted.

Francis shook his head.

Solomon noticed, "Nothing is too stupid, Francis. If you have an idea, let's hear it."

The boy cleared his throat. "I know my sister. She's going to try to find the controller *no matter what you tell her*. Instead of wasting time trying to change her mind, why don't you let me *help* her?"

havencosm

Nkiru licked her lips. "Think of it like a game. The controller won't be easy to find, but there will be clues. There may also be traps. We only get one shot, so *be careful*."

Clues? Se-Jong scanned the room. One wall was completely covered with consoles and screens, all active, all displaying a bewildering array of complex diagrams and data. The area around the blast door was mostly empty except for a worktable scattered with unrecognizable tools. The wall opposite the blast door was lined with tall metal storage lockers and the exit door through which they would escape. The only decoration was a row of colorful tiles forming a border that circled the room at ceiling level.

Whooooooooooooooom . . .

The overhead lights flickered. All the consoles and screens went dark for a moment before rebooting. The pulsating rumble from the harvester had risen to a smooth, uninterrupted roar. Se-Jong glanced at the snowglobe. Vague static, indistinct moving figures.

"What does the controller look like?" Littlefeather shouted.

"I'm not sure. I think it might look like a VR headset."

"A what?"

"Something you wear on your head. It covers your eyes."

"Like eyeglasses?"

"Bigger. More like snow goggles with metal lenses." She pointed to the row of storage lockers at the rear of the room. "It's probably locked inside one of those."

Se-Jong and Toroni rushed to the lockers. The doors were numbered but otherwise featureless, with no handle, latch, or hinge. Se-Jong tried pressing random places, hammering with his fist, prying the seams. He and Toroni battered the lockers with their shoulders. Toroni risked a laser shot at one of the locker doors, but his rifle was still disabled by the harvester's powerfield.

"It won't be obvious," Nkiru called. She was scurrying around the periphery of the room, examining the consoles and wall screens. She moved to the worktable on the front wall, quickly picking up each tool and examining it. Then she moved back to the wall of consoles, her eyes flitting across the screens and controls. Through the thick blast door, the cry of the harvester sounded like the atmospheric jets of an orbital shuttle spooling up for takeoff.

Toroni was wiring a small explosive charge from his tactical kit when a flicker caught Se-Jong's eye. The snowglobe had changed appearance. In the static were symbols. He dug it out of his pocket, squinted. Not symbols, but indistinct writing.

He held it up. "Look at this!"

Nkiru grabbed the sphere and cradled it in her palm. "Rupe! Rupe, can you hear me? It's too blurry. I can't read it." She shook the snowglobe. No change. "Can you write bigger? Make the letters bigger."

Movement in the snowglobe. Nkiru's focus was fierce.

Letters formed as if someone was writing them on a white surface. This time, instead of a line of text, only a few letters were visible:

S1E9. HURRY! LUV, GEO

Nkiru scowled at the message.

"What does it mean?" said Littlefeather.

A smile bent Nkiru's lips. "It's from my brother. It means season 1, episode 9." She lifted the snowglobe, spoke loudly and distinctly, "Got it, Francis. The 'Escape Room' episode. I'm on it."

She pushed the snowglobe into Se-Jong's hands. Her eyes searched the room, fell on the worktable near the blast door. She rushed to the table, grabbed one of the scattered tools, then moved to the bank of consoles and inserted the tool's nose into a small hole beneath the largest screen. An image of four symbols appeared on the screen: a square, a triangle, a circle, and an X.

□ △ ○ ✕

When she spun the crank, a number appeared below the first symbol, the square. It changed to a *1*, then a *2*, then a *3*.

"See the row of tiles around the walls?" she shouted. Se-Jong looked up. Just below the ceiling and extending around the periphery of the room was a decorative border, a single row of colorful ceramic tiles. "The symbols on this screen match the symbols on those tiles. Look at the tiles. Do you see a pattern in the symbols?"

He looked up at the band of tiles. "What's that got to do with opening the lockers?"

"Goddamn it, Lieutenant, this is a *game*. I know what I'm doing. Do you see a pattern or not?"

He scanned the wall. Each tile contained one of the four symbols. To Se-Jong the distribution of symbols seemed random.

A new sound came from beyond the blast door, accompanied by a burning smell and a strong metallic taste on his tongue. The floor shuddered. He steadied himself against one of the lockers.

Nkiru's eyes flew around the room. "Count the tiles of each symbol. Hurry! How many have a square symbol?"

They all froze, counting.

"Twelve," called Littlefeather.

Nkiru busied herself at the console. The number beneath the square on the screen increased as she turned the tool's handle.

"No, there's thirteen!" shouted Toroni. "Thirteen!"

The floor shuddered again.

"He's right. Thirteen squares," agreed Littlefeather.

Nkiru spun the tool until the number below the square was *13*. She pressed a prominent gray button on the console below the screen. The square flashed, and a *0* symbol appeared below the triangle on the screen.

"Yes! How many triangles?" Nkiru cried.

"Stand by. Uh, sixteen, seventeen, *eighteen* triangles!"

"*How* many?"

"*Eighteen*," shouted Toroni and Littlefeather in unison.

Se-Jong was counting the X symbols, which seemed most numerous.

. . . *17, 18, 19, 20, 21* . . .

The floor suddenly fell at least a meter, and Se-Jong went to his knees. With a great, ringing crash, the blast door buckled.

Toroni gestured toward the exit door. "Time to go!"

Nkiru gave them a look of wild desperation. "No! Count the symbols. How many circles?"

"Shit, I lost count," Littlefeather cried.

"I'll count the X's; you count the circles," Se-Jong called.

He started over.

1, 2, 3, 4 . . .

Another crash at the blast door. He didn't allow his eyes to be torn from his task.

. . . 11, 12, 13 . . .

"Twenty-two circles," said Littlefeather.

Nkiru spun the handle of the tool until the number *22* appeared beneath the circle symbol on her screen. "What about X's? How many X's?"

Se-Jong whispered each number as he counted, more intensely focused on this task than any other in his life.

14, 15, 16, 17, 18, 19, 20, 21, 22, 23, 24, 25, 26 . . .

He heard Littlefeather's voice, but it was distant, as if she were calling out from across a vast space. "Seekers! They're coming through the door!"

"We have to go, *now!*" cried Toroni.

27, 28, 29, 30 . . .

Toroni shouldered his laser rifle and pointed it at the seekers, but it would not fire. He shook it in frustration, then pulled what looked like a grenade from his tacsuit.

WHOOOOOOOOM!

The roar of the harvester quadrupled in intensity. The floor shook. Everyone froze except Nkiru.

"How many X's?" she screamed. Her eyes were wild, desperate.

He'd lost count. "Fuck!"

He saw her face fall. She took a soft, measured breath, gave him a smile that chilled his soul. They were out of time.

Se-Jong let himself slump. He lowered his gaze, noticed an unexpected change.

The snowglobe. Someone had replaced the previous message with a new one.

```
Sq:13 Tri:18 O:22 X:33
```

He stared at it.

X:33
X:33

"Thirty-three!" Se-Jong shrieked. "Nkiru, thirty-three X's!"

Nkiru jerked upright, gave him an incredulous glance, then cranked the tool and slammed her palm on the gray button.

The storage lockers opened, and at the center of the room, the bars of the cage surrounding the motive core slid into the floor. In the same instant, the volume of the harvester's engines climbed to a thunderous crescendo.

Nkiru flew to the lockers at the rear of the room. She tore through the shelves, tossing the priceless relics to the ground like unwanted children's toys. Gleaming weapons. Armor. Ancient coins and jewels. Handheld devices of unknown function. A magnificent iron-clasped book. Littlefeather's eyes burned as she pulled out her komnic and swept it across the priceless trove of avatar relics, recording the moment of their discovery.

"Here it is!" Nkiru held up a pliable band of metal obviously designed to fit around a humanoid head. Without hesitation she slipped it on her eyes. Several small lights appeared around the edges of the opaque eyepieces.

"Wait. Is that a good idea?"

She ignored Se-Jong. Twisting her head from side to side, she said, "I can see something, but it's not . . . I can't find a way to . . . there aren't any . . . wait." She made a gesture of frustration. "It's like looking through muddy water at an abstract painting."

Se-Jong glanced at the exit door, then at the battered blast door. Blue light shone through widening seams.

"Wait, wait," Nkiru said, a measure of hope creeping into her voice. "I think maybe I can—"

The blast door crumpled like metal foil and the harvester exploded through.

A mass of seekers flooded the room, a tidal wave of glowing blue kelp, blindingly fast and moving with deliberate intent toward the motive core.

Se-Jong flung himself at Nkiru, tackled her toward the rear of the room.

Toroni flung a grenade into the roaring tumult, to no noticeable effect. He stumbled and was lost behind the thick sea of seekers.

Se-Jong consolidated his hold on Nkiru. He felt other hands and realized Littlefeather was embracing both of them. In this alien place, simple human contact made their impending deaths more bearable.

The seekers swallowed the motive core, severed the cables that connected it with the other equipment in the room, and withdrew back out the blast door with spectacular swiftness.

A split second of silence, then the ignition of the harvester's thruster nodes blistered the room with light and heat. Se-Jong huddled with Nkiru and Littlefeather beneath the open lockers, their screams lost in the din of the harvester's departure.

Once again, the floor seemed to fall away beneath them. With a chest-crushing shock wave, the room filled with superheated dust. Gigatons of rock were displaced as the monster broke through the top of the mountain. In an instant of suspended time, Se-Jong felt Nkiru's face pressed into his neck; then, the shattered remains of the mountaintop avalanched back down into the space created by the harvester's sudden vacancy.

meatspace

A chaotic roar overloaded the speaker. Light exploded from the video screen, filling the conference room and illuminating the upturned faces surrounding Rupe. The video spun as the force of the harvester's attack threw the Orb across Jaspaar's lab.

The Orb rolled to a stop. Gobbets of dirt and debris spotted the image. Dust streamed and whirlpooled across the field of view. The roar from the speakers diminished and was gone.

Silence.

Rupe wasn't breathing, and he suspected that nobody else was, either. The haze cleared. Incredibly, Jaspaar's lab was still at least partially intact.

"Oh, god," breathed Francis.

A boot, covered by filth, toe upturned toward the ceiling, blocked most of the view.

"It's not moving," Zia said.

"Are they alive?" Solomon said.

Rupe stared at the screen. At the boot. Something was still producing light in the lab, though the light looked . . . different. Brighter than it should be. He shook his head to clear it. This deep in the mountain, the harvester's departure should have obliterated Jaspaar's lab and everything in it.

"Our transmission isn't being blocked anymore," Chun called from her laptop. "They should be able to see us now."

He took a step toward the teleconference microphone mounted below the screen. "Hello? Hello, can anybody hear me? Gaia, are you there?"

Silence.

Francis moved to Rupe's side. "Fi, it's me. Say something, please!"

The boot moved.

havencosm

Dream-words cut through a dullness of sound. The Mucktu queen glares at him.

> *"Wake up! Is she alive?"*

Utter blackness. The taste of burning dirt. Everything hurt. *Everything.*

Nkiru was in his arms. He could feel her body convulse with coughs, but he couldn't hear anything but a numbing whine.

She's alive, he tried to whisper, but his mouth was filled with grit.

He cracked open his good eye, saw a shaft of light angling through the pall of dust. He blinked away the grimy crust that threatened to cement his eyelid shut. The light was filtering through the ragged hole of what had once been the blast door.

Sunlight.

Motion next to him. Littlefeather, also coughing violently. No sign of Toroni.

Hints of artificial light. Some of the consoles were still powered; some of the displays still glowed with complex diagrams and symbols.

The controller goggles were askew on Nkiru's face. He pulled them off, stroked her brow. Her eyes opened.

"Are you okay?" The cadence of his words sounded like dull hammer strikes within his skull.

She nodded and began to uncurl away from him.

Faint sounds trickled into his damaged ears. A clatter of rocks, boulders. The repeating *whoop* of an alarm siren. And words.

Curses, like only a Solar Marine could produce.

"Ah, you mother-fucking heaping pile of gods-damned bartchin' shitheap uselessness, I am sick and garl-shatting tired of this place."

Toroni sat on the floor, leaning against one of the consoles, his rifle at his side. He coughed ferociously. When he saw Se-Jong, he gave a weak thumbs-up.

The four of them crept to shredded remains of the blast door and looked out through the pall of smoke and dust. The catwalk and stairs were gone. The floor of the boss chamber had collapsed a hundred meters or more, leaving them staring out from a sheer cliff face at a deep, rubble-filled crater. The floor shook as gargantuan boulders shifted within the newly formed void.

The roof of the mountain had been blown away. Above, the late evening sky was visible through a ragged opening half a kilometer across, beyond which an impossibly tall column of black smoke traced the harvester's path of ascent.

They had loosed a First Epoch monster into the Known Arc.

Se-Jong's fingers found Nkiru's. His voice sounded distant, muffled in his battered eardrums. "Well, that's not good."

"No, it's really not," she said.

He scanned the crater floor, barely visible through the settling dust. Somewhere down there beneath tons of broken rock lay the remains of his grandmother. They would never find her body. She would remain on Grone for all eternity, with this broken mountain as her gravestone. Private McCloud, too, and Arni and Kaiin and the marines and militans.

Nkiru squeezed his hand. "I'm so sorry."

"What's going to happen now?" Toroni asked.

Her eyes wandered the debris field in the bowl of the crater. "I'm not sure. The harvester will probably head for the nearest rocky planet and start . . . harvesting."

"There's a gas giant with big icy moons in the Grone system," said Littlefeather. "Outside this system, I don't know what's closest. Wald, maybe? Caerini Prime?"

Se-Jong couldn't remember the population of Wald, but it would be in the tens of millions at least. Caerini Prime was Earth's biggest and fastest-growing colony, with almost a billion human inhabitants. He turned to Toroni. "Contact the *Columbia* in orbit. Warn them about the harvester. Get them to track its path. Tell them to send a hypervee probe to follow it." When he saw the surprise in Toroni's face, he realized he'd just barked orders in the same tone used by Grandmother.

Toroni looked to Littlefeather for confirmation. She nodded, and the marine lifted his komnic and typed furiously.

"If they can track it, maybe they can nuke it," Se-Jong said. "Stop it before it does any damage."

Nkiru shook her head. "It won't be that easy. Whole avatar fleets were lost trying to kill those things." She tensed, released Se-Jong's hand. "What happened to the Orb? Where is it?"

Se-Jong slapped at the empty utility pocket in which he'd stashed the snowglobe during his headlong dash up the catwalk. "It must've fallen out."

"Shit. We have to find it, now!" She turned to the others. "Help me find the Orb!"

The room was filled with rocks and debris. Everything was coated in thick dust. They spread out.

From across the room, Toroni shouted, "Quiet! Listen."

A sound came from one of the battered wall consoles. A man's voice, tinny and indistinct.

No, not from the console. From underneath the console. Nkiru rushed to the console, knelt, and sifted through the debris. Something was emitting light. She picked it up.

The snowglobe.

They clustered around her as she frantically wiped it clean. The static was gone, replaced by a wide view of a room with a long table and scattered chairs. A group of humans was clustered at the head of the table, staring anxiously.

Se-Jong felt suddenly empty. Since he'd met her, it had been just the two of them, he and Nkiru, against the cosmos. Now, here were the people from her life before. They knew her secrets. They knew her past.

One of them was the ruddy, wild-eyed man with the bushy beard. Rupe, Nkiru had called him. He was jabbering, and in tears.

"Gaia. You're alive. I knew it." He turned to the people around him. "I told you. Didn't I tell you? She survived the Grone boss. She did it."

LEVEL UP

meatspace

So many questions. So many.

Everyone was babbling.

"What happened to Arni?"

"How old are you now?"

"Was that Wolfe? What was wrong with him?"

"What does it feel like?"

"Did you find Analise Novak?"

"Who are those people with you? Are they bots?"

Francis was beaming with joy, clutching his mother by the shoulders. Ms. Martinez was smiling, too, but her face was also twisted with confusion and concern.

Rupe was crying as hard as he'd ever cried. Bawling. Blubbering. His beard was soaked. He could only smile as he stared at the image of Gaia's face on the wall screen. She was bruised and filthy; her chest was heaving as if she'd just completed some mighty physical exertion; but she was grinning triumphantly. She'd come through. She'd survived. He'd convinced Solomon, Chun, the lot of them, that Fiona was their only chance. And he'd been right.

Solomon raised his arms and demanded silence. The room quieted.

"Fiona, I think I speak for everyone in this room when I say I'm delighted to see your face."

She nodded, unable to speak. She was crying, too, Rupe saw. Her chest was heaving from exertion and relief. Suddenly she jerked, as if she was being pulled away. Zia gasped until it became clear that she was being grabbed and embraced by her team bots. They were crying, too, even the big one who looked like a commando.

Others were pouring into the conference room, drawn by the commotion. Lieberman, Howe, two soldiers, the FBI guard, and several of the JEEB engineers.

Solomon shouted at the screen. "Fiona! Fiona, can you give us a status report?"

"That's not Fiona," Rupe murmured. "Fiona is on the table back in the lab. That's Gaia."

Solomon gave him a pained look. On the screen, Gaia's boisterous comrades had released her.

Solomon tried again. "Gaia, it appears that you managed to resynchronize the timestream, but the firewall is still up. What's going on?"

Gaia's grin faded. "That's, um, that's a little hard to explain."

"Give us the thirty-second version."

"Well, uh, let me see. The situation in here is . . . complicated." She paused. "It's like you said it would be. It feels real, completely real. My body is . . . whole. I feel . . . *alive*. I don't know how else to explain it. The game is *alive*, Rupe. The places and the people are *alive*. I can smell the air and taste the food and when I stub my toe it hurts. I get hungry. I have a period every month, and I catch colds and my hair grows."

Solomon interrupted. "We'll get a full debrief later. For now, it appears you made it to Grone. What happened there? Just a thirty-second summary, please."

She laughed. "Thirty seconds, huh? Okay, uh, well, it took me five years to find a way off JEEB Earth, then two more years to collect the items I needed and figure out how to get to Grone. I found Arni on Grone—or rather, he found me. There's something wrong with him. He has trouble remembering, and sometimes he acts like he's lost his mind. He helped me get to Atum's Lair. I managed to reprogram the scancorder and get the software fix into the holobox, but something happened to the emora. When I put the holobox into the machine at

Atum's Lair, it malfunctioned and Arni . . . Arni got killed. There were some people chasing us, so we didn't have time to try and fix it. Our only way out was through the boss chamber. We ran into Roland Wolfe in the boss chamber. He tried to—"

Zia blurted, "Wait. You found Wolfe?"

"He was one of the bad guys chasing me."

"Wolfe is a bad guy?"

"Yes. He didn't remember who he was, or where he came from."

"Where is he now?"

"He didn't make it out of the boss chamber."

Solomon grimaced.

"What about Analise?" Zia said.

"I never found her."

Solomon held up his hand. "We'll get into the details later. Keep going."

"Yeah, okay. Let's see, we made it past the boss, barely. A lot of people were killed in the fight trying to help me. Important people, good people. We made it to Jaspaar's lab just a few minutes ago, but I couldn't find the controller headset in time, and the harvester blew a hole in the top of the mountain and escaped. I think I managed to use the controller to keep it from killing us, but then again, we might've just been lucky." She paused, held the Orb close so that her face filled the screen. "Wait. Wait. Francis? Is that you?"

Francis shouldered his way to Rupe's side, tugging his mother by her arm. "I'm here, Fi. We're both here."

Tears streaked the grime on Gaia's cheeks. "Mama! Francis!"

Francis and Ms. Martinez were crying now, too. "You're so grown up," said Ms. Martinez.

"You look completely bad ass," said Francis. "What's it like in there?"

"It's incredible. It's dangerous. It's amazing. It's horrifying. There's so much I need to tell you. It's so good to see you. Both of you."

"Are you okay?" said Ms. Martinez.

"Mama, I'm okay. I've had lots of help. These are my friends."

There were three bots with Gaia: a man and a woman wearing military gear, and a young man in a filthy orange coverall with bloodshot eyes and bandages on half his face.

Rupe recognized the injured man in the orange coverall. It was the smiling boy from the selfie Gaia had sent Francis from the viewpoint overlooking the crater on Grone. Bad things had happened to the boy in the time between the selfie and now.

Gaia turned the Orb toward the man in combat gear. "This is Sergeant Toroni. He's a Solar Marine." She turned to the woman. "This is Ensign Littlefeather; she's an officer in the Solar Guard, which is the space navy for JEEB Earth. She's a female version of Indiana Jones."

Rupe searched his memory. Solar Marines, Solar Guard? The organizations weren't from the *Longstar's Rangers* fictional canon, nor from any of the world-building additions he and Arni had developed to flesh out the game universe.

Gaia turned to the bot with the bloody face. "This is Kwon Se-Jong. He's been helping me. I wouldn't have made it here without him. He's . . . he's my . . . he's my best friend."

The injured bot winced. "Uh, hello."

"Se-Jong, this is my brother, Francis, and my mom, Roberta."

The bot named Se-Jong nodded, but he was clearly disconcerted. From her tone of voice, Rupe wondered if he was Gaia's boyfriend. Given the time elapsed in the havencosm, she'd be almost twenty-two years old. A grown woman, no longer the scared fifteen-year-old to whom he'd said goodbye just a few minutes earlier.

Zia said, "So they *are* sentient. Analise was right."

Gaia nodded. "They're people. Real people. Just like us. *Exactly* like us."

On the screen, the three bots looked at each other, disoriented by the tone of the conversation. Rupe wondered how much she'd told them. Obviously not everything.

"How much time is left?" Gaia said.

"Three hours, nine minutes," said Chun.

"You just left," said Francis.

Gaia shook her head. "Unbelievable. It's been seven years for me. So much has happened."

"Yeah, you grew up. Guess that makes you my big sister now."

"Yeah, I guess it does." She paused. "Uh, Francis, you saved us all. If you hadn't given me the clue about the 'Escape Room' episode, we wouldn't have made it."

Francis wiped moisture off his cheek. "We're a team, Fi. Always."

Rupe allowed himself a grin. He'd modeled the puzzle in Jaspaar's lab after an episode of *Longstar's Rangers*, season 2, episode 9, titled "The Escape Room."

Fiona's mother turned to Solomon. "You need to get her out of there. Bring her home."

Chun shook her head. "We can't, not until the firewall comes down."

Solomon turned back to the screen. "Fiona, what exactly happened when you tried to lower the firewall?"

"I did the thing with the spit and teardrops, just like you told me. It seemed to work. The scancorder transferred the code to the holobox. But the blood thing, it didn't work. When I put a drop of blood on the emora, it didn't turn black like you said it would. It turned purple instead. Arni freaked out. He said I was . . . he said there was something wrong with my blood chemistry."

"Describe exactly what happened," prompted Zia.

"When I touched the emora, the kernel interface activated, just like you said it would, but it malfunctioned. It blew up. It killed Arni."

Next to Rupe, Chun stiffened. So did Zia. But death was transient in the havencosm, wasn't it? It had to be. For as long as Arni had been inside, he must have died and respawned several times.

"I'm sorry; that must have been difficult," said Solomon. "What happened next?"

"Um, there were some people chasing us. We had to run from them. We ended up in the boss chamber."

"Who was chasing you?"

Gaia shook her head. "That's a long story. You wouldn't believe this place. There are whole societies, civilizations, religions. Nasty politics. It's not a peaceful place."

"Can you get back to Atum's Lair?"

"No. The harvester blew up the mountain when it escaped. Atum's Lair is gone."

Chun edged to the front of the group. "Do you still have the holobox?"

"Yes." Gaia rummaged in a backpack, pulled it out.

"What happened to it?"

"It got a little singed, but it's intact."

"What about the emora?"

"It didn't work. Like I said, something was wrong with my blood."

"But you still have it?"

"Yes."

Relief flooded Rupe. At least Gaia still had the tools she needed to lower the firewall. If they could somehow remotely fix the emora, she could try again. Even with Atum's Lair destroyed, there were other ways in the havencosm to access and update the Haven machine's kernel. Now that he and Chun could coach Gaia in real time, there were many more options. If they could repair the emora, they could get Gaia into the Foundation Core itself, where she could apply the patch directly to the kernel instead of to a remote node.

Chun was apparently having similar thoughts. She turned to Lieberman. "What could have happened to her capatar's blood that would cause the emora to malfunction?"

He shook his head. "No idea."

"Could the changes we're seeing in her meatspace body's DNA be related?"

"How should I know? Seems impossible, but then all this seems impossible."

Solomon addressed Gaia. "You did well. Very well. And now that we can talk to you, we can support you directly. From this moment forward, you'll have all the resources of the JEEB program and the entire United States Department of Defense behind you. The smartest people in the world. We'll figure it out together and get you home safely."

"I'd prefer it if you sent an avatar army to help us. Rupe, don't forget: you said you'd show up with a warfleet and an army of avatars if I managed to get to Grone."

"You better believe it, baby. As soon as we get that firewall down, I'm there," he said. "As long as we can communicate, everything will be okay."

"Fi, do *not* lose the Orb," said Francis.

"I won't, believe me."

A cascade of beeps and chimes came from the screen. Two of Gaia's companion bots, the ones wearing combat gear, were receiving messages on handheld devices attached to their belts. The one named Toroni looked at Gaia.

"The interference from the harvester is gone. The dropship has our location. It's on its way. Five minutes."

"What does that mean?" asked Solomon.

Gaia grimaced. "Remember I told you we were being chased? Well, there are two starships here from two different factions, each one trying to get to us first."

"Show us your situation," Solomon said. "Pan around the room."

Everything was covered in thick dust, but Rupe recognized the lab he'd created based on the set from the "Game Changer" episode. The motive core enclosure was open, and the core was missing. The rear door he'd provided as an escape route was closed but undamaged. As she panned past the blast door, the destruction wrought by the harvester's violent departure was revealed.

"What's that?" Zia said. She moved to Rupe's side and pointed at something on the screen.

"Back up, Gaia. Show us the view out the blast door again."

The image shifted as Gaia pointed the Orb out the blast door. Sheer crater walls. Tumbled boulders, as big as skyscrapers. Smoke.

"There," said Zia. "What is that thing?"

A silver needle was rising above the jagged rim of the crater. For it to be visible at this distance, it must be huge.

Gaia saw it too, and so did her companions. The bot named Littlefeather said, "It's the *Navis Sacris*."

"What's a *Navis Sacris*?" Rupe asked.

Nkiru's voice was thin. "It's one of bad guys' starships."

"What do they want?"

"Me. They want me."

havencosm

Se-Jong watched Nkiru's face as she interacted with the people inside the Orb. Her expression was filled with enormous relief, pride, and also something he'd never seen: acceptance of authority.

They're calling her Gaia, or Fiona. Not a single one of them has called her Nkiru. Who is she, really, and who are they? Her mother. Her brother. The guy named Rupe. The Department of Defense. The Jeeb program. What are they?

There was no longer any question: she was a part of some massive conspiracy. She'd said she'd been helped by Janga monks, but the people in the snowglobe certainly weren't Jangas, nor were they monks.

Toroni and Littlefeather were listening to Nkiru's conversation with the people in the Orb, too, and they both looked as freaked out as Se-Jong felt. He tugged Nkiru's arm, whispered in her ear.

"We need to talk for a minute."

She shrugged him off. The man named Rupe was advising her to collect some of the items from the storage cabinets there in the lab.

Se-Jong dug his fingers into her arm, turned her forcibly toward him. "Please put that thing down so we can talk in private."

Nkiru seemed about to curse until she saw the expressions on the faces of Littlefeather and Toroni.

"Rupe, stand by. I need a minute." She placed the snowglobe on the lab table and strode to the other side of the room. Se-Jong and the others clustered around her.

"Who are these people?" hissed Toroni.

"They're my friends from . . . before. They sent me here. I don't have time to explain, but I promise I will. They're good people; you have to believe me. They're trying to save all of us. They're in danger, too."

"Where are they?"

"They're on . . . Earth."

"That's impossible."

"No, actually, they *are* on Earth. They're in Palo Alto, California."

"So, this Orb really is an avatar ansible? Instant interstellar communications?"

"Sort of, yes."

A sound drew Toroni's attention. He stiffened and ran to the blast door opening. "I see the dropship. Four minutes."

Littlefeather's voice was urgent, demanding. "I don't know what your deal is, Nkiru Anaya, but Captain Kwon was right: you're the most dangerous person alive. The Father Regis will do anything to get his hands on you. Anything. And gods help us if the Mucktu find out you exist. If I take you to the ship, the XO will turn you over to Command, and Command will turn you over to the church. But if I let you go, who knows what you and your friends in the crystal ball will do? You talked to Captain-Brother Kaiin back there like he was an old friend, too. How do I know that you aren't an agent of the church? Or something worse?" She sighed. "You say you're trying to save the world. Tell me—how is the world going to end?"

"You want the truth?" Nkiru looked toward the opening, through which the jets of the approaching dropship were much louder. "Okay, here goes. Ten thousand years ago, an avatar came here to Grone and found Atum's Lair and tinkered with the machine that controls the natural laws of the universe. She screwed up the clock that runs time. I know it sounds ridiculous, but it's what caused the Cataclysm and created the Devastation. Reality is out of sync with itself. I was sent here to repair the damage using the holobox and the emora back at Atum's Lair, but it didn't work. If I can't find another way to fix the damage, then at some point soon, space and time will become so unstable they'll tear reality apart. My friends, they understand the problem, and they're the only ones who can help me."

Littlefeather shook her head angrily. "You know how delusional that sounds, right?" When Nkiru didn't answer, she grew more insistent. "Damn it, Anaya, why should I believe you? I mean, isn't it more likely that you're some kind of Caeren terrorist? They've been trying to breed a race of false avatars for the past couple of centuries. Maybe they finally cracked the code. Maybe you've been stealing our relics so they can use them against us." She waved her arms around at the walls of the dungeon. "How do you know so much about this place? Why should we believe all your bullshit about the emora and Atum's Lair and the end of the world?"

Nkiru's response was flat and emotionless. "Because it was me."

She opened her blood-red eyes and locked them on Se-Jong. The veil of deception that had surrounded her from the moment they'd first met was gone. She took a deep breath, and he was suddenly afraid of what she was about to say.

"It was me. *I* was here ten thousand years ago. *I* was the avatar that broke the universe. *I* caused the Cataclysm. And those people in the Orb? They're the Oa. They created this cosmos we're in. Only, they're not gods. They're just people. And they're scared, just like us."

She didn't break her gaze. She believed what she was saying. Her eyes held only the fire of truth.

Or more likely, the fire of insanity.

But . . . there was no doubt she was avatar. He'd seen her skin glow with a million stars. The gobsmacker she held clutched in her arms was lit up and humming. She'd just led them through an unexplored avatar dungeon, survived a battle with a monster from First Epoch legends.

He stammered, "How . . . how old are you?"

"I'm twenty-one years old." When he shook his head in disbelief, she said, "Listen to me, Se-Jong. Time is broken. Space is broken. *I* broke them. And if I can't fix the problem, everything, everywhere, is going to end."

Without any warning, her face flooded with anguish as if some long-held emotional dam had finally burst from the pressure. She bent at the waist and let out a silent, gasping sob. Her filthy, tangled hair fell over her face.

Through the ragged gap that had once been the blast door, the dropship's jets were louder.

"Three minutes," shouted Toroni from the opening.

Se-Jong knelt next to Nkiru, but she turned violently away.

Littlefeather had been watching Nkiru with a clenched jaw. It suddenly tightened even more. She spun to Toroni. "Delay the dropship!"

"What? Why?"

"Just do it. Make something up."

The marine hesitated, then began speaking earnestly into his komnic.

Littlefeather turned to Se-Jong.

"Gods help us all. If she's lying or delusional, I'll kill her myself. I swear I will."

meatspace

Everyone was huddled at the front of the conference room table, staring up at the screen, watching as Gaia argued with the three bots. Rupe could hear snatches of their conversation. Gaia was crying.

The bot called Se-Jong, the one with the injured face, gathered Gaia into his arms and kissed her. After a moment she responded, wrapping her arms around him and pressing herself into him. He spoke to her in quiet tones while the other two bots looked on anxiously.

Rupe glanced at Zia. Her jaw was open. Francis too seemed speechless. Gaia had just kissed a computer-generated non-player character.

On the screen, Gaia nodded, wiped her face, seemed to collect herself. The bot called Littlefeather said something to her, and they all glanced toward the Orb. Se-Jong said something else, and Gaia nodded.

They approached the Orb. Littlefeather picked it up. Her face filled the wall screen, a mix of indecision and bravado. "Uh, which one of you is in charge?"

Solomon stepped forward. "I am. Colonel Jacob Solomon, United States Air Force."

Littlefeather struggled for composure. "United States . . . Air Force," she repeated slowly. She closed her eyes, shook her head, had some sort of internal battle with herself, came to a decision. Based on her wild-eyed expression, she'd just taken a massive leap of faith.

"I'm Ensign Littlefeather, Master Reliquist, Solar Guard. Nkiru Anaya tells me that you can help us escape this place and avoid our pursuers."

"Nkiru Anaya?"

Littlefeather pointed to Gaia.

Solomon cleared his throat. "Yes. We have detailed maps and inside knowledge of your current location. What's your situation?"

The young bot was nervous, but she seemed encouraged by Solomon's calm military composure. "We've got one injured, but he's stable and mobile. There's a squad of Solar Marines in a dropship that will arrive at any moment. We won't be able to resist them, and if they find us, we'll have no choice but to surrender Anaya. There's also a church ship here with Dei Militans who also want to capture her. We need to avoid both groups and find a way to get her out of this mountain undetected."

"Stand by, Ensign." Solomon turned to Rupe. "Can you get them out?"

"The only exit from Jaspaar's lab is through the red door. What happens next depends on the condition of the dungeon. Different sections were designed to collapse when the harvester escaped, based of different game variables. I can get them out, but how it happens depends on which routes are blocked."

Solomon nodded. "Ensign Littlefeather, this man is Rupe Schroeder. He's the architect of the Grone dungeon. He'll guide you out."

Littlefeather blinked. She cleared her throat. "The . . . *architect?* Of . . . *Grone?*"

Rupe felt a surge of pride. On the screen, Gaia put her hand on Littlefeather's shoulder. "It's like I said. They're the Oa, but they're *not* gods."

"This is so fucked up," muttered Littlefeather.

"Steady, Ensign," said Solomon. "We'll explain everything later, after we've gotten Fion—, uh, Nkiru to safety." He nodded to Rupe. "It's your show, Mr. Schroeder. Get them out of there."

Rupe took a deep breath. "Gaia, you're going to have to go through the rear exit door. It's the only way out, other than back through the blast door. You'll need the blue access card to open it. There's still power to the lab, right?"

"I think so. Some of the consoles are still lit up."

"Good. Get your things together and get ready. I see you have a gobsmacker. Is it charged?"

"Not really. It's got one shot left, maybe two."

"Good. You may need it. There are a few other things you should take from the lab. I'll explain as we go."

Rupe turned to the group surrounding him. "Francis, you and I are the only two gamers here. I'm going to need you. Take a seat at the table. You and I will use those two laptops. Dr. Chun, please monitor the Haven engine for any timestream instability, and do whatever you can to maintain synchronization. Zia, keep the link to the Orb steady. We can't afford to lose contact with them. Dr. Lieberman, get back to the lab and keep an eye on Fiona's vitals. Let us know the instant anything changes." He turned to Solomon. "Colonel, I need you to . . . just, be you."

Solomon chuckled. "Easy enough. And, Rupe, calm down. You're a steely-eyed gamer. You got this."

"Yeah. I got this."

havencosm

While Toroni monitored the location of the dropship from the ruined blast door, Se-Jong followed Littlefeather and Nkiru to the lockers at the rear of the room. Nkiru began rifling through the shelves and the items already scattered on the floor, stuffing items into her pack as directed by the man in the snowglobe. She took four items: a pewter ring, identical to one she already wore on her finger; a pair of steel forearm bracers, which beeped and re-formed themselves to the contours of her wrists when she donned them; a webbed bag of clear glass marbles that she attached to her utility belt; and a coil of thin climbing rope, which she shoved in her backpack along with the controller headset for the harvester.

"Okay, Rupe, we're ready."

"Now, get to the rear door—wait, what's that sound?"

The throaty roar of dropship jets filled the room. From the blast door, Toroni said, "They're here. Hovering outside, twenty meters." He motioned out the door toward the dropship, giving the hand signal that Se-Jong knew meant "Stand by." Toroni turned to Littlefeather. "Ensign, are you sure about this?"

"I'm not sure, okay? I'm not sure at all, but the captain gave me explicit orders," Littlefeather replied. "*Keep Anaya out of the hands of the church, and of the Mucktu, at any and all costs.* It's your choice, Sergeant. Stay here if you like. I won't blame you, but I trust Captain Kwon's judgment."

Toroni grimaced. After a moment's hesitation, he spun back into the room and shouldered his pack. "Garl-monking fuggerbitten murd," he cursed. "Let's do this."

They clustered behind Nkiru at the red exit door. She pulled out the access card.

"Rupe, are you ready?"

"Go, Gaia."

Nkiru pressed the card against the reader. The door opened.

They all leaped backward as stones tumbled through the doorway. The corridor beyond was blocked by a cave-in.

"Shit," said Toroni.

"Rupe, we're screwed," wailed Nkiru. "Should I use the gobsmacker?"

The roar of the dropship grew louder as the hovering craft crept closer to the blast-door entrance.

"Um, let me think," shouted Rupe. "No. Don't waste your gobsmacker's charge. Wave your right hand at the doorway and say *parandicus*."

"Parandicus?"

"Wave at the door. Say it."

Nkiru flapped her hand toward the cave-in. "Parandicus."

With a pop of displaced air, the tumbled barrier vanished, revealing a clean, well-lit corridor. Littlefeather gasped.

"What just happened?" said Gaia.

"It's a developer's cheat code," said Rupe. "It won't work on strategic barriers, only random, incidental barriers like this. Hurry through. The cheat only lasts sixty seconds."

"How come Arni didn't know about this cheat code?"

"I'm the Gamemaster, and the Gamemaster has his secrets, okay?"

"You got any other secrets?"

"What do you think? Get moving."

The roar of the dropship fell to a whisper when the door closed behind them. The corridor proceeded straight and level for a hundred meters. Se-Jong jogged alongside Nkiru. She held the snowglobe in both hands, arms extended, giving the people inside it a clear view of the path ahead. Rupe spoke continuously.

"Okay, when you get to the corridor junction ahead, you'll want to make a left, assuming it's not blocked by another cave-in. It'll lead to the cargo warehouse adjacent to the flitter pad. Your blue access card will open the doors. Inside the warehouse, you'll need to find your way through a maze of cargo containers that the earthquake tumbled when the harvester escaped; I'll tell you which path to take. Be careful: some of the broken containers spilled proximity mines and flashchasers. They'll be scattered everywhere. Try to avoid them. You'll have to detonate the mines you can't avoid. Use the popbangs for that: those are the little marble thingies you collected in Jaspaar's lab. If a flashchaser locks onto you, use your bracers to deflect it. Gaia, you go first and protect the bots. When you reach the end of the maze, you'll be at the entrance to the flitter hangar. If we can find a flitter that still works, you can fly it out. Most of them are armed, and if you fly low in ground-hugging mode, you shouldn't have trouble getting away from anything trying to chase you."

"What if the flitters are all dead? They've been sitting here for a hundred centuries, you know."

"Your gobsmacker still works. The scancorder and holobox worked. Hopefully at least one of the flitters will work. If not, there's a beamrider station in the hangar. We'll get you out, one way or another."

At the junction, the way to the left was clear. Everyone was huffing. Se-Jong was determined not to fall behind, even though with every step it felt like the skin was being jostled off his injured cheek.

Behind him, Toroni said, "Kwon, you okay?"

Se-Jong nodded. Toroni gave him an encouraging smile. "Your grandmother would be proud of you."

Too winded to reply, Se-Jong nodded again.

They reached a door. Nkiru swiped the access card. Just as Rupe had described, they were confronted by a warehouse filled with cargo containers, each the size of a school bus.

At one time the containers had been neatly stacked, four high, in long rows extending to the opposite wall of the warehouse. Now, as Rupe had predicted, they were a tumbled mess. Many were broken, their contents spilled and mixed in great heaps. Parts of the ceiling had collapsed, bringing down most of the lights. The warehouse was dark, full of echoes.

"Go straight, between the blue and orange containers. There's a tunnel beneath that will take you through to the next row. Watch for mines and flashchasers. They're scattered randomly by the game physics, so I can't predict where they'll be."

"What do they look like?" Toroni asked.

"The mines look like metal tea saucers. The flashchasers look like little fireworks rockets, and they have a light in the nose that alerts you when you get too close. If it blinks once, back away. If it blinks twice, you have half a second to react. You don't get a warning with the mines. If you pass within a meter, they detonate. A single detonation does fifteen points damage to anyone within a two-meter radius, so don't take any chances."

"Fifteen points damage?"

The boy, Nkiru's brother, said, "He means it'll probably kill you, unless you're wearing armor. Most bots have between five and fifteen hit points. You can't let even a single one of the mines explode or you'll die." He paused. "Hey, Fi, bots still don't respawn, do they?"

Nkiru glanced at Se-Jong. "No, Francis. They don't respawn."

Respawn? Toroni and Littlefeather exchanged an uneasy glance.

Rupe continued. "Get moving, but slowly, carefully."

—

The mines were everywhere. The boy, Francis, was particularly good at seeing them and pointing them out, so much so that Rupe eventually fell silent and let him lead the group.

"There's one: six feet ahead, to your left. See it?"

"Yes," said Nkiru.

"There's another mine—no, two of them—up on that ledge there. Hug the left side to pass."

"No. There's not enough room."

"You sure?"

"Damn it, Francis, I'm sure."

"Okay." The boy and Rupe held a whispered conference. Francis said, "Use a popbang."

Nkiru fumbled with the webbed pouch at her waist and removed one of the clear marbles.

"Toss it at the two mines on the ledge. You have to hit them. Don't miss."

"I *know*, Francis. We used popbangs on Bosporan, remember?" Nkiru swallowed, licked her lips. She took aim and threw. The glass marble traced a shallow arc and hit the uppermost of the two mines.

Both mines detonated, but instead of an explosion, there was only a muffled *pop* as the popbang contained the energy of the detonations in a beachball-size sphere. The sphere quickly dissipated into acrid-smelling smoke.

"Nice," said Francis. "Just like in the game."

They continued through the maze of fallen containers, following Francis's directions, detonating three more mines. Halfway across the warehouse, Se-Jong's eye was drawn to movement on top of one of the container stacks. A mere shimmer, maybe just a trick of his battered eyes. He paused, stared at the spot for a long moment before satisfying himself it was nothing.

Sixty seconds later he saw it again.

"Toroni," he said quietly. He pointed up to where he'd seen the shimmer. The marine fixed his rifle in the direction Se-Jong had indicated. Littlefeather and Nkiru stopped, stared.

"I thought I saw something move, twice."

Toroni nodded, peered through his scope. Nkiru held up the Orb. "Rupe, we may not be alone," Se-Jong said.

"I don't see anything," said Nkiru.

"Arni disabled the adversary bots for the dungeon," said Rupe, "so if something's there, it's not part of the scene's combat scenario. Could it be one of the groups chasing you?"

"Not likely, after what happened in the boss chamber," said Toroni.

"I don't see anything either," said Littlefeather.

"It could be an animal," said Rupe. "We designed a whole ecosystem for Grone, including a few cave dwellers."

Nkiru looked at Se-Jong. He shrugged. "I didn't get a clear look at it. It looked like a heat shimmer."

"Maybe a stealthshield?" suggested Francis.

Rupe shook his head. "That's not possible. Gaia is the only person in the havencosm who can use a stealthshield. Analise and Wolfe don't have her, uh, enhancements."

"Let's keep moving," said Littlefeather. "And keep your eyes open."

Something blinked in the darkness a couple of meters ahead.

"Stop!" Se-Jong cried.

Everyone froze.

"Now what?" whispered Toroni.

He pointed. "I saw something blink. Is that a flashchaser?"

Nkiru squinted. "Good eyes. Rupe, what should I do?"

"Are all the bots behind you?"

She looked back at Se-Jong. Her face was filled with tension. "Yes."

"Okay, listen carefully. There's no way past it without setting it off, so you'll have to use your bracers to deflect it. Gaia, when you take your next step, it'll probably launch. They're *fast*, like bottle rockets. Go ahead and cross your bracers in front of you like Wonder Woman does in the movies. As long as you're facing the flashchaser, it'll be deflected."

Nkiru assumed a wide stance, crossed her forearms in an X. The metal bracers clinked together.

"Okay, take a step forward."

The flashchaser blinked again.

"Take another step."

Blink-blink.

It launched with a sizzling whoosh, crossing the intervening space in a split second, faster than Se-Jong expected, and ricocheted off Nkiru's bracers. It shot upward and exploded against one of the cargo containers.

"Murd," cursed Toroni.

Nkiru lowered her bracers, looked into the snowglobe. "I've done that a thousand times with a controller, but it's a whole lot scarier when it's in person."

"I can imagine," said Rupe. "You did great. Now, stay alert. You might not see the next one before it launches. Be ready with your bracers."

"Hey, Rupe?" she said.

"Yeah?"

"Thank you. This is so much easier with your help."

"Gaia, it's my honor. You're the bravest person I've ever known."

"I second that," said her brother.

Nkiru gave the Orb a half smile. She turned to Se-Jong. Her eyes were bright, and the relief in her face was vast. She no longer bore her burden alone. The cavalry had finally arrived.

"We're almost there," urged Littlefeather.

meatspace

Gaia and her team of bots were about to emerge from the maze of cargo containers and head for the door to the flitter hangar. Rupe studied the image on the screen, his mind racing ahead to the next steps. There were two options. If Gaia could get a flitter to work, she could fly it anywhere within a couple thousand kilometers. Within that radius were two minor dungeons, both well hidden in the mountainous chain of craters that girdled the planet's equator. She could hide in one of them until they could figure out what to do next. Both sites held useful loot Gaia could use to improve her situation. If he could get her properly outfitted with high-level weapons and defensive gear, she would essentially be invulnerable to anything in the havencosm other than another avatar.

The other escape option was the beamrider station. Using a beamrider pod, Gaia could get off-planet immediately, though the destination options would be limited, and she would be jumping blindly into a completely unknown situation on another world. Plus, the beamrider pod seated two people, so Gaia would only be able to take one of her companions with her. Better a flitter, then.

The wide door from the warehouse to the hangar was partially open. It shouldn't have been. This entire section of the dungeon should have been inaccessible to anyone and anything except the first team to make it past the boss. He scowled at the screen. As he'd expected, the ceiling had partially collapsed, damaging all but three of the twelve aircraft parked in the hangar. He felt a wave of relief. The harvester's escape scenario had played out just as he'd designed it. Gaia was nearing the end of the preprogrammed dungeon encounter. There were no more threats.

On the screen, Gaia approached one of the undamaged flitters, the bots following her closely.

"Can she fly that thing?" said Solomon.

"The flying craft in the game were designed to be piloted by teen gamers with no knowledge of aerodynamics whatsoever. Yes, she can fly it." Rupe turned to Francis. "She's flown them before, in the game, right?"

Francis shook his head. "No, she couldn't fly with a trackball controller. I did all the flying; she was always the navigator."

"Doesn't matter. She'll be fine."

Fiona glared into the Orb. "You guys realize I can hear everything you say, right?"

"Yeah, sorry. Do you think you can fly a flitter?"

"Sure I can," she smirked. "They were designed for a twelve-year-old, right?"

Rupe chuckled. He and Arni had designed the flitter based on an air-car design from the TV show, a sort of George Jetson–inspired platform with fins and a big four-seat bubble cockpit. It even made a *Jetsons*-style trilling sound when activated and in flight. It couldn't fly very high, but it was fast and . . .

Wait. Something was wrong.

"Hold up, Gaia," he said.

He stared at the image on the screen. Something was off about the flitter.

"What is it?" said Nkiru.

"Give me a second. Point the Orb at the flitter."

He studied the image. The craft was right where it was supposed to be. It was covered in dust from the recent cave-in, but that was by design.

"Um, Gaia, is that a handprint on the flitter door?"

"Looks like it."

Rupe licked his lips. He glanced at Zia, then back at the screen. "The first team to survive the boss encounter are supposed to be the first people in the flitter hangar. Who left that handprint?"

Gaia considered this. "It's been ten thousand years. Is it possible that in that time somebody got in here? A local, maybe?"

"Maybe, but the ceiling was designed to collapse only when the harvester escaped. That dust should be fresh, less than an hour old."

"Murd," said the bot marine. He whipped his rifle to the ready, glared around the chamber.

"What do you want me to do?" said Gaia.

"Uh, check out the flitter, carefully."

Gaia handed the Orb to the bot named Se-Jong, who held it at arm's length in front of him, giving Rupe and the others a clear view of Nkiru.

She raised the gobsmacker and slowly approached the aircraft. There were no footprints in the dust on the hangar floor surrounding the flitter, which made the handprint even more odd. Grime covered the side window, masking any threats that might lurk inside. She stepped on the landing skid, then with one hand, slowly opened the flitter door.

"Oh, no," she said.

havencosm

Se-Jong joined Nkiru on the flitter's skid. He held the Orb inside the open door so her friends from . . . *meatspace* . . . could see.

The control panel was smashed, burned. Wisps of smoke rose from the debris.

"This just happened." He spun to Toroni. "We're definitely not alone."

The marine clicked his optical scanner down over his eye and swung his rifle in a wide arc, taking in every corner of the hangar.

"I don't see anything."

Nkiru looked into the Orb. "Rupe, this flitter isn't going anywhere. Something trashed the controls."

Se-Jong pointed to the handprint on the flitter door: four fingers and a very human-looking thumb. "Not a some*thing*," he said, "a some*body*."

"Check the others," said Rupe. "Be careful."

The remaining pair of flitters had suffered the same fate. The controls were bashed, useless.

Rupe said, "What about the beamriders? See the line of alcoves on the north wall of the hangar? Get there. Quickly."

Nkiru went first, gobsmacker ready. Se-Jong followed her, then Littlefeather. Toroni took the rear, walking backward, rifle raised, alert for any movement. They hurried to the alcoves. Se-Jong counted twelve of them, each containing an egg-shaped glass pod. Each pod sat atop a pedestal base and held two seats.

They were all smashed, save one. Smoke bubbled from the damaged pods.

"Oh, shit," said Rupe.

"What should I do?" said Nkiru.

Se-Jong turned in a circle, examining the hangar. "Is there another way out?"

"The only way out is a flitter or a beamrider," said Rupe.

Littlefeather pointed to the ribbed-metal expanse of the exterior hangar door, which led out to the mountainside. "If we can open that, maybe we can make a run for it on foot."

"The only way to open the outer door is using a flitter's control panel," said Rupe. "You might blast a hole in it with the gobsmacker, but it's a sheer cliff on the other side, and those people out there looking for you would see you trying to climb down the mountainside."

"We could go back to the dropship," suggested Toroni. "Take our chances with the XO."

Littlefeather eyed the undamaged pod. "What about that one?"

Toroni shook his head in warning. "Whoever smashed the other pods may have left this one undamaged for a reason."

"You think it's a trap?" said Nkiru.

He shrugged. "Sure looks that way to me. Let's go back to the dropship. We explain the situation to the XO when we get back to the *Columbia*."

"The XO will turn Nkiru over to the militans," insisted Littlefeather.

"You don't know that. She's loyal to the captain."

"She won't have a choice, Sergeant. She doesn't have the political clout of Captain Kwon." Littlefeather hesitated, then nodded to herself as if she'd come to a difficult internal decision. "Listen. You all need to know this. For the past six years, the church has been quietly transferring avatar relics from the chapels and temples of almost every world into the big reliquaries of the central cathedrals on Earth and Assinni. It went on for a long time before anyone in the Solar Guard noticed it. Captain Kwon gave me the job of tracking the movements of the relics. And guess what I found? They're stockpiling anything that might possibly be an avatar weapon in their most secure reliquaries."

"Six years," muttered Nkiru. "Just after I arrived."

"It can't be a coincidence," said Littlefeather. "They also started ramping up membership in the Cataclyst Youth, especially on the outlying agricultural worlds. They've been focused on recruiting kids approaching military age."

"Shit," said Toroni.

Littlefeather nodded glumly. "You marines are a pretty devout bunch, aren't you, Sergeant? You have a church-appointed military priest in every unit, don't you? What do you think would happen if the Father Regis called on the entire corps of marines to betray their Solar Guard commanders?"

Toroni clenched his jaw. "We're Solar Marines. We took an oath."

"What's more important: your oath to the Solar Alliance or the oath you made to the gods as a part of the Cataclyst Covenant?" Before he could answer, she continued. "I know what you'd do, Sergeant. There's a reason Captain Kwon chose you for her security detail. It's the same reason she chose me. But do you really believe everybody in the Solar Guard will be as loyal?" Her tone softened into regret. "Of course you don't."

"It'll be a nightmare," he said quietly.

"Yes, it will." She gave Nkiru an appraising look. "The Regium has been looking for you for years, and it's willing to go to war to get you. If the Father Regis calls the faithful to arms, half the human population will revolt against the civil government, especially on the rural colony worlds and the Alliance planets. That's why Captain Kwon and a few other officers have been making contingency plans to preserve the Guard fleet and keep it out of the church's hands."

Toroni's knuckles had whitened around the stock of his rifle. "If the church gets Nkiru, it'll trigger the biggest war the Known Arc has ever seen."

Littlefeather nodded.

A long silence.

"Yeah, that's not gonna happen." Nkiru chewed her lip, looked up at the row of beamriders. "Could Arni have smashed the pods? He said he spent the last hundred years making tunnels all through the mountain."

"It wasn't Arni," said Littlefeather. "Arni died back in Atum's Lair. These pods were destroyed in the past few minutes, since the harvester escaped. Just like the flitters."

Nkiru turned to the Orb. "Rupe, is it possible that Arni could have already respawned and gotten back here in time to do this?"

"It's not likely. He's a capatar, so if he respawned, he probably would've respawned on JEEB Earth. There's no way he could've gotten back to Grone so quickly. I suppose it's possible he could have found a way to activate a beamrider, but none of these pods connects to JEEB Earth."

Jeeb Earth? Respawned? What?

It was avatarspeak. Se-Jong had a million questions, but now was not the time to ask them.

"I say we use the beamrider," said Littlefeather. "It can go anywhere, right? Get to a safe planet. Askelon, maybe, or back to Earth."

"They don't work that way," said Francis. "Each pod is linked to another specific pod. You can't change the destination."

To Se-Jong, the transparent egg seemed menacing. Littlefeather echoed his thoughts. "What if it links to a pod on a planet that was lost in the Devastation? Or a world on the opposite rim of the Halo? If we use it, we may never find our way back to the Known Arc."

Nkiru examined an inscription on the pod's pedestal base. "Uh, it says it links to Orus. I don't recognize that. Rupe?"

"Orus is a planetoid not far from Grone. It has a dungeon that was taken over by privateers loyal to Emperor Torax. They use it as a secret base. It's gravitationally bound at the center of a cluster of spinning neutron stars, and it's really hard to get to with a starship without getting incinerated."

"Rupe, that was ten thousand years ago. Torax is long gone."

"The dungeon should still be there, though."

"What if we get to Orus, and we're stuck there?"

"We could always come back here to Grone," suggested Littlefeather. "Right, uh, Mr. Rupe? These pods are two-way, right?"

"Theoretically, yes. You could beam back here using the linked pod on Orus."

Toroni objected. "We're assuming that whoever smashed the other pods won't smash this one after we leave. Then we'd be stranded."

"I can't hold off the entire Solar Guard or the Dei Militans with a barely charged gobsmacker," said Nkiru. "If I stay here, I'll end up a prisoner on Earth or Assinni. They'll capture me and send me to one of their research facilities and take me apart to figure out how I work." She paused. "There might be another way. Rupe, what happens if I take the suicide express?"

"No way," blurted Francis. "No way."

Nkiru made a slashing motion with her hand. "Shut up, both of you! Rupe, what about it?"

Rupe's expression was troubled, thoughtful.

meatspace

Rupe turned to Chun, lowered his voice. "What do you think? If Gaia dies, what are the chances she'll respawn somewhere safe?"

"Who knows? Capatars are constructs of the jeebcosm, which is the military's version of the game environment. They were never designed to respawn like avatars. In fact, capatars were never intended to exist in the havencosm at all. Some software mod Analise created made it possible: some kind of patch that merged the capatar code from the jeebcosm with the avatar and bot code from the havencosm."

"What does that mean?" asked Solomon.

"It means we have no idea what happens when a capatar dies in the havencosm."

Rupe nodded, turned to the screen. "Gaia, we don't think the suicide express is a good idea. There's no telling where you'll respawn, or what condition you'll be in. There's a good chance you might not respawn at all."

"But Wolfe's capatar has respawned—many times. So has Arni's. You just said they probably respawned on JEEB Earth."

"We don't know that for sure," said Zia. "That's the initial spawn point for all capatars, but who knows what happened to the respawn code when Wolfe migrated JEEB Earth? Plus, you're different. The DNA mods we made to your capatar could affect the respawn procedure. It's possible you'll respawn like an avatar, at the designated save point near the location where you were killed, at the same age and with the same characteristics as the moment you died. Or maybe you'll birth-spawn as a naked infant, like a bot, on some random world. If so, will your infant capatar have all the memories of its earlier incarnation? Maybe not; you said that Wolfe appeared to have no memory of the JEEB project."

"Arni had memories," said Nkiru. "He remembered me."

"But he was also highly unstable, was he not?"

Nkiru fell silent.

Zia continued. "Look, we just don't know what will happen if you die. Capatars were never intended to respawn, never intended be in the havencosm environment at all." She paused, and her eyes narrowed in thought. "Plus, even if you do respawn somewhere as an adult with all your memories, you'll lose your item inventory, including the emora and the holobox, and you may not be able to find them again. I say you go to Orus, and we can help you the rest of the way."

havencosm

Nkiru lowered the Orb, looked at Se-Jong.

"You're absolutely *not* going to kill yourself," he said.

"Yeah, really bad idea," agreed Toroni.

Littlefeather remained thoughtfully silent.

In the Orb, Rupe cleared his throat. "All right then, looks like we're going to Orus. Gaia, listen up. It's a two-seat pod, and it'll only work for you. You can only take one person with you at a time. You'll have to make three round trips to get everybody across."

Littlefeather stared at the pod. "One of us needs to stay here. If the rest of us get stuck on Orus, we're going to need rescue." She turned to Toroni. "That's you, Sergeant. Get back to the dropship. Don't tell the XO or anybody else what happened. Tell her instead that we got separated, and you think we were killed along with Captain Kwon and the other marines. Blame it on the militans. When you get back to Trumbull Station, contact a Janga monk there named Monardi. Tell him everything."

"Monardi?"

"Yes. He's a friend of the captain's. You can trust him."

Toroni looked doubtful. "I don't like this."

Littlefeather tried to sound reassuring. "Once you deliver the message, you can forget all of this ever happened. Go back to your duties, knowing that you did everything you could to help Captain Kwon. Monardi will take it from there."

"If anybody goes with the avatar, it should be me," Toroni said. "What if Orus is a trap? She'll need a marine for protection. You know this Monardi: *you* go talk to him."

Littlefeather shook her head. "I've studied avatar relics and dungeons my whole life. I know more about the history of the Known Arc than all of you combined. If this pod goes to a ten-thousand-year-old avatar dungeon, Nkiru's best chance for survival is if I go."

Toroni seemed ready to argue, but Nkiru put her hand on his arm. "She's right. I need the reliquist with me, but I'm trusting my life to whoever stays behind. We all are. I'd rather trust my life to a Solar Marine."

"We'll be with her, too," said Rupe. "As long as she has the Orb, she won't be alone. We'll guide her the whole way. I have a few tricks on Orus."

The colonel named Solomon spoke. "Gaia, I've postponed the deadline we set before you entered the havencosm. The quakes have stopped for now, thanks to you. We still aren't in the clear, but for now we'll hold until we learn more about the situation."

Nkiru held the Orb close to her face. "Francis, where's Mama?"

"She's back with your, uh, your body, in the lab. She's holding your hand."

Nkiru smiled. "Tell her I can feel her, and that I love her. And Francis?"

"Yeah?"

"I love you, too. I'm glad you're with me now."

"Me too, Fi. I wish I was there in person."

"You'd love it."

"I know."

Nkiru turned wistfully to Toroni. "Sergeant, thank you, too, for everything. I'm so sorry about Private McCloud."

The marine grimaced. "I still think I should go with you."

"I promise I will contact you once we get off Orus."

"Better not call my komnic. They'll be watching me, for sure."

"Don't worry. I'm good at being sneaky."

He chuckled. "That's an understatement."

Nkiru gave him an awkward hug, which he returned even more awkwardly.

"Take care, Sergeant."

"Take care . . . Gaia."

Colonel Solomon's voice sounded from the Orb. "Thank you for your service, Sergeant. I hope we meet again."

"Me too, sir."

Nkiru turned to face Se-Jong and Littlefeather. "Which one of you is going with me on the first trip?"

Se-Jong brusquely shouldered Littlefeather to the side.

"That would be me."

Nkiru laughed. "I figured as much. Come on, Lieutenant, let's do this."

Littlefeather stuck her lip out. "Better you than me, Kwon. That thing is ten thousand years old. I'll let you test it to make sure it works."

"Gee, thanks."

"My pleasure." She took his hand, changed her mind, and embraced him. "I'll see you on the other side. If something goes wrong, take good care of our avatar."

"You know I will."

"I'm sorry about your grandmother," she whispered in his ear, "I loved her too."

"Better get going," said Toroni. "They're tracking my komnic."

Se-Jong released Littlefeather and turned to Nkiru.

"Are you ready for this?" she asked.

"I suppose." He hefted his pack, slung it across his shoulders.

Unexpectedly, Nkiru hugged him.

"You stink," she whispered.

"Somebody sprayed me with Yok-Stop."

"Sorry about that."

He moved his mouth to her ear. "I love you."

She laughed softly. "That's been obvious for a while, Lieutenant." She nestled her face into his shoulder.

He stroked her tangled silver hair, her extraordinary skin, scratched, bruised, and filthy. This person in his arms was, as Littlefeather had said, the most important person alive. Not just an avatar, which was mind-boggling enough, but something different and far more significant. Something new.

Part woman, part goddess.

In his mind he saw a vision of this day's events had he never met her. His grandmother would still be alive, going about her regular daily routine, as would the marines and the militans. He'd be in classes at the War College, completely oblivious to the great secrets and ancient conspiracies of the Cataclyst Church and the Mucktu Bloodline. Oblivious to the world-eating monster lurking beneath a mountain on faraway Grone. Oblivious to the fact that the Oa and the archangels of the scriptures might actually be *real*.

Because of Nkiru, he would never sleep soundly in blissful ignorance of the true shape of things. She had expanded the envelope of his mind, bent his perception of reality, and it could never be returned to its original form.

He should be angry at her. He should hate her for causing what had transpired. Instead, he felt only awe.

Epochs were measured by the lives of figures like Nkiru Anaya. Religions were started, wars were fought. She was myth. She was legend. She was song.

And he was a part of it all.

He held her tightly, reluctant to end the embrace, knowing that when he did, it would mark the beginning of an entirely new life for him. He looked up at the beamrider pod, preparing himself for the biggest leap of faith of his entire life. Who knew what might lie at the beamrider's destination? As Toroni feared, it might be a deadly trap, set by an unknown assailant. They might beam into a hard vacuum. The receiving pod might be buried under a miles-deep cave-in. It might be at the bottom of an ocean. It might be surrounded by flesh-eating dungeon monsters. There might be no receiving pod at all, only oblivion at the end of the line.

He looked down at the fabric of his coldsuit, drenched with grime and drying blood. *My blood, Arni's blood, McCloud's blood, my grandmother's blood. The blood of her Solar Marines. The blood of Captain-Brother Kaiin and his Dei Militans. All mingled in a dark stain, just like in the Sacraments of the Covenant. The church was born in blood. It feeds on blood. Today, it had feasted, and it might feast yet again before the day's end.*

"Let's do this," he said. He pulled away, and she released him.

Nkiru inhaled deeply, looked once again at Littlefeather and Toroni. Their faces were grim but determined. She turned back to Bryson. "Hold these." She handed him the Orb and her backpack, clicked open the glass door panel, and climbed into the pod. She did something to a small panel between the seats. The pedestal beneath the beamrider pod began to hum. "Now, hand me my things," she said.

He wedged himself against the pod door, held up the backpack containing her relics. She buckled herself into the pod seat and reached for the backpack.

———

Se-Jong saw the shimmer from the corner of his eye in the instant before it hit him, slamming him away from the pod. He fell hard on the concrete floor, losing his grip on the backpack and the Orb. The Orb bounced away. Pain flared grotesquely in his injured cheek.

He scrambled upright, lurched back toward the pod. From her seat in the beamrider, he saw Nkiru raise the gobsmacker and fire it at the insubstantial shimmer, point-blank range.

The impact should have jellied the attacker and blasted its remains out the open pod door. Instead, the shimmer absorbed the energy of the gobsmacker with a searing flash.

He staggered toward the pod, both arms raised, blinded.

His palms struck smooth, curved glass.

The blinding light faded, but the retinal afterimage obscured everything except a thin ring around the edge of his visual field.

Indistinct shapes, colors.

A voice he recognized.

Snarling, clear and distinct:

"Get back!"

He blinked, cried out incoherently, blinked again.

A sound: the pod door slamming shut with a hermetic *thunk*.

Movement in the pod. Se-Jong squeezed his eyes, opened them, tried to make out the scene details at the edge of his sight. Inside the pod, the shimmer field was gone, and in its place was a small humanoid figure with long dark braids spilling over a threadbare gray cloak. Something was wrong with its face. Nkiru was still buckled into her seat, reeling away from the intruder in horror.

The attacker reached for the beamrider controls.

A whine and the strong electrical smell of ozone, then a soft vacuum-pop, and suddenly the beamrider pod was empty.

Nkiru was gone.

Se-Jong felt his soul tear away from his body and begin freefalling into an abyss. Impossibly, he knew both the face and the voice of Nkiru's attacker. He'd seen her before, hidden within Leodiva's ancient *Reveal of Creation* fresco in the rotunda of the Torax Chapel on Assinni.

He'd seen her since, too, and heard her voice, in his nightmares.

The witch queen of the Mucktu Bloodline.

meatspace

The image on the wall screen reeled as the Orb rolled across the floor. It steadied at a drunken angle. A part of the pod was visible.

It was empty.

"What the fuck just happened," cried Zia.

"Did you see that? Who was that?"

"Are the bots still alive? Wait, I see one of them moving."

Rupe shushed the others and directed his voice toward the wall screen. "Hello? Can anyone hear me? Hello?"

No answer. The three bots were milling around the base of the pedestal, stunned. The Orb had rolled too far away for them to hear his calls.

"Please tell me we've been recording the video feed from the Orb," said Solomon.

Zia rushed to her laptop. "Yes. Stand by. Let me go back a couple of minutes earlier in the footage, we can watch it again in slow motion."

Rupe continued to try to attract a bot's attention. The boy called Se-Jong climbed into the pod and worked the controls, perhaps trying to follow Gaia. He was shouting something to the other bots. Rupe couldn't make out the words, but his tone was filled with desperation, anguish.

"Okay, got it," said Zia from her laptop. Rupe rushed to her side. Chun, Solomon and Francis pressed closely into his shoulders, all eyes on Zia's computer.

On the screen, a jostling replay of events recorded by the Orb. The bot named Se-Jong had been holding it clutched in his hand, so most of the image was obscured by his palm and fingers.

Zia scrolled forward in the footage.

Kwon was holding the Orb up to Gaia, for her to take it so he could climb into the pod next to her. The image suddenly went akilter as the Orb flew out of Kwon's hand.

Zia slowed the image, began advancing frame by frame. The individual stills were streaked and blurred from the spinning motion of the Orb. Rupe couldn't make anything out.

The Orb struck the floor, bounced, and began rolling. The image was less indistinct. Zia continuously clicked a key on her keyboard to advance the frames.

Click click click.

On her screen he saw the ceiling, the floor, a blurred glimpse of the edge of the pod pedestal. The Orb's rolling motion began to slow, the image becoming less blurred with every revolution.

Click click click.

One of the bot's boots, the ceiling again, then a tantalizing glimpse of the pod and the two figures within.

"Hold it there," said Solomon. "That looks like the same creature that killed Wolfe's capatar at the end of the Orb video he sent us."

They all leaned close over Zia's shoulder. Nkiru's attacker did indeed resemble the blue-faced humanoid from Wolfe's video, but the picture was too blurred to make out details

"Keep going," said Solomon.

Click click click.

Click click click.

Click click click.

"There!" cried Francis.

Zia froze the frame. The attacker's face was clear.

Shocked silence.

Deep skin. A silvery tattoo of leaves and vines crawled across her neck and cheeks. A milky jewel glowed from a wide dimple in the center of her forehead. Most horrifyingly, her eyes were missing, leaving only smooth, shadowed sockets.

"Holy fuck," Rupe said. Next to him, Francis shuddered.

Chun squinted at the screen. "Is that . . . *Analise?*"

"It's her," whispered Zia. "It's *definitely* her."

"Christ on a stick," muttered Chun.

havencosm | *MANHATTAN*

The ritual Mantra of the Rapture, sung during Exilemass, was one of the Universal Cataclyst Church's most ancient traditions, first conducted by the disciples of Andrik the Redeemer in the days following the Rapture of the Avatars. The ceremony was a particular favorite of Brother Jerome's, especially in its Mass Chant form, as it was today, when thousands of the faithful had gathered inside Earth's largest cathedral for the performance.

It began with the Highfather ringing the big bronze gong behind the pit-altar, symbolizing the primal toll of the Cosmic Clock, the Elemental Sound that had accompanied both the Creation and the Cataclysm. The assembled masses closed their eyes and began softly chanting the Sacred Syllables, which were the Oa, the Names of the Gods.

OhhhhhhhhhhAhhhhhhhhh

Brother Jerome chanted in the form he'd practiced since childhood. The First Syllable began with silence, gradually building and prolonging the deep-throated *Oh* sound until his chest vibrated with power. The transition to the Second Syllable, *Ah*, was achieved by slowly moving his tongue toward the back of his throat and widening his mouth. Finally, the shift to the Third Syllable, also known as the Silent Syllable, was formed by lowering the volume until the *Ah* sound became a whisper and then dissolved into nothingness. He then took a slow breath in total silence and repeated the mantra, over and over, and would continue until the Highfather was moved to ring the gong a second time.

OhhhhhhhhhhAhhhhhhhhh

The sound of nine thousand voices in harmony and unison, echoing up into the high arches of the choir and nave, was thunderous and awe-inspiring. The Mass Chant usually lasted an hour, but to Jerome the experience had a completely timeless quality.

He let his mind slip away, which he knew was the point of the mantra. After twenty minutes of ritual sound, he began to feel his soul vibrating in harmony with the recitations. He was approaching the state of qui, the ecstasy, when his soul would commune with the cosmos.

He focused on the sensation. It was most intense during the stillness of the Silent Syllable, the emptiness between the repetitions of the sacred mantra. Something lived in that silence. Something older, bigger, and even more primal than the Oa.

A buzz, deep in the innermost pocket of his cape. Caught up in the building enchantment of qui, he barely registered it.

It buzzed again. Next to him, Brother O'Lear gave him an unbelieving glare.

Jerome's heart stuttered, and the ecstasy of the qui melted like a sandcastle beneath a wave. He'd turned his komnic to do-not-disturb mode. The fact that it was alerting him during this most holy of ceremonies meant the notification was beyond urgent.

As surreptitiously as possible, his hand wandered into his cape and retrieved the device. He glanced at the notification through lowered eyelids, shielding it from the prying eyes of O'Lear.

The message was from Brother Monardi, and it was sealed with the church's strongest encryption. Jerome typed the unlock code and quickly read the message in the ten seconds allotted before the security routines erased it:

Starlight sighted on Orus. Come with me.

Without breaking the ceremonial posture of prayer, he surveyed his surroundings. Monardi was standing in the cathedral's southern transept, next to the doors that led out to Fiftieth Street. He was wearing street clothes.

Jerome nodded. Monardi nodded back, then quickly turned and exited the sanctuary.

A Janga Adept leaving the cathedral in the midst of the Mass Chant was unheard of. It would cause a stir and arouse unwanted interest. Had Monardi's facial expression been less urgent, or his message less compelling, Jerome would have stayed until the end.

He made the sign of the Linked Trinity; then, as softly as possible, he left the prayer circle surrounding the altar and made his way down the central aisle toward the transept. The eyes of the worshippers followed him incredulously, but thankfully, nobody broke prayer form to challenge him.

Monardi was waiting outside, and as soon as Jerome emerged, he hurried west toward Fifth Avenue. Jerome followed at a safe distance, wishing he were less conspicuous. His black-and-yellow Janga robe was hard to ignore.

Monardi caught a taxi on Fifth, and Jerome followed suit. They sped down Fifth Avenue, passing the broken stump of the Empire State Building. It veered onto Twenty-Third at the Flatiron, then south again on Park Avenue, then onto Broadway, passing Union Square and depositing him on the corner of Broadway and East Twelfth.

The safepoint was secreted in a basement beneath the corner bookstore. In an alley adjacent to the building, pressure on one of the discolored bricks behind a dumpster caused a steel plate on the filthy alley floor to open silently.

He took the ladder to the bottom, ducking through the dripping sewer pipe until he reached another unmarked metal door, seemingly rusted shut since the building's nineteenth-century origins.

Epilogue

It opened at his coded taps. Monardi gave him a grim look, beckoned him inside. The safepoint was a collection of four rooms, outfitted as a primitive emergency shelter. Jangas were barely tolerated these days and often needed to meet in secret to avoid church scrutiny.

Three people were waiting in the rearmost room. A young woman and two young men. They looked up at Jerome. He saw expectation, suspicion, hostility. Also hope, and a terrible fear.

He turned to Monardi. "What's this about?"

Monardi gestured at the strangers. One of them, the youngest, an earnest-looking boy of nineteen or twenty, stood and faced Jerome. His face had a nasty scar on the cheek, still bruised and raw, just beginning to heal. He was holding an object in both hands, wrapped in a cloth.

The boy unwrapped the object. It was a translucent sphere, about the size of a softball. It was glowing as if an image was being projected within it.

"What is this?"

Jerome reached out for the Orb, but the boy jerked it back.

"I'll hold it," the boy snapped. "You just look."

Jerome nodded. The boy slowly extended his arm, letting the Orb rest in his palm.

Jerome startled when a strangely accented voice came from the Orb. A face appeared in its depths.

"Hello? Hello? Are you Brother Jerome?"

"Who's asking?"

"My name is Rupert Schroeder. I'm a friend of Nkiru Anaya. She's in trouble, and we need your help."

Monardi made the sign of the Linked Trinity over his chest. Jerome felt the urge to make the sign as well but refrained. He clutched his hands together so the trembling wouldn't be obvious.

Somehow, he found the courage to speak. "She told me of you. You're her friend from . . . meatspace."

"You know about meatspace?"

The moment felt utterly surreal. The rumblings of the Mass Chant still echoed in Jerome's mind, and the weight of history and legend pressed upon his shoulders.

OhhhhhhhhhhAhhhhhhhhh

"She told me of it, yes."
"Then you understand how important she is?"
"I do."
"And you'll help us?"
Jerome drew himself up and spoke through clenched teeth.
"If I have to travel through hell itself."

Here ends GRONE. The story continues in ORUS, in which a fellowship is forged across two worlds and fights to save both, and science and magic converge to reveal an astonishing truth.

NEXT STEPS

Please take a few moments to rate GRONE on Amazon.
Ratings are a book's lifeblood and are GREATLY appreciated.

THE LEGENDS OF THE KNOWN ARC TRILOGY

GRONE — Everything we thought we knew about the **game** was wrong. — PATRICK CUMBY

ORUS — Our worlds are broken and the avatars are gone, but the **game** goes on. — PATRICK CUMBY

PHADE — Only at the broken edge of reality can the **game** be ended. — PATRICK CUMBY

Learn more and get updates on sequels, standalone novels, and short stories set in the Known Arc universe:

PatrickCumby.com/LOKAVERSE

Acknowledgements

A book of this scale and scope is a team project. First and foremost, I extend an entire universe of thanks to my wife Jeanne, who has suffered through the anguish of every plot hole and rewrite with stubborn confidence and optimism. There is as much of her heart in this book as my own. Same with my daughter, Maggie, without whose unflagging willingness to read and reread every version of the manuscripts-in-progress this book wouldn't exist. My son Thomas and my son-in-law Sergei, both avid gamers, gave soul and accuracy to the *Longstar* gameplay. They know their stuff, and if there are any inaccuracies, they are my fault alone.

My editor, the remarkable Christine Crabb, deserves my special thanks. Her sharp red pen and her deep knowledge of the subject matter has made me a much better writer. I'm hugely indebted to my beta readers who opened my eyes to the possibilities in this story: Maggie Kornaev, Lee Waldron (whose ideas resulted in a far better ending), Chris Chadwick, Dennis Ashworth, Bruce Clendenning, Elliot Clendenning, Mila Clendenning, Mike Luciano, and Thomas Cumby (if I've forgotten anyone, please forgive me). Thanks are due to Stanley Dankoski for refining the earliest version of the manuscript, and to all those who encouraged, supported, and most importantly, taught me along the way, including Jane Cumby, Lenny Bernstein, Abigail Dewitt, Heather Newton, Beth Revis, Anne Wertz Garvin, and everyone at the Great Smokies Writing Program at the University of North Carolina Asheville.

If you think there may be a puzzle hidden somewhere in this book, go to:

patrickcumby.com/grone-puzzle.

□ △ ○ ✕

Printed in Great Britain
by Amazon